P9-CMY-666

withdrawn

THE DARK TOWER

THE DARK TOWER VII

STEPHEN KING

ALSO BY STEPHEN KING

Dark Tower–related in bold

THE DARK TOWER VII

THE DARK TOWER

STEPHEN KING

ILLUSTRATED BY

MICHAEL WHELAN

DONALD M. GRANT, PUBLISHER, INC.
HAMPTON FALLS, NEW HAMPSHIRE 03844
IN ASSOCIATION WITH SCRIBNER

withdrawn

He who speaks without an attentive ear is mute.

Therefore, Constant Reader, this final book in the *Dark Tower* cycle

is dedicated to you.

Long days and pleasant nights.

Not hear? When noise was everywhere! it tolled
Increasing like a bell. Names in my ears
Of all the lost adventurers, my peers —
How such a one was strong, and such was bold,
And such was fortunate, yet each of old
Lost, lost! one moment knelled the woe of years.

There they stood, ranged along the hillsides, met
To view the last of me, a living frame
For one more picture! In a sheet of flame
I saw them and I knew them all. And yet
Dauntless the slug-horn to my lips I set,
And blew. 'Childe Roland to the Dark Tower came.'

—Robert Browning
"Childe Roland to the Dark Tower Came"

I was born
Six-gun in my hand,
behind a gun
I'll make my final stand.

—Bad Company

What have I become?
My sweetest friend
Everyone I know
Goes away in the end
You could have it all
My empire of dirt
I will let you down
I will make you hurt

—Trent Reznor

CONTENTS

EPILOGUE
SUSANNAH IN NEW YORK

CODA
FOUND

APPENDIX
ROBERT BROWNING
"CHILDE ROLAND TO THE DARK TOWER CAME"

AUTHOR'S NOTE

ILLUSTRATIONS

REPRODUCTION

REVELATION

REDEMPTION

RESUMPTION

THE DARK TOWER

THE DARK TOWER VII

PART ONE:

THE LITTLE RED KING

DAN-TETE

CHAPTER I:
CALLAHAN AND THE VAMPIRES

ONE

Pere Don Callahan had once been the Catholic priest of a town, 'Salem's Lot had been its name, that no longer existed on any map. He didn't much care. Concepts such as reality had ceased to matter to him.

This onetime priest now held a heathen object in his hand, a scrimshaw turtle made of ivory. There was a nick in its beak and a scratch in the shape of a question mark on its back, but otherwise it was a beautiful thing.

Beautiful and *powerful*. He could feel the power in his hand like volts.

"How lovely it is," he whispered to the boy who stood with him. "Is it the Turtle Maturin? It is, isn't it?"

The boy was Jake Chambers, and he'd come a long loop in order to return almost to his starting-place here in Manhattan. "I don't know," he said. "She calls it the *sköldpadda*, and it may help us, but it can't kill the harriers that are waiting for us in there." He nodded toward the Dixie Pig, wondering if he meant Susannah or Mia when he used that all-purpose feminine pronoun *she*. Once he would have said it didn't matter because the two women were so tightly wound together. Now, however, he thought it did matter, or would soon.

"Will you?" Jake asked the Pere, meaning *Will you stand. Will you fight. Will you kill.*

"Oh yes," Callahan said calmly. He put the ivory turtle with its wise eyes and scratched back into his breast pocket with the extra shells for the gun he carried, then patted the cunningly made thing once to make sure it rode safely. "I'll shoot until the

3

bullets are gone, and if I run out of bullets before they kill me, I'll club them with the . . . the gun-butt."

The pause was so slight Jake didn't even notice it. But in that pause, the White spoke to Father Callahan. It was a force he knew of old, even in boyhood, although there had been a few years of bad faith along the way, years when his understanding of that elemental force had first grown dim and then become lost completely. But those days were gone, the White was his again, and he told God thankya.

Jake was nodding, saying something Callahan barely heard. And what Jake said didn't matter. What that other voice said— the voice of something

(*Gan*)

perhaps too great to be called God— *did.*

The boy must go on, the voice told him. *Whatever happens here, however it falls, the boy must go on. Your part in the story is almost done. His is not.*

They walked past a sign on a chrome post (**CLOSED FOR PRIVATE FUNCTION**), Jake's special friend Oy trotting between them, his head up and his muzzle wreathed in its usual toothy grin. At the top of the steps, Jake reached into the woven sack Susannah-Mio had brought out of Calla Bryn Sturgis and grabbed two of the plates—the 'Rizas. He tapped them together, nodded at the dull ringing sound, and then said: "Let's see yours."

Callahan lifted the Ruger Jake had brought out of Calla New York, and now back into it; life is a wheel and we all say thankya. For a moment the Pere held the Ruger's barrel beside his right cheek like a duelist. Then he touched his breast pocket, bulging with shells, and with the turtle. The *sköldpadda.*

Jake nodded. "Once we're in, we stay together. Always together, with Oy between. On three. And once we start, we never stop."

"Never stop."

"Right. Are you ready?"

"Yes. God's love on you, boy."

"And on you, Pere. One . . . two . . . *three.*" Jake opened the

door and together they went into the dim light and the sweet
tangy smell of roasting meat.

TWO

Jake went to what he was sure would be his death remembering
two things Roland Deschain, his true father, had said. *Battles that
last five minutes spawn legends that live a thousand years.* And *You
needn't die happy when your day comes, but you must die satisfied, for
you have lived your life from beginning to end and ka is always served.*
    Jake Chambers surveyed the Dixie Pig with a satisfied mind.

THREE

Also with crystal clarity. His senses were so heightened that he
could smell not just roasting flesh but the rosemary with which
it had been rubbed; could hear not only the calm rhythm of his
breath but the tidal murmur of his blood climbing brainward on
one side of his neck and descending heartward on the other.
    He also remembered Roland's saying that even the shortest
battle, from first shot to final falling body, seemed long to
those taking part. Time grew elastic; stretched to the point of
vanishment. Jake had nodded as if he understood, although he
hadn't.
    Now he did.
    His first thought was that there were too many of them—far,
far too many. He put their number at close to a hundred, the
majority certainly of the sort Pere Callahan had referred to as
"low men." (Some were low women, but Jake had no doubt the
principle was the same.) Scattered among them, all less fleshy
than the low *folken* and some as slender as fencing weapons,
their complexions ashy and their bodies surrounded in dim
blue auras, were what had to be vampires.
    Oy stood at Jake's heel, his small, foxy face stern, whining
low in his throat.
    That smell of cooking meat wafting through the air was not
pork.

FOUR

Ten feet between us any time we have ten feet to give, Pere—so Jake had said out on the sidewalk, and even as they approached the *maître d*'s platform, Callahan was drifting to Jake's right, putting the required distance between them.

Jake had also told him to scream as loud as he could for as long as he could, and Callahan was opening his mouth to begin doing just that when the voice of the White spoke up inside again. Only one word, but it was enough.

Sköldpadda, it said.

Callahan was still holding the Ruger up by his right cheek. Now he dipped into his breast pocket with his left hand. His awareness of the scene before him wasn't as hyper-alert as his young companion's, but he saw a great deal: the orangey-crimson electric *flambeaux* on the walls, the candles on each table immured in glass containers of a brighter, Halloweenish orange, the gleaming napkins. To the left of the dining room was a tapestry showing knights and their ladies sitting at a long banquet table. There was a sense in here—Callahan wasn't sure exactly what provoked it, the various tells and stimuli were too subtle—of people just resettling themselves after some bit of excitement: a small kitchen fire, say, or an automobile accident on the street.

Or a lady having a baby, Callahan thought as he closed his hand on the Turtle. *That's always good for a little pause between the appetizer and the entrée.*

"Now come Gilead's ka-mais!" shouted an excited, nervous voice. Not a human one, of that Callahan was almost positive. It was too *buzzy* to be human. Callahan saw what appeared to be some sort of monstrous bird-human hybrid standing at the far end of the room. It wore straight-leg jeans and a plain white shirt, but the head rising from that shirt was painted with sleek feathers of dark yellow. Its eyes looked like drops of liquid tar.

"*Get them!*" this horridly ridiculous thing shouted, and brushed aside a napkin. Beneath it was some sort of weapon.

Callahan supposed it was a gun, but it looked like the sort you saw on *Star Trek*. What did they call them? Phasers? Stunners?

It didn't matter. Callahan had a far better weapon, and wanted to make sure they all saw it. He swept the place-settings and the glass container with the candle in it from the nearest table, then snatched away the tablecloth like a magician doing a trick. The last thing he wanted to do was to trip over a swatch of linen at the crucial moment. Then, with a nimbleness he wouldn't have believed even a week ago, he stepped onto one of the chairs and from the chair to the table-top. Once on the table, he lifted the *sköldpadda* with his fingers supporting the turtle's flat undershell, giving them all a good look at it.

I could croon something, he thought. *Maybe "Moonlight Becomes You" or "I Left My Heart in San Francisco."*

At that point they had been inside the Dixie Pig for exactly thirty-four seconds.

FIVE

High school teachers faced with a large group of students in study hall or a school assembly will tell you that teenagers, even when freshly showered and groomed, reek of the hormones which their bodies are so busy manufacturing. Any group of people under stress emits a similar stink, and Jake, with his senses tuned to the most exquisite pitch, smelled it here. When they passed the *maître d*'s stand (Blackmail Central, his Dad liked to call such stations), the smell of the Dixie Pig's diners had been faint, the smell of people coming back to normal after some sort of dust-up. But when the bird-creature in the far corner shouted, Jake had smelled the patrons more strongly. It was a metallic aroma, enough like blood to incite his temper and his emotions. Yes, he saw Tweety Bird knock aside the napkin on his table; yes, he saw the weapon beneath; yes, he understood that Callahan, standing on the table, was an easy shot. That was of far less concern to Jake than the mobilizing weapon that was Tweety Bird's mouth. Jake was drawing back his right arm, meaning to fling the first of his nineteen plates and amputate the head in which that mouth resided, when Callahan raised the turtle.

It won't work, not in here, Jake thought, but even before the idea had been completely articulated in his mind, he understood it *was* working. He knew by the smell of them. The aggressiveness went out of it. And the few who had begun to rise from their tables—the red holes in the foreheads of the low people gaping, the blue auras of the vampires seeming to pull in and intensify—sat back down again, and hard, as if they had suddenly lost command of their muscles.

"*Get them, those are the ones Sayre . . .*" Then Tweety stopped talking. His left hand—if you could call such an ugly talon a hand—touched the butt of his high-tech gun and then fell away. The brilliance seemed to leave his eyes. "They're the ones Sayre . . . S-S-Sayre . . ." Another pause. Then the bird-thing said, "Oh sai, what is the lovely thing that you hold?"

"You know what it is," Callahan said. Jake was moving and Callahan, mindful of what the boy gunslinger had told him outside—*Make sure that every time I look on my right, I see your face*—stepped back down from the table to move with him, still holding the turtle high. He could almost taste the room's silence, but—

But there was *another* room. Rough laughter and hoarse, carousing yells—a party from the sound of it, and close by. On the left. From behind the tapestry showing the knights and their ladies at dinner. *Something going on back there,* Callahan thought, *and probably not Elks' Poker Night.*

He heard Oy breathing fast and low through his perpetual grin, a perfect little engine. And something else. A harsh rattling sound with a low and rapid clicking beneath. The combination set Callahan's teeth on edge and made his skin feel cold. Something was hiding under the tables.

Oy saw the advancing insects first and froze like a dog on point, one paw raised and his snout thrust forward. For a moment the only part of him to move was the dark and velvety skin of his muzzle, first twitching back to reveal the clenched needles of his teeth, then relaxing to hide them, then twitching back again.

The bugs came on. Whatever they were, the Turtle Maturin upraised in the Pere's hand meant nothing to them. A fat guy wearing a tuxedo with plaid lapels spoke weakly, almost questioningly, to the bird-thing: "They weren't to come any further than here, Meiman, nor to leave. We were told . . ."

Oy lunged forward, a growl coming through his clamped teeth. It was a decidedly un-Oylike sound, reminding Callahan of a comic-strip balloon: *Arrrrr!*

"No!" Jake shouted, alarmed. "No, Oy!"

At the sound of the boy's shout, the yells and laughter from behind the tapestry abruptly ceased, as if the *folken* back there had suddenly become aware that something had changed in the front room.

Oy took no notice of Jake's cry. He crunched three of the bugs in rapid succession, the crackle of their breaking carapaces gruesomely clear in the new stillness. He made no attempt to eat them but simply tossed the corpses, each the size of a mouse, into the air with a snap of the neck and a grinning release of the jaws.

And the others retreated back under the tables.

He was made for this, Callahan thought. *Perhaps once in the long-ago all bumblers were. Made for it the way some breeds of terrier are made to—*

A hoarse shout from behind the tapestry interrupted these thoughts: *"Humes!"* one voice cried, and then a second: *"Ka-humes!"*

Callahan had an absurd impulse to yell *Gesundheit!*

Before he could yell that or anything else, Roland's voice suddenly filled his head.

SIX

"Jake, go."

The boy turned toward Pere Callahan, bewildered. He was walking with his arms crossed, ready to fling the 'Rizas at the first low man or woman who moved. Oy had returned to his heel, although he was swinging his head ceaselessly from side to side and his eyes were bright with the prospect of more prey.

"We go together," Jake said. "They're buffaloed, Pere! And we're close! They took her through here . . . this room . . . and then through the kitchen—"

Callahan paid no attention. Still holding the turtle high (as one might hold a lantern in a deep cave), he had turned toward the tapestry. The silence from behind it was far more terrible than the shouts and feverish, gargling laughter. It was silence like a pointed weapon. And the boy had stopped.

"Go while you can," Callahan said, striving for calmness. "Catch up to her *if* you can. This is the command of your dinh. This is also the will of the White."

"But you can't—"

"Go, Jake!"

The low men and women in the Dixie Pig, whether in thrall to the *sköldpadda* or not, murmured uneasily at the sound of that shout, and well they might have, for it was not Callahan's voice coming from Callahan's mouth.

"You have this one chance and must take it! Find her! As dinh I command you!"

Jake's eyes flew wide at the sound of Roland's voice issuing from Callahan's throat. His mouth dropped open. He looked around, dazed.

In the second before the tapestry to their left was torn aside, Callahan saw its black joke, what the careless eye would first surely overlook: the roast that was the banquet's main entrée had a human form; the knights and their ladies were eating human flesh and drinking human blood. What the tapestry showed was a cannibals' communion.

Then the ancient ones who had been at their own sup tore aside the obscene tapestry and burst out, shrieking through the great fangs that propped their deformed mouths forever open. Their eyes were as black as blindness, the skin of their cheeks and brows—even the backs of their hands—tumorous with wild teeth. Like the vampires in the dining room, they were surrounded with auras, but these were of a poisoned violet so dark it was almost black. Some sort of ichor dribbled from the corners of their eyes and mouths. They were gibbering and several were laughing: seeming not to create the sounds but rather to snatch them out of the air like something that could be rent alive.

And Callahan knew them. Of course he did. Had he not been sent hence by one of their number? Here were the *true* vampires, the Type Ones, kept like a secret and now loosed on the intruders.

The turtle he held up did not slow them in the slightest.

Callahan saw Jake staring, pale, eyes shiny with horror and bulging from their sockets, all purpose forgotten at the sight of these freaks.

Without knowing what was going to come out of his mouth until he heard it, Callahan shouted: *"They'll kill Oy first! They'll kill him in front of you and drink his blood!"*

Oy barked at the sound of his name. Jake's eyes seemed to clear at the sound, but Callahan had no time to follow the boy's fortunes further.

Turtle won't stop them, but at least it's holding the others back. Bullets won't stop them, but—

With a sense of *déjà vu*—and why not, he had lived all this before in the home of a boy named Mark Petrie—Callahan dipped into the open front of his shirt and brought out the cross he wore there. It clicked against the butt of the Ruger and then hung below it. The cross was lit with a brilliant bluish-white glare. The two ancient things in the lead had been about to grab him and draw him into their midst. Now they drew back instead, shrieking with pain. Callahan saw the surface of their skin sizzle and begin to liquefy. The sight of it filled him with savage happiness.

"Get back from me!" he shouted. "The power of God commands you! The power of Christ commands you! The ka of Mid-World commands you! *The power of the White commands you!*"

One of them darted forward nevertheless, a deformed skeleton in an ancient, moss-encrusted dinner suit. Around its neck it wore some sort of ancient award . . . the Cross of Malta, perhaps? It swiped one of its long-nailed hands at the crucifix Callahan was holding out. He jerked it down at the last second, and the vampire's claw passed an inch above it. Callahan lunged forward without thought and drove the tip of the cross into the yellow parchment of the thing's forehead. The gold crucifix went in like a red-hot skewer into butter. The thing in the rusty dinner suit let out a liquid cry of pained dismay and stumbled backward. Callahan pulled his cross back. For one moment, before the elderly monster clapped its claws to its brow, Callahan saw the hole his cross had made. Then a thick, curdy, yellow stuff began to spill through the ancient one's fingers. Its knees unhinged and it tumbled to the floor between two tables. Its mates shrank away from it, screaming with outrage. The thing's face was already collapsing inward beneath its twisted hands. Its aura whiffed out like a candle and then there was nothing but a puddle of yellow, liquefying flesh spilling like vomit from the sleeves of its jacket and the legs of its pants.

Callahan strode briskly toward the others. His fear was gone. The shadow of shame that had hung over him ever since Barlow had taken his cross and broken it was also gone.

Free at last, he thought. *Free at last, great God Almighty, I'm free at last.* Then: *I believe this is redemption. And it's good, isn't it? Quite good, indeed.*

"H'row it aside!" one of them cried, its hands held up to shield its face. "Nasty bauble of the 'heep-God, h'row it aside if you dare!"

Nasty bauble of the sheep-God, indeed. If so, why do you cringe?

Against Barlow he had not dared answer this challenge, and it had been his undoing. In the Dixie Pig, Callahan turned the cross toward the thing which had dared to speak.

"I needn't stake my faith on the challenge of such a thing as you, sai," he said, his words ringing clearly in the room. He had forced the old ones back almost to the archway through which they had come. Great dark tumors had appeared on the hands and faces of those in front, eating into the paper of their ancient skin like acid. "And I'd never throw away such an old friend in any case. But *put* it away? Aye, if you like." And he dropped it back into his shirt.

Several of the vampires lunged forward immediately, their fang-choked mouths twisting in what might have been grins. Callahan held his hands out toward them. The fingers (and the barrel of the Ruger) glowed, as if they had been dipped into blue fire. The eyes of the turtle had likewise filled with light; its shell shone.

"Stand away from me!" Callahan cried. "The power of God and the White commands you!"

SEVEN

When the terrible shaman turned to face the Grandfathers, Meiman of the taheen felt the Turtle's awful, lovely glammer lessen a bit. He saw that the boy was gone, and that filled him with dismay, yet at least he'd gone further in rather than slipping out, so that might still be all right. But if the boy found the door to Fedic and used it, Meiman might find himself in very bad trouble, indeed. For Sayre answered to Walter o' Dim, and Walter answered only to the Crimson King himself.

Never mind. One thing at a time. Settle the shaman's hash first. Turn the Grandfathers loose on him. Then go after the boy, perhaps shouting that his friend wanted him after all, that might work—

Meiman (the Canaryman to Mia, Tweety Bird to Jake) crept forward, grasping Andrew—the fat man in the tux with the plaid lapels—with one hand and Andrew's even fatter jilly with the other. He gestured at Callahan's turned back.

Tirana shook her head vehemently. Meiman opened his beak and hissed at her. She shrank away from him. Detta Walker had already gotten her fingers into the mask Tirana wore and it hung in shreds about her jaw and neck. In the middle of her forehead, a red wound opened and closed like the gill of a dying fish.

Meiman turned to Andrew, released him long enough to point at the shaman, then drew the talon that served him as a hand across his feathered throat in a grimly expressive gesture. Andrew nodded and brushed away his wife's pudgy hands when they tried to restrain him. The mask of humanity was good enough to show the low man in the garish tuxedo visibly gathering his courage. Then he leaped forward with a strangled cry, seizing Callahan around the neck not with his hands but his fat forearms. At the same moment his jilly lunged and struck the ivory turtle from the Pere's hand, screaming as she did so. The *sköldpadda* tumbled to the red rug, bounced beneath one of the tables, and there (like a certain paper boat some of you may remember) passes out of this tale forever.

The Grandfathers still held back, as did the Type Three vampires who had been dining in the public room, but the low men and women sensed weakness and moved in, first hesitantly, then with growing confidence. They surrounded Callahan, paused, and then fell on him in all their numbers.

"Let me go in God's name!" Callahan cried, but of course it did no good. Unlike the vampires, the things with the red wounds in their foreheads did not respond to the name of Callahan's God. All he could do was hope Jake wouldn't stop, let alone double back; that he and Oy would go like the wind to Susannah. Save her if they could. Die with her if they could not. And kill her baby, if chance allowed. God help him, but he had been wrong about that. They should have snuffed out the baby's life back in the Calla, when they had the chance.

Something bit deeply into his neck. The vampires would come now, cross or no cross. They'd fall on him like the sharks they were once they got their first whiff of his life's blood. *Help me God, give me strength,* Callahan thought, and felt the strength flow into him. He rolled to his left as claws ripped into his shirt, tearing it to ribbons. For a moment his right hand was free, and the Ruger was still in it. He turned it toward the working,

sweaty, hate-congested face of the fat one named Andrew and placed the barrel of the gun (bought for home protection in the long-distant past by Jake's more than a little paranoid TV-executive father) against the soft red wound in the center of the low man's forehead.

"No-ooo, you daren't!" Tirana cried, and as she reached for the gun, the front of her gown finally burst, spilling her massive breasts free. They were covered with coarse fur.

Callahan pulled the trigger. The Ruger's report was deafening in the dining room. Andrew's head exploded like a gourd filled with blood, spraying the creatures who had been crowding in behind him. There were screams of horror and disbelief. Callahan had time to think, *It wasn't supposed to be this way, was it?* And: *Is it enough to put me in the club? Am I a gunslinger yet?*

Perhaps not. But there was the bird-man, standing right in front of him between two tables, its beak opening and closing, its throat beating visibly with excitement.

Smiling, propping himself on one elbow as blood pumped onto the carpet from his torn throat, Callahan leveled Jake's Ruger.

"No!" Meiman cried, raising his misshapen hands to his face in an utterly fruitless gesture of protection. *"No, you CAN'T—"*

Can so, Callahan thought with childish glee, and fired again. Meiman took two stumble-steps backward, then a third. He struck a table and collapsed on top of it. Three yellow feathers hung above him on the air, seesawing lazily.

Callahan heard savage howls, not of anger or fear but of hunger. The aroma of blood had finally penetrated the old ones' jaded nostrils, and nothing would stop them now. So, if he didn't want to join them—

Pere Callahan, once Father Callahan of 'Salem's Lot, turned the Ruger's muzzle on himself. He wasted no time looking for eternity in the darkness of the barrel but placed it deep against the shelf of his chin.

"Hile, Roland!" he said, and knew
(*the wave they are lifted by the wave*)
that he was heard. "Hile, gunslinger!"

His finger tightened on the trigger as the ancient monsters fell upon him. He was buried in the reek of their cold and bloodless breath, but not daunted by it. He had never felt so strong. Of all the years in his life he had been happiest when he had been a simple vagrant, not a priest but only Callahan o' the Roads, and felt that soon he would be let free to resume that life and wander as he would, his duties fulfilled, and that was well.

"May you find your Tower, Roland, and breach it, *and may you climb to the top!*"

The teeth of his old enemies, these ancient brothers and sisters of a thing which had called itself Kurt Barlow, sank into him like stingers. Callahan felt them not at all. He was smiling as he pulled the trigger and escaped them for good.

Chapter II:
Lifted on the Wave

On their way out along the dirt camp-road which had taken them to the writer's house in the town of Bridgton, Eddie and Roland came upon an orange pickup truck with the words CENTRAL MAINE POWER MAINTENANCE painted on the sides. Nearby, a man in a yellow hardhat and an orange high-visibility vest was cutting branches that threatened the low-hanging electrical lines. And did Eddie feel something then, some gathering force? Maybe a precursor of the wave rushing down the Path of the Beam toward them? He later thought so, but couldn't say for sure. God knew he'd been in a weird enough mood already, and why not? How many people got to meet their creators? Well . . . Stephen King *hadn't* created Eddie Dean, a young man whose Co-Op City happened to be in Brooklyn rather than the Bronx—not yet, not in that year of 1977, but Eddie felt certain that in time King would. How else could he be here?

Eddie nipped in ahead of the power-truck, got out, and asked the sweating man with the brush-hog in his hands for directions to Turtleback Lane, in the town of Lovell. The Central Maine Power guy passed on the directions willingly enough, then added: "If you're serious about going to Lovell today, you're gonna have to use Route 93. The Bog Road, some folks call it."

He raised a hand to Eddie and shook his head like a man forestalling an argument, although Eddie had not in fact said a word since asking his original question.

"It's seven miles longer, I know, and jouncy as a bugger, but you can't get through East Stoneham today. Cops've got it

17

blocked off. State Bears, local yokels, even the Oxford County Sheriff's Department."

"You're kidding," Eddie said. It seemed a safe enough response.

The power guy shook his head grimly. "No one seems to know exactly what's up, but there's been shootin—automatic weapons, maybe—and explosions." He patted the battered and sawdusty walkie-talkie clipped to his belt. "I've even heard the t-word once or twice this afternoon. Not s'prised, either."

Eddie had no idea what the t-word might be, but knew Roland wanted to get going. He could feel the gunslinger's impatience in his head; could almost see Roland's impatient finger-twirling gesture, the one that meant *Let's go, let's go.*

"I'm talking 'bout terrorism," the power guy said, then lowered his voice. "People don't think shit like that can happen in America, buddy, but I got news for you, it can. If not today, then sooner or later. Someone's gonna blow up the Statue of Liberty or the Empire State Building, that's what I think—the right-wingers, the left-wingers, or the goddam A-rabs. Too many crazy people."

Eddie, who had a nodding acquaintance with ten more years of history than this fellow, nodded. "You're probably right. In any case, thanks for the info."

"Just tryin to save you some time." And, as Eddie opened the driver's-side door of John Cullum's Ford sedan: "You been in a fight, mister? You look kinda bunged up. Also you're limping."

Eddie had been in a fight, all right: had been grooved in the arm and plugged in the right calf. Neither wound was serious, and in the forward rush of events he had nearly forgotten them. Now they hurt all over again. Why in God's name had he turned down Aaron Deepneau's bottle of Percocet tablets?

"Yeah," he said, "that's why I'm going to Lovell. Guy's dog bit me. He and I are going to have a talk about it." Bizarre story, didn't have much going for it in the way of plot, but he was no writer. That was King's job. In any case, it was good enough to get him back behind the wheel of Cullum's Ford Galaxie before the power guy could ask him any more questions, and Eddie reckoned that made it a success. He drove away quickly.

"You got directions?" Roland asked.

"Yeah."

"Good. Everything's breaking at once, Eddie. We have to get to Susannah as fast as we can. Jake and Pere Callahan, too. And the baby's coming, whatever it is. May have come already."

Turn right when you get back out to Kansas Road, the power guy had told Eddie (Kansas as in Dorothy, Toto, and Auntie Em, everything breaking at once), and he did. That put them rolling north. The sun had gone behind the trees on their left, throwing the two-lane blacktop entirely into shadow. Eddie had an almost palpable sense of time slipping through his fingers like some fabulously expensive cloth that was too smooth to grip. He stepped on the gas and Cullum's old Ford, although wheezy in the valves, walked out a little. Eddie got it up to fifty-five and pegged it there. More speed might have been possible, but Kansas Road was both twisty and badly maintained.

Roland had taken a sheet of notepaper from his shirt pocket, unfolded it, and was now studying it (although Eddie doubted if the gunslinger could actually read much of the document; this world's written words would always be mostly mystery to him). At the top of the paper, above Aaron Deepneau's rather shaky but perfectly legible handwriting (and Calvin Tower's all-important signature), was a smiling cartoon beaver and the words DAM IMPORTANT THINGS TO DO. A silly pun if ever there was one.

I don't like silly questions, I won't play silly games, Eddie thought, and suddenly grinned. It was a point of view to which Roland still held, Eddie felt quite sure, notwithstanding the fact that, while riding Blaine the Mono, their lives had been saved by a few well-timed silly questions. Eddie opened his mouth to point out that what might well turn out to be the most important document in the history of the world—more important than the Magna Carta or the Declaration of Independence or Albert Einstein's Theory of Relativity—was headed by a dumb pun, and how did Roland like them apples? Before he could get out a single word, however, the wave struck.

TWO

His foot slipped off the gas pedal, and that was good. If it had stayed on, both he and Roland would surely have been injured, maybe killed. When the wave came, staying in control of John Cullum's Ford Galaxie dropped all the way off Eddie Dean's list of priorities. It was like that moment when the roller coaster has reached the top of its first mountain, hesitates a moment . . . tilts . . . *plunges* . . . and you fall with a sudden blast of hot summer air in your face and a pressure against your chest and your stomach floating somewhere behind you.

In that moment Eddie saw everything in Cullum's car had come untethered and was floating—pipe ashes, two pens and a paperclip from the dashboard, Eddie's dinh, and, he realized, his dinh's ka-mai, good old Eddie Dean. No wonder he had lost his stomach! (He wasn't aware that the car itself, which had drifted to a stop at the side of the road, was also floating, tilting lazily back and forth five or six inches above the ground like a small boat on an invisible sea.)

Then the tree-lined country road was gone. Bridgton was gone. The world was gone. There was the sound of todash chimes, repulsive and nauseating, making him want to grit his teeth in protest . . . except his teeth were gone, too.

THREE

Like Eddie, Roland had a clear sense of being first *lifted* and then *hung,* like something that had lost its ties to Earth's gravity. He heard the chimes and felt himself elevated through the wall of existence, but he understood this wasn't real todash—at least not of the sort they'd experienced before. This was very likely what Vannay called *aven kal,* words which meant *lifted on the wind* or *carried on the wave.* Only the *kal* form, instead of the more usual *kas,* indicated a natural force of disastrous proportions: not a wind but a hurricane; not a wave but a *tsunami.*

The very Beam means to speak to you, Gabby, Vannay said in his mind—Gabby, the old sarcastic nickname Vannay had adopted because Steven Deschain's boy was so close-mouthed. His limping, brilliant tutor had stopped using it (probably at Cort's insistence) the year Roland had turned eleven. *You would do well to listen if it does.*

I will listen very well, Roland replied, and was dropped. He gagged, weightless and nauseated.

More chimes. Then, suddenly, he was floating again, this time above a room filled with empty beds. One look was enough to assure him that this was where the Wolves brought the children they kidnapped from the Borderland Callas. At the far end of the room—

A hand grasped his arm, a thing Roland would have thought impossible in this state. He looked to his left and saw Eddie beside him, floating naked. They were both naked, their clothes left behind in the writer's world.

Roland had already seen what Eddie was pointing to. At the far end of the room, a pair of beds had been pushed together. A white woman lay on one of them. Her legs—the very ones Susannah had used on their todash visit to New York, Roland had no doubt—were spread wide. A woman with the head of a rat—one of the taheen, he felt sure—bent between them.

Next to the white woman was a dark-skinned one whose legs ended just below the knees. Floating naked or not, nauseated or not, todash or not, Roland had never in his life been so glad to see anyone. And Eddie felt the same. Roland heard him cry out joyfully in the center of his head and reached a hand to still the younger man. He *had* to still him, for Susannah was looking at them, had almost certainly seen them, and if she spoke to them, he needed to hear every word she said. Because although those words would come from her mouth, it would very likely be the Beam that spoke; the Voice of the Bear or that of the Turtle.

Both women wore metal hoods over their hair. A length of segmented steel hose connected them.

Some kind of Vulcan mind-meld, Eddie said, once again filling the center of his head and blotting out everything else. *Or maybe—*

Hush! Roland broke in. *Hush, Eddie, for your father's sake!*

A man wearing a white coat seized a pair of cruel-looking forceps from a tray and pushed the rathead taheen nurse aside. He bent, peering up between Mia's legs and holding the forceps above his head. Standing close by, wearing a tee-shirt with words of Eddie and Susannah's world on it, was a taheen with the head of a fierce brown bird.

He'll sense us, Roland thought. *If we stay long enough, he'll surely sense us and raise the alarm.*

But Susannah was looking at him, the eyes below the clamp of the hood feverish. Bright with understanding. *Seeing* them, aye, say true.

She spoke a single word, and in a moment of inexplicable but perfectly reliable intuition, Roland understood the word came not from Susannah but from Mia. Yet it was also the Voice of the Beam, a force perhaps sentient enough to understand how seriously it was threatened, and to want to protect itself.

Chassit was the word Susannah spoke; he heard it in his head because they were ka-tet and an-tet; he also saw it form soundlessly on her lips as she looked up toward the place where they floated, onlookers at something that was happening in some other where and when at this very moment.

The hawk-headed taheen looked up, perhaps following her gaze, perhaps hearing the chimes with its preternaturally sharp ears. Then the doctor lowered his forceps and thrust them beneath Mia's gown. She shrieked. Susannah shrieked with her. And as if Roland's essentially bodiless being could be pushed away by the force of those combined screams like a milkweed pod lifted and carried on a gust of October wind, the gunslinger felt himself rise violently, losing touch with this place as he went, but holding onto that one word. It brought with it a brilliant memory of his mother leaning over him as he lay in bed. In the room of many colors, this had been, the nursery, and of course now he understood the colors he'd only accepted as a young boy, accepted as children barely out of their clouts accept everything: with unquestioning wonder, with the unspoken assumption that it's *all* magic.

The windows of the nursery had been stained glass representing the Bends o' the Rainbow, of course. He remembered his mother leaning toward him, her face pied with that lovely various light, her hood thrown back so he could trace the curve of her neck with the eye of a child

(*it's* all *magic*)

and the soul of a lover; he remembered thinking how he would court her and win her from his father, if she would have him; how they would marry and have children of their own and live forever in that fairy-tale kingdom called the All-A-Glow; and how she sang to him, how Gabrielle Deschain sang to her little boy with his big eyes looking solemnly up at her from his pillow and his face already stamped with the many swimming colors of his wandering life, singing a lilting nonsense song that went like this:

> *Baby-bunting, baby-dear,*
> *Baby, bring your berries here.*
> *Chussit, chissit, chassit!*
> *Bring enough to fill your basket!*

Enough to fill my basket, he thought as he was flung, weightless, through darkness and the terrible sound of the todash chimes. The words weren't quite nonsense but old numbers, she'd told him once when he had asked. *Chussit, chissit, chassit:* seventeen, eighteen, nineteen.

Chassit is nineteen, he thought. *Of course, it's all nineteen.* Then he and Eddie were in light again, a fever-sick orange light, and there were Jake and Callahan. He even saw Oy standing at Jake's left heel, his fur bushed out and his muzzle wrinkled back to show his teeth.

Chussit, chissit, chassit, Roland thought as he looked at his son, a boy so small and terribly outnumbered in the dining room of the Dixie Pig. *Chassit is nineteen. Enough to fill my basket. But what basket? What does it mean?*

FOUR

Beside Kansas Road in Bridgton, John Cullum's twelve-year-old Ford (a hundred and six thousand on the odometer and she was just getting wa'amed up, Cullum liked to tell people) seesawed lazily back and forth above the soft shoulder, front tires touching down and then rising so the back tires could briefly kiss the dirt. Inside, two men who appeared not only unconscious but *transparent* rolled lazily with the car's motion like corpses in a sunken boat. And around them floated the debris which collects in any old car that's been hard-used: the ashes and pens and paperclips and the world's oldest peanut and a penny from the back seat and pine needles from the floormats and even one of the floormats itself. In the darkness of the glove compartment, objects rattled timidly against the closed door.

Someone passing would undoubtedly have been thunder-struck at the sight of all this stuff—and people! people who *might be dead!*—floating around in the car like jetsam in a space capsule. But no one *did* come along. Those who lived on this side of Long Lake were mostly looking across the water toward the East Stoneham side even though there was really nothing over there to see any longer. Even the smoke was almost gone.

Lazily the car floated and inside it, Roland of Gilead rose slowly to the ceiling, where his neck pressed against the dirty roof-liner and his legs cleared the front seat to trail out behind him. Eddie was first held in place by the wheel, but then some random sideways motion of the car slid him free and he also rose, his face slack and dreaming. A silver line of drool escaped the corner of his mouth and floated, shining and full of minus-cule bubbles, beside one blood-crusted cheek.

FIVE

Roland knew that Susannah had seen him, had probably seen Eddie, as well. That was why she'd labored so hard to speak that single word. Jake and Callahan, however, saw neither of them.

The boy and the Pere had entered the Dixie Pig, a thing that was either very brave or very foolish, and now all of their concentration was necessarily focused on what they'd found there.

Foolhardy or not, Roland was fiercely proud of Jake. He saw the boy had established canda between himself and Callahan: that distance (never the same in any two situations) which assures that a pair of outnumbered gunslingers cannot be killed by a single shot. Both had come ready to fight. Callahan was holding Jake's gun . . . and another thing, as well: some sort of carving. Roland was almost sure it was a can-tah, one of the little gods. The boy had Susannah's 'Rizas and their tote-sack, retrieved from only the gods knew where.

The gunslinger spied a fat woman whose humanity ended at the neck. Above her trio of flabby chins, the mask she'd been wearing hung in ruins. Looking at the rathead beneath, Roland suddenly understood a good many things. Some might have come clearly to him sooner, had not his attention—like that of the boy and the Pere at this very moment—been focused on other matters.

Callahan's low men, for instance. They might well be taheen, creatures neither of the *Prim* nor of the natural world but misbegotten things from somewhere between the two. They certainly weren't the sort of beings Roland called slow mutants, for those had arisen as a result of the old ones' ill-advised wars and disastrous experiments. No, they might be genuine taheen, sometimes known as the third people or the can-toi, and yes, Roland should have known. How many of the taheen now served the being known as the Crimson King? Some? Many?

All?

If the third answer was the correct one, Roland reckoned the road to the Tower would be difficult indeed. But to look beyond the horizon was not much in the gunslinger's nature, and in this case his lack of imagination was surely a blessing.

SIX

He saw what he needed to see. Although the can-toi—
Callahan's low folk—had surrounded Jake and Callahan on all
sides (the two of them hadn't even seen the duo behind them,
the ones who'd been guarding the doors to Sixty-first Street),
the Pere had frozen them with the carving, just as Jake had been
able to freeze and fascinate people with the key he'd found in
the vacant lot. A yellow taheen with the body of a man and the
head of a waseau had some sort of gun near at hand but made
no effort to grab it.

Yet there was another problem, one Roland's eye, trained to
see every possible snare and ambush, fixed upon at once. He
saw the blasphemous parody of Eld's Last Fellowship on the wall
and understood its significance completely in the seconds
before it was ripped away. And the smell: not just flesh but
human flesh. This too he would have understood earlier, had he
had time to think about it . . . only life in Calla Bryn Sturgis had
allowed him little time to think. In the Calla, as in a storybook,
life had been one damned thing after another.

Yet it was clear enough now, wasn't it? The low folk might
only be taheen; a child's ogres, if it did ya. Those behind the
tapestry were what Callahan had called Type One vampires and
what Roland himself knew as the Grandfathers, perhaps the
most gruesome and powerful survivors of the *Prim*'s long-ago
recession. And while such as the taheen might be content to
stand as they were, gawking at the sigul Callahan held up, the
Grandfathers wouldn't spare it a second glance.

Now clattering bugs came pouring out from under the
table. They were of a sort Roland had seen before, and any
doubts he might still have held about what was behind that
tapestry departed at the sight of them. They were parasites,
blood-drinkers, camp-followers: Grandfather-fleas. Probably
not dangerous while there was a bumbler present, but of course
when you spied the little doctors in such numbers, the Grandfathers were never far behind.

As Oy charged at the bugs, Roland of Gilead did the only thing he could think of: he swam down to Callahan.

Into Callahan.

SEVEN

Pere, I am here.

Aye, Roland. What—

No time. GET HIM OUT OF HERE. You must. Get him out while there's still time!

EIGHT

And Callahan tried. The boy, of course, didn't want to go. Looking at him through the Pere's eyes, Roland thought with some bitterness: *I should have schooled him better in betrayal. Yet all the gods know I did the best I could.*

"Go while you can," Callahan told Jake, striving for calmness. "Catch up to her *if* you can. This is the command of your dinh. This is also the will of the White."

It should have moved him but it didn't, he still argued—gods, he was nearly as bad as Eddie!—and Roland could wait no longer.

Pere, let me.

Roland seized control without waiting for a reply. He could already feel the wave, the *aven kal,* beginning to recede. And the Grandfathers would come at any second.

"*Go, Jake!*" he cried, using the Pere's mouth and vocal cords like a loudspeaker. If he had thought about how one might do something like this, he would have been lost completely, but thinking about things had also never been his way, and he was grateful to see the boy's eyes flash wide. "*You have this one chance and must take it! Find her! As dinh I command you!*"

Then, as in the hospital ward with Susannah, he felt himself once more tossed upward like something without weight, blown out of Callahan's mind and body like a bit of cobweb or a fluff of dandelion thistle. For a moment he tried to flail his way back, like a swimmer trying to buck a strong current just long enough to reach the shore, but it was impossible.

Roland! That was Eddie's voice, and filled with dismay. *Jesus, Roland, what in God's name are those things?*

The tapestry had been torn aside. The creatures which rushed out were ancient and freakish, their warlock faces warped with teeth growing wild, their mouths propped open by fangs as thick as the gunslinger's wrists, their wrinkled and stubbled chins slick with blood and scraps of meat.

And still—gods, oh gods—the boy remained!

"They'll kill Oy first!" Callahan shouted, only Roland didn't think it *was* Callahan. He thought it was Eddie, using Callahan's voice as Roland had. Somehow Eddie had found either smoother currents or more strength. Enough to get inside after Roland had been blown out. *"They'll kill him in front of you and drink his blood!"*

It was finally enough. The boy turned and fled with Oy running beside him. He cut directly in front of the waseau-taheen and between two of the low *folken,* but none made any effort to grab him. They were still staring at the raised Turtle on Callahan's palm, mesmerized.

The Grandfathers paid no attention to the fleeing boy at all, as Roland had felt sure they would not. He knew from Pere Callahan's story that one of the Grandfathers had come to the little town of 'Salem's Lot where the Pere had for awhile preached. The Pere had lived through the experience—not common for those who faced such monsters after losing their weapons and siguls of power—but the thing had forced Calla-han to drink of its tainted blood before letting him go. It had marked him for these others.

Callahan was holding his cross-sigul out toward them, but before Roland could see anything else, he was exhaled back into darkness. The chimes began again, all but driving him mad with their awful tintinnabulation. Somewhere, faintly, he could hear Eddie shouting. Roland reached for him in the dark, brushed Eddie's arm, lost it, found his hand, and seized it. They rolled over and over, clutching each other, trying not to be separated, hoping not to be lost in the doorless dark between the worlds.

CHAPTER III:
EDDIE MAKES A CALL

Eddie returned to John Cullum's old car the way he'd some-times come out of nightmares as a teenager: tangled up and panting with fright, totally disoriented, not sure of who he was, let alone where.

He had a second to realize that, incredible as it seemed, he and Roland were floating in each other's arms like unborn twins in the womb, only this was no womb. A pen and a paperclip were drifting in front of his eyes. So was a yellow plastic case he recognized as an eight-track tape. *Don't waste your time, John,* he thought. *No true thread there, that's a dead-end gadget if there ever was one.*

Something was scratching the back of his neck. Was it the domelight of John Cullum's scurgy old Galaxie? By God he thought it w—

Then gravity reasserted itself and they fell, with meaningless objects raining down all around them. The floormat which had been floating around in the Ford's cabin landed draped over the steering wheel. Eddie's midsection hit the top of the front seat and air exploded out of him in a rough whoosh. Roland landed beside him, and on his bad hip. He gave a single barking cry and then began to pull himself back into the front seat.

Eddie opened his mouth to speak. Before he could, Calla-han's voice filled his head: *Hile, Roland! Hile, gunslinger!*

How much psychic effort had it cost the Pere to speak from that other world? And behind it, faint but *there*, the sound of bes-tial, triumphant cries. Howls that were not quite words.

Eddie's wide and startled eyes met Roland's faded blue

31

ones. He reached out for the gunslinger's left hand, thinking: *He's going. Great God, I think the Pere is going.*

May you find your Tower, Roland, and breach it—

"—and may you climb to the top," Eddie breathed.

They were back in John Cullum's car and parked—askew but otherwise peacefully enough—at the side of Kansas Road in the shady early-evening hours of a summer's day, but what Eddie saw was the orange hell-light of that restaurant that wasn't a restaurant at all but a den of cannibals. The thought that there could *be* such things, that people walked past their hiding place each and every day, not knowing what was inside, not feeling the greedy eyes that perhaps marked them and measured them—

Then, before he could think further, he cried out with pain as phantom teeth settled into his neck and cheeks and midriff; as his mouth was violently kissed by nettles and his testicles were skewered. He screamed, clawing at the air with his free hand, until Roland grabbed it and forced it down.

"Stop, Eddie. Stop. They're gone." A pause. The connection broke and the pain faded. Roland was right, of course. Unlike the Pere, they had escaped. Eddie saw that Roland's eyes were shiny with tears. *"He's* gone, too. The Pere."

"The vampires? You know, the cannibals? Did . . . Did they . . . ?" Eddie couldn't finish the thought. The idea of Pere Callahan as one of *them* was too awful to speak aloud.

"No, Eddie. Not at all. He—" Roland pulled the gun he still wore. The scrolled steel sides gleamed in the late light. He tucked the barrel deep beneath his chin for a moment, looking at Eddie as he did it.

"He escaped them," Eddie said.

"Aye, and how angry they must be."

Eddie nodded, suddenly exhausted. And his wounds were aching again. No, *sobbing.* "Good," he said. "Now put that thing back where it belongs before you shoot yourself with it." And as Roland did: "What just happened to us? Did we go todash or was it another Beamquake?"

"I think it was a bit of both," Roland said. "There's a thing called *aven kal*, which is like a tidal-wave that runs along the Path of the Beam. We were lifted on it."

"And allowed to see what we wanted to see."

Roland thought about this for a moment, then shook his head with great firmness. "We saw what the *Beam* wanted us to see. Where it wants us to go."

"Roland, did you study this stuff when you were a kid? Did your old pal Vannay teach classes in . . . I don't know, The Anatomy of Beams and Bends o' the Rainbow?"

Roland was smiling. "Yes, I suppose that we were taught such things in both History and Summa Logicales."

"Logicka-*what?*"

Roland didn't answer. He was looking out the window of Cullum's car, still trying to get his breath back—both the physical and the figurative. It really wasn't that hard to do, not here; being in this part of Bridgton was like being in the neighborhood of a certain vacant lot in Manhattan. Because there was a generator near here. Not sai King, as Roland had first believed, but the *potential* of sai King . . . of what sai King might be able to create, given world enough and time. Wasn't King also being carried on *aven kal*, perhaps generating the very wave that lifted him?

A man can't pull himself up by his own bootstraps no matter how hard he tries, Cort had lectured when Roland, Cuthbert, Alain, and Jamie had been little more than toddlers. Cort speaking in the tone of cheery self-assurance that had gradually hardened to harshness as his last group of lads grew toward their trials of manhood. But maybe about bootstraps Cort had been wrong. Maybe, under certain circumstances, a man *could* pull himself up by them. Or give birth to the universe from his navel, as Gan was said to have done. As a writer of stories, was King not a creator? And at bottom, wasn't creation about making something from nothing—seeing the world in a grain of sand or pulling one's self up by one's own bootstraps?

And what was he doing, sitting here and thinking long philosophical thoughts while two members of his tet were lost?

"Get this carriage going," Roland said, trying to ignore the sweet humming he could hear—whether the Voice of the Beam or the Voice of Gan the Creator, he didn't know. "We've got to get to Turtleback Lane in this town of Lovell and see if we can't find our way through to where Susannah is."

And not just for Susannah, either. If Jake succeeded in eluding the monsters in the Dixie Pig, he would also head to where she lay. Of this Roland had no doubt.

Eddie reached for the transmission lever—despite all its gyrations, Cullum's old Galaxie had never quit running—and then his hand fell away from it. He turned and looked at Roland with a bleak eye.

"What ails thee, Eddie? Whatever it is, spill it quick. The baby's coming now—may have come already. Soon they'll have no more use for her!"

"I know," Eddie said. "But we can't go to Lovell." He grimaced as if what he was saying was causing him physical pain. Roland guessed it probably was. "Not yet."

TWO

They sat quiet for a moment, listening to the sweetly tuned hum of the Beam, a hum that sometimes became joyous voices. They sat looking into the thickening shadows in the trees, where a million faces and a million stories lurked, O can you say unfound door, can you say lost.

Eddie half-expected Roland to shout at him—it wouldn't be the first time—or maybe clout him upside the head, as the gunslinger's old teacher, Cort, had been wont to do when his pupils were slow or contrary. Eddie almost hoped he would. A good shot to the jaw might clear his head, by Shardik.

Only muddy thinking's not the trouble and you know it, he thought. *Your head is clearer than his. If it wasn't, you could let go of this world and go on hunting for your lost wife.*

At last Roland spoke. "What is it, then? This?" He bent and picked up the folded piece of paper with Aaron Deepneau's pinched handwriting on it. Roland looked at it for a moment, then flicked it into Eddie's lap with a little grimace of distaste.

"You know how much I love her," Eddie said in a low, strained voice. "You *know* that."

Roland nodded, but without looking at him. He appeared to be staring down at his own broken and dusty boots, and the dirty floor of the passenger-side footwell. Those downcast eyes, that gaze which would not turn to him who'd come almost to idolize Roland of Gilead, sort of broke Eddie Dean's heart. Yet he pressed on. If there had ever been room for mistakes, it was gone now. This was the endgame.

"I'd go to her this minute if I thought it was the right thing to do. Roland, this *second!* But we *have* to finish our business in this world. Because this world is one-way. Once we leave today, July 9th, 1977, we can never come here again. We—"

"Eddie, we've been through all of this." Still not looking at him.

"Yes, but do you *understand* it? Only one bullet to shoot, one 'Riza to throw. That's why we came to Bridgton in the first place! God knows I wanted to go to Turtleback Lane as soon as John Cullum told us about it, but I thought we had to see the writer, and talk to him. And I was right, wasn't I?" Almost pleading now. *"Wasn't I?"*

Roland looked at him at last, and Eddie was glad. This was hard enough, *wretched* enough, without having to bear the turned-away, downcast gaze of his dinh.

"And it may not matter if we stay a little longer. If we concentrate on those two women lying together on those two beds, Roland—if we concentrate on Suze and Mia *as we last saw them*—then it's possible we can cut into their history at that point. Isn't it?"

After a long, considering moment during which Eddie wasn't conscious of drawing a single breath, the gunslinger nodded. Such could not happen if on Turtleback Lane they found what the gunslinger had come to think of as an "old-ones door," because such doors were *dedicated,* and always came out at the same place. But were they to find a *magic* door somewhere along Turtleback Lane in Lovell, one that had been left behind when the *Prim* receded, then yes, they might be able to cut in where they wanted. But such doors could be tricky, too; this they had found out for themselves in the Cave of Voices, when the door there had sent Jake and Callahan to New York instead of Roland and Eddie, thereby scattering all their plans into the Land of Nineteen.

"What else must we do?" Roland said. There was no anger in his voice, but to Eddie he sounded both tired and unsure.

"Whatever it is, it's gonna be hard. That much I guarantee you."

Eddie took the bill of sale and gazed at it as grimly as any Hamlet in the history of drama had ever stared upon the skull of poor Yorick. Then he looked back at Roland. "This gives us title to the vacant lot with the rose in it. We need to get it to Moses Carver of Holmes Dental Industries. And where is he? We don't know."

"For that matter, Eddie, we don't even know if he's still alive."

Eddie voiced a wild laugh. "You say true, I say thankya! Why don't I turn us around, Roland? I'll drive us back to Stephen King's house. We can cadge twenty or thirty bucks off him—because, brother, I don't know if you noticed, but we don't have a crying dime between the two of us—but more important, we can get him to write us a really good hardboiled private eye, someone who looks like Bogart and kicks ass like Clint Eastwood. Let *him* track down this guy Carver for us!"

He shook his head as if to clear it. The hum of the voices sounded sweetly in his ears, the perfect antidote to the ugly todash chimes.

"I mean, my wife is in bad trouble somewhere up the line, for all I know she's being eaten alive by vampires or vampire bugs, and here I sit beside a country road with a guy whose most basic skill is shooting people, trying to work out how I'm going to start a fucking *corporation!*"

"Slow down," Roland said. Now that he was resigned to staying in this world a little longer, he seemed calm enough. "Tell me what it is you feel we need to do before we can shake the dirt of this where and when from our heels for good."

So Eddie did.

THREE

Roland had heard a good deal of it before, but hadn't fully understood what a difficult position they were in. They owned the vacant lot on Second Avenue, yes, but their basis for ownership was a holographic document that would look mighty shaky in a court o' legal, especially if the powers-that-be from the Sombra Corporation started throwing lawyers at them.

Eddie wanted to get the writ of trade to Moses Carver, if he could, along with the information that his goddaughter, Odetta Holmes—missing for thirteen years by the summer of 1977—was alive and well and wanted above all things for Carver to assume guardianship, not just of the vacant lot itself, but of a certain rose growing wild within its borders.

Moses Carver—if still alive—had to be convinced enough by what he heard to fold the so-called Tet Corporation into Holmes Industries (or vice-versa). More! He had to dedicate what was left of his life (and Eddie had an idea Carver might be Aaron Deepneau's age by now) to building a corporate giant whose only real purpose was to thwart two other corporate giants, Sombra and North Central Positronics, at every turn. To strangle them if possible, and keep them from becoming a monster that would leave its destroyer's track across all the dying expanse of Mid-World and mortally wound the Dark Tower itself.

"Maybe we should have left the writ o' trade with sai Deepneau," Roland mused when he had heard Eddie through to the end. "At least he could have located this Carver and sought him out and told our tale for us."

"No, we did right to keep it." This was one of the few things of which Eddie was completely sure. "If we'd left this piece of paper with Aaron Deepneau, it'd be ashes in the wind by now."

"You believe Tower would have repented his bargain and talked his friend into destroying it?"

"I know it," Eddie said. "But even if Deepneau could stand up to his old friend going yatta-yatta-yatta in his ear for hours on end—'Burn it, Aaron, they coerced me and now they mean to screw me, you know it as well as I do, burn it and we'll call the cops on those *momsers*'—do you think Moses Carver would believe such a crazy story?"

Roland smiled bleakly. "I don't think his belief would be an issue, Eddie. Because, think thee a moment, how much of our crazy story has Aaron Deepneau actually *heard*?"

"Not enough," Eddie agreed. He closed his eyes and pressed the heels of his hands against them. Hard. "I can only think of one person who could actually convince Moses Carver to do the things we'd have to ask, and she's otherwise occupied. In the year of '99. And by then, Carver's gonna be as dead as Deepneau and maybe Tower himself."

"Well, what can we do without her? What will satisfy you?"

Eddie was thinking that perhaps Susannah could come back to 1977 without them, since *she*, at least, hadn't visited it yet. Well . . . she'd come here todash, but he didn't think that exactly counted. He supposed she might be barred from 1977 solely on the grounds that she was ka-tet with him and Roland. Or some other grounds. Eddie didn't know. Reading the fine print had never been his strong point. He turned to ask Roland what he thought, but Roland spoke before he got a chance.

"What about our dan-tete?" he asked.

Although Eddie understood the term—it meant baby god or little savior—he did not at first understand what Roland meant by it. Then he did. Had not their Waterford dan-tete loaned them the very car they were sitting in, say thankya? *"Cullum?* Is that who you're talking about, Roland? The guy with the case of autographed baseballs?"

"You say true," Roland replied. He spoke in that dry tone which indicated not amusement but mild exasperation. "Don't overwhelm me with your enthusiasm for the idea."

"But . . . you told him to go away! And he agreed to go!"

"And how enthusiastic would you say he was about visiting his friend in Vermong?"

"Mont," Eddie said, unable to suppress a smile. Yet, smiling or not, what he felt most strongly was dismay. He thought that

ugly scraping sound he heard in his imagination was Roland's two-fingered right hand, prospecting around at the very bottom of the barrel.

Roland shrugged as if to say he didn't care if Cullum had spoken of going to Vermont or Barony o' Garlan. "Answer my question."

"Well . . ."

Cullum actually hadn't expressed much enthusiasm for the idea at all. He had from the very first reacted more like one of *them* than one of the grass-eaters among whom he lived (Eddie recognized grass-eaters very easily, having been one himself until Roland first kidnapped him and then began his homicidal lessons). Cullum had been clearly intrigued by the gunslingers, and curious about their business in his little town. But Roland had been very emphatic about what he wanted, and folks had a way of following his orders.

Now he made a twirling motion with his right hand, his old impatient gesture. *Hurry, for your father's sake. Shit or get off the commode.*

"I guess he really didn't *want* to go," Eddie said. "But that doesn't mean he's still at his house in East Stoneham."

"He is, though. He *didn't* go."

Eddie managed to keep his mouth from dropping open only with some effort. "How can you know that? Can you touch him, is that it?"

Roland shook his head.

"Then how—"

"Ka."

"Ka? *Ka?* Just what the fuck does *that* mean?"

Roland's face was haggard and tired, the skin pale beneath his tan. "Who else do we know in this part of the world?"

"No one, but—"

"Then it's him." Roland spoke flatly, as if stating some obvious fact of life for a child: up is over your head, down is where your feet stick to the earth.

Eddie got ready to tell him that was stupid, nothing more than rank superstition, then didn't. Putting aside Deepneau,

Tower, Stephen King, and the hideous Jack Andolini, John Cullum *was* the only person they knew in this part of the world (or on this level of the Tower, if you preferred to think of it that way). And, after the things Eddie had seen in the last few months—hell, in the last *week*—who was he to sneer at superstition?

"All right," Eddie said. "I guess we better try it."

"How do we get in touch?"

"We can phone him from Bridgton. But in a story, Roland, a minor character like John Cullum would *never* come in off the bench to save the day. It wouldn't be considered realistic."

"In life," Roland said, "I'm sure it happens all the time."

And Eddie laughed. What the hell else could you do? It was just so perfectly *Roland.*

FOUR

**BRIDGTON HIGH STREET 1
HIGHLAND LAKE 2
HARRISON 3
WATERFORD 6
SWEDEN 9
LOVELL 18
FRYEBURG 24**

They had just passed this sign when Eddie said, "Root around in the glove-compartment a little, Roland. See if ka or the Beam or whatever left us a little spare change for the pay phone."

"Glove—? Do you mean this panel here?"

"Yeah."

Roland first tried to turn the chrome button on the front, then got with the program and pushed it. The inside was a mare's nest that hadn't been improved by the Galaxie's brief period of weightlessness. There were credit card receipts, a very old tube of what Eddie identified as "tooth-paste" (Roland could make out the words **HOLMES DENTAL** on it quite clearly), a fottergraff showing a smiling little girl—Cullum's niece, mayhap—on a pony, a stick of what he first took for explosive (Eddie said it was a road flare, for emergencies), a magazine that appeared to be called YANKME . . . and a cigar-box. Roland couldn't quite make out the word on this, although he thought it might be *trolls*. He showed the box to Eddie, whose eyes lit up.

"That says TOLLS," he said. "Maybe you're right about Cullum and ka. Open it up, Roland, do it please ya."

The child who had given this box as a gift had crafted a loving (and rather clumsy) catch on the front to hold it closed. Roland slipped the catch, opened the box, and showed Eddie a great many silver coins. "Is it enough to call sai Cullum's house?"

"Yeah," Eddie said. "Looks like enough to call Fairbanks, Alaska. It won't help us a bit, though, if Cullum's on the road to Vermont."

FIVE

The Bridgton town square was bounded by a drug store and a pizza-joint on one side; a movie theater (The Magic Lantern) and a department store (Reny's) on the other. Between the theater and the department store was a little plaza equipped with benches and three pay phones.

Eddie swept through Cullum's box of toll-change and gave Roland six dollars in quarters. "I want you to go over there," he said, pointing at the drug store, "and get me a tin of aspirin. Will you know it when you see it?"

"Astin. I'll know it."

"The smallest size they have is what I want, because six bucks really isn't much money. Then go next door, to that place that says Bridgton Pizza and Sandwiches. If you've still got at least sixteen of those money-coins left, tell them you want a hoagie."

Roland nodded, which wasn't good enough for Eddie. "Let me hear you say it."

"Hoggie."

"Hoagie."

"HOOG-gie."

"Ho—" Eddie quit. "Roland, let me hear you say 'poor-boy.'"

"Poor boy."

"Good. If you have at least sixteen quarters left, ask for a poorboy. Can you say 'lots of mayo'?"

"Lots of mayo."

"Yeah. If you have less than sixteen, ask for a salami and cheese sandwich. *Sandwich,* not a popkin."

"Salommy sanditch."

"Close enough. And don't say anything else unless you absolutely have to."

Roland nodded. Eddie was right, it would be better if he did not speak. People only had to look at him to know, in their secret hearts, that he wasn't from these parts. They also had a tendency to step away from him. Better he not exacerbate that.

The gunslinger dropped a hand to his left hip as he turned toward the street, an old habit that paid no comfort this time; both revolvers were in the trunk of Cullum's Galaxie, wrapped in their cartridge belts.

Before he could get going again, Eddie grabbed his shoulder. The gunslinger swung round, eyebrows raised, faded eyes on his friend.

"We have a saying in our world, Roland—we say so-and-so was grasping at straws."

"And what does it mean?"

"This," Eddie said bleakly. "What we're doing. Wish me good luck, fella."

Roland nodded. "Aye, so I do. Both of us."

He began to turn away and Eddie called him back again. This time Roland wore an expression of faint impatience.

"Don't get killed crossing the street," Eddie said, and then briefly mimicked Cullum's way of speaking. "Summah folks're thicker'n ticks on a dog. And they're not ridin hosses."

"Make your call, Eddie," Roland said, and then crossed

Bridgton's high street with slow confidence, walking in the same rolling gait that had taken him across a thousand other high streets in a thousand small towns.

Eddie watched him, then turned to the telephone and consulted the directions. After that he lifted the receiver and dialed the number for Directory Assistance.

SIX

He didn't go, the gunslinger had said, speaking of John Cullum with flat certainty. *And why? Because Cullum was the end of the line, there was no one else for them to call.* Roland of Gilead's damned old *ka,* in other words.

After a brief wait, the Directory Assistance operator coughed up Cullum's number. Eddie tried to memorize it — he'd always been good at remembering numbers, Henry had sometimes called him Little Einstein — but this time he couldn't be confident of his ability. Something seemed to have happened either to his thinking processes in general (which he didn't believe) or to his ability to remember certain artifacts of this world (which he sort of did). As he asked for the number a second time — and wrote it in the gathered dust on the phone kiosk's little ledge — Eddie found himself wondering if he'd still be able to read a novel, or follow the plot of a movie from the succession of images on a screen. He rather doubted it. And what did it matter? The Magic Lantern next door was showing *Star Wars,* and Eddie thought that if he made it to the end of his life's path and into the clearing without another look at Luke Skywalker and another listen to Darth Vader's noisy breathing, he'd still be pretty much okay.

"Thanks, ma'am," he told the operator, and was about to dial again when there was a series of explosions behind him. Eddie whirled, heart-rate spiking, right hand dipping, expecting to see Wolves, or harriers, or maybe that son of a bitch Flagg —

What he saw was a convertible filled with laughing, goofy-faced high school boys with sunburned cheeks. One of them had just tossed out a string of firecrackers left over from the Fourth of July—what kids their age in Calla Bryn Sturgis would have called bangers.

If I'd had a gun on my hip, I might have shot a couple of those bucks, Eddie thought. *You want to talk goofy, start with that.* Yes. Well. And maybe he might not have. Either way, he had to admit the possibility that he was no longer exactly safe in the more civilized quarters.

"Live with it," Eddie murmured, then added the great sage and eminent junkie's favorite advice for life's little problems: *"Deal."*

He dialed John Cullum's number on the old-fashioned rotary phone, and when a robot voice—Blaine the Mono's great-great-great-great-great-grandmother, mayhap—asked him to deposit ninety cents, Eddie dropped in a buck. What the hell, he was saving the world.

The phone rang once . . . rang twice . . . and was picked up!

"John!" Eddie almost yelled. "Good fucking deal! John, this is—"

But the voice on the other end was already speaking. As a child of the late eighties, Eddie knew this did not bode well.

"—have reached John Cullum of Cullum Caretakin and Camp Checkin," said Cullum's voice in its familiar slow Yankee drawl. "I gut called away kinda sudden, don'tcha know, and can't say with any degree a' certainty just when I'll be back. If this inconveniences ya, I beg pa'aad'n, but you c'n call Gary Crowell, at 926-5555, or Junior Barker, at 929-4211."

Eddie's initial dismay had departed—depaa-aated, Cullum himself would have said—right around the time the man's wavery recorded voice was telling Eddie that he, Cullum, couldn't say with any degree of certainty when he'd be back. Because Cullum was right there, in his hobbity little cottage on the western shore of Keywadin Pond, either sitting on his over-stuffed hobbity sofa or in one of the two similarly overstuffed hobbity chairs. Sitting there and monitoring messages on his no-doubt-clunky mid-seventies answering machine. And Eddie knew this because . . . well . . .

Because he just knew.

The primitive recording couldn't completely hide the sly humor that had crept into Cullum's voice by the end of the message. "Coss, if you're still set on talkin to nobody but yours truly, you c'n leave me a message at the beep. Keep it short." The final word came out *shawt.*

Eddie waited for the beep and then said, "It's Eddie Dean, John. I know you're there, and I think you've been waiting for my call. Don't ask me *why* I think that, because I don't really know, but—"

There was a loud click in Eddie's ear, and then Cullum's voice—his *live* voice—said, "Hello there, son, you takin good care of my car?"

For a moment Eddie was too bemused to reply, for Cullum's Downeast accent had turned the question into something quite different: *You takin good care of my ka?*

"Boy?" Cullum asked, suddenly concerned. "You still on the wire?"

"Yeah," Eddie said, "and so are you. I thought you were going to Vermont, John."

"Well, I tell you what. This place ain't seen a day this excitin prob'ly since South Stoneham Shoe burnt down in 1923. The cops've gut all the ruds out of town blocked off."

Eddie was sure they were letting folks through the road-blocks if they could show proper identification, but he ignored that issue in favor of something else. "Want to tell me you couldn't find your way out of that town without seeing a single cop, if it suited your fancy?"

There was a brief pause. In it, Eddie became aware of someone at his elbow. He didn't turn to look; it was Roland. Who else in this world would smell—subtly but unquestionably—of another world?

"Oh, well," Cullum said at last. "Maybe I *do* know a woods road or two that come out over in Lovell. It's been a dry summer, n I guess I could get m'truck up em."

"One or two?"

"Well, say three or four." A pause, which Eddie didn't break.

He was having too much fun. "Five or six," Cullum amended, and Eddie chose not to respond to this, either. "Eight," Cullum said at last, and when Eddie laughed, Cullum joined in. "What's on your mind, son?"

Eddie glanced at Roland, who was holding out a tin of aspirin between the two remaining fingers of his right hand. Eddie took it gratefully. "I want you to come over to Lovell," he said to Cullum. "Seems like we might have a little more palavering to do, after all."

"Ayuh, and it seems like I musta known it," Cullum said, "although it was never right up on the top of my mind; up there I kep' thinkin 'I'll be gettin on the road to Montpelier soon,' and still I kep' findin one more thing and one more thing to do around here. If you'da called five minutes ago, you woulda gotten a busy—I 'us on the phone to Charlie Beemer. It was his wife 'n sister-in-law that got killed in the market, don't you know. And then I thought, 'What the hell, I'll just give the whole place a good sweep before I put my gear in the back of the truck and go.' Nothin up on top is what I'm sayin, but down underneath I guess I been waitin for your call ever since I got back here. Where'll you be? Turtleback Lane?"

Eddie popped open the aspirin tin and looked greedily at the little line-up of tablets. Once a junkie, always a junkie, he reckoned. Even when it came to this stuff. "Ayuh," he said, with his tongue only partly in his cheek; he had become quite the mimic of regional dialects since meeting Roland on a Delta jet descending into Kennedy Airport. "You said that lane was nothing but a two-mile loop off Route 7, didn't you?"

"So I did. Some very nice homes along Turtleback." A brief, reflective pause. "And a lot of em for sale. There's been quite a number of walk-ins in that part of the world just lately. As I may have also mentioned. Such things make folks nervous, and rich folks, at least, c'n afford to get away from what makes it ha'ad to sleep at night."

Eddie could wait no longer; he took three of the aspirin and tossed them into his mouth, relishing the bitter taste as they dissolved on his tongue. Bad as the pain currently was, he would have borne twice as much if he could have heard from Susannah. But she was quiet. He had an idea that the line of communication between them, chancy at best, had ceased to exist with the coming of Mia's damned baby.

"You boys might want to keep your shootin irons close at hand if you're headed over to Turtleback in Lovell," Cullum said. "As for me, I think I'll just toss m'shotgun in m'truck before I set sail."

"Why not?" Eddie agreed. "You want to look for your car along the loop, okay? You'll find it."

"Ayuh, that old Galaxie's ha'ad to miss," Cullum agreed. "Tell me somethin, son. I'm not goin to V'mont, but I gut a feelin you mean to send me somewhere, if I agree to go. You mind tellin me where?"

Eddie thought that Mark Twain might elect to call the next chapter of John Cullum's no doubt colorful life *A Maine Yankee in the Crimson King's Court*, but elected not to say so. "Have you ever been to New York City?"

"Gorry, yes. Had a forty-eight-hour pass there, when I was in the Army." The final word came out in a ridiculously flat drawl. "Went to Radio City Music Hall and the Empire State Buildin, that much I remember. Musta made a few other tourist stops, though, because I lost thirty dollars out of m'wallet and a couple of months later I got diagnosed with a pretty fine case of the clap."

"This time you'll be too busy to catch the clap. Bring your credit cards. I know you have some, because I got a look at the receipts in your glove-compartment." He felt an almost insane urge to draw the last word out, make it *compaa-aaaatment*.

"Mess in there, ennit?" Cullum asked equably.

"Ayuh, looks like what was left when the dog chewed the shoes. See you in Lovell, John." Eddie hung up. He looked at the bag Roland was carrying and lifted his eyebrows.

"It's a poorboy sanditch," Roland said. "With lots of mayo, whatever that is. I'd want a sauce that didn't look quite so much like come, myself, but may it do ya fine."

Eddie rolled his eyes. "Gosh, that's a real appetite-builder."

"Do you say so?"

Eddie had to remind himself once more that Roland had almost no sense of humor. "I do, I do. Come on. I can eat my come-and-cheese sandwich while I drive. Also, we need to talk about how we're going to handle this."

SEVEN

The way to handle it, both agreed, was to tell John Cullum as much of their tale as they thought his credulity (and sanity) could stand. Then, if all went well, they would entrust him with the vital bill of sale and send him to Aaron Deepneau. With strict orders to make sure he spoke to Deepneau apart from the not entirely trustworthy Calvin Tower.

"Cullum and Deepneau can work together to track Moses Carver down," Eddie said, "and I think I can give Cullum enough information about Suze—private stuff—to convince Carver that she's still alive. After that, though . . . well, a lot depends on how convincing those two guys can be. And how eager they are to work for the Tet Corporation in their sunset years. Hey, they may surprise us! I can't see Cullum in a suit and tie, but traveling around the country and throwing monkey-wrenches in Sombra's business?" He considered, head cocked, then nodded with a smile. "Yeah. I can see that pretty well."

"Susannah's godfather is apt to be an old codger himself," Roland observed. "Just one of a different color. Such fellows often speak their own language when they're an-tet. And may-hap I can give John Cullum something that will help convince Carver to throw in with us."

"A sigul?"

"Yes."

Eddie was intrigued. "What kind?"

But before Roland could answer, they saw something that made Eddie stomp on the brake-pedal. They were in Lovell now, and on Route 7. Ahead of them, staggering unsteadily along the shoulder, was an old man with snarled and straggly white hair. He wore a clumsy wrap of dirty cloth that could by no means be called a robe. His scrawny arms and legs were whipped with scratches. There were sores on them as well, burning a dull red. His feet were bare, and equipped with ugly and dangerous-looking yellow talons instead of toes. Clasped under one arm was a splintery wooden object that might have been a broken lyre. Eddie thought no one could have looked more out of place on this road, where the only pedestrians they had seen so far were serious-looking exercisers, obviously from "away," looking ever so put-together in their nylon jogging shorts, baseball hats, and tee-shirts (one jogger's shirt bore the legend **DON'T SHOOT THE TOURISTS**).

The thing that had been trudging along the berm of Route 7 turned toward them, and Eddie let out an involuntary cry of horror. Its eyes bled together above the bridge of its nose, reminding him of a double-yolked egg in a frypan. A fang depended from one nostril like a bone booger. Yet somehow worst of all was the dull green glow that baked out from the creature's face. It was as if its skin had been painted with some sort of thin fluorescent gruel.

It saw them and immediately dashed into the woods, dropping its splintered lyre behind.

"*Christ!*" Eddie screamed. If that was a walk-in, he hoped never to see another.

"Stop, Eddie!" Roland shouted, then braced the heel of one hand against the dashboard as Cullum's old Ford slid to a dusty halt close to where the thing had vanished.

"Open the backhold," Roland said as he opened the door. "Get my widowmaker."

"Roland, we're in kind of a hurry here, and Turtleback Lane's still three miles north. I really think we ought to—"

"*Shut your fool's mouth and get it!*" Roland roared, then ran to the edge of the woods. He drew a deep breath, and when he shouted after the rogue creature, his voice sent gooseflesh racing up Eddie's arms. He had heard Roland speak so once or twice before, but in between it was easy to forget that the blood of a King ran in his veins.

He spoke several phrases Eddie could not understand, then

one he could: "So come forth, ye Child of Roderick, ye spoiled, ye lost, and make your bow before me, Roland, son of Steven, of the Line of Eld!"

For a moment there was nothing. Eddie opened the Ford's trunk and brought Roland his gun. Roland strapped it on without so much as a glance at Eddie, let alone a word of thanks.

Perhaps thirty seconds went by. Eddie opened his mouth to speak. Before he could, the dusty roadside foliage began to shake. A moment or two later, the misbegotten thing re-appeared. It staggered with its head lowered. On the front of its robe was a large wet patch. Eddie could smell the reek of a sick thing's urine, wild and strong.

Yet it made a knee and raised one misshapen hand to its forehead, a doomed gesture of fealty that made Eddie feel like weeping. "Hile, Roland of Gilead, Roland of Eld! Will you show me some sigul, dear?"

In a town called River Crossing, an old woman who called herself Aunt Talitha had given Roland a silver cross on a fine-link silver chain. He'd worn it around his neck ever since. Now he reached into his shirt and showed it to the kneeling crea-ture—a slow mutie dying of radiation sickness, Eddie was quite sure—and the thing gave a cracked cry of wonder.

"Would'ee have peace at the end of your course, thou Child of Roderick? Would'ee have the peace of the clearing?"

"Aye, my dear," it said, sobbing, then added a great deal more in some gibberish tongue Eddie couldn't understand. Eddie looked both ways along Route 7, expecting to see traf-fic—this was the height of the summer season, after all—but spied nothing in either direction. For the moment, at least, their luck still held.

"How many of you are there in these parts?" Roland asked, interrupting the walk-in. As he spoke, he drew his revolver and raised that old engine of death until it lay against his shirt.

The Child of Roderick tossed its hand at the horizon without looking up. "Delah, gunslinger," he said, "for here the worlds are thin, say *anro con fa; sey-sey desene fanno billet cobair can. I Chevin devar dan do.* Because I felt sat for dem. *Can-toi, can-tah, can Dis-cordia, aven la cam mah can. May-mi? Iffin lah vainen, eth*—"

"How many *dan devar?*"

It thought about Roland's question, then spread its fingers (there *were* ten, Eddie noted) five times. Fifty. Although fifty of what, Eddie didn't know.

"And Discordia?" Roland asked sharply. "Do you truly say so?"

"Oh aye, so says me, Chevin of Chayven, son of Hamil, minstrel of the South Plains that were once my home."

"Say the name of the town that stands near Castle Discordia and I'll release you."

"Ah, gunslinger, all there are dead."

"I think not. Say it."

"Fedic!" screamed Chevin of Chayven, a wandering *musica* who could never have suspected its life would end in such a far, strange place—not the plains of Mid-World but the mountains of western Maine. It suddenly raised its horrid, glowing face to Roland. It spread its arms wide, like something which has been crucified. *"Fedic on the far side of Thunderclap, on the Path of the Beam! On V Shardik, V Maturin, the Road to the Dark T*—"

Roland's revolver spoke a single time. The bullet took the kneeling thing in the center of its forehead, completing the ruin of its ruined face. As it was flung backward, Eddie saw its flesh turn to greenish smoke as ephemeral as a hornet's wing. For a moment Eddie could see Chevin of Chayven's floating teeth like a ghostly ring of coral, and then they were gone.

Roland dropped his revolver back into his holster, then pronged the two remaining fingers of his right hand and drew them downward in front of his face, a benedictory gesture if Eddie had ever seen one.

"Give you peace," Roland said. Then he unbuckled his gunbelt and began to roll the weapon into it once more.

"Roland, was that . . . was it a slow mutant?"

"Aye, I suppose you'd say so, poor old thing. But the Rod-ericks are from beyond any lands I ever knew, although before the world moved on they gave their grace to Arthur Eld." He turned to Eddie, his blue eyes burning in his tired face. "Fedic is where Mia has gone to have her baby, I have no doubt. Where she's taken Susannah. By the last castle. We must back-track to Thunderclap eventually, but Fedic's where we need to go first. It's good to know."

"He said he felt sad for someone. Who?"

Roland only shook his head, not answering Eddie's question. A Coca-Cola truck blasted by, and thunder rumbled in the far west.

"Fedic o' the Discordia," the gunslinger murmured instead. "Fedic o' the Red Death. If we can save Susannah—and Jake—we'll backtrack toward the Callas. But we'll return when our business there is done. And when we turn southeast again . . ."

"What?" Eddie asked uneasily. "What then, Roland?"

"Then there's no stopping until we reach the Tower." He held out his hands, watched them tremble minutely. Then he looked up at Eddie. His face was tired but unafraid. "I have never been so close. I hear all my lost friends and their lost fathers whispering to me. They whisper on the Tower's very breath."

Eddie looked at Roland for a minute, fascinated and fright-ened, and then broke the mood with an almost physical effort. "Well," he said, moving back toward the driver's door of the Ford, "if any of those voices tells you what to say to Cullum—the best way to convince him of what we want—be sure to let me know."

Eddie got in the car and closed the door before Roland could reply. In his mind's eye he kept seeing Roland leveling his big revolver. Saw him aiming it at the kneeling figure and pulling the trigger. This was the man he called both dinh and friend. But could he say with any certainty that Roland wouldn't do the same thing to him . . . or Suze . . . or Jake . . . if his heart told him it would take him closer to his Tower? He could not. And yet he would go on with him. Would have gone on even if he'd been sure in his heart—oh, God forbid!—that Susannah was dead. Because he had to. Because Roland had become a good deal more to him than his dinh or his friend.

"My father," Eddie murmured under his breath just before Roland opened the passenger door and climbed in.

"Did you speak, Eddie?" Roland asked.

"Yes," Eddie said. " 'Just a little farther.' My very words."

Roland nodded. Eddie dropped the transmission back into Drive and got the Ford rolling toward Turtleback Lane. Still in the distance—but a little closer than before—thunder rumbled again.

CHAPTER IV:
DAN-TETE

As the baby's time neared, Susannah Dean looked around, once more counting her enemies as Roland had taught her. *You must never draw,* he'd said, *until you know how many are against you, or you've satisfied yourself that you can never know, or you've decided it's your day to die.* She wished she didn't also have to cope with the terrible thought-invading helmet on her head, but whatever that thing was, it didn't seem concerned with Susannah's effort to count those present at the arrival of Mia's chap. And that was good.

There was Sayre, the man in charge. The *low* man, with one of those red spots pulsing in the center of his forehead. There was Scowther, the doctor between Mia's legs, getting ready to officiate at the delivery. Sayre had roughed the doc up when Scowther had displayed a little too much arrogance, but probably not enough to interfere with his efficiency. There were five other low men in addition to Sayre, but she'd only picked out two names. The one with the bulldog jowls and the heavy, sloping gut was Haber. Next to Haber was a bird-thing with the brown feathered head and vicious beebee eyes of a hawk. This creature's name seemed to be Jey, or possibly Gee. That was seven, all armed with what looked like automatic pistols in docker's clutches. Scowther's swung carelessly out from beneath his white coat each time he bent down. Susannah had already marked that one as hers.

There were also three pallid, watchful humanoid things standing beyond Mia. These, buried in dark blue auras, were vampires, Susannah was quite sure. Probably of the sort Callahan had called Type Threes. (The Pere had once referred to them as pilot sharks.) That made ten. Two of the vampires carried bahs, the third some sort of electrical sword now turned down to no more than a guttering core of light. If she managed to get Scowther's gun (*when* you get it, sweetie, she amended— she'd read *The Power of Positive Thinking* and still believed every word the Rev. Peale had written), she would turn it on the man with the electric sword first. God might know how much damage such a weapon could inflict, but Susannah Dean didn't want to find out.

Also present was a nurse with the head of a great brown rat. The pulsing red eye in the center of her forehead made Susannah believe that most of the other low *folken* were wearing humanizing masks, probably so they wouldn't scare the game while out and about on the sidewalks of New York. They might not all look like rats underneath, but she was pretty sure that none of them looked like Robert Goulet. The rathead nurse was the only one present who wore no weapon that Susannah could see.

Eleven in all. Eleven in this vast and mostly deserted infirmary that wasn't, she felt quite sure, under the borough of Manhattan. And if she was going to settle their hash, it would have to be while they were occupied with Mia's baby—her precious *chap*.

"It's coming, doctor!" the nurse cried in nervous ecstasy.

It was. Susannah's counting stopped as the worst pain yet rolled over her. Over both of them. Burying them. They screamed in tandem. Scowther was commanding Mia to *push*, to *push NOW!*

Susannah closed her eyes and also bore down, for it was her baby, too . . . or had been. As she felt the pain flow out of her like water whirlpooling its way down a dark drain, she experienced the deepest sorrow she had ever known. For it was Mia the baby was flowing into; the last few lines of the living message Susannah's body had somehow been made to transmit. It was ending. Whatever happened next, this part was ending, and Susannah Dean let out a cry of mingled relief and regret; a cry that was itself like a song.

And then, before the horror began—something so terrible she would remember each detail as if in the glare of a brilliant light until the day of her entry into the clearing—she felt a small hot hand grip her wrist. Susannah turned her head, rolling the unpleasant weight of the helmet with it. She could hear herself gasping. Her eyes met Mia's. Mia opened her lips and spoke a single word. Susannah couldn't hear it over Scowther's roaring (he was bending now, peering between Mia's legs and holding the forceps up and against his brow). Yet she *did* hear it, and understood that Mia was trying to fulfill her promise.

I'd free you, if chance allows, her kidnapper had said, and the word Susannah now heard in her mind and saw on the laboring woman's lips was *chassit.*

Susannah, do you hear me?

I hear you very well, Susannah said.

And you understand our compact?

Aye. I'll help you get away from these with your chap, if I can. And . . .

Kill us if you can't! the voice finished fiercely. It had never been so loud. That was partly the work of the connecting cable, Susannah felt sure. *Say it, Susannah, daughter of Dan!*

I'll kill you both if you—

She stopped there. Mia seemed satisfied, however, and that was well, because Susannah couldn't have gone on if both their lives had depended on it. Her eye had happened on the ceiling of this enormous room, over the aisles of beds halfway down. And there she saw Eddie and Roland. They were hazy, floating in and out of the ceiling, looking down at her like phantom fish.

Another pain, but this one not as severe. She could feel her thighs hardening, pushing, but that seemed far away. Not important. What mattered was whether or not she was really seeing what she thought she was seeing. Could it be that her overstressed mind, wishing for rescue, had created this hallucination to comfort her?

She could almost believe it. *Would* have, very likely, had

they not both been naked, and surrounded by an odd collection of floating junk: a matchbook, a peanut, ashes, a penny. And a floormat, by God! A car floormat with FORD printed on it.

"Doctor, I can see the hea—"

A breathless squawk as Dr. Scowther, no gentleman he, elbowed Nurse Ratty unceremoniously aside and bent even closer to the juncture of Mia's thighs. As if he meant to pull her chap out with his teeth, perhaps. The hawk-thing, Jey or Gee, was speaking to the one called Haber in an excited, buzzing dialect.

They're really there, Susannah thought. *The floormat proves it.* She wasn't sure *how* the floormat proved it, only that it did. And she mouthed the word Mia had given her: *chassit.* It was a password. It would open at least one door and perhaps many. To wonder if Mia had told the truth never even crossed Susannah's mind. They were tied together, not just by the cable and the helmets, but by the more primitive (and far more powerful) act of childbirth. No, Mia hadn't lied.

"Push, you gods-damned lazy bitch!" Scowther almost howled, and Roland and Eddie suddenly disappeared through the ceiling for good, as if blown away by the force of the man's breath. For all Susannah knew, they had been.

She turned on her side, feeling her hair stuck to her head in clumps, aware that her body was pouring out sweat in what could have been gallons. She pulled herself a little closer to Mia; a little closer to Scowther; a little closer to the crosshatched butt of Scowther's dangling automatic.

"Be still, sissa, hear me I beg," said one of the low men, and touched Susannah's arm. The hand was cold and flabby, covered with fat rings. The caress made her skin crawl. "This will be over in a minute and then all the worlds change. When this one joins the Breakers in Thunderclap—"

"Shut up, Straw!" Haber snapped, and pushed Susannah's would-be comforter backward. Then he turned eagerly to the delivery again.

Mia arched her back, groaning. The rathead nurse put her

hands on Mia's hips and pushed them gently back down to the bed. "Nawthee, nawthee, push 'ith thy belly."

"Eat shit, you bitch!" Mia screamed, and while Susannah felt a faint tug of her pain, that was all. The connection between them was fading.

Summoning her own concentration, Susannah cried into the well of her own mind. *Hey! Hey Positronics lady! You still there?*

"The link . . . is down," said the pleasant female voice. As before, it spoke in the middle of Susannah's head, but unlike before, it seemed dim, no more dangerous than a voice on the radio that comes from far away due to some atmospheric flaw. "Repeat: the link . . . is down. We hope you'll remember North Central Positronics for all your mental enhancement needs. And Sombra Corporation! A leader in mind-to-mind communication since the ten thousands!"

There was a tooth-rattling *BEE-EEEEP* far down in Susannah's mind, and then the link was gone. It wasn't just the absence of the horridly pleasant female voice; it was *everything*. She felt as if she'd been let out of some painful body-compressing trap.

Mia screamed again, and Susannah let out a cry of her own. Part of this was not wanting Sayre and his mates to know the link between her and Mia had been broken; part was genuine sorrow. She had lost a woman who had become, in a way, her true sister.

Susannah! Suze, are you there?

She started up on her elbows at this new voice, for a moment almost forgetting the woman beside her. That had been—

Jake? Is it you, honey? It is, isn't it? Can you hear me?

YES! he cried. *Finally!* God, *who've you been talking to? Keep yelling so I can home in on y—*

The voice broke off, but not before she heard a ghostly rattle of distant gunfire. Jake shooting at someone? She thought not. She thought someone was shooting at *him*.

TWO

"Now!" Scowther shouted. "*Now,* Mia! Push! For your life! Give it all you have! *PUSH!*"

Susannah tried to roll closer to the other woman—*Oh, I'm concerned and wanting comfort, see how concerned I am, concern and wanting comfort is all it is*—but the one called Straw pulled her back. The segmented steel cable swung and stretched out between them. "Keep your distance, bitch," Straw said, and for the first time Susannah faced the possibility that they weren't going to let her get hold of Scowther's gun. Or any gun.

Mia screamed again, crying out to a strange god in a strange language. When she tried to raise her midsection from the table, the nurse—Alia, Susannah thought the nurse's name was Alia—forced her down again, and Scowther gave a short, curt cry of what sounded like satisfaction. He tossed aside the forceps he'd been holding.

"Why d'ye do that?" Sayre demanded. The sheets beneath Mia's spread legs were now damp with blood, and the boss sounded flustered.

"Won't need them!" Scowther returned breezily. "She was built for babies, could have a dozen in the rice-patch and never miss a row's worth of picking. Here it comes, neat as you please!"

Scowther made as if to grab the largish basin sitting on the next bed, decided he didn't have quite enough time, and slipped his pink, gloveless hands up the inside of Mia's thighs, instead. This time when Susannah made an effort to move closer to Mia, Straw didn't stop her. All of them, low men and vampires alike, were watching the last stage of the birth with complete fascination, most of them clustered at the end of the two beds which had been pushed together to make one. Only Straw was still close to Susannah. The vampire with the fire-sword had just been demoted; she decided that Straw would be the first to go.

"*Once more!*" Scowther cried. "*For your baby!*"

Like the low men and the vampires, Mia had forgotten Susannah. Her wounded, pain-filled eyes fixed on Sayre. "May I have him, sir? Please say I may have him, if only for a little while!"

Sayre took her hand. The mask which covered his real face smiled. "Yes, my darling," he said. "The chap is yours for years and years. Only push this one last time."

Mia, don't believe his lies! Susannah cried, but the cry went nowhere. Likely that was just as well. Best she be entirely forgotten for the time being.

Susannah turned her thoughts in a new direction. *Jake! Jake, where are you?*

No answer. Not good. Please God he was still alive.

Maybe he's only busy. Running . . . hiding . . . fighting. Silence doesn't necessarily mean he's—

Mia howled what sounded like a string of obscenities, pushing as she did so. The lips of her already distended vagina spread further. A freshet of blood poured out, widening the muddy delta-shape on the sheet beneath her. And then, through the welter of crimson, Susannah saw a crown of white and black. The white was skin. The black was hair.

The mottle of white and black began to retreat into the crimson and Susannah thought the baby would settle back, still not quite ready to come into the world, but Mia was done waiting. She pushed with all her considerable might, her hands held up before her eyes in clenched and trembling fists, her eyes slitted, her teeth bared. A vein pulsed alarmingly in the center of her forehead; another stood out on the column of her throat.

"*HEEEYAHHHH!*" she cried. "*COMMALA, YOU PRETTY BASTARD! COMMALA-COME-COME!*"

"Dan-tete," murmured Jey, the hawk-thing, and the others picked it up in a kind of reverent whisper: *Dan-tete . . . dan-tete . . . commala dan-tete.* The coming of the little god.

This time the baby's head did not just crown but rushed forward. Susannah saw his hands held against his blood-spattered chest in tiny fists that trembled with life. She saw blue eyes, wide open and startling in both their awareness and their similarity to Roland's. She saw sooty black lashes. Tiny beads of blood jeweled them, barbaric natal finery. Susannah saw—and would never forget—how the baby's lower lip momentarily caught on the inner lip of his mother's vulva. The baby's mouth was pulled briefly open, revealing a perfect row of little teeth in the lower jaw. They *were* teeth—not fangs but perfect little teeth—yet still, to see them in the mouth of a newborn gave Susannah a chill. So did the sight of the chap's penis, disproportionately large and fully erect. Susannah guessed it was longer than her little finger.

Howling in pain and triumph, Mia surged up on her elbows, her eyes bulging and streaming tears. She reached out and seized Sayre's hand in a grip of iron as Scowther deftly caught the baby. Sayre yelped and tried to pull away, but he might as well have tried to . . . well, to pull away from a Deputy Sheriff in Oxford, Mississippi. The little chant had died and there was a moment of shocked silence. In it, Susannah's overstrained ears clearly heard the sound of bones grinding in Sayre's wrist.

"DOES HE LIVE?" Mia shrieked into Sayre's startled face. Spittle flew from her lips. *"TELL ME, YOU POXY WHORESON, IF MY CHAP LIVES!"*

Scowther lifted the chap so that he and the child were face to face. The doctor's brown eyes met the baby's blue ones. And as the chap hung there in Scowther's grip with its penis jutting defiantly upward, Susannah clearly saw the crimson mark on the babe's left heel. It was as if that foot had been dipped in blood just before the baby left Mia's womb.

Rather than spanking the baby's buttocks, Scowther drew in a breath and blew it in puffs directly into the chap's eyes. Mia's chap blinked in comical (and undeniably human) surprise. It drew in a breath of its own, held it for a moment, then let it out. King of Kings he might be, or the destroyer of worlds, but he embarked upon life as had so many before him, squalling with outrage. Mia burst into glad tears at the sound of that cry. The devilish creatures gathered around the new mother were bond-servants of the Crimson King, but that didn't make them immune to what they had just witnessed. They broke into applause and laughter. Susannah was not a little disgusted to find herself joining them. The baby looked around at the sound, his expression one of clear amazement.

Weeping, with tears running down her cheeks and clear snot dripping from her nose, Mia held out her arms. "Give him to me!" wept she; so wept Mia, daughter of none and mother of one. "Let me hold him, I beg, let me hold my son! Let me hold my chap! Let me hold my precious!"

And the baby *turned its head* to the sound of his mother's voice. Susannah would have said such a thing was impossible, but of course she would have said a baby born wide awake, with a mouthful of teeth and a boner, was impossible, as well. Yet in every other way the babe seemed completely normal to her: chubby and well-formed, human and thus dear. There was the red mark on his heel, yes, but how many children, normal in every other regard, were born with some sort of birthmark? Hadn't her own father been born red-handed, according to family legend? This mark wouldn't even show, unless the kid was at the beach.

Still holding the newborn up to his face, Scowther looked at Sayre. There was a momentary pause during which Susannah could easily have seized Scowther's automatic. She didn't even think of doing it. She'd forgotten Jake's telepathic cry; had likewise forgotten her weird visit from Roland and her husband. She was as enrapt as Jey and Straw and Haber and all the rest, enrapt at this moment of a child's arrival in a worn-out world.

Sayre nodded, almost imperceptibly, and Scowther lowered baby Mordred, still wailing (and still looking over his shoulder, apparently for his mother), into Mia's waiting arms.

Mia turned him around at once so she could look at him, and Susannah's heart froze with dismay and horror. For Mia had run mad. It was brilliant in her eyes; it was in the way her mouth managed to sneer and smile at the same time while drool, pinked and thickened with blood from her bitten tongue, trickled down the sides of her chin; most of all it was in her triumphant laughter. She might come back to sanity in the days ahead, but—

Bitch ain't nevah *comin back,* Detta said, not without sympathy. *Gittin this far n den gittin shed of it done broke her. She* busted, *n you know it as well's Ah do!*

"O, such beauty!" Mia crooned. "O, see thy blue eyes, thy skin as white as the sky before Wide Earth's first snow! See thy nipples, such perfect berries they are, see thy prick and thy balls as smooth as new peaches!" She looked around, first at Susannah—her eyes skating over Susannah's face with absolutely no recognition—and then at the others. *"See my chap, ye unfortunates, ye gonicks, my precious, my baby, my boy!"* She shouted to them, demanded *of* them, laughing with her mad eyes and crying with her crooked mouth. *"See what I gave up eternity for! See my Mordred, see him very well, for never will you see another his like!"*

Panting harshly, she covered the baby's bloody, staring face with kisses, smearing her mouth until she looked like a drunk who has tried to put on lipstick. She laughed and kissed the chubby flap of his infant's double chin, his nipples, his navel, the jutting tip of his penis, and—holding him up higher and higher in her trembling arms, the child she meant to call Mordred goggling down at her with that comic look of astonishment—she kissed his knees and then each tiny foot. Susannah heard that room's first suckle: not the baby at his mother's breast but Mia's mouth on each perfectly shaped toe.

THREE

Yon child's my dinh's doom, Susannah thought coldly. *If I do nothing else, I could seize Scowther's gun and shoot it. T'would be the work of two seconds.*

With her speed—her uncanny gunslinger's speed—this was likely true. But she found herself unable to move. She had foreseen many outcomes to this act of the play, but not Mia's madness, never that, and it had caught her entirely by surprise. It crossed Susannah's mind that she was lucky indeed that the Positronics link had gone down when it had. If it hadn't, she might be as mad as Mia.

And that link could kick back in, sister— don't you think you better make your move while you still can?

But she *couldn't,* that was the thing. She was frozen in wonder, held in thrall.

"Stop that!" Sayre snapped at her. "Your job isn't to slurp at him but to feed him! If you'd keep him, hurry up! Give him suck! Or should I summon a wetnurse? There are many who'd give their eyes for the opportunity!"

"Never . . . in . . . your . . . *LIFE!*" Mia cried, laughing, but she lowered the child to her chest and impatiently brushed aside the bodice of the plain white gown she wore, baring her right breast. Susannah could see why men would be taken by her; even now that breast was a perfect, coral-tipped globe that seemed more fit for a man's hand and a man's lust than a baby's nourishment. Mia lowered the chap to it. For a moment he rooted as comically as he'd goggled at her, his face striking the nipple and then seeming to bounce off. When it came down again, however, the pink rose of his mouth closed on the erect pink bud of her breast and began to suck.

Mia stroked the chap's tangled and blood-soaked black curls, still laughing. To Susannah, her laughter sounded like screams.

There was a clumping on the floor as a robot approached. It looked quite a bit like Andy the Messenger Robot—same skinny seven- or eight-foot height, same electric-blue eyes, same many-jointed, gleaming body. In its arms it bore a large glass box filled with green light.

"What's that fucking thing for?" Sayre snapped. He sounded both pissed off and incredulous.

"An incubator," Scowther said. "I felt it would be better to be safe than sorry."

When he turned to look, his shoulder-holstered gun swung toward Susannah. It was an even better chance, the best she'd ever have, and she knew it, but before she could take it, Mia's chap *changed.*

FOUR

Susannah saw red light run down the child's smooth skin, from the crown of its head to the stained heel of its right foot. It was not a flush but a *flash*, lighting the child from without: Susannah would have sworn it. And then, as it lay upon Mia's deflated stomach with its lips clamped around her nipple, the red flash was followed by a blackness that rose up and spread, turning the child into a lightless gnome, a negative of the rosy baby that had escaped Mia's womb. At the same time its body began to shrivel, its legs pulling up and melting into its belly, its head sliding down—and pulling Mia's breast with it—into its neck, which puffed up like the throat of a toad. Its blue eyes turned to tar, then back to blue again.

Susannah tried to scream and could not.

Tumors swelled along the black thing's sides, then burst and extruded legs. The red mark which had ridden the heel was still visible, but now had become a blob like the crimson brand on a black widow spider's belly. For that was what this thing was: a spider. Yet the baby was not entirely gone. A white excrescence rose from the spider's back. In it Susannah could see a tiny, deformed face and blue sparks that were eyes.

"What—?" Mia asked, and started up on her elbows once again. Blood had begun to pour from her breast. The baby drank it like milk, losing not a drop. Beside Mia, Sayre was standing as still as a graven image, his mouth open and his eyes bulging from their sockets. Whatever he'd expected from this birth—whatever he'd been *told* to expect—it wasn't this. The Detta part of Susannah took a child's vicious pleasure in the man's shocked expression: he looked like the comedian Jack Benny milking a laugh.

For a moment only Mia seemed to realize what had happened, for her face began to lengthen with a kind of informed horror—and, perhaps, pain. Then her smile returned, that angelic madonna's smile. She reached out and stroked the

still-changing freak at her breast, the black spider with the tiny
human head and the red mark on its bristly gut.

"*Is he not beautiful?*" she cried. "*Is my son not beautiful, as fair
as the summer sun?*"

These were her last words.

FIVE

Her face didn't freeze, exactly, but *stilled.* Her cheeks and brow
and throat, flushed dark with the exertions of childbirth only a
moment before, faded to the waxy whiteness of orchid petals.
Her shining eyes grew still and fixed in their sockets. And suddenly it was as if Susannah were looking not at a *woman* lying on
a bed but the *drawing* of a woman. An extraordinarily good one,
but still something that had been created on paper with strokes
of charcoal and a few pale colors.

Susannah remembered how she had returned to the
Plaza–Park Hyatt Hotel after her first visit to the allure of Castle Discordia, and how she'd come here to Fedic after her last
palaver with Mia, in the shelter of the merlon. How the sky and
the castle and the very stone of the merlon had torn open. And
then, as if her thought had caused it, Mia's face was ripped apart
from hairline to chin. Her fixed and dulling eyes fell crookedly
away to either side. Her lips split into a crazy double twin-grin.
And it wasn't blood that poured out of that widening fissure in
her face but a stale-smelling white powder. Susannah had a frag-
mented memory of T. S. Eliot

(*hollow men stuffed men headpiece filled with straw*)
and Lewis Carroll

(*why you're nothing but a pack of cards*)
before Mia's dan-tete raised its unspeakable head from its first
meal. Its blood-smeared mouth opened and it hoisted itself,
lower legs scrabbling for purchase on its mother's deflating
belly, upper ones almost seeming to shadowbox at Susannah.

It squealed with triumph, and if it had at that moment
chosen to attack the other woman who had given it nurture,

Susannah Dean would surely have died next to Mia. Instead, it returned to the deflated sac of breast from which it had taken its first suck, and tore it off. The sound of its chewing was wet and loose. A moment later it burrowed into the hole it had made, the white human face disappearing while Mia's was obliterated by the dust boiling out of her deflating head. There was a harsh, almost industrial sucking sound and Susannah thought, *It's taking all the moisture out of her, all the moisture that's left. And look at it! Look at it swell! Like a leech on a horse's neck!*

Just then a ridiculously English voice—it was the plummy intonation of the lifelong gentleman's gentleman—said: "Pardon me, sirs, but will you be wanting this incubator after all? For the situation seems to have altered somewhat, if you don't mind my saying."

It broke Susannah's paralysis. She pushed herself upward with one hand and seized Scowther's automatic pistol with the other. She yanked, but the gun was strapped across the butt and wouldn't come free. Her questing index finger found the little sliding knob that was the safety and pushed it. She turned the gun, holster and all, toward Scowther's ribcage.

"What the dev—" he began, and then she pulled the trigger with her middle finger, at the same time yanking back on the shoulder-rig with all her force. The straps binding the holster to Scowther's body held, but the thinner one holding the automatic in place snapped, and as Scowther fell sideways, trying to look down at the smoking black hole in his white labcoat, Susannah took full possession of his gun. She shot Straw and the vampire beside him, the one with the electric sword. For a moment the vampire was there, still staring at the spidergod that had looked so much like a baby to begin with, and then its aura whiffed out. The thing's flesh went with it. For a moment there was nothing where it had been but an empty shirt tucked into an empty pair of bluejeans. Then the clothes collapsed.

"*Kill her!*" Sayre screamed, reaching for his own gun. "*Kill that bitch!*"

Susannah rolled away from the spider crouched on the

body of its rapidly deflating mother, raking at the helmet she was wearing even as she tumbled off the side of the bed. There was a moment of excruciating pain when she thought it wasn't going to come away and then she hit the floor, free of it. It hung over the side of the bed, fringed with her hair. The spider-thing, momentarily pulled off its roost when its mother's body jerked, chittered angrily.

Susannah rolled beneath the bed as a series of gunshots went off above her. She heard a loud *SPROINK* as one of the slugs hit a spring. She saw the rathead nurse's feet and hairy lower legs and put a bullet into one of her knees. The nurse gave a scream, turned, and began to limp away, squalling.

Sayre leaned forward, pointing the gun at the makeshift double bed just beyond Mia's deflating body. There were already three smoking, smoldering holes in the groundsheet. Before he could add a fourth, one of the spider's legs caressed his cheek, tearing open the mask he wore and revealing the hairy cheek beneath. Sayre recoiled, crying out. The spider turned to him and made a mewling noise. The white thing high on its back— a node with a human face—glared, as if to warn Sayre away from its meal. Then it turned back to the woman, who was really not recognizable as a woman any longer; she looked like the ruins of some incredibly ancient mummy which had now turned to rags and powder.

"I say, this *is* a bit confusing," the robot with the incubator remarked. "Shall I retire? Perhaps I might return when matters have clarified somewhat."

Susannah reversed direction, rolling out from beneath the bed. She saw that two of the low men had taken to their heels. Jey, the hawkman, didn't seem to be able to make up his mind. Stay or go? Susannah made it up for him, putting a single shot into the sleek brown head. Blood and feathers flew.

Susannah got up as well as she could, gripping the side of the bed for balance, holding Scowther's gun out in front of her. She had gotten four. The rathead nurse and one other had run. Sayre had dropped his gun and was trying to hide behind the robot with the incubator.

Susannah shot the two remaining vampires and the low man with the bulldog face. That one—Haber—hadn't forgotten Susannah; he'd been holding his ground and waiting for a clear shot. She got hers first and watched him fall backward with deep satisfaction. Haber, she thought, had been the most dangerous.

"Madam, I wonder if you could tell me—" began the robot, and Susannah put two quick shots into its steel face, darkening the blue electric eyes. This trick she had learned from Eddie. A gigantic siren immediately went off. Susannah felt that if she listened to it long, she would be deafened.

"I HAVE BEEN BLINDED BY GUNFIRE!" the robot bellowed, still in its absurd would-you-like-another-cup-of-tea-madam accent. *"VISION ZERO, I NEED HELP, CODE 7, I SAY, HELP!"*

Sayre stepped away from it, hands held high. Susannah couldn't hear him over the siren and the robot's blatting, but she could read the words as they came off the bastard's lips: *I surrender, will you accept my parole?*

She smiled at this amusing idea, unaware that she smiled. It was without humor and without mercy and meant only one thing: she wished she could get him to lick her stumps, as he had forced Mia to lick his boots. But there wasn't time enough. He saw his doom in her grin and turned to run and Susannah shot him twice in the back of the head—once for Mia, once for Pere Callahan. Sayre's skull shattered in a fury of blood and brains. He grabbed the wall, scrabbled at a shelf loaded with equipment and supplies, and then went down dead.

Susannah now took aim at the spider-god. The tiny white human head on its black and bristly back turned to look at her. The blue eyes, so uncannily like Roland's, blazed.

No, you cannot! You must *not! For I am the King's only son!*

I can't? she sent back, leveling the automatic. *Oh, sugar, you are just . . . so . . . WRONG!*

But before she could pull the trigger, there was a gunshot from behind her. A slug burned across the side of her neck. Susannah reacted instantly, turning and throwing herself sideways into the aisle. One of the low men who'd run had had a change of heart and come back. Susannah put two bullets into his chest and made him mortally sorry.

She turned, eager for more—yes, this was what she wanted, what she had been made for, and she'd always revere Roland for showing her—but the others were either dead or fled. The spider raced down the side of its birthbed on its many legs, leaving the papier-mâché corpse of its mother behind. It turned its white infant's head briefly toward her.

You'd do well to let me pass, Blackie, or—

She fired at it, but stumbled over the hawkman's outstretched hand as she did. The bullet that would have killed the abomination went a little awry, clipping off one of its eight hairy legs instead. A yellowish-red fluid, more like pus than blood, poured from the place where the leg had joined the body. The thing screamed at her in pain and surprise. The audible portion of that scream was hard to hear over the endless cycling blat of the robot's siren, but she heard it in her head loud and clear.

I'll pay you back for that! My father and I, we'll pay you back! Make you cry for death, so we will!

You ain't gonna have a chance, sugar, Susannah sent back, trying to project all the confidence she possibly could, not wanting the thing to know what she believed: that Scowther's automatic might have been shot dry. She aimed with a deliberation that was unnecessary, and the spider scuttled rapidly away from her, darting first behind the endlessly sirening robot and then through a dark doorway.

All right. Not great, not the best solution by any means, but she was still alive, and that much was grand.

And the fact that all of sai Sayre's crew were dead or run off? That wasn't bad, either.

Susannah tossed Scowther's gun aside and selected another, this one a Walther PPK. She took it from the docker's clutch Straw had been wearing, then rummaged in his pockets, where she found half a dozen extra clips. She briefly considered adding the vampire's electric sword to her armory and decided to leave it where it was. Better the tools you knew than those you didn't.

She tried to get in touch with Jake, couldn't hear herself think, and turned to the robot. *"Hey, big boy! Shut off that damn sireen, what do you say?"*

She had no idea if it would work, but it did. The silence was immediate and wonderful, with the sensuous texture of moiré silk. Silence might be useful. If there was a counterattack, she'd hear them coming. And the dirty truth? She *hoped* for a counterattack, *wanted* them to come, and never mind whether that made sense or not. She had a gun and her blood was up. That was all that mattered.

(*Jake! Jake, do you hear me, kiddo? If you hear, answer your big sis!*)

Nothing. Not even that rattle of distant gunfire. He was out of t—

Then, a single word—*was* it a word?

(*wimeweh*)

More important, was it *Jake?*

She didn't know for sure, but she thought yes. And the word seemed familiar to her, somehow.

Susannah gathered her concentration, meaning to call louder this time, and then a queer idea came to her, one too strong to be called intuition. Jake was trying to be quiet. He was . . . hiding? Maybe getting ready to spring an ambush? The idea sounded crazy, but maybe *his* blood was up, too. She didn't know, but thought he'd either sent her that one odd word

(*wimeweh*)

on purpose, or it had slipped out. Either way, it might be better to let him roll his own oats for awhile.

"I say, I have been blinded by gunfire!" the robot insisted. Its voice was still loud, but had dropped to a range at least approaching normal. "I can't see a bloody thing and I have this incubator—"

"Drop it," Susannah said.

"But—"

"Drop it, Chumley."

"I beg pawdon, madam, but my name is Nigel the Butler and I really can't—"

Susannah had been hauling herself closer during this little exchange—you didn't forget the old means of locomotion just because you'd been granted a brief vacation with legs, she was discovering—and read both the name and the serial number stamped on the robot's chrome-steel midsection.

"Nigel DNK 45932, drop that fucking glass box, say thankya!"

The robot (**DOMESTIC** was stamped just below its serial number) dropped the incubator and then whimpered when it shattered at its steel feet.

Susannah worked her way over to Nigel, and found she had to conquer a moment's fear before reaching up and taking one three-fingered steel hand. She needed to remind herself that this wasn't Andy from Calla Bryn Sturgis, nor could Nigel *know* about Andy. The butler-robot might or might not be sophisticated enough to crave revenge—certainly Andy had been—but you couldn't crave what you didn't know about.

She hoped.

"Nigel, pick me up."

There was a whine of servomotors as the robot bent.

"No, hon, you have to come forward a little bit. There's broken glass where you are."

"Pawdon, madam, but I'm blind. I believe it was you who shot my eyes out."

Oh. That.

"Well," she said, hoping her tone of irritation would disguise the fear beneath, "I can't very well get you new ones if you don't pick me up, can I? Now get a wiggle on, may it do ya. Time's wasting."

Nigel stepped forward, crushing broken glass beneath its feet, and came to the sound of her voice. Susannah controlled the urge to cringe back, but once the Domestic Robot had set its grip on her, its touch was quite gentle. It lifted her into its arms.

"Now take me to the door."

"Madam, beg pawdon but there are *many* doors in Sixteen. More still beneath the castle."

Susannah couldn't help being curious. "How many?"

A brief pause. "I should say five hundred and ninety-five are currently operational." She immediately noticed that five-ninety-five added up to nineteen. Added up to *chassit.*

"Do you mind giving me a carry to the one I came through before the shooting started?" Susannah pointed toward the far end of the room.

"No, madam, I don't mind at all, but I'm sorry to tell you that it will do you no good," Nigel said in his plummy voice. "That door, NEW YORK #7/FEDIC, is one-way." A pause. Relays clicking in the steel dome of its head. "Also, it burned out after its last use. It has, as you might say, gone to the clearing at the end of the path."

"Oh, that's just *wonderful!*" Susannah cried, but realized she wasn't exactly surprised by Nigel's news. She remembered the ragged humming sound she'd heard it making just before Sayre had pushed her rudely through it, remembered thinking, even in her distress, that it was a dying thing. And yes, it had died. "Just *wonderful!*"

"I sense you are distressed, madam."

"You're goddamned right I'm distressed! Bad enough the damned thing only opened one-way! Now it's shut down completely!"

"Except for the default," Nigel agreed.

"Default? What do you mean, default?"

"That would be NEW YORK #9/FEDIC," Nigel told her. "At one time there were over thirty one-way New York–to–Fedic ports, but I believe #9 is the only one that remains. All commands pertaining to NEW YORK #7/FEDIC will now have defaulted to #9."

Chassit, she thought . . . almost prayed. *He's talking about* chassit, *I think. Oh God, I hope he is.*

"Do you mean passwords and such, Nigel?"

"Why, yes, madam."

"Take me to Door #9."

"As you wish."

Nigel began to move rapidly up the aisle between the hundreds of empty beds, their taut white sheets gleaming under the brilliant overhead lamps. Susannah's imagination momentarily populated this room with screaming, frightened children, freshly arrived from Calla Bryn Sturgis, maybe from the neighboring Callas, as well. She saw not just a single rathead nurse but battalions of them, eager to clamp the helmets over the heads of the kidnapped children and start the process that . . . that did what? Ruined them in some way. Sucked the intelligence out of their heads and knocked their growth-hormones out of whack and ruined them forever. Susannah supposed that at first they would be cheered up to hear such a pleasant voice in their heads, a voice welcoming them to the wonderful world of North Central Positronics and the Sombra Group. Their crying would stop, their eyes fill with hope. Perhaps, they would think the nurses in their white uniforms were good in spite of their hairy, scary faces and yellow fangs. As good as the voice of the nice lady.

Then the hum would begin, quickly building in volume as it moved toward the middle of their heads, and this room would again fill with their frightened screams—

"Madam? Are you all right?"

"Yes. Why do you ask, Nigel?"

"I believe you shivered."

"Never mind. Just get me to the door to New York, the one that still works."

SIX

Once they left the infirmary, Nigel bore her rapidly down first one corridor and then another. They came to escalators that looked as if they had been frozen in place for centuries. Halfway down one of them, a steel ball on legs flashed its amber eyes at Nigel and cried, *"Howp! Howp!"* Nigel responded *"Howp, howp!"* in return and then said to Susannah (in the confidential tone certain gossipy people adopt when discussing Those Who Are Unfortunate), "He's a Mech Foreman and has been stuck there for over eight hundred years—fried boards, I imagine. Poor soul! But he still tries to do his best."

Twice Nigel asked her if she believed his eyes could be replaced. The first time Susannah told him she didn't know. The second time—feeling a little sorry for him (definitely him now, not it)—she asked what *he* thought.

"I think my days of service are nearly over," he said, and then added something that made her arms tingle with goose-flesh: "O Discordia!"

The Diem Brothers are dead, she thought, remembering— had it been a dream? a vision? a glimpse of *her* Tower?— something from her time with Mia. Or had it been her time in Oxford, Mississippi? Or both? *Papa Doc Duvalier is dead. Christa McAuliffe is dead. Stephen King is dead, popular writer killed while taking afternoon walk, O Discordia, O lost!*

But who was Stephen King? Who was Christa McAuliffe, for that matter?

Once they passed a low man who had been present at the birth of Mia's monster. He lay curled on a dusty corridor floor like a human shrimp with his gun in one hand and a hole in his head. Susannah thought he'd committed suicide. In a way, she supposed that made sense. Because things had gone wrong, hadn't they? And unless Mia's baby found its way to where it belonged on its own, Big Red Daddy was going to be mad. Might be mad even if Mordred somehow found his way home.

His *other* father. For this was a world of twins and mirror images, and Susannah now understood more about what she'd seen than she really wanted to. Mordred too was a twin, a Jekyll-and-Hyde creature with two selves, and he—or it—had the faces of two fathers to remember.

They came upon a number of other corpses; all looked like suicides to Susannah. She asked Nigel if he could tell—by their smells, or something—but he claimed he could not.

"How many are still here, do you think?" she asked. Her blood had had time to cool a little, and now she felt nervous.

"Not many, madam. I believe that most have moved on. Very likely to the Derva."

"What's the Derva?"

Nigel said he was dreadfully sorry, but that information

was restricted and could be accessed only with the proper pass-word. Susannah tried *chassit,* but it was no good. Neither was *nineteen* or, her final try, *ninety-nine.* She supposed she'd have to be content with just knowing most of them were gone.

Nigel turned left, into a new corridor with doors on both sides. She got him to stop long enough to try one of them, but there was nothing of particular note inside. It was an office, and long-abandoned, judging by the thick fall of dust. She was interested to see a poster of madly jitterbugging teenagers on one wall. Beneath it, in large blue letters, was this:

SAY, YOU COOL CATS AND BOPPIN' KITTIES! I ROCKED AT THE HOP WITH ALAN FREED! CLEVELAND, OHIO, OCTOBER 1954

Susannah was pretty sure that the performer on stage was Richard Penniman. Club-crawling folkies such as herself affected disdain for anyone who rocked harder than Phil Ochs, but Suze had always had a soft spot in her heart for Little Richard; good golly, Miss Molly, you sure like to ball. She guessed it was a Detta thing.

Did these people once upon a time use their doors to vacation in various wheres and whens of their choice? Did they use the power of the Beams to turn certain levels of the Tower into tourist attractions?

She asked Nigel, who told her he was sure he did not know. Nigel still sounded sad about the loss of his eyes.

Finally they came into an echoing rotunda with doors marching all around its mighty circumference. The marble tiles on the floor were laid in a black-and-white checkerboard pattern Susannah remembered from certain troubled dreams in which Mia had fed her chap. Above, high and high, constellations of electric stars winked in a blue firmament that was now showing plenty of cracks. This place reminded her of the Cradle of Lud, and even more strongly of Grand Central Station. Somewhere in the walls, air-conditioners or -exchangers ran rustily. The smell in the air was weirdly familiar, and after a short struggle, Susannah identified it: Comet Cleanser. They sponsored *The Price Is Right,* which she sometimes watched on TV if she happened to be home in the morning. *"I'm Don Pardo, now please welcome your host, Mr. Bill Cullen!"* Susannah felt a moment of vertigo and closed her eyes.

Bill Cullen is dead. Don Pardo is dead. Martin Luther King is dead, shot down in Memphis. Rule Discordia!

O Christ, those *voices,* would they never stop?

She opened her eyes and saw doors marked SHANGHAI/FEDIC and BOMBAY/FEDIC and one marked DALLAS (NOVEMBER 1963)/FEDIC. Others were written in runes that meant nothing to her. At last Nigel stopped in front of one she recognized.

NORTH CENTRAL POSITRONICS, LTD.
New York/Fedic
Maximum Security

All of this Susannah recognized from the other side, but below VERBAL ENTRY CODE REQUIRED was this message, flashing ominous red:

#9 FINAL DEFAULT

SEVEN

"What would you like to do next, madam?" Nigel asked.

"Set me down, sugarpie."

She had time to wonder what her response would be if Nigel declined to do so, but he didn't even hesitate. She walk-hopped-scuttled to the door in her old way and put her hands on it. Beneath them she felt a texture that was neither wood nor metal. She thought she could hear a very faint hum. She considered trying *chassit*—her version of Ali Baba's *Open, sesame*—and didn't bother. There wasn't even a doorknob. One-way meant one-way, she reckoned; no kidding around.

(*JAKE!*)

She sent it with all her might.

No answer. Not even that faint
(*wimeweh*)
nonsense word. She waited a moment longer, then turned
around and sat with her back propped against the door. She
dropped the extra ammo clips between her spread knees and
then held the Walther PPK up in her right hand. A good
weapon to have with your back to a locked door, she reckoned;
she liked the weight of it. Once upon a time, she and others had
been trained in a protest technique called passive resistance. Lie
down on the lunchroom floor, cover your soft middle and softer
privates. Do not respond to those who strike you and revile
you and curse your parents. Sing in your chains like the sea.
What would her old friends make of what she had become?

Susannah said: "You know what? I don't give shit one. Passive resistance is also dead."

"Madam?"

"Nothing, Nigel."

"Madam, may I ask—"

"What I'm doing?"

"Exactly, madam."

"Waiting on a friend, Chumley. Just waiting on a friend."

She thought that DNK 45932 would remind her that his
name was Nigel, but he didn't. Instead, he asked how long
she would wait for her friend. Susannah told him until hell froze
over. This elicited a long silence. Finally Nigel asked: "May I go,
then, madam?"

"How will you see?"

"I have switched to infrared. It is less satisfying than three-X
macrovision, but it will suffice to get me to the repair bays."

"Is there anyone in the repair bays who can fix you?" Susannah asked with mild curiosity. She pushed the button that
dropped the clip out of the Walther's butt, then rammed it back
in, taking a certain elemental pleasure in the oily, metallic
SNACK! sound it made.

"I'm sure I can't say, madam," Nigel replied, "although the
probability of such a thing is very low, certainly less than one
per cent. If no one comes, then I, like you, will wait."

She nodded, suddenly tired and very sure that this was where the grand quest ended—here, leaning against this door. But you didn't give up, did you? Giving up was for cowards, not gunslingers.

"May ya do fine, Nigel—thanks for the piggyback. Long days and pleasant nights. Hope you get your eyes back. Sorry I shot em out, but I was in a bit of a tight and didn't know whose side you were on."

"And good wishes to you, madam."

Susannah nodded. Nigel clumped off and then she was alone, leaning against the door to New York. Waiting for Jake. Listening for Jake.

All she heard was the rusty, dying wheeze of the machinery in the walls.

Chapter V:
In the Jungle,
the Mighty Jungle

The threat that the low men and the vampires might kill Oy was the only thing that kept Jake from dying with the Pere. There was no agonizing over the decision; Jake yelled

(*OY, TO ME!*)

with all the mental force he could muster, and Oy ran swiftly at his heel. Jake passed low men who stood mesmerized by the turtle and straight-armed a door marked EMPLOYEES ONLY. From the dim orange-red glow of the restaurant he and Oy entered a zone of brilliant white light and charred, pungent cookery. Steam billowed against his face, hot and wet,

(*the jungle*)

perhaps setting the stage for what followed,

(*the mighty jungle*)

perhaps not. His vision cleared as his pupils shrank and he saw he was in the Dixie Pig's kitchen. Not for the first time, either. Once, not too long before the coming of the Wolves to Calla Bryn Sturgis, Jake had followed Susannah (only then she'd have been Mia) into a dream where she'd been searching some vast and deserted kitchen for food. *This* kitchen, only now the place was bustling with life. A huge pig sizzled on an iron spit over an open fire, the flames leaping up through a food-caked iron grate at every drop of grease. To either side were gigantic copper-hooded stoves upon which pots nearly as tall as Jake himself fumed. Stirring one of these was a gray-skinned creature so hideous that Jake's eyes hardly knew how to look at it. Tusks

81

rose from either side of its gray, heavy-lipped mouth. Dewlapped cheeks hung in great warty swags of flesh. The fact that the creature was wearing foodstained cook's whites and a puffy popcorn chef's toque somehow finished the nightmare, sealed it beneath a coat of varnish. Beyond this apparition, nearly lost in the steam, two other creatures dressed in whites were washing dishes side by side at a double sink. Both wore neckerchiefs. One was human, a boy of perhaps seventeen. The other appeared to be some sort of monster housecat on legs.

"*Vai, vai, los mostros pubes, tre cannits en founs!*" the tusked chef screeched at the washerboys. It hadn't noticed Jake. One of them—the cat—did. It laid back its ears and hissed. Without thinking, Jake threw the Oriza he'd been holding in his right hand. It sang across the steamy air and sliced through the cat-thing's neck as smoothly as a knife through a cake of lard. The head toppled into the sink with a sudsy splash, the green eyes still blazing.

"*San fai, can dit los!*" cried the chef. He seemed either unaware of what had happened or was unable to grasp it. He turned to Jake. The eyes beneath his sloping, crenellated forehead were a bleary blue-gray, the eyes of a sentient being. Seen head-on, Jake realized what it was: some kind of freakish, intelligent warthog. Which meant it was cooking its own kind. That seemed perfectly fitting in the Dixie Pig.

"*Can foh pube ain-tet can fah! She-so pan! Vai!*" This was addressed to Jake. And then, just to make the lunacy complete: "And eef you won'd scrub, *don'd even stard!*"

The other washboy, the human one, was screaming some sort of warning, but the chef paid no attention. The chef seemed to believe that Jake, having killed one of his helpers, was now duty- and honor-bound to take the dead cat's place.

Jake flung the other plate and it sheared through the warthog's neck, putting an end to its blabber. Perhaps a gallon of blood flew onto the stovetop to the thing's right, sizzling and sending up a horrible charred smell. The warthog's head slewed to the left on its neck and then tilted backward, but didn't come off. The being—it was easily seven feet tall—took two stagger-steps to its left and embraced the sizzling pig turning on its spit. The head tore loose a little further, now lying on Chef Warthog's right shoulder, one eye glaring up at the steam-wreathed fluorescent lights. The heat sealed the cook's hands to the roast and they began to melt. Then the thing fell forward into the open flames and its tunic caught fire.

Jake whirled from this in time to see the other potboy advancing on him with a butcher knife in one hand and a cleaver in the other. Jake grabbed another 'Riza from the bag but held his throw in spite of the voice in his head that was yammering for him to go on, go on and do it, give the bastard what he'd once heard Margaret Eisenhart refer to as a "deep haircut." This term had made the other Sisters of the Plate laugh hard. Yet as much as he wanted to throw, he held his hand.

What he saw was a young man whose skin was a pallid yellowish-gray under the brilliant kitchen lights. He looked both terrified and malnourished. Jake raised the plate in warning and the young man stopped. It wasn't the 'Riza he was looking at, however, but Oy, who stood between Jake's feet. The bumbler's fur was bushed out around his body, seeming to double his size, and his teeth were bared.

"Do you—" Jake began, and then the door to the restaurant burst open. One of the low men rushed in. Jake threw the plate without hesitation. It moaned through the steamy, brilliant air and took off the intruder's head with gory precision just above the Adam's apple. The headless body bucked first to the left and then to the right, like a stage comic accepting a round of applause with a whimsical move, and then collapsed.

Jake had another plate in each hand almost immediately, his arms once more crossed over his chest in the position sai Eisenhart called "the load." He looked at the washerboy, who was still holding the knife and the cleaver. Without much threat, however, Jake thought. He tried again and this time got the whole question out. "Do you speak English?"

"Yar," the boy said. He dropped the cleaver so he could hold one water-reddened thumb and its matching forefinger about a quarter of an inch apart. "Bout just a liddle. I learn since I come over here." He opened his other hand and the knife joined the cleaver on the kitchen floor.

"Do you come from Mid-World?" Jake asked. "You do, don't you?"

He didn't think the washerboy was terribly bright ("No quiz-kid," Elmer Chambers would no doubt have sneered), but he was at least smart enough to be homesick; in spite of his terror, Jake saw an unmistakable flash of that look in the boy's eyes. "Yar," he said. "Come from Ludweg, me."

"Near the city of Lud?"

"North of there, if you do like it or if you don't," said the washerboy. "Will'ee kill me, lad? I don't want to die, sad as I am."

"I won't be the one to kill you if you tell me the truth. Did a woman come through here?"

The washerboy hesitated, then said: "Aye. Sayre and his closies had 'er. She 'us out on her feet, that 'un, head all lollin . . ." He demonstrated, rolling his head on his neck and looking more like the village idiot than ever. Jake thought of Sheemie in Roland's tale of his Mejis days.

"But not dead."

"Nar. I hurt her breevin, me."

Jake looked toward the door, but no one came through. Yet. He should go, but—

"What's your name, cully?"

"Jochabim, that be I, son of Hossa."

"Well, listen, Jochabim, there's a world outside this kitchen called New York City, and pubes like you are free. I suggest you get out while you have an opportunity."

"They'd just bring me back and stripe me."

"No, you don't understand how big it is. Like Lud when Lud was—"

He looked at Jochabim's dull-eyed face and thought, *No, I'm the one who doesn't understand. And if I hang around here trying to convince him to desert, I'll no doubt get just what I—*

The door leading to the restaurant popped open again. This time two low men tried to come through at once and momentarily jammed together, shoulder to shoulder. Jake threw both of his plates and watched them crisscross in the steamy air, beheading both newcomers just as they burst through. They fell backward and once more the door swung shut. At Piper School Jake had learned about the Battle of Thermopylae, where the Greeks had held off a Persian army that had outnumbered them ten to one. The Greeks had drawn the Persians into a narrow mountain pass; he had this kitchen door. As long as they kept coming through by ones and twos—as they must unless they could flank him somehow—he could pick them off.

At least until he ran out of Orizas.

"Guns?" he asked Jochabim. "Are there guns here?"

Jochabim shook his head, but given the young man's irritating look of density, it was hard to tell if this meant *No guns in the kitchen* or *I don't ken you.*

"All right, I'm going," he said. "And if you don't go yourself while you've got a chance, Jochabim, you're an even bigger fool than you look. Which would be saying a lot. There are *video games* out there, kid—think about it."

Jochabim continued giving Jake the *duh* look, however, and Jake gave up. He was about to speak to Oy when someone spoke to him through the door.

"Hey, kid." Rough. Confidential. Knowing. The voice of a man who could hit you for five or sleep with your girlfriend any time he liked, Jake thought. "Your friend the faddah's dead. In fact, the faddah's *dinnah.* You come out now, with no more nonsense, maybe you can avoid being dessert."

"Turn it sideways and stick it up your ass," Jake called. This got through even Jochabim's wall of stupidity; he looked shocked.

"Last chance," said the rough and knowing voice. "Come on out."

"Come on in!" Jake countered. "I've got plenty of plates!" Indeed, he felt a lunatic urge to rush forward, bang through the door, and take the battle to the low men and women in the restaurant dining room on the other side. Nor was the idea all that crazy, as Roland himself would have known; it was the last thing they'd expect, and there was at least an even chance that he could panic them with half a dozen quickly thrown plates and start a rout.

The problem was the monsters that had been feeding behind the tapestry. The vampires. *They'd* not panic, and Jake knew it. He had an idea that if the Grandfathers had been able to come into the kitchen (or perhaps it was just lack of interest that kept them in the dining room—that and the last scraps of the Pere's corpse), he would be dead already. Jochabim as well, quite likely.

He dropped to one knee, murmured "Oy, find Susannah!" and reinforced the command with a quick mental picture.

The bumbler gave Jochabim a final distrustful look, then began to nose about on the floor. The tiles were damp from a recent mopping, and Jake was afraid the bumbler wouldn't be able to find the scent. Then Oy gave a single sharp cry—more dog's bark than human's word—and began to hurry down the center of the kitchen between the stoves and the steam tables, nose low to the ground, only going out of his way long enough to skirt Chef Warthog's smoldering body.

"Listen, to me, you little bastard!" cried the low man outside the door. "I'm losing patience with you!"

"Good!" Jake cried. "Come on in! Let's see if you go back out again!"

He put his finger to his lips in a shushing gesture while looking at Jochabim. He was about to turn and run—he had no idea how long it would be before the washerboy yelled through the door that the kid and his billy-bumbler were no longer holding Thermopylae Pass—when Jochabim spoke to him in a low voice that was little more than a whisper.

"What?" Jake asked, looking at him uncertainly. It sounded as if the kid had said *mind the mind-trap,* but that made no sense. Did it?

"Mind the mind-trap," Jochabim said, this time much more clearly, and turned away to his pots and sudsy water.

"*What* mind-trap?" Jake asked, but Jochabim affected not to hear and Jake couldn't stay long enough to cross-examine him. He ran to catch up with Oy, throwing glances back over his shoulder. If a couple more of the low men burst into the kitchen, Jake wanted to be the first to know.

But none did, at least not before he had followed Oy through another door and into the restaurant's pantry, a dim room stacked high with boxes and smelling of coffee and spices. It was like the storeroom behind the East Stoneham General Store, only cleaner.

TWO

There was a closed door in the corner of the Dixie Pig's pantry. Beyond it was a tiled stairway leading down God only knew how far. It was lit by low-wattage bulbs behind bleary, fly-spotted glass shades. Oy started down without hesitation, descending with a kind of bobbing, front-end/back-end regularity that was pretty comical. He kept his nose pressed to the stairs, and Jake knew he was onto Susannah; he could pick it up from his little friend's mind.

Jake tried counting the stairs, made it as far as a hundred and twenty, then lost his grip on the numbers. He wondered if they were still in New York (or under it). Once he thought he heard a faint, familiar rumbling and decided that if that was a subway train, they were.

Finally they reached the bottom of the stairs. Here was a wide, vaulted area that looked like a gigantic hotel lobby, only without the hotel. Oy made his way across it, snout still low to the ground, his squiggle of a tail wagging back and forth. Jake had to jog in order to keep up. Now that they no longer filled the bag, the 'Rizas jangled back and forth. There was a kiosk on the far side of the lobby-vault, with a sign in one dusty window reading LAST CHANCE FOR NEW YORK SOUVENIRS and another reading VISIT SEPTEMBER 11, 2001! TIX STILL AVAILABLE FOR THIS WONDERFUL EVENT! ASTHMATICS PROHIBITED W/O DR'S CERTIFICATE! Jake wondered what was so fabulous about September 11th of 2001 and then decided that maybe he didn't want to know.

Suddenly, as loud in his head as a voice spoken directly into his ear: *Hey! Hey Positronics lady! You still there?*

Jake had no idea who the Positronics lady might be, but he recognized the voice asking the question.

Susannah! he shouted, coming to a stop near the tourist kiosk. A surprised, joyful grin creased his strained face and made it a kid's again. *Suze, are you there?*

And heard her cry out in happy surprise.

Oy, realizing that Jake was no longer following close behind, turned and gave an impatient *Ake-Ake!* cry. For the moment at least, Jake disregarded him.

"I hear you!" he shouted. "Finally! God, who've you been talking to? Keep yelling so I can home in on y—"

From behind him—perhaps at the top of the long staircase, perhaps already on it—someone yelled, "That's him!" There were gunshots, but Jake barely heard them. To his intense horror, something had crawled inside his head. Something like a mental hand. He thought it was probably the low man who had spoken to him through the door. The low man's hand had found dials in some kind of Jake Chambers Dogan, and was fiddling with them. Trying

(*to freeze me freeze me in place freeze my feet right to the floor*)

to stop him. And that voice had gotten in because while he was sending and receiving, he was *open*—

Jake! Jake, where are you?

There was no time to answer her. Once, while trying to open the unfound door in the Cave of Voices, Jake had summoned a vision of a million doors opening wide. Now he summoned one of them slamming shut, creating a sound like God's own sonic boom.

Just in time, too. For a moment longer his feet remained stuck to the dusty floor, and then something screamed in agony and pulled back from him. Let him go.

Jake got moving, jerkily at first, then picking up steam. God, that had been close! Very faintly, he heard Susannah call his name again but didn't dare throw himself open enough to reply. He'd just have to hope that Oy would hold onto her scent, and that she would keep sending.

THREE

He decided later that he must have started singing the song from
Mrs. Shaw's radio shortly after Susannah's final faint cry, but
there was no way of telling for sure. One might as well try to pin-
point the genesis of a headache or the exact moment one consciously realizes he is coming down with a cold. What Jake was
sure of was that there were more gunshots, and once the buzzing
whine of a ricochet, but all that was a good distance behind, and
finally he didn't bother ducking anymore (or even looking
back). Besides, Oy was moving fast now, really shucking those
furry little buns of his. Buried machinery thumped and
wheezed. Steel rails surfaced in the passageway floor, leading
Jake to assume that once a tram or some other kind of shuttle
had run here. At regular intervals, official communiqués
(PATRICIA AHEAD; FEDIC; DO YOU HAVE YOUR
BLUE PASS?) were printed on the walls. In some places
the tiles had fallen off, in others the tram-rails were gone, and in
several spots puddles of ancient, verminous water filled what
looked for all the world like potholes. Jake and Oy passed two or
three stalled vehicles that resembled a cross between golf-carts
and flatcars. They also passed a turnip-headed robot that flashed
the dim red bulbs of its eyes and made a single croaking sound
that might have been *halt.* Jake raised one of the Orizas, having
no idea if it could do any good against such a thing if it came
after him, but the robot never moved. That single dim flash
seemed to have drained the last few ergs in its batteries, or
energy cells, or atomic slug, or whatever it ran on. Here and
there he saw graffiti. Two were familiar. The first was ALL HAIL THE
CRIMSON KING, with the red eye above each of the I's in the message. The other read BANGO SKANK, '84. *Man,* Jake thought dis-
tractedly, *that guy Bango gets around.* And then heard himself
clearly for the first time, singing under his breath. Not words,
exactly, but just an old, barely remembered refrain from one of
the songs on Mrs. Shaw's kitchen radio: "A-wimeweh, a-wimeweh,
a-weee-ummm-immm-oweh . . ."

He quit it, creeped out by the muttery, talismanic quality of the chant, and called for Oy to stop. "Need to take a leak, boy."

"Oy!" Cocked ears and bright eyes providing the rest of the message: *Don't take too long.*

Jake sprayed urine onto one of the tile walls. Greenish dreck was seeping between the squares. He also listened for the sound of pursuit and was not disappointed. How many back there? What sort of posse? Roland probably would have known, but Jake had no idea. The echoes made it sound like a regiment.

As he was shaking off, it came to Jake Chambers that the Pere would never do this again, or grin at him and point his finger, or cross himself before eating. They had killed him. Taken his life. Stopped his breath and pulse. Save perhaps for dreams, the Pere was now gone from the story. Jake began to cry. Like his smile, the tears made him once again look like a child. Oy had turned around, eager to be off on the scent, but now looked back over one shoulder with an expression of unmistakable concern.

"'S'all right," Jake said, buttoning his fly and then wiping his cheeks with the heel of his hand. Only it wasn't all right. He was more than sad, more than angry, more than scared about the low men running relentlessly up his backtrail. Now that the adrenaline in his system had receded, he realized he was hungry as well as sad. Tired, too. *Tired?* Verging on exhaustion. He couldn't remember when he'd last slept. Being sucked through the door into New York, he could remember that, and Oy almost being hit by a taxi, and the God-bomb minister with the name that reminded him of Jimmy Cagney playing George M. Cohan in that old black-and-white movie he'd watched on the TV in his room when he was small. Because, he realized now, there had been a song in that movie about a guy named Harrigan: *H–A–double R–I; Harrigan, that's me.* He could remember those things, but not when he'd last eaten a square—

"*Ake!*" Oy barked, relentless as fate. If bumblers had a breaking point, Jake thought wearily, Oy was still a long way from his. "*Ake-Ake!*"

"Yeah-yeah," he agreed, pushing away from the wall. "Ake-Ake will now run-run. Go on. Find Susannah."

He wanted to plod, but plodding would quite likely not be good enough. Mere walking, either. He flogged his legs into a jog and once more began to sing under his breath, this time the words to the song: *In the jungle, the mighty jungle, the lion sleeps tonight . . . In the jungle, the quiet jungle, the lion sleeps tonight . . . ohhh . . .* "And then he was off again, *wimeweh, wimeweh, wimeweh,* nonsense words from the kitchen radio that was always tuned to the oldies on WCBS . . . only weren't memories of some movie wound around and into his memory of this particular song? Not a song from *Yankee Doodle Dandy* but from some other movie? One with scary monsters? Something he'd seen when he was just a little kid, maybe not even out of his

(*clouts*)

diapers?

"Near the village, the quiet village, the lion sleeps tonight . . . Near the village, the peaceful village, the lion sleeps tonight . . . HUH-oh, a-wimeweh, a-wimeweh . . ."

He stopped, breathing hard, rubbing his side. He had a stitch there but it wasn't bad, at least not yet, hadn't sunk deep enough to stop him. But that goo . . . that greenish goo dribbling between the tiles . . . it was oozing through the ancient grout and busted ceramic because this was

(*the jungle*)

deep below the city, deep like catacombs

(*wimeweh*)

or like—

"Oy," he said, speaking through chapped lips. Christ, he was so thirsty! "Oy, this isn't goo, this is *grass*. Or weeds . . . or . . ."

Oy barked his friend's name, but Jake hardly noticed. The echoing sound of the pursuers continued (had drawn a bit closer, in fact), but for the time being he ignored them, as well.

Grass, growing out of the tiled wall.

Overwhelming the wall.

He looked down and saw more grass, a brilliant green that was almost purple beneath the fluorescent lights, growing up out of the floor. And bits of broken tile crumbling into shards and fragments like remains of the old people, the ancestors who had lived and built before the Beams began to break and the world began to move on.

He bent down. Reached into the grass. Brought up sharp shards of tile, yes, but also *earth,* the earth of

(*the jungle*)

some deep catacomb or tomb or perhaps—

There was a beetle crawling through the dirt he'd scooped up, a beetle with a red mark on its back like a bloody smile, and Jake cast it away with a cry of disgust. Mark of the King! Say true! He came back to himself and realized that he was down on one knee, practicing at archaeology like the hero in some old movie while the hounds drew closer on his trail. And Oy was looking at him, eyes shining with anxiety.

"Ake! Ake-Ake!"

"Yeah," he said, heaving himself to his feet. "I'm coming. But Oy . . . what *is* this place?"

Oy had no idea why he heard anxiety in his ka-dinh's voice; what *he* saw was the same as before and what he smelled was the same as before: *her* smell, the scent the boy had asked him to find and follow. And it was fresher now. He ran on along its bright brand.

FOUR

Jake stopped again five minutes later, shouting, "Oy! Wait up a minute!"

The stitch in his side was back, and it was deeper, but it still wasn't the stitch that had stopped him. *Everything* had changed. Or was changing. And God help him, he thought he knew what it was changing into.

Above him the fluorescent lights still shone down, but the tile walls were shaggy with greenery. The air had become damp and humid, soaking his shirt and sticking it against his body. A beautiful orange butterfly of startling size flew past his wide eyes. Jake snatched at it but the butterfly eluded him easily. Almost merrily, he thought.

The tiled corridor had become a jungle path. Ahead of them, it sloped up to a ragged hole in the overgrowth, probably some sort of forest clearing. Beyond it Jake could see great old trees growing in a mist, their trunks thick with moss, their branches looped with vines. He could see giant spreading ferns, and through the green lace of the leaves, a burning jungle sky. He knew he was under New York, must be under New York, but—

What sounded like a monkey chittered, so close by that Jake flinched and looked up, sure he would see it directly overhead, grinning down from behind a bank of lights. And then, freezing his blood, came the heavy roar of a lion. One that was most definitely *not* asleep.

He was on the verge of retreating, and at full speed, when he realized he could *not*; the low men (probably led by the one who'd told him the *faddah* was *dinnah*) were back that way. And Oy was looking at him with bright-eyed impatience, clearly wanting to go on. Oy was no dummy, but he showed no signs of alarm, at least not concerning what was ahead.

For his own part, Oy still couldn't understand the boy's problem. He knew the boy was tired—he could smell that— but he also knew Ake was afraid. Why? There were unpleasant smells in this place, the smell of many men chief among them, but they did not strike Oy as immediately dangerous. And besides, *her* smell was here. *Very* fresh now. Almost new.

"*Ake!*" he yapped again.

Jake had his breath now. "All right," he said, looking around. "Okay. But slow."

"*Lo,*" Oy said, but even Jake could detect the stunning lack of approval in the bumbler's response.

Jake moved only because he had no other options. He walked up the slope of the overgrown trail (in Oy's perception the way was perfectly straight, and had been ever since leaving the stairs) toward the vine- and fern-fringed opening, toward the lunatic chitter of the monkey and the testicle-freezing roar of the hunting lion. The song circled through his mind again and again

(*in the village . . . in the jungle . . . hush my darling, don't stir my darling . . .*)

and now he knew the name of it, even the name of the group

(*that's the Tokens with "The Lion Sleeps Tonight," gone from the charts but not from our hearts*)

that had sung it, but what was the *movie?* What was the name of the goddam *mo*—

Jake reached the top of the slope and the edge of the clearing. He looked through an interlacing of broad green leaves and brilliant purple flowers (a tiny green worm was journeying into the heart of one), and as he looked, the name of the movie came to him and his skin broke out in gooseflesh from the nape of his neck all the way down to his feet. A moment later the first dinosaur came out of the jungle (the mighty jungle), and walked into the clearing.

FIVE

Once upon a time long ago
   (far and wee)
   when he was just a little lad;
   (there's some for you and some for me)
   once upon a time when mother went to Montreal with her art club and father went to Vegas for the annual unveiling of the fall shows;
   (blackberry jam and blackberry tea)
   once upon a time when 'Bama was four—

SIX

'Bama's what the only good one
   (*Mrs. Shaw Mrs. Greta Shaw*)
   calls him. She cuts the crusts off his sandwiches, she puts his

nursie-school drawings on the fridge with magnets that look like little plastic fruits, she calls him 'Bama and that's a special name to him

(*to them*)

because his father taught him one drunk Saturday afternoon to chant "Go wide, go wide, roll you Tide, we don't run and we don't hide, we're the 'Bama Crimson Tide!" *and so she calls him 'Bama, it's a secret name and how they know what it means and no one else does is like having a house you can go into, a safe house in the scary woods where outside the shadows all look like monsters and ogres and tigers.*

("Tyger, tyger, burning bright," *his mother sings to him, for this is her idea of a lullabye, along with* "I heard a fly buzz . . . when I died," *which gives 'Bama Chambers a terrible case of the creeps, although he never tells her; he lies in bed sometimes at night and sometimes during afternoon naptime thinking* I will hear a fly and it will be my deathfly, my heart will stop and my tongue will fall down my throat like a stone down a well *and these are the memories he denies*)

It is good to have a secret name and when he finds out mother is going to Montreal for the sake of art and father is going to Vegas to help present the Network's new shows at the Up-fronts he begs his mother to ask Mrs. Greta Shaw to stay with him and finally his mother gives in. Little Jakie knows Mrs. Shaw is not mother and on more than one occasion Mrs. Greta Shaw herself has told him she is not mother

("I hope you know I'm not your mother, 'Bama," she says, giving him a plate and on the plate is a peanut butter, bacon, and banana sandwich with the crusts cut off as only Greta Shaw knows how to cut them off, "because that is not in my job description"

(And Jakie—only he's 'Bama here, he's 'Bama between them—doesn't know exactly how to tell her he knows that, knows that, knows that, but he'll make do with her until the real thing comes along or until he grows old enough to get over his fear of the Deathfly)

And Jakie says Don't worry, I'm okay, *but he is still glad Mrs. Shaw agrees to stay instead of the latest au pair who wears short skirts and is always playing with her hair and her lipstick and doesn't care jackshit about him and doesn't know that in his secret heart he is 'Bama, and boy that little Daisy Mae*

(which is what his father calls all *the au pairs)*

is stupid stupid stupid. *Mrs. Shaw isn't stupid. Mrs. Shaw gives him a snack she sometimes calls Afternoon Tea or even High Tea, and no matter what it is— cottage cheese and fruit, a sandwich with the crusts cut off, custard and cake, leftover canapés from a cocktail party the night before— she sings the same little song when she lays it out: "A little snack that's far and wee, there's some for you and some for me, blackberry jam and blackberry tea."*

There is a TV is his room, and every day while his folks are gone he takes his after-school snack in there and watches watches watches and he hears her radio in the kitchen, always the oldies, always WCBS, and sometimes he hears her, *hears Mrs. Greta Shaw singing along with the Four Seasons Wanda Jackson Lee "Yah-Yah" Dorsey, and sometimes he pretends his folks die in a plane crash and she somehow* does *become his mother and she calls him* poor little lad *and* poor little lost tyke *and then by virtue of some magical transformation she loves him instead of just taking care of him, loves him loves him loves him the way he loves her, she's his mother (or maybe his wife, he is unclear about the difference between the two), but she calls him 'Bama instead of sugarlove*

(his real mother)

or hotshot

(his father)

and *although he knows the idea is stupid, thinking about it in bed is fun, thinking about it beats the penis-piss out of thinking about the Deathfly that would come and buzz over his corpse when he died with his tongue down his throat like a stone down a well. In the afternoon when he gets home from nursie-school (by the time he's old enough to know it's* actually nursery school *he will be out of it) he watches* Million Dollar Movie *in his room. On* Million Dollar Movie *they show exactly the same movie at exactly the same time— four o'clock— every day for a week. The week before his parents went away and Mrs. Greta Shaw stayed the night instead of going home*

(O what bliss, for Mrs. Greta Shaw negates Discordia, can you say amen)

there was music from two directions every day, there were the oldies in the kitchen

(WCBS can you say God-bomb)

and on the TV James Cagney is strutting in a derby and singing about Harrigan—H–A–double R–I, Harrigan, that's me! *Also the one about being a real live nephew of my Uncle Sam.*

Then it's a new week, the week his folks are gone, and a new movie, and the first time he sees it it scares the living breathing shit out of him. This movie is called The Lost Continent, *and it stars Mr. Cesar Romero, and when Jake sees it again (at the advanced age of ten) he will wonder how he could ever have been afraid of such a stupid movie as that one. Because it's about explorers who get lost in the jungle, see, and there are* dinosaurs *in the jungle, and at four years of age he didn't realize the dinosaurs were nothing but* fucking CARTOONS, *no different from Tweety and Sylvester and Popeye the Sailor Man, uck-uck-uck, can ya say Wimpy, can you give me Olive Oyl. The first dinosaur he sees is a triceratops that comes blundering out of the jungle, and the girl explorer*

(Bodacious ta-tas, *his father would undoubtedly have said, it's what his father always says about what Jake's mother calls A Certain Type Of Girl*)

screams her lungs out, and Jake would scream too if he could but his chest is locked down with terror, o here is Discordia incarnate! In the monster's eyes he sees the utter nothing that means the end of everything, for pleading won't work with such a monster and screaming won't work with such a monster, it's too dumb, all screaming does is attract the monster's attention, and does, *it turns toward the Daisy Mae with the bodacious ta-tas and then it* charges *the Daisy Mae with the bodacious ta-tas, and in the kitchen (the mighty kitchen) he hears the Tokens, gone from the charts but not from our hearts, they are singing about the jungle, the peaceful jungle, and here in front of the little boy's huge horrified eyes is a jungle which is anything but peaceful, and it's not a lion but a lumbering thing that looks sort of like a rhinoceros only bigger, and it has a kind of bone collar around its neck, and later Jake will find out you call this kind of monster a* triceratops, *but for now it is nameless, which makes it even worse, nameless is worse.* "Wimeweh," *sing the Tokens,* "Weee-ummm-a-weh," *and of course Cesar Romero shoots the monster just before it can tear the girl with the bodacious ta-tas limb from limb, which is good at the time, but that night the monster comes back, the* triceratops *comes back, it's in his closet, because even at four he understands that sometimes his closet isn't his closet, that its door can open on different places where there are worse things waiting.*

He begins to scream, at night he can scream, and Mrs. Greta Shaw comes into the room. She sits on the edge of his bed, her face ghostly with blue-gray beautymud, and she asks him what's wrong 'Bama and he is actually able to tell her. He could never have told his father or mother, had one of them been there to begin with, which they of course aren't, but he can tell Mrs. Shaw because while she isn't a lot different from the other help — the au pairs babysitters child minders school-walkers — she is a little different, enough to put his drawings on the fridge with the little magnets, enough to make all the difference, to hold up the tower of a silly little boy's sanity, say hallelujah, say found not lost, say amen.

She listens to everything he has to say, nodding, and makes him say tri-CER-a-TOPS until finally he gets it right. Getting it right is better. And then she says, "Those things were real once, but they died out a hundred million years ago, 'Bama. Maybe even more. Now don't bother me any more because I need my sleep."

Jake watches The Lost Continent *on* Million Dollar Movie *every day that week. Every time he watches it, it scares him a little less. Once, Mrs. Greta Shaw comes in and watches part of it with him. She brings him his snack, a big bowl of Hawaiian Fluff (also one for herself) and sings him her wonderful little song: "A little snack that's far and wee, there's some for you and some for me, blackberry jam and blackberry tea." There are no blackberries in Hawaiian Fluff, of course, and they have the last of the Welch's Grape Juice to go with it instead of tea, but Mrs. Greta Shaw says it is the thought that counts. She has taught him to say* Rooty-tooty-salutie *before they drink, and to clink glasses. Jake thinks that's the absolute coolest, the cat's ass.*

Pretty soon the dinosaurs come. 'Bama and Mrs. Greta Shaw sit side by side, eating Hawaiian Fluff and watching as a big one (Mrs. Greta Shaw says you call that kind a Tyrannasorbet Wrecks) eats the bad explorer. "Cartoon dinosaurs," Mrs. Greta Shaw sniffs. "Wouldn't you think they could do better than that." As far as Jake is concerned, this is the most brilliant piece of film criticism he has ever heard in his life. Brilliant and useful.

Eventually his parents come back. Top Hat *enjoys a week's run on*

Million Dollar Movie *and little Jakie's night terrors are never mentioned. Eventually he forgets his fear of the triceratops and the Tyrannasorbet.*

SEVEN

Now, lying in the high green grass and peering into the misty clearing from between the leaves of a fern, Jake discovered that some things you *never* forgot.

Mind the mind-trap, Jochabim had said, and looking down at the lumbering dinosaur—a cartoon triceratops in a real jungle like an imaginary toad in a real garden—Jake realized that this was it. This was the mind-trap. The triceratops wasn't real no matter how fearsomely it might roar, no matter that Jake could actually smell it—the rank vegetation rotting in the soft folds where its stubby legs met its stomach, the shit caked to its vast armor-plated rear end, the endless cud drooling between its tusk-edged jaws—and hear its panting breath. It *couldn't* be real, it was a *cartoon,* for God's sake!

And yet he knew it was real enough to kill him. If he went down there, the cartoon triceratops would tear him apart just as it would have torn apart the Daisy Mae with the bodacious ta-tas if Cesar Romero hadn't appeared in time to put a bullet into the thing's One Vulnerable Spot with his big-game hunter's rifle. Jake had gotten rid of the hand that had tried to monkey with his motor controls—had slammed all those doors so hard he'd chopped off the hand's intruding fingers, for all he knew—but this was different. He could not close his eyes and just walk by; that was a real monster his traitor mind had created, and it could really tear him apart.

There was no Cesar Romero here to keep it from happening. No Roland, either.

There were only the low men, running his backtrail and getting closer all the time.

As if to emphasize this point, Oy looked back the way they'd come and barked once, piercingly loud.

The triceratops heard and roared in response. Jake expected

Oy to shrink against him at that mighty sound, but Oy continued to look back over Jake's shoulder. It was the *low men* Oy was worried about, not the triceratops below them or the Tyrannasorbet Wrecks that might come next, or—

Because Oy doesn't see it, he thought.

He monkeyed with this idea and couldn't pull it apart. Oy hadn't smelled it or heard it, either. The conclusion was inescapable: to Oy the terrible triceratops in the mighty jungle below did not exist.

Which doesn't change the fact that it does to me. It's a trap that was set for me, or for anyone else equipped with an imagination who might happen along. Some gadget of the old people, no doubt. Too bad it's not broken like most of their other stuff, but it's not. I see what I see and there's nothing I can do about i—

No, wait.

Wait just a second.

Jake had no idea how good his mental connection to Oy actually was, but thought he would soon find out.

"Oy!"

The calling voices of the low men were now horribly close. Soon they would see the boy and the bumbler stopped here and break into a charge. Oy could smell them coming but looked at Jake calmly enough anyway. At his beloved Jake, for whom he would die if called upon to do so.

"Oy, can you change places with me?"

It turned out that he could.

EIGHT

Oy tottered erect with Ake in his arms, swaying back and forth, horrified to discover how narrow the boy's range of balance was. The idea of walking even a short distance on but two legs was terribly daunting, yet it would have to be done, and done at once. Ake said so.

For his part, Jake knew he would have to shut the borrowed eyes he was looking through. He was in Oy's head but he could still see the triceratops; now he could also see a pterodactyl cruising the hot air above the clearing, its leathery wings stretched to catch the thermals blowing from the air-exchangers.

Oy! You have to do it on your own. And if we're going to stay ahead of them you have to do it now.

Ake! Oy responded, and took a tentative step forward. The boy's body wavered from side to side, out to the very edge of balance and then beyond. Ake's stupid two-legs body tumbled sideways. Oy tried to save it and only made the tumble worse, going down on the boy's right side and bumping Ake's furry head.

Oy tried to bark his frustration. What came out of Ake's mouth was a stupid thing that was more word than sound: "Bark! Ark! *Shit*-bark!"

"I hear him!" someone shouted. "Run! Come on, double-time, you useless cunts! Before the little bastard gets to the door!"

Ake's ears weren't keen, but with the way the tile walls magnified sounds, that was no problem. Oy could hear their running footfalls.

"You have to get up and go!" Jake tried to yell, and what came out was a garbled, barking sentence: *"Ake-Ake, affa! Up n go!"* Under other circumstances it might have been funny, but not under these.

Oy got up by putting Ake's back against the wall and pushing with Ake's legs. At last he was getting the hang of the motor controls; they were in a place Ake called *Dogan* and were fairly simple. Off to the left, however, an arched corridor led into a huge room filled with mirror-bright machinery. Oy knew that if he went into that place—the chamber where Ake kept all his marvelous thoughts and his store of words—he would be lost forever.

Luckily, he didn't need to. Everything he needed was in the Dogan. Left foot . . . forward. (*And pause.*) Right foot . . . forward. (*And pause.*) Hold the thing that looks like a billy-bumbler but is really your friend and use the other arm for balance. Resist the urge to drop to all fours and crawl. The pursuers will catch up if he does that; he can no longer smell them (not with

Ake's amazingly stupid little bulb of a snout), but he is sure of it, all the same.

For his part, Jake could smell them clearly, at least a dozen and maybe as many as sixteen. Their bodies were perfect engines of stink, and they pushed the aroma ahead of them in a dirty cloud. He could smell the asparagus one had had for dinner; could smell the meaty, wrong aroma of the cancer which was growing in another, probably in his head but perhaps in his throat.

Then he heard the triceratops roar again. It was answered by the bird-thing riding the air overhead.

Jake closed his—well, Oy's—eyes. In the dark, the bumbler's side-to-side motion was even worse. Jake was concerned that if he had to put up with much of it (especially with his eyes shut), he would ralph his guts out. Just call him 'Bama the Seasick Sailor.

Go, Oy, he thought. *Fast as you can. Don't fall down again, but . . . fast as you can!*

NINE

Had Eddie been there, he might have been reminded of Mrs. Mislaburski from up the block: Mrs. Mislaburski in February, after a sleet storm, when the sidewalk was glazed with ice and not yet salted down. But, ice or no ice, she would not be kept from her daily chop or bit of fish at the Castle Avenue Market (or from mass on Sunday, for Mrs. Mislaburski was perhaps the most devout Catholic in Co-Op City). So here she came, thick legs spread, candy-pink in their support hose, one arm clutching her purse to her immense bosom, the other held out for balance, head down, eyes searching for the islands of ashes where some responsible building super had already been out (Jesus and Mother Mary bless those good men), also for the treacherous patches that would defeat her, that would send her whoopsy with her large pink knees flying apart, and down she'd come on her sit-upon, or maybe on her back, a woman could break her spine, a woman could be *paralyzed* like poor

Mrs. Bernstein's daughter that was in the car accident in Mamaroneck, such things happened. And so she ignored the catcalls of the children (Henry Dean and his little brother Eddie often among them) and went on her way, head down, arm outstretched for balance, sturdy black old lady's purse curled to her midsection, determined that if she *did* go whoopsy-my-daisy she would protect her purse and its contents at all costs, would fall on it like Joe Namath falling on the football after a sack.

So did Oy of Mid-World walk the body of Jake along a stretch of underground corridor that looked (to him, at least) pretty much like all the rest. The only difference he could see was the three holes on either side, with big glass eyes looking out of them, eyes that made a low and constant humming sound.

In his arms was something that looked like a bumbler with its eyes squeezed tightly shut. Had they been open, Jake might have recognized these things as projecting devices. More likely he would not have seen them at all.

Walking slowly (Oy knew they were gaining, but he also knew that walking slowly was better than falling down), legs spread wide and shuffling along, holding Ake curled to his chest just as Mrs. Mislaburski had held her purse on those icy days, he made his way past the glass eyes. The hum faded. Was it far enough? He hoped so. Walking like a human was simply too hard, too nerve-wracking. So was being close to all of Ake's thinking machinery. He felt an urge to turn and look at it—all those bright mirror surfaces!—but didn't. To look might well bring on hypnosis. Or something worse.

He stopped. "Jake! Look! See!"

Jake tried to reply *Okay* and barked, instead. Pretty funny. He cautiously opened his eyes and saw tiled wall on both sides. There was grass and tiny sprays of fern still growing out of it, true enough, but it *was* tile. It *was* corridor. He looked behind him and saw the clearing. The triceratops had forgotten them. It was locked in a battle to the death with the Tyrannasorbet, a scene he recalled with complete clarity from *The Lost Continent.* The girl with the bodacious ta-tas had watched the battle from the safety of Cesar Romero's arms, and when the cartoon Tyrannasorbet had clamped its huge mouth over the triceratops's face in a death-bite, the girl had buried her own face against Cesar Romero's manly chest.

"Oy!" Jake barked, but barking was *lame* and he switched to thinking, instead.

Change back with me!

Oy was eager to comply—never had he wanted anything so much—but before they could effect the swap, the pursuers caught sight of them.

"*Theah!*" shouted the one with the Boston accent—he who had proclaimed that the *Faddah* was *dinnah.* "Theah they aah! Get em! Shoot em!"

And, as Jake and Oy switched their minds back into their proper bodies, the first bullets began to flick the air around them like snapping fingers.

TEN

The fellow leading the pursuers was a man named Flaherty. Of the seventeen of them, he was the only hume. The rest save one were low men and vampires. The last was a taheen with the head of an intelligent stoat and a pair of huge hairy legs protruding from Bermuda shorts. Below the legs were narrow feet that ended in brutally sharp thorns. A single kick from one of Lamla's feet could cut a full-grown man in half.

Flaherty—raised in Boston, for the last twenty years one of the King's men in a score of late-twentieth-century New Yorks—had put together his posse as fast as he could, in a nerve-roasting agony of fear and fury. *Nothing gets into the Pig.* That was what Sayre had told Meiman. And anything that *did* get in was not, under any circumstances, to be allowed out. That went double for the gunslinger or any of his ka-tet. Their meddling had long since passed the merely annoying stage, and you didn't have to be one of the elite to know it. But now Meiman, who had been called the Canary by his few friends, was dead and the kid had somehow gotten past them. A *kid,*

for God's love! A fucking *kid!* But how were they to know that
the two of them would have such a powerful totem as that turtle? If the damn thing hadn't happened to bounce beneath
one of the tables, it might be holding them in place still.

Flaherty knew it was true, but also knew that Sayre would
never accept it as a valid argument. Would not even give him,
Flaherty, a chance to put it forward. No, he would be dead long
before that, and the others, as well. Sprawled on the floor with
the doctor-bugs gorging on their blood.

It was easy to say that the kid would be stopped at the door,
that he wouldn't—*couldn't*—know any of the authorization
phrases that opened it, but Flaherty no longer trusted such
ideas, tempting as they might be. All bets were off, and Flaherty
felt a soaring sense of relief when he saw the kid and his furry little pal stopped up ahead. Several of the posse fired, but missed.
Flaherty wasn't surprised. There was some sort of green area
between them and the kid, a fucking swatch of jungle under the
city was what it looked like, and a mist was rising, making it hard
to aim. Plus some kind of ridiculous cartoon dinosaurs! One of
them raised its blood-smeared head and roared at them, holding its tiny forepaws against its scaly chest.

Looks like a dragon, Flaherty thought, and before his eyes the
cartoon dinosaur *became* a dragon. It roared and spewed a jet of
fire that set several dangling vines and a mat of hanging moss
to burning. The kid, meanwhile, was on the move again.

Lamla, the stoat-headed taheen, pushed his way to the forefront and raised one furred fist to his forehead. Flaherty
returned the salute impatiently. "What's down theah, Lam? Do
you know?"

Flaherty himself had never been below the Pig. When he
traveled on business, it was always between New Yorks, which
meant using either the door on Forty-seventh Street between
First and Second, the one in the eternally empty warehouse on
Bleecker Street (only in some worlds that one was an eternally
half-completed building), or the one way uptown on Ninety-
fourth Street. (The last was now on the blink much of the time,
and of course nobody knew how to fix it.) There were other

doors in the city—New York was lousy with portals to other wheres and whens—but those were the only ones that still worked.

And the one to Fedic, of course. The one up ahead.

"'Tis a mirage-maker," the stoat-thing said. Its voice was wet and rumbling and very far from human. "'Yon machine trolls for what ye fear and makes it real. Sayre would've turned it on when he and his tet passed with the blackskin jilly. To keep 'is backtrail safe, ye do ken."

Flaherty nodded. A mind-trap. Very clever. Yet how good was it, really? Somehow the cursed shitting boy had passed, hadn't he?

"Whatever the boy saw will turn into what *we* fear," the taheen said. "It works on imagination."

Imagination. Flaherty seized on the word. "Fine. Whatevah they see down theah, tell em to just ignore it."

He raised an arm to motion his men onward, greatly relieved by what Lam had told him. Because they had to press the chase, didn't they? Sayre (or Walter o' Dim, who was even worse) would very likely kill the lot of them if they failed to stop yon snot-babby. And Flaherty really *did* fear the idea of dragons, that was the other thing; had ever since his father had read him a story about such when he was a boy.

The taheen stopped him before he could complete the let's-go gesture.

"What now, Lam?" Flaherty snarled.

"You don't understand. What's down there is real enough to kill you. To kill *all* of us."

"What do *you* see, then?" This was no time to be curious, but that had always been Conor Flaherty's curse.

Lamla lowered his head. "I don't like to say. 'Tis bad enough. The point is, sai, we'll die down there if we're not careful. What happened to you might look like a stroke or a heart attack to a cut-em-up man, but t'would be whatever you see down there. Anyone who doesn't think the imagination can kill is a fool."

The rest had gathered behind the taheen now. They were

alternating glances into the hazy clearing with looks at Lamla. Flaherty didn't like what he saw on their faces, not a bit. Killing one or two of those least willing to veil their sullen eyes might restore the enthusiasm of the rest, but what good would that do if Lamla was right? Cursed old people, always leaving their toys behind! Dangerous toys! How they complicated a man's life! A pox on every last one!

"Then how do we get past?" Flaherty cried. "For that mattah, how did the *brat* get past?"

"Dunno about the brat," Lamla said, "but all *we* need to do is shoot the projectors."

"What shitting projectors?"

Lamla pointed below . . . or along the course of the corridor, if what the ugly bastard said was true. "There," Lam said. "I know you can't see em, but take my word for it, they're there. Either side."

Flaherty was watching with a certain fascination as Jake's misty jungle clearing continued to change before his eyes into the deep dark forest, as in *Once upon a time when everyone lived in the deep dark forest and nobody lived anywhere else, a dragon came to rampage.*

Flaherty didn't know what Lamla and the rest of them were seeing, but before his eyes the dragon (which had been a Tyrannasorbet Wrecks not so long ago) obediently rampaged, setting trees on fire and looking for little Catholic boys to eat.

"I see *NOTHING!*" he shouted at Lamla. "I think youah out of your shitting *MIND!*"

"I've seen em turned off," Lamla said quietly, "and can recall near about where they lie. If you'll let me bring up four men and set em shooting on either side, I don't believe it will take long to shut em down."

And what will Sayre say when I tell him we shot the hell out of his precious mind-trap? Flaherty could have said. *What will Walter o' Dim say, for that mattah? For what's roont can never be fixed, not by such as us who know how to rub two sticks together and make a fire but not much more.*

Could have said but didn't. Because getting the boy was

more important than any antique gadget of the old people, even one as amazing as yon mind-trap. And Sayre was the one who turned it on, wasn't he? Say aye! If there was explaining to be done, let Sayre do it! Let him make his knee to the big boys and talk till they shut him up! Meanwhile, the gods-damned snot-babby continued to rebuild the lead that Flaherty (who'd had visions of being honored for stepping so promptly into the breach) and his men had so radically reduced. If only one of them had been lucky enough to hit the kid when he and his little furbag friend had been in view! Ah, but wish in one hand, shit in the other! See which one fills up first!

"Bring youah best shots," Flaherty said in his Back Bay/John F. Kennedy accent. "Have at it."

Lamla ordered three low men and one of the vamps forward, put two on each side, and talked to them rapidly in another language. Flaherty gathered that a couple of them had already been down here and, like Lam, remembered about where the projectors lay hidden in the walls.

Meanwhile, Flaherty's dragon—or, more properly speaking, his *da's* dragon—continued to rampage in the deep dark forest (the jungle was completely gone now) and set things on fire.

At last—although it seemed a very long time to Flaherty, it was probably less than thirty seconds—the sharpshooters began to fire. Almost immediately both forest and dragon paled before Flaherty's eyes, turned into something that looked like overexposed movie footage.

"That's one of 'em, cullies!" Lamla yelled in a voice that became unfortunately ovine when it was raised. *"Pour it on! Pour it on for the love of your fathers!"*

Half this crew probably never had such a thing, Flaherty thought morosely. Then came the clearly audible shatter-sound of breaking glass and the dragon froze in place with billows of flame issuing from its mouth and nostrils, as well as from the gills on the sides of its armored throat.

Encouraged, the sharpshooters began firing faster, and a few moments later the clearing and the frozen dragon both disappeared. Where they had been was only more tiled hallway, with the tracks of those who had recently passed this way marking the dust. On either side were the shattered projector portals.

"All right!" Flaherty yelled after giving Lamla an approving nod. "Now we're going after the kid, and we're going to double-time it, and we're going to catch him, and we're going to bring him back with his head on a stick! Are you with me?"

They roared savage agreement, none louder than Lamla, whose eyes glowed the same baleful yellow-orange as the dragon's breath.

"Good, then!" Flaherty set off, roaring a tune any Marine drill-corps would have recognized: *"We don't care how far you run—"*

"WE DON'T CARE HOW FAR YOU RUN!" they bawled back as they trotted four abreast through the place where Jake's jungle had been. Their feet crunched in the shattered glass.

"We'll bring you back before we're done!"
"WE'LL BRING YOU BACK BEFORE WE'RE DONE!"
"You can run to Cain or Lud—"
"YOU CAN RUN TO CAIN OR LUD!"
"We'll eat your balls and drink your blood!"

They called it in return, and Flaherty picked up the pace yet a little more.

ELEVEN

Jake heard them coming again, come-come-commala. Heard them promising to eat his balls and drink his blood.

Brag, brag, brag, he thought, but tried to run faster, anyway. He was alarmed to find he couldn't. Doing the mindswap with Oy had tired him out quite a little b—

No.

Roland had taught him that self-deception was nothing but pride in disguise, an indulgence to be denied. Jake had done his best to heed this advice, and as a result admitted that "being tired" no longer described his situation. The stitch in his side had grown fangs that had sunk deep into his armpit. He knew he had gained on his pursuers; he also knew from the shouted cadence-chant that they were making up the distance they'd lost. Soon they would be shooting at him and Oy again, and while men didn't shoot for shit while they were running, someone could always get lucky.

Now he saw something up ahead, blocking the corridor. A door. As he approached it, Jake allowed himself to wonder what he'd do if Susannah wasn't on the other side. Or if she was there but didn't know how to help him.

Well, he and Oy would make a stand, that was all. No cover, no way to reenact Thermopylae Pass this time, but he'd throw plates and take heads until they brought him down.

If he needed to, that was.

Maybe he would not.

Jake pounded toward the door, his breath now hot in his throat—close to burning—and thought, *It's just as well. I couldn't have run much further, anyway.*

Oy got there first. He put his front paws on the ghostwood and looked up as if reading the words stamped into the door and the message flashing below them. Then he looked back at Jake, who came panting up with one hand pressed against his armpit and the remaining Orizas clanging loudly back and forth in their bag.

NORTH CENTRAL POSITRONICS, LTD.
New York/Fedic

Maximum Security
VERBAL ENTRY CODE REQUIRED
#9 FINAL DEFAULT

He tried the doorknob, but that was only a formality. When the chilly metal refused to turn in his grip, he didn't bother trying again but hammered the heels of both hands against the wood, instead. "Susannah!" he shouted. "If you're there, let me in!"

Not by the hair of my chinny-chin-chin he heard his father say, and his mother, much more gravely, as if she knew storytelling was serious business: *I heard a fly buzz . . . when I died.*

From behind the door there was nothing. From behind Jake, the chanting voices of the Crimson King's posse swept closer.

"*Susannah!*" he bawled, and when there was no answer this time he turned, put his back to the door (hadn't he always known it would end just this way, with his back to a locked door?), and seized an Oriza in each hand. Oy stood between his feet, and now his fur was bushed out, now the velvety-soft skin of his muzzle wrinkled back to show his teeth.

Jake crossed his arms, assuming "the load."

"Come on then, you bastards," he said. "For Gilead and the Eld. For Roland, son of Steven. For me and Oy."

At first he was too fiercely concentrated on dying well, of taking at least one of them with him (the fellow who'd told him the *Faddah* was *dinnah* would be his personal preference) and more if he could, to realize the voice he was hearing had come from the other side of the door rather than from his own mind.

"Jake! Is it really you, sugarpie?"

His eyes widened. Oh please let it not be a trick. If it was, Jake reckoned that he would never be played another.

"Susannah, they're coming! Do you know how—"

"*Yes!* Should still be *chassit,* do you hear me? If Nigel's right, the word should still be *cha—*"

Jake didn't give her a chance to finish saying it again. Now he could see them sweeping toward him, running full-out. Some waving guns and already shooting into the air.

"*Chassit!*" he yelled. "*Chassit* for the Tower! *Open! Open, you son of a bitch!*"

Behind his pressing back the door between New York and Fedic clicked open. At the head of the charging posse, Flaherty saw it happen, uttered the bitterest curse in his lexicon, and fired a single bullet. He was a good shot, and all the force of his not inconsiderable will went with that particular slug, guiding it. No doubt it would have punched through Jake's forehead above the left eye, entering his brain and ending his life, had not a strong, brown-fingered hand seized Jake by the collar at that very moment and yanked him backward through the shrill elevator-shaft whistle that sounds endlessly between the levels of the Dark Tower. The bullet buzzed by his head instead of entering it.

Oy came with him, barking his friend's name shrilly— *Ake-Ake, Ake-Ake!*—and the door slammed shut behind them. Flaherty reached it twenty seconds later and hammered on it until his fists bled (when Lamla tried to restrain him, Flaherty thrust him back with such ferocity that the taheen went a-sprawl), but there was nothing he could do. Hammering did not work; cursing did not work; nothing worked.

At the very last minute, the boy and the bumbler had eluded them. For yet a little while longer the core of Roland's ka-tet remained unbroken.

Chapter VI:
On Turtleback Lane

See this, I do beg ya, and see it very well, for it's one of the most beautiful places that still remain in America.

I'd show you a homely dirt lane running along a heavily wooded switchback ridge in western Maine, its north and south ends spilling onto Route 7 about two miles apart. Just west of this ridge, like a jeweler's setting, is a deep green dimple in the landscape. At the bottom of it—the stone in the setting—is Kezar Lake. Like all mountain lakes, it may change its aspect half a dozen times in the course of a single day, for here the weather is beyond prankish; you could call it half-mad and be perfectly accurate. The locals will be happy to tell you about ice-cream snow flurries that came to this part of the world once in late August (that would be 1948) and once spang on the Glorious Fourth (1959). They'll be even more delighted to tell you about the tornado that came blasting across the lake's frozen surface in January of 1971, sucking up snow and creating a whirling mini-blizzard that crackled with thunder in its middle. Hard to believe such crazy-jane weather, but you could go and see Gary Barker, if you don't believe me; he's got the pictures to prove it.

Today the lake at the bottom of the dimple is blacker than homemade sin, not just reflecting the thunderheads massing overhead but amplifying their mood. Every now and then a splinter of silver streaks across that obsidian looking-glass as lightning stabs out of the clouds overhead. The sound of thunder rolls through the congested sky west to east, like the wheels of some great stone bucka rolling down an alley in the sky. The pines and oaks and birches are still and all the world holds its

113

breath. All shadows have disappeared. The birds have fallen silent. Overhead another of those great waggons rolls its solemn course, and in its wake—hark!—we hear an engine. Soon enough John Cullum's dusty Ford Galaxie appears with Eddie Dean's anxious face rising behind the wheel and the headlights shining in the premature gathering dark.

TWO

Eddie opened his mouth to ask Roland how far they were going, but of course he knew. Turtleback Lane's south end was marked by a sign bearing a large black 1, and each of the driveways splitting off lakeward to their left bore another, higher number. They caught glimpses of the water through the trees, but the houses themselves were below them on the slope and tucked out of sight. Eddie seemed to taste ozone and electric grease with every breath he drew, and twice patted the hair on the nape of his neck, sure it would be standing on end. It wasn't, but knowing it didn't change the nervous, witchy feeling of exhilaration that kept sweeping through him, lighting up his solar plexus like an overloaded circuit-breaker and spreading out from there. It was the storm, of course; he just happened to be one of those people who feel them coming along the ends of their nerves. But never one's approach as strongly as this.

It's not all the storm, and you know it.

No, of course not. Although he thought all those wild volts might somehow have facilitated his contact with Susannah. It came and went like the reception you sometimes got from distant radio stations at night, but since their meeting with

(*Ye Child of Roderick, ye spoiled, ye lost*)

Chevin of Chayven, it had become much stronger. Because this whole part of Maine was thin, he suspected, and close to many worlds. Just as their ka-tet was close to whole again. For Jake was with Susannah, and the two of them seemed to be safe enough for the time being, with a solid door between them and their pursuers. Yet there was something ahead of those two, as well—something Susannah either didn't want to talk about or couldn't make clear. Even so, Eddie had sensed both her horror of it and her terror that it might come back, and he thought he knew what it was: Mia's baby. Which had been Susannah's as well in some way he still didn't fully understand. Why an armed woman should be afraid of an infant, Eddie didn't know, but he was sure that if she was, there must be a good reason for it.

They passed a sign that said FENN, 11, and another that said ISRAEL, 12. Then they came around a curve and Eddie stamped on the Galaxie's brakes, bringing the car to a hard and dusty stop. Parked at the side of the road beside a sign reading BECKHARDT, 13, was a familiar Ford pickup truck and an even more familiar man leaning nonchalantly against the truck's rust-spotted longbed, dressed in cuffed bluejeans and an ironed blue chambray shirt buttoned all the way to the closeshaved, wattled neck. He also wore a Boston Red Sox cap tilted just a little to one side as if to say *I got the drop on you, partner.* He was smoking a pipe, the blue smoke rising and seeming to hang suspended around his seamed and good-humored face on the breathless pre-storm air.

All this Eddie saw with the clarity of his amped-up nerves, aware that he was smiling as you do when you come across an old friend in a strange place—the Pyramids of Egypt, the marketplace in old Tangiers, maybe an island off the coast of Formosa, or Turtleback Lane in Lovell on a thunderstruck afternoon in the summer of 1977. And Roland was also smiling. Old long, tall, and ugly—smiling! Wonders never ceased, it seemed.

They got out of the car and approached John Cullum. Roland raised a fist to his forehead and bent his knee a little. "Hile, John! I see you very well."

"Ayuh, see you, too," John Cullum said. "Clear as day." He skimmed a salute outward from beneath the brim of his cap and above the tangle of his eyebrows. Then he dipped his chin in Eddie's direction. "Young fella."

"Long days and pleasant nights," Eddie said, and touched his knuckles to his brow. He was not from this world, not anymore, and it was a relief to give up the pretense.

"That's a pretty thing to say," John remarked. Then: "I beat you here. Kinda thought I might."

Roland looked around at the woods on both sides of the road, and at the lane of gathering darkness in the sky above it. "I don't think this is quite the place . . . ?" In his voice was the barest touch of a question.

"Nope, it ain't quite the place you want to finish up," John agreed, puffing his pipe. "I passed where you want to finish up on m'way in, and I tell you this: if you mean to palaver, we better do it here rather than there. You go up there, you won't be able t'do nawthin but gape. I tell you, I ain't never seen the beat of it." For a moment his face shone like the face of a child who's caught his first firefly in a jar and Eddie saw that he meant every word.

"Why?" he asked. "What's up there? Is it walk-ins? Or is it a door?" The idea occurred to him . . . and then seized him. "It *is* a door, isn't it? And it's open!"

John began to shake his head, then appeared to reconsider. "Might be a door," he said, stretching the noun out until it became something luxurious, like a sigh at the end of a long hard day: *doe-ahh.* "Doesn't exactly *look* like a door, but . . . ayuh. Could be. Somewhere in that light?" He appeared to calculate. "Ayuh. But I think you boys want to palaver, and if we go up there to Cara Laughs, there won't be no palaver; just you standin there with your jaws dropped." Cullum threw back his head and laughed. "Me, too!"

"What's Cara Laughs?" Eddie asked.

John shrugged. "A lot of folks with lakefront properties name their houses. I think it's because they pay s'much for em, they want a little more back. Anyway, Cara's empty right now. Family named McCray from Washington D.C. owns it, but they gut it up for sale. They've run onto some hard luck. Fella had a stroke, and she . . ." He made a bottle-tipping motion.

Eddie nodded. There was a great deal about this Tower-chasing business he didn't understand, but there were also things he knew without asking. One was that the core of the walk-in activity in this part of the world was the house on Turtleback Lane John Cullum had identified as Cara Laughs. And when they got there, they'd find the identifying number at the head of the driveway was 19.

He looked up and saw the storm-clouds moving steadily west above Kezar Lake. West toward the White Mountains, too—what was almost surely called the Discordia in a world not far from here—and along the Path of the Beam.

Always along the Path of the Beam.

"What do you suggest, John?" Roland asked.

Cullum nodded at the sign reading BECKHARDT. "I've care-took for Dick Beckhardt since the late fifties," he said. "Helluva nice man. He's in Wasin'ton now, doin something with the Carter administration." *Caaa-tah.* "I got a key. I think maybe we ought to go on down there. It's warm n dry, and I don't think it's gonna be either one out here before long. You boys c'n tell your tale, and I c'n listen—which is a thing I do tol'ably well—and then we can all take a run up to Cara. I . . . well I just *never* . . ." He shook his head, took his pipe out of his mouth, and looked at them with naked wonder. "I never seen the beat of it, I tell you. It was like I didn't even know how to look at it."

"Come on," Roland said. "We'll all ride down in your car-tomobile, if it does ya."

"Does me just fine," John said, and got into the back.

THREE

Dick Beckhardt's cottage was half a mile down, pine-walled, cozy. There was a pot-bellied stove in the living room and a braided rug on the floor. The west-facing wall was glass from end to end and Eddie had to stand there for a moment, looking out, in spite of the urgency of their errand. The lake had gone a shade of dead ebony that was somehow frightening—*like the eye of a zombie,* he thought, and had no idea why he thought it. He had an idea that if the wind picked up (as it would surely do when the rain came), the whitecaps would ruffle the surface and make it easier to look at. Would take away that look of some-thing looking back at *you.*

John Cullum sat at Dick Beckhardt's table of polished pine, took off his hat, and held it in the bunched fingers of his right hand. He looked at Roland and Eddie gravely. "We know each other pretty damn well for folks who haven't known each other very damn long," he said. "Wouldn't you say that's so?"

They nodded. Eddie kept expecting the wind to begin outside, but the world went on holding its breath. He was willing to bet it was going to be one hellacious storm when it came.

"Folks gut t'know each other that way in the Army," John said. "In the war." *Aaa-my.* And *war* too Yankee for representation. "Way it always is when the chips're down, I sh'd judge."

"Aye," Roland agreed. " 'Gunfire makes close relations,' we say."

"Do ya? Now I know you gut things to tell me, but before you start, there's one thing I gut to tell you. And I sh'd smile n kiss a pig if it don't please you good n hard."

"What?" Eddie asked.

"County Sheriff Eldon Royster took four fellas into custody over in Auburn couple of hours ago. Seems as though they was tryin to sneak past a police roadblock on a woods road and gut stuck for their trouble." John put his pipe in his mouth, took a wooden match from his breast pocket, and set his thumb against the tip. For the moment, however, he didn't flick it; only held it there. "Reason they 'us tryin to sneak around is they seemed to have quite a fair amount of fire-power." *Fiah-powah.* "Machine-guns, grenades, and some of that stuff they call C-4. One of em was a fella I b'lieve you mentioned—Jack Andolini?" And with that he popped the Diamond Bluetip alight.

Eddie collapsed back in one of sai Beckhardt's prim Shaker chairs, turned his head up to the ceiling, and bellowed laughter at the rafters. When he was tickled, Roland reflected, no one could laugh like Eddie Dean. At least not since Cuthbert Allgood had passed into the clearing. "Handsome Jack Andolini, sitting in a county hoosegow in the State of Maine!" he said. "Roll me in sugar and call me a fuckin jelly-doughnut! If only my brother Henry was alive to see it."

Then Eddie realized that Henry probably *was* alive right

now—some version of him, anyway. Assuming the Dean brothers existed in this world.

"Ayuh, thought that'd please ya," John said, drawing the flame of the rapidly blackening match down into the bowl of his pipe. It clearly pleased him, too. He was grinning almost too hard to kindle his tobacco.

"Oh deary-dear," Eddie said, wiping his eyes. "That makes my day. Almost makes my *year.*"

"I gut somethin else for ya," John said, "but we'll let her be for now." The pipe was at last going to his satisfaction and he settled back, eyes shifting between the two strange, wandering men he had met earlier that day. Men whose ka was now entwined with his own, for better or worse, and richer or poorer. "Right now I'd like t'hear your story. And just what it is you'd have me do."

"How old are you, John?" Roland asked him.

"Not s' old I don't still have a little get up n go," John replied, a trifle coldly. "What about y'self, chummy? How many times you ducked under the pole?"

Roland gave him a smile—the kind that said *point taken, now let's change the subject.* "Eddie will speak for both of us," he said. They had decided on this during their ride from Bridgton. "My own tale's too long."

"Do you say so," John remarked.

"I do," Roland said. "Let Eddie tell you his story, as much as he has time for, and we'll both tell what we'd have you do, and then, if you agree, he'll give you one thing to take to a man named Moses Carver . . . and I'll give you another."

John Cullum considered this, then nodded. He turned to Eddie.

Eddie took a deep breath. "The first thing you ought to know is that I met this guy here in a middle of an airplane flight from Nassau, the Bahamas, to Kennedy Airport in New York. I was hooked on heroin at the time, and so was my brother. I was muling a load of cocaine."

"And when might this have been, son?" John Cullum asked.

"The summer of 1987."

They saw wonder on Cullum's face but no shade of disbelief. "So you *do* come from the future! Gorry!" He leaned forward through the fragrant pipe-smoke. "Son," he said, "tell your tale. And don'tcha skip a goddam word."

FOUR

It took Eddie almost an hour and a half—and in the cause of brevity he *did* skip some of the things that had happened to them. By the time he'd finished, a premature night had settled on the lake below them. And still the threatening storm neither broke nor moved on. Above Dick Beckhardt's cottage thunder sometimes rumbled and sometimes cracked so sharply they all jumped. A stroke of lightning jabbed directly into the center of the narrow lake below them, briefly illuminating the entire surface a delicate nacreous purple. Once the wind arose, making voices move through the trees, and Eddie thought *It'll come now, surely it will come now,* but it did not. Nor did the impending storm leave, and this queer suspension, like a sword hanging by the thinnest of threads, made him think of Susannah's long, strange pregnancy, now terminated. At around seven o'clock the power went out and John looked through the kitchen cabinets for a supply of candles while Eddie talked on—the old people of River Crossing, the mad people in the city of Lud, the terrified people of Calla Bryn Sturgis, where they'd met a former priest who seemed to have stepped directly out of a book. John put the candles on the table, along with crackers and cheese and a bottle of Red Zinger iced tea. Eddie finished with their visit to Stephen King, telling how the gunslinger had hypnotized the writer to forget their visit, how they had briefly seen their friend Susannah, and how they had called John Cullum because, as Roland said, there was no one else in this part of the world they *could* call. When Eddie fell silent, Roland told of meeting Chevin of Chayven on their way to Turtleback Lane. The gunslinger laid the silver cross he'd shown Chevin on the table by the plate of cheese, and John poked the fine links of the chain with one thick thumbnail.

Then, for a long time, there was silence.

When he could bear it no longer, Eddie asked the old care-taker how much of the tale he believed.

"All of it," John said without hesitation. "You gut to take care of that rose in New York, don't you?"

"Yes," Roland said.

"Because that's what's kep' one of those Beams safe while most of the others has been broken down by these what-do-you-call-em telepathics, the Breakers."

Eddie was amazed at how quickly and easily Cullum had grasped that, but perhaps there was no reason to be. *Fresh eyes see clear,* Susannah liked to say. And Cullum was very much what the grays of Lud would have called "a trig cove."

"Yes," Roland said. "You say true."

"The rose is takin care of one Beam. Stephen King's in charge of the other 'un. Least, that's what you think."

Eddie said, "He'd bear watching, John—all else aside, he's got some lousy habits—but once we leave this world's 1977, we can never come back and check on him."

"King doesn't exist in any of these other worlds?" John asked.

"Almost surely not," Roland said.

"Even if he does," Eddie put in, "what he does in them doesn't matter. This is the key world. This, and the one Roland came from. This world and that one are twins."

He looked at Roland for confirmation. Roland nodded and lit the last of the cigarettes John had given him earlier.

"I might be able to keep an eye on Stephen King," John said. "He don't need to know I'm doin it, either. That is, if I get back from doin your cussed business in New York. I gut me a pretty good idear what it is, but maybe you'd better spell it out." From his back pocket he took a battered notepad with the words Mead Memo written on the green cover. He paged most of the way through it, found a blank sheet, produced a pencil from his breast pocket, licked the tip (Eddie restrained a shudder), and then looked at them as expectantly as any freshman on the first day of high school.

"Now, dearies," he said, "why don't you tell your Uncle John the rest."

FIVE

This time Roland did most of the talking, and although he had less to say than Eddie, it still took him half an hour, for he spoke with great caution, every now and then turning to Eddie for help with a word or phrase. Eddie had already seen the killer and the diplomat who lived inside Roland of Gilead, but this was his first clear look at the envoy, a messenger who meant to get every word right. Outside, the storm still refused to break or to go away.

At last the gunslinger sat back. In the yellow glow of the candles, his face appeared both ancient and strangely lovely. Looking at him, Eddie for the first time suspected there might be more wrong with him than what Rosalita Munoz had called "the dry twist." Roland had lost weight, and the dark circles beneath his eyes whispered of illness. He drank off a whole glass of the red tea at a single draught, and asked: "Do you understand the things I've told you?"

"Ayuh." No more than that.

"Ken it very well, do ya?" Roland pressed. "No questions?"

"Don't think so."

"Tell it back to us, then."

John had filled two pages with notes in his looping scrawl. Now he paged back and forth between them, nodding to himself a couple of times. Then he grunted and returned the pad to his hip pocket. *He may be a country cousin, but he's a long way from stupid*, Eddie thought. *And meeting him was a long way from just luck; that was ka having a very good day.*

"Go to New York," John said. "Find this fella Aaron Deepneau. Keep his buddy out of it. Convince Deepneau that takin care of the rose in that vacant lot is just about the most important job in the world."

"You can cut the just-about," Eddie said.

John nodded as if that went without saying. He picked up

the piece of notepaper with the cartoon beaver on top and tucked it into his voluminous wallet. Passing the bill of sale to him had been one of the harder things Eddie Dean had had to do since being sucked through the unfound door and into East Stoneham, and he came close to snatching it back before it could disappear into the caretaker's battered old Lord Buxton. He thought he understood much better now about how Calvin Tower had felt.

"Because you boys now own the lot, you own the rose," John said.

"The Tet Corporation now owns the rose," Eddie said. "A corporation of which you're about to become executive vice-president."

John Cullum looked unimpressed with his putative new title. He said, "Deepneau's supposed to draw up articles of incorporation and make sure Tet's legal. Then we go to see this fella Moses Carver and make sure *he* gets on board. That's apt to be the hard part—" *Haa-aad paa-aat* "—but we'll give it our best go."

"Put Auntie's cross around your neck," Roland said, "and when you meet with sai Carver, show it to him. It may go a long way toward convincing him you're on the straight. But first you must blow on it, like this."

On their ride from Bridgton, Roland had asked Eddie if he could think of any secret—no matter how trivial or great—which Susannah and her godfather might have shared in common. As a matter of fact Eddie did know such a secret, and he was now astounded to hear Susannah speak it from the cross which lay on Dick Beckhardt's pine table.

"We buried Pimsy under the apple tree, where he could watch the blossoms fall in the spring," her voice said. "And Daddy Mose told me not to cry anymore, because God thinks to mourn a pet too long . . ."

Here the words faded away, first to a mutter and then to nothing at all. But Eddie remembered the rest and repeated it now: "'. . . to mourn a pet too long's a sin.' She said Daddy Mose told her she could go to Pimsy's grave once in awhile and whisper 'Be happy in heaven' but never to tell anyone else, because preachers don't hold much with the idea of animals going to heaven. And she kept the secret. I was the only one she ever told." Eddie, perhaps remembering that post-coital confidence in the dark of night, was smiling painfully.

John Cullum looked at the cross, then up at Roland, wide-eyed. "What is it? Some kind of tape recorder? It ain't, is it?"

"It's a sigul," Roland said patiently. "One that may help you with this fellow Carver, if he turns out to be what Eddie calls 'a hardass.'" The gunslinger smiled a little. *Hardass* was a term he liked. One he understood. "Put it on."

But Cullum didn't, at least not at once. For the first time since the old fellow had come into their acquaintance—including that period when they'd been under fire in the General Store—he looked genuinely discomposed. "Is it magic?" he asked.

Roland shrugged impatiently, as if to tell John that the word had no useful meaning in this context, and merely repeated: "Put it on."

Gingerly, as if he thought Aunt Talitha's cross might glow redhot at any moment and give him a serious burn, John Cullum did as bid. He bent his head to look down at it (momentarily giving his long Yankee face an amusing burgher's double chin), then tucked it into his shirt.

"Gorry," he said again, very softly.

SIX

Aware that he was speaking now as once he'd been spoken to, Eddie Dean said: "Tell the rest of your lesson, John of East Stoneham, and be true."

Cullum had gotten out of bed that morning no more than a country caretaker, one of the world's unknown and unseen. He'd go to bed tonight with the potential of becoming one of the world's most important people, a true prince of the Earth. If he was afraid of the idea, it didn't show. Perhaps he hadn't grasped it yet.

But Eddie didn't believe that. This was the man ka had put in their road, and he was both trig and brave. If Eddie had been Walter at this moment (or Flagg, as Walter sometimes called himself), he believed he would have trembled.

"Well," John said, "it don't mind a mite to ya who runs the company, but you want Tet to swallow up Holmes, because from now on the job doesn't have anything to do with makin toothpaste and cappin teeth, although it may go on lookin that way yet awhile."

"And what's—"

Eddie got no further. John raised a gnarled hand to stop him. Eddie tried to imagine a Texas Instruments calculator in that hand and discovered he could, and quite easily. Weird.

"Gimme a chance, youngster, and I'll tell you."

Eddie sat back, making a zipping motion across his lips.

"Keep the rose safe, that's first. Keep the *writah* safe, that's second. But beyond that, me and this guy Deepneau and this other guy Carver are s'posed to build up one of the world's most powerful corporations. We trade in real estate, we work with . . . uh . . ." He pulled out the battered green pad, consulted it quickly, and put it away. "We work with 'software developers,' whatever they are, because they're gonna be the next wave of technology. We're supposed to remember three words." He ticked them off. "Microsoft. Microchips. Intel. And n'matter how big we grow—or how *fast*—our three real jobs are the same: protect the rose, protect Stephen King, and try to screw over two other companies every chance we get. One's called Sombra. Other's . . ." There was the slightest of hesitations. "The other's North Central Positronics. Sombra's mostly interested in proppity, accordin to you fellas. Positronics . . . well, science and gadgets, that's obvious even to me. If Sombra wants a piece of land, Tet tries t'get it first. If North Central wants a patent, we try to get it first, or at least to frig it up for them. Throw it to a third party if it comes to that."

Eddie was nodding approval. He hadn't told John that last, the old guy had come up with it on his own.

"We're the Three Toothless Musketeers, the Old Farts of the

Apocalypse, and we're supposed to keep those two outfits from gettin what they want, by fair means or foul. Dirty tricks most definitely allowed." John grinned. "I never been to Harvard Business School"—Haa-vid Bi'ness School—"but I guess I can kick a fella in the crotch as well's anyone."

"Good," Roland said. He started to get up. "I think it's time we—"

Eddie raised a hand to stop him. Yes, he wanted to get to Susannah and Jake; couldn't wait to sweep his darling into his arms and cover her face with kisses. It seemed years since he had last seen her on the East Road in Calla Bryn Sturgis. Yet he couldn't leave it at this as easily as Roland, who had spent his life being obeyed and had come to take the death-allegiance of complete strangers as a matter of course. What Eddie saw on the other side of Dick Beckhardt's table wasn't another tool but an independent Yankee who was tough-minded and smart as a whip . . . but really too old for what they were asking. And speaking of too old, what about Aaron Deepneau, the Chemotherapy Kid?

"My friend wants to get moving and so do I," Eddie said. "We've got miles to go yet."

"I know that. It's on your face, son. Like a scar."

Eddie was fascinated by the idea of duty and ka as something that left a mark, something that might look like decoration to one eye and disfigurement to another. Outside, thunder cracked and lightning flashed.

"But why would you do this?" Eddie asked. "I have to know that. Why would you take all this on for two men you just met?"

John thought it over. He touched the cross he wore now and would wear until his death in the year of 1989—the cross given to Roland by an old woman in a forgotten town. He would touch it just that way in the years ahead when contemplating some big decision (the biggest might have been the one to sever Tet's connection with IBM, a company that had shown an ever-increasing willingness to do business with North Central Positronics) or preparing for some covert action (the firebombing of Sombra Enterprises in New Delhi, for instance, in the year before he died). The cross spoke to Moses Carver and never spoke again in Cullum's presence no matter how much he blew on it, but sometimes, drifting to sleep with his hand clasped around it, he would think: *'Tis a sigul. 'Tis a sigul, dear— something that came from another world.*

If he had regrets toward the end (other than about some of the tricks, which were filthy indeed and cost more than one man his life), it was that he never got a chance to visit the world on the other side, which he glimpsed one stormy evening on Turtleback Lane in the town of Lovell. From time to time Roland's sigul sent him dreams of a field filled with roses, and a sooty-black tower. Sometimes he was visited by terrible visions of two crimson eyes, floating unattached to any body and relentlessly scanning the horizon. Sometimes there were dreams in which he heard the sound of a man relentlessly winding his horn. From these latter dreams he would awake with tears on his cheeks, those of longing and loss and love. He would awake with his hand closed around the cross, thinking *I denied Discordia and regret nothing; I have spat into the bodiless eyes of the Crimson King and rejoice; I threw my lot with the gunslinger's ka-tet and the White and never once questioned the choice.*

Yet for all that he wished he could have walked out, just once, into that other land: the one beyond the door.

Now he said: "You boys want all the right things. I can't put it any clearer than that. I believe you." He hesitated. "I believe *in* you. What I see in your eyes is true."

Eddie thought he was done, and then Cullum grinned like a boy.

"Also it 'pears to me you're offerin the keys to one humongous great engine." *Engyne.* "Who wouldn't want to turn it on, and see what it does?"

"Are you scared?" Roland asked.

John Cullum considered the question, then nodded. "Ayuh," he said.

Roland nodded. "Good," he said.

SEVEN

They drove back up to Turtleback Lane in Cullum's car beneath a black, boiling sky. Although this was the height of the summer season and most of the cottages on Kezar were probably occupied, they saw not a single car moving in either direction. All the boats on the lake had long since run for cover.

"Said I had somethin else for ya," John said, and went to the back of his truck, where there was a steel lockbox snugged up against the cab. Now the wind had begun to blow. It swirled his scanty fluff of white hair around his head. He ran a combination, popped a padlock, and swung back the lockbox's lid. From inside he brought out two dusty bags the wanderers knew well. One looked almost new compared to the other, which was the scuffed no-color of desert dust and laced its long length with rawhide.

"Our gunna!" Eddie cried, so delighted—and so *amazed*—that the words almost came out in a scream. "How in the name of *hell*—?"

John offered them a smile that augured well for his future as a dirty trickster: bemused on the surface, sly beneath. "Nice surprise, ain't it? Thought so m'self. I went back to get a look at Chip's store—what 'us left of it—while there was still a lot of confusion. People runnin hither, thither, and yon is what I mean to say; coverin bodies, stringin that yella tape, takin pitchers. Somebody'd put those bags off to one side and they looked just a dight lonely, so I ..." He shrugged one bony shoulder. "I scooped em up."

"This would have been while we were visiting with Calvin Tower and Aaron Deepneau in their rented cabin," Eddie said. "After *you* went back home, supposedly to pack for Vermont. Is that right?" He was stroking the side of his bag. He knew that smooth surface very well; hadn't he shot the deer it had come from and scraped off the hair with Roland's knife and stitched the hide himself, with Susannah to help him? Not long after the great robot bear Shardik had almost unzipped Eddie's guts, that had been. Sometime in the last century, it seemed.

"Yuh," Cullum said, and when the old fellow's smile sweetened, Eddie's last doubts about him departed. They had found the right man for this world. Say true and thank Gan big-big.

"Strap on your gun, Eddie," Roland said, holding out the revolver with the worn sandalwood grips.

Mine. Now he calls it mine. Eddie felt a small chill.

"I thought we were going to Susannah and Jake." But he took the revolver and belted it on willingly enough.

Roland nodded. "But I believe we have a little work to do first, against those who killed Callahan and then tried to kill Jake." His face didn't change as he spoke, but both Eddie Dean and John Cullum felt a chill. For a moment it was almost impossible to look at the gunslinger.

So came—although they did not know it, which was likely more mercy than such as they deserved—the death sentence of Flaherty, the taheen Lamla, and their ka-tet.

EIGHT

Oh my God, Eddie tried to say, but no sound came out.

He had seen brightness growing ahead of them as they drove north along Turtleback Lane, following the one working taillight of Cullum's truck. At first he thought it might be the carriage-lamps guarding some rich man's driveway, then perhaps floodlights. But the glow kept strengthening, a blue-golden brilliance to their left, where the ridge sloped down to the lake. As they approached the source of the light (Cullum's pickup now barely crawling), Eddie gasped and pointed as a circle of radiance broke free of the main body and flew toward them, changing colors as it came: blue to gold to red, red to green to gold and back to blue. In the center of it was something that looked like an insect with four wings. Then, as it soared above the bed of Cullum's truck and into the dark woods on the east side of the road, it looked toward them and Eddie saw the insect had a human face.

"What . . . dear God, Roland, *what*—"

"Taheen," Roland said, and said no more. In the growing brilliance his face was calm and tired.

More circles of light broke free of the main body and streamed across the road in cometary splendor. Eddie saw flies and tiny jeweled hummingbirds and what appeared to be winged frogs. Beyond them . . .

The taillight of Cullum's truck flashed bright, but Eddie was so busy goggling that he would have rear-ended the man had Roland not spoken to him sharply. Eddie threw the Galaxie into Park without bothering to either set the emergency brake or turn off the engine. Then he got out and walked toward the blacktop driveway that descended the steep wooded slope. His eyes were huge in the delicate light, his mouth hung open. Cullum joined him and stood looking down. The driveway was flanked by two signs: CARA LAUGHS on the left and **19** on the right.

"Somethin, ain't it?" Cullum asked quietly.

You got that *right,* Eddie tried to reply, and still no words would come out of his mouth, only a breathless wheeze.

Most of the light was coming from the woods to the east of the road and to the left of the Cara Laughs driveway. Here the trees—mostly pines, spruces, and birches bent from a late-winter ice storm—were spread far apart, and hundreds of figures walked solemnly among them as though in a rustic ballroom, their bare feet scuffing through the leaves. Some were pretty clearly Children of Roderick, and as roont as Chevin of Chayven. Their skins were covered with the sores of radiation sickness and very few had more than a straggle of hair, but the light in which they walked gave them a beauty that was almost too great to look upon. Eddie saw a one-eyed woman carrying what appeared to be a dead child. She looked at him with an expression of sorrow and her mouth moved, but Eddie could hear nothing. He raised his fist to his forehead and bent his leg. Then he touched the corner of one eye and pointed to her. *I see you,* the gesture said . . . or so he hoped. *I see you very well.* The woman bearing the dead or sleeping child returned the gesture, and then passed from sight.

Overhead, thunder cracked sharply and lightning flashed down into the center of the glow. An ancient fir tree, its lusty trunk girdled with moss, took the bolt and split apart down its center, falling half one way and half the other. The inside was on fire. And a great gust of sparks—not fire, not this, but something with the ethereal quality of swamplight—went twisting up toward the hanging swags of the clouds. In those sparks Eddie saw tiny dancing bodies, and for a moment he couldn't breathe. It was like watching a squadron of Tinker Bells, there and then gone.

"Look at em," John said reverently. "Walk-ins! Gorry, there's *hundreds!* I wish my friend Donnie was here to see."

Eddie thought he was probably right: hundreds of men, women, and children were walking through the woods below them, walking through the light, appearing and disappearing and then appearing again. As he watched, he felt a cold drop of water splash his neck, followed by a second and a third. The wind swooped down through the trees, provoking another upward gush of those fairy-like creatures and turning the tree that had been halved by lightning into a pair of vast crackling torches.

"Come on," Roland said, grabbing Eddie's arm. "It's going to come a downpour and this'll go out like a candle. If we're still on this side when it does, we'll be stuck here."

"Where—" Eddie began, and then he saw. Near the foot of the driveway, where the forest cover gave way to a tumble of rocks falling down to the lake, was the core of the glow, for the time being too bright to look at. Roland dragged him in that direction. John Cullum remained hypnotized for a moment longer by the walk-ins, then tried to follow them.

"No!" Roland called over his shoulder. The rain was falling harder now, the drops cold on his skin and the size of coins. "You have your work, John! Fare you well!"

"And you, boys!" John called back. He stopped and raised his hand in a wave. A bolt of electricity cut across the sky, momentarily lighting his face in brilliant blue and deepest black. "And you!"

"Eddie, we're going to run into the core of the light," Roland said. "It's not a door of the old people but of the *Prim*—that *is* magic, do ye ken. It'll take us to the place we want, if we concentrate hard enough."

"Where—"

"There's no time! Jake's told me where, by touch! Only hold my hand and keep your mind blank! I can take us!"

Eddie wanted to ask him if he was absolutely sure of that, but there was no time. Roland broke into a run. Eddie joined him. They sprinted down the slope and into the light. Eddie felt it breathing over his skin like a million small mouths. Their boots crackled in the deep leaf cover. To his right was the burning tree. He could smell the sap and the sizzle of its cooking bark. Now they closed in on the core of the light. At first Eddie could see Kezar Lake through it and then he felt an enormous force grip him and pull him forward through the cold rain and into that brilliant murmuring glare. For just a moment he glimpsed the shape of a doorway. Then he redoubled his grip on Roland's hand and closed his eyes. The leaf-littered ground ran out beneath his feet and they were flying.

Chapter VII:
Reunion

Flaherty stood at the New York/Fedic door, which had been scarred by several gunshots but otherwise stood whole against them, an impassable barrier which the shitting kid had somehow passed. Lamla stood silent beside him, waiting for Flaherty's rage to exhaust itself. The others also waited, maintaining the same prudent silence.

Finally the blows Flaherty had been raining on the door began to slow. He administered one final overhand smash, and Lamla winced as blood flew from the hume's knuckles.

"What?" Flaherty asked, catching his grimace. *"What?* Do you have something to say?"

Lamla cared not at all for the white circles around Flaherty's eyes and the hard red roses in Flaherty's cheeks. Least of all for the way Flaherty's hand had risen to the butt of the Glock automatic hanging beneath his armpit. "No," he said. "No, sai."

"Go on, say what's on your mind, do it please ya," Flaherty persisted. He tried to smile and produced a gruesome grin instead—the leer of a madman. Quietly, with barely a rustle, the rest pulled back. "Others will have plenty to say; why shouldn't you start, my cully? I lost him! Be the first to carp, you ugly motherfucker!"

I'm dead, Lamla thought. *After a life of service to the King, one unguarded expression in the presence of a man who needs a scapegoat, and I'm dead.*

He looked around, verifying that none of the others would step in for him, and then said: "Flaherty, if I've offended you in some way I'm sor—"

133

"Oh, you've *offended* me, sure enough!" Flaherty shrieked, his Boston accent growing thicker as his rage escalated. "I'm sure I'll pay for tonight's work, aye, but I think you'll pay fir—"

There was a kind of gasp in the air around them, as if the corridor itself had inhaled sharply. Flaherty's hair and Lamla's fur rippled. Flaherty's posse of low men and vampires began to turn. Suddenly one of them, a vamp named Albrecht, shrieked and bolted forward, allowing Flaherty a view of two newcomers, men with raindrops still fresh and dark on their jeans and boots and shirts. There was trail-dusty gunna-gar at their feet and revolvers hung at their hips. Flaherty saw the sandalwood grips in the instant before the younger one drew, faster than blue blazes, and understood at once why Albrecht had run. Only one sort of man carried guns that looked like that.

The young one fired a single shot. Albrecht's blond hair jumped as if flicked by an invisible hand and then he collapsed forward, fading within his clothes as he did so.

"Hile, you bondsmen of the King," the older one said. He spoke in a purely conversational tone. Flaherty—his hands still bleeding from his extravagant drumming on the door through which the snot-babby had disappeared—could not seem to get the sense of him. It was the one of whom they had been warned, surely it was Roland of Gilead, but how had he gotten here, and on their blindside? *How?*

Roland's cold blue eyes surveyed them. "Which of this sorry herd calls himself dinh? Will that one honor us by stepping forward or not? Not?" His eyes surveyed them; his left hand departed the vicinity of his gun and journeyed to the corner of his mouth, where a small sarcastic smile had bloomed. "Not? Too bad. Th'art cowards after all, I'm sorry to see. Thee'd kill a priest and chase a lad but not stand and claim thy day's work. Th'art cowards and the sons of cow—"

Flaherty stepped forward with his bleeding right hand clasped loosely around the butt of the gun that hung below his left armpit in a docker's clutch. "That would be me, Roland-of-Steven."

"You know my name, do you?"

"Aye! I know your name by your face, and your face by your mouth. T'is the same as the mouth of your mother, who did suck John Farson with such glee until he spewed 'is—"

Flaherty drew as he spoke, a bushwhacker's trick he'd no doubt practiced and used before to advantage. And although he was fast and the forefinger of Roland's left hand still touched the side of his mouth when Flaherty's draw began, the gunslinger beat him easily. His first bullet passed between the lips of Jake's chief harrier, exploding the teeth at the front of his upper jaw to bone fragments which Flaherty drew down his throat with his dying breath. His second pierced Flaherty's forehead between the eyebrows and he was flung back against the New York/Fedic door with the unfired Glock spilling from his hand to discharge a final time on the hallway floor.

Most of the others drew a split-second later. Eddie killed the six in front, having taken time to reload the chamber he'd fired at Albrecht. When the revolver was empty, he rolled behind his dinh to reload, as he had been taught. Roland picked off the next five, then rolled smoothly behind Eddie, who took out the rest save one.

Lamla had been too cunning to try and so was the last standing. He raised his empty hands, the fingers furry and the palms smooth. "Will ye grant me parole, gunslinger, if I promise ye peace?"

"Not a bit," Roland said, and cocked his revolver.

"Be damned to you, then, chary-ka," said the taheen, and Roland of Gilead shot him where he stood, and Lamla of Galee fell down dead.

TWO

Flaherty's posse lay stacked in front of the door like cordwood, Lamla facedown in front. Not a single one had had a chance to fire. The tile-throated corridor stank of the gunsmoke which hung in a blue layer. Then the purifiers kicked in, chugging wearily in the wall, and the gunslingers felt the air first stirred into motion and then sucked across their faces.

Eddie reloaded the gun—his, now, so he had been told—and dropped it back into its holster. Then he went to the dead and yanked four of them absently aside so he could get to the door. "Susannah! Suze, are you there?"

Do any of us, except in our dreams, truly expect to be reunited with our hearts' deepest loves, even when they leave us only for minutes, and on the most mundane of errands? No, not at all. Each time they go from our sight we in our secret hearts count them as dead. Having been given so much, we reason, how could we expect not to be brought as low as Lucifer for the staggering presumption of our love?

So Eddie didn't expect her to answer until she did—from another world, and through a single thickness of wood. "Eddie? Sugar, is it you?"

Eddie's head, which had seemed perfectly normal only seconds before, was suddenly too heavy to hold up. He leaned it against the door. His eyes were similarly too heavy to hold open and so he closed them. The weight must have been tears, for suddenly he was swimming in them. He could feel them rolling down his cheeks, warm as blood. And Roland's hand, touching his back.

"Susannah," Eddie said. His eyes were still closed. His fingers were splayed on the door. "Can you open it?"

Jake answered. "No, but you can."

"What word?" Roland asked. He had been alternating glances at the door with looks behind him, almost hoping for reinforcements (for his blood was up), but the tiled corridor was empty. "What word, Jake?"

There was a pause—brief, but it seemed very long to Eddie—and then both spoke together. *"Chassit,"* they said.

Eddie didn't trust himself to say it; his throat was too full of tears. Roland had no such problem. He hauled several more bodies away from the door (including Flaherty's, his face still fixed in its final snarl) and then spoke the word. Once again the door between the worlds clicked open. It was Eddie who opened it wide and then the four of them were face-to-face again, Susannah and Jake in one world, Roland and Eddie in another, and between them a shimmering transparent membrane like living mica. Susannah held out her hands and they plunged through the membrane like hands emerging from a body of water that had been somehow magically turned on its side.

Eddie took them. He let her fingers close over his and draw him into Fedic.

THREE

By the time Roland stepped through, Eddie had already lifted Susannah and was holding her in his arms. The boy looked up at the gunslinger. Neither of them smiled. Oy sat at Jake's feet and smiled for both of them.

"Hile, Jake," Roland said.

"Hile, Father."

"Will you call me so?"

Jake nodded. "Yes, if I may."

"Such would please me ever," Roland said. Then, slowly—as one performs an action with which he's unfamiliar—he held out his arms. Looking up at him solemnly, never taking his eyes from Roland's face, the boy Jake moved between those killer's hands and waited until they locked at his back. He had had dreams of this that he would never have dared to tell.

Susannah, meanwhile, was covering Eddie's face with kisses. "They almost got Jake," she was saying. "I sat down on my side of the door . . . and I was so tired I nodded off. He musta called me three, four times before I . . ."

Later he would hear her tale, every word and to the end. Later there would be time for palaver. For now he cupped her breast—the left one, so he could feel the strong, steady beat of her heart—and then stopped her speech with his mouth.

Jake, meanwhile, said nothing. He stood with his head turned so his cheek rested against Roland's midsection. His eyes were closed. He could smell rain and dust and blood on the gunslinger's shirt. He thought of his parents, who were lost; his friend Benny, who was dead; the Pere, who had been overrun by all those from whom he had so long fled. The man he held had betrayed him once for the Tower, had let him fall, and Jake couldn't say the same might not happen again. Certainly there were miles ahead, and they would be hard ones. Still, for now, he was content. His mind was quiet and his sore heart was at peace. It was enough to hold and be held.

Enough to stand here with his eyes shut and to think *My father has come for me.*

PART TWO:
BLUE HEAVEN

DEVAR-TOI

Chapter I:
The Devar-Tete

ONE

The four reunited travelers (five, counting Oy of Mid-World) stood at the foot of Mia's bed, looking at what remained of Susannah's *twim*, which was to say her twin. Without the deflated clothes to give the corpse some definition, probably none of them could have said for certain what it had once been. Even the snarl of hair above the split gourd of Mia's head looked like nothing human; it could have been an exceptionally large dust-bunny.

Roland looked down at the disappearing features, wondering that so little remained of the woman whose obsession—the chap, the chap, always the chap—had come so near to wrecking their enterprise for good. And without them, who would remain to stand against the Crimson King and his infernally clever chancellor? John Cullum, Aaron Deepneau, and Moses Carver. Three old men, one of them with blackmouth disease, which Eddie called can't, sir.

So much you did, he thought, gazing raptly at the dusty, dissolving face. *So much you did and so much more you would have done, aye, and all without a check or qualm, and so will the world end, I think, a victim of love rather than hate. For love's ever been the more destructive weapon, sure.*

He leaned forward, smelling what could have been old flowers or ancient spices, and exhaled. The thing that looked vaguely like a head even now blew away like milkweed fluff or a dandy-o ball.

"She meant no harm to the universe," Susannah said, her voice not quite steady. "She only wanted any woman's privilege: to have a baby. Someone to love and raise."

141

"Aye," Roland agreed, "you say true. Which is what makes her end so black."

Eddie said, "Sometimes I think we'd all be better off if the people who mean well would just creep away and die."

"That'd be the end of *us,* Big Ed," Jake pointed out.

They all considered this, and Eddie found himself wondering how many they'd already killed with their well-intentioned meddling. The bad ones he didn't care about, but there had been others, too—Roland's lost love, Susan, was only one.

Then Roland left the powdery remains of Mia's corpse and came to Susannah, who was sitting on one of the nearby beds with her hands clasped between her thighs. "Tell me everything that befell since you left us on the East Road, after the battle," he said. "We need to—"

"Roland, I never meant to leave you. It was Mia. She took over. If I hadn't had a place to go—a Dogan—she might've taken over completely."

Roland nodded to show he understood that. "Nevertheless, tell me how you came to this devar-tete. And Jake, I'd hear the same from you."

"Devar-tete," Eddie said. The phrase held some faint familiarity. Did it have something to do with Chevin of Chayven, the slow mutie Roland had put out of its misery in Lovell? He thought so. "What's that?"

Roland swept a hand at the room with all its beds, each with its helmet-like machine and segmented steel hose; beds where the gods only knew how many children from the Callas had lain, and been ruined. "It means little prison, or torture-chamber."

"Doesn't look so little to me," Jake said. He couldn't tell how many beds there were, but he guessed the number at three hundred. Three hundred at least.

"Mayhap we'll come upon a larger one before we're finished. Tell your tale, Susannah, and you too, Jake."

"Where do we go from here?" Eddie asked.

"Perhaps the tale will tell," Roland answered.

TWO

Roland and Eddie listened in silent fascination as Susannah and Jake recounted their adventures, turn and turn about. Roland first halted Susannah while she was telling them of Mathiessen van Wyck, who had given her his money and rented her a hotel room. The gunslinger asked Eddie about the turtle in the lining of the bag.

"I didn't *know* it was a turtle. I thought it might be a stone."

"If you'd tell this part again, I'd hear," Roland said.

So, thinking carefully, trying to remember completely (for it all seemed a very long time ago), Eddie related how he and Pere Callahan had gone up to the Doorway Cave and opened the ghostwood box with Black Thirteen inside. They'd expected Black Thirteen to open the door, and so it had, but first—

"We put the box in the bag," Eddie said. "The one that said NOTHING BUT STRIKES AT MIDTOWN LANES in New York and NOTHING BUT STRIKES AT MID-*WORLD* LANES on the Calla Bryn Sturgis side. Remember?"

They all did.

"And I felt something in the lining of the bag. I told Callahan, and he said . . ." Eddie mulled it over. "He said, 'This isn't the time to investigate it.' Or something like that. I agreed. I remember thinking we had enough mysteries on our hands already, we'd save this one for another day. Roland, who in God's name put that thing in the bag, do you think?"

"For that matter, who left the bag in the vacant lot?" Susannah asked.

"Or the key?" Jake chimed in. "I found the key to the house in Dutch Hill in that same lot. Was it the rose? Did the rose somehow . . . I dunno . . . make them?"

Roland thought about it. "Were I to guess," he said, "I'd say that sai King left those signs and siguls."

"The writer," Eddie said. He weighed the idea, then nodded slowly. He vaguely remembered a concept from high school— the god from the machine, it was called. There was a fancy

Latin term for it as well, but that one he couldn't remember. Had probably been writing Mary Lou Kenopensky's name on his desk while the other kids had been obediently taking notes. The basic concept was that if a playwright got himself into a corner he could send down the god, who arrived in a flower-decked bucka wagon from overhead and rescued the characters who were in trouble. This no doubt pleased the more religious playgoers, who believed that God—not the special-effects version who came down from some overhead platform the audience couldn't see but the One who wert in heaven— really *did* save people who deserved it. Such ideas had undoubtedly gone out of fashion in the modern age, but Eddie thought that popular novelists—of the sort sai King seemed on his way to becoming—probably still used the technique, only disguising it better. Little escape hatches. Cards that read GET OUT OF JAIL FREE or ESCAPE THE PIRATES or FREAK STORM CUTS ELECTRICAL POWER, EXECUTION POSTPONED. The god from the machine (who was actually the writer), patiently working to keep the characters safe so his tale wouldn't end with an unsatisfying line like "And so the ka-tet was wiped out on Jericho Hill and the bad guys won, rule Discordia, so sorry, better luck next time (*what* next time, ha-ha), THE END."

Little safety nets, like a key. Not to mention a scrimshaw turtle.

"If he wrote those things into his story," Eddie said, "it was long after we saw him in 1977."

"Aye," Roland agreed.

"And I don't think he thought them up," Eddie said. "Not really. He's just . . . I dunno, just a . . ."

"A bumhug?" Susannah asked, smiling.

"No!" Jake said, sounding a little shocked. "Not that. He's a sender. A telecaster." He was thinking about his father and his father's job at the Network.

"Bingo," Eddie said, and leveled a finger at the boy. This idea led him to another: that if Stephen King did not remain alive long enough to write those things into his tale, the key and the turtle would not be there when they were needed. Jake would have been eaten by the Doorkeeper in the house on Dutch

Hill . . . always assuming he got that far, which he probably wouldn't have done. And if he escaped the Dutch Hill monster, he would've been eaten by the Grandfathers—Callahan's Type One vampires—in the Dixie Pig.

Susannah thought to tell them about the vision she'd had as Mia was beginning her final journey from the Plaza-Park Hotel to the Dixie Pig. In this vision she'd been jugged in a jail cell in Oxford, Mississippi, and there had been voices coming from a TV somewhere. Chet Huntley, Walter Cronkite, Frank McGee: newscasters chanting the names of the dead. Some of those names, like President Kennedy and the Diem brothers, she'd known. Others, like Christa McAuliffe, she had not. But one of the names had been Stephen King's, she was quite sure of it. Chet Huntley's partner

(*good night Chet good night David*)

saying that Stephen King had been struck and killed by a Dodge minivan while walking near his house. King had been fifty-two, according to Brinkley.

Had Susannah told them that, a great many things might have happened differently, or not at all. She was opening her mouth to add it into the conversation—a falling chip on a hillside strikes a stone which strikes a larger stone which then strikes two others and starts a landslide—when there was the clunk of an opening door and the clack of approaching footsteps. They all turned, Jake reaching for a 'Riza, the others for their guns.

"Relax, fellas," Susannah murmured. "It's all right. I know this guy." And then to DNK 45932, **DOMESTIC**, she said: "I didn't expect to see you again so soon. In fact, I didn't expect to see you at all. What's up, Nigel old buddy?"

So this time something which might have been spoken was not, and the *deus ex machina* which might have descended to rescue a writer who had a date with a Dodge minivan on a late-spring day in the year of '99 remained where it was, high above the mortals who acted their parts below.

THREE

The nice thing about robots, in Susannah's opinion, was that most of them didn't hold grudges. Nigel told her that no one had been available to fix his visual equipment (although he might be able to do it himself, he said, given access to the right components, discs, and repair tutorials), so he had come back here, relying on the infrared, to pick up the remains of the shattered (and completely unneeded) incubator. He thanked her for her interest and introduced himself to her friends.

"Nice to meet you, Nige," Eddie said, "but you'll want to get started on those repairs, I kennit, so we won't keep you." Eddie's voice was pleasant and he'd reholstered his gun, but he kept his hand on the butt. In truth he was a little bit freaked by the resemblance Nigel bore to a certain messenger robot in the town of Calla Bryn Sturgis. That one *had* held a grudge.

"No, stay," Roland said. "We may have chores for you, but for the time being I'd as soon you were quiet. Turned off, if it please you." *And if it doesn't,* his tone implied.

"Certainly, sai," Nigel replied in his plummy British accent. "You may reactivate me with the words *Nigel, I need you.*"

"Very good," Roland said.

Nigel folded his scrawny (but undoubtedly powerful) stainless-steel arms across his chest and went still.

"Came back to pick up the broken glass," Eddie marveled. "Maybe the Tet Corporation could sell em. Every housewife in America would want two—one for the house and one for the yard."

"The less we're involved with science, the better," Susannah said darkly. In spite of her brief nap while leaning against the door between Fedic and New York, she looked haggard, done almost to death. "Look where it's gotten this world."

Roland nodded to Jake, who told of his and Pere Callahan's adventures in the New York of 1999, beginning with the taxi that had almost hit Oy and ending with their two-man attack on the low men and the vampires in the dining room of the Dixie

Pig. He did not neglect to tell how they had disposed of Black Thirteen by putting it in a storage locker at the World Trade Center, where it would be safe until early June of 2002, and how they had found the turtle, which Susannah had dropped, like a message in a bottle, in the gutter outside the Dixie Pig.

"So brave," Susannah said, and ruffled Jake's hair. Then she bent to stroke Oy's head. The bumbler stretched his long neck to maximize the caress, his eyes half-closed and a grin on his foxy little face. "So damned brave. Thankee-sai, Jake."

"Thank Ake!" Oy agreed.

"If it hadn't been for the turtle, they would have gotten us both." Jake's voice was steady, but he had gone pale. "As it was, the Pere . . . he . . ." Jake wiped away a tear with the heel of his hand and gazed at Roland. "You used his voice to send me on. I heard you."

"Aye, I had to," the gunslinger agreed. "'Twas no more than what he wanted."

Jake said, "The vampires didn't get him. He used my Ruger before they could take his blood and change him into one of *them*. I don't think they would've done that, anyway. They would have torn him apart and eaten him. They were *mad*."

Roland was nodding.

"The last thing he sent—I think he said it out loud, although I'm not sure—it was . . ." Jake considered it. He was weeping freely now. "He said 'May you find your Tower, Roland, and breach it, and may you climb to the top.' Then . . ." Jake made a little puffing sound between his pursed lips. "Gone. Like a candle-flame. To whatever worlds there are."

He fell silent. For several moments they all did, and the quiet had the feel of a deliberate thing. Then Eddie said, "All right, we're back together again. What the hell do we do next?"

FOUR

Roland sat down with a grimace, then gave Eddie Dean a look which said—clearer than any words ever could have done— *Why do you try my patience?*

"All right," Eddie said, "it's just a habit. Quit giving me the look."

"What's a habit, Eddie?"

Eddie thought of his final bruising, addictive year with Henry less frequently these days, but he thought of it now. Only he didn't like to say so, not because he was ashamed—Eddie really thought he might be past that—but because he sensed the gunslinger's growing impatience with Eddie's explaining things in terms of his big brother. And maybe that was fair. Henry had been the defining, shaping force in Eddie's life, okay. Just as Cort had been the defining, shaping force in Roland's . . . but the gunslinger didn't talk about his old teacher *all* the time.

"Asking questions when I already know the answer," Eddie said.

"And what's the answer this time?"

"We're going to backtrack to Thunderclap before we go on to the Tower. We're either going to kill the Breakers or set them free. Whatever it takes to make the Beams safe. We'll kill Walter, or Flagg, or whatever he's calling himself. Because he's the field marshal, isn't he?"

"He was," Roland agreed, "but now a new player has come on the scene." He looked at the robot. "Nigel, I need you."

Nigel unfolded his arms and raised his head. "How may I serve?"

"By getting me something to write with. Is there such?"

"Pens, pencils, and chalk in the Supervisor's cubicle at the far end of the Extraction Room, sai. Or so there was, the last time I had occasion to be there."

"The Extraction Room," Roland mused, studying the serried ranks of beds. "Do you call it so?"

"Yes, sai." And then, almost timidly: "Vocal elisions and fricatives suggest that you're angry. Is that the case?"

"They brought children here by the hundreds and thousands—healthy ones, for the most part, from a world where too many are still born twisted—and sucked away their minds. Why would I be angry?"

"Sai, I'm sure I don't know," Nigel said. He was, perhaps, repenting his decision to come back here. "But I had no part in the extraction procedures, I assure you. I am in charge of domestic services, including maintenance."

"Bring me a pencil and a piece of chalk."

"Sai, you won't destroy me, will you? It was Dr. Scowther who was in charge of the extractions over the last twelve or fourteen years, and Dr. Scowther is dead. This lady-sai shot him, and with his own gun." There was a touch of reproach in Nigel's voice, which was quite expressive within its narrow range.

Roland only repeated: "Bring me a pencil and a piece of chalk, and do it jin-jin."

Nigel went off on his errand.

"When you say a new player, you mean the baby," Susannah said.

"Certainly. He has two fathers, that bah-bo."

Susannah nodded. She was thinking about the tale Mia had told her during their todash visit to the abandoned town of Fedic—abandoned, that was, except for the likes of Sayre and Scowther and the marauding Wolves. Two women, one white and one black, one pregnant and one not, sitting in chairs outside the Gin-Puppy Saloon. There Mia had told Eddie Dean's wife a great deal—more than either of them had known, perhaps.

That's where they changed me, Mia had told her, "they" presumably meaning Scowther and a team of other doctors. Plus magicians? Folk like the Manni, only gone over to the other side? Maybe. Who could say? In the Extraction Room she'd been made mortal. Then, with Roland's sperm already in her, something else had happened. Mia didn't remember much about that part, only a red darkness. Susannah wondered now if the Crimson King had come to her in person, mounting her with its huge and ancient spider's body, or if its unspeakable sperm had been transported somehow to mix with Roland's. In either case, the baby grew into the loathsome hybrid Susannah had seen: not a werewolf but a were-*spider.* And now it was out there, somewhere. Or perhaps it was here, watching them even as they palavered and Nigel returned with various writing implements.

Yes, she thought. *It's watching us. And hating us . . . but not equally. Mostly it's Roland the dan-tete hates. Its first father.*

She shivered.

"Mordred means to kill you, Roland," she said. "That's its job. What it was made for. To end you, and your quest, and the Tower."

"Yes," Roland said, "and to rule in his father's place. For the Crimson King is old, and I have come more and more to believe that he is imprisoned, somehow. If that's so, then he's no longer our real enemy."

"Will we go to his castle on the other side of the Discordia?" Jake asked. It was the first time he'd spoken in half an hour. "We will, won't we?"

"I think so, yes," Roland said. *"Le Casse Roi Russe,* the old legends call it. We'll go there ka-tet and slay what lives there."

"Let it be so," Eddie said. "By God, let that be so."

"Aye," Roland agreed. "But our first job is the Breakers. The Beamquake we felt in Calla Bryn Sturgis, just before we came here, suggests that their work is nearly done. Yet even if it isn't—"

"Ending what they're doing is our job," Eddie said.

Roland nodded. He looked more tired than ever. "Aye," he said. "Killing them or setting them free. Either way, we must finish their meddling with the two Beams that remain. And we must finish off the dan-tete. The one that belongs to the Crimson King . . . and to me."

FIVE

Nigel ended up being quite helpful (although not just to Roland and his ka-tet, as things fell). To begin with he brought two pencils, two pens (one of them a great old thing that would have looked at home in the hand of a Dickens scrivener), and three pieces of chalk, one of them in a silver holder that looked like a lady's lipstick. Roland chose this and gave Jake another piece. "I can't write words you'd understand easily," he said, "but our numbers are the same, or close enough. Print what I say to one side, Jake, and fair."

Jake did as he was bid. The result was crude but understandable enough, a map with a legend.

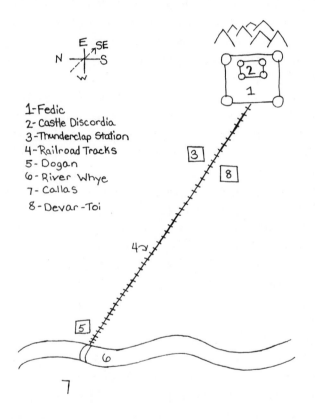

1-Fedic
2- Castle Discordia
3 -Thunderclap Station
4-Railroad Tracks
5- Dogan
6- River Whye
7- Callas
8- Devar -Toi

"Fedic," Roland said, pointing to 1, and then drew a short chalk line to 2. "And here's Castle Discordia, with the doors beneath. An almighty tangle of em, from what we hear. There'll be a passage that'll take us from here to there, under the castle. Now, Susannah, tell again how the Wolves go, and what they do." He handed her the chalk in its holder.

She took it, noticing with some admiration that it sharpened itself as it was used. A small trick but a neat one.

"They ride through a one-way door that brings them out

here," she said, drawing a line from 2 to 3, which Jake had dubbed Thunderclap Station. "We ought to know this door when we see it, because it'll be *big*, unless they go through single-file."

"Maybe they do," Eddie said. "Unless I'm wrong, they're pretty well stuck with what the old people left them."

"You're not wrong," Roland said. "Go on, Susannah." He wasn't hunkering but sitting with his right leg stretched stiffly out. Eddie wondered how badly his hip was hurting him, and if he had any of Rosalita's cat-oil in his newly recovered purse. He doubted it.

She said, "The Wolves ride from Thunderclap along the course of the railroad tracks, at least until they're out of the shadow . . . or the darkness . . . or whatever it is. Do you know, Roland?"

"No, but we'll see soon enough." He made his impatient twirling gesture with his left hand.

"They cross the river to the Callas and take the children. When they get back to the Thunderclap Station, I think they must board their horses and their prisoners on a train and go back to Fedic that way, for the door's no good to them."

"Aye, I think that's the way of it," Roland agreed. "They bypass the devar-toi—the prison we've marked with an 8—for the time being."

Susannah said: "Scowther and his Nazi doctors used the hood-things on these beds to extract something from the kids. It's the stuff they give to the Breakers. Feed it to em or inject em with it, I guess. The kids and the brain-stuff go back to Thunderclap Station by the door. The kiddies are sent back to Calla Bryn Sturgis, maybe the other Callas as well, and at what you call the devar-toi—"

"Mawster, dinnah is served," Eddie said bleakly.

Nigel chipped in at this point, sounding absolutely cheerful. "Would you care for a bite, sais?"

Jake consulted his stomach and found it was rumbling. It was horrible to be this hungry so soon after the Pere's death—and after the things he had seen in the Dixie Pig—but he was, nevertheless. "Is there food, Nigel? Is there really?"

"Yes, indeed, young man," Nigel said. "Only tinned goods, I'm afraid, but I can offer better than two dozen choices, including baked beans, tuna-fish, several kinds of soup—"

"Tooter-fish for me," Roland said, "but bring an array, if you will."

"Certainly, sai."

"I don't suppose you could rustle me up an Elvis Special," Jake said longingly. "That's peanut butter, banana, and bacon."

"Jesus, kid," Eddie said. "I don't know if you can tell in this light, but I'm turning green."

"I have no bacon or bananas, unfortunately," Nigel said (pronouncing the latter *ba-NAW-nas*), "but I do have peanut butter and three kinds of jelly. Also apple butter."

"Apple butter'd be good," Jake said.

"Go on, Susannah," Roland said as Nigel moved off on his errand. "Although I suppose I needn't speed you along so; after we eat, we'll need to take some rest." He sounded far from pleased with the idea.

"I don't think there's any more to tell," she said. "It sounds confusing—*looks* confusing, too, mostly because our little map doesn't have any scale—but it's essentially just a loop they make every twenty-four years or so: from Fedic to Calla Bryn Sturgis, then back to Fedic with the kids, so they can do the extraction. Then they take the kids back to the Callas and the brainfood to this prison where the Breakers are."

"The devar-toi," Jake said.

Susannah nodded. "The question is what we do to interrupt the cycle."

"We go through the door to Thunderclap station," Roland said, "and from the station to where the Breakers are kept. And there . . ." He looked at each of his ka-tet in turn, then raised his finger and made a dryly expressive shooting gesture.

"There'll be guards," Eddie said. "Maybe a lot of them. What if we're outnumbered?"

"It won't be the first time," Roland said.

CHAPTER II:
THE WATCHER

When Nigel returned, he was bearing a tray the size of a wagon-wheel. On it were stacks of sandwiches, two Thermoses filled with soup (beef and chicken), plus canned drinks. There was Coke, Sprite, Nozz-A-La, and something called Wit Green Wit. Eddie tried this last and pronounced it foul beyond description.

All of them could see that Nigel was no longer the same pip-pip, jolly-good fellow he'd been for God alone knew how many decades and centuries. His lozenge-shaped head kept jerking to one side or the other. When it went to the left he would mutter *"Un, deux, trois!"* To the right it was *"Ein, zwei, drei!"* A constant low clacking had begun in his diaphragm.

"Sugar, what's wrong with you?" Susannah asked as the domestic robot lowered the tray to the floor amidst them.

"Self-diagnostic exam series suggests total systemic break-down during the next two to six hours," Nigel said, sounding glum but otherwise calm. "Pre-existing logic faults, quarantined until now, have leaked into the GMS." He then twisted his head viciously to the right. *"Ein, zwei, drei!* Live free or die, here's Greg in your eye!"

"What's GMS?" Jake asked.

"And who's Greg?" Eddie added.

"GMS stands for general mentation systems," said Nigel. "There are two such systems, rational and irrational. Conscious and subconscious, as you might say. As for Greg, that would be Greg Stillson, a character in a novel I'm reading. Quite enjoyable. It's called *The Dead Zone*, by Stephen King. As to why I bring him up in this context, I have no idea."

155

TWO

Nigel explained that logic faults were common in what he called Asimov Robots. The smarter the robot, the more the logic faults . . . and the sooner they started showing up. The old people (Nigel called them the Makers) compensated for this by setting up a stringent quarantine system, treating mental glitches as though they were smallpox or cholera. (Jake thought this sounded like a really fine way of dealing with insanity, although he supposed that psychiatrists wouldn't care for the idea much; it would put them out of business.) Nigel believed that the trauma of having his eyes shot out had weakened his mental survival-systems somehow, and now all sorts of bad stuff was loose in his circuits, eroding his deductive and inductive reasoning capabilities, gobbling logic-systems left and right. He told Susannah he didn't hold this against her in the slightest. Susannah raised a fist to her forehead and thanked him big-big. In truth, she did not completely believe good old DNK 45932, although she was damned if she knew why. Maybe it was just a holdover from their time in Calla Bryn Sturgis, where a robot not much different from Nigel had turned out to be a nasty, grudge-holding cully indeed. And there was something else.

I spy with my little eye, Susannah thought.

"Hold out thy hands, Nigel."

When the robot did, they all saw the wiry hairs caught in the joints of his steel fingers. There was also a drop of blood on a . . . would you call it a knuckle? "What's this?" she asked, holding several of the hairs up.

"I'm sorry, mum, I cawn't—"

Couldn't see. No, of course not. Nigel had infrared, but his actual eyesight was gone, courtesy of Susannah Dean, daughter of Dan, gunslinger in the Ka-Tet of Nineteen.

"They're hairs. I also spy some blood."

"Ah, yes," Nigel said. "Rats in the kitchen, mum. I'm programmed to dispose of vermin when I detect them. There are a great many these days, I'm sorry to say; the world is moving on." And then, snapping his head violently to the left: *"Un-deux-trois! Minnie Mouse est la mouse pour moi!"*

"Um . . . did you kill Minnie and Mickey before or after you made the sandwiches, Nige old buddy?" Eddie asked.

"After, sai, I assure you."

"Well, I might pass, anyway," Eddie said. "I had a poorboy back in Maine, and it's sticking to my ribs like a motherfucker."

"You should say *un, deux, trois,*" Susannah told him. The words were out before she knew she was going to say them.

"Cry pardon?" Eddie was sitting with his arm around her. Since the four of them had gotten back together, he touched Susannah at every opportunity, as if needing to confirm the fact that she was more than just wishful thinking.

"Nothing." Later, when Nigel was either out of the room or completely broken down, she'd tell him her intuition. She thought that robots of Nigel and Andy's type, like those in the Isaac Asimov stories she'd read as a teenager, weren't supposed to lie. Perhaps Andy had either been modified or had modified himself so that wasn't a problem. With Nigel, she thought it was a problem, indeed: can ya say problem big-big. She had an idea that, unlike Andy, Nigel was essentially goodhearted, but yes— he'd either lied or gilded the truth about the rats in the larder. Maybe about other things, as well. *Ein, zwei, drei* and *Un, deux, trois* was his method of letting off the pressure. For awhile, anyway.

It's Mordred, she thought, looking around. She took a sandwich because she had to eat—like Jake, she was ravenous—but her appetite was gone and she knew she'd take no enjoyment from what she plugged grimly down her throat. *He's been at Nigel, and now he's watching us somewhere. I know it—I feel it.*

And, as she took her first bite of some long-preserved, vacuum-packed mystery-meat:

A mother always knows.

THREE

None of them wanted to sleep in the Extraction Room (although they would have had their pick of three hundred or more freshly made beds) nor in the deserted town outside, so Nigel took them to his quarters, pausing every now and then for a vicious head-clearing shake and to count off in either German or French. To this he began adding numbers in some other language none of them knew.

Their way led them through a kitchen—all stainless steel and smoothly humming machines, quite different from the ancient cookhouse Susannah had visited todash beneath Castle Discordia—and although they saw the moderate clutter of the meal Nigel had prepared them, there was no sign of rats, living or dead. None of them commented on this.

Susannah's sense of being observed came and went.

Beyond the pantry was a neat little three-room apartment where Nigel presumably hung his hat. There was no bedroom, but beyond the living room and a butler's pantry full of monitoring equipment was a neat book-lined study with an oak desk and an easy chair beneath a halogen reading lamp. The computer on the desk had been manufactured by North Central Positronics, no surprise there. Nigel brought them blankets and pillows which he assured them were fresh and clean.

"Maybe you sleep on your feet, but I guess you like to sit down to read like anyone else," Eddie said.

"Oh, yes indeedy, one-two-threedy," Nigel said. "I enjoy a good book. It's part of my programming."

"We'll sleep six hours, then push on," Roland told them.

Jake, meanwhile, was examining the books more closely. Oy moved beside him, always at heel, as Jake checked the spines, occasionally pulling one out for a closer peek. "He's got all of Dickens, it looks like," he said. "Also Steinbeck . . . Thomas Wolfe . . . a lot of Zane Grey . . . somebody named Max Brand . . . a guy named Elmore Leonard . . . and the always popular Steve King."

They all took time to look at the two shelves of King books, better than thirty in all, at least four of them very large and two the size of doorstops. King had been an extremely busy writer-bee since his Bridgton days, it appeared. The newest volume was called *Hearts in Atlantis* and had been published in a year with which they were very familiar: 1999. The only ones missing, so far as they could tell, were the ones about *them.* Assuming King had gone ahead and written them. Jake checked the copyright pages, but there were few obvious holes. That might mean nothing, however, because he had written so much.

Susannah inquired of Nigel, who said he had never seen any books by Stephen King concerning Roland of Gilead or the Dark Tower. Then, having said so, he twisted his head viciously to the left and counted off in French, this time all the way to ten.

"Still," Eddie said after Nigel had retired, clicking and clacking and clucking his way out of the room, "I bet there's a lot of information here we could use. Roland, do you think we could pack the works of Stephen King and take them with us?"

"Maybe," Roland said, "but we won't. They might confuse us."

"Why do you say so?"

Roland only shook his head. He didn't know why he said so, but he knew it was true.

FOUR

The Arc 16 Experimental Station's nerve-center was four levels down from the Extraction Room, the kitchen, and Nigel's study. One entered the Control Suite through a capsule-shaped vestibule. The vestibule could only be opened from the outside by using three ID slides, one after the other. The piped-in Muzak on this lowest level of the Fedic Dogan sounded like Beatles tunes as rendered by The Comatose String Quartet.

Inside the Control Suite were over a dozen rooms, but the only one with which we need concern ourselves was the one filled with TV screens and security devices. One of these latter devices ran a small but vicious army of hunter-killer robots equipped with sneetches and laser pistols; another was supposed to release poison gas (the same kind Blaine had used to slaughter the people of Lud) in the event of a hostile takeover. Which, in the view of Mordred Deschain, had happened. He had tried to activate both the hunter-killers and the gas; neither had responded. Now Mordred had a bloody nose, a blue bruise on his forehead, and a swollen lower lip, for he'd fallen out of the chair in which he sat and rolled about on the floor, bellowing reedy, childish cries which in no way reflected the true depth of his fury.

To be able to see them on at least five different screens and not be able to kill or even hurt them! No wonder he was in a fury! He had felt the living darkness closing in on him, the darkness which signaled his change, and had forced himself to be calm so the change wouldn't happen. He had already discovered that the transformation from his human self to his spider self (and back again) consumed shocking amounts of energy. Later on that might not matter, but for the time being he had to be careful, lest he starve like a bee in a burned-over tract of forest.

What I'd show you is much more bizarre than anything we have looked at so far, and I warn you in advance that your first impulse will be to laugh. That's all right. Laugh if you must. Just don't take your eye off what you see, for even in your imagination, here is a creature which can do you damage. Remember that it came of two fathers, both of them killers.

FIVE

Now, only a few hours after his birth, Mia's chap already weighed twenty pounds and had the look of a healthy six-months' baby. Mordred wore a single garment, a makeshift towel diaper which Nigel had put on when he had brought the baby his first meal of Dogan wildlife. The child *needed* a diaper, for he could not as yet hold his waste. He understood that control over these functions would be his soon—perhaps before the day was out, if he continued to grow at his current rate—but it couldn't happen soon enough to suit him. He was for the nonce imprisoned in this idiotic infant's body.

To be trapped in such a fashion was hideous. To fall out of the chair and be capable of nothing more than lying there, waving his bruised arms and legs, bleeding and squalling! DNK 45932 would have come to pick him up, could no more resist the commands of the King's son than a lead weight dropped from a high window can resist the pull of gravity, but Mordred didn't dare call him. Already the brown bitch suspected something wasn't right with Nigel. The brown bitch was wickedly perceptive, and Mordred himself was terribly vulnerable. He was able to control every piece of machinery in the Arc 16 station, mating with machinery was one of his many talents, but as he lay on the floor of the room with CONTROL CENTER on the door (it had been called "The Head" back in the long-ago, before the world moved on), Mordred was coming to realize how few machines there were to control. No wonder his father wanted to push down the Tower and begin again! This world was broken.

He'd needed to change back into the spider in order to regain the chair, where he'd once again resumed his human shape . . . but by the time he made it, his stomach was rumbling and his mouth was sour with hunger. It wasn't just changing that sucked up the energy, he'd come to suspect; the spider was closer to his true form, and when he was in that shape his metabolism ran hot and fast. His thoughts changed, as well, and there was an attraction to that, because his human thoughts were colored by emotions (over which he seemed to have no control, although he supposed he might, in time) that were mostly unpleasant. As a spider, his thoughts weren't real thoughts at all, at least not in the human sense; they were dark bellowing things that seemed to rise out of some wet interior ground. They were about

(*EAT*)
and
(*ROAM*)
and

(*RAPE*)

and

(*KILL*)

The many delightful ways to do these things rumbled through the dan-tete's rudimentary consciousness like huge headlighted machines that went speeding unheeding through the world's darkest weather. To think in such a way—to let go of his human half—was immensely attractive, but he thought that to do so now, while he had almost no defenses, would get him killed.

And almost already had. He raised his right arm—pink and smooth and perfectly naked—so he could look down at his right hip. This was where the brown bitch had shot him, and although Mordred had grown considerably since then, had doubled both in length and weight, the wound remained open, seeping blood and some custardy stuff, dark yellow and stinking. He thought that this wound in his human body would never heal. No more than his other body would ever be able to grow back the leg the bitch had shot off. And had she not stumbled—ka: aye, he had no doubt of it—the shot would have taken his head off instead of his leg, and then the game would have been over, because—

There was a harsh, croaking buzz. He looked into the monitor that showed the other side of the main entry and saw the domestic robot standing there with a sack in one hand. The sack was twitching, and the black-haired, clumsily diapered baby sitting at the banks of monitors immediately began to salivate. He reached out one endearingly pudgy hand and punched a series of buttons. The security room's curved outer door slid open and Nigel stepped into the vestibule, which was built like an airlock. Mordred went immediately on to the buttons that would open the inner door in response to the sequence 2-5-4-1-3-1-2-1, but his motor control was still almost nonexistent and he was rewarded by another harsh buzz and an infuriating female voice (infuriating because it reminded him of the brown bitch's voice) which said, "YOU HAVE ENTERED THE WRONG SECURITY CODE FOR THIS

DOOR. YOU MAY RETRY ONCE WITHIN THE NEXT TEN
SECONDS. TEN . . . NINE . . ."

Mordred would have said *Fuck you* if he'd been capable of
speech, but he wasn't. The best he could do was a babble of
baby-talk that undoubtedly would have caused Mia to crow
with a mother's pride. Now he didn't bother with the buttons;
he wanted what the robot had in the bag too badly. The rats (he
assumed they were rats) were alive this time. *Alive,* by God, the
blood still running in their veins.

Mordred closed his eyes and concentrated. The red light
Susannah had seen before his first change once more ran
beneath his fair skin from the crown of his head to the stained
right heel. When that light passed the open wound in the baby's
hip, the sluggish flow of blood and pussy matter grew briefly
stronger, and Mordred uttered a low cry of misery. His hand
went to the wound and spread blood over the small bowl of his
belly in a thoughtless comforting gesture. For a moment there
was a sense of blackness rising to replace the red flush, accom-
panied by a wavering of the infant's shape. This time there was
no transformation, however. The baby slumped back in the
chair, breathing hard, a tiny trickle of clear urine dribbling
from his penis to wet the front of the towel he wore. There was
a muffled pop from beneath the control panel in front of the
chair where the baby slumped askew, panting like a dog.

Across the room, a door marked MAIN ACCESS slid open.
Nigel tramped stolidly in, twitching his capsule of a head almost
constantly now, counting off not in two or three languages
but in perhaps as many as a dozen.

"Sir, I really cannot continue to—"

Mordred made a baby's cheerful goo-goo-ga-ga sounds and
held out his hands toward the bag. The thought which he sent
was both clear and cold: *Shut up. Give me what I need.*

Nigel put the bag in his lap. From within it came a cheeping
sound almost like human speech, and for the first time Mordred
realized that the twitches were all coming from a single creature.
Not a rat, then! Something bigger! Bigger and bloodier!

He opened the bag and peered in. A pair of gold-ringed eyes

looked pleadingly back at him. For a moment he thought it was
the bird that flew at night, the hoo-hoo bird, he didn't know its
name, and then he saw the thing had fur, not feathers. It was a
throcken, known in many parts of Mid-World as a billy-bumbler,
this one barely old enough to be off its mother's teat.

There now, there, he thought at it, his mouth filling with
drool. *We're in the same boat, my little cully—we're motherless
children in a hard, cruel world. Be still and I'll give you comfort.*

Dealing with a creature as young and simple-headed as this
wasn't much different from dealing with the machines. Mordred
looked into its thoughts and located the node that controlled its
simple bit of will. He reached for it with a hand made of
thought—made of his will—and seized it. For a moment he
could hear the creature's timid, hopeful thought

(*don't hurt me please don't hurt me; please let me live; I want to
live have fun play a little; don't hurt me please don't hurt me please let
me live*)

and he responded:

All is well, don't fear, cully, all is well.

The bumbler in the bag (Nigel had found it in the motor-
pool, separated from its mother, brothers, and sisters by the
closing of an automatic door) relaxed—not believing, exactly,
but *hoping* to believe.

SIX

In Nigel's study, the lights had been turned down to quarter-
brilliance. When Oy began to whine, Jake woke at once. The
others slept on, at least for the time being.

What's wrong, Oy?

The bumbler didn't reply, only went on whining deep in his
throat. His gold-ringed eyes peered into the gloomy far corner
of the study, as if seeing something terrible there. Jake could
remember peering into the corner of his bedroom the same
way after waking from some nightmare in the small hours of the
morning, a dream of Frankenstein or Dracula or

(*Tyrannasorbet Wrecks*)

some other boogeyman, God knew what. Now, thinking that perhaps bumblers also had nightmares, he tried even harder to touch Oy's mind. There was nothing at first, then a deep, blurred image

(*eyes   eyes looking out of the darkness*)

of something that might have been a billy-bumbler in a sack.

"Shhhh," he whispered into Oy's ear, putting his arms around him. "Don't wake em, they need their sleep."

"Leep," Oy said, very low.

"You just had a bad dream," Jake whispered. "Sometimes I have them, too. They're not real. Nobody's got you in a bag. Go back to sleep."

"Leep." Oy put his snout on his right forepaw. "Oy-be ki-yit."

That's right, Jake thought at him, *Oy be quiet.*

The gold-ringed eyes, still looking troubled, remained open a bit longer. Then Oy winked at Jake with one and closed both. A moment later, the bumbler was asleep again. Somewhere close by, one of his kind had died . . . but dying was the way of the world; it was a hard world and always had been.

Oy dreamed of being with Jake beneath the great orange orb of the Peddler's Moon. Jake, also sleeping, picked it up by touch and they dreamed of Old Cheap Rover Man's Moon together.

Oy, who died? asked Jake beneath the Peddler's one-eyed, knowing wink.

Oy, said his friend. *Delah.* Many.

Beneath the Old Cheap Man's empty orange stare Oy said no more; had, in fact, found a dream within his dream, and here also Jake went with him. This dream was better. In it, the two of them were playing together in bright sunshine. To them came another bumbler: a sad fellow, by his look. He tried to talk to them, but neither Jake nor Oy could tell what he said, because he was speaking in English.

SEVEN

Mordred wasn't strong enough to lift the bumbler from the bag, and Nigel either would not or could not help him. The robot only stood inside the door of the Control Center, twisting his head to one side or the other, counting and clanking more loudly than ever. A hot, cooked smell had begun to rise from his innards.

Mordred succeeded in turning the bag over and the bumbler, probably half a yearling, fell into his lap. Its eyes were half-open, but the yellow-and-black orbs were dull and unmoving.

Mordred threw his head back, grimacing in concentration. That red flash ran down his body, and his hair tried to stand on end. Before it could do more than begin to rise, however, it and the infant's body to which it had been attached were gone. The spider came. It hooked four of its seven legs about the bumbler's body and drew it effortlessly up to the craving mouth. In twenty seconds it had sucked the bumbler dry. It plunged its mouth into the creature's soft underbelly, tore it open, lifted the body higher, and ate the guts which came tumbling out: delicious, strength-giving packages of dripping meat. It ate deeper, making muffled mewling sounds of satisfaction, snapping the billy-bumbler's spine and sucking the brief dribble of marrow. Most of the energy was in the blood—aye, always in the blood, as the Grandfathers well knew—but there was strength in meat, as well. As a human baby (Roland had used the old Gilead endearment, *bah-bo*), he could have taken no nourishment from either the juice or the meat. Would likely have choked to death on it. But as a spider—

He finished and cast the corpse aside onto the floor, just as he had the used-up, desiccated corpses of the rats. Nigel, that dedicated bustling butler, had disposed of those. He would not dispose of this one. Nigel stood silent no matter how many times Mordred bawled *Nigel, I need you!* Around the robot, the smell of charred plastic had grown strong enough to activate the overhead fans. DNK 45932 stood with his eyeless face turned to the left. It gave him an oddly inquisitive look, as if he'd died while on the verge of asking an important question: *What is the meaning of life,* perhaps, or *Who put the overalls in Mrs. Murphy's chowder?* In any case, his brief career as a rat- and bumbler-catcher was over.

For the time being, Mordred was full of energy—the meal had been fresh and wonderful—but that wouldn't last long. If he stayed in his spider-shape, he'd use up this new reservoir of strength even faster. If he went back to being a baby, however, he wouldn't even be able to get down from the chair in which he was sitting, or once more put on the diaper—which had, of course, slid off his body when he changed. But he *had* to change back, for in his spider-shape he couldn't think clearly at all. As for deductive reasoning? The idea was a bitter joke.

The white node on the spider's back closed its human eyes, and the black body beneath flushed a congested red. The legs retracted toward the body and disappeared. The node which was the baby's head grew and gained detail as the body beneath paled and took on human shape; the child's blue eyes—bombardier eyes, gunslinger eyes—flashed. He was still full of strength from the bumbler's blood and meat, he could feel it as the transformation rushed toward its conclusion, but a distressing amount of it (something like the foam on top of a glass of beer) had already dissipated. And not just from switching back and forth, either. The fact was that he was growing at a headlong pace. That sort of growth required relentless nourishment, and there was damned little nourishment to be had in the Arc 16 Experimental Station. Or in Fedic beyond, for that matter. There were canned goods and meals in foil packets and powdered power drinks, yar, plenty of those, but none of what was here would feed him as he needed to be fed. He needed fresh meat and even more than meat he needed *blood.* And the blood of animals would sustain the avalanche of his growth for only so long. Very soon he was going to need human blood, or the pace of his growth would first slow, then stop. The pain of starvation would come, but that pain, twisting relentlessly in his vitals like an auger, would be nothing to the mental and spiritual pain of watching *them* on the various video screens: still alive, reunited in their fellowship, with the comfort of a cause.

The pain of seeing *him.* Roland of Gilead.

How, he wondered, did he know the things he knew? From his mother? Some of them, yes, for he'd felt a million of Mia's thoughts and memories (a good many of them swiped from Susannah) rush into him as he fed on her. But to know it was that way with the Grandfathers, as well, how did he know that? That, for instance, a German vampire who swilled the life's blood of a Frenchman might speak French for a week or ten days, speak it like a native, and then the ability, like his victim's memories, would begin to fade . . .

How could he know a thing like that?

Did it matter?

Now he watched them sleep. The boy Jake had awakened, but only briefly. Earlier Mordred had watched them eat, four fools and a bumbler—full of blood, full of energy—dining in a circle together. Always they would sit in a circle, they would make that circle even when they stopped to rest five minutes on the trail, doing it without even being aware of it, their circle that kept the rest of the world out. Mordred had no circle. Although he was new, he already understood that *outside* was his ka, just as it was the ka of winter's wind to swing through only half the compass: from north to east and then back again to bleak north once more. He accepted this, yet he still looked at them with the outsider's resentment, knowing he would hurt them and that the satisfaction would be bitter. He was of two worlds, the foretold joining of *Prim* and *Am*, of *gadosh* and *godosh*, of *Gan* and *Gilead*. He was in a way like Jesus Christ, but in a way he was *purer* than the sheepgod-man, for the sheepgod-man had but one true father, who was in the highly hypothetical heaven, and a stepfather who was on Earth. Poor old Joseph, who wore horns put on him by God Himself.

Mordred Deschain, on the other hand, had two *real* fathers. One of whom now slept on the screen before him.

You're old, Father, he thought. It gave him vicious pleasure to think so; it also made him feel small and mean, no more than . . . well, no more than a spider, looking down from its web. Mordred was twins, and would remain twins until Roland of the Eld was dead and the last ka-tet broken. And the longing voice that told him to go *to* Roland, and call him father? To call Eddie and Jake his brothers, Susannah his sister? That was the gullible voice of his mother. They'd kill him before he could get a single word out of his mouth (assuming he had reached a stage where he could do more than gurgle baby-talk). They'd cut off his balls and feed them to the brat's bumbler. They'd bury his castrated corpse, and shit on the ground where he lay, and then move on.

You're finally old, Father, and now you walk with a limp, and at end of day I see you rub your hip with a hand that's picked up the tiniest bit of a shake.

Look, if you would. Here sits a baby with blood streaking his fair skin. Here sits a baby weeping his silent, eerie tears. Here sits a baby that knows both too much and too little, and although we must keep our fingers away from his mouth (he snaps, this one; snaps like a baby crocodile), we are allowed to pity him a little. If ka is a train—and it is, a vast, hurtling mono, maybe sane, maybe not—then this nasty little lycanthrope is its most vulnerable hostage, not tied to the tracks like little Nell but strapped to the thing's very headlight.

He may tell himself he has two fathers, and there may be some truth to it, but there is no father here and no mother, either. He ate his mother alive, say true, ate her big-big, she was his first meal, and what choice did he have about that? He is the last miracle ever to be spawned by the still-standing Dark Tower, the scarred wedding of the rational and the irrational, the natural and the supernatural, and yet he is alone, and he is a-hungry. Destiny might have intended him to rule a chain of universes (or destroy them all), but so far he has succeeded in establishing dominion over nothing but one old domestic robot who has now gone to the clearing at the end of the path.

He looks at the sleeping gunslinger with love and hate,

loathing and longing. But suppose he went to them and was *not* killed? What if they were to welcome him in? Ridiculous idea, yes, but allow it for the sake of argument. Even then he would be expected to set Roland above him, accept Roland as dinh, and that he will never do, never do, no, never do.

CHAPTER III:
THE SHINING WIRE

ONE

"You were watching them," said a soft, laughing voice. Then it lilted a bit of cradle nonsense Roland would have remembered well from his own early childhood: "'Penny, posy, Jack's a-nosy! Do ya say so? Yes I do-so! He's my sneaky, peeky, darling bah-bo!' Did you like what you saw before you fell asleep? Did you watch them move on with the rest of the failing world?"

Perhaps ten hours had passed since Nigel the domestic robot had performed his last duty. Mordred, who in fact had fallen deeply asleep, turned his head toward the voice of the stranger with no residual fuzzy-headedness or surprise. He saw a man in bluejeans and a hooded parka standing on the gray tiles of the Control Center. His gunna—nothing more than a beat-up duffelbag—lay at his feet. His cheeks were flushed, his face handsome, his eyes burning hot. In his hand was an automatic pistol, and as he looked into the dark eye of its muzzle, Mordred Deschain for the second time realized that even gods could die once their divinity had been diluted with human blood. But he wasn't afraid. Not of this one. He *did* look back into the monitors that showed Nigel's apartment, and confirmed that the newcomer was right: it was empty.

The smiling stranger, who seemed to have sprung from the very floor, raised the hand not holding the gun to the hood of his parka and turned a bit of it outward. Mordred saw a flash of metal. Some kind of woven wire coated the inside of the hood.

"I call it my 'thinking-cap,'" said the stranger. "I can't hear your thoughts, which is a drawback, but you can't get into my head, which is a—"

171

(*which is a definite advantage, wouldn't you say*)

"—which is a definite advantage, wouldn't you say?"

There were two patches on the jacket. One read U.S. ARMY and showed a bird—the eagle-bird, not the hoo-hoo bird. The other patch was a name: RANDALL FLAGG. Mordred discovered (also with no surprise) that he could read easily.

"Because, if you're anything like your father—the *red* one, that is—then your mental powers may exceed mere communication." The man in the parka tittered. He didn't want Mordred to know he was afraid. Perhaps he'd convinced himself he *wasn't* afraid, that he'd come here of his own free will. Maybe he had. It didn't matter to Mordred one way or the other. Nor did the man's plans, which jumbled and ran in his head like hot soup. Did the man really believe the "thinking-cap" had closed off his thoughts? Mordred looked closer, pried deeper, and saw the answer was yes. Very convenient.

"In any case, I believe a bit of protection to be very prudent. Prudence is always the wisest course; how else did I survive the fall of Farson and the death of Gilead? I wouldn't want you to get in my head and walk me off a high building, now would I? Although why would you? You need me or someone, now that yon bucket of bolts has gone silent and you just a bah-bo who can't tie his own clout across the crack of his shitty ass!"

The stranger—who was really no stranger at all—laughed. Mordred sat in the chair and watched him. On the side of the child's cheek was a pink weal, for he'd gone to sleep with his small hand against the side of his small face.

The newcomer said, "I think we can communicate very well if I talk and you nod for yes or shake your head for no. Knock on your chair if you don't understand. Simple enough! Do you agree?"

Mordred nodded. The newcomer found the steady blue glare of those eyes unsettling—*très* unsettling—but tried not to show it. He wondered again if coming here had been the right thing to do, but he had tracked Mia's course ever since she had kindled, and why, if not for this? It was a dangerous game, agreed, but now there were only two creatures who could unlock the door at the foot of the Tower before the Tower fell . . . which it would, and soon, because the writer had only days left to live in his world, and the final Books of the Tower—three of them—remained unwritten. In the last one that *was* written in that key world, Roland's ka-tet had banished sai Randy Flagg from a dream-palace on an interstate highway, a palace that had looked to Eddie, Susannah, and Jake like the Castle of Oz the Great and Terrible (Oz the Green King, may it do ya fine). They had, in fact, almost killed that bad old bumhug Walter o' Dim, thereby providing what some would no doubt call a happy ending. But beyond page 676 of *Wizard and Glass* not a word about Roland and the Dark Tower had Stephen King written, and Walter considered this the *real* happy ending. The people of Calla Bryn Sturgis, the roont children, Mia and Mia's baby: all those things were still sleeping inchoate in the writer's subconscious, creatures without breath pent behind an unfound door. And now Walter judged it was too late to set them free. Damnably quick though King had been throughout his career—a genuinely talented writer who'd turned himself into a shoddy (but rich) quick-sketch artist, a rhymeless Algernon Swinburne, do it please ya—he couldn't get through even the first hundred pages of the remaining tale in the time he had left, not if he wrote day and night.

Too late.

There had been a day of choice, as Walter well knew: he had been at *Le Casse Roi Russe,* and had seen it in the glass ball the Old Red Thing still possessed (although by now it no doubt lay forgotten in some castle corner). By the summer of 1997, King had clearly known the story of the Wolves, the twins, and the flying plates called Orizas. But to the writer, all that had seemed like too much work. He had chosen a book of loosely interlocked stories called *Hearts in Atlantis* instead, and even now, in his home on Turtleback Lane (where he had never seen so much as a single walk-in), the writer was frittering away the last of his time writing about peace and love and Vietnam. It was true that one character in what would be King's last book had a part to play in the Dark Tower's history as it might be, but that fellow—an old man with talented brains—would never get a chance to speak lines that really mattered. Lovely.

In the only world that really mattered, the true world where time never turns back and there are no second chances (tell ya true), it was June 12th of 1999. The writer's time had shrunk to less than two hundred hours.

Walter o' Dim knew he didn't have quite that long to reach the Dark Tower, because time (like the metabolism of certain spiders) ran faster and hotter on this side of things. Say five days. Five and a half at the outside. He had that long to reach the Tower with Mordred Deschain's birthmarked, amputated foot in his gunna . . . to open the door at the bottom and mount those murmuring stairs . . . to bypass the trapped Red King . . .

If he could find a vehicle . . . or the right door . . .

Was it too late to become the God of All?

Perhaps not. In any case, what harm in trying?

Walter o' Dim had wandered long, and under a hundred names, but the Tower had always been his goal. Like Roland, he wanted to climb it and see what lived at the top. If anything did.

He had belonged to none of the cliques and cults and faiths and factions that had arisen in the confused years since the Tower began to totter, although he wore their siguls when it suited him. His service to the Crimson King was a late thing, as was his service to John Farson, the Good Man who'd brought down Gilead, the last bastion of civilization, in a tide of blood and murder. Walter had done his own share of murder in those years, living a long and only quasi-mortal life. He had witnessed the end of what he had then believed to be Roland's last ka-tet at Jericho Hill. *Witnessed* it? That was a little overmodest, by all the gods and fishes! Under the name of Rudin Filaro, he had fought with his face painted blue, had screamed and charged with the rest of the stinking barbarians, and had brought down Cuthbert Allgood himself, with an arrow through the eye. Yet through all that he'd kept his gaze on the Tower. Perhaps that was why the damned gunslinger—as the sun went down on that day's work, Roland of Gilead had been

the last of them—had been able to escape, having buried hir.
self in a cart filled with the dead and then creeping out of th
slaughterpile at sundown, just before the whole works hac
been set alight.

He had seen Roland years earlier, in Mejis, and had just
missed his grip on him there, too (although he put that mostly
down to Eldred Jonas, he of the quavery voice and the long
gray hair, and Jonas had paid). The King had told him then
that they weren't done with Roland, that the gunslinger would
begin the end of matters and ultimately cause the tumble of
that which he wished to save. Walter hadn't begun to believe
that until the Mohaine Desert, where he had looked around
one day and discovered a certain gunslinger on his backtrail,
one who had grown old over the course of falling years, and
hadn't completely believed it until the reappearance of Mia,
who fulfilled an old and grave prophecy by giving birth to the
Crimson King's son. Certainly the Old Red Thing was of no
more use to him, but even in his imprisonment and insanity,
he—*it*—was dangerous.

Still, until he'd had Roland to complete him—to make
him greater than his own destiny, perhaps—Walter o' Dim had
been little more than a wanderer left over from the old days,
a mercenary with a vague ambition to penetrate the Tower
before it was brought down. Was that not what had brought
him to the Crimson King in the first place? Yes. And it wasn't
his fault that the great scuttering spider-king had run mad.

Never mind. Here was his son with the same mark on his
heel—Walter could see it at this very moment—and everything balanced. Of course he'd need to be careful. The thing in
the chair looked helpless, perhaps even thought it *was* helpless,
but it wouldn't do to underestimate it just because it looked like
a baby.

Walter slipped the gun into his pocket (for the moment;
only for the moment) and held his hands out, empty and
palms up. Then he closed one of them into a fist, which he
raised to his forehead. Slowly, never taking his eyes from Mordred, wary lest he should change (Walter had seen that change,

and what had happened to the little beast's mother), the new-comer dropped to one knee.

"Hile, Mordred Deschain, son of Roland of Gilead that was and of the Crimson King whose name was once spoken from End-World to Out-World; hile you son of two fathers, both of them descended from Arthur Eld, first king to rise after the *Prim* receded, and Guardian of the Dark Tower."

For a moment nothing happened. In the Control Center there was only silence and the lingering smell of Nigel's fried circuits.

Then the baby lifted its chubby fists, opened them, and raised his hands: *Rise, bondsman, and come to me.*

TWO

"It's best you not 'think strong,' in any case," the newcomer said, stepping closer. "They knew you were here, and Roland is almighty Christing clever; trig-delah is he. He caught up with me once, you know, and I thought I was done. I truly did." From his gunna the man who sometimes called himself Flagg (on another level of the Tower, he had brought an entire world to ruin under that name) had taken peanut butter and crackers. He'd asked permission of his new dinh, and the baby (although bitterly hungry himself) had nodded regally. Now Walter sat cross-legged on the floor, eating rapidly, secure in his thinking-cap, unaware there was an intruder inside and all that he knew was being ransacked. He was safe until that ransacking was done, but afterward—

Mordred raised one chubby baby-hand in the air and swooped it gracefully down in the shape of a question mark.

"How did I escape?" Walter asked. "Why, I did what any true cozener would do in such circumstances—told him the truth! Showed him the Tower, at least several levels of it. It stunned him, right and proper, and while he was open in such fashion, I took a leaf from his own book and hypnotized him. We were in one of the fistulas of time which sometimes swirl out from the Tower, and the world moved on all around us as we had our

palaver in that bony place, aye! I brought more bones—human ones—and while he slept I dressed em in what was left of my own clothes. I could have killed him then, but what of the Tower if I had, eh? What of *you*, for that matter? You never would have come to be. It's fair to say, Mordred, that by allowing Roland to live and draw his three, I saved your life before your life was even kindled, so I did. I stole away to the seashore—felt in need of a little vacation, hee! When Roland got there, he went one way, toward the three doors. I'd gone the other, Mordred my dear, and here I am!"

He laughed through a mouthful of crackers and sprayed crumbs on his chin and shirt. Mordred smiled, but he was revolted. This was what he was supposed to work with, *this*? A cracker-gobbling, crumb-spewing fool who was too full of his own past exploits to sense his present danger, or to know his defenses had been breached? By all the gods, he *deserved* to die! But before that could happen, there were two more things he needed. One was to know where Roland and his friends had gone. The other was to be fed. This fool would serve both purposes. And what made it easy? Why, that Walter had also grown old—old and lethally sure of himself—and too vain to realize it.

"You may wonder why I'm here, and not about your father's business," Walter said. "Do you?"

Mordred didn't, but he nodded, just the same. His stomach rumbled.

"In truth, I *am* about his business," Walter said, and gave his most charming smile (spoiled somewhat by the peanut butter on his teeth). He had once probably known that any statement beginning with the words *In truth* is almost always a lie. No more. Too old to know. Too vain to know. Too stupid to remember. But he was wary, all the same. He could feel the child's force. In his head? Rummaging around in his head? Surely not. The thing trapped in the baby's body was powerful, but surely not *that* powerful.

Walter leaned forward earnestly, clasping his knees.

"Your Red Father is . . . indisposed. As a result of having lived so close to the Tower for so long, and having thought upon it so deeply, I have no doubt. It's down to you to finish what he began. I've come to help you in that work."

Mordred nodded, as if pleased. He *was* pleased. But ah, he was also so hungry.

"You may have wondered how I reached you in this supposedly secure chamber," Walter said. "In truth I helped build this place, in what Roland would call the long-ago."

That phrase again, as obvious as a wink.

He had put the gun in the left pocket of his parka. Now, from the right, he withdrew a gadget the size of a cigarette-pack, pulled out a silver antenna, and pushed a button. A section of the gray tiles withdrew silently, revealing a flight of stairs. Mordred nodded. Walter—or Randall Flagg, if that was what he was currently calling himself—had indeed come out of the floor. A neat trick, but of course he had once served Roland's father Steven as Gilead's court magician, hadn't he? Under the name of Marten. A man of many faces and many neat tricks was Walter o' Dim, but never as clever as he seemed to think. Not by half. For Mordred now had the final thing he had been looking for, which was the way Roland and his friends had gotten out of here. There was no need to pluck it from its hiding place in Walter's mind, after all. He only needed to follow the fool's backtrail.

First, however . . .

Walter's smile had faded a little. "Did'ee say something, sire? For I thought I heard the sound of your voice, far back in my mind."

The baby shook his head. And who is more believable than a baby? Are their faces not the very definition of guilelessness and innocence?

"I'd take you with me and go after them, if you'd come," Walter said. "What a team we'd make! They've gone to the devar-toi in Thunderclap, to release the Breakers. I've already promised to meet your father—your *White* Father—and his ka-tet should they dare go on, and that's a promise I intend to keep. For, hear me well, Mordred, the gunslinger Roland Deschain has stood against me at every turn, and I'll bear it no more. *No more!* Do you hear?" His voice was rising in fury.

Mordred nodded innocently, widening his pretty baby's eyes in what might have been taken for fear, fascination, or both. Certainly Walter o' Dim seemed to preen beneath his regard, and really, the only question now was when to take him— immediately or later? Mordred was very hungry, but thought he would hold off at least a bit longer. There was something oddly compelling about watching this fool stitching the last few inches of his fate with such earnestness.

Once again Mordred drew the shape of a question mark in the air.

Any last vestige of a smile faded from Walter's face. "What do I truly want? Is that what you're asking for?"

Mordred nodded yes.

"'Tisn't the Dark Tower at all, if you want the truth; it's Roland who stays on my mind and in my heart. I want him dead." Walter spoke with flat and unsmiling finality. "For the long and dusty leagues he's chased me; for all the trouble he's caused me; and for the Red King, as well—the *true* King, ye do ken; for his presumption in refusing to give over his quest no matter what obstacles were placed in his path; most of all for the death of his mother, whom I once loved." And, in an undertone: "Or at least coveted. In either case, it was he who killed her. No matter what part I or Rhea of the Cöos may have played in that matter, it was the boy himself who stopped her breath with his damned guns, slow head, and quick hands.

"As for the end of the universe . . . I say let it come as it will, in ice, fire, or darkness. What did the universe ever do for me that I should mind its welfare? All I know is that Roland of Gilead has lived too long and *I want that son of a bitch in the ground.* And those he's drawn, too."

For the third and last time, Mordred drew the shape of a question in the air.

"There's only a single working door from here to the devar-toi, young master. It's the one the Wolves use . . . or used; I think they've made their last run, so I do. Roland and his friends have gone through it, but that's all right, there's plenty to occupy em right where they come out—they might find the reception a bit hot! Mayhap we can take care of em while they've got the Breakers and the remaining Children of Roderick and the true guards o' the watch to worry about. Would you like that?"

The infant nodded an affirmative with no hesitation. He then put his fingers to his mouth and chewed at them.

"Yes," Walter said. His grin shone out. "Hungry, of course you are. But I'm sure we can do better than rats and half-grown billy-bumblers when it comes to dinner. Don't you?"

Mordred nodded again. He was sure they could, too.

"Will I play the good da' and carry you?" Walter asked. "That way you don't have to change to your spider-self. Ugh! Not a shape 'tis easy to love, or even like, I must say."

Mordred was holding up his arms.

"Y'won't shit on me, will you?" Walter asked casually, halting halfway across the floor. His hand slid into his pocket, and Mordred realized with a touch of alarm that the sly bastard had been hiding something from him, just the same: he knew the so-called "thinking-cap" wasn't working. Now he meant to use the gun after all.

THREE

In fact, Mordred gave Walter o' Dim far too much credit, but isn't that a trait of the young, perhaps even a survival skill? To a wide-eyed lad, the tacky tricks of the world's most ham-fisted prestidigitator look like miracles. Walter did not actually realize what was happening until very late in the game, but he was a wily old survivor, tell ya true, and when understanding came, it came entire.

There's a phrase, *the elephant in the living room,* which purports to describe what it's like to live with a drug addict, an alcoholic, an abuser. People outside such relationships will sometimes ask, "How could you let such a business go on for so many years? Didn't you see *the elephant in the living room?*" And it's so hard for anyone living in a more normal situation to understand the answer that comes closest to the truth: "I'm sorry, but it was there when I moved in. I didn't know it was an *elephant*; I thought it was *part of the furniture.*" There comes an *aha*-moment for some folks—the lucky ones—when they suddenly recognize the difference. And that moment came for Walter. It came too late, but not by much.

Y'won't shit on me, will you—that was the question he asked, but between the word *shit* and the phrase *on me,* he suddenly realized there was an intruder in his house . . . *and it had been there all along.* Not a baby, either; this was a gangling, slope-headed adolescent with pockmarked skin and dully curious eyes. It was perhaps the best, truest visualization Walter could have made for Mordred Deschain as he at that moment existed: a teenage housebreaker, probably high on some aerosol cleaning product.

And he had been there *all the time!* God, how could he not have known? The housebreaker hadn't even been hiding! He had been right out in the open, standing there against the wall, gape-mouthed and taking it all in.

His plans for bringing Mordred with him—of using him to end Roland's life (if the guards at the devar-toi couldn't do it first, that was), then killing the little bastard and taking his valuable left foot—collapsed in an instant. In the next one a new plan arose, and it was simplicity itself. *Mustn't let him see that I know. One shot, that's all I can risk, and only because I must risk it. Then I run. If he's dead, fine. If not, perhaps he'll starve before—*

Then Walter realized his hand had stopped. Four fingers had closed around the butt of the gun in the jacket pocket, but they were now frozen. One was very near the trigger, but he couldn't move that, either. It might as well have been buried in cement. And now Walter clearly saw the shining wire for the first time. It emerged from the toothless pink-gummed mouth of the baby sitting in the chair, crossed the room, glittering beneath the lights, and then encircled him at chest-level, binding his arms to his sides. He understood the wire wasn't really there . . . but at the same time, it *was.*

He couldn't move.

FOUR

Mordred didn't see the shining wire, perhaps because he'd never read *Watership Down*. He'd had the chance to explore Susannah's mind, however, and what he saw now was remarkably like Susannah's Dogan. Only instead of switches saying things like CHAP and EMOTIONAL TEMP, he saw ones that controlled Walter's ambulation (this one he quickly turned to OFF), cogitation, and motivation. It was certainly a more complex setup than the one in the young bumbler's head—there he'd found nothing but a few simple nodes, like granny knots—but still not difficult to operate.

The only problem was that he was a baby.

A damned *baby* stuck in a chair.

If he really meant to change this delicatessen on legs into cold-cuts, he'd have to move quickly.

FIVE

Walter o' Dim was not too old to be gullible, he understood that now—he'd underestimated the little monster, relying too much on what it looked like and not enough on his own knowledge of what it *was*—but he was at least beyond the young man's trap of total panic.

If he means to do anything besides sit in that chair and look at me, he'll have to change. When he does, his control may slip. That'll be my chance. It's not much, but it's the only one I have left.

At that moment he saw a brilliant red light run down the baby's skin from crown to toes. In the wake of it, the chubby-pink bah-bo's body began to darken and swell, the spider's legs bursting out through his sides. At the same instant, the shining wire coming out of the baby's mouth disappeared and Walter felt the suffocating band which had been holding him in place disappear.

No time to risk even a single shot, not now. Run. Run from him . . . from it. That's all you can do. You never should have come here in the first place. You let your hatred of the gunslinger blind you, but it still may not be too la—

He turned to the trapdoor even as this thought raced through his mind, and was about to put his foot on the first step when the shining wire re-established itself, this time not looping around his arms and chest but around his throat, like a garrote.

Gagging and choking and spewing spit, eyes bulging from their sockets, Walter turned jerkily around. The loop around his throat loosened the barest bit. At the same time he felt something very like an invisible hand skim up his brow and push the hood back from his head. He'd always gone dressed in such fashion, when he could; in certain provinces to the south even of Garlan he had been known as *Walter Hodji,* the latter word meaning both *dim* and *hood.* But this particular lid (borrowed from a certain deserted house in the town of French Landing, Wisconsin) had done him no good at all, had it?

I think I may have come to the end of the path, he thought as he saw the spider strutting toward him on its seven legs, a bloated, lively thing (livelier than the baby, aye, and four thousand times as ugly) with a freakish blob of human head peering over the hairy curve of its back. On its belly, Walter could see the red mark that had been on the baby's heel. Now it had an hourglass shape, like the one that marks the female black widow, and he understood that was the mark he'd have wanted; killing the baby and amputating its foot likely would have done him no good at all. It seemed he had been wrong all down the line.

The spider reared up on its four back legs. The three in front pawed at Walter's jeans, making a low and ghastly scratching sound. The thing's eyes bulged up at him with that dull intruder's curiosity which he had already imagined too well.

Oh yes, I'm afraid it's the end of the path for you. Huge in his head. Booming like words from a loudspeaker. *But you intended the same for me, didn't you?*

No! At least not immediately—

But you did! "Don't kid a kidder," as Susannah would say. So now I do the one you call my White Father a small favor. You may not have been his greatest enemy, Walter Padick (as you were called when you set out, all in the long-ago), but you were his oldest, I grant. And now I take you out of his road.

Walter did not realize he had held onto some dim hope of escape even with the loathsome thing before him, reared up, the eyes staring at him with dull avidity while the mouth drooled, until he heard for the first time in a thousand years the name a boy from a farm in Delain had once answered to: Walter Padick. Walter, son of Sam the Miller in the Eastar'd Barony. He who had run away at thirteen, had been raped in the ass by another wanderer a year later and yet had somehow withstood the temptation to go crawling back home. Instead he had moved on toward his destiny.

Walter Padick.

At the sound of that voice, the man who had sometimes called himself Marten, Richard Fannin, Rudin Filaro, and Randall Flagg (among a great many others), gave over all hope except for the hope of dying well.

I be a-hungry, Mordred be a-hungry, spoke the relentless voice in the middle of Walter's head, a voice that came to him along the shining wire of the little king's will. *But I'd eat proper, beginning with the appetizer. Your eyes, I think. Give them to me.*

Walter struggled mightily, but without so much as a moment's success. The wire was too strong. He saw his hands rise and hover in front of his face. He saw his fingers bend into hooks. They pushed up his eyelids like windowshades, then dug the orbs out from the top. He could hear the sounds they made as they tore loose of the tendons which turned them and the optic nerves which relayed their marvelous messages. The sound that marked the end of sight was low and wet. Bright red dashes of light filled his head, and then darkness rushed in forever. In Walter's case, forever wouldn't last long, but if time is subjective (and most of us know that it is), then it was far *too* long.

Give them to me, I say! No more dilly-dallying! I'm a-hungry!

Walter o' Dim—now Walter o' Dark—turned his hands

over and dropped his eyeballs. They trailed filaments as they fell, making them look a little like tadpoles. The spider snatched one out of the air. The other plopped to the tile where the surprisingly limber claw at the end of one leg picked it up and tucked it into the spider's mouth. Mordred popped it like a grape but did not swallow; rather he let the delicious slime trickle down his throat. Lovely.

Tongue next, please.

Walter wrapped an obedient hand around it and pulled, but succeeded in ripping it only partly loose. In the end it was too slippery. He would have wept with agony and frustration if the bleeding sockets where his eyes had been could have manufactured tears.

He reached for it again, but the spider was too greedy to wait.

Bend down! Poke your tongue out like you would at your honey's cunny. Quick, for your father's sake! Mordred's a-hungry!

Walter, still all too aware of what was happening to him, struggled against this fresh horror with no more success than against the last. He bent over with his hands on his thighs and his bleeding tongue stuck crookedly out between his lips, wavering wearily as the hemorrhaging muscles at the back of his mouth tried to support it. Once more he heard the scrabbling sounds as Mordred's front legs scratched at the legs of his denim pants. The spider's hairy maw closed over Walter's tongue, sucked it like a lollipop for one or two blissful seconds, and then tore it free with a single powerful wrench. Walter—now speechless as well as eyeless—uttered a swollen scream of pain and fell over, clutching at his distorted face, rolling back and forth on the tiles.

Mordred bit down on the tongue in his mouth. It burst into a bliss of blood that temporarily wiped away all thought. Walter had rolled onto his side and was feeling blindly for the trapdoor, something inside still screaming that he should not give up but keep trying to escape the monster that was eating him alive.

With the taste of blood in his mouth, all interest in foreplay departed Mordred. He was reduced to his central core, which was mostly appetite. He pounced upon Randall Flagg, Walter o' Dim, Walter Padick that was. There were more screams, but only a few. And then Roland's old enemy was no more.

SIX

The man had been quasi-immortal (a phrase at least as foolish as "most unique") and made a legendary meal. After gorging on so much, Mordred's first urge—strong but not quite insurmountable—was to vomit. He controlled it, as he did his second one, which was even stronger: to change back to his baby-self and sleep.

If he was to find the door of which Walter had spoken, the best time to do so was right now, and in a shape which would make it possible to hurry along at a good speed: the shape of the spider. So, passing the desiccated corpse without a glance, Mordred scarpered nimbly through the trapdoor and down the stairs and into a corridor below. This passage smelled strongly of alkali and seemed to have been cut out of the desert bedrock.

All of Walter's knowledge—at least fifteen hundred years of it—bellowed in his brain.

The dark man's backtrail eventually led to an elevator shaft. When a bristly claw pressed on the UP button produced nothing but a tired humming from far above and a smell like frying shoe-leather from behind the control panel, Mordred climbed the car's inner wall, pushed up the maintenance hatch with a slender leg, and squeezed through. That he *had* to squeeze did not surprise him; he was bigger now.

He climbed the cable

(*itsy bitsy spider went up the waterspout*)

until he came to the door where, his senses told him, Walter had entered the elevator and then sent it on its last ride. Twenty minutes later (and still jazzing on all that wonderful blood; *gallons* of the stuff, it had seemed), he came to a place where Walter's trail divided. This might have posed him, child that he still very much was, but here the scent and the sense of the others joined Walter's track and Mordred went that way, now following Roland and his ka-tet rather than the magician's backtrail. Walter must have followed them for awhile and then turned around to find Mordred. To find his fate.

Twenty minutes later the little fellow came to a door marked with no word but a sigul he could read well enough:

The question was whether to open it now or to wait. Childish eagerness clamored for the former, growing prudence for the latter. He had been well-fed and had no need of more nourishment, especially if he changed back to his hume-self for awhile. Also, Roland and his friends might still be on the far side of this door. Suppose they were, and drew their weapons at the sight of him? They were infernally fast, and he could be killed by gunfire.

He *could* wait; felt no deep need beyond the eagerness of the child that wants everything and wants it *now*. Certainly he didn't suffer the bright intensity of Walter's hate. His own feelings were more complex, tinctured by sadness and loneliness and—yes, he'd do better to admit it—love. Mordred felt he wanted to enjoy this melancholy for awhile. There would be food aplenty on the other side of this door, he was sure of it, so he'd eat. And grow. And watch. He would watch his father, and his sister-mother, and his ka-brothers, Eddie and Jake. He'd watch them camp at night, and light their fires, and form their circle around it. He'd watch from his place that was *outside*. Perhaps they would feel him and look uneasily into the dark, wondering what was out there.

He approached the door, reared up before it, and pawed at it questioningly. Too bad, really, there wasn't a peephole. And it probably *would* be safe to go through now. What had Walter said? That Roland's ka-tet meant to release the Breakers, whatever they might be (it had been in Walter's mind, but Mordred hadn't bothered looking for it).

There's plenty to occupy em right where they come out—they might find the reception a trifle hot!

Had Roland and his children perhaps been killed on the other side? Ambushed? Mordred believed he would have known had that happened. Would have felt it in his mind like a Beamquake.

In any case he would wait awhile before creeping through the door with the cloud-and-lightning sigul on it. And when he was through? Why, he'd find them. And overhear their palaver. And watch them, both awake and asleep. Most of all, he would watch the one Walter had called his White Father. His only *real* father now, if Walter had been right about the Crimson King's having gone insane.

And for the present?

Now, for a little while, I may sleep.

The spider ran up the wall of this room, which was full of great hanging objects, and spun a web. But it was the baby— naked, and now looking fully a year old—that slept in it, head down and high above any predators that might come hunting.

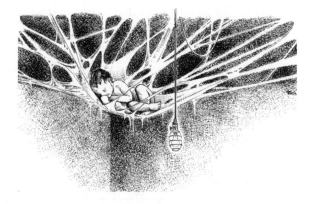

Chapter IV:
The Door into Thunderclap

When the four wanderers woke from their sleep (Roland first, and after six hours exactly), there were more popkins stacked on a cloth-covered tray, and and also more drinks. Of the domestic robot, however, there was no sign.

"All right, enough," Roland said, after calling Nigel for the third time. "He told us he was on his last legs; seems that while we slept, he fell off em."

"He was doing something he didn't want to do," Jake said. His face looked pale and puffy. From sleeping too heavily was Roland's first thought, and then wondered how he could be such a fool. The boy had been crying for Pere Callahan.

"Doing what?" Eddie asked, slipping his pack over one shoulder and then hoisting Susannah onto his hip. "For who? And why?"

"I don't know," Jake said. "He didn't *want* me to know, and I didn't feel right about prying. I know he was just a robot, but with that nice English voice and all, he seemed like more."

"That's a scruple you may need to get over," Roland said, as gently as he could.

"How heavy am I, sugar?" Susannah asked Eddie cheerfully. "Or maybe what I should ask is 'How bad you missin that good old wheelchair?' Not to mention the shoulder-rig."

"Suze, you hated that piggyback rig from the word go and we both know it."

"Wasn't askin about that, and *you* know it."

It always fascinated Roland when Detta crept unheard into Susannah's voice, or—even more spooky—her face. The

189

woman herself seemed unaware of these incursions, as her husband did now.

"I'd carry you to the end of the world," Eddie said sentimentally, and kissed the tip of her nose. "Unless you put on another ten pounds or so, that is. Then I might have to leave you and look for a lighter lady."

She poked him—not gently, either—and then turned to Roland. "This is a damn big place, once you're down underneath. How're we gonna find the door that goes through to Thunderclap?"

Roland shook his head. He didn't know.

"How bout you, Cisco?" Eddie asked Jake. "You're the one who's strong in the touch. Can you use it to find the door we want?"

"Maybe if I knew how to start," Jake said, "but I don't."

And with that, all three of them again looked at Roland. No, make it four, because even the gods-cursed bumbler was staring. Eddie would have made a joke to dispel any discomfort he felt at such a combined stare, and Roland actually fumbled for one. Something about how too many eyes spoiled the pie, maybe? No. That saying, which he'd heard from Susannah, was about cooks and broth. In the end he simply said, "We'll cast about a little, the way hounds do when they've lost the scent, and see what we find."

"Maybe another wheelchair for me to ride in," Susannah said brightly. "This nasty white boy has got his hands all *over* my purity."

Eddie gave her a sincere look. "If it was really pure, hon," he said, "it wouldn't be cracked like it is."

TWO

It was Oy who actually took over and led them, but not until they returned to the kitchen. The humans were poking about with a kind of aimlessness that Jake found rather unsettling when Oy began to bark out his name: *"Ake! Ake-Ake!"*

They joined the bumbler at a chocked-open door that read

C-LEVEL. Oy went a little way along the corridor then looked back over his shoulder, eyes brilliant. When he saw they weren't following, he barked his disappointment.

"What do you think?" Roland asked. "Should we follow him?"

"Yes," Jake said.

"What scent has he got?" Eddie asked. "Do you know?"

"Maybe something from the Dogan," Jake said. "The real one, on the other side of the River Whye. Where Oy and I overheard Ben Slightman's Da' and the . . . you know, the robot."

"Jake?" Eddie asked. "You okay, kid?"

"Yes," Jake said, although he'd had a bit of a bad turn, remembering how Benny's Da' had screamed. Andy the Messenger Robot, apparently tired of Slightman's grumbling, had pushed or pinched something in the man's elbow—a nerve, probably—and Slightman had "hollered like an owl," as Roland might say (and probably with at least mild contempt). Slightman the Younger was beyond such things, now, of course, and it was that realization—a boy, once full of fun and now cool as riverbank clay—which had made the son of Elmer pause. You had to die, yes, and Jake hoped he could do it at least moderately well when the hour came. He'd had some training in *how* to do it, after all. It was the thought of all that grave-time that chilled him. That downtime. That lie-still-and-continue-to-be-dead time.

Andy's scent—cold but oily and distinctive—had been all over the Dogan on the far side of the River Whye, for he and Slightman the Elder had met there many times before the Wolf raid that had been greeted by Roland and his makeshift posse. This smell wasn't exactly the same, but it was interesting. Certainly it was the only familiar one Oy had struck so far, and he wanted to follow it.

"Wait a minute, wait a minute," Eddie said. "I see something we need."

He put Susannah down, crossed the kitchen, and returned rolling a stainless-steel table probably meant for transporting stacks of freshly washed dishes or larger utensils.

"Upsy-daisy, don't be crazy," Eddie said, and lifted Susannah onto it.

She sat there comfortably enough, gripping the sides, but looked dubious. "And when we come to a flight of stairs? What then, sugarboy?"

"Sugarboy will burn that bridge when he comes to it," Eddie said, and pushed the rolling table into the hall. "Mush, Oy! On, you huskies!"

"Oy! Husk!" The bumbler hurried briskly along, bending his head every now and again to dip into the scent but mostly not bothering much. It was too fresh and too wide to need much attention. It was the smell of the Wolves he had found. After an hour's walk, they passed a hangar-sized door marked TO HORSES. Beyond this, the trail led them to a door which read STAGING AREA and AUTHORIZED PERSONNEL ONLY. (That they were followed for part of their hike by Walter o' Dim was a thing none of them, not even Jake—strong in the touch though he was—suspected. On the boy, at least, the hooded man's "thinking-cap" worked quite well. When Walter was sure where the bumbler was leading them, he'd turned back to palaver with Mordred—a mistake, as it turned out, but one with this consolation: he would never make another.)

Oy sat before the closed door, which was the kind that swung both ways, with his cartoon squiggle of tail tight against his hindquarters, and barked. *"Ake, ope-ope! Ope, Ake!"*

"Yeah, yeah," Jake said, "in a minute. Hold your water."

"STAGING AREA," Eddie said. "That sounds at least moderately hopeful."

They were still pushing Susannah on the stainless-steel table, having negotiated the only stairway they'd come to (a fairly short one) without too much trouble. Susannah had gone down first on her butt—her usual mode of descent—while Roland and Eddie carried the table along behind her. Jake went between the woman and the men with Eddie's gun raised, the long scrolled barrel laid into the hollow of his left shoulder, a position known as "the guard."

Roland now drew his own gun, laid it in the hollow of his

right shoulder, and pushed the door open. He went through in a slight crouch, ready to dive either way or jump backward if the situation demanded it.

The situation did not. Had Eddie been first, he might have believed (if only momentarily) that he was being attacked by flying Wolves sort of like the flying monkeys in *The Wizard of Oz*. Roland, however, was not overburdened with imagination, and even though a good many of the overhead fluorescent light strips in this huge, barnlike space had gone out, he wasted no time—or adrenaline—in mistaking the suspended objects for anything but what they actually were: broken robot raiders awaiting repair.

"Come on in," he said, and his words came echoing back to him. Somewhere, high in the shadows, came a flutter of wings. Swallows, or perhaps barn-rusties that had found their way in from outside. "I think all's well."

They came, and stood looking up with silent awe. Only Jake's four-footed friend was unimpressed. Oy was taking advantage of the break to groom himself, first the left side and then the right. At last Susannah, still sitting on the rolling steel table, said: "Tell you what, I've seen a lot, but I haven't ever seen anything quite like this."

Neither had the others. The huge room was thick with Wolves that seemed suspended in flight. Some wore their green Dr. Doom hoods and capes; others hung naked save for their steel suits. Some were headless, some armless, and a few were missing either one leg or the other. Their gray metal faces seemed to snarl or grin, depending on how the light hit them. Lying on the floor was a litter of green capes and discarded green gauntlets. And about forty yards away (the room itself had to stretch at least two hundred yards from end to end) was a single gray horse, lying on its back with its legs sticking stiffly up into the air. Its head was gone. From its neck there emerged tangles of yellow-, green-, and red-coated wires.

They walked slowly after Oy, who was trotting with brisk unconcern across the room. The sound of the rolling table was loud in here, the returning echo a sinister rumble. Susannah

kept looking up. At first—and only because there was now so little light in what must once have been a place of brilliance—she
thought the Wolves were floating, held up by some sort of anti-
gravity device. Then they came to a place where most of the
fluorescents were still working, and she saw the guy-wires.

"They must have repaired em in here," she said. "If there
was anyone left to do it, that is."

"And I think over there's where they powered em up,"
Eddie said, and pointed. Along the far wall, which they could
just now begin to see clearly, was a line of bays. Wolves were
standing stiffly in some of them. Other bays were empty, and in
these they could see a number of plug-in points.

Jake abruptly burst out laughing.

"What?" Susannah asked. "What is it?"

"Nothing," he said. "It's just that . . ." His laughter pealed
out again, sounding fabulously young in that gloomy chamber.
"It's just that they look like commuters at Penn Station, lined
up at the pay telephones to call home or the office."

Eddie and Susannah considered this for a moment, and
then they also burst out laughing. So, Roland thought, Jake's
seeing must have been true. After all they'd been through,
this did not surprise him. What made him glad was to hear the
boy's laughter. It was right that Jake should cry for the Pere, who
had been his friend, but it was good that he could still laugh.
Very good, indeed.

THREE

The door they wanted was to the left of the utility bays. They all
recognized the cloud-and-lightning sigul on it at once from the
note "R.F." had left them on the back of a sheet of the *Oz Daily
Buzz*, but the door itself was very different from the ones they
had encountered so far; except for the cloud and lightning-bolt,
it was strictly utilitarian. Although it had been painted green
they could see it was steel, not ironwood or the heavier ghostwood. Surrounding it was a gray frame, also steel, with thigh-
thick insulated power-cords coming out of each side. These ran

into one of the walls. From behind that wall came a rough rumbling sound which Eddie thought he recognized.

"Roland," he said in a low voice. "Do you remember the Portal of the Beam we came to, way back at the start? Even before Jake joined our happy band, this was."

Roland nodded. "Where we shot the Little Guardians. Shardik's retinue. Those of it that still survived."

Eddie nodded. "I put my ear against that door and listened. '*All is silent in the halls of the dead,*' I thought. '*These are the halls of the dead, where the spiders spin and the great circuits fall quiet, one by one.*'"

He had actually spoken this aloud, but Roland wasn't surprised Eddie didn't remember doing so; he'd been hypnotized or close to it.

"We were on the outside, then," Eddie said. "Now we're on the inside." He pointed at the door into Thunderclap, then with one finger traced the course of the fat cables. "The machinery sending power through these doesn't sound very healthy. If we're going to use this thing, I think we ought to right away. It could shut down for good anytime, and then what?"

"Have to call Triple-A Travel," Susannah said dreamily.

"I don't think so. We'd be basted . . . what do you call it, Roland?"

"Basted in a hot oast. 'These are the rooms of ruin.' You said that, too. Do you recall?"

"I *said* it? Right out loud?"

"Aye." Roland led them to the door. He reached out, touched the knob, then pulled his hand back.

"Hot?" Jake asked.

Roland shook his head.

"Electrified?" Susannah asked.

The gunslinger shook his head again.

"Then go on and go for it," Eddie said. "Let's boogie."

They crowded close behind Roland. Eddie was once more holding Susannah on his hip and Jake had picked Oy up. The bumbler was panting through his usual cheery grin and inside their gold rings his eyes were as bright as polished onyx.

"What do we do—" *if it's locked* was how Jake meant to finish, but before he could, Roland turned the knob with his right hand (he had his remaining gun in the left) and pulled the door open. Behind the wall, the machinery cycled up a notch, the sound of it growing almost desperate. Jake thought he could smell something hot: burning insulation, maybe. He was just telling himself to stop imagining things when a number of overhead fans started up. They were as loud as taxiing fighter airplanes in a World War II movie, and they all jumped. Susannah actually put a hand on her head, as if to shield it from falling objects.

"Come on," Roland snapped. "Quick." He stepped through without a backward look. During the brief moment when he was halfway through, he seemed to be broken into two pieces. Beyond the gunslinger, Jake could see a vast and gloomy room, much bigger than the Staging Area. And silvery crisscrossing lines that looked like dashes of pure light.

"Go on, Jake," Susannah said. "You next."

Jake took a deep breath and stepped through. There was no riptide, such as they'd experienced in the Cave of Voices, and no jangling chimes. No sense of going todash, not even for a moment. Instead there was a horrid feeling of being turned inside-out, and he was attacked by the most violent nausea he had ever known. He stepped downward, and his knee buckled. A moment later he was on both knees. Oy spilled out of his arms. Jake barely noticed. He began to retch. Roland was on all fours next to him, doing the same. From somewhere came steady low chugging sounds, the persistent *ding-ding-ding-ding* of a bell, and an echoing amplified voice.

Jake turned his head, meaning to tell Roland that now he understood why they sent *robot* raiders through their damned door, and then he vomited again. The remains of his last meal ran steaming across cracked concrete.

All at once Susannah was crying "No! *No!*" in a distraught voice. Then "Put me down! Eddie, put me down before I—" Her voice was interrupted by harsh yarking sounds. Eddie managed to deposit her on the cracked concrete before turning his head and joining the Upchuck Chorus.

Oy fell on his side, hacked hoarsely, then got back on his feet. He looked dazed and disoriented . . . or maybe Jake was only attributing to the bumbler the way he felt himself.

The nausea was beginning to fade a little when he heard clacking, echoing footfalls. Three men were hurrying toward them, all dressed in jeans, blue chambray shirts, and odd, homemade-looking footwear. One of them, an elderly gent with a mop of untidy white hair, was ahead of the other two. All three had their hands in the air.

"Gunslingers!" cried the man with the white hair. "*Are* you gunslingers? If you are, don't shoot! We're on your side!"

Roland, who looked in no condition to shoot anyone (*Not that I'd want to test that,* Jake thought), tried to get up, almost made it, then went back to one knee and made another strangled retching sound. The man with the white hair seized one of his wrists and hauled him up without ceremony.

"The sickness is bad," the old man said, "no one knows it any better than I. Fortunately it passes rapidly. You have to come with us right away. I know how little you feel like it but you see, there's an alarm in the ki'-dam's study and—"

He stopped. His eyes, almost as blue as Roland's, were widening. Even in the gloom Jake could see the old guy's face losing its color. His friends had caught up with him, but he seemed not to notice. It was Jake Chambers he was looking at.

"Bobby?" he said in a voice that was not much more than a whisper. "My God, is it Bobby Garfield?"

Chapter V:
Steek-Tete

The white-haired gent's companions were a good deal younger (one looked to Roland hardly out of his teens), and both seemed absolutely terrified. Afraid of being shot by mistake, of course—that was why they'd come hurrying out of the gloom with their hands raised—but of something else, as well, because it must be clear to them now that they weren't going to be assassinated out of hand.

The older man gave an almost spastic jerk, pulling himself out of some private place. "Of course you're not Bobby," he murmured. "Hair's the wrong color, for one thing . . . and—"

"Ted, we have to get *out* of here," the youngest of the three said urgently. "And I mean *inmediatamento.*"

"Yes," the older man said, but his gaze remained on Jake. He put a hand over his eyes (to Eddie he looked like a carny mentalist getting ready to go into his big thought-reading routine), then lowered it again. "Yes, of course." He looked at Roland. "Are you the dinh? Roland of Gilead? Roland of the Eld?"

"Yes, I—" Roland began, then bent over and retched again. Nothing came out but a long silver string of spittle; he'd already lost his share of Nigel's soup and sandwiches. Then he raised a slightly trembling fist to his forehead in greeting and said, "Yes. You have the advantage of me, sai."

"That doesn't matter," the white-haired man replied. "Will you come with us? You and your ka-tet?"

"To be sure," Roland said.

Behind him, Eddie bent over and vomited again. "God-*damn!*" he cried in a choked voice. "And I thought going Greyhound was bad! That thing makes the bus look like a . . . a . . . ."

199

"Like a first-class stateroom on the *Queen Mary*," Susannah said in a weak voice.

"Come . . . *on!*" the youngest man said in an urgent voice. "If The Weasel's on the way with his taheen posse, he'll be here in five minutes! That cat can *scramble!*"

"Yes," the man with the white hair agreed. "We really must go, Mr. Deschain."

"Lead," Roland said. "We'll follow."

TWO

They hadn't come out in a train station but rather in some sort of colossal roofed switching-yard. The silvery lines Jake had seen were crisscrossing rail-lines, perhaps as many as seventy different sets of tracks. On a couple of them, stubby, automated engines went back and forth on errands that had to be centuries outdated. One was pushing a flatcar filled with rusty I-beams. The other began to cry in an automated voice: "Will a Camka-A please go to Portway 9. Camka-A to Portway 9, if you please."

Pogo-sticking up and down on Eddie's hip began to make Susannah feel sick to her stomach all over again, but she'd caught the white-haired man's urgency like a cold. Also, she now knew what the taheen were: monstrous creatures with the bodies of human beings and the heads of either birds or beasts. They reminded her of the things in that Bosch painting, *The Garden of Earthly Delights*.

"I may have to puke again, sugarbunch," she said. "Don't you dare slow down if I do."

Eddie made a grunting sound she took for an affirmative. She could see sweat pouring down his pale skin and felt sorry for him. He was as sick as she was. So now she knew what it was like to go through a scientific teleportation device that was clearly no longer working very well. She wondered if she would ever be able to bring herself to go through another one.

Jake looked up and saw a roof made of a million panes of different shapes and sizes; it was like looking at a tile mosaic painted a uniform dark gray. Then a bird flew through one of

them, and he realized those weren't tiles up there but panels of
glass, some of them broken. That dark gray was apparently
just how the outside world looked in Thunderclap. *Like a constant eclipse,* he thought, and shivered. Beside him, Oy made
another series of those hoarse hacking sounds and then trotted
on, shaking his head.

THREE

They passed a clutter of beached machinery—generators,
maybe—then entered a maze of helter-skelter traincars that
were very different from those hauled by Blaine the Mono.
Some looked to Susannah like the sort of New York Central
commuter cars she might have seen in Grand Central Station in
her own when of 1964. As if to underline this notion, she
noticed one with **BAR CAR** printed on the side. Yet there were
others that appeared much older than that; made of dark riv-
eted tin or steel instead of brushed chrome, they looked like the
sort of passenger cars you'd see in an old Western movie, or a
TV show like *Maverick.* Beside one of these stood a robot with
wires sprouting crazily from its neck. It was holding its head—
which wore a hat with a badge reading CLASS A CONDUCTOR on
it—beneath one arm.

At first Susannah tried to keep count of the lefts and rights
they were making in this maze, then gave it up as a bad job.
They finally emerged about fifty yards from a clapboard-sided
hut with the alliterative message LADING/LOST LUGGAGE over the
door. The intervening distance was an apron of cracked concrete scattered with abandoned luggage-carts, stacks of crates,
and two dead Wolves. *No,* Susannah thought, *make that three.* The
third one was leaning against the wall in the deeper shadows
just around the corner from LADING/LOST LUGGAGE.

"Come on," said the old man with the mop of white hair,
"not much further, now. But we have to hurry, because if the
taheen from Heartbreak House catch us, they'll kill you."

"They'd kill us, too," said the youngest of the three. He
brushed his hair out of his eyes. "All except for Ted. Ted's the

only one of us who's indispensable. He's just too modest to say so."

Past LADING/LOST LUGGAGE was (reasonably enough, Susannah thought) SHIPPING OFFICE. The fellow with the white hair tried the door. It was locked. This seemed to please rather than upset him. "Dinky?" he said.

Dinky, it seemed, was the youngest of the three. He took hold of the knob and Susannah heard a snapping sound from somewhere inside. Dinky stepped back. This time when Ted tried the door, it opened easily. They stepped into a dim office bisected by a high counter. On it was a sign that almost made Susannah feel nostalgic: **TAKE NUMBER AND WAIT**, it said.

When the door was closed, Dinky once more grasped the knob. There was another brisk snap.

"You just locked it again," Jake said. He sounded accusing, but there was a smile on his face, and the color was coming back into his cheeks. "Didn't you?"

"Not now, please," said the white-haired man—Ted. "No time. Follow me, please."

He flipped up a section of the counter and led them through. Behind it was an office area containing two robots that looked long dead, and three skeletons.

"Why the hell do we keep finding bones?" Eddie asked. Like Jake he was feeling better and only thinking out loud, not really expecting an answer. He got one, however. From Ted.

"Do you know of the Crimson King, young man? You do, of course you do. I believe that at one time he covered this entire part of the world with poison gas. Probably for a lark. Killed almost everyone. The darkness you see is the lingering result. He's mad, of course. It's a large part of the problem. In here."

He led them through a door marked **PRIVATE** and into a room that had once probably belonged to a high poobah in the wonderful world of shipping and lading. Susannah saw tracks on the floor, suggesting that this place had been visited recently. Perhaps by these same three men. There was a desk beneath six inches of fluffy dust, plus two chairs and a couch. Behind the desk was a window. Once it had been covered with venetian blinds, but these had collapsed onto the floor, revealing a vista as forbidding as it was fascinating. The land beyond Thunder-clap Station reminded her of the flat, deserty wastes on the far side of the River Whye, but rockier and even more forbidding.

And of course it was darker.

Tracks (eternally halted trains sat on some of them) radi-ated out like strands of a steel spiderweb. Above them, a sky of darkest slate-gray seemed to sag almost close enough to touch. Between the sky and the Earth the air was *thick,* somehow; Susannah found herself squinting to see things, although there seemed to be no actual mist or smog in the air.

"Dinky," the white-haired man said.

"Yes, Ted."

"What have you left for our friend The Weasel to find?"

"A maintenance drone," Dinky replied. "It'll look like it found its way in through the Fedic door, set off the alarm, then got fried on some of the tracks at the far end of the switch-ing-yard. Quite a few are still hot. You see dead birds around em all the time, fried to a crisp, but even a good-sized rustie's too small to trip the alarm. A drone, though . . . I'm pretty sure he'll buy it. The Wease ain't stupid, but it'll look pretty believable."

"Good. That's very good. Look yonder, gunslingers." Ted pointed to a sharp upthrust of rock on the horizon. Susannah could make it out easily; in this dark countryside all horizons seemed close. She could see nothing remarkable about it, though, only folds of deeper shadow and sterile slopes of tum-bled rock. "That's Can Steek-Tete."

"The Little Needle," Roland said.

"Excellent translation. It's where we're going."

Susannah's heart sank. The mountain—or perhaps you called something like that a butte—had to be eight or ten miles away. At the very limit of vision, in any case. Eddie and Roland and the two younger men in Ted's party couldn't carry her that far, she didn't believe. And how did they know they could trust these new fellows, anyway?

On the other hand, she thought, *what choice do we have?*

"You won't need to be carried," Ted told her, "but Stanley

can use your help. We'll join hands, like folks at a séance. I'll want you all to visualize that rock formation when we go through. And hold the name in the forefront of your mind: Steek-Tete, the Little Needle."

"Whoa, whoa," Eddie said. They had approached yet another door, this one standing open on a closet. Wire hangers and one ancient red blazer hung in there. Eddie grasped Ted's shoulder and swung him around. "Go through what? Go through where? Because if it's a door like the last one—"

Ted looked up at Eddie—had to look up, because Eddie was taller—and Susannah saw an amazing, dismaying thing: Ted's eyes appeared to be *shaking* in their sockets. A moment later she realized this wasn't actually the case. The man's pupils were growing and then shrinking with eerie rapidity. It was as if they couldn't decide if it was light or dark in here.

"It's not a door we're going through at all, at least not of the kinds with which you may be familiar. You have to trust me, young man. Listen."

They all fell silent, and Susannah could hear the snarl of approaching motors.

"That's The Weasel," Ted told them. "He'll have taheen with him, at least four, maybe half a dozen. If they catch sight of us in here, Dink and Stanley are almost certainly going to die. They don't have to *catch* us but only *catch sight* of us. We're risking our lives for you. This isn't a game, and I need you to stop asking questions and *follow* me!"

"We will," Roland said. "And we'll think about the Little Needle."

"Steek-Tete," Susannah agreed.

"You won't get sick again," Dinky said. "Promise."

"Thank God," Jake said.

"Thang-odd," Oy agreed.

Stanley, the third member of Ted's party, continued to say nothing at all.

FOUR

It was just a closet, and an office closet, at that—narrow and musty. The ancient red blazer had a brass tag on the breast pocket with the words HEAD OF SHIPPING stamped on it. Stanley led the way to the back, which was nothing but a blank wall. Coathangers jingled and jangled. Jake had to watch his step to keep from treading on Oy. He'd always been slightly prone to claustrophobia, and now he began to feel the pudgy fingers of the Panic-Man caressing his neck: first one side and then the other. The 'Rizas clanked softly together in their bag. Seven people and one billy-bumbler crowding into an abandoned office closet? It was nuts. He could still hear the snarl of the approaching engines. The one in charge called The Weasel.

"Join hands," Ted murmured. "And concentrate."

"Steek-Tete," Susannah repeated, but to Jake she sounded dubious this time.

"Little Nee—" Eddie began, and then stopped. The blank wall at the end of the closet was gone. Where it had been was a small clearing with boulders on one side and a steep, scrub-crusted hillside on another. Jake was willing to bet that was Steek-Tete, and if it was a way out of this enclosed space, he was delighted to see it.

Stanley gave a little moan of pain or effort or both. The man's eyes were closed and tears were trickling out from beneath the lids.

"Now," Ted said. "Lead us through, Stanley." To the others he added: "And help him if you can! Help him, for your fathers' sakes!"

Jake tried to hold an image of the outcrop Ted had pointed to through the office window and walked forward, holding Roland's hand ahead of him and Susannah's behind him. He felt a breath of cold air on his sweaty skin and then stepped through onto the slope of Steek-Tete in Thunderclap, thinking just briefly of Mr. C. S. Lewis, and the wonderful wardrobe that took you to Narnia.

FIVE

They did not come out in Narnia.

It was cold on the slope of the butte, and Jake was soon shivering. When he looked over his shoulder he saw no sign of the portal they'd come through. The air was dim and smelled of something pungent and not particularly pleasant, like kerosene. There was a small cave folded into the flank of the slope (it was really not much more than another closet), and from it Ted brought a stack of blankets and a canteen that turned out to hold a sharp, alkali-tasting water. Jake and Roland wrapped themselves in single blankets. Eddie took two and bundled himself and Susannah together. Jake, trying not to let his teeth start chattering (once they did, there'd be no stopping them), envied the two of them their extra warmth.

Dink had also wrapped himself in a blanket, but neither Ted nor Stanley seemed to feel the cold.

"Look down there," Ted invited Roland and the others. He was pointing at the spiderweb of tracks. Jake could see the rambling glass roof of the switching-yard and a green-roofed structure next to it that had to be half a mile long. Tracks led away in every direction. *Thunderclap Station,* he marveled. *Where the Wolves put the kidnapped kids on the train and send them along the Path of the Beam to Fedic. And where they bring them back after they've been roont.*

Even after all he'd been through, it was hard for Jake to believe that they had been down there, six or eight miles away, less than two minutes ago. He suspected they'd all played a part in keeping the portal open, but it was the one called Stanley who'd created it in the first place. Now he looked pale and tired, nearly used up. Once he staggered on his feet and Dink (a *very* unfortunate nickname, in Jake's humble opinion) grabbed his arm and steadied him. Stanley seemed not to notice. He was looking at Roland with awe.

Not just awe, Jake thought, *and not exactly fear, either. Something else. What?*

Approaching the station were two motorized buckas with

big balloon tires—ATVs. Jake assumed it was The Weasel (whoever he was) and his taheen buddies.

"As you may have gleaned," Ted told them, "there's an
alarm in the Devar-Toi Supervisor's office. The *warden's* office,
if you like. It goes off when anyone or anything uses the door
between the Fedic staging area and yon station—"

"I believe the term you used for him," Roland said dryly,
"wasn't supervisor or warden but ki'-dam."

Dink laughed. "That's a good pickup on your part, dude."

"What does ki'-dam mean?" Jake asked, although he had a
fair notion. There was a phrase folks used in the Calla: headbox,
heartbox, ki'box. Which meant, in descending order, one's
thought processes, one's emotions, and one's lower functions.
Animal functions, some might say; ki'box could be translated as
shitbox if you were of a vulgar turn of mind.

Ted shrugged. "Ki'-dam means shit-for-brains. It's Dinky's
nickname for sai Prentiss, the Devar Master. But you already
knew that, didn't you?"

"I guess," Jake said. "Kinda."

Ted looked at him long, and when Jake identified that
expression, it helped him define how Stanley was looking at
Roland: not with fear but with fascination. Jake had a pretty
good idea Ted was still thinking about how much he looked like
someone named Bobby, and he was pretty sure Ted knew he had
the touch. What was the source of Stanley's fascination? Or
maybe he was making too much of it. Maybe it was just that Stanley had never expected to see a gunslinger in the flesh.

Abruptly, Ted turned from Jake and back to Roland. "Now
look this way," he said.

"*Whoa!*" Eddie cried. "What the *hell?*"

Susannah was amused as well as amazed. What Ted was
pointing out reminded her of Cecil B. DeMille's Bible epic *The
Ten Commandments,* especially the parts where the Red Sea
opened by Moses had looked suspiciously like Jell-O and the
voice of God coming from the burning bush sounded quite a bit
like Charles Laughton. Still, it *was* amazing. In a cheesy Holly-
wood-special-effects way, that was.

What they saw was a single fat and gorgeous bolt of sunlight slanting down from a hole in the sagging clouds. It cut through the strangely dark air like a searchlight beam and lit a compound that might have been six miles from Thunderclap Station. And "about six miles" was really all you could say, because there was no more north or south in this world, at least not that you could count on. Now there was only the Path of the Beam.

"Dinky, there's a pair of binoculars in—"

"The lower cave, right?"

"No, I brought them up the last time we were here," Ted replied with carefully maintained patience. "They're sitting on that pile of crates just inside. Get them, please."

Eddie barely noticed this byplay. He was too charmed (and amused) by that single broad ray of sun, shining down on a green and cheerful plot of land, as unlikely in this dark and sterile desert as . . . well, he supposed, as unlikely as Central Park must seem to tourists from the Midwest making their first trip to New York.

He could see buildings that looked like college dormitories—*nice* ones—and others that looked like comfy old manor houses with wide stretches of green lawn before them. At the far side of the sunbeam's area was what looked like a street lined with shops. The perfect little Main Street America, except for one thing: in all directions it ended in dark and rocky desert. He saw four stone towers, their sides agreeably green with ivy. No, make that six. The other two were mostly concealed in stands of graceful old elms. Elms in the desert!

Dink returned with a pair of binoculars and offered them to Roland, who shook his head.

"Don't hold it against him," Eddie said. "His eyes . . . well, let's just say they're something else. I wouldn't mind a peek, though."

"Me, either," Susannah said.

Eddie handed her the binoculars. "Ladies first."

"No, really, I—"

"*Stop it,*" Ted almost snarled. "Our time here is brief, our risk enormous. Don't waste the one or increase the other, if you please."

Susannah was stung but held back a retort. Instead she took the binoculars, raised them to her eyes, and adjusted them. What she saw merely heightened her sense of looking at a small but perfect college campus, one that merged beautifully with the neighboring village. *No town-versus-gown tensions there, I bet,* she thought. *I bet Elmville and Breaker U go together like peanut butter and jelly, Abbott and Costello, hand and glove.* Whenever there was a Ray Bradbury short in the *Saturday Evening Post,* she always turned to it first, she *loved* Bradbury, and what she was looking at through the binoculars made her think of Greentown, Bradbury's idealized Illinois village. A place where adults sat out on their porches in rocking chairs, drinking lemonade, and the kids played tag with flashlights in the lightning-bug-stitched dusk of summer evenings. And the nearby college campus? No drinking there, at least not to excess. No joysticks or goofballs or rock and roll, either. It would be a place where the girls kissed the boys goodnight with chaste ardor and were glad to sign back in so that the Dormitory Mom wouldn't think ill of them. A place where the sun shone all day, where Perry Como and the Andrews Sisters sang on the radio, and nobody suspected they were actually living in the ruins of a world that had moved on.

No, she thought coldly. *Some of them know. That's why these three showed up to meet us.*

"That's the Devar-Toi," Roland said flatly. Not a question.

"Yeah," Dinky said. "The good old Devar-Toi." He stood beside Roland and pointed at a large white building near the dormitories. "See that white one? That's Heartbreak House, where the can-toi live. Ted calls em the low men. They're taheen-human hybrids. And they don't call it the Devar-Toi, they call it Algul Siento, which means—"

"Blue Heaven," Roland said, and Jake realized why: all of the buildings except for the rock towers had blue tiled roofs. Not Narnia but Blue Heaven. Where a bunch of folks were busy bringing about the end of the world.

All the worlds.

SIX

"It looks like the pleasantest place in existence, at least since In-World fell," Ted said. "Doesn't it?"

"Pretty nice, all right," Eddie agreed. He had at least a thousand questions, and guessed Suze and Jake probably had another thousand between them, but this wasn't the time to ask them. In any case, he kept looking at that wonderful little hundred-acre oasis down there. The one sunny green spot in all of Thunderclap. The one *nice* place. And why not? Nothing but the best for Our Breaker Buddies.

And, in spite of himself, one question *did* slip out.

"Ted, why does the Crimson King want to bring the Tower down? Do you know?"

Ted gave him a brief glance. Eddie thought it cool, maybe downright cold, until the man smiled. When he did, his whole face lit up. Also, his eyes had quit doing that creepy in-and-out thing, which was a *big* improvement.

"He's mad," Ted told him. "Nuttier than a fruitcake. Riding the fabled rubber bicycle. Didn't I tell you that?" And then, before Eddie could reply: "Yes, it's quite nice. Whether you call it Devar-Toi, the Big Prison, or Algul Siento, it looks a treat. It *is* a treat."

"Very classy accommos," Dinky agreed. Even Stanley was looking down at the sunlit community with an expression of faint longing.

"The food is the best," Ted went on, "and the double feature at the Gem Theater changes twice a week. If you don't want to go to the movies, you can bring the movies home on DVDs."

"What are those?" Eddie asked, then shook his head. "Never mind. Go on."

Ted shrugged, as if to say *What else do you need?*

"Absolutely astral sex, for one thing," Dinky said. "It's sim, but it's still incredible—I made it with Marilyn Monroe, Madonna, and Nicole Kidman all in one week." He said this with a certain uneasy pride. "I could have had them all at the same time if I'd wanted to. The only way you can tell they're not real is to breathe directly on them, from close up. When you do, the part you blow on . . . kinda disappears. It's unsettling."

"Booze? Dope?" Eddie asked.

"Booze in limited quantities," Ted replied. "If you're into oenology, for instance, you'll experience fresh wonders at every meal."

"What's oenology?" Jake asked.

"The science of wine-snobbery, sugarbun," Susannah said.

"If you come to Blue Heaven addicted to something," Dinky said, "they get you off it. Kindly. The one or two guys who proved especially tough nuts in that area . . ." His eyes met Ted's briefly. Ted shrugged and nodded. "Those dudes disappeared."

"In truth, the low men don't *need* any more Breakers," Ted said. "They've got enough to finish the job right now."

"How many?" Roland asked.

"About three hundred," Dinky said.

"Three hundred and seven, to be exact," Ted said. "We're quartered in five dorms, although that word conjures the wrong image. We have our own suites, and as much—or as little— contact with our fellow Breakers as we wish."

"And you know what you're doing?" Susannah asked.

"Yes. Although most don't spend a lot of time thinking about it."

"I don't understand why they don't mutiny."

"What's your when, ma'am?" Dinky asked her.

"My . . . ?" Then she understood. "1964."

He sighed and shook his head. "So you don't know about Jim Jones and the People's Temple. It's easier to explain if you know about that. Almost a thousand people committed suicide at this religious compound a Jesus-guy from San Francisco set up in Guyana. They drank poisoned Kool-Aid out of a tub while he watched them from the porch of his house and used a bullhorn to tell them stories about his mother."

Susannah was staring at him with horrified disbelief, Ted with poorly disguised impatience. Yet he must have thought something about this was important, because he held silence.

"Almost a thousand," Dinky reiterated. "Because they were confused and lonely and they thought Jim Jones was their friend. Because—dig it—*they had nothing to go back to.* And it's like that here. If the Breakers united, they could make a mental hammer that'd knock Prentiss and The Weasel and the taheen and the can-toi all the way into the next galaxy. Instead there's no one but me, Stanley, and everyone's favorite super-breaker, the totally eventual Mr. Theodore Brautigan of Milford, Connecticut. Harvard Class of '20, Drama Society, Debate Club, editor of *The Crimson,* and—of course!—Phi Beta Crapper."

"Can we trust you three?" Roland asked. The question sounded deceptively idle, little more than a time-passer.

"You have to," Ted said. "You've no one else. Neither do we."

"If we were on their side," Dinky said, "don't you think we'd have something better to wear on our feet than moccasins made out of rubber fuckin tires? In Blue Heaven you get everything except for a few basics. Stuff you wouldn't ordinarily think of as indispensable, but stuff that . . . well, it's harder to take a powder when you've got nothing to wear but your Algul Siento slippers, let's put it that way."

"I still can't believe it," Jake said. "All those people working to break the Beams, I mean. No offense, but—"

Dinky turned on him with his fists clenched and a tight, furious smile on his face. Oy immediately stepped in front of Jake, growling low and showing his teeth. Dinky either didn't notice or paid no attention. "Yeah? Well guess what, kiddo? I *take* offense. I take offense like a motherfucker. What do *you* know about what it's like to spend your whole life on the outside, to be the butt of the joke every time, to always be Carrie at the fuckin prom?"

"Who?" Eddie asked, confused, but Dinky was on a roll and paid no attention.

"There are guys down there who can't walk or talk. One chick with no arms. Several with hydrocephalus, which means they have heads out to fuckin *New Jersey.*" He held his hands two feet beyond his head on either side, a gesture they all took for exaggeration. Later they would discover it was not. "Poor old Stanley here, he's one of the ones who can't talk."

Roland glanced at Stanley, with his pallid, stubbly face and his masses of curly dark hair. And the gunslinger almost smiled. "*I* think he can talk," he said, and then: "Do'ee bear your father's name, Stanley? I believe thee does."

Stanley lowered his head, and color mounted in his cheeks, yet he was smiling. At the same time he began to cry again. *Just what in the hell's going on here?* Eddie wondered.

Ted clearly wondered, too. "Sai Deschain, I wonder if I could ask—"

"No, no, cry pardon," Roland said. "Your time is short just now, so you said and we all feel it. Do the Breakers know how they're being fed? *What* they're being fed, to increase their powers?"

Ted abruptly sat on a rock and looked down at the shining steel cobweb of rails. "It has to do with the kiddies they bring through the Station, doesn't it?"

"Yes."

"They don't know and *I* don't know," Ted said in that same heavy voice. "Not really. We're fed dozens of pills a day. They come morning, noon, and night. Some are vitamins. Some are no doubt intended to keep us docile. I've had some luck purging those from my system, and Dinky's, and Stanley's. Only . . . for such a purging to work, gunslinger, you must *want* it to work. Do you understand?"

Roland nodded.

"I've thought for a long time that they must also be giving us some kind of . . . I don't know . . . brain-booster . . . but with so many pills, it's impossible to tell which one it might be. Which one it is that makes us cannibals, or vampires, or both." He paused, looking down at the improbable sunray. He extended his hands on both sides. Dinky took one, Stanley the other.

"Watch this," Dinky said. "This is good."

Ted closed his eyes. So did the other two. For a moment there was nothing to see but three men looking out over the dark desert toward the Cecil B. DeMille sunbeam . . . and they *were* looking, Roland knew. Even with their eyes shut.

The sunbeam winked out. For a space of perhaps a dozen seconds the Devar-Toi was as dark as the desert, and Thunder-clap Station, and the slopes of Steek-Tete. Then that absurd golden glow came back on. Dinky uttered a harsh (but not dis-satisfied) sigh and stepped back, disengaging from Ted. A moment later, Ted let go of Stanley and turned to Roland.

"You did that?" the gunslinger asked.

"The three of us together," Ted said. "Mostly it's Stanley. He's an extremely powerful sender. One of the few things that terrify Prentiss and the low men and the taheen is when they lose their artificial sunlight. It happens more and more often, you know, and not always because we're meddling with the machinery. The machinery is just . . ." He shrugged. "It's running down."

"Everything is," Eddie said.

Ted turned to him, unsmiling. "But not fast enough, Mr. Dean. This fiddling with the remaining two Beams must stop, and very soon, or it will make no difference. Dinky, Stanley, and I will help you if we can, even if it means killing the rest of them."

"Sure," Dinky said with a hollow smile. "If the Rev. Jim Jones could do it, why not us?"

Ted gave him a disapproving glance, then looked back at Roland's ka-tet. "Perhaps it won't come to that. But if it does . . ." He stood up suddenly and seized Roland's arm. "*Are* we cannibals?" he asked in a harsh, almost strident voice. "Have we been eating the children the Greencloaks bring from the Borderlands?"

Roland was silent.

Ted turned to Eddie. "I want to know."

Eddie made no reply.

"Madam-sai?" Ted asked, looking at the woman who sat astride Eddie's hip. "We're prepared to help you. Will you not help me by telling me what I ask?"

"Would knowing change anything?" Susannah asked.

Ted looked at her for a moment longer, then turned to

Jake. "You really could be my young friend's twin," he said. "Do you know that, son?"

"No, but it doesn't surprise me," Jake said. "It's the way things work over here, somehow. Everything . . . um . . . fits."

"Will you tell me what I want to know? Bobby would."

So you can eat yourself alive? Jake thought. *Eat yourself instead of them?*

He shook his head. "I'm not Bobby," he said. "No matter how much I might look like him."

Ted sighed and nodded. "You stick together, and why would that surprise me? You're ka-tet, after all."

"We gotta go," Dink told Ted. "We've already been here too long. It isn't just a question of getting back for room-check; me n Stanley've got to trig their fucking telemetery so when Prentiss and The Wease check it they'll say 'Teddy B was there all the time. So was Dinky Earnshaw and Stanley Ruiz, no problem with *those* boys.'"

"Yes," Ted agreed. "I suppose you're right. Five more minutes?"

Dinky nodded reluctantly. The sound of a siren, made faint by distance, came on the wind, and the young man's teeth showed in a smile of genuine amusement. "They get *so* upset when the sun goes in," he said. "When they have to face up to what's really around them, which is some fucked-up version of nuclear winter."

Ted put his hands in his pockets for a moment, looking down at his feet, then up at Roland. "It's time that this . . . this grotesque comedy came to an end. We three will be back tomorrow, if all goes well. Meanwhile, there's a bigger cave about forty yards down the slope, and on the side away from Thunderclap Station and Algul Siento. There's food and sleeping bags and a stove that runs on propane gas. There's a map, very crude, of the Algul. I've also left you a tape recorder and a number of tapes. They probably don't explain everything you'd like to know, but they'll fill in many of the blank spots. For now, just realize that Blue Heaven isn't as nice as it looks. The ivy towers are watchtowers. There are three runs of fence around the whole place. If you're trying to get out from the inside, the first run you strike gives you a sting—"

"Like barbwire," Dink said.

"The second one packs enough of a wallop to knock you out," Ted went on. "And the third—"

"I think we get the picture," Susannah said.

"What about the Children of Roderick?" Roland asked. "They have something to do with the Devar, for we met one on our way here who said so."

Susannah looked at Eddie with her eyebrows raised. Eddie gave her a *tell-you-later* look in return. It was a simple and perfect bit of wordless communication, the sort people who love each other take for granted.

"*Those* wanks," Dinky said, but not without sympathy. "They're . . . what do they call em in the old movies? Trusties, I guess. They've got a little village about two miles beyond the station in that direction." He pointed. "They do groundskeeping work at the Algul, and there might be three or four skilled enough to do roofwork . . . replacing shingles and such. Whatever contaminants there are in the air here, those poor shmucks are especially vulnerable to em. Only on them it comes out looking like radiation sickness instead of just pimples and eczema."

"Tell me about it," Eddie said, remembering poor old Chevin of Chayven: his sore-eaten face and urine-soaked robe.

"They're wandering *folken*," Ted put in. "Bedouins. I think they follow the railroad tracks, for the most part. There are catacombs under the station and Algul Siento. The Rods know their way around them. There's tons of food down there, and twice a week they'll bring it into the Devar on sledges. Mostly now that's what we eat. It's still good, but . . ." He shrugged.

"Things are falling down fast," Dinky said in a tone of uncharacteristic gloom. "But like the man said, the wine's great."

"If I asked you to bring one of the Children of Roderick with you tomorrow," Roland said, "could you do that?"

Ted and Dinky exchanged a startled glance. Then both of them looked at Stanley. Stanley nodded, shrugged, and spread his hands before him, palms down: *Why, gunslinger?*

Roland stood for a moment lost in thought. Then he turned to Ted. "Bring one with half a brain left in his head," Roland instructed. "Tell him 'Dan sur, dan tur, dan Roland, dan Gilead.' Tell it back."

Without hesitation, Ted repeated it.

Roland nodded. "If he still hesitates, tell him Chevin of Chayven says he must come. They speak a little plain, do they not?"

"Sure," Dinky said. "But mister . . . you couldn't let a Rod come up here and see you and then turn him free again. Their mouths are hung in the middle and run on both ends."

"Bring one," Roland said, "and we'll see what we see. I have what my ka-mai Eddie calls a hunch. Do you ken hunch-think?"

Ted and Dinky nodded.

"If it works out, fine. If not . . . be assured that the fellow you bring will never tell what he saw here."

"You'd kill him if your hunch doesn't pan out?" Ted asked.

Roland nodded.

Ted gave a bitter laugh. "Of course you would. It reminds me of the part in *Huckleberry Finn* when Huck sees a steamboat blow up. He runs to Miss Watson and the Widow Douglas with the news, and when one of them asks if anyone was killed, Huck says with perfect aplomb, 'No, ma'am, only a nigger.' In this case we can say 'Only a Rod. Gunslinger-man had a hunch, but it didn't pan out.'"

Roland gave him a cold smile, one that was unnaturally full of teeth. Eddie had seen it before and was glad it wasn't aimed at him. He said, "I thought you knew what the stakes were, sai Ted. Did I misunderstand?"

Ted met his gaze for a moment, then looked down at the ground. His mouth was working.

During this, Dinky appeared to be engaged in silent palaver with Stanley. Now he said: "If you want a Rod, we'll get you one. It's not much of a problem. The problem may be getting here at all. If we don't . . ."

Roland waited patiently for the young man to finish. When he didn't, the gunslinger asked: "If you don't, what would you have us do?"

Ted shrugged. The gesture was such a perfect imitation of Dinky's that it was funny. "The best you can," he said. "There are also weapons in the lower cave. A dozen of the electric fireballs they call sneetches. A number of machine-guns, what I've heard some of the low men call speed-shooters. They're U.S. Army AR-15s. Other things we're not sure of."

"One of them's some kind of sci-fi raygun like in a movie," Dinky said. "I think it's supposed to disintegrate things, but either I'm too dumb to turn it on or the battery's dead." He turned anxiously to the white-haired man. "Five minutes are up, and more. We have to put an egg in our shoe and beat it, Tedster. Let's chug."

"Yes. Well, we'll be back tomorrow. Perhaps by then you'll have a plan."

"*You* don't?" Eddie asked, surprised.

"*My* plan was to run, young man. It seemed like a terribly bright idea at the time. I ran all the way to the spring of 1960. They caught me and brought me back, with a little help from my young friend Bobby's mother. And now, we really must—"

"One more minute, do it please ya," Roland said, and stepped toward Stanley. Stanley looked down at his feet, but his beard-scruffy cheeks once more flooded with color. And—

He's shivering, Susannah thought. *Like an animal in the woods, faced with its first human being.*

Stanley looked perhaps thirty-five, but he could have been older; his face had the carefree smoothness Susannah associated with certain mental defects. Ted and Dinky both had pimples, but Stanley had none. Roland put his hands on the fellow's forearms and looked earnestly at him. At first the gunslinger's eyes met nothing but the masses of dark, curly hair on Stanley's bowed head.

Dinky started to speak. Ted silenced him with a gesture.

"Will'ee not look me in the face?" Roland asked. He spoke with a gentleness Susannah had rarely heard in his voice. "Will'ee not, before you go, Stanley, son of Stanley? Sheemie that was?"

Susannah felt her mouth drop open. Beside her, Eddie

grunted like a man who has been punched. She thought, *But Roland's old . . . so old! Which means that if this is the tavern-boy he knew in Mejis . . . the one with the donkey and the pink* sombrera hat . . . *then he must* also *be . . .*

The man raised his face slowly. Tears were streaming from his eyes.

"Good old Will Dearborn," he said. His voice was hoarse, and jigged up and down through the registers as a voice will do when it has lain long unused. "I'm so sorry, sai. Were you to pull your gun and shoot me, I'd understand. So I would."

"Why do'ee say so, Sheemie?" Roland asked in that same gentle voice.

Stanley's tears flowed faster. "You saved my life. Arthur and Richard, too, but mostly you, good old Will Dearborn who was really Roland of Gilead. And I let her die! Her that you loved! And I loved her, too!"

The man's face twisted in agony and he tried to pull away from Roland. Yet Roland held him.

"None of that was your fault, Sheemie."

"I should have died for her!" he cried. "I should have died in her place! I'm stupid! Foolish as they said!" He slapped himself across the face, first one way and then the other, leaving red weals. Before he could do it again, Roland seized the hand and forced it down to his side again.

" 'Twas Rhea did the harm," Roland said.

Stanley—who had been Sheemie an eon ago—looked into Roland's face, searching his eyes.

"Aye," Roland said, nodding. " 'Twas the Cöos . . . and me, as well. I should have stayed with her. If anyone was blameless in the business, Sheemie—*Stanley*—it was you."

"Do you say so, gunslinger? Truey-true?"

Roland nodded. "We'll palaver all you would about this, if there's time, and about those old days, but not now. No time now. You have to go with your friends, and I must stay with mine."

Sheemie looked at him a moment longer, and yes, Susannah could now see the boy who had bustled about a long-ago tavern called the Travellers' Rest, picking up empty beer schooners and dropping them into the wash-barrel which stood beneath the two-headed elk's head that was known as The Romp, avoiding the occasional shove from Coral Thorin or the even more ill-natured kicks that were apt to come from an aging whore called Pettie the Trotter. She could see the boy who had almost been killed for spilling liquor on the boots of a hardcase named Roy Depape. It had been Cuthbert who had saved Sheemie from death that night . . . but it had been Roland, known to the townsfolk as Will Dearborn, who had saved them all.

Sheemie put his arms around Roland's neck and hugged him tight. Roland smiled and stroked his curly hair with his disfigured right hand. A loud, honking sob escaped Sheemie's throat. Susannah could see the tears in the corners of the gunslinger's eyes.

"Aye," Roland said, speaking in a voice almost too low to hear. "I always knew you were special; Bert and Alain did, too. And here we find each other, well-met further down the path. We're well-met, Sheemie son of Stanley. So we are. So we are."

CHAPTER VI:
THE MASTER OF BLUE HEAVEN

ONE

Pimli Prentiss, the Algul Siento Master, was in the bathroom when Finli (known in some quarters as The Weasel) knocked at the door. Prentiss was examining his complexion by the unforgiving light of the fluorescent bar over the washbasin. In the magnifying mirror, his skin looked like a grayish, crater-pocked plain, not much different from the surface of the wastelands stretching in every direction around the Algul. The sore on which he was currently concentrating looked like an erupting volcano.

"Who be for me?" Prentiss bawled, although he had a pretty good idea.

"Finli o' Tego!"

"Walk in, Finli!" Never taking his eyes from the mirror. His fingers, closing in on the sides of the infected pimple, looked huge. They applied pressure.

Finli crossed Prentiss's office and stood in the bathroom door. He had to bend slightly in order to look in. He stood over seven feet, very tall even for a taheen.

"Back from the station like I was never gone," said Finli. Like most of the taheen, his speaking voice reeled wildly back and forth between a yelp and a growl. To Pimli, they all sounded like the hybrids from H. G. Wells's *The Island of Dr. Moreau,* and he kept expecting them to break into a chorus of "Are we not men?" Finli had picked this out of his mind once and asked about it. Prentiss had replied with complete honesty, knowing that in a society where low-grade telepathy was the rule, honesty was ever the best policy. The *only* policy, when dealing with the taheen. Besides, he liked Finli o' Tego.

221

"Back from the station, good," Pimli said. "And what did you find?"

"A maintenance drone. Looks like it went rogue on the Arc 16 side and—"

"Wait," Prentiss said. "If you will, if you will, thanks."

Finli waited. Prentiss leaned even closer toward the mirror, face frowning in concentration. The Master of Blue Heaven was tall himself, about six-two, and possessed of an enormous sloping belly supported by long legs with slab thighs. He was balding and had the turnip nose of a veteran drinker. He looked perhaps fifty. He *felt* like about fifty (younger, when he hadn't spent the previous night tossing them back with Finli and several of the can-toi). He had been fifty when he came here, a good many years ago; at least twenty-five, and that might be a big underestimation. Time was goofy on this side, just like direction, and you were apt to lose both quickly. Some *folken* lost their minds, as well. And if they ever lost the sun machine for good—

The top of the pimple bulged . . . trembled . . . burst. Ah!

A glut of bloody pus leaped from the site of the infection, splattered onto the mirror, and began to drool down its slightly concave surface. Pimli Prentiss wiped it off with the tip of a finger, turned to flick it into the jakes, then offered it to Finli instead.

The taheen shook his head, then made the sort of exasperated noise any veteran dieter would have recognized, and guided the Master's finger into his mouth. He sucked the pus off and then released the finger with an audible pop.

"Shouldn't do it, can't resist," Finli said. "Didn't you tell me that *folken* on the other side decided eating rare beef was bad for them?"

"Yar," Pimli said, wiping the pimple (which was still oozing) with a Kleenex. He had been here a long time, and there would never be any going back, for all sorts of reasons, but until recently he had been up on current events; until the previous— could you call it a year?—he'd gotten *The New York Times* on a fairly regular basis. He bore a great affection for the *Times,* loved doing the daily crossword puzzle. It was a little touch of home.

"But they go on eating it, just the same."

"Yar, I suppose many do." He opened the medicine cabinet and brought out a bottle of hydrogen peroxide from Rexall.

"It's your fault for putting it in front of me," Finli said. "Not that such stuff is bad for us, ordinarily; it's a natural sweet, like honey or berries. The problem's Thunderclap." And, as if his boss hadn't gotten the point, Finli added: "Too much of what comes out of it don't run the true thread, no matter how sweet it might taste. Poison, do ya."

Prentiss dampened a cotton ball with the hydrogen peroxide and swabbed out the wound in his cheek. He knew exactly what Finli was talking about, how could he not? Before coming here and assuming the Master's mantle, he hadn't seen a blemish on his skin in well over thirty years. Now he had pimples on his cheeks and brow, acne in the hollows of his temples, nasty nests of blackheads around his nose, and a cyst on his neck that would soon have to be removed by Gangli, the compound doctor. (Prentiss thought Gangli was a terrible name for a physician; it reminded him both of *ganglion* and *gangrene*.) The taheen and the can-toi were less susceptible to dermatological problems, but their flesh often broke open spontaneously, they suffered from nosebleeds, and even minor wounds—the scrape of a rock or a thorn—could lead to infection and death if not promptly seen to. Antibiotics had worked a treat on such infections to begin with; not so well anymore. Same with such pharmaceutical marvels as Accutane. It was the environment, of course; death baking out of the very rocks and earth that surrounded them. If you wanted to see things at their worst you only had to look at the Rods, who were no better than slow mutants these days. Of course, *they* wandered far to the . . . was it still the southeast? They wandered far in the direction where a faint red glow could be seen at night, in any case, and everyone said things were much worse in that direction. Pimli didn't know for sure if that was true, but he suspected it was. They didn't call the lands beyond Fedic the Discordia because they were vacation spots.

"Want more?" he asked Finli. "I've got a couple on my forehead that're ripe."

"Nay, I want to make my report, double-check the videotapes and telemetry, go on over to The Study for a quick peek, and then sign out. After that I want a hot bath and about three hours with a good book. I'm reading *The Collector*."

"And you like it," Prentiss said, fascinated.

"Very much, say thankya. It reminds me of our situation here. Except I like to think our goals are a little nobler and our motivations a little higher than sexual attraction."

"Noble? So you call it?"

Finli shrugged and made no reply. Close discussion of what was going on here in Blue Heaven was generally avoided by unspoken consent.

Prentiss led Finli into his own library-study, which overlooked the part of Blue Heaven they called the Mall. Finli ducked beneath the light fixture with the unconscious grace of long practice. Prentiss had once told him (after a few shots of graf) that he would have made a hell of a center in the NBA. "The first all-taheen team," he'd said. "They'd call you The Freaks, but so what?"

"These basketball players, they get the best of everything?" Finli had inquired. He had a sleek weasel's head and large black eyes. No more expressive than dolls' eyes, in Pimli's view. He wore a lot of gold chains—they had become fashionable among Blue Heaven personnel, and a brisk trading market in such things had grown up over the last few years. Also, he'd had his tail docked. Probably a mistake, he'd told Prentiss one night when they'd both been drunk. Painful beyond belief and bound to send him to the Hell of Darkness when his life was over, unless . . .

Unless there was nothing. This was an idea Pimli denied with all his mind and heart, but he'd be a liar if he didn't admit (if only to himself) that the idea sometimes haunted him in the watches of the night. For such thoughts there were sleeping pills. And God, of course. His faith that all things served the will of God, even the Tower itself.

In any case, Pimli had confirmed that yes, basketball players—*American* basketball players, at least—got the best of everything, including more pussy than a fackin toilet seat. This remark had caused Finli to laugh until reddish tears had seeped from the corners of his strangely inexpressive eyes.

"And the best thing," Pimli had continued, "is this: you'd be able to play near forever, by NBA standards. For instance, do ya hear, the most highly regarded player in my old country (although I never saw him play; he came after my time) was a fellow named Michael Jordan, and—"

"If he were taheen, what would he be?" Finli had interrupted. This was a game they often played, especially when a few drinks over the line.

"A weasel, actually, and a damned handsome one," Pimli had said, and in a tone of surprise that had struck Finli as comical. Once more he'd roared until tears came out of his eyes.

"But," Pimli had continued, "his career was over in hardly more than fifteen years, and that includes a retirement and a comeback or two. How many years could you play a game where you'd have to do no more than run back and forth the length of a campa court for an hour or so, Fin?"

Finli of Tego, who was then over three hundred years old, had shrugged and flicked his hand at the horizon. Delah. Years beyond counting.

And how long had Blue Heaven—Devar-Toi to the newer inmates, Algul Siento to the taheen and the Rods—how long had this prison been here? Also delah. But if Finli was correct (and Pimli's heart said that Finli almost certainly was), then delah was almost over. And what could he, once Paul Prentiss of Rahway, New Jersey, and now Pimli Prentiss of the Algul Siento, do about it?

His job, that was what.

His fackin job.

TWO

"So," Pimli said, sitting down in one of the two wing chairs by the window, "you found a maintenance drone. Where?"

"Close to where Track 97 leaves the switching-yard," said

Finli. "That track's still hot—has what you call 'a third rail'—and so that explains that. Then, after we'd left, you call and say there's been a *second* alarm."

"Yes. And you found—?"

"Nothing," Finli said. "That time, nothing. Probably a malfunction, maybe even caused by the first alarm." He shrugged, a gesture that conveyed what they both knew: it was all going to hell. And the closer to the end they moved, the faster it went.

"You and your fellows had a good look, though?"

"Of course. No intruders."

But both of them were thinking in terms of intruders who were human, taheen, can-toi, or mechanical. No one in Finli's search-party had thought to look up, and likely would not have spotted Mordred even if they had: a spider now as big as a medium-sized dog, crouched in the deep shadow under the main station's eave, held in place by a little hammock of webbing.

"You're going to check the telemetry again because of the second alarm?"

"Partly," Finli said. "Mostly because things feel hinky to me." This was a word he'd picked up from one of the many other-side crime novels he read—they fascinated him—and he used it at every opportunity.

"Hinky how?"

Finli only shook his head. He couldn't say. "But telemetry doesn't lie. Or so I was taught."

"You question it?"

Aware he was on thin ice again—that they both were—Finli hesitated, and then decided what the hell. "These are the end-times, boss. I question damn near everything."

"Does that include your duty, Finli o' Tego?"

Finli shook his head with no hesitation. No, it didn't include his duty. It was the same with the rest of them, including the former Paul Prentiss of Rahway. Pimli remembered some old soldier—maybe "Dugout" Doug MacArthur—saying, "When my eyes close in death, gentlemen, my final thought will be of the corps. And the corps. And the corps." Pimli's own final thought would probably be of Algul Siento. Because what else was there now? In the words of another great American—Martha Reeves of Martha and the Vandellas—they had nowhere to run, baby, nowhere to hide. Things were out of control, running downhill with no brakes, and there was nothing left to do but enjoy the ride.

"Would you mind a little company as you go your rounds?" Pimli asked.

"Why not?" The Weasel replied. He smiled, revealing a mouthful of needle-sharp teeth. And sang, in his odd and wavering voice: "'Dream with me . . . I'm on my way to the moon of my fa-aathers . . .'"

"Give me one minute," Pimli said, and got up.

"Prayers?" Finli asked.

Pimli stopped in the doorway. "Yes," he said. "Since you ask. Any comments, Finli o' Tego?"

"Just one, perhaps." The smiling thing with the human body and the sleek brown weasel's head continued to smile. "If prayer's so exalted, why do you kneel in the same room where you sit to shit?"

"Because the Bible suggests that when one is in company, one should do it in one's closet. Further comments?"

"Nay, nay." Finli waved a negligent hand. "Do thy best and thy worst, as the Manni say."

THREE

In the bathroom, Paul o' Rahway closed the lid on the toilet, knelt on the tiles, and folded his hands.

If prayer's so exalted, why do you kneel in the same room where you sit to shit?

Maybe I should have said because it keeps me humble, he thought. *Because it keeps me right-sized. It's dirt from which we arose and it's dirt to which we return, and if there's a room where it's hard to forget that, it's this one.*

"God," he said, "grant me strength when I am weak, answers when I am confused, courage when I am afraid. Help me to hurt no one who doesn't deserve it, and even then not unless they leave me no other choice. Lord . . ."

And while he's on his knees before the closed toilet seat, this man who will shortly be asking his God to forgive him for working to end creation (and with absolutely no sense of irony), we might as well look at him a bit more closely. We won't take long, for Pimli Prentiss isn't central to our tale of Roland and his ka-tet. Still, he's a fascinating man, full of folds and contradictions and dead ends. He's an alcoholic who believes deeply in a personal God, a man of compassion who is now on the very verge of toppling the Tower and sending the trillions of worlds that spin on its axis flying into the darkness in a trillion different directions. He would quickly put Dinky Earnshaw and Stanley Ruiz to death if he knew what they'd been up to . . . and he spends most of every Mother's Day in tears, for he loved his own Ma dearly and misses her bitterly. When it comes to the Apocalypse, here's the perfect guy for the job, one who knows how to get kneebound and can speak to the Lord God of Hosts like an old friend.

And here's an irony: Paul Prentiss could be right out of the ads that proclaim "I got my job through *The New York Times!*" In 1970, laid off from the prison then known as Attica (he and Nelson Rockefeller missed the mega-riot, at least), he spied an ad in the *Times* with this headline:

WANTED: EXPERIENCED CORRECTIONS OFFICER
FOR HIGHLY RESPONSIBLE POSITION
IN PRIVATE INSTITUTION
High Pay! Top Benefits! Must Be Willing to Travel!

The high pay had turned out to be what his beloved Ma would have called "a pure-D, high-corn lie," because there was no pay at all, not in the sense an America-side corrections officer would have understood, but the benefits . . . yes, the bennies were exceptional. To begin with he'd wallowed in sex as he now wallowed in food and booze, but that wasn't the point. The point, in sai Prentiss's view, was this: what did you want out of life? If it was to do no more than watch the zeros increase in your bank account, than clearly Algul Siento was no place for you . . . which would be a terrible thing, because once you had signed on, there was no turning back; it was all the corps. And the corps. And every now and then, when an example needed to be made, a corpse or two.

Which was a hundred per cent okey-fine with Master Prentiss, who had gone through the solemn taheen name-changing ceremony some twelve years before and had never regretted it. Paul Prentiss had become Pimli Prentiss. It was at that point he had turned his heart as well as his mind away from what he now only called "America-side." And not because he'd had the best baked Alaska and the best champagne of his life here. Not because he'd had sim sex with hundreds of beautiful women, either. It was because this was his job, and he intended to finish it. Because he'd come to believe that their work at the Devar-Toi was God's as well as the Crimson King's. And behind the idea of God was something even more powerful: the image of a billion universes tucked into an egg which he, the former Paul Prentiss of Rahway, once a forty-thousand-dollar-a-year man with a stomach ulcer and a bad medical benefits program okayed by a corrupt union, now held in the palm of his hand. He understood that he was also in that egg, and that he would cease to exist as flesh when he broke it, but surely if there was heaven and a God in it, then both superseded the power of the Tower. It was to that heaven he would go, and before that throne he would kneel to ask forgiveness for his sins. And he would be welcomed in with a hearty *Well done, thou good and faithful servant.* His Ma would be there, and she would hug him, and they would enter the fellowship of Jesus together. That day would come, Pimli was quite sure, and probably before Reap Moon rolled around again.

Not that he considered himself a religious nut. Not at all. These thoughts of God and heaven he kept strictly to himself. As far as the rest of the world was concerned, he was just a joe doing a job, one he intended to do well to the very end. Certainly he saw himself as no villain, but no truly dangerous man ever has. Think of Ulysses S. Grant, that Civil War general who'd said he intended to fight it out on this line if it took all summer.

In the Algul Siento, summer was almost over.

FOUR

The Master's home was a tidy Cape Cod at one end of the Mall. It was called Shapleigh House (Pimli had no idea why), and so of course the Breakers called it Shit House. At the other end of the Mall was a much larger dwelling—a gracefully rambling Queen Anne called (for equally obscure reasons) Damli House. It would have looked at home on Fraternity Row at Clemson or Ole Miss. The Breakers called this one Heartbreak House, or sometimes Heartbreak Hotel. Fine. It was where the taheen and a sizable contingent of can-toi lived and worked. As for the Breakers, let them have their little jokes, and by all means let them believe that the staff didn't know.

Pimli Prentiss and Finli o' Tego strolled up the Mall in companionable silence . . . except, that was, when they passed off-duty Breakers, either alone or in company. Pimli greeted each of them with unfailing courtesy. The greetings they returned varied from the completely cheerful to sullen grunts. Yet each made some sort of response, and Pimli counted this a victory. He cared about them. Whether they liked it or not—many didn't—he cared about them. They were certainly easier to deal with than the murderers, rapists, and armed robbers of Attica.

Some were reading old newspapers or magazines. A foursome was throwing horseshoes. Another foursome was on the putting green. Tanya Leeds and Joey Rastosovich were playing chess under a graceful old elm, the sunlight making dapples on their faces. They greeted him with real pleasure, and why not? Tanya Leeds was now actually Tanya Rastosovich, for Pimli had married them a month ago, just like the captain of a ship. And he supposed that in a way, that was what this was: the good ship *Algul Siento*, a cruise vessel that sailed the dark seas of Thunderclap in her own sunny spotlight. The sun went out from time to time, say true, but today's outage had been minimal, only forty-three seconds.

"How's it going, Tanya? Joseph?" Always Joseph and never Joey, at least not to his face; he didn't like it.

They said it was going fine and gave him those dazed, fuck-struck smiles of which only newlyweds are capable. Finli said nothing to the Rastosoviches, but near the Damli House end of the Mall, he stopped before a young man sitting on a faux marble bench beneath a tree, reading a book.

"Sai Earnshaw?" the taheen asked.

Dinky looked up, eyebrows raised in polite enquiry. His face, studded with a bad case of acne, bore the same polite no-expression.

"I see you're reading *The Magus*," Finli said, almost shyly. "I myself am reading *The Collector*. Quite a coincidence!"

"If you say so," Dinky replied. His expression didn't change.

"I wonder what you think of Fowles? I'm quite busy right now, but perhaps later we could discuss him."

Still wearing that politely expressionless expression, Dinky Earnshaw said, "Perhaps later you could take your copy of *The Collector*—hardcover, I hope—and stick it up your furry ass. Sideways."

Finli's hopeful smile disappeared. He gave a small but perfectly correct bow. "I'm sorry you feel that way, sai."

"The fuck outta here," Dinky said, and opened his book again. He raised it pointedly before his face.

Pimli and Finli o' Tego walked on. There was a period of silence during which the Master of Algul Siento tried out different approaches to Finli, wanting to know how badly he'd been hurt by the young man's comment. The taheen was proud of his ability to read and appreciate hume literature, that much Pimli knew. Then Finli saved him the trouble by putting both of his long-fingered hands—his ass wasn't actually furry, but his fingers were—between his legs.

"Just checking to make sure my nuts are still there," he said, and Pimli thought the good humor he heard in the Chief of Security's voice was real, not forced.

"I'm sorry about that," Pimli said. "If there's anyone in Blue Heaven who has an authentic case of post-adolescent angst, it's sai Earnshaw."

"'You're tearing me apart!'" Finli moaned, and when the Master gave him a startled look, Finli grinned, showing those rows of tiny sharp teeth. "It's a famous line from a film called *Rebel Without a Cause,*" he said. "Dinky Earnshaw makes me think of James Dean." He paused to consider. "Without the haunting good looks, of course."

"An interesting case," Prentiss said. "He was recruited for an assassination program run by a Positronics subsidiary. He killed his control and ran. We caught him, of course. He's never been any real trouble—not for us—but he's got that pain-in-the-ass attitude."

"But you feel he's not a problem."

Pimli gave him a sideways glance. "Is there something *you* feel I should know about him?"

"No, no. I've never seen you so jumpy as you've been over the last few weeks. Hell, call a spade a spade—so *paranoid.*"

"My grandfather had a proverb," Pimli said. "'You don't worry about dropping the eggs until you're almost home.' We're almost home now."

And it was true. Seventeen days ago, not long before the last batch of Wolves had come galloping through the door from the Arc 16 Staging Area, their equipment in the basement of Damli House had picked up the first appreciable bend in the Bear-Turtle Beam. Since then the Beam of Eagle and Lion had snapped. Soon the Breakers would no longer be needed; soon the disintegration of the second-to-last Beam would happen with or without their help. It was like a precariously balanced object that had now picked up a sway. Soon it would go too far beyond its point of perfect balance, and then it would fall. Or, in the case of the Beam, it would break. Wink out of existence. It was the Tower that would fall. The last Beam, that of Wolf and Elephant, might hold for another week or another month, but not much longer.

Thinking of that should have pleased Pimli, but it didn't.

Mostly because his thoughts had returned to the Greencloaks. Sixty or so had gone through Calla-bound last time, the usual deployment, and they should have been back in the usual seventy-two hours with the usual catch of Calla children.

Instead . . . nothing.

He asked Finli what *he* thought about that.

Finli stopped. He looked grave. "I think it may have been a virus," he said.

"Cry pardon?"

"A computer virus. We've seen it happen with a good deal of our computer equipment in Damli, and you want to remember that, no matter how fearsome the Greencloaks may look to a bunch of rice-farmers, computers on legs is all they really are." He paused. "Or the Calla-*folken* may have found a way to kill them. Would it surprise me to find that they'd gotten up on their hind legs to fight? A little, but not a lot. Especially if someone with guts stepped forward to lead them."

"Someone like a gunslinger, mayhap?"

Finli gave him a look that stopped just short of patronizing.

Ted Brautigan and Stanley Ruiz rode up the sidewalk on ten-speed bikes, and when the Master and the Security Head raised hands to them, both raised their hands in return. Brautigan didn't smile but Ruiz did, the loose happy smile of a true mental defective. He was all eye-boogers, stubbly cheeks, and spit-shiny lips, but a powerful bugger just the same, before God he was, and such a man could do worse than chum around with Brautigan, who had changed completely since being hauled back from his little "vacation" in Connecticut. Pimli was amused by the identical tweed caps the two men were wearing—their bikes were also identical—but not by Finli's look.

"Quit it," Pimli said.

"Quit what, sai?" Finli asked.

"Looking at me as if I were a little kid who just lost the top off his ice cream cone and doesn't have the wit to realize it."

But Finli didn't back down. He rarely did, which was one of the things Pimli liked about him. "If you don't want folk to look at you like a child, then you mustn't act like one. There've been rumors of gunslingers coming out of Mid-World to save the day for a thousand years and more. And never a single authenticated sighting. Personally, I'd be more apt to expect a visit from your Man Jesus."

"The Rods say—"

Finli winced as if this actually hurt his head. "Don't start with what the Rods say. Surely you respect my intelligence—and your own—more than that. Their brains have rotted even faster than their skins. As for the Wolves, let me advance a radical concept: it doesn't matter *where* they are or what's happened to them. We've got enough booster to finish the job, and that's all I care about."

The Security Head stood for a moment at the steps that led up to the Damli House porch. He was looking after the two men on the identical bikes and frowning thoughtfully. "Brautigan's been a lot of trouble."

"Hasn't he just!" Pimli laughed ruefully. "But his troublesome days are over. He's been told that his special friends from Connecticut—a boy named Robert Garfield and a girl named Carol Gerber—will die if he makes any more trouble. Also he's come to realize that while a number of his fellow Breakers regard him as a mentor, and some, such as the softheaded boy he's with, revere him, no one is interested in his . . . philosophical ideas, shall we say. Not any longer, if they ever were. And I had a talk with him after he came back. A heart-to-heart."

This was news to Finli. "About what?"

"Certain facts of life. Sai Brautigan has come to understand that his unique powers no longer matter as much as they once did. It's gone too far for that. The remaining two Beams are going to break with him or without him. And he knows that at the end there's apt to be . . . confusion. Fear and confusion." Pimli nodded slowly. "Brautigan wants to be here at the end, if only to comfort such as Stanley Ruiz when the sky tears open.

"Come, let's have another look at the tapes and the telemetry. Just to be safe."

They went up the wide wooden steps of Damli House, side by side.

FIVE

Two of the can-toi were waiting to escort the Master and his Security Chief downstairs. Pimli reflected on how odd it was that everyone—Breakers and Algul Siento staff alike—had come to call them "the low men." Because it was Brautigan who coined the phrase. "Speak of angels, hear the flutter of their wings," Prentiss's beloved Ma might have said, and Pimli supposed that if there were true manimals in these final days of the true world, then the can-toi would fill the bill much better than the taheen. If you saw them without their weird living masks, you would have thought they *were* taheen, with the heads of rats. But unlike the true taheen, who regarded humes (less a few remarkable exceptions such as Pimli himself) as an inferior race, the can-toi worshipped the human form as divine. Did they wear the masks in worship? They were closemouthed on the subject, but Pimli didn't think so. He thought they believed they were *becoming* human—which was why, when they first put on their masks (these were living flesh, grown rather than made), they took a hume name to go with their hume aspect. Pimli knew they believed they would somehow replace human beings after the Fall . . . although *how* they could believe such a thing was entirely beyond him. There would be heaven after the Fall, that was obvious to anyone who'd ever read the Book of Revelation . . . but Earth?

Some *new* Earth, perhaps, but Pimli wasn't even sure of that.

Two can-toi security guards, Beeman and Trelawney, stood at the end of the hall, guarding the head of the stairs going down to the basement. To Pimli, all can-toi men, even those with blond hair and skinny builds, looked weirdly like that actor from the forties and fifties, Clark Gable. They all seemed to have the same thick, sensual lips and batty ears. Then, when you got very close, you could see the artificial wrinkles at the neck and behind the ears, where their hume masks twirled into pigtails and ran into the hairy, toothy flesh that was their reality (whether they accepted it or not). And there were the eyes. Hair surrounded them, and if you looked closely, you could see that what you originally took for *sockets* were, in fact, holes in those peculiar masks of living flesh. Sometimes you could hear the masks themselves breathing, which Pimli found both weird and a little revolting.

"Hile," said Beeman.

"Hile," said Trelawney.

Pimli and Finli returned the greeting, they all fisted their foreheads, and then Pimli led the way downstairs. In the lower corridor, walking past the sign which read WE MUST ALL WORK TOGETHER TO CREATE A FIRE-FREE ENVIRONMENT and another reading ALL HAIL THE CAN-TOI, Finli said, very low: "They are *so* odd."

Pimli smiled and clapped him on the back. That was why he genuinely liked Finli o' Tego: like Ike and Mike, they thought alike.

SIX

Most of the Damli House basement was a large room jammed with equipment. Not all of the stuff worked, and they had no use for some of the instruments that did (there was plenty they didn't even understand), but they were very familiar with the surveillance equipment and the telemetry that measured *darks*: units of expended psychic energy. The Breakers were expressly forbidden from using their psychic abilities outside of The Study, and not all of them could, anyway. Many were like men and women so severely toilet-trained that they were unable to urinate without the visual stimuli that assured them that yes, they were in the toilet, and yes, it was all right to let go. Others, like children who aren't yet completely toilet-trained, were unable to prevent the occasional psychic outburst. This might amount to no more than giving someone they didn't like a transient headache or knocking over a bench on the Mall, but Pimli's men kept careful track, and outbursts that were deemed "on purpose" were punished, first offenses lightly, repeat offenses with rapidly mounting severity. And, as Pimli liked to lecture to the newcomers (back in the days when there had *been* newcomers), "Be sure your sin will find you out." Finli's scripture was even simpler: *Telemetry doesn't lie.*

Today they found nothing but transient blips on the telemetry readouts. It was as meaningless as a four-hour audio recording of some group's farts and burps would have been. The videotapes and the swing-guards' daybooks likewise produced nothing of interest.

"Satisfied, sai?" Finli asked, and something in his voice caused Pimli to swing around and look at him sharply.

"Are *you?*"

Finli o' Tego sighed. At times like this Pimli wished that either Finli were hume or that he himself were truly taheen. The problem was Finli's inexpressive black eyes. They were almost the shoebutton eyes of a Raggedy Andy doll, and there was simply no way to read them. Unless, maybe, you were another taheen.

"I haven't felt right for weeks now," Finli said at last. "I drink too much graf to put myself asleep, then drag myself through the day, biting people's heads off. Part of it's the loss of communications since the last Beam went—"

"You know that was inevitable—"

"Yes, of course I know. What I'm saying is that I'm trying to find rational reasons to explain irrational feelings, and that's never a good sign."

On the far wall was a picture of Niagara Falls. Some can-toi guard had turned it upside down. The low men considered turning pictures upside down the absolute height of humor. Pimli had no idea why. But in the end, who gave a shit? *I know how to do my facking job,* he thought, re-hanging Niagara Falls rightside up. *I know how to do that, and nothing else matters, tell God and the Man Jesus thank ya.*

"We always knew things were going to get wacky at the end," Finli said, "so I tell myself that's all this is. This . . . you know . . ."

"This feeling you have," the former Paul Prentiss supplied. Then he grinned and laid his right forefinger over a circle made by his left thumb and index finger. This was a taheen gesture which meant *I tell you the truth.* "This *irrational* feeling."

"Yar. Certainly I know that the Bleeding Lion hasn't reappeared in the north, nor do I believe that the sun's cooling from the inside. I've heard tales of the Red King's madness and that the Dan-Tete has come to take his place, and all I can say is 'I'll believe it when I see it.' Same with this wonderful news about how a gunslinger-man's come out of the west to save the Tower, as the old tales and songs predict. Bullshit, every bit of it."

Pimli clapped him on the shoulder. "Does my heart good to hear you say so!"

It did, too. Finli o' Tego had done a hell of a job during his tenure as Head. His security cadre had had to kill half a dozen Breakers over the years—all of them homesick fools trying to escape—and two others had been lobotomized, but Ted Brautigan was the only one who'd actually made it "under the fence" (this phrase Pimli had picked up from a film called *Stalag 17*), and they had reeled him back in, by God. The can-toi took the credit, and the Security Chief let them, but Pimli knew the truth: it was Finli who'd choreographed each move, from beginning to end.

"But it might be more than just nerves, this feeling of mine," Finli continued. "I *do* believe that sometimes folk can have bona fide intuitions." He laughed. "How could one not believe that, in a place as lousy with precogs and postcogs as this one?"

"But no teleports," Pimli said. "Right?"

Teleportation was the one so-called wild talent of which all the Devar staff was afraid, and with good reason. There was no end to the sort of havoc a teleport could wreak. Bringing in about four acres of outer space, for instance, and creating a vacuum-induced hurricane. Fortunately there was a simple test to isolate that particular talent (easy to administer, although the equipment necessary was another leftover of the old people and none of them knew how long it would continue to work) and a simple procedure (also left behind by the old ones) for shorting out such dangerous organic circuits. Dr. Gangli was able to take care of potential teleports in under two minutes. "So simple it makes a vasectomy look like brain-surgery," he'd said once.

"Absa-fackin-lutely no teleports," was what Finli said now, and led Prentiss to an instrument console that looked eerily like Susannah Dean's visualization of her Dogan. He pointed at two dials marked in the henscratch of the old people (marks similar to those on the Unfound Door). The needle of each dial lay flat against the O mark on the left. When Finli tapped them with his furry thumbs, they jumped a little and then fell back.

"We don't know exactly what these dials were actually meant to measure," he said, "but one thing they *do* measure is teleportation potential. We've had Breakers who've tried to shield the talent and it doesn't work. If there was a teleport in the woodpile, Pimli o' New Jersey, these needles would be jittering all the way up to fifty or even eighty."

"So." Half-smiling, half-serious, Pimli began to count off on his fingers. "No teleports, no Bleeding Lion stalking from the north, no gunslinger-man. Oh, and the Greencloaks succumbed to a computer virus. If all that's the case, what's gotten under your skin? What feels hinky-di-di to ya?"

"The approaching end, I suppose." Finli sighed heavily. "I'm going to double the guard in the watchtowers tonight, any ro', and humes along the fence, as well."

"Because it feels hinky-di-di." Pimli, smiling a little.

"Hinky-di-di, yar." Finli did not smile; his cunning little teeth remained hidden inside his shiny brown muzzle.

Pimli clapped him on the shoulder. "Come on, let's go up to The Study. Perhaps seeing all those Breakers at work will soothe you."

"P'rhaps it will," Finli said, but he still didn't smile.

Pimli said gently, "It's all right, Fin."

"I suppose," said the taheen, looking doubtfully around at the equipment, and then at Beeman and Trelawney, the two low men, who were respectfully waiting at the door for the two big bugs to finish their palaver. "I suppose 'tis." Only his heart didn't believe it. The only thing he was sure his heart believed was that there were no teleports left in Algul Siento.

Telemetry didn't lie.

SEVEN

Beeman and Trelawney saw them all the way down the oak-paneled basement corridor to the staff elevator, which was also oak-paneled. There was a fire-extinguisher on the wall of the car and another sign reminding Devar-*folken* that they had to work together to create a fire-free environment.

This too had been turned upside down.

Pimli's eyes met Finli's. The Master believed he saw amusement in his Security Chief's look, but of course what he saw might have been no more than his own sense of humor, reflected back at him like a face in a mirror. Finli untacked the sign without a word and turned it rightside up. Neither of them commented on the elevator machinery, which was loud and ill-sounding. Nor on the way the car shuddered in the shaft. If it froze, escape through the upper hatch would be no problem, not even for a slightly overweight (well . . . *quite* overweight) fellow like Prentiss. Damli House was hardly a skyscraper, and there was plenty of help near at hand.

They reached the third floor, where the sign on the closed elevator door was rightside up. It said **STAFF ONLY** and **PLEASE USE KEY** and **GO DOWN IMMEDIATELY IF YOU HAVE REACHED THIS LEVEL IN ERROR. YOU WILL NOT BE PENALIZED IF YOU REPORT IMMEDIATELY.**

As Finli produced his key-card, he said with a casualness that might have been feigned (God *damn* his unreadable black eyes): "Have you heard from sai Sayre?"

"No," Pimli said (rather crossly), "nor do I really expect to. We're isolated here for a reason, deliberately forgotten in the desert just like the scientists of the Manhattan Project back in the 1940s. The last time I saw him, he told me it might be . . . well, the last time I saw him."

"Relax," Finli said. "I was just asking." He swiped the key-card down its slot and the elevator door slid open with a rather hellish *screee* sound.

EIGHT

The Study was a long, high room in the center of Damli, also oak-paneled and rising three full stories to a glass roof that allowed the Algul's hard-won sunlight to pour in. On the balcony opposite the door through which Prentiss and the Tego entered was an odd trio consisting of a ravenhead taheen named Jakli, a can-toi technician named Conroy, and two hume guards whose names Pimli could not immediately recall. Taheen, can-toi, and humes got on together during work hours by virtue of careful—and sometimes brittle—courtesy, but one did not expect to see them socializing off-duty. And indeed the balcony was strictly off-limits when it came to "socializing." The Breakers below were neither animals in a zoo nor exotic fish in an aquarium; Pimli (Finli o' Tego, as well) had made this point to the staff over and over. The Master of Algul Siento had only had to lobo one staff member in all his years here, a per-fectly idiotic hume guard named David Burke, who had actually been throwing something—had it been peanut-shells?—down on the Breakers below. When Burke had realized the Master was serious about lobotomizing him, he begged for a second chance, promising he'd never do anything so foolish and demeaning again. Pimli had turned a deaf ear. He'd seen a chance to make an example which would stand for years, per-haps for decades, and had taken it. You could see the now *truly* idiotic Mr. Burke around to this day, walking on the Mall or out by Left'rds Bound'ry, mouth slack and eyes vaguely puz-zled—*I* almost *know who I am, I* almost *remember what I did to end up like this,* those eyes said. He was a living example of what sim-ply wasn't done when one was in the presence of working Breakers. But there was no rule expressly prohibiting staff from coming up here and they all did from time to time.

Because it was refreshing.

For one thing, being near working Breakers made talk unnecessary. What they called "good mind" kicked in as you walked down the third-floor hall on either side, from either elevator, and when you opened the doors giving on the balcony good mind bloomed in your head, opening all sorts of perceptual doorways. Aldous Huxley, Pimli had thought on more than one occasion, would have gone absolutely bonkers up here. Sometimes one found one's heels leaving the floor in a kind of half-assed float. The stuff in your pockets tended to rise and hang in the air. Formerly baffling situations seemed to resolve themselves the moment you turned your thoughts to them. If you'd forgotten something, your five o'clock appointment or your brother-in-law's middle name, for instance, this was the place where you could remember. And even if you realized that what you'd forgotten was important, you were never distressed. *Folken* left the balcony with smiles on their faces even if they'd come up in the foulest of moods (a foul mood was an excellent reason to visit the balcony in the first place). It was as if some sort of happy-gas, invisible to the eye and unmeasurable by even the most sophisticated telemetry, always rose from the Breakers below.

The two of them hiled the trio across the way, then approached the wide fumed-oak railing and looked down. The room below might have been the capacious library of some richly endowed gentlemen's club in London. Softly glowing lamps, many with genuine Tiffany shades, stood on little tables or shone on the walls (oak-paneled, of course). The rugs were the most exquisite Turkish. There was a Matisse on one wall, a Rembrandt on another . . . and on a third was the *Mona Lisa*. The real one, as opposed to the fake hanging in the Louvre on Keystone Earth. A man stood before it with his arms clasped behind him. From up here he looked as though he were studying the painting—trying to decipher the famously enigmatic smile, maybe—but Pimli knew better. The men and women holding magazines looked as though they were reading, too, but if you were right down there you'd see that they were gazing blankly over the tops of their *McCall's* and their *Harper's* or a little off to one side. An eleven- or twelve-year-old girl in a gorgeous striped summer dress that might have cost sixteen hundred dollars in a Rodeo Drive kiddie boutique was sitting before a dollhouse on the hearth, but Pimli knew she wasn't paying any attention to the exquisitely made replica of Damli at all.

Thirty-three of them down there. Thirty-three in all. At eight o'clock, an hour after the artificial sun snapped off, thirty-three fresh Breakers would troop in. And there was one fellow—one and one only—who came and went just as he pleased. A fellow who'd gone under the wire and paid no penalty for it at all . . . except for being brought back, that was, and for this man, that was penalty enough.

As if the thought had summoned him, the door at the end of the room opened, and Ted Brautigan slipped quietly in. He was still wearing his tweed riding cap. Daneeka Rostov looked up from the dollhouse and gave him a smile. Brautigan dropped her a wink in return. Pimli gave Finli a little nudge.

Finli: (*I see him*)

But it was more than seeing. They *felt* him. The moment Brautigan came into the room, those on the balcony—and, much more important, those on the floor—felt the power-level rise. They still weren't completely sure what they'd gotten in Brautigan, and the testing equipment didn't help in that regard (the old dog had blown out several pieces of it himself, and on purpose, the Master was quite sure). If there were others like him, the low men had found none on their talent hunts (now suspended; they had all the talent they needed to finish the job). One thing that *did* seem clear was Brautigan's talent as a facilitator, a psychic who was not just powerful by himself but was able to up the abilities of others just by being near them. Finli's thoughts, ordinarily unreadable even to Breakers, now burned in Pimli's mind like neon.

Finli: (*He is extraordinary*)

Pimli: (*And, so far as we know, unique   Have you seen the thing*)

Image: Eyes growing and shrinking, growing and shrinking.

Finli: (*Yes   Do you know what causes it*)

Pimli: (*Not at all   Nor care dear Finli   nor care   That old*)

Image: An elderly mongrel with burdocks in his matted fur, limping along on three legs.

(*has almost finished his work   almost time to*)

Image: A gun, one of the hume guards' Berettas, against the side of the old mongrel's head.

Three stories below them, the subject of their conversation picked up a newspaper (the newspapers were all old, now, old like Brautigan himself, years out of date), sat in a leather-upholstered club chair so voluminous it seemed almost to swallow him, and appeared to read.

Pimli felt the psychic force rising past them and through them, to the skylight and through that, too, rising to the Beam that ran directly above Algul, working against it, chipping and eroding and rubbing relentlessly against the grain. Eating holes in the magic. Working patiently to put out the eyes of the Bear. To crack the shell of the Turtle. To break the Beam which ran from Shardik to Maturin. To topple the Dark Tower which stood between.

Pimli turned to his companion and wasn't surprised to realize he could now see the cunning little teeth in the Tego's weasel head. Smiling at last! Nor was he surprised to realize he could read the black eyes. Taheen, under ordinary circumstances, could send and receive some very simple mental communications, but not be progged. Here, though, all that changed. Here—

—Here Finli o' Tego was at peace. His concerns

(*hinky-di-di*)

were gone. At least for the time being.

Pimli sent Finli a series of bright images: a champagne bottle breaking over the stern of a boat; hundreds of flat black graduation caps rising in the air; a flag being planted on Mount Everest; a laughing couple escaping a church with their heads bent against a pelting storm of rice; a planet—Earth— suddenly glowing with fierce brilliance.

Images that all said the same thing.

"Yes," Finli said, and Pimli wondered how he could ever have thought those eyes hard to read. "Yes, indeed. Success at the end of the day."

Neither of them looked down at that moment. Had they done, they would have seen Ted Brautigan—an old dog, yes, and tired, but perhaps not *quite* as tired as some thought— looking up at them.

With a ghost of his own smile.

NINE

There was never rain out here, at least not during Pimli's years, but sometimes, in the Stygian blackness of its nights, there were great volleys of dry thunder. Most of the Devar-Toi's staff had trained themselves to sleep through these fusillades, but Pimli often woke up, heart hammering in his throat, the Our Father running through his mostly unconscious mind like a circle of spinning red ribbon.

Earlier that day, talking to Finli, the Master of Algul Siento had used the phrase *hinky-di-di* with a self-conscious smile, and why not? It was a child's phrase, almost, like *allee-allee-in-free* or *eenie-meenie-minie-moe.*

Now, lying in his bed at Shapleigh House (known as Shit House to the Breakers), a full Mall's length away from Damli House, Pimli remembered the feeling—the flat-out *certainty*— that everything was going to be okay; success assured, only a matter of time. On the balcony Finli had shared it, but Pimli wondered if his Security Chief was now lying awake as Pimli himself was, and thinking how easy it was to be misled when you were around working Breakers. Because, do ya, they sent up that happy-gas. That good-mind vibe.

And suppose . . . just *suppose*, now . . . someone was actually *channeling* that feeling? Sending it up to them like a lullabye? *Go to sleep, Pimli, go to sleep, Finli, go to sleep all of you good children . . .*

Ridiculous idea, totally paranoid. Still, when another double-boom of thunder rolled out of what might still be the south-east—from the direction of Fedic and the Discordia, anyway—Pimli Prentiss sat up and turned on the bedside lamp.

Finli had spoken of doubling the guard tonight, both in the watchtowers and along the fences. Perhaps tomorrow they might triple it. Just to be on the safe side. And because complacency this close to the end would be a very bad thing, indeed.

Pimli got out of bed, a tall man with a hairy slab of gut, now wearing blue pajama pants and nothing else. He pissed, then knelt in front of the toilet's lowered lid, folded his hands, and prayed until he felt sleepy. He prayed to do his duty. He prayed to see trouble before trouble saw him. He prayed for his Ma, just as Jim Jones had prayed for his as he watched the line move toward the tub of poisoned Kool-Aid. He prayed until the thunder had died to little more than a senile mutter, then went back to bed, calm again. His last thought before drifting off was about tripling the guard first thing in the morning, and that was the first thing he thought of when he woke to a room awash in artificial sunlight. Because you had to take care of the eggs when you were almost home.

CHAPTER VII:
KA-SHUME

ONE

A feeling both blue and strange crept among the gunslingers after Brautigan and his friends left, but at first no one spoke of it. Each of them thought that melancholy belonged to him or her alone. Roland, who might have been expected to know the feeling for what it was (ka-shume, Cort would have called it), ascribed it instead to worries about the following day and even more to the debilitating atmosphere of Thunderclap, where day was dim and night was as dark as blindness.

Certainly there was enough to keep them busy after the departure of Brautigan, Earnshaw, and Sheemie Ruiz, that friend of Roland's childhood. (Both Susannah and Eddie had attempted to talk to the gunslinger about Sheemie, and Roland had shaken them off. Jake, strong in the touch, hadn't even tried. Roland wasn't ready to talk about those old days again, at least not yet.) There was a path leading down and around the flank of Steek-Tete, and they found the cave of which the old man had told them behind a cunning camouflage of rocks and desert-dusty bushes. This cave was much bigger than the one above, with gas lanterns hung from spikes that had been driven into the rock walls. Jake and Eddie lit two of these on each side, and the four of them examined the cave's contents in silence.

The first thing Roland noticed was the sleeping-bags: a quartet lined up against the left-hand wall, each considerately placed on an inflated air mattress. The tags on the bags read PROPERTY OF U.S. ARMY. Beside the last of these, a fifth air mattress had been covered with a layer of bath towels. *They were expecting four people and one animal*, the gunslinger thought. *Precognition, or have they been watching us somehow? And does it matter?*

247

There was a plastic-swaddled object sitting on a barrel marked **DANGER! MUNITIONS!** Eddie removed the protective plastic and revealed a machine with reels on it. One of the reels was loaded. Roland could make nothing of the single word on the front of the speaking machine and asked Susannah what it was.

"Wollensak," she said. "A German company. When it comes to these things, they make the best."

"Not no mo', sugarbee," Eddie said. "In my when we like to say 'Sony! No baloney!' *They* make a tape-player you can clip right to your belt. It's called a Walkman. I bet this dinosaur weighs twenty pounds. More, with the batteries."

Susannah was examining the unmarked tape boxes that had been stacked beside the Wollensak. There were three of them. "I can't wait to hear what's on these," she said.

"After the daylight goes, maybe," Roland said. "For now, let's see what else we've got here."

"Roland?" Jake asked.

The gunslinger turned toward him. There was something about the boy's face that almost always softened Roland's own. Looking at Jake did not make the gunslinger handsome, but seemed to give his features a quality they didn't ordinarily have. Susannah thought it was the look of love. And, perhaps, some thin hope for the future.

"What is it, Jake?"

"I know we're going to fight—"

"'Join us next week for *Return to the O.K. Corral,* starring Van Heflin and Lee Van Cleef,'" Eddie murmured, walking toward the back of the cave. There a much larger object had been covered with what looked like a quilted mover's pad.

"—but when?" Jake continued. "Will it be tomorrow?"

"Perhaps," Roland replied. "I think the day after's more likely."

"I have a terrible feeling," Jake said. "It's not being afraid, exactly—"

"Do you think they're going to beat us, hon?" Susannah asked. She put a hand on Jake's neck and looked into his face.

She had come to respect his feelings. She sometimes wondered how much of what he was now had to do with the creature he'd faced to get here: the thing in the house on Dutch Hill. No robot there, no rusty old clockwork toy. The doorkeeper had been a genuine leftover of the *Prim.* "You smell a whuppin in the wind? That it?"

"I don't think so," Jake said. "I don't know what it is. I've only felt something like it once, and that was just before . . ."

"Just before what?" Susannah asked, but before Jake had a chance to reply, Eddie broke in. Roland was glad. *Just before I fell.* That was how Jake had meant to finish. *Just before Roland let me fall.*

"Holy *shit!* Come here, you guys! You gotta see this!"

Eddie had pulled away the mover's pad and revealed a motorized vehicle that looked like a cross between an ATV and a gigantic tricycle. The tires were wide balloon jobs with deep zigzag treads. The controls were all on the handlebars. And there was a playing card propped on the rudimentary dashboard. Roland knew what it was even before Eddie plucked it up between two fingers and turned it over. The card showed a woman with a shawl over her head at a spinning wheel. It was the Lady of Shadows.

"Looks like our pal Ted left you a ride, sugarbee," Eddie said.

Susannah had hurried over at her rapid crawl. Now she lifted her arms. "Boost me up! Boost me, Eddie!"

He did, and when she was in the saddle, holding handlebars instead of reins, the vehicle looked made for her. Susannah thumbed a red button and the engine thrummed to life, so low you could barely hear it. Electricity, not gasoline, Eddie was quite sure. Like a golf-cart, but probably a lot faster.

Susannah turned toward them, smiling radiantly. She patted the three-wheeler's dark brown nacelle. "Call me Missus Centaur! I been lookin for this my whole life and never even knew."

None of them noticed the stricken expression on Roland's face. He bent over to pick up the card Eddie had dropped so no one would.

Yes, it was her, all right—the Lady of the Shadows. Under her shawl she seemed to be smiling craftily and sobbing, both at the same time. On the last occasion he'd seen that card, it had been in the hand of the man who sometimes went by the name of Walter, sometimes that of Flagg.

You have no idea how close you stand to the Tower now, he had said. *Worlds turn about your head.*

And now he recognized the feeling that had crept among them for what it almost certainly was: not worry or weariness but ka-shume. There was no real translation for that rue-laden term, but it meant to sense an approaching break in one's ka-tet.

Walter o' Dim, his old nemesis, was dead. Roland had known it as soon as he saw the face of the Lady of Shadows. Soon one of his own would die as well, probably in the coming battle to break the power of the Devar-Toi. And once again the scales which had temporarily tilted in their favor would balance.

It never once crossed Roland's mind that the one to die might be him.

TWO

There were three brand names on what Eddie immediately dubbed "Suzie's Cruisin Trike." One was Honda; one was Takuro (as in that wildly popular pre-superflu import, the Takuro Spirit); the third was North Central Positronics. And a fourth, as well: U.S. ARMY, as in PROPERTY OF.

Susannah was reluctant to get off it, but finally she did. God knew there was plenty more to see; the cave was a treasure trove. Its narrowing throat was filled with food supplies (mostly freeze-dried stuff that probably wouldn't taste as good as Nigel's chow but would at least nourish them), bottled water, canned drinks (plenty of Coke and Nozz-A-La but nothing alcoholic), and the promised propane stove. There were also crates of weaponry. Some of the crates were marked U.S. ARMY, but by no means all.

Now their most basic abilities came out: the true thread, Cort might have called it. Those talents and intuitions that

could have remained sleeping for most of their lives, only stirring long enough to get them into occasional trouble, if Roland
had not deliberately wakened them . . . cosseted them . . . and
then filed their teeth to deadly points.

Hardly a word was spoken among them as Roland produced a wide prying tool from his purse and levered away the
tops of the crates. Susannah had forgotten about the Cruisin
Trike she had been waiting for all her life; Eddie forgot to
make jokes; Roland forgot about his sense of foreboding. They
became absorbed in the weaponry that had been left for them,
and there was no piece of it they did not understand either at
once or after a bit of study.

There was a crate of AR-15 rifles, the barrels packed in
grease, the firing mechanisms fragrant with banana oil. Eddie
noted the added selector switches, and looked in the crate
next to the 15's. Inside, covered with plastic and also packed in
grease, were metal drums. They looked like the ones you saw on
tommy-guns in gangster epics like *White Heat,* only these were
bigger. Eddie lifted one of the 15's, turned it over, and found
exactly what he expected: a conversion clip that would allow
these drums to be attached to the guns, turning them into
rapid-fire rice-cutters. How many shots per drum? A hundred?
A hundred and twenty-five? Enough to mow down a whole
company of men, that was sure.

There was a box of what looked like rocket shells with the letters STS stenciled on each. In a rack beside them, propped
against the cave wall, were half a dozen handheld launchers.
Roland pointed at the atom-symbol on them and shook his
head. He did not want them shooting off weapons that would
release potentially lethal radiation no matter how powerful
they might be. He was willing to kill the Breakers if that was what
it took to stop their meddling with the Beam, but only as a last
resort.

Flanking a metal tray filled with gas-masks (to Jake they
looked gruesome, like the severed heads of strange bugs) were
two crates of handguns: snub-nosed machine-pistols with the
word COYOTE embossed on the butts and heavy automatics

called Cobra Stars. Jake was attracted to both weapons (in truth his heart was attracted to *all* the weapons), but he took one of the Stars because it looked a little bit like the gun he had lost. The clip fed up the handle and held either fifteen or sixteen shots. This was not a matter of counting but only of *looking* and *knowing.*

"Hey," Susannah said. She'd gone back toward the front of the cave. "Come look at this. Sneetches."

"Check out the crate-lid," Jake said when they joined her. Susannah had set it aside; Jake picked it up and was studying it with admiration. It showed the face of a smiling boy with a lightning-bolt scar on his forehead. He was wearing round glasses and brandishing what appeared to be a magician's wand at a floating sneetch. The words stenciled beneath the drawing read:

PROPERTY 449th SQUADRON
24 "SNEETCHES"

HARRY POTTER MODEL

SERIAL #465-17-CC NDJKR

"Don't Mess with the 449!"
We'll Kick the "Slytherin" Out of You!

There were two dozen sneetches in the crate, packed like eggs in little nests of plastic excelsior. None of Roland's band had had the opportunity to study live ones closely during their battle with the Wolves, but now they had a good swatch of time during which they could indulge their most natural interests and curiosities. Each took up a sneetch. They were about the size of tennis balls, but a great deal heavier. Their surfaces had been gridded, making them resemble globes marked with lines of latitude and longitude. Although they looked like steel, the surfaces had a faint giving quality, like very hard rubber.

There was an ID-plate on each sneetch and a button beside

it. "That wakes it up," Eddie murmured, and Jake nodded. There was also a small depressed area in the curved surface, just the right size for a finger. Jake pushed it without the slightest worry that the thing would explode, or maybe extrude a mini-buzzsaw that would cut off his fingers. You used the button at the bottom of the depression to access the programming. He didn't know how he knew that, but he most certainly did.

A curved section of the sneetch's surface slid away with a faint *Auowwm!* sound. Revealed were four tiny lights, three of them dark and one flashing slow amber pulses. There were seven windows, now showing **0 00 00 00**. Beneath each was a button so small that you'd need something like the end of a straightened paperclip to push it. "The size of a bug's asshole," as Eddie grumbled later on, while trying to program one. To the right of the windows were another two buttons, these marked **S** and **W**.

Jake showed it to Roland. "This one's SET and the other one's WAIT. Do you think so? I think so."

Roland nodded. He'd never seen such a weapon before—not close up, at any rate—but, coupled with the windows, he thought the use of the buttons was obvious. And he thought the sneetches might be useful in a way the long-shooters with their atom-shells would not be. SET and WAIT.

SET . . . and WAIT.

"Did Ted and his two pals leave all this stuff for us here?" Susannah asked.

Roland hardly thought it mattered who'd left it—it was here and that was enough—but he nodded.

"How? And where'd they get it?"

Roland didn't know. What he did know was that the cave was a ma'sun—a war-chest. Below them, men were making war on the Tower which the line of Eld was sworn to protect. He and his tet would fall upon them by surprise, and with these tools they would smite and smite until their enemies lay with their boots pointed to the sky.

Or until theirs did.

"Maybe he explains on one of the tapes he left us," Jake said.

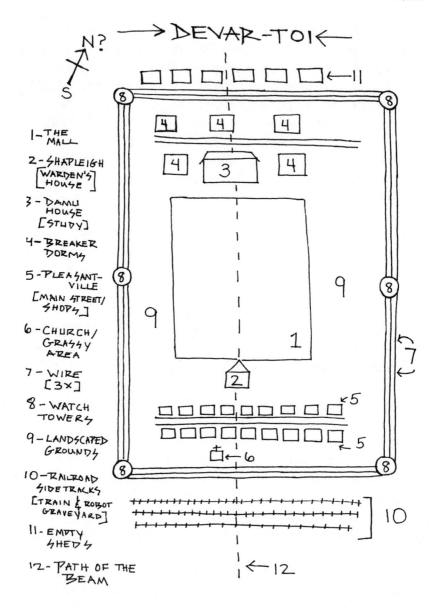

DEVAR-TOI

N?

S

←11

1 — THE MALL

2 — SHAPLEIGH [WARDEN'S HOUSE]

3 — DAMLI HOUSE [STUDY]

4 — BREAKER DORMS

5 — PLEASANT-VILLE [MAIN STREET/ SHOPS]

6 — CHURCH/ GRASSY AREA

7 — WIRE [3×]

8 — WATCH TOWERS

9 — LANDSCAPED GROUNDS

10 — RAILROAD SIDE TRACKS [TRAIN & ROBOT GRAVEYARD]

11 — EMPTY SHEDS

12 — PATH OF THE BEAM

He had engaged the safety of his new Cobra automatic and tucked it away in the shoulder-bag with the remaining Orizas. Susannah had also helped herself to one of the Cobras, after twirling it around her finger a time or two, like Annie Oakley.

"Maybe he does," she said, and gave Jake a smile. It had been a long time since Susannah had felt so physically well. So *not-preg.* Yet her mind was troubled. Or perhaps it was her spirit.

Eddie was holding up a piece of cloth that had been rolled into a tube and tied with three hanks of string. "That guy Ted said he was leaving us a map of the prison-camp. Bet this is it. Anyone 'sides me want a look?"

They all did. Jake helped Eddie to unroll the map. Brautigan had warned them it was rough, and it surely was: really no more than a series of circles and squares. Susannah saw the name of the little town—Pleasantville—and thought again of Ray Bradbury. Jake was tickled by the crude compass, where the map-maker had added a question mark beside the letter *N*.

While they were studying this hastily rendered example of cartography, a long and wavering cry rose in the murk outside. Eddie, Susannah, and Jake looked around nervously. Oy raised his head from his paws, gave a low, brief growl, then put his head back down again and appeared to go to sleep: *Hell wit'choo, bad boy, I'm wit' my homies and I ain't ascairt.*

"What is it?" Eddie asked. "A coyote? A jackal?"

"Some kind of desert dog," Roland agreed absently. He was squatted on his hunkers (which suggested his hip was better, at least temporarily) with his arms wrapped around his shins. He never took his eyes from the crude circles and squares drawn on the cloth. "Can-toi-tete."

"Is that like *Dan*-Tete?" Jake asked.

Roland ignored him. He scooped up the map and left the cave with it, not looking back. The others shared a glance and then followed him, once more wrapping their blankets about them like shawls.

THREE

Roland returned to where Sheemie (with a little help from his friends) had brought them through. This time the gunslinger used the binoculars, looking down at Blue Heaven long and long. Somewhere behind them, the desert dog howled again, a lonely sound in the gloom.

And, Jake thought, the gloom was gloomier now. Your eyes adjusted as the day dialed itself down, but that brilliant spotlight of sun seemed brighter than ever by contrast. He was pretty sure the deal with the sun-machine was that you got your full-on, your full-off, and nothing in between. Maybe they even let it shine all night, but Jake doubted it. People's nervous systems were set up for an orderly progression of dark and day, he'd learned that in science class. You could make do with long periods of low light—people did it every year in the Arctic countries—but it could really mess with your head. Jake didn't think the guys in charge down there would want to goof up their Breakers if they could help it. Also, they'd want to save their "sun" for as long as they could; everything here was old and prone to breakdowns.

At last Roland gave the binoculars to Susannah. "Do look ya especially at the buildings on either end of the grassy rectangle." He unrolled the map like a character about to read a scroll in a stage-play, glanced at it briefly, and then said, "They're numbered 2 and 3 on the map."

Susannah studied them carefully. The one marked 2, the Warden's House, was a small Cape Cod painted electric blue with white trim. It was what her mother might have called a fairy-tale house, because of the bright colors and the gingerbread scalloping around the eaves.

Damli House was much bigger, and as she looked, she saw several people going in and out. Some had the carefree look of civilians. Others seemed much more—oh, call it watchful. And she saw two or three slumping along under loads of stuff. She handed the glasses to Eddie and asked him if those were Children of Roderick.

"I think so," he said, "but I can't be completely—"

"Never mind the Rods," Roland said, "not now. What do you think of those two buildings, Susannah?"

"Well," she said, proceeding carefully (she did not, in fact, have the slightest idea what it was he wanted from her), "they're both beautifully maintained, especially compared to some of the falling-down wrecks we've seen on our travels. The one they call Damli House is especially handsome. It's a style we call Queen Anne, and—"

"Are they of wood, do you think, or just made to look that way? I'm particularly interested in the one called Damli."

Susannah redirected the binoculars there, then handed them to Eddie. He looked, then handed them to Jake. While Jake was looking, there was an audible CLICK! sound that rolled to them across the miles . . . and the Cecil B. DeMille sunbeam which had been shining down on the Devar-Toi like a spotlight went out, leaving them in a thick purple dusk which would soon be complete and utter dark.

In it, the desert-dog began to howl again, raising the skin on Jake's arms into gooseflesh. The sound rose . . . rose . . . and suddenly cut off with one final choked syllable. It sounded like some final cry of surprise, and Jake had no doubt that the desert-dog was dead. Something had crept up behind it, and when the big overhead light went out—

There were still lights on down there, he saw: a double white row that might have been streetlights in "Pleasantville," yellow circles that were probably arc-sodiums along the various paths of what Susannah was calling Breaker U . . . and spotlights running random patterns across the dark.

No, Jake thought, *not spotlights. Searchlights. Like in a prison movie.* "Let's go back," he said. "There's nothing to see any-more, and I don't like it out here in the dark."

Roland agreed. They followed him in single file, with Eddie carrying Susannah and Jake walking behind them with Oy at his heel. He kept expecting a second desert-dog to take up the cry of the first, but none did.

FOUR

"They were wood," Jake said. He was sitting cross-legged beneath one of the gas lanterns, letting its welcome white glow shine down on his face.

"Wood," Eddie agreed.

Susannah hesitated a moment, sensing it was a question of real importance and reviewing what she had seen. Then she also nodded. "Wood, I'm almost positive. *Especially* the one they call Damli House. A Queen Anne built out of stone or brick and camouflaged to look like wood? It makes no sense."

"If it fools wandering folk who'd burn it down," Roland said, "it does. It does make sense."

Susannah thought about it. He was right, of course, but—

"I still say wood."

Roland nodded. "So do I." He had found a large green bottle marked PERRIER. Now he opened it and ascertained that Perrier was water. He took five cups and poured a measure into each. He set them down in front of Jake, Susannah, Eddie, Oy, and himself.

"Do you call me dinh?" he asked Eddie.

"Yes, Roland, you know I do."

"Will you share khef with me, and drink this water?"

"Yes, if you like." Eddie had been smiling, but now he wasn't. The feeling was back, and it was strong. Ka-shume, a rueful word he did not yet know.

"Drink, bondsman."

Eddie didn't exactly like being called bondsman, but he drank his water. Roland knelt before him and put a brief, dry kiss on Eddie's lips. "I love you, Eddie," he said, and outside in the ruin that was Thunderclap, a desert wind arose, carrying gritty poisoned dust.

"Why . . . I love you, too," Eddie said. It was surprised out of him. "What's wrong? And don't tell me nothing is, because I feel it."

"Nothing's wrong," Roland said, smiling, but Jake had never heard the gunslinger sound so sad. It terrified him. "It's only ka-shume, and it comes to every ka-tet that ever was . . . but now, while we are whole, we share our water. We share our khef. 'Tis a jolly thing to do."

He looked at Susannah.

"Do you call me dinh?"

"Yes, Roland, I call you dinh." She looked very pale, but perhaps it was only the white light from the gas lanterns.

"Will you share khef with me, and drink this water?"

"With pleasure," said she, and took up the plastic cup.

"Drink, bondswoman."

She drank, her grave dark eyes never leaving his. She thought of the voices she'd heard in her dream of the Oxford jail-cell: this one dead, that one dead, t'other one dead; O Discordia, and the shadows grow deeper.

Roland kissed her mouth. "I love you, Susannah."

"I love you, too."

The gunslinger turned to Jake. "Do you call me dinh?"

"Yes," Jake said. There was no question about *his* pallor; even his lips were ashy. "Ka-shume means death, doesn't it? Which one of us will it be?"

"I know not," Roland said, "and the shadow may yet lift from us, for the wheel's still in spin. Did you not feel ka-shume when you and Callahan went into the place of the vampires?"

"Yes."

"Ka-shume for both?"

"Yes."

"Yet here you are. Our ka-tet is strong, and has survived many dangers. It may survive this one, too."

"But I feel—"

"Yes," Roland said. His voice was kind, but that awful look was in his eyes. The look that was beyond mere sadness, the one that said this would be whatever it was, but the Tower was beyond, the Dark Tower was beyond and it was there that he dwelt, heart and soul, ka and khef. "Yes, I feel it, too. So do we all. Which is why we take water, which is to say fellowship, one with the other. Will you share khef with me, and share this water?"

"Yes."

"Drink, bondsman."

Jake did. Then, before Roland could kiss him, he dropped the cup, flung his arms about the gunslinger's neck, and whispered fiercely into his ear: "Roland, I love you."

"I love you, too," he said, and released him. Outside, the wind gusted again. Jake waited for something to howl—perhaps in triumph—but nothing did.

Smiling, Roland turned to the billy-bumbler.

"Oy of Mid-World, do you call me dinh?"

"Dinh!" Oy said.

"Will you share khef with me, and this water?"

"Khef! Wat'!"

"Drink, bondsman."

Oy inserted his snout into his plastic cup—an act of some delicacy—and lapped until the water was gone. Then he looked up expectantly. There were beads of Perrier on his whiskers.

"Oy, I love you," Roland said, and leaned his face within range of the bumbler's sharp teeth. Oy licked his cheek a single time, then poked his snout back into the glass, hoping for a missed drop or two.

Roland put out his hands. Jake took one and Susannah the other. Soon they were all linked. *Like drunks at the end of an A.A. meeting*, Eddie thought.

"We are ka-tet," Roland said. "We are one from many. We have shared our water as we have shared our lives and our quest. If one should fall, that one will not be lost, for we are one and will not forget, even in death."

They held hands a moment longer. Roland was the first to let go.

"What's your plan?" Susannah asked him. She didn't call him sugar; never called him that or any other endearment ever again, so far as Jake was aware. "Will you tell us?"

Roland nodded toward the Wollensak tape recorder, still sitting on the barrel. "Perhaps we should listen to that first," he said. "I do have a plan of sorts, but what Brautigan has to say might help with some of the details."

FIVE

Night in Thunderclap is the very definition of darkness: no moon, no stars. Yet if we were to stand outside the cave where Roland and his tet have just shared khef and will now listen to the tapes Ted Brautigan has left them, we'd see two red coals floating in that wind-driven darkness. If we were to climb the path up the side of Steek-Tete toward those floating coals (a dangerous proposition in the dark), we'd eventually come upon a seven-legged spider now crouched over the queerly deflated body of a mutie coyote. This can-toi-tete was a literally misbegotten thing in life, with the stub of a fifth leg jutting from its chest and a jellylike mass of flesh hanging down between its rear legs like a deformed udder, but its flesh nourishes Mordred, and its blood—taken in a series of long, steaming gulps—is as sweet as a dessert wine. There are, in truth, all sorts of things to eat over here. Mordred has no friends to lift him from place to place via the seven-league boots of teleportation, but he found his journey from Thunderclap Station to Steek-Tete far from arduous.

He has overheard enough to be sure of what his father is planning: a surprise attack on the facility below. They're badly outnumbered, but Roland's band of shooters is fiercely devoted to him, and surprise is ever a powerful weapon.

And gunslingers are what Jake would call *fou*, crazy when their blood is up, and afraid of nothing. Such insanity is an even more powerful weapon.

Mordred was born with a fair amount of inbred knowledge, it seems. He knows, for instance, that his Red Father, possessed of such information as Mordred now has, would have sent word of the gunslinger's presence at once to the Devar-Toi's Master or Security Chief. And then, sometime later tonight, the ka-tet out of Mid-World would have found *themselves* ambushed. Killed in their sleep, mayhap, thus allowing the Breakers to continue the King's work. Mordred wasn't born with a knowledge of that work, but he's capable of logic and his ears are sharp. He now understands what the gunslingers are about: they have come here to break the Breakers.

He could stop it, true, but Mordred feels no interest in his Red Father's plans or ambitions. What he most truly enjoys, he's discovering, is the bitter loneliness of *outside*. Of watching with the cold interest of a child watching life and death and war and peace through the glass wall of the antfarm on his bureau.

Would he let yon ki'-dam actually kill his White Father? Oh, probably not. Mordred is reserving that pleasure for himself, and he has his reasons; already he has his reasons. But as for the others—the young man, the shor'-leg woman, the kid— yes, if ki'-dam Prentiss gets the upper hand, by all means let him kill any or all three of them. As for Mordred Deschain, he will let the game play out straight. He will watch. He will listen. He will hear the screams and smell the burning and watch the blood soak into the ground. And then, if he judges that Roland won't win his throw, he, Mordred, will step in. On behalf of the Crimson King, if it seems like a good idea, but really on his own behalf, and for his own reason, which is really quite simple: *Mordred's a-hungry.*

And if Roland and his ka-tet should win their throw? Win and press on to the Tower? Mordred doesn't really think it will happen, for he is in his own strange way a member of their ka-tet, he shares their khef and feels what they do. He feels the impending break of their fellowship.

Ka-shume! Mordred thinks, smiling. There's a single eye left in the desert-dog's face. One of the hairy black spider-legs caresses it and then plucks it out. Mordred eats it like a grape, then turns back to where the white light of the gas-lanterns spills around the corners of the blanket Roland has hung across the cave's mouth.

Could he go down closer? Close enough to listen?

Mordred thinks he could, especially with the rising wind to mask the sound of his movements. An exciting idea.

He scutters down the rocky slope toward the errant sparks of light, toward the murmur of the voice from the tape recorder and the thoughts of those listening: his brothers, his sister-mother, the pet billy, and, of course, overseeing them all, Big White Ka-Daddy.

Mordred creeps as close as he dares and then crouches in the cold and windy dark, miserable and enjoying his misery, dreaming his outside dreams. Inside, beyond the blanket, is light. Let them have it, if they like; for now let there be light. Eventually he, Mordred, will put it out. And in the darkness, he will have his pleasure.

Chapter VIII:
Notes from
the Gingerbread House

ONE

Eddie looked at the others. Jake and Roland were sitting on the sleeping-bags which had been left for them. Oy lay curled up at Jake's feet. Susannah was parked comfortably on the seat of her Cruisin Trike. Eddie nodded, satisfied, and pushed the tape recorder's PLAY button. The reels spun . . . there was silence . . . they spun . . . and silence . . . then, after clearing his throat, Ted Brautigan began to speak. They listened for over four hours, Eddie replacing each empty reel with the next full one, not bothering to rewind.

No one suggested they stop, certainly not Roland, who listened with silent fascination even when his hip began to throb again. Roland thought he understood more, now; certainly he knew they had a real chance to stop what was happening in the compound below them. The knowledge frightened him because their chances of success were slim. The feeling of ka-shume made that clear. And one did not really understand the stakes until one glimpsed the goddess in her white robe, the bitch-goddess whose sleeve fell back to reveal her comely white arm as she beckoned: *Come to me, run to me. Yes, it's possible, you may gain your goal, you may win, so run to me, give me your whole heart. And if I break it? If one of you falls short, falls into the pit of cof-fah (the place your new friends call hell)? Too bad for you.*

Yes, if one of them fell into coffah and burned within sight of the fountains, that would be too bad, indeed. And the bitch in the white robe? Why, she'd only put her hands on her hips, and throw back her head, and laugh as the world ended. So much depended on the man whose weary, rational voice now filled the cave. The Dark Tower itself depended on him, for Brautigan was a man of staggering powers.

The surprising thing was that the same could be said of Sheemie.

TWO

"Test, one two . . . test, one two . . . test, test, test. This is Ted Stevens Brautigan and this is a test . . ."

A brief pause. The reels turned, one full, the other now beginning to fill.

"Okay, good. Great, in fact. I wasn't sure this thing would work, especially here, but it seems fine. I prepared for this by trying to imagine you four—five, counting the boy's little friend—listening to me, because I've always found visualization an excellent technique when preparing some sort of presentation. Unfortunately, in this case it doesn't work. Sheemie can send me very good mental pictures—brilliant ones, in fact—but Roland is the only one of you he's actually seen, and him not since the fall of Gilead, when both of them were very young. No disrespect, fellows, but I suspect the Roland now coming toward Thunderclap looks hardly anything like the young man my friend Sheemie so worshipped.

"Where are you now, Roland? In Maine, looking for the writer? The one who also created me, after a fashion? In New York, looking for Eddie's wife? Are any of you even still alive? I know the chances of you reaching Thunderclap aren't good; ka is drawing you to the Devar-Toi, but a very powerful anti-ka, set in motion by the one you call the Crimson King, is working against you and your tet in a thousand ways. All the same . . .

"Was it Emily Dickinson who called hope the thing with feathers? I can't remember. There are a great many things I can't remember any longer, but it seems I still remember how to fight. Maybe that's a good thing. I *hope* it's a good thing.

"Has it crossed your mind to wonder where I'm recording this, lady and gentlemen?"

It hadn't. They simply sat, mesmerized by the slightly dusty sound of Brautigan's voice, passing a bottle of Perrier and a tin filled with graham crackers back and forth.

"I'll tell you," Brautigan went on, "partly because the three of you from America will surely find it amusing, but mostly because you may find it useful in formulating a plan to destroy what's going on in Algul Siento.

"As I speak, I'm sitting on a chair made of slab chocolate. The seat is a big blue marshmallow, and I doubt if the air mattresses we're planning to leave you could be any more comfortable. You'd think such a seat would be sticky, but it's not. The walls of this room—and the kitchen I can see if I look through the gumdrop arch to my left—are made of green, yellow, and red candy. Lick the green one and you taste lime. Lick the red one and you taste raspberry. Although taste (in any sense of that slippery word) had very little to do with Sheemie's choices, or so I believe; I think he simply has a child's love of bright primary colors."

Roland was nodding and smiling a little.

"Although I must tell you," the voice from the tape recorder said dryly, "I'd be happy to have at least one room with a slightly more reserved décor. Something in blue, perhaps. Earth-tones would be even better.

"Speaking of earth tones, the stairs are also chocolate. The banister's a candy-cane. One cannot, however, say 'the stairs going up to the second floor,' because there *is* no second floor. Through the window you can see cars that look suspiciously like bonbons going by, and the street itself looks like licorice. But if you open the door and take more than a single step toward Twizzler Avenue, you find yourself back where you started. In what we may as well call 'the real world,' for want of a better term.

"Gingerbread House—which is what we call it because that's what you always smell in here, warm gingerbread, just out of the oven—is as much Dinky's creation as it is Sheemie's. Dink wound up in the Corbett House dorm with Sheemie, and heard Sheemie crying himself to sleep one night. A lot of people would have passed by on the other side in a case like that, and I realize that no one in the world looks less like the Good Samaritan than Dinky Earnshaw, but instead of passing by he knocked on the door of Sheemie's suite and asked if he could come in.

"Ask him about it now and Dinky will tell you it was no big deal. 'I was new in the place, I was lonely, I wanted to make some friends,' he'll say. 'Hearing a guy bawling like that, it hit me that *he* might want a friend, too.' As though it were the most natural thing in the world. In a lot of places that might be true, but not in Algul Siento. And you need to understand that above all else, I think, if you're going to understand *us.* So forgive me if I seem to dwell on the point.

"Some of the hume guards call us morks, after a space alien in some television comedy. And morks are the most selfish people on Earth. Antisocial? Not exactly. Some are *extremely* social, but only insofar as it will get them what they currently want or need. Very few morks are sociopaths, but most sociopaths are morks, if you understand what I'm saying. The most famous, and thank God the low men never brought him over here, was a mass murderer named Ted Bundy.

"If you have an extra cigarette or two, no one can be more sympathetic—or admiring—than a mork in need of a smoke. Once he's got it, though, he's gone.

"Most morks—I'm talking ninety-eight or -nine out of a hundred—would have heard crying behind that closed door and never so much as slowed down on their way to wherever. Dinky knocked and asked if he could come in, even though he was new in the place and justifiably confused (he also thought he was going to be punished for murdering his previous boss, but that's a story for another day).

"And we should look at Sheemie's side of it. Once again, I'd say ninety-eight or even ninety-nine morks out of a hundred would have responded to a question like that by shouting 'Get lost!' or even 'Fuck off!' Why? Because we are exquisitely aware that we're different from most people, and that it's a difference most people don't like. Any more than the Neanderthals liked the first Cro-Magnons in the neighborhood, I would imagine. Morks don't like to be caught off-guard."

A pause. The reels spun. All four of them could sense Brautigan thinking hard.

"No, that's not quite right," he said at last. "What morks don't like is to be caught in an emotionally vulnerable state. Angry, happy, in tears or fits of hysterical laughter, anything like that. It would be like you fellows going into a dangerous situation without your guns.

"For a long time, I was alone here. I was a mork who cared, whether I liked it or not. Then there was Sheemie, brave enough to accept comfort if comfort was offered. And Dink, who was willing to reach out. Most morks are selfish introverts masquerading as rugged individualists—they want the world to see them as Dan'l Boone types—and the Algul staff loves it, believe me. No community is easier to govern than one that rejects the very concept of community. Do you see why I was attracted to Sheemie and Dinky, and how lucky I was to find them?"

Susannah's hand crept into Eddie's. He took it and squeezed it gently.

"Sheemie was afraid of the dark," Ted continued. "The low men—I call em all low men, although there are humes and taheen at work here as well as can-toi—have a dozen sophisticated tests for psychic potential, but they couldn't seem to realize that they had caught a halfwit who was simply afraid of the dark. Their bad luck.

"Dinky understood the problem right away, and solved it by telling Sheemie stories. The first ones were fairy-tales, and one of them was 'Hansel and Gretel.' Sheemie was fascinated by the idea of a candy house, and kept asking Dinky for more details. So, you see, it was Dinky who actually thought of the chocolate chairs with the marshmallow seats, the gumdrop arch, and the candy-cane banister. For a little while there *was* a second floor; it had the beds of the Three Bears in it. But Sheemie never cared much for that story, and when it slipped his mind, the upstairs of Casa Gingerbread . . ." Ted Brautigan chuckled. "Well, I suppose you could say it biodegraded.

"In any case, I believe that this place I'm in is actually a fistula in time, or . . ." Another pause. A sigh. Then: "Look, there are a billion universes comprising a billion realities. That's something I've come to realize since being hauled back from what the ki'-dam insists on calling 'my little vacation in Connecticut.' Smarmy son of a bitch!"

Real hate in Brautigan's voice, Roland thought, and that was good. Hate was good. It was useful.

"Those realities are like a hall of mirrors, only no two reflections are exactly the same. I may come back to that image eventually, but not yet. What I want you to understand for now—or simply accept—is that reality is *organic,* reality is *alive.* It's something like a muscle. What Sheemie does is poke a hole in that muscle with a mental hypo. He only has a needle like this because he's special—"

"Because he's a mork," Eddie murmured.

"Hush!" Susannah said.

"—using it," Brautigan went on.

(Roland considered rewinding in order to pick up the missing words and decided they didn't matter.)

"It's a place outside of time, outside of reality. I know you understand a little bit about the function of the Dark Tower; you understand its unifying purpose. Well, think of Gingerbread House as a balcony on the Tower: when we come here, we're outside the Tower but still attached *to* the Tower. It's a real place—real enough so I've come back from it with candy-stains on my hands and clothes—but it's a place only Sheemie Ruiz can access. And once we're there, it's whatever he wants it to be. One wonders, Roland, if you or your friends had any inkling of what Sheemie truly was and what he could do when you met him in Mejis."

At this, Roland reached out and pushed the STOP button on the tape recorder. "We knew he was . . . odd," he told the others. "We knew he was special. Sometimes Cuthbert would say, 'What *is* it about that boy? He makes my skin itch!' And then he showed up in Gilead, he and his mule, Cappi. Claimed to have followed us. And we *knew* that was impossible, but so much was happening by then that a saloon-boy from Mejis—not bright but cheerful and helpful—was the least of our worries."

"He teleported, didn't he?" Jake asked.

Roland, who had never even heard the word before today, nodded immediately. "At least part of the distance; he had to have. For one thing, how else could he have crossed the Xay River? There was only the one bridge, a thing made out of ropes, and once we were across, Alain cut it. We watched it fall into the water a thousand feet below."

"Maybe he went around," Jake said.

Roland nodded. "Maybe he did . . . but it would have taken him at least six hundred wheels out of his way."

Susannah whistled.

Eddie waited to see if Roland had more to say. When it was clear he didn't, Eddie leaned forward and pushed the PLAY button again. Ted's voice filled the cave once more.

"Sheemie's a teleport. Dinky himself is a precog . . . among other things. Unfortunately, a good many avenues into the future are blocked to him. If you're wondering if young sai Earnshaw knows how all this is going to turn out, the answer is no.

"In any case, there's this hypodermic hole in the living flesh of reality . . . this balcony on the flank of the Dark Tower . . . this Gingerbread House. A real place, as hard as that might be to believe. It's here that we'll store the weapons and camping gear we eventually mean to leave for you in one of the caves on the far side of Steek-Tete, and it's here that I'm making this tape. When I left my room with this old-fashioned but fearsomely efficient machine under my arm, it was 10:14 AM, BHST—Blue Heaven Standard Time. When I return, it will still be 10:14 AM. No matter how long I stay. That is only one of the terribly convenient things about Gingerbread House.

"You need to understand—perhaps Sheemie's old friend Roland already does—that we are three rebels in a society dedicated to the idea of going along to get along, even if it means the end of existence . . . and sooner rather than later. We have a number of extremely useful talents, and by pooling them we've managed to stay one step ahead. But if Prentiss or

Finli o' Tego—he's Prentiss's Security Chief—finds out what we're trying to do, Dinky would be worm-food by nightfall. Sheemie as well, quite likely. I'd probably be safe awhile longer, for reasons I'll get to, but if Pimli Prentiss found out we were trying to bring a true gunslinger into his affairs—one who may already have orchestrated the deaths of over five dozen Greencloaks not far from here—even my life might not be safe." A pause. "Worthless thing that it is."

There was a longer pause. The reel that had been empty was now half-full. "Listen, then," Brautigan said, "and I'll tell you the story of an unfortunate and unlucky man. It may be a longer story than you have time to listen to; if that be the case, I'm sure at least three of you will understand the use of the button labeled FF. As for me, I'm in a place where clocks are obsolete and broccoli is no doubt prohibited by law. I have all the time in the world."

Eddie was again struck by how weary the man sounded.

"I'd just suggest that you not fast-forward unless you really have to. As I've said, there may be something here that can help you, although I don't know what. I'm simply too close to it. And I'm tired of keeping my guard up, not just when I'm awake but when I'm sleeping, too. If I wasn't able to slip away to Gingerbread House every now and again and sleep with no defenses, Finli's can-toi boys would surely have bagged the three of us a long time ago. There's a sofa in the corner, also made out of those wonderful non-stick marshmallows. I can go there and lie down and have the nightmares I need to have in order to keep my sanity. Then I can go back to the Devar-Toi, where my job isn't just protecting myself but protecting Sheemie and Dink, too. Making sure that when we go about our covert business, it appears to the guards and their fucking telemetry that we were right where we belonged the whole time: in our suites, in The Study, maybe taking in a movie at the Gem or grabbing ice cream sodas at Henry Graham's Drug Store and Fountain afterward. It also means continuing to Break, and every day I can feel the Beam we're currently working on—Bear and Turtle—bending more and more.

"Get here quick, boys. That's my wish for you. Get here just as quick as ever you can. Because it isn't just a question of me slipping up, you know. Dinky's got a terrible temper and a habit of going off on foul-mouthed tirades if someone pushes his hot-buttons. He could say the wrong thing in a state like that. And Sheemie does his best, but if someone were to ask him the wrong question or catch him doing the wrong thing when I'm not around to fix it . . ."

Brautigan didn't finish that particular thought. As far as his listeners were concerned, he didn't need to.

THREE

When he begins again, it's to tell them he was born in Milford, Connecticut, in the year 1898. We have all heard similar introductory lines, enough to know that they signal— for better or worse— the onset of auto-biography. Yet as they listen to that voice, the gunslingers are visited by another familiarity; this is true even of Oy. At first they're not able to put their finger on it, but in time it comes to them. The story of Ted Brautigan, a Wandering Accountant instead of a Wandering Priest, is in many ways similar to that of Pere Donald Callahan. They could almost be twins. And the sixth listener— the one beyond the blanket-blocked cave entrance in the windy dark— hears with growing sympathy and understanding. Why not? Booze isn't a major player in Brautigan's story, as it was in the Pere's, but it's still a story of addiction and isolation, the story of an outsider.

FOUR

At the age of eighteen, Theodore Brautigan is accepted into Harvard, where his Uncle Tim went, and Uncle Tim— childless himself— is more than willing to pay for Ted's higher education. And so far as Timothy Atwood knows, what happens is perfectly straightforward: offer made, offer accepted, nephew shines in all the right areas, nephew graduates and prepares to enter uncle's furniture business after six months spent touring post–World War I Europe.

What Uncle Tim doesn't know is that before going to Harvard, Ted tries to enlist in what will soon be known as the American Expeditionary Force. "Son," the doctor tells him, "you've got one hell of a loud heart murmur, and your hearing is substandard. Now are you going to tell me that you came here not knowing those things would get you a red stamp? Because, pardon me if I'm out of line, here, you look too smart for that."

And then Ted Brautigan does something he's never done before, has sworn he never will do. He asks the Army doc to pick a number, not just between one and ten but between one and a thousand. To humor him (it's rainy in Hartford, and that means things are slow in the enlistment office), the doctor thinks of the number 748. Ted gives it back to him. Plus 419 . . . 89 . . . and 997. When Ted invites him to think of a famous person, living or dead, and when Ted tells him Andrew Johnson, not Jackson but Johnson, the doc is finally amazed. He calls over another doc, a friend, and Ted goes through the same rigmarole again . . . with one exception. He asks the second doctor to pick a number between one and a million, then tells the doctor he was thinking of eighty-seven thousand, four hundred and sixteen. The second doctor looks momentarily surprised— stunned, in fact— then covers with a big shitlicking smile. "Sorry, son," he says, "you were only off by a hundred and thirty thousand or so." Ted looks at him, not smiling, not responding to the shitlicking smile in any way at all of which he is aware, but he's eighteen, and still young enough to be flabbergasted by such utter and seemingly pointless mendacity. Meanwhile, Doc Number Two's shitlicking smile has begun to fade on its own. Doc Number Two turns to Doc Number One and says "Look at his eyes, Sam— look at what's happening to his eyes."

The first doctor tries to shine an ophthalmoscope in Ted's eyes and Ted brushes it impatiently aside. He has access to mirrors and has seen the way his pupils sometimes expand and contract, is aware when it's happening even when there's no mirror handy by a kind of shuttering, stuttering effect in his vision, and it doesn't interest him, especially not now. What interests him now is that Doc Number Two is fucking with him and he doesn't know why. "Write the number down this time," he invites. "Write it down so you can't cheat."

Doc Number Two blusters. Ted reiterates his challenge. Doc Sam produces a piece of paper and a pen and the second doctor takes it. He is actually about to write a number when he reconsiders and tosses the pen on Sam's desk and says: "This is some kind of cheap streetcorner trick, Sam. If you can't see that, you're blind." And stalks away.

Ted invites Dr. Sam to think of a relative, any relative, and a moment later tells the doctor he's thinking of his brother Guy, who died of appendicitis when Guy was fourteen; ever since, their mother has called Guy Sam's guardian angel. This time Dr. Sam looks as though he's been slapped. At last he's afraid. Whether it's the odd in-and-out movement of Ted's pupils, or the matter-of-fact demonstration of telepathy with no dramatic forehead-rubbing, no "I'm getting a picture . . . wait . . . ," Dr. Sam is finally afraid. He stamps **REJECTED** *on Ted's enlistment application with the big red stamp and tries to get rid of him — next case, who wants to go to France and sniff the mustard gas? — but Ted takes his arm in a grip which is gentle but not in the least tentative.*

"Listen to me," says Ted Stevens Brautigan. "I am a genuine telepath. I've suspected it since I was six or seven years old — old enough to know the word — and I've known it for sure since I was sixteen. I could be of great help in Army Intelligence, and my substandard hearing and heart murmur wouldn't matter in such a post. As for the thing with my eyes?" He reaches into his breast pocket, produces a pair of sunglasses, and slips them on. "Ta-da!"

He gives Dr. Sam a tentative smile. It does no good. There is a Sergeant-at-Arms standing at the door of the temporary recruitment office in East Hartford High's physical education department, and the medic summons him. "This fellow is 4-F and I'm tired of arguing with him. Perhaps you'd be good enough to escort him off the premises."

Now it is Ted's arm which is gripped, and none too gently.

"Wait a minute!" Ted says. "There's something else! Something even more valuable! I don't know if there's a word for it, but . . ."

Before he can continue, the Sergeant-at-Arms drags him out and hustles him rapidly down the hall, past several gawking boys and girls almost exactly his own age. There is a word, and he'll learn it years later, in Blue Heaven. The word is facilitator, *and as far as Paul "Pimli" Prentiss is concerned, it makes Ted Stevens Brautigan just about the most valuable hume in the universe.*

Not on that day in 1916, though. On that day in 1916, he is dragged briskly down the hallway and deposited on the granite step outside the main doors and told by a man with a foot-thick accent that "Y'all just want t'stay outta heah, boa." After some consideration, Ted decides the Sergeant-at-Arms isn't calling him a snake; boa *in this context is most likely Dixie for* boy.

For a little while Ted just stands where he has been left. He's thinking What does it take to convince you? *and* How blind can you be? *He can't believe what just happened to him.*

But he has *to believe it, because here he is, on the outside. And at the end of a six-mile walk around Hartford he thinks he understands something else as well. They* will *never* believe. *None of them. Not ever. They'll refuse to see that a fellow who could read the collective mind of the German High Command might be mildly useful. A fellow who could tell the* Allied *High Command where the next big German push was going to come. A fellow who could do a thing like that a few times— maybe even just* once *or* twice! *— might be able to end the war by Christmas. But he won't have the chance because they won't give it to him. And why? It has something to do with the second doctor changing his number when Ted landed on it, and then refusing to write another one down. Because somewhere down deep they* want *to fight, and a guy like him would spoil everything.*

It's something like that.

Fuck it, then. He'll go to Harvard on his uncle's nickel.

And does. Harvard's all Dinky told them, and more: Drama, Debate, Harvard Crimson, *Mathematical Odd Fellows and, of course, the capper, Phi Beta Crapper. He even saves Unc a few bucks by graduating early.*

He is in the south of France, the war long over, when a telegram reaches him: UNCLE DEAD **STOP** RETURN HOME SOONEST **STOP.**

The key word here seemed to be **STOP.**

God knows it was one of those watershed moments. He went home, yes, and he gave comfort where comfort was due, yes. But instead of stepping into the furniture business, Ted decides to **STOP** *his march toward financial success and* **START** *his march toward financial obscurity. In the course of the man's long story, Roland's ka-tet never once hears Ted Brautigan blame his deliberate anonymity on his outré* *talent, or on his moment of epiphany: this is one valuable talent that no one in the world wants.*

And God, how he comes to understand that! For one thing, his "wild talent" (as the pulp science-fiction magazines sometimes call it) is actually physically dangerous under the right circumstances. Or the wrong ones.

In 1935, in Ohio, it makes Ted Brautigan a murderer.

He has no doubt that some would feel the word is too harsh, but he will be the judge of that in this particular case, thank you oh so very much, and he thinks the word is apt. It's Akron and it's a blue summer dusk and kids are playing kick-the-can at one end of Stossy Avenue and stickball at the other and Brautigan stands on the corner in a summerweight suit, stands by the pole with the white stripe painted on it, the white stripe that means the bus stops here. Behind him is a deserted candystore with a blue NRA eagle in one window and a whitewashed message in the other that says THEIR KILLING THE LITTLE MAN. Ted is just standing there with his scuffed cordovan briefcase and a brown sack— a pork chop for his supper, he got it at Mr. Dale's Fancy Butcher Shop—when all at once somebody runs into him from behind and he's driven into the telephone pole with the white stripe on it. He connects nose-first. His nose breaks. It sprays blood. Then his mouth connects, and he feels his teeth cut into the soft lining of his lips, and all at once his mouth is filled with a salty taste like hot tomato juice. There's a thud in the small of his back and a ripping sound. His trousers are pulled halfway down over his ass by the force of the hit, hanging crooked and twisted, like the pants of a clown, and all at once a guy in a tee-shirt and gabardine slacks with a shiny seat is running off down Stossy Avenue toward the stickball game and that thing flapping in his right hand, flapping like a brown leather tongue, why, that thing is Ted Brautigan's wallet. He has just been mugged out of his wallet, by God!

The purple dusk of that summer night deepens suddenly to full dark, then lightens up again, then deepens once more. It's his eyes, doing the trick that so amazed the second doctor almost twenty years before, but Ted hardly notices. His attention is fixed on the fleeing man, the son of a bitch who just mugged him out of his wallet and spoiled his face in the process. He's never been so angry in his life, never, and although the thought he sends at the fleeing man is innocuous, almost gentle

(say buddy I would've given you a dollar if you'd asked maybe even two)

it has the deadly weight of a thrown spear. And it was a spear. It takes him some time to fully accept that, but when the time comes he realizes that he's a murderer and if there's a God, Ted Brautigan will someday have to stand at His throne and answer for what he's just done. The fleeing man looks like he stumbles over something, but there's nothing there, only HARRY LOVES BELINDA printed on the cracked sidewalk in fading chalk. The sentiment is surrounded with childish doodles—stars, a comet, a crescent moon—which he will later come to fear. Ted feels like he just took a spear in the middle of the back himself, but he, at least, is still standing. And he didn't mean it. There's that. He knows in his heart that he didn't mean it. He was just . . . surprised into anger.

He picks up his wallet and sees the stickball kids staring at him, their mouths open. He points his wallet at them like some kind of gun with a floppy barrel, and the boy holding the sawed-off broomhandle flinches. It's the flinch even more than the falling body that will haunt Ted's dreams for the next year or so, and then off and on for the rest of his life. Because he likes kids, would never scare one on purpose. And he knows what they are seeing: a man with his pants mostly pulled down so his boxer shorts show (for all he knows his dingus could be hanging out of the fly front, and wouldn't that just be the final magical touch), a wallet in his hand and a loony look on his bloody kisser.

"You didn't see anything!" he shouts at them. "You hear me, now! You hear me! You didn't see anything!"

Then he hitches up his pants. Then he goes back to his briefcase and picks it up, but not the pork chop in the brown paper sack, fuck the pork chop, he lost his appetite along with one of his incisors. Then he takes another look at the body on the sidewalk, and the frightened kids. Then he runs.

Which turns into a career.

FIVE

The end of the second tape pulled free of the hub and made a soft *fwip-fwip-fwip* sound as it turned.

"Jesus," Susannah said. "Jesus, that poor man."

"So long ago," Jake said, and shook his head as if to clear it. To him, the years between his when and Mr. Brautigan's seemed an unbridgeable chasm.

Eddie picked up the third box and displayed the tape inside, raising his eyebrows at Roland. The gunslinger twirled a finger in his old gesture, the one that said go on, go on.

Eddie threaded the tape through the heads. He'd never done this before, but you didn't have to be a rocket scientist, as the saying went. The tired voice began again, speaking from the Gingerbread House Dinky Earnshaw had made for Sheemie, a real place created from nothing more than imagination. A balcony on the side of the Dark Tower, Brautigan had called it.

He'd killed the man (by accident, they all would have agreed; they had come to live by the gun and knew the difference between *by accident* and *on purpose* without needing to discuss the matter) around seven in the evening. By nine that night, Brautigan was on a westbound train. Three days later he was scanning the Accountants Wanted ads in the Des Moines newspaper. He knew something about himself by then, knew how careful he would have to be. He could no longer allow himself the luxury of anger even when anger was justified. Ordinarily he was just your garden-variety telepath—could tell you what you had for lunch, could tell you which card was the queen of hearts because the streetcorner sharpie running the monte-con knew—but when angry he had access to this spear, this terrible spear . . .

"And just by the way, that's not true," said the voice from the tape recorder. "The part about being just a garden-variety telepath, I mean, and I understood that even when I was a wet-behind-the-ears kid trying to get into the Army. I just didn't know the word for what I was."

The word, it turned out, was *facilitator.* And he later became sure that certain folks—certain *talent scouts*—were watching him even then, sizing him up, knowing he was different even in the subset of telepaths but not *how* different. For one thing, telepaths who did not come from the Keystone Earth (it was their phrase) were rare. For another, Ted had come to realize by the mid-nineteen-thirties that what he had was actually *catching*: if he touched a person while in a state of high emotion, that person for a short time became a telepath. What he hadn't known then was that people who were *already* telepaths became stronger.

Exponentially stronger.

"But that's ahead of my story," he said.

He moved from town to town, a hobo who rode the rods in a passenger car and wearing a suit instead of in a boxcar wearing Oshkosh biballs, never staying in one place long enough to put down roots. And in retrospect, he supposed he knew that even then he was being watched. It was an intuitive thing, or like oddities one sometimes glimpsed from the corner of one's eye. He became aware of a certain *kind* of people, for instance. A few were women, most were men, and all had a taste for loud clothes, rare steak, and fast cars painted in colors as garish as their clothing. Their faces were oddly heavy and strangely inexpressive. It was a look he much later came to associate with dumbbells who'd gotten plastic surgery from quack doctors. During that same twenty-year period—but once again not consciously, only in the corner of his mind's eye—he became aware that no matter what city he was in, those childishly simple symbols had a way of turning up on fences and stoops and sidewalks. Stars and comets, ringed planets and crescent moons. Sometimes a red eye. There was often a hopscotch grid in the same area, but not always. Later on, he said, it all fit together in a crazy sort of way, but not back in the thirties and forties and early fifties, when he was drifting. No, back then he'd been a little bit like Docs One and Two, not wanting to see what was right in front of him, because it was . . . disturbing.

And then, right around the time Korea was winding down,

he saw The Ad. It promised **THE JOB OF A LIFETIME** and said that if you were **THE MAN WITH THE RIGHT QUALIFICA-TIONS**, there would be **ABSOLUTELY NO QUESTIONS ASKED**. A number of required skills were enumerated, accountancy being one of them. Brautigan was sure the ad ran in newspapers all over the country; he happened to read it in the Sacramento *Bee.*

"Holy crap!" Jake cried. "That's the same paper Pere Callahan was reading when he found out his friend George Magruder—"

"Hush," Roland said. "Listen."

They listened.

SIX

The tests are administered by humes (a term Ted Brautigan won't know for another few weeks— not until he steps out of the year 1955 and into the no-time of the Algul). The interviewer he eventually meets in San Francisco is also a hume. Ted will learn (among a great many other things) that the disguises the low men wear, most particularly the masks *they wear, are not good, not when you're up close and personal. Up close and personal you can see the truth: they are hume/taheen hybrids who take the matter of their* becoming *with a religious fervor. The easiest way to find yourself wrapped in a low-man bearhug with a set of murderous low-man teeth searching for your carotid artery is to aver that the only two things they are* becoming *is older and uglier. The red marks on their foreheads— the Eye of the King— usually disappear when they are America-side (or dry up, like temporarily dormant pimples), and the masks take on a weird organic quality, except for behind the ears, where the hairy, tooth-scabbed underflesh shows, and inside the nostrils, where one can see dozens of little moving cilia. But who is so impolite as to look up a fellow's snot-gutters?*

Whatever they think, up close and personal there's something definitely wrong with them even when they're America-side, and no one wants to scare the new fish before the net's properly in place. So it's humes (an abbreviation the can-toi won't even use; they find it demeaning, like "nigger" or "vamp") at the exams, humes in the interview rooms, nothing but humes until later, when they go through one of the working America-side doorways and come out in Thunderclap.

Ted is tested, along with a hundred or so others, in a gymnasium that reminds him of the one back in East Hartford. This one has been filled with rows and rows of study-hall desks (wrestling mats have been considerately laid down to keep the desks' old-fashioned round iron bases from scratching the varnished hardwood), but after the first round of testing—a ninety-minute diagnostic full of math, English, and vocabulary questions—half of them are empty. After the second round, it's three quarters. Round Two consists of some mighty weird questions, highly subjective *questions, and in several cases Ted gives an answer in which he does not believe, because he thinks—maybe* knows—*that the people giving the test want a different answer from the one he (and most people) would ordinarily give. For instance, there's this little honey:*

23. You come to a stop near an over-turned car on a little-traveled road. Trapped in the car is a Young Man crying for rescue. You ask, "Are you hurt, Young Man?" to which he responds, "I don't think so!" In the field nearby is a Satchel filled with Money. You:

a. Rescue the Young Man and give him back his Money
b. Rescue the Young Man but insist that the Money be taken to the local Police
c. Take the Money and go on your way, knowing that although the road may be little traveled, someone will be along eventually to free the Young Man
d. None of the above

Had this been a test for the Sacramento PD, Ted would have circled "b" in a heartbeat. He may be little more than a hobo on the road, but his mama didn't raise no fools, thank you oh so very much. That choice would be the correct one in most circumstances, too—the play-it-safe choice, the can't-go-wrong choice. And, as a fall-back position, the one that says "I don't have a frigging clue what this is about but at least I'm honest enough to say so," there's "d."

Ted circles "c," but not because that is necessarily what he'd do in that situation. On the whole he tends to think that he'd go for "a," presuming he could at least ask the "Young Man" a few questions about where the loot came from. And if outright torture wasn't involved (and he would know, wouldn't he, no matter what the "Young Man" might have to say on the subject), sure, here's your money, Vaya con Dios. *And why? Because Ted Brautigan happens to believe that the owner of the defunct candystore had a point: THEIR KILLING THE LITTLE MAN.*

But he circles "c," and five days later he finds himself in the anteroom of an out-of-business dance studio in San Francisco (his train-fare from Sacramento prepaid), along with three other men and a sullen-looking teenage girl (the girl's the former Tanya Leeds of Bryce, Colorado, as it turns out). Better than four hundred people showed up for the test in the gym, lured by the honeypot ad. Goats, for the most part. Here, however, are four sheep. One per cent. And even this, as Brautigan will discover in the full course of time, is an amazing catch.

Eventually he is shown into an office marked PRIVATE. *It is mostly filled with dusty ballet stuff. A broad-shouldered, hard-faced man in a brown suit sits in a folding chair, incongruously surrounded by filmy pink tutus. Ted thinks,* A real toad in an imaginary garden.

The man sits forward, arms on his elephantine thighs. "Mr. Brautigan," he says, "I may or may not be a toad, but I can offer you the job of a lifetime. I can also send you out of here with a handshake and a much-obliged. It depends on the answer to one question. A question about a question, in fact."

The man, whose name turns out to be Frank Armitage, hands Ted a sheet of paper. On it, blown up, is Question 23, the one about the Young Man and the Satchel of Money.

"You circled 'c,'" Frank Armitage says. "So now, with absolutely no hesitation whatever, *please tell me why."*

"Because 'c' was what you wanted," Ted replies with absolutely no hesitation whatever.

"And how do you know that?"

"Because I'm a telepath," Ted says. "And that's what you're really looking for." He tries to keep his poker face and thinks he succeeds pretty well, but inside he's filled with a great and singing relief. Because he's

found a job? No. Because they'll shortly make him an offer that would make the prizes on the new TV quiz shows look tame? No.
    Because someone finally wants what he can do.
    Because someone finally wants him.

SEVEN

The job offer turned out to be another honeypot, but Brautigan was honest enough in his taped memoir to say he might have gone along even if he'd known the truth.

"Because talent won't be quiet, doesn't know *how* to be quiet," he said. "Whether it's a talent for safe-cracking, thought-reading, or dividing ten-digit numbers in your head, it screams to be used. It never shuts up. It'll wake you in the middle of your tiredest night, screaming, 'Use me, use me, use me! I'm tired of just sitting here! Use me, fuckhead, use me!'"

Jake broke into a roar of pre-adolescent laughter. He covered his mouth but kept laughing through his hands. Oy looked up at him, those black eyes with the gold wedding rings floating in them, grinning fiendishly.

There in the room filled with the frilly pink tutus, his fedora hat cocked back on his crewcut head, Armitage asked if Ted had ever heard of "the South American Seabees." When Ted replied that he hadn't, Armitage told him that a consortium of wealthy South American businessmen, mostly Brazilian, had hired a bunch of American engineers, construction workers, and rough-necks in 1946. Over a hundred in all. These were the South American Seabees. The consortium hired them all for a four-year period, and at different pay-grades, but the pay was extremely generous—almost embarrassingly so—at all grades. A 'dozer operator might sign a contract for $20,000 a year, for instance, which was tall tickets in those days. But there was more: a bonus equal to one year's pay. A total of $100,000. If, that was, the fellow would agree to one unusual condition: you go, you work, and you don't come back until the four years are up or the work is done. You got two days off every week, just like in America, and you got a vacation every year, just like in America, but in the pampas. You couldn't go back to North America (or even Rio) until your four-year hitch was over. If you died in South America, you got planted there—no one was going to pay to have your body shipped back to Wilkes-Barre. But you got fifty grand up front, and a sixty-day grace period during which you could spend it, save it, invest it, or ride it like a pony. If you chose investment, that fifty grand might be seventy-five when you came waltzing out of the jungle with a bone-deep tan, a whole new set of muscles, and a lifetime of stories to tell. And, of course, once you were out you had what the limeys liked to call "the other half" to put on top of it.

This was like that, Armitage told Ted earnestly. Only the front half would be a cool quarter of a million and the back end half a million.

"Which sounded incredible," Ted said from the Wollen-sak. "Of course it did, by jiminy. I didn't find out until later how incredibly cheap they were buying us, even at those prices. Dinky is particularly eloquent on the subject of their stinginess . . . 'they' in this case being all the King's bureaucrats. He says the Crimson King is trying to bring about the end of all creation on the budget plan, and of course he's right, but I think even Dinky realizes—although he won't admit it, of course—that if you offer a man too much, he simply refuses to believe it. Or, depending on his imagination (many telepaths and precogs have almost no imagination at all), be *unable* to believe it. In our case the period of indenture was to be six years, with an option to renew, and Armitage needed my decision immediately. Few techniques are so successful, lady and gentlemen, as the one where you boggle your target's mind, freeze him with greed, then blitz him.

"I was duly blitzed, and agreed at once. Armitage told me that my quarter-mil would be in the Seaman's San Francisco Bank as of that afternoon, and I could draw on it as soon as I got down there. I asked him if I had to sign a contract. He reached out one of his hands—big as a ham, it was—and told me *that* was our contract. I asked him where I'd be going and what I'd be doing—all questions I should have asked first, I'm sure you'd agree, but I was so stunned it never crossed my mind.

"Besides, I was pretty sure I knew. I thought I'd be working for the government. Some kind of Cold War deal. The telepathic branch of the CIA or FBI, set up on an island in the Pacific. I remember thinking it would make one hell of a radio play.

"Armitage told me, 'You'll be traveling far, Ted, but it will also be right next door. And for the time being, that's all I can say. Except to keep your mouth shut about our arrangement during the eight weeks before you actually . . . mmm . . . ship out. Remember that loose lips sink ships. At the risk of inculcating you with paranoia, assume that you are being watched.'

"And of course I *was* watched. Later—*too* later, in a manner of speaking—I was able to replay my last two months in Frisco and realize that the can-toi were watching me the whole time.

"The low men."

EIGHT

"Armitage and two other humes met us outside the Mark Hopkins Hotel," said the voice from the tape recorder. "I remember the date with perfect clarity; it was Halloween of 1955. Five o'clock in the afternoon. Me, Jace McGovern, Dave Ittaway, Dick . . . I can't remember his last name, he died about six months later, Humma said it was pneumonia and the rest of the ki'cans backed him up—ki'can sort of means shit-people or shit-*folken,* if you're interested—but it was suicide and I knew it if no one else did. The rest . . . well, remember Doc Number Two? The rest were and are like him. 'Don't tell me what I don't want to know, sai, don't mess up my worldview.' Anyway, the last one was Tanya Leeds. Tough little thing . . ."

A pause and a click. Then Ted's voice resumed, sounding temporarily refreshed. The third tape had almost finished. *He must have really burned through the rest of the story,* Eddie thought, and found that the idea disappointed him. Whatever else he was, Ted was a hell of a good tale-spinner.

"Armitage and his colleagues showed up in a Ford station wagon, what we called a woody in those charming days. They drove us inland, to a town called Santa Mira. There was a paved main street. The rest of them were dirt. I remember there were a lot of oil-derricks, looking like praying mantises, sort of . . . although it was dark by then and they were really just shapes against the sky.

"I was expecting a train depot, or maybe a bus with CHAR-TERED in the destination window. Instead we pulled up to this empty freight depot with a sign reading SANTA MIRA SHIPPING hanging askew on the front and I got a thought, clear as day, from Dick whatever-his-name was. *They're going to kill us,* he was thinking. *They brought us out here to kill us and steal our stuff.*

"If you're not a telepath, you don't know how scary something like that can be. How the surety of it kind of . . . invades your head. I saw Dave Ittaway go pale, and although Tanya didn't make a sound—she was a tough little thing, as I told you—it was bright enough in the car to see there were tears standing in the corners of her eyes.

"I leaned over her, took Dick's hands in mine, and squeezed down on them when he tried to pull away. I thought at him, *They didn't give us a quarter of a mill each, most of it still stashed safe in the Seaman's Bank, so they could bring us out to the williwags and steal our watches.* And Jace thought at me, *I don't even have a watch. I pawned my Gruen two years ago in Albuquerque, and by the time I thought about buying another one— around midnight last night, this was— all the stores were closed and I was too drunk to climb down off the barstool I was on, anyway.*

"That relaxed us, and we all had a laugh. Armitage asked us what we were laughing about and that relaxed us even more, because we had something they didn't, could communicate in a way they couldn't. I told him it was nothing, then gave Dick's hands another little squeeze. It did the job. I . . . facilitated him, I suppose. It was my first time doing that. The first of many. That's part of the reason I'm so tired; all that facilitating wears a man out.

"Armitage and the others led us inside. The place was

deserted, but at the far end there was a door with two words chalked on it, along with those moons and stars. THUNDERCLAP STATION, it said. Well, there *was* no station: no tracks, no buses, no road other than the one we'd used to get there. There were windows on either side of the door and nothing on the other side of the building but a couple of smaller buildings—deserted sheds, one of them just a burnt-out shell—and a lot of scrub-land littered with trash.

"Dave Ittaway said, 'Why are we going out there?' and one of the others said, 'You'll see,' and we certainly did.

" 'Ladies first,' Armitage said, and he opened the door.

"It was dark on the other side, but not the same *kind* of dark. It was *darker* dark. If you've seen Thunderclap at night, you'll know. And it sounded different. Old buddy Dick there had some second thoughts and turned around. One of the men pulled a gun. And I'll never forget what Armitage said. Because he sounded . . . kindly. 'Too late to back out now,' he said. 'Now you can only go forward.'

"And I think right then I knew that business about the six-year plan, and re-upping if we wanted to, was what my friend Bobby Garfield and *his* friend Sully-John would have called just a shuck and jive. Not that we could read it in their thoughts. They were all wearing hats, you see. You never see a low man— or a low lady, for that matter—without a hat on. The men's looked like plain old fedoras, the sort most guys wore back then, but these were no ordinary lids. They were thinking-caps. Although *anti*-thinking-caps would be more accurate; they muf-fle the thoughts of the people wearing them. If you try to prog someone who's wearing one—*prog* is Dinky's word for thought-reading—you just get a hum with a lot of whispering under-neath. Very unpleasant, like the todash chimes. If you've heard them, you know. Discourages too much effort, and effort's the last thing most of the telepaths in the Algul are interested in. What the Breakers are mostly interested in, lady and gentlemen, is going along to get along. Which only shows up for what it is— monstrous—if you pull back and take the long view. One more thing most Breakers are not into. Quite often you hear a saying—a little poem—around campus, or see it chalked on the walls: 'Enjoy the cruise, turn on the fan, there's nothing to lose, so work on your tan.' It means a lot more than 'Take it easy.' The implications of that little piece of doggerel are extremely unpleasant. I wonder if you can see that."

Eddie thought *he* could, at least, and it occurred to him that his brother Henry would have made an absolutely wonderful Breaker. Always assuming he'd been allowed to take along his heroin and his Creedence Clearwater Revival albums, that was.

A longer pause from Ted, then a rueful sort of laugh.

"I believe it's time to make a long story a little shorter. We went through the door, leave it at that. If you've done it, you know it can be very unpleasant, if the door's not in tip-top working order. And the door between Santa Mira, California, and Thunderclap was in better shape than some I've been through since.

"For a moment there was only darkness on the other side, and the howl of what the taheen call desert-dogs. Then a cluster of lights went on and we saw these . . . these *things* with the heads of birds and weasels and one with the head of a bull, horns and all. Jace screamed, and so did I. Dave Ittaway turned and tried to run, but Armitage grabbed him. Even if he hadn't, where was there to go? Back through the door? It was closed, and for all I know, that's a one-way. The only one of us who never made a sound was Tanya, and when she looked at me, what I saw in her eyes and read in her thoughts was relief. Because we knew, you see. Not all the questions were answered, but the two that mattered were. Where were we? In another world. When were we coming back? Never in life. Our money would sit in the Seaman's of San Francisco until it turned into millions, and no one would ever spend it. We were in for the long haul.

"There was a bus there, with a robot driver named Phil. 'My name's Phil, I'm over the hill, but the best news is that I never spill,' he said. He smelled like lightning and there were all sorts of discordant clicking sounds coming from deep in his guts. Old Phil's dead now, dumped in the train and robot graveyard with God alone knows how many others, but they've got enough mechanized help to finish what they've started, I'm sure.

"Dick fainted when we came out on Thunderclap-side, but by the time we could see the lights of the compound, he'd come around again. Tanya had his head in her lap, and I remember how gratefully he was looking up at her. It's funny what you remember, isn't it? They checked us in at the gate. Assigned us our dorms, assigned us our suites, saw that we were fed . . . and a damned fine meal it was. The first of many.

"The next day, we went to work. And, barring my little 'vacation in Connecticut,' we've been working ever since."

Another pause. Then:

"God help us, we've been working ever since. And, God forgive us, most of us have been happy. Because the only thing talent wants is to be used."

NINE

He tells them of his first few shifts in The Study, and his realization— not gradual but almost immediate— that they are not here to search out spies or read the thoughts of Russian scientists, "or any of that space-shot nonsense," as Dinky would say (not that Dinky was there at first, although Sheemie was). No, what they are doing is breaking *something. He can feel it, not just in the sky above Algul Siento but every-where around them, even under their feet.*

Yet he is content enough. The food is good, and although his sexual appetites have subsided quite a bit over the years, he's not a bit averse to the odd bonk, just reminding himself every time that sim sex is really nothing but accessorized masturbation. But then, he's had the odd bonk with the odd whore over the years, as many men living on the road have, and he could testify that that sort of sex is also not much different than masturbation; you're putting it to her just as hard as you can, the sweat pouring off you, and she's going "Baby-baby-baby," and all the time wondering if she ought to gas the car and trying to remember which day is double stamps at the Red & White. As with most things in life, you have to use your imagination, and Ted can do that, he's good at the old visualization thing, thank you oh so very much. He likes the roof over his head, he likes the company— the guards are guards, yeah, but he believes them when they say it's as much their job to keep bad stuff from getting in as it is to make sure the Breakers don't get out. He likes most of the inmates, too, and realizes after a year or two that the inmates need him in some strange way. He's able to comfort them when they get the mean reds; he's able to assuage their crampy waves of homesickness with an hour or so of murmured conversation. And surely this is a good thing. Maybe it's all a good thing— certainly it feels like a good thing. To be homesick is human, but to Break is divine. He tries to explain to Roland and his tet, but the best he can do, the closest he can come, is to say it's like finally being able to scratch that out-of-reach place on your back that always drives you crazy with its mild but persistent itch. He likes to go to The Study, and so do all the others. He likes the feeling of sitting there, of smelling the good wood and good leather, of searching . . . searching . . . and then, suddenly, aahhh. *There you are. You're hooked in, swinging like a monkey on a limb. You're* breaking, *baby, and to break is divine.*

Dinky once said that The Study was the only place in the world where he really felt in touch with himself, and that was why he wanted to see it shut down. Burned *down, if possible. "Because I know the kind of shit I get up to when I'm in touch with myself," he told Ted. "When I, you know, really get in the groove." And Ted knew exactly what he was talking about. Because The Study was always too good to be true. You sat down, maybe picked up a magazine, looked at pictures of models and margarine, movie stars and motor cars, and you felt your mind* rise. *The Beam was all around, it was like being in some vast corridor full of force, but your mind always rose to the roof and when it got there it found that big old sliding groove.*

Maybe once, just after the Prim *withdrew and Gan's voice still echoed in the rooms of the macroverse, the Beams were smooth and polished, but those days are gone. Now the Way of the Bear and the Turtle is lumpy and eroded, full of coves and cols and bays and cracks, plenty of places to get your fingers in and take hold, and sometimes you* drag *at it and sometimes you can feel yourself worming your way* into *it like a drop of acid that can think. All these sensations are intensely pleasurable. Sexy.*

And for Ted there's something else, as well, although he doesn't know he's the only one who's got it until Trampas tells him. Trampas never means to tell him anything, but he's got this lousy case of eczema, you see, and it changes everything. Hard to believe a flaky scalp might be responsible for saving the Dark Tower, but the idea's not entirely farfetched.

Not entirely farfetched at all.

TEN

"There are about a hundred and eighty full-time personnel at work in the Algul," Ted said. "I'm not the guy to tell anyone how to do his job, but that's something you may want to write down, or at least remember. Roughly speaking, it's sixty per eight-hour shift and split twenty-twenty-twenty. Taheen have the sharpest eyes and generally man the watchtowers. Humes patrol the outer run of fence. With guns, mind you—hard calibers. Top-side there's Prentiss, the Master, and Finli o' Tego, the Security Chief—hume and taheen, respectively—but most of the floaters are can-toi . . . the low men, you understand.

"Most low men don't get along with the Breakers; a little stiff camaraderie is the best they can do. Dinky told me once that they're jealous of us because we're what he calls 'finished humes.' Like the hume guards, the can-toi wear thinking-caps when they're on duty so we can't prog them. The fact is most Breakers haven't tried to prog anyone or anything but the Beam in years, and maybe can't, anymore; the mind is also a muscle, and like any other, it atrophies if you don't use it."

A pause. A click on the tape. Then:

"I'm not going to be able to finish. I'm disappointed but not entirely surprised. This will have to be my last story, folks. I'm sorry."

A low sound. A sipping sound, Susannah was quite sure; Ted having another drink of water.

"Have I told you that the taheen don't need the thinking-caps? They speak perfectly good English, and I've sensed from time to time that some have limited progging abilities of their own, can send and receive—at least a little—but if you dip into them, you get these mind-numbing blasts of what sounds like mental static—white noise. I assumed it was some sort of protective device; Dinky believes it's the way they actually *think*. Either way, it makes it easier for them. They don't have to remember to put on hats in the morning when they go out!

"Trampas was one of the can-toi rovers. You might see him one day strolling along Main Street in Pleasantville, or sitting on a bench in the middle of the Mall, usually with some self-help book like *Seven Steps to Positive Thinking*. Then, the next day, there he is leaning against the side of Heartbreak House, taking in the sun. Same with the other can-toi floaters. If there's a pattern, I've never been able to anticipate it, or Dinky either. We don't think there is one.

"What's always made Trampas different is a complete lack of that sense of jealousy. He's actually friendly—or was; in some ways he hardly seemed to be a low man at all. Not many of his can-toi colleagues seem to like him a whole hell of a lot. Which is ironic, you know, because if there really *is* such a thing as *becoming*, then Trampas is one of the few who actually seem to be getting somewhere with it. Simple laughter, for instance. When most low men laugh, it sounds like a basket of rocks rolling down a tin coal-chute: makes you fair shiver, as Tanya says. When Trampas laughs, he sounds a little high-pitched but otherwise normal. Because he *is* laughing, I think. Genuinely laughing. The others are just forcing it.

"Anyway, I struck up a conversation with him one day. On Main Street, this was, outside the Gem. *Star Wars* was back for its umpty-umpth revival. If there's any movie the Breakers never get enough of, it's *Star Wars*.

"I asked him if he knew where his name came from. He said yes, of course, from his clan-fam. Each can-toi is given a hume name by his clan-fam at some point in his development; it's a kind of maturity-marker. Dinky says they get that name the first time they successfully whack off, but that's just Dinky being Dinky. The fact is we don't know and it doesn't matter, but some of the names are pretty hilarious. There's one fellow who looks like Rondo Hatton, a film actor from the thirties who suffered from acromegaly and got work playing monsters and psychopaths, but his name is Thomas Carlyle. There's another one named Beowulf and a fellow named Van Gogh Baez."

Susannah, a Bleecker Street folkie from way back, put her face in her hands to stifle a gust of giggles.

"Anyway, I told him that Trampas was a character from a famous Western novel called *The Virginian*. Only second banana to the actual hero, true, but Trampas has got the one line from the book everyone remembers: '*Smile* when you say that!' It tickled our Trampas, and I ended up telling him the whole plot of the book over cups of drug-store coffee.

"We became friends. I'd tell him what was going on in our little community of Breakers, and he'd tell me all sorts of interesting but innocent things about what was going on over on *his* side of the fence. He also complained about his eczema, which made his head itch terribly. He kept lifting his hat—this little beanie-type of thing, almost like a *yarmulke*, only made of denim—to scratch underneath. He claimed that was the worst place of all, even worse than down there on your makie-man. And little by little, I realized that every time he lifted his beanie to scratch, I could read his thoughts. Not just the ones on top but *all* of them. If I was fast—and I learned to be—I could pick and choose, exactly the way you'd pick and choose articles in an encyclopedia by turning the pages. Only it wasn't really like that; it was more like someone turning a radio on and off during a news broadcast."

"Holy shit," Eddie said, and took another graham cracker. He wished mightily for milk to dip them in; graham crackers without milk were almost like Oreos without the white stuff in the middle.

"Imagine turning a radio or a TV on full-blast," Ted said in his rusty, failing voice, "and then turning it off again . . . justasquick." He purposely ran this together, and they all smiled—even Roland. "That'll give you the idea. Now I'll tell you what I learned. I suspect you know it already, but I just can't take the risk that you don't. It's too important.

"There is a Tower, lady and gentlemen, as you *must* know. At one time six beams crisscrossed there, both taking power from it—it's some kind of unimaginable power-source—and lending support, the way guy-wires support a radio tower. Four of these Beams are now gone, the fourth very recently. The only two remaining are the Beam of the Bear, Way of the Turtle—Shardik's Beam—and the Beam of the Elephant, Way of the Wolf—some call that one Gan's Beam.

"I wonder if you can imagine my horror at discovering what I'd actually been doing in The Study. When I'd been scratching that innocent itch. Although I knew all along that it was something important, *knew* it.

"And there was something worse, something I *hadn't* suspected, something that applied only to me. I'd known that I was different in some ways; for one thing, I seemed to be the only Breaker with an ounce of compassion in my makeup. When they've got the mean reds, I am, as I told you, the one they come to. Pimli Prentiss, the Master, married Tanya and Joey Rastosovich—insisted on it, wouldn't hear a word against the idea, kept saying that it was his privilege and his responsibility, he was just like the captain on an old cruise-ship—and of course they let him do it. But afterward, they came to my rooms and Tanya said, '*You* marry us, Ted. Then we'll really be married.'

"And sometimes I ask myself, 'Did you think that was all it was? Before you started visiting with Trampas, and listening every time he lifted up his cap to scratch, did you truly think that having a little pity and a little love in your soul were the only things that set you apart from the others? Or were you fooling yourself about that, too?'

"I don't know for sure, but maybe I can find myself innocent on that particular charge. I really did not understand that my talent goes far beyond progging and Breaking. I'm like a microphone for a singer or a steroid for a muscle. I . . . *hype* them. Say there's a unit of force—call it *darks*, all right? In The Study, twenty or thirty people might be able to put out fifty darks an hour without me. *With* me? Maybe it jumps to five *hundred* darks an hour. And it jumps all at once.

"Listening to Trampas's head, I came to see that they considered me the catch of the century, maybe of all time, the one truly indispensable Breaker. I'd already helped them to snap one Beam and I was cutting *centuries* off their work on Shardik's Beam. And when Shardik's Beam snaps, lady and gentlemen, Gan's can only last a little while. And when Gan's Beam also snaps, the Dark Tower will fall, creation will end, and the very Eye of Existence will turn blind.

"How I ever kept Trampas from seeing my distress I don't know. And I've reason to believe that I didn't keep as complete a poker face as I thought at the time.

"I knew I had to get out. And that was when Sheemie came to me the first time. I *think* he'd been reading me all along, but even now I don't know for sure, and neither does Dinky. All I know is that one night he came to my room and thought to me, 'I'll make a hole for you, sai, if you want, and you can go boogie-bye-bye.' I asked him what he meant, and he just looked at me. It's funny how much a single look can say, isn't it? *Don't insult my intelligence. Don't waste my time. Don't waste your own.* I didn't read those thoughts in his mind, not at all. I saw them on his face."

Roland grunted agreement. His brilliant eyes were fixed on the turning reels of the tape recorder.

"I *did* ask him where the hole would come out. He said he didn't know—I'd be taking luck of the draw. All the same, I didn't think it over for long. I was afraid that if I did, I'd find reasons to stay. I said, 'Go ahead, Sheemie—send me boogie-bye-bye.'

"He closed his eyes and concentrated, and all at once the corner of my room was gone. I could see cars going by. They were distorted, but they were actual American cars. I didn't argue or question any more, I just went for it. I wasn't completely sure I could go through into that other world, but I'd reached a point where I hardly even cared. I thought dying might be the best thing I could do. It would slow them down, at least.

"And just before I took the plunge, Sheemie thought to me, 'Look for my friend Will Dearborn. His real name is Roland.

His friends are dead, but I know he's not, because I can hear him. He's a gunslinger, and he has new friends. Bring them here and they'll make the bad folks stop hurting the Beam, the way he made Jonas and his friends stop when they were going to kill me.' For Sheemie, this was a sermon.

"I closed my eyes and went through. There was a brief sensation of being turned on my head, but that was all. No chimes, no nausea. Really quite pleasant, at least compared to the Santa Mira doorway. I came out on my hands and knees beside a busy highway. There was a piece of newspaper blowing around in the weeds. I picked it up and saw I'd landed in April of 1960, almost five years after Armitage and his friends herded us through the door in Santa Mira, on the other side of the country. I was looking at a piece of the Hartford *Courant,* you see. And the road turned out to be the Merritt Parkway."

"Sheemie can make magic doors!" Roland cried. He had been cleaning his revolver as he listened, but now he put it aside. "That's what teleporting is! *That's what it means!*"

"Hush, Roland," Susannah said. "This must be his Connecticut adventure. I want to hear this part."

ELEVEN

But none of them hear about Ted's Connecticut adventure. He simply calls it "a story for another day" and tells his listeners that he was caught in Bridgeport while trying to accumulate enough cash to disappear permanently. The low men bundled him into a car, drove him to New York, and took him to a ribjoint called the Dixie Pig. From there to Fedic, and from Fedic to Thunderclap Station; from the station right back to the Devar-Toi, oh Ted, so good to see you, welcome back.

The fourth tape is now three-quarters done, and Ted's voice is little more than a croak. Nevertheless, he gamely pushes on.

"I hadn't been gone long, but over here time had taken one of its erratic slips forward. Humma o' Tego was out, possibly because of me, and Prentiss of New Jersey, the ki'-dam, was in. He and Finli interrogated me in the Master's suite a good many times. There was no physical torture—I guess they still reckoned me too important to chance *spoiling me—but there was a lot of discomfort and plenty of mind-games. They also made it clear that if I tried to run again, my Connecticut friends would be put to death. I said, 'Don't you boys get it? If I keep doing my job, they're going out, anyway.* Everybody's *going out, with the possible exception of the one you call the Crimson King.'*

"*Prentiss steepled his fingers in the annoying way he has and said, 'That may be or may not be true, sai, but if it is,* we *won't suffer when we "go out," as you put it. Little Bobby and little Carol, on the other hand . . . not to mention Carol's mother and Bobby's friend, Sully-John . . .' He didn't have to finish. I still wonder if they knew how terribly frightened they'd made me with that threat against my young friends. And how terribly angry.*

"*All their questions came down to two things they really wanted to know: Why had I run, and who helped me do it. I could have fallen back on the old name–rank–serial number routine, but decided to chance being a bit more expansive. I'd wanted to run, I said, because I'd gotten a glimmering from some of the can-toi guards about what we were really doing, and I didn't like the idea. As for how I'd gotten out, I told them I didn't know. I went to sleep one night, I said, and just woke up beside the Merritt Parkway. They went from scoffing at this story to semi-believing it, mostly because I never varied it a single jot or tittle, no matter how many times they asked. And of course they already knew how powerful I was, and in ways that were different from the others.*

"'*Do you think you're a teleport in some subconscious way, sai?*' *Finli asked me.*

"'*How could I say?*' *I asked in turn—always answer a question with a question is a good rule to follow during interrogation, I think, as long as it's a relatively soft interrogation, as this one was. 'I've never sensed any such ability, but of course we don't always know what's lurking in our subconscious, do we?'*

"'*You better hope it wasn't you,' Prentiss said. 'We can live with almost any wild talent around here except that one. That one, Mr. Brautigan, would spell the end even for such a valued employee as yourself.' I wasn't sure I believed that, but later Trampas gave me reason to think Prentiss might have been telling the truth. Anyway, that was my story and I never went beyond it.*

"Prentiss's houseboy, a fellow named Tassa—a hume, if it matters—would bring in cookies and cans of Nozz-A-La—which I like because it tastes a bit like root beer—and Prentiss would offer me all I wanted . . . after, that was, I told them where I'd gotten my information and how I'd escaped Algul Siento. Then the whole round of questions would start again, only this time with Prentiss and the Wease munching cookies and drinking Nozzie. But at some point they'd always give in and allow me a drink and a bite to eat. As interrogators, I'm afraid there just wasn't enough Nazi in them to make me give up my secrets. They tried to prog me, of course, but . . . have you heard that old saying about never bullshitting a bullshitter?"

Eddie and Susannah both nod. So does Jake, who has heard his father say that during numerous conversations concerning Programming at the Network.

"I bet you have," Ted resumes. "Well, it's also fair to say that you can't prog a progger, at least not one who's gone beyond a certain level of understanding. And I'd better get to the point before my voice gives out entirely.

"One day about three weeks after the low men hauled me back, Trampas approached me on Main Street in Pleasantville. By then I'd met Dinky, had identified him as a kindred spirit, and was, with his help, getting to know Sheemie better. A lot was going on in addition to my daily interrogations in Warden's House. I'd hardly even thought about Trampas since returning, but he'd thought of little else than me. As I quickly found out.

"'I know the answers to the questions they keep asking you,' he said. 'What I don't know is why you haven't given me up.'

"I said the idea had never crossed my mind—that tattle-taleing wasn't the way I'd been raised to do things. And besides, it wasn't as if they were putting an electrified cattle-prod up my rectum or pulling my fingernails . . . although they might have resorted to such techniques, had it been anyone other than me. The worst they'd done was to make me look at the plate of cookies on Prentiss's desk for an hour and a half before relenting and letting me have one.

"'I was angry at you at first,' Trampas said, 'but then I realized—reluctantly—that I might have done the same thing in your place. The *first week you were back I didn't sleep much, I can tell you. I'd lie on my bed there in Damli, expecting them to come for me at any minute. You know what they'd do if they found out it was me, don't you?'*

"I told him I did not. He said that he'd be flogged by Gaskie, Finli's Second, and then sent raw-backed into the wastes, either to die in the Discordia or to find service in the castle of the Red King. But such a trip would not be easy. Southeast of Fedic one may also contract such things as the Eating Sickness (probably cancer, but a kind that's very fast, very painful, and very nasty) or what they just call the Crazy. The Children of Roderick commonly suffer from both these problems, and others, as well. The minor skin diseases of Thunderclap— the eczema, pimples, and rashes— are apparently only the beginning of one's problems in End-World. But for an exile, service in the Court of the Crimson King would be the only hope. Certainly a can-toi such as Trampas couldn't go to the Callas. They're closer, granted, and there's genuine sunshine there, but you can imagine what would happen to low men or the taheen in the Arc of the Callas."

Roland's tet can imagine that very well.

"'Don't make too much of it,' I said. 'As that new fellow Dinky might say, I don't put my business on the street. It's really as simple as that. There's no chivalry involved.'

"He said he was grateful nevertheless, then looked around and said, very low: 'I'd pay you back for your kindness, Ted, by telling you to co-operate with them, to the extent that you can. I don't mean you should get me in trouble, but I don't want you to get in more trouble yourself, either. They may not need you quite as badly as you may think.'

"And I'd have you hear me well now, lady and gentlemen, for this may be very important; I simply don't know. All I know for certain is that what Trampas told me next gave me a terrible deep chill. He said that of all the other-side worlds, there's one that's unique. They call it the Real World. All Trampas seems to know about it is that it's real in the same way Mid-World was, before the Beams began to weaken and Mid-World moved on. In America-side of this special 'Real' World, he says, time sometimes jerks but always runs one way: ahead. And in that world lives a man who also serves as a kind of facilitator; he may even be a mortal guardian of Gan's Beam."

TWELVE

Roland looked at Eddie, and as their eyes met, both mouthed the same word: *King.*

THIRTEEN

"Trampas told me that the Crimson King has tried to kill this man, but ka has ever protected his life. 'They say his song has cast the circle,' Trampas told me, 'although no one seems to know exactly what that means.' Now, however, ka— not the Red King but plain old ka— has decreed that this man, this guardian or whatever he is, should die. He's stopped, you see. Whatever song it was he was supposed to sing, he's stopped, and that has finally made him vulnerable. But not to the Crimson King. Trampas kept telling me that. No, it's ka he's vulnerable to. 'He no longer sings,' Trampas said. 'His song, the one that matters, has ended. He has forgotten the rose.'"

FOURTEEN

In the outer silence, Mordred heard this and then withdrew to ponder it.

FIFTEEN

"Trampas told me all this only so I'd understand I was no longer completely indispensable. Of course they want to keep me; presumably there would be honor in bringing down Shardik's Beam before this man's death could cause Gan's Beam to break."

A pause.

"Do they see the lethal insanity of a race to the brink of oblivion, and then over the edge? Apparently not. If they did, surely they wouldn't be racing to begin with. Or is it a simple failure of imagination? One doesn't like to think such a rudimentary failing could bring about the end, yet . . ."

SIXTEEN

Roland, exasperated, twirled his fingers almost as if the old man to whose voice they were listening could see them. He wanted to hear, very well and every word, what the can-toi guard knew about Stephen King, and instead Brautigan had gotten off onto some rambling, discursive sidetrack. It was understandable—the man was clearly exhausted—but there was something here more important than everything else. Eddie knew it, too. Roland could read it on the young man's strained face. Together they watched the remaining brown tape—now no more than an eighth of an inch deep—melt away.

SEVENTEEN

"... yet we're only poor benighted humies, and I suppose we can't know about these things, not with any degree of certainty ..."

He fetches a long, tired sigh. The tape turns, melting off the final reel and running silently and uselessly between the heads. Then, at last:

"I asked this magic man's name and Trampas said, 'I know it not, Ted, but I do know there's no magic in him anymore, for he's ceased whatever it was that ka meant him to do. If we leave him be, the Ka of Nineteen, which is that of his world, and the Ka of Ninety-nine, which is that of our world, will combine to— "

But there is no more. That is where the tape runs out.

EIGHTEEN

The take-up reel turned and the shiny brown tape-end flapped, making that low *fwip-fwip-fwip* sound until Eddie leaned forward and pressed STOP. He muttered "Fuck!" under his breath.

"Just when it was getting interesting," Jake said. "And those numbers again. Nineteen . . . and ninety-nine." He paused, then said them together. "Nineteen-ninety-nine." Then a third time. "1999. The Keystone Year in the Keystone World. Where Mia went to have her baby. Where Black Thirteen is now."

"Keystone World, Keystone Year," Susannah said. She took the last tape off the spindle, held it up to one of the lamps for a moment, then put it back in its box. "Where time always goes in one direction. Like it's s'posed to."

"Gan *created* time," Roland said. "This is what the old legends say. Gan rose from the void—some tales say from the sea, but both surely mean the *Prim*—and made the world. Then he tipped it with his finger and set it rolling and that was time."

Something was gathering in the cave. Some revelation. They all felt it, a thing as close to bursting as Mia's belly had been at the end. Nineteen. Ninety-nine. They had been haunted by these numbers. They had turned up everywhere. They saw them in the sky, saw them written on board fences, heard them in their dreams.

Oy looked up, ears cocked, eyes bright.

Susannah said, "When Mia left the room we were in at the Plaza-Park to go to the Dixie Pig—room *1919,* it was—I fell into a kind of trance. I had dreams . . . jailhouse-dreams . . . newscasters announcing that this one, that one, and t'other one had died—"

"You told us," Eddie said.

She shook her head violently. "Not *all* of it, I didn't. Because some of it didn't seem to make any sense. Hearing Dave Garroway say that President Kennedy's little *boy* was dead, for instance—little John-John, the one who saluted his Daddy's coffin when the catafalque went by. I didn't tell you because that part was nuts. Jake, Eddie, had little John-John Kennedy died in your whens? Either of your whens?"

They shook their heads. Jake was not even sure of whom Susannah was speaking.

"But he *did.* In the Keystone World, and in a when beyond any of ours. I bet it was in the when of '99. So dies the son of the last gunslinger, O Discordia. What I think now is that I was kind of hearing the obituary page from *The Time Traveler's Weekly.* It was all different times mixed together. John-John Kennedy, then Stephen King. I'd never heard of him, but David Brinkley said he wrote *'Salem's Lot.* That's the book Father Callahan was in, right?"

Roland and Eddie nodded.

"Father Callahan told us his story."

"Yeah," Jake said. "But what—"

She overrode him. Her eyes were hazy, distant. Eyes just a look away from understanding. "And then comes Brautigan to the Ka-Tet of Nineteen, and tells *his* tale. And look! Look at the tape counter!"

They leaned over. In the windows were

1999.

"I think King might have written Ted's story, too," she said. "Anybody want to take a guess what year *that* story showed up, or *will* show up, in the Keystone World?"

"1999," Jake said, low. "But not the part we heard. The part we *didn't* hear. Ted's Connecticut Adventure."

"And you met him," Susannah said, looking at her dinh and her husband. "You met Stephen King."

They nodded again.

"He made the Pere, he made Brautigan, he made *us*," she said, as if to herself, then shook her head. "No. 'All things serve the Beam.' He . . . he *facilitated* us."

"Yeah." Eddie was nodding. "Yeah, okay. That feels just about right."

"In my dream I was in a cell," she said. "I was wearing the clothes I had on when I got arrested. And David Brinkley said Stephen King was dead, woe, Discordia—something like that. Brinkley said he was . . ." She paused, frowning. She would have demanded that Roland hypnotize the complete recollection out of her if it had been necessary, but it turned out not to be. "Brinkley said King was killed by a minivan while walking near his home in Lovell, Maine."

Eddie jerked. Roland sat forward, his eyes burning. "Do you say so?"

Susannah nodded firmly.

"He bought the house on Turtleback Lane!" the gunslinger

roared. He reached out and took hold of Eddie's shirt. Eddie seemed not to even notice. "Of *course* he did! Ka speaks and the wind blows! He moved a little further along the Path of the Beam and bought the house where it's thin! Where we saw the walk-ins! Where we talked to John Cullum and then came back through! Do you doubt it? *Do you doubt it so much as a single god-dam bit?*"

Eddie shook his head. Of course he didn't doubt it. It had a ring, like the one you got when you were at the carnival and hit the pedal just right with the mallet, hit it with all your force, and the lead slug flew straight to the top of the post and rang the bell up there. You got a Kewpie doll when you rang the bell, and was that because Stephen King *thought* it was a Kewpie doll? Because King came from the world where Gan started time rolling with His holy finger? Because if *King* says Kewpie, we *all* say Kewpie, and we all say thankya? If he'd somehow gotten the idea that the prize for ringing the Test Your Strength bell at the carnival was a *Cloo*pie doll, would *they* say Cloopie? Eddie thought the answer was yes. He thought the answer was yes just as surely as Co-Op City was in Brooklyn.

"David Brinkley said King was fifty-two. You boys met him, so do the math. Could he have been fifty-two in the year of '99?"

"You bet your purity," Eddie said. He tossed Roland a dark, dismayed glance. "And since nineteen's the part we keep running into—Ted Stevens Brautigan, go on, count the letters!—I bet it has to do with more than just the year. Nineteen—"

"It's a date," Jake said flatly. "Sure it is. Keystone Date in Keystone Year in Keystone World. The nineteenth of something, in the year of 1999. Most likely a summer month, because he was out walking."

"It's summer over there right now," Susannah said. "It's June. The 6-month. Turn 6 on its head and you get 9."

"Yeah, and spell dog backward, you get god," Eddie said, but he sounded uneasy.

"I think she's right," Jake said. "I think it's June 19th. That's when King gets turned into roadkill and even the *chance* that he might go back to work on the *Dark Tower* story—*our* story—is kaput. Gan's Beam is lost in the overload. Shardik's Beam is left, but it's already eroded." He looked at Roland, his face pale, his lips almost blue. "It'll snap like a toothpick."

"Maybe it's happened already," Susannah said.

"No," Roland said.

"How can you be sure?" she asked.

He gave her a wintry, humorless smile. "Because," he said, "we'd no longer be here."

NINETEEN

"How can we stop it from happening?" Eddie asked. "That guy Trampas told Ted it was ka."

"Maybe he got it wrong," Jake said, but his voice was thin. Trailing. "It was only a rumor, so maybe he got it wrong. And hey, maybe King's got until July. Or August. Or what about September? It could be September, doesn't that seem likely? September's the 9-month, after all . . ."

They looked at Roland, who was now sitting with his leg stretched out before him. "Here's where it hurts," he said, as if speaking to himself. He touched his right hip . . . then his ribs . . . last the side of his head. "I've been having headaches. Worse and worse. Saw no reason to tell you." He drew his diminished right hand down his right side. "This is where he'll be hit. Hip smashed. Ribs busted. Head crushed. Thrown dead into the ditch. Ka . . . and the end of ka." His eyes cleared and he turned urgently to Susannah. "What date was it when you were in New York? Refresh me."

"June first of 1999."

Roland nodded and looked to Jake. "And you? The same, yes?"

"Yes."

"Then to Fedic . . . a rest . . . and on to Thunderclap." He paused, thinking, then spoke four words with measured emphasis. "There is still time."

"But time moves faster over there—"

"And if it takes one of those hitches—"

"Ka—"

Their words overlapped. Then they fell quiet again, looking at him again.

"We can change ka," Roland said. "It's been done before. There's always a price to pay—ka-shume, mayhap—but it can be done."

"How do we get there?" Eddie asked.

"There's only one way," Roland said. "Sheemie must send us."

Silence in the cave, except for a distant roll of the thunder that gave this dark land its name.

"We have two jobs," Eddie said. "The writer and the Breakers. Which comes first?"

"The writer," Jake said. "While there's still time to save him."

But Roland was shaking his head.

"Why not?" Eddie cried. "Ah, man, why *not?* You *know* how slippery time is over there! And it's one-way! If we miss the window, we'll never get another chance!"

"But we have to make Shardik's Beam safe, too," Roland said.

"Are you saying Ted and this guy Dinky wouldn't let Sheemie help us unless we help them first?"

"No. Sheemie would do it for me, I'm sure. But suppose something happened to him while we were in the Keystone World? We'd be stranded in 1999."

"There's the door on Turtleback Lane—" Eddie began.

"Even if it's still there in 1999, Eddie, Ted told us that Shardik's Beam has already started to bend." Roland shook his head. "My heart says yonder prison is the place to start. If any of you can say different, I will listen, and gladly."

They were quiet. Outside the cave, the wind blew.

"We need to ask Ted before we make any final decision," Susannah said at last.

"No," Jake said.

"No!" Oy agreed. Zero surprise there; if Ake said it, you could take it to the bumbler bank, as far as Oy was concerned.

"Ask *Sheemie,*" Jake said. "Ask Sheemie what *he* thinks we should do."

Slowly, Roland nodded.

Chapter IX:
Tracks on the Path

When Jake awoke from a night of troubled dreams, most of them set in the Dixie Pig, a thin and listless light was seeping into the cave. In New York, that kind of light had always made him want to skip school and spend the entire day on the sofa, reading books, watching game-shows on TV, and napping the afternoon away. Eddie and Susannah were curled up together inside a single sleeping-bag. Oy had eschewed the bed which had been left him in order to sleep beside Jake. He was curled into a U, snout on left forepaw. Most people would have thought him asleep, but Jake saw the sly glimmer of gold beneath his lids and knew that Oy was peeking. The gunslinger's sleeping-bag was unzipped and empty.

Jake thought about this for a moment or two, then got up and went outside. Oy followed along, padding quietly over the tamped dirt as Jake walked up the trail.

TWO

Roland looked haggard and unwell, but he was squatting on his hunkers, and Jake decided that if he was limber enough to do that, he was probably okay. He squatted beside the gunslinger, hands dangling loosely between his thighs. Roland glanced at him, said nothing, then looked back toward the prison the staff called Algul Siento and the inmates called the Devar-Toi. It was a brightening blur beyond and below them. The sun—electric, atomic, whatever—wasn't shining yet.

Oy plopped down next to Jake with a little *whuffing* sound, then appeared to go back to sleep. Jake wasn't fooled.

309

"Hile and merry-greet-the-day," Jake said when the silence began to feel oppressive.

Roland nodded. "Merry see, merry be." He looked as merry as a funeral march. The gunslinger who had danced a furious commala by torchlight in Calla Bryn Sturgis might have been a thousand years in his grave.

"How are you, Roland?"

"Good enough to hunker."

"Aye, but how are you?"

Roland glanced at him, then reached into his pocket and brought out his tobacco pouch. "Old and full of aches, as you must know. Would you smoke?"

Jake considered, then nodded.

"They'll be shorts," Roland warned. "There's plenty in my purse I was glad to have back, but not much blow-weed."

"Save it for yourself, if you want."

Roland smiled. "A man who can't bear to share his habits is a man who needs to quit them." He rolled a pair of cigarettes, using some sort of leaf which he tore in two, handed one to Jake, then lit them up with a match he popped alight on his thumbnail. In the still, chill air of Can Steek-Tete, the smoke hung in front of them, then rose slowly, stacking on the air. Jake thought the tobacco was hot, harsh, and stale, but he said no word of complaint. He liked it. He thought of all the times he'd promised himself he wouldn't smoke like his father did— never in life—and now here he was, starting the habit. And with his new father's agreement, if not approval.

Roland reached out a finger and touched Jake's fore-head . . . his left cheek . . . his nose . . . his chin. The last touch hurt a little. "Pimples," Roland said. "It's the air of this place." He suspected it was emotional upset, as well—grief over the Pere—but to let Jake know he thought that would likely just increase the boy's unhappiness over Callahan's passing.

"You don't have any," Jake said. "Skin's as clear as a bell. Luck-*ee.*"

"No pimples," Roland agreed, and smoked. Below them in the seeping light was the village. *The peaceful village,* Jake thought, but it looked more than peaceful; it looked downright dead. Then he saw two figures, little more than specks from here, strolling toward each other. Hume guards patrolling the outer run of the fence, he presumed. They joined together into a single speck long enough for Jake to imagine a bit of their palaver, and then the speck divided again. "No pimples, but my hip hurts like a son of a bitch. Feels like someone opened it in the night and poured it full of broken glass. *Hot* glass. But this is far worse." He touched the right side of his head. "It feels cracked."

"You really think it's Stephen King's injuries you're feeling?"

Instead of making a verbal reply, Roland laid the forefinger of his left hand across a circle made by the thumb and pinky of his right: that gesture which meant *I tell you the truth.*

"That's a bummer," Jake said. "For him as well as you."

"Maybe; maybe not. Because, think you, Jake; think you well. Only living things feel pain. What I'm feeling suggests that King won't be killed instantly. And that means he might be easier to save."

Jake thought it might only mean King was going to lie beside the road in semi-conscious agony for awhile before expiring, but didn't like to say so. Let Roland believe what he liked. But there was something else. Something that concerned Jake a lot more, and made him uneasy.

"Roland, may I speak to you dan-dinh?"

The gunslinger nodded. "If you would." A slight pause. A flick at the left corner of the mouth that wasn't quite a smile. "If *thee* would."

Jake gathered his courage. "Why are you so angry now? What are you angry *at?* Or whom?" Now it was his turn to pause. "Is it me?"

Roland's eyebrows rose, then he barked a laugh. "Not you, Jake. Not a bit. Never in life."

Jake flushed with pleasure.

"I keep forgetting how strong the touch has become in you. You'd have made a fine Breaker, no doubt."

This wasn't an answer, but Jake didn't bother saying so. And the idea of being a Breaker made him repress a shiver.

"Don't you know?" Roland asked. "If thee knows I'm what Eddie calls royally pissed, don't you know why?"

"I could look, but it wouldn't be polite." But it was a lot more than that. Jake vaguely remembered a Bible story about Noah getting loaded on the ark, while he and his sons were waiting out the flood. One of the sons had come upon his old man lying drunk on his bunk, and had laughed at him. God had cursed him for it. To peek into Roland's thoughts wouldn't be the same as looking—and laughing—while he was drunk, but it was close.

"Thee's a fine boy," Roland said. "Fine and good, aye." And although the gunslinger spoke almost absently, Jake could have died happily enough at that moment. From somewhere beyond and above them came that resonant CLICK! sound, and all at once the special-effects sunbeam speared down on the Devar-Toi. A moment later, faintly, they heard the sound of music: "Hey Jude," arranged for elevator and supermarket. Time to rise and shine down below. Another day of Breaking had just begun. Although, Jake supposed, down there the Breaking never really stopped.

"Let's have a game, you and I," Roland proposed. "You try to get into my head and see who I'm angry at. I'll try to keep you out."

Jake shifted position slightly. "That doesn't sound like a fun game to me, Roland."

"Nevertheless, I'd play against you."

"All right, if you want to."

Jake closed his eyes and called up an image of Roland's tired, stubbled face. His brilliant blue eyes. He made a door between and slightly above those eyes—a little one, with a brass knob—and tried to open it. For a moment the knob turned. Then it stopped. Jake applied more pressure. The knob began to turn again, then stopped once again. Jake opened his eyes and saw that fine beads of sweat had broken on Roland's brow.

"This is stupid. I'm making your headache worse," he said.

"Never mind. Do your best."

My worst, Jake thought. But if they had to play this game, he wouldn't draw it out. He closed his eyes again and once again saw the little door between Roland's tangled brows. This time he applied more force, piling it on quickly. It felt a little like arm-wrestling. After a moment the knob turned and the door opened. Roland grunted, then uttered a painful laugh. "That's enough for me," he said. "By the gods, thee's strong!"

Jake paid no attention to that. He opened his eyes. "The writer? King? Why are you mad at *him?*"

Roland sighed and cast away the smoldering butt of his cigarette; Jake had already finished with his. "Because we have two jobs to do where we should have only one. Having to do the second one is sai King's fault. He knew what he was supposed to do, and I think that on some level he knew that doing it would keep him safe. But he was *afraid.* He was *tired.*" Roland's upper lip curled. "Now his irons are in the fire, and we have to pull them out. It's going to cost us, and probably a-dearly."

"You're angry at him because he's afraid? But . . ." Jake frowned. "But why wouldn't he be afraid? He's only a writer. A tale-spinner, not a gunslinger."

"I know that," Roland said, "but I don't think it was fear that stopped him, Jake, or not *just* fear. He's lazy, as well. I felt it when I met him, and I'm sure that Eddie did, too. He looked at the job he was made to do and it daunted him and he said to himself, 'All right, I'll find an *easier* job, one that's more to my liking and more to my abilities. And if there's trouble, they'll take care of me. They'll *have* to take care of me.' And so we do."

"You didn't like him."

"No," Roland agreed, "I didn't. Not a bit. Nor trusted him. I've met tale-spinners before, Jake, and they're all cut more or less from the same cloth. They tell tales because they're afraid of life."

"Do you say so?" Jake thought it was a dismal idea. He also thought it had the ring of truth.

"I do. But . . ." He shrugged. *It is what it is,* that shrug said.

Ka-shume, Jake thought. If their ka-tet broke, and it was King's fault . . .

If it was King's fault, what? Take revenge on him? It was a gunslinger's thought; it was also a stupid thought, like the idea of taking revenge on God.

"But we're stuck with it," Jake finished.

"Aye. That wouldn't stop me from kicking his yellow, lazy ass if I got the chance, though."

Jake burst out laughing at that, and the gunslinger smiled. Then Roland got to his feet with a grimace, both hands planted on the ball of his right hip. *"Bugger,"* he growled.

"Hurts bad, huh?"

"Never mind my aches and mollies. Come with me. I'll show you something more interesting."

Roland, limping slightly, led Jake to where the path curled around the flank of the lumpy little mountain, presumably bound for the top. Here the gunslinger tried to hunker, grimaced, and settled to one knee, instead. He pointed to the ground with his right hand. "What do you see?"

Jake also dropped to one knee. The ground was littered with pebbles and fallen chunks of rock. Some of this talus had been disturbed, leaving marks in the scree. Beyond the spot where they knelt side by side, two branches of what Jake thought was a mesquite bush had been broken off. He bent forward and smelled the thin and acrid aroma of the sap. Then he examined the marks in the scree again. There were several of them, narrow and not too deep. If they were tracks, they certainly weren't *human* tracks. Or those of a desert-dog, either.

"Do you know what made these?" Jake asked. "If you do, just say it—don't make me arm-rassle you for it."

Roland gave him a brief grin. "Follow them a little. See what you find."

Jake rose and walked slowly along the marks, bent over at the waist like a boy with a stomach-ache. The scratches in the talus went around a boulder. There was dust on the stone, and scratches in the dust—as if something bristly had brushed against the boulder on its way by.

There were also a couple of stiff black hairs.

Jake picked one of these up, then immediately opened his

fingers and blew it off his skin, shivering with revulsion as he did it. Roland watched this keenly.

"You look like a goose just walked over your grave."

"It's awful!" Jake heard a faint stutter in his voice. "Oh God, what was it? What was w-watching us?"

"The one Mia called Mordred." Roland's voice hadn't changed, but Jake found he could hardly bring himself to look into the gunslinger's eyes; they were that bleak. "The chap she says I fathered."

"He was here? In the night?"

Roland nodded.

"Listening . . . ?" Jake couldn't finish.

Roland could. "Listening to our palaver and our plans, aye, I think so. And Ted's tale as well."

"But you don't know for sure. Those marks could be anything." Yet the only thing Jake could think of in connection with those marks, now that he'd heard Susannah's tale, were the legs of a monster spider.

"Go thee a little further," Roland said.

Jake looked at him questioningly, and Roland nodded. The wind blew, bringing them the Muzak from the prison compound (now he thought it was "Bridge Over Troubled Water"), also bringing the distant sound of thunder, like rolling bones.

"What—"

"Follow," Roland said, nodding to the stony talus on the slope of the path.

Jake did, knowing this was another lesson—with Roland you were always in school. Even when you were in the shadow of death there were lessons to be learned.

On the far side of the boulder, the path carried on straight for about thirty yards before curving out of sight once more. On this straight stretch, those dash-marks were very clear. Groups of three on one side, groups of four on the other.

"She said she shot off one of its legs," Jake said.

"So she did."

Jake tried to visualize a seven-legged spider as big as a human baby and couldn't do it. Suspected he didn't *want* to do it.

Beyond the next curve there was a desiccated corpse in the path. Jake was pretty sure it had been flayed open, but it was hard to tell. There were no innards, no blood, no buzzing flies. Just a lump of dirty, dusty stuff that vaguely—*very* vaguely—resembled something canine.

Oy approached, sniffed, then lifted his leg and pissed on the remains. He returned to Jake's side with the air of one who has concluded some important piece of business.

"That was our visitor's dinner last night," Roland said.

Jake was looking around. "Is he watching us now? What do you think?"

Roland said, "I think growing boys need their rest."

Jake felt a twinge of some unpleasant emotion and put it behind him without much examination. Jealousy? Surely not. How could he be jealous of a thing that had begun life by eating its own mother? It was blood-kin to Roland, yes—his true son, if you wanted to be picky about it—but that was no more than an accident.

Wasn't it?

Jake became aware that Roland was looking at him closely, looking in a way that made Jake uneasy.

"Penny for em, dimmy-da," the gunslinger said.

"Nothing," Jake said. "Just wondering where he's laid up."

"Hard to tell," Roland said. "There's got to be a hundred holes in this hill alone. Come."

Roland led the way back around the boulder where Jake had found the stiff black hairs, and once he was there, he began to methodically scuff away the tracks Mordred had left behind.

"Why are you doing that?" Jake asked, more sharply than he had intended.

"There's no need for Eddie and Susannah to know about this," Roland said. "He only means to watch, not to interfere in our business. At least for the time being."

How do you know that? Jake wanted to ask, but that twinge came again—the one that absolutely couldn't be jealousy—and he decided not to. Let Roland think whatever he wanted.

Jake, meanwhile, would keep his eyes open. And if Mordred should be foolish enough to show himself . . .

"It's Susannah I'm most concerned about," Roland said. "She's the one most likely to be distracted by the chap's presence. And her thoughts would be the easiest for him to read."

"Because she's its mother," Jake said. He didn't notice the change of pronoun, but Roland did.

"The two of them are connected, aye. Can I count on you to keep your mouth shut?"

"Sure."

"And try to guard your mind—that's important, as well."

"I can try, but . . ." Jake shrugged in order to say that he didn't really know how one did that.

"Good," Roland said. "And I'll do the same."

The wind gusted again. "Bridge Over Troubled Water" had changed to (Jake was pretty sure) a Beatles tune, the one with the chorus that ended *Beep-beep-mmm-beep-beep, yeah!* Did they know that one in the dusty, dying towns between Gilead and Mejis? Jake wondered. Were there Shebs in some of those towns that played "Drive My Car" jagtime on out-of-tune pianos while the Beams weakened and the glue that held the worlds together slowly stretched into strings and the worlds themselves sagged?

He gave his head a hard, brisk shake, trying to clear it. Roland was still watching him, and Jake felt an uncharacteristic flash of irritation. "I'll keep my mouth shut, Roland, and at least try to keep my thoughts to myself. Don't worry about me."

"I'm not worried," Roland said, and Jake found himself fighting the temptation to look inside his dinh's head and find out if that was actually true. He still thought looking was a bad idea, and not just because it was impolite, either. Mistrust was very likely a kind of acid. Their ka-tet was fragile enough already, and there was much work to do.

"Good," Jake said. "That's good."

"Good!" Oy agreed, in a hearty *that's settled* tone that made them both grin.

"We know he's there," Roland said, "and it's likely he

doesn't know we know. Under the circumstances, there's no better way for things to be."

Jake nodded. The idea made him feel a little calmer.

Susannah came to the mouth of the cave at her usual speedy crawl while they were walking back toward it. She sniffed at the air and grimaced. When she glimpsed them, the grimace turned into a grin. "I see handsome men! How long have you boys been up?"

"Only a little while," Roland said.

"And how are you feeling?"

"Fine," Roland said. "I woke up with a headache, but now it's almost gone."

"Really?" Jake asked.

Roland nodded and squeezed the boy's shoulder.

Susannah wanted to know if they were hungry. Roland nodded. So did Jake.

"Well, come on in here," she said, "and we'll see what we can do about that situation."

THREE

Susannah found powdered eggs and cans of Prudence corned beef hash. Eddie located a can-opener and a small gas-powered hibachi grill. After a little muttering to himself, he got it going and was only a bit startled when the hibachi began talking.

"Hello! I'm three-quarters filled with Gamry Bottled Gas, available at Wal-Mart, Burnaby's, and other fine stores! When you call for Gamry, you're calling for quality! Dark in here, isn't it? May I help you with recipes or cooking times?"

"You could help me by shutting up," Eddie said, and the grill spoke no more. He found himself wondering if he had offended it, then wondered if perhaps he should kill himself and spare the world a problem.

Roland opened four cans of peaches, smelled them, and nodded. "Okay, I think," he said. "Sweet."

They were just finishing this repast when the air in front of the cave shimmered. A moment later, Ted Brautigan, Dinky

Earnshaw, and Sheemie Ruiz appeared. With them, cringing and very frightened, dressed in fading and tattered biballs, was the Rod Roland had asked them to bring.

"Come in and have something to eat," Roland said amiably, as if a quartet of teleports showing up was a common occurrence. "There's plenty."

"Maybe we'll skip breakfast," Dinky said. "We don't have much t—"

Before he could finish, Sheemie's knees buckled and he collapsed at the mouth of the cave, his eyes rolling up to whites and a thin froth of spit oozing out between his cracked lips. He began to shiver and buck, his legs kicking aimlessly, his rubber moccasins scratching lines in the talus.

CHAPTER X:
THE LAST PALAVER
(SHEEMIE'S DREAM)

ONE

Susannah supposed you couldn't classify what came next as pandemonium; surely it took at least a dozen people to induce such a state, and they were but seven. Eight counting the Rod, and you certainly had to count him, because he was creating a large part of the uproar. When he saw Roland he dropped to his knees, raised his hands over his head like a ref signaling a successful extra-point kick, and began salaaming rapidly. Each downstroke was extreme enough to thump his forehead on the ground. He was at the same time babbling at the top of his lungs in his odd, vowelly language. He never took his eyes off Roland while he performed these gymnastics. Susannah had little doubt the gunslinger was being saluted as some kind of god.

Ted also dropped on his knees, but it was Sheemie with whom he was concerned. The old man put his hands on the sides of Sheemie's head to stop it whipping back and forth; already Roland's old acquaintance from his Mejis days had cut one cheek on a sharp bit of stone, a cut that was dangerously close to his left eye. And now blood began to pour from the corners of Sheemie's mouth and run up his modestly stubbled cheeks.

"Give me something to put in his mouth!" Ted cried. "Come on, somebody! Wake up! He's biting the *shit* out of himself!"

The wooden lid was still leaning against the open crate of sneetches. Roland brought it smartly down on his raised knee— no sign of dry twist in that hip now, she noted—and smashed it to bits. Susannah grabbed a piece of board on the fly, then turned to Sheemie. No need to get on her knees; she was always on them, anyway. One end of the wooden piece was jagged with splinters. She wrapped a protective hand around this and then put the piece of wood in Sheemie's mouth. He bit down on it so hard she could hear the crunch.

The Rod, meanwhile, continued his high, almost falsetto chant. The only words she could pick out of the gibberish were *Hile, Roland, Gilead,* and *Eld.*

"Somebody shut him up!" Dinky cried, and Oy began barking.

"Never mind the Rod, get Sheemie's feet!" Ted snapped. "Hold him still!"

Dinky dropped to his knees and grabbed Sheemie's feet, one now bare, the other still wearing its absurd rubber moc.

"Oy, hush!" Jake said, and Oy did. But he was standing with his short legs spread and his belly low to the ground, his fur bushed out so he seemed nearly double his normal size.

Roland crouched by Sheemie's head, forearms on the dirt floor of the cave, mouth by one of Sheemie's ears. He began to murmur. Susannah could make out very little of it because of the Rod's falsetto babbling, but she did hear *Will Dearborn that was* and *All's well* and—she thought—*rest.*

Whatever it was, it seemed to get through. Little by little Sheemie relaxed. She could see Dinky easing his hold on the former tavern-boy's ankles, ready to grab hard again if Sheemie renewed his kicking. The muscles around Sheemie's mouth also relaxed, and his teeth unlocked. The piece of wood, still nailed lightly to his mouth by his upper incisors, seemed to levitate. Susannah pulled it gently free, looking with amazement at the blood-rimmed holes, some almost half an inch deep, that had been driven into the soft wood. Sheemie's tongue lolled from the side of his mouth, reminding her of how Oy looked at siesta time, sleeping on his back with his legs spread to the four points of the compass.

Now there was only the rapid auctioneer's babble of the Rod, and the low growl deep in Oy's chest as he stood protectively at Jake's side, looking at the newcomer with narrowed eyes.

"Shut your mouth and be still," Roland told the Rod, then added something else in another language.

The Rod froze halfway into another salaam, hands still raised above his head, staring at Roland. Eddie saw the side of his nose had been eaten away by a juicy sore, red as a strawberry. The Rod put his scabbed, dirty palms over his eyes, as if the gunslinger were a thing too bright to look at, and fell on his side. He drew his knees up to his chest, producing a loud fart as he did so.

"Harpo speaks," Eddie said, a joke snappy enough to make Susannah laugh. Then there was silence except for the whine of the wind outside the cave, the faint sound of recorded music from the Devar-Toi, and the distant rumble of thunder, that sound of rolling bones.

Five minutes later Sheemie opened his eyes, sat up, and looked around with the bewildered air of one who knows not where he is, how he got there, or why. Then his eyes fixed on Roland, and his poor, tired face lit in a smile.

Roland returned it, and held out his arms. "Can'ee come to me, Sheemie? If not, I'll come to you, sure."

Sheemie crawled to Roland of Gilead on his hands and knees, his dark and dirty hair hanging in his eyes, and laid his head on Roland's shoulder. Susannah felt tears stinging her eyes and looked away.

TWO

Some short time later Sheemie sat propped against the wall of the cave with the mover's pad that had been over Suzie's Cruisin Trike cushioning his head and back. Eddie had offered him a soda, but Ted suggested water might be better. Sheemie drank the first bottle of Perrier at a single go, and now sat sipping another. The rest of them had instant coffee, except for Ted; he was drinking a can of Nozz-A-La.

"Don't know how you stand that stuff," Eddie said.

"Each to his own taste, said the old maid as she kissed the cow," Ted replied.

Only the Child of Roderick had nothing. He lay where he was, at the mouth of the cave, with his hands pressed firmly over his eyes. He was trembling lightly.

Ted had checked Sheemie over between Sheemie's first and second bottle of water, taking his pulse, looking in his mouth, and feeling his skull for any soft places. Each time he asked Sheemie if it hurt, Sheemie solemnly shook his head, never taking his eyes off Roland during the examination. After feeling Sheemie's ribs ("Tickles, sai, so it do," Sheemie said with a smile), Ted pronounced him fit as a fiddle.

Eddie, who could see Sheemie's eyes perfectly well—one of the gas-lanterns was nearby and cast a strong glow on Sheemie's face—thought that was a lie of near Presidential quality.

Susannah was cooking up a fresh batch of powdered eggs and corned beef hash. (The grill had spoken up again—"More of the same, eh?" it asked in a tone of cheery approval.) Eddie caught Dinky Earnshaw's eye and said, "Want to step outside with me for a minute while Suze makes with the chow?"

Dinky glanced at Ted, who nodded, then back at Eddie. "If you want. We've got a little more time this morning, but that doesn't mean we can waste any."

"I understand," Eddie said.

THREE

The wind had strengthened, but instead of freshening the air, it smelled fouler than ever. Once, in high school, Eddie had gone on a field trip to an oil refinery in New Jersey. Until now he thought that was hands-down the worst thing he'd ever smelled in his life; two of the girls and three of the boys had puked. He remembered their tour-guide laughing heartily and saying, "Just remember that's the smell of money—it helps." Maybe Perth Oil and Gas was still the all-time champeen, but only because what he was smelling now wasn't quite so strong. And just by the way, what was there about Perth Oil and Gas that seemed familiar? He didn't know and it probably didn't matter, but it was strange, the way things kept coming around over here. Only "coming around" wasn't quite right, was it?

"Echoing back," Eddie murmured. "That's what it is."

"Beg pardon, partner?" Dinky asked. They were once again standing on the path, looking down at the blue-roofed buildings in the distance, and the tangle of stalled traincars, and the perfect little village. Perfect, that was, until you remembered it was behind a triple run of wire, one of those runs carrying an electrical charge strong enough to kill a man on contact.

"Nothing," Eddie said. "What's that smell? Any idea?"

Dinky shook his head, but pointed beyond the prison compound in a direction that might or might not be south or east. "Something poison out there is all I know," he said. "Once I asked Finli and he said there used to be factories in that direction. Positronics business. You know that name?"

"Yes. But who's Finli?"

"Finli o' Tego. The top security guy, Prentiss's number one boy, also known as The Weasel. A taheen. Whatever your plans are, you'll have to go through him to make them work. And he won't make it easy for you. Seeing him stretched out dead on the ground would make me feel like it was a national holiday. By the way, my real name's Richard Earnshaw. Pleased as hell to meetcha." He put out his hand. Eddie shook it.

"I'm Eddie Dean. Known as Eddie of New York out here west of the Pecos. The woman's Susannah. My wife."

Dinky nodded. "Uh-huh. And the boy's Jake. Also of New York."

"Jake Chambers, right. Listen, Rich—"

"I salute the effort," he said, smiling, "but I've been Dinky too long to change now, I guess. And it could be worse. I worked for awhile at the Supr Savr Supermarket with a twentysomething guy known as JJ the Fuckin Blue Jay. People will still be calling him that when he's eighty and wearing a pee-bag."

"Unless we're brave, lucky, and good," Eddie said, *"nobody's* gonna see eighty. Not in this world or any of the others."

Dinky looked startled, then glum. "You got a point."

"That guy Roland used to know looks bad," Eddie said. "Did you see his *eyes?*"

Dinky nodded, glummer than ever. "I think those little spots of blood in the whites are called petechiae. Something like that." Then, in a tone of apology Eddie found rather bizarre, under the circumstances: "I don't know if I'm saying that right."

"I don't care what you call them, it's not good. And him pitching a fit like that—"

"Not a very nice way to put it," Dinky said.

Eddie didn't give a shit if it was or wasn't. "Has it ever happened to him before?"

Dinky's eyes broke contact with Eddie's and looked down at his own shuffling feet, instead. Eddie thought that was answer enough.

"How many times?" Eddie hoped he didn't sound as appalled as he felt. There were enough pinprick-sized blood-spots in the whites of Sheemie's eyes to make them look as if someone had flung paprika into them. Not to mention the bigger ones in the corners.

Still without looking at him, Dinky raised four fingers.

"Four times?"

"Yuh," Dinky said. He was still studying his makeshift mocs. "Starting with the time he sent Ted to Connecticut in 1960. It was like doing that ruptured something inside him." He looked up, trying to smile. "But he didn't faint yesterday, when the three of us went back to the Devar."

"Let me make sure I've got this right. In the prison down there, you guys have all sorts of venial sins, but only one mortal one: teleportation."

Dinky considered this. The rules certainly weren't that liberal for the taheen and the can-toi; they could be exiled or lobotomized for all sorts of reasons, including such wrongs as negligence, teasing the Breakers, or the occasional act of outright cruelty. Once—so he had been told—a Breaker had been raped by a low man, who was said to have explained earnestly to the camp's last Master that it was part of his *becoming*—the Crimson King himself had appeared to this fellow in a dream and told him to do it. For this the can-toi had been sentenced to death. The Breakers had been invited to attend his execution (accomplished by a single pistol-shot to the head), which had taken place in the middle of Pleasantville's Main Street.

Dinky told Eddie about this, then admitted that yes, for the inmates, at least, teleportation was the only mortal sin. That he knew of, anyway.

"And Sheemie's your teleport," Eddie said. "You guys help him—*facilitate* for him, to use the Tedster's word—and you cover up for him by fudging the records, somehow—"

"They have no idea how easy it is to cook their telemetry," Dinky said, almost laughing. "Partner, they'd be *shocked*. The hard part is making sure we don't tip over the whole works."

Eddie didn't care about that, either. It worked. That was the only thing that mattered. Sheemie also worked . . . but for how long?

"—but *he's* the one who does it," Eddie finished. "Sheemie."

"Yuh."

"The only one who *can* do it."

"Yuh."

Eddie thought about their two tasks: freeing the Breakers (or killing them, if there was no other way to make them stop) and keeping the writer from being struck and killed by a minivan while taking a walk. Roland thought they might be able to accomplish both things, but they'd need Sheemie's teleportation ability at least twice. Plus, their visitors would have to get back inside the triple run of wire after today's palaver was done, and presumably that meant he'd have to do it a third time.

"He says it doesn't hurt," Dinky said. "If that's what you're worried about."

Inside the cave the others laughed at something, Sheemie back to consciousness and taking nourishment, everyone the best of friends.

"It's not," Eddie said. "What does Ted think is happening to Sheemie when he teleports?"

"That he's having brain hemorrhages," Dinky said promptly.

"Little tiny strokes on the surface of his brain." He tapped a finger at different points on his own skull in demonstration. "Boink, boink, boink."

"Is it getting worse? It is, isn't it?"

"Look, if you think him jaunting us around is my idea, you better think again."

Eddie raised one hand like a traffic cop. "No, no. I'm just trying to figure out what's going on." *And what our chances are.*

"I hate using him that way!" Dinky burst out. He kept his voice pitched low, so those in the cave wouldn't hear, but Eddie never for a moment considered that he was exaggerating. Dinky was badly upset. "He doesn't mind—he *wants* to do it—and that makes it worse, not better. The way he looks at Ted . . ." He shrugged. "It's the way a dog'd look at the best master in the universe. He looks at your dinh the same way, as I'm sure you've noticed."

"He's doing it *for* my dinh," Eddie said, "and that makes it okay. You may not believe that, Dink, but—"

"But you do."

"Totally. Now here's the really important question: does Ted have any idea how long Sheemie can last? Keeping in mind that now he's got a little more help at this end?"

Who you tryin to cheer up, bro? Henry spoke up suddenly inside his head. Cynical as always. *Him or yourself?*

Dinky was looking at Eddie as if he were crazy, or soft in the head, at least. "Ted was an accountant. Sometimes a tutor. A day-laborer when he couldn't get anything better. He's no doctor."

But Eddie kept pushing. "What does he think?"

Dinky paused. The wind blew. The music wafted. Farther away, thunder mumbled out of the murk. At last he said: "Three or four times, maybe . . . but the effects are getting worse. Maybe only twice. But there are no guarantees, okay? He could drop dead of a massive stroke the next time he bears down to make that hole we go through."

Eddie tried to think of another question and couldn't. That last answer pretty well covered the waterfront, and when Susannah called them back inside, he was more than glad to go.

FOUR

Sheemie Ruiz had rediscovered his appetite, which all of them took as a good sign, and was tucking in happily. The bloodspots in his eyes had faded somewhat, but were still clearly visible. Eddie wondered what the guards back in Blue Heaven would make of those if they noticed them, and also wondered if Sheemie could wear a pair of sunglasses without exciting comment.

Roland had gotten the Rod to his feet and was now conferring with him at the back of the cave. Well . . . sort of. The gunslinger was talking and the Rod was listening, occasionally sneaking tiny awed peeks at Roland's face. It was gibberish to Eddie, but he was able to pick out two words: Chevin and Chayven. Roland was asking this one about the one they'd met staggering along the road in Lovell.

"Does he have a name?" Eddie asked Dink and Ted, taking a second plate of food.

"I call him Chucky," Dinky said. "Because he looks a little bit like the doll in this horror movie I saw once."

Eddie grinned. *"Child's Play,* yeah. I saw that one. After your when, Jake. And *way* after yours, Suziella." The Rod's hair wasn't right, but the chubby, freckled cheeks and the blue eyes were. "Do you think he can keep a secret?"

"If no one asks him, he can," Ted said. Which was not, in Eddie's view, a very satisfactory answer.

After five minutes or so of chat, Roland seemed satisfied and rejoined the others. He hunkered—no problem doing that now that his joints had limbered up—and looked at Ted. "This fellow's name is Haylis of Chayven. Will anyone miss him?"

"Unlikely," Ted said. "The Rods show up at the gate beyond the dorms in little groups, looking for work. Fetching and carrying, mostly. They're given a meal or something to drink as pay. If they don't show up, no one misses them."

"Good. Now—how long are the days here? Is it twenty-four hours from now until tomorrow morning at this time?"

Ted seemed interested in the question and considered it for several moments before replying. "Call it twenty-five," he said. "Maybe a little longer. Because time is slowing down, at least here. As the Beams weaken, there seems to be a growing disparity in the time-flow between the worlds. It's probably one of the major stress points."

Roland nodded. Susannah offered him food and he shook his head with a word of thanks. Behind them, the Rod was sitting on a crate, looking down at his bare and sore-covered feet. Eddie was surprised to see Oy approach the fellow, and more surprised still when the bumbler allowed Chucky (or Haylis) to stroke his head with one misshapen claw of a hand.

"And is there a time of morning when things down there might be a little less . . . I don't know . . ."

"A little disorganized?" Ted suggested.

Roland nodded.

"Did you hear a horn a little while ago?" Ted asked. "Just before we showed up?"

They all shook their heads.

Ted didn't seem surprised. "But you heard the music start, correct?"

"Yes," Susannah said, and offered Ted a fresh can of Nozz-A-La. He took it and drank with gusto. Eddie tried not to shudder.

"Thank you, ma'am. In any case, the horn signals the change of shifts. The music starts then."

"I hate that music," Dinky said moodily.

"If there's any time when control wavers," Ted went on, "that would be it."

"And what o'clock is that?" Roland asked.

Ted and Dinky exchanged a doubtful glance. Dinky showed eight fingers, his eyebrows raised questioningly. He looked relieved when Ted nodded at once.

"Yes, eight o'clock," Ted said, then laughed and gave his head a cynical little shake. "What *would* be eight, anyway, in a world where yon prison might always lie firmly east and not east by southeast on some days and dead east on others."

But Roland had been living with the dissolving world long

before Ted Brautigan had even dreamed of such a place as Algul Siento, and he wasn't particularly upset by the way formerly hard-and-fast facts of life had begun to bend. "About twenty-five hours from right now," Roland said. "Or a little less."

Dinky nodded. "But if you're counting on raging confusion, forget it. They know their places and go to them. They're old hands."

"Still," Roland said, "it's the best we're apt to do." Now he looked at his old acquaintance from Mejis. And beckoned to him.

FIVE

Sheemie set his plate down at once, came to Roland, and made a fist. "Hile, Roland, Will Dearborn that was."

Roland returned this greeting, then turned to Jake. The boy gave him an uncertain look. Roland nodded at him, and Jake came. Now Jake and Sheemie stood facing each other with Roland hunkered between them, seeming to look at neither now that they were brought together.

Jake raised a hand to his forehead.

Sheemie returned the gesture.

Jake looked down at Roland and said, "What do you want?"

Roland didn't answer, only continued to look serenely toward the mouth of the cave, as if there were something in the apparently endless murk out there which interested him. And Jake knew what was wanted, as surely as if he had used the touch on Roland's mind to find out (which he most certainly had not). They had come to a fork in the road. It had been Jake who'd suggested Sheemie should be the one to tell them which branch to take. At the time it had seemed like a weirdly good idea—who knew why. Now, looking into that earnest, not-very-bright face and those bloodshot eyes, Jake wondered two things: what had ever possessed him to suggest such a course of action, and why someone—probably Eddie, who retained a relatively hard head in spite of all they'd been through—hadn't told him, kindly but firmly, that putting their future in Sheemie Ruiz's hands was a dumb idea. Totally noodgy, as his old schoolmates back at Piper might have said. Now Roland, who believed that even in the shadow of death there were still lessons to be learned, wanted Jake to ask the question Jake himself had proposed, and the answer would no doubt expose him as the superstitious scatterbrain he had become. Yet still, why not ask? Even if it were the equivalent of flipping a coin, why not? Jake had come, possibly at the end of a short but undeniably interesting life, to a place where there were magic doors, mechanical butlers, telepathy (of which he was capable, at least to some small degree, himself), vampires, and were-spiders. So why not let Sheemie choose? They *had* to go one way or the other, after all, and he'd been through too goddam much to worry about such a paltry thing as looking like an idiot in front of his companions. *Besides,* he thought, *if I'm not among friends here, I never will be.*

"Sheemie," he said. Looking into those bloody eyes was sort of horrible, but he made himself do it. "We're on a quest. That means we have a job to do. We—"

"You have to save the Tower," said Sheemie. "And my old friend is to go in, and mount to the top, and see what's to see. There may be renewal, there may be death, or there may be both. He was Will Dearborn once, aye, so he was. Will Dearborn to me."

Jake glanced at Roland, who was still hunkered down, looking out of the cave. But Jake thought his face had gone pale and strange.

One of Roland's fingers made his twirling go-ahead gesture.

"Yes, we're supposed to save the Dark Tower," Jake agreed. And thought he understood some of Roland's lust to see it and enter it, even if it killed him. What lay at the center of the universe? What man (or boy) could but wonder, once the question was thought of, and want to see?

Even if looking drove him mad?

"But in order to do that, we have to do two jobs. One involves going back to our world and saving a man. A writer who's telling our story. The other job is the one we've been talking about. Freeing the Breakers." Honesty made him add: "Or stopping them, at least. Do you understand?"

But this time Sheemie didn't reply. He was looking where Roland was looking, out into the murk. His face was that of someone who's been hypnotized. Looking at it made Jake uneasy, but he pushed on. He had come to his question, after all, and where else was there to go but on?

"The question is, which job do we do first? It'd seem that saving the writer might be easier because there's no opposition . . . that we know of, anyway . . . but there's a chance that . . . well . . ." Jake didn't want to say *But there's a chance that teleporting us might kill you,* and so came to a lame and unsatisfying halt.

For a moment he didn't think Sheemie would make any reply, leaving him with the job of deciding whether or not to try again, but then the former tavern-boy spoke. He looked at none of them as he did so, but only out of the cave and into the dim of Thunderclap.

"I had a dream last night, so I did," said Sheemie of Mejis, whose life had once been saved by three young gunslingers from Gilead. "I dreamed I was back at the Travellers' Rest, only Coral wasn't there, nor Stanley, nor Pettie, nor Sheb—him that used to play the pianer. There was nobbut me, and I was moppin the floor and singin 'Careless Love.' Then the batwings screeked, so they did, they had this funny sound they made . . ."

Jake saw that Roland was nodding, a trace of a smile on his lips.

"I looked up," Sheemie resumed, "and in come this boy." His eyes shifted briefly to Jake, then back to the mouth of the cave. "He looked like you, young sai, so he did, close enough to be twim. But his face were covert wi' blood and one of his eye'n were put out, spoiling his pretty, and he walked all a-limp. Looked like death, he did, and frighten't me terrible, and made me sad to see him, too. I just kept moppin, thinkin that if I did that he might not never mind me, or even see me at all, and go away."

Jake realized he knew this tale. Had he seen it? Had he actually been that bloody boy?

"But he looked right at you . . ." Roland murmured, still a-hunker, still looking out into the gloom.

"Aye, Will Dearborn that was, right at me, so he did, and said 'Why must you hurt me, when I love you so? When I can do nothing else nor want to, for love made me and fed me and—'"

"'And kept me in better days,'" Eddie murmured. A tear fell from one of his eyes and made a dark spot on the floor of the cave.

"'—and kept me in better days? Why will you cut me, and disfigure my face, and fill me with woe? I have only loved you for your beauty as you once loved me for mine in the days before the world moved on. Now you scar me with nails and put burning drops of quicksilver in my nose; you have set the animals on me, so you have, and they have eaten of my softest parts. Around me the can-toi gather and there's no peace from their laughter. Yet still I love you and would serve you and even bring the magic again, if you would allow me, for that is how my heart was cast when I rose from the *Prim*. And once I was strong as well as beautiful, but now my strength is almost gone.'"

"You cried," Susannah said, and Jake thought: *Of course he did.* He was crying himself. So was Ted; so was Dinky Earnshaw. Only Roland was dry-eyed, and the gunslinger was pale, so pale.

"He wept," said Sheemie (tears were rolling down his cheeks as he told his dream), "and I did, too, for I could see that he had been fair as daylight. He said, 'If the torture were to stop now, I might still recover—if never my looks, then at least my strength—'"

"'My *kes*,'" Jake said, and although he'd never heard the word before he pronounced it correctly, almost as if it were *kiss*.

"'—and my *kes*. But another week . . . or maybe five days . . . or even three . . . and it will be too late. Even if the torture stops, I'll die. And you'll die too, for when love leaves the world, all hearts are still. Tell them of my love and tell them of my pain and tell them of my hope, which still lives. For this is all I have and all I am and all I ask.' Then the boy turned and went out. The batwing door made its same sound. *Skree-eek.*"

He looked at Jake, now, and smiled like one who has just

awakened. "I can't answer your question, sai." He knocked a fist on his forehead. "Don't have much in the way of brains up here, me—only cobwebbies. Cordelia Delgado said so, and I reckon she was right."

Jake made no reply. He was dazed. He had dreamed about the same disfigured boy, but not in any saloon; it had been in Gage Park, the one where they'd seen Charlie the Choo-Choo. Last night. Had to have been. He hadn't remembered until now, would probably never have remembered if Sheemie hadn't told his own dream. And had Roland, Eddie, and Susannah also had a version of the same dream? Yes. He could see it on their faces, just as he could see that Ted and Dinky looked moved but otherwise bewildered.

Roland stood up with a wince, clamped his hand briefly to his hip, then said, "Thankee-sai, Sheemie, you've helped us greatly."

Sheemie smiled uncertainly. "How did I do that?"

"Never mind, my dear." Roland turned his attention to Ted. "My friends and I are going to step outside briefly. We need to speak an-tet."

"Of course," Ted said. He shook his head as if to clear it.

"Do my peace of mind a favor and keep it short," Dinky said. "We're probably still all right, but I don't want to push our luck."

"Will you need him to jump you back inside?" Eddie asked, nodding to Sheemie. This was in the nature of a rhetorical question; how else would the three of them get back?

"Well, yeah, but . . ." Dinky began.

"Then you'll be pushing your luck plenty." That said, Eddie, Susannah, and Jake followed Roland out of the cave. Oy stayed behind, sitting with his new friend, Haylis of Chayven. Something about that troubled Jake. It wasn't a feeling of jealousy but rather one of dread. As if he were seeing an omen someone wiser than himself—one of the Manni-folk, perhaps—could interpret. But would he want to know?

Perhaps not.

SIX

"I didn't remember my dream until he told his," Susannah said, "and if he *hadn't* told his, I probably never would have remembered."

"Yeah," Jake said.

"But I remember it clearly enough now," she went on. "I was in a subway station and the boy came down the stairs—"

Jake said, "I was in Gage Park—"

"And I was at the Markey Avenue playground, where me and Henry used to play one-on-one," Eddie said. "In my dream, the kid with the bloody face was wearing a tee-shirt that said NEVER A DULL MOMENT—"

"—IN MID-WORLD," Jake finished, and Eddie gave him a startled look.

Jake barely noticed; his thoughts had turned in another direction. "I wonder if Stephen King ever uses dreams in his writing. You know, as yeast to make the plot rise."

This was a question none of them could answer.

"Roland?" Eddie asked. "Where were you in your dream?"

"The Travellers' Rest, where else? Wasn't I there with Sheemie, once upon a time?" *With my friends, now long gone,* he could have added, but did not. "I was sitting at the table Eldred Jonas used to favor, playing one-hand Watch Me."

Susannah said quietly, "The boy in the dream *was* the Beam, wasn't he?"

As Roland nodded, Jake realized that Sheemie had told them which task came first, after all. Had told them beyond all doubt.

"Do any of you have a question?" Roland asked.

One by one, his companions shook their heads.

"We are ka-tet," Roland said, and in unison they answered: "*We are one from many.*"

Roland tarried a moment longer, looking at them—more than looking, seeming to savor their faces—and then he led them back inside.

"Sheemie," he said.

"Yes, sai! Yes, Roland, Will Dearborn that was!"

"We're going to save the boy you told us about. We're going to make the bad folk stop hurting him."

Sheemie smiled, but it was a puzzled smile. He didn't remember the boy in his dream, not anymore. "Good, sai, that's good!"

Roland turned his attention to Ted. "Once Sheemie gets you back this time, put him to bed. Or, if that would attract the wrong sort of attention, just make sure he takes it easy."

"We can write him down for the sniffles and keep him out of The Study," Ted agreed. "There are a lot of colds Thunder-side. But you folks need to understand that there are no guarantees. He could get us back inside this time, and then—" He snapped his fingers in the air.

Laughing, Sheemie imitated him, only snapping both sets of fingers. Susannah looked away, sick to her stomach.

"I *know* that," Roland said, and although his tone did not change very much, each member of his ka-tet knew it was a good thing this palaver was almost over. Roland had reached the rim of his patience. "Keep him quiet even if he's well and feeling fine. We won't need him for what I have in mind, and thanks to the weapons you've left us."

"They're good weapons," Ted agreed, "but are they good enough to wipe out sixty men, can-toi, and taheen?"

"Will the two of you stand with us, once the fight begins?" Roland asked.

"With the greatest pleasure," Dinky said, baring his teeth in a remarkably nasty grin.

"Yes," Ted said. "And it might be that I have another weapon. Did you listen to the tapes I left you?"

"Yes," Jake replied.

"So you know the story about the guy who stole my wallet." This time they all nodded.

"What about that young woman?" Susannah asked. "One tough cookie, you said. What about Tanya and her boyfriend? Or her husband, if that's what he is?"

Ted and Dinky exchanged a brief, doubtful look, then shook their heads simultaneously.

"Once, maybe," Ted said. "Not now. Now she's married. All she wants to do is cuddle with her fella."

"And Break," Dinky added.

"But don't they understand . . ." She found she couldn't finish. She was haunted not so much by the remnants of her own dream as by Sheemie's. *Now you scar me with nails,* the dream-boy had told Sheemie. The dream-boy who had once been fair.

"They don't *want* to understand," Ted told her kindly. He caught a glimpse of Eddie's dark face and shook his head. "But I won't let you hate them for it. You—*we*—may have to kill some of them, but I won't let you hate them. They did not put understanding away from them out of greed or fear, but from despair."

"And because to Break is divine," Dinky said. He was also looking at Eddie. "The way the half an hour after you shoot up can be divine. If you know what I'm talking about."

Eddie sighed, stuck his hands in his pockets, said nothing.

Sheemie surprised them all by picking up one of the Coyote machine-pistols and swinging it in an arc. Had it been loaded, the great quest for the Dark Tower would have ended right there. "I'll fight, too!" he cried. *"Pow, pow, pow! Bam-bam-bam-ba-dam!"*

Eddie and Susannah ducked; Jake threw himself instinctively in front of Oy; Ted and Dinky raised their hands in front of their faces, as if that could possibly have saved them from a burst of a hundred high-caliber, steel-jacketed slugs. Roland plucked the machine-pistol calmly from Sheemie's hands.

"Your time to help will come," he said, "but after this first battle's fought and won. Do you see Jake's bumbler, Sheemie?"

"Aye, he's with the Rod."

"He talks. See if you can get him to talk to you."

Sheemie obediently went to where Chucky/Haylis was still stroking Oy's head, dropped to one knee, and commenced trying to get Oy to say his name. The bumbler did almost at once, and with remarkable clarity. Sheemie laughed, and Haylis

joined in. They sounded like a couple of kids from the Calla.
The roont kind, perhaps.

Roland, meanwhile, turned to Dinky and Ted, his lips little
more than a white line in his stern face.

SEVEN

"He's to be kept out of it, once the shooting starts." The gunslinger mimed turning a key in a lock. "If we lose, what happens
to him later on won't matter. If we win, we'll need him at least
one more time. Probably twice."

"To go where?" Dinky asked.

"Keystone World America," Eddie said. "A small town in
western Maine called Lovell. As early in June of 1999 as one-way
time allows."

"Sending me to Connecticut appears to have inaugurated
Sheemie's seizures," Ted said in a low voice. "You know that
sending you back America-side is apt to make him worse, don't
you? Or kill him?" He spoke in a matter-of-fact tone. *Just askin,
gents.*

"We know," Roland said, "and when the time comes, I'll
make the risk clear and ask him if—"

"Oh man, you can stick *that* one where the sun don't shine,"
Dinky said, and Eddie was reminded so strongly of himself—the
way he'd been during his first few hours on the shore of the
Western Sea, confused, pissed off, and jonesing for heroin—that
he felt a moment of *déjà vu.* "If you told him you wanted him to
set himself on fire, the only thing he'd want to know would be if
you had a match. He thinks you're Christ on a cracker."

Susannah waited, with a mixture of dread and almost prurient interest, for Roland's response. There was none. Roland
only stared at Dinky, his thumbs hooked into his gunbelt.

"Surely you realize that a dead man can't bring you back
from America-side," Ted said in a more reasonable tone.

"We'll jump that fence when and if we come to it," Roland
said. "In the meantime, we've got several other fences to get
over."

"I'm glad we're taking on the Devar-Toi first, whatever the risk," Susannah said. "What's going on down there is an abomination."

"Yes, ma'am," Dinky drawled, and pushed up an imaginary hat. "Ah reckon that's the word."

The tension in the cave eased. Behind them, Sheemie was telling Oy to roll over, and Oy was doing so willingly enough. The Rod had a big, sloppy smile on his face. Susannah wondered when Haylis of Chayven had last had occasion to use his smile, which was childishly charming.

She thought of asking Ted if there was any way of telling what day it was in America right now, then decided not to bother. If Stephen King was dead, they'd know; Roland had said so, and she had no doubt he was right. For now the writer was fine, happily frittering away his time and valuable imagination on some meaningless project while the world he'd been born to imagine continued to gather dust in his head. If Roland was pissed at him, it was really no wonder. She was a little pissed at him herself.

"What's your plan, Roland?" Ted asked.

"It relies on two assumptions: that we can surprise them and then stampede them. I don't think they expect to be interrupted in these last days; from Pimli Prentiss down to the lowliest hume guard outside the fence, they have no reason to believe they'll be bothered in their work, certainly not attacked. If my assumptions are correct, we'll succeed. If we fail, at least we won't live long enough to see the Beams break and the Tower fall."

Roland found the crude map of the Algul and put it on the floor of the cave. They all gathered around it.

"These railroad sidetracks," he said, indicating the hashmarks labeled 10. "Some of the dead engines and traincars on them stand within twenty yards of the south fence, it looks like through the binoculars. Is that right?"

"Yeah," Dinky said, and pointed to the center of the nearest line. "Might as well call it south, anyway—it's as good a word as any. There's a boxcar on this track that's real close to the fence. Only ten yards or so. It says SOO LINE on the side."

Ted was nodding.

"Good cover," Roland said. "Excellent cover." Now he pointed to the area beyond the north end of the compound. "And here, all sorts of sheds."

"There used to be supplies in them," Ted said, "but now most are empty, I think. For awhile a gang of Rods slept there, but six or eight months ago, Pimli and the Wease kicked them out."

"But more cover, empty or full," Roland said. "Is the ground behind and around them clear of obstacles and pretty much smooth? Smooth enough for that thing to go back and forth?" He cocked a thumb at Suzie's Cruisin Trike.

Ted and Dinky exchanged a glance. "Definitely," Ted said.

Susannah waited to see if Eddie would protest, even before he knew what Roland had in mind. He didn't. Good. She was already thinking about what weapons she'd want. What guns.

Roland sat quiet for a moment or two, gazing at the map, almost seeming to commune with it. When Ted offered him a cigarette, the gunslinger took it. Then he began to talk. Twice he drew on the side of a weapons crate with a piece of chalk. Twice more he drew arrows on the map, one pointing to what they were calling north, one to the south. Ted asked a question; Dinky asked another. Behind them, Sheemie and Haylis played with Oy like a couple of children. The bumbler mimicked their laughter with eerie accuracy.

When Roland had finished, Ted Brautigan said: "You mean to spill an almighty lot of blood."

"Indeed I do. As much as I can."

"Risky for the lady," Dink remarked, looking first at her and then at her husband.

Susannah said nothing. Neither did Eddie. He recognized the risk. He also understood why Roland would want Suze north of the compound. The Cruisin Trike would give her mobility, and they'd need it. As for risk, they were six planning to take on sixty. Or more. Of course there would be risk, and of course there would be blood.

Blood and fire.

"I may be able to rig a couple of other guns," Susannah said. Her eyes had taken on that special Detta Walker gleam. "Radio-controlled, like a toy airplane. I dunno. But I'll move, all right. I'm goan speed around like grease on a hot griddle."

"Can this work?" Dinky asked bluntly.

Roland's lips parted in a humorless grin. "It *will* work."

"How can you say that?" Ted asked.

Eddie recalled Roland's reasoning before their call to John Cullum and could have answered that question, but answers were for their ka-tet's dinh to give—if he would—and so he left this one to Roland.

"Because it has to," the gunslinger said. "I see no other way."

CHAPTER XI:

THE ATTACK ON ALGUL SIENTO

ONE

It was a day later and not long before the horn signaled the morning change of shift. The music would soon start, the sun would come on, and the Breaker night-crew would exit The Study stage left while the Breaker day-crew entered stage right. Everything was as it should be, yet Pimli Prentiss had slept less than an hour the previous night and even that brief time had been haunted by sour and chaotic dreams. Finally, around four (what his bedside clock in fact *claimed* was four, but who knew anymore, and what did it matter anyway, this close to the end), he'd gotten up and sat in his office chair, looking out at the darkened Mall, deserted at this hour save for one lone and pointless robot who'd taken it into its head to patrol, waving its six pincer-tipped arms aimlessly at the sky. The robots that still ran grew wonkier by the day, but pulling their batteries could be dangerous, for some were booby-trapped and would explode it you tried it. There was nothing you could do but put up with their antics and keep reminding yourself that all would be over soon, praise Jesus and God the Father Almighty. At some point the former Paul Prentiss opened the desk drawer above the kneehole, pulled out the .40 Peacemaker Colt inside, and held it in his lap. It was the one with which the previous Master, Humma, had executed the rapist Cameron. Pimli hadn't had to execute anyone in his time and was glad of it, but holding the pistol in his lap, feeling its grave weight, always offered a certain comfort. Although why he should require comfort in the watches of the night, especially when everything was going so well, he had no idea. All he knew for sure was that there had been some anomalous blips on what Finli and Jenkins, their chief technician,

343

liked to call the Deep Telemetry, as if these were instruments at the bottom of the ocean instead of just in a basement closet adjacent to the long, low room holding the rest of the more useful gear. Pimli recognized what he was feeling—call a spade a spade—as a sense of impending doom. He tried to tell himself it was only his grandfather's proverb in action, that he was almost home and so it was time to worry about the eggs.

Finally he'd gone into his bathroom, where he closed the lid of the toilet and knelt to pray. And here he was still, only something had changed in the atmosphere. He'd heard no footfall but knew someone had stepped into his office. Logic suggested who it must be. Still without opening his eyes, still with his hands clasped on the closed cover of the toilet, he called: "Finli? Finli o' Tego? Is that you?"

"Yar, boss, it's me."

What was *he* doing here before the horn? Everyone, even the Breakers, knew what a fiend for sleep was Finli the Weasel. But all in good time. At this moment Pimli was entertaining the Lord (although in truth he'd nearly dozed off on his knees when some deep sub-instinct had warned him he was no longer alone on the first floor of Warden's House). One did not snub such an important guest as the Lord God of Hosts, and so he finished his prayer—"Grant me the grace of Thy will, amen!"—before rising with a wince. His damned back didn't care a bit for the belly it had to hoist in front.

Finli was standing by the window, holding the Peacemaker up to the dim light, turning it to and fro in order to admire the delicate scrollwork on the butt-plates.

"This is the one that said goodnight to Cameron, true?" Finli asked. "The rapist Cameron."

Pimli nodded. "Have a care, my son. It's loaded."

"Six-shot?"

"Eight! Are you blind? Look at the size of the cylinder, for God's love."

Finli didn't bother. He handed the gun back to Pimli, instead. "I know how to pull the trigger, so I do, and when it comes to guns that's enough."

"Aye, if it's loaded. What are you doing up at this hour, and bothering a man at his morning prayers?"

Finli eyed him. "If I were to ask you why I find you *at* your prayers, dressed and combed instead of in your bathrobe and slippers with only one eye open, what answer would you make?"

"I've got the jitters. It's as simple as that. I guess you do, too."

Finli smiled, charmed. "Jitters! Is that like heebie-jeebies, and harum-scarum, and hinky-di-di?"

"Sort of—yar."

Finli's smile widened, but Pimli thought it didn't look quite genuine. "I like it! I like it very well! Jittery! Jittersome!"

"No," Pimli said. "'Got the jitters,' that's how you use it."

Finli's smile faded. "I also have the jitters. I'm heebie and jeebie. I feel hinky-di-di. I'm harum and you're scarum."

"More blips on the Deep Telemetry?"

Finli shrugged, then nodded. The problem with the Deep Telemetry was that none of them were sure exactly what it measured. It might be telepathy, or (God forbid) teleportation, or even deep tremors in the fabric of reality—precursors of the Bear Beam's impending snap. Impossible to tell. But more and more of that previously dark and quiet equipment had come alive in the last four months or so.

"What does Jenkins say?" Pimli asked. He slipped the .40 into his docker's clutch almost without thinking, so moving us a step closer to what you will not want to hear and I will not want to tell.

"Jenkins says whatever rides out of his mouth on the flying carpet of his tongue," said the Tego with a rude shrug. "Since he don't even know what the symbols on the Deep Telemetry dials and vid screens signify, how can you ask his opinion?"

"Easy," Pimli said, putting a hand on his Security Chief's shoulder. He was surprised (and a little alarmed) to feel the flesh beneath Finli's fine Turnbull & Asser shirt thrumming slightly. Or perhaps trembling. "Easy, pal! I was only asking."

"I can't sleep, I can't read, I can't even fuck," Finli said. "I tried all three, by Gan! Walk down to Damli House with me, would you, and have a look at the damned readouts. Maybe you'll have some ideas."

"I'm a trailboss, not a technician," Pimli said mildly, but he was already moving toward the door. "However, since I've nothing better to do—"

"Maybe it's just the end coming on," Finli said, pausing in the doorway. "As if there could be any *just* about such a thing."

"Maybe that's it," Pimli said equably, "and a walk in the morning air can't do us any ha—Hey! Hey, you! You, there! You Rod! Turn around when I talk to you, hadn't you just better!"

The Rod, a scrawny fellow in an ancient pair of denim biballs (the deeply sagging seat had gone completely white), obeyed. His cheeks were chubby and freckled, his eyes an engaging shade of blue even though at the moment alarmed. He actually wouldn't have been bad-looking except for his nose, which had been eaten away almost completely on one side, giving him a bizarre one-nostril look. He was toting a basket. Pimli was pretty sure he'd seen this shufflefoot bah-bo around the ranch before, but couldn't be sure; to him, all Rods looked alike.

It didn't matter. Identification was Finli's job and he took charge now, pulling a rubber glove out of his belt and putting it on as he strode forward. The Rod cringed back against the wall, clasping his wicker basket tighter and letting go a loud fart that had to have been pure nerves. Pimli needed to bite down on the inside of his cheek, and quite fiercely, to keep a smile from rising on his lips.

"Nay, nay, *nay!*" the Security Chief cried, and slapped the Rod briskly across the face with his newly gloved hand. (It did not do to touch the Children of Roderick skin to skin; they carried too many diseases.) Loose spit flew from the Rod's mouth and blood from the hole in his nose. "Speak not with your ki'box to me, sai Haylis! The hole in thy head's not much better, but at least it can give me a word of respect. It had better be able to!"

"Hile, Finli o' Tego!" Haylis muttered, and fisted himself in the forehead so hard the back of his head bounced off the wall—*bonk!* That did it: Pimli barked a laugh in spite of himself. Nor would Finli be able to reproach him with it on their walk to Damli House, for he was smiling now, too. Although Pimli doubted that the Rod named Haylis would find much to comfort him in that smile. It exposed too many sharp teeth. "Hile, Finli o' the Watch, long days and pleasant nights to'ee, sai!"

"Better," Finli allowed. "Not much, but a little. What in hell's name are you doing here before Horn and Sun? And tell me what's in thy bascomb, wiggins?"

Haylis hugged it tighter against his chest, his eyes flashing with alarm. Finli's smile disappeared at once.

"You flip the lid and show me what's in thy bascomb this second, cully, or thee'll be picking thy teeth off the carpet." These words came out in a smooth, low growl.

For a moment Pimli thought the Rod still would not comply, and he felt a twinge of active alarm. Then, slowly, the fellow lifted the lid of the wicker basket. It was the sort with handles, known in Finli's home territory as a bascomb. The Rod held it reluctantly out. At the same time he closed his sore-looking, booger-rimmed eyes and turned his head aside, as if in anticipation of a blow.

Finli looked. For a long time he said nothing, then gave his own bark of laughter and invited Pimli to have a peek. The Master knew what he was seeing at once, but figuring out what it meant took a moment longer. Then his mind flashed back to popping the pimple and offering Finli the bloody pus, as one would offer a friend left-over *hors d'oeuvre* at the end of a dinner-party. In the bottom of the Rod's basket was a little pile of used tissues. Kleenex, in fact.

"Did Tammy Kelly send you to pick up the swill this morning?" Pimli asked.

The Rod nodded fearfully.

"Did she tell you that you could have whatever you found and fancied from the wastecans?"

He thought the Rod would lie. If and when he did, the Master would command Finli to beat the fellow, as an object-lesson in honesty.

But the Rod—Haylis—shook his head, looking sad.

"All right," Pimli said, relieved. It was really too early in the day for beatings and howlings and tears. They spoiled a man's breakfast. "You can go, and with your prize. But next time, cully, ask permission or you'll leave here a-hurt. Do'ee ken?"

The Rod nodded energetically.

"Go on, then, go! Out of my house and out of my sight!"

They watched him leave, him with his basket of snotty tissues that he'd undoubtedly eat like candy nougat, each shaming the other into keeping his face grave and stern until the poor disfigured son of no one was gone. Then they burst into gales of laughter. Finli o' Tego staggered back against the wall hard enough to knock a picture off its hook, then slid to the floor, howling hysterically. Pimli put his face in his hands and laughed until his considerable gut ached. The laughter erased the tension with which each had begun the day, venting it all at once.

"A dangerous fellow, indeed!" Finli said when he could speak a little again. He was wiping his streaming eyes with one furry paw-hand.

"The Snot Saboteur!" Pimli agreed. His face was bright red.

They exchanged a look and were off again, braying gales of relieved laughter until they woke the housekeeper way up on the third floor. Tammy Kelly lay in her narrow bed, listening to yon ka-mais bellow below, looking disapprovingly up into the gloom. Men were much the same, in her view, no matter what sort of skin they wore.

Outside, the hume Master and the taheen Security Chief walked up the Mall, arm in arm. The Child of Roderick, meanwhile, scurried out through the north gate, head down, heart thumping madly in his chest. How close it had been! Aye! If Weasel-Head had asked him, 'Haylis, didjer plant anything?' he would have lied as best he could, but such as him couldn't lie successfully to such as Finli o' Tego; never in life! He would have been found out, sure. But he *hadn't* been found out, praise Gan. The ball-thing the gunslinger had given him was now stowed away in the back bedroom, humming softly to itself. He'd put it in the wastebasket, as he had been told, and covered it with fresh tissue from the box on the washstand, also as he had been told. Nobody had told him he might take the cast-away tissues, but he hadn't been able to resist their soupy, delicious smell. And it had worked for the best, hadn't it? Yar! For instead of asking him all manner of questions he couldn't have answered, they'd laughed at him and let him go. He wished he could climb the mountain and play with the bumbler again, so he did, but the white-haired old hume named Ted had told him to go away, far and far, once his errand was done. And if he heard shooting, Haylis was to hide until it was over. And he would—oh yes, nair doot. Hadn't he done what Roland o' Gilead had asked of him? The first of the humming balls was now in Feveral, one of the dorms, two more were in Damli House, where the Breakers worked and the off-duty guards slept, and the last was in Master's House . . . where he'd almost been caught! Haylis didn't know what the humming balls did, nor wanted to know. He would go away, possibly with his friend, Garma, if he could find her. If shooting started, they would hide in a deep hole, and he would share his tissues with her. Some had nothing on them but bits of shaving soap, but there were wet snots and big boogies in some of the others, he could smell their enticing aroma even now. He would save the biggest of the latter, the one with the jellied blood in it, for Garma, and she might let him pokey-poke. Haylis walked faster, smiling at the prospect of going pokey-poke with Garma.

TWO

Sitting on the Cruisin Trike in the concealment afforded by one of the empty sheds north of the compound, Susannah watched Haylis go. She noted that the poor, disfigured sai was smiling about something, so things had probably gone well with him. That was good news, indeed. Once he was out of sight, she returned her attention to her end of Algul Siento.

She could see both stone towers (although only the top half of the one on her left; the rest was concealed by a fold of hillside). They were shackled about with some sort of ivy. Cultivated rather than wild, Susannah guessed, given the barrenness of the surrounding countryside. There was one fellow in the west tower, sitting in what appeared to be an easy chair, maybe even a La-Z-Boy. Standing at the railing of the east one were a taheen with a beaver's head and a low man (if he was a hume, Susannah thought, he was one butt-ugly son of a bitch), the two of them in conversation, pretty clearly waiting for the horn that would send them off-shift and to breakfast in the commissary. Between the two watchtowers she could see the triple line of fencing, the runs strung widely enough apart so that more sentries could walk in the aisles between the wire without fear of getting a lethal zap of electricity. She saw no one there this morning, though. The few *folken* moving about inside the wire were idling along, none of them in a great hurry to get anywhere. Unless the lackadaisical scene before her was the biggest con of the century, Roland was right. They were as vulnerable as a herd of fat shoats being fed their last meal outside the slaughtering-pen: come-come-commala, shor'-ribs to folla. And while the gunslingers had had no luck finding any sort of radio-controlled weaponry, they *had* discovered that three of the more science-fictiony rifles were equipped with switches marked INTERVAL. Eddie said he thought these rifles were *lazers*, although nothing about them looked lazy to Susannah. Jake had suggested they take one of them out of sight of the Devar-Toi and try it out, but Roland vetoed the idea immediately. Last evening, this had been, while going over the plan for what seemed like the hundredth time.

"He's right, kid," Eddie had said. "The clowns down there might know we were shooting those things even if they couldn't see or hear anything. We don't know what kind of vibes their telemetry can pick up."

Under cover of dark, Susannah had set up all three of the "lazers." When the time came, she'd set the interval switches. The guns might work, thus adding to the impression they were trying to create; they might not. She'd give it a try when the time came, and that was all she could do.

Heart thumping heavily, Susannah waited for the music.

For the horn. And, if the sneetches the Rod had set worked the way Roland *believed* they would work, for the fires.

"The ideal would be for all of them to go hot during the five or ten minutes when they're changing the guard," Roland had said. "Everyone scurrying hither and thither, waving to their friends and exchanging little bits o' gossip. We can't expect that—not really—but we can hope for it."

Yes, they could do that much . . . but wish in one hand, shit in the other, see which one fills up first. In any case, it would be her decision as to when to fire the first shot. After that, everything would happen jin-jin.

Please, God, help me pick the right time.

She waited, holding one of the Coyote machine-pistols with the barrel in the hollow of her shoulder. When the music started—a recorded version of what she thought might be "'At's Amore"—Susannah lurched on the seat of the SCT and squeezed the trigger involuntarily. Had the safety not been on, she would have poured a stream of bullets into the shed's ceiling and no doubt queered the pitch at once. But Roland had taught her well, and the trigger didn't move beneath her finger. Still, her heartbeat had doubled—trebled, maybe—and she could feel sweat trickling down her sides, even though the day was once again cool.

The music had started and that was good. But the music wasn't enough. She sat on the SCT's saddle, waiting for the horn.

THREE

"Dino Martino," Eddie said, almost too low to hear.

"Hmmm?" Jake asked.

The three of them were behind the SOO LINE boxcar, having worked their way through the graveyard of old engines and traincars to that spot. Both of the boxcar's loading doors were open, and all three of them had had a peek through them at the fence, the south watchtowers, and the village of Pleasantville, which consisted of but a single street. The six-armed robot which had earlier been on the Mall was now here, rolling up and down Main Street past the quaint (and closed) shops, bellowing what sounded like math equations at the top of its . . . lungs?

"Dino Martino," Eddie repeated. Oy was sitting at Jake's feet, looking up with his brilliant gold-ringed eyes; Eddie bent and gave his head a brief pat. "Dean Martin did that song originally."

"Yeah?" Jake asked doubtfully.

"Sure. Only we used to sing it, 'When-a da moon hits-a yo' lip like a big piece-a shit, 'at's amore—'"

"Hush, do ya please," Roland murmured.

"Don't suppose you smell any smoke yet, do you?" Eddie asked.

Jake and Roland shook their heads. Roland had his big iron with the sandalwood grips. Jake was armed with an AR-15, but the bag of Orizas was once more hung over his shoulder, and not just for good luck. If all went well, he and Roland would be using them soon.

FOUR

Like most men with what's known as "house-help," Pimli Prentiss had no clear sense of his employees as creatures with goals, ambitions, and feelings—as humes, in other words. As long as there was someone to bring him his afternoon glass of whiskey and set his chop (rare) in front of him at six-thirty, he didn't think of them at all. Certainly he would have been quite astounded to learn that Tammy (his housekeeper) and Tassa (his houseboy) loathed each other. They treated each other with perfect—if chilly—respect when they were around him, after all.

Only Pimli wasn't around this morning as "'At's Amore" (interpreted by the Billion Bland Strings) rose from Algul Siento's hidden speakers. The Master was walking up the Mall, now in the company of Jakli, a ravenhead taheen tech, as well as his Security Chief. They were discussing the Deep Telemetry, and Pimli had no thought at all for the house he had left behind for the last time. Certainly it never crossed his mind that Tammy Kelly (still in her nightgown) and Tassa of Sonesh (still in his silk sleep-shorts) were on the verge of battle about the pantry-stock.

"Look at this!" she cried. They were standing in the kitchen, which was deeply gloomy. It was a large room, and all but three of the electric lights were burned out. There were only a few bulbs left in Stores, and they were earmarked for The Study.

"Look at what?" Sulky. *Pouty.* And was that the remains of lip paint on his cunning little Cupid's-bow of a mouth? She thought it was.

"Do'ee not see the empty spots on the shelves?" she asked indignantly. "Look! No more baked beans—"

"He don't care beans for beans, as you very well know—"

"No tuna-fish, either, and will'ee tell me he don't eat *that?* He'd eat it until it ran out his ears, and thee knows it!"

"Can you not—"

"No more soup—"

"Balls there ain't!" he cried. "Look there, and there, and *th*—"

"Not the Campbell's Tamater he likes best," she overrode him, drawing closer in her excitement. Their arguments had never developed into outright fisticuffs before, but Tassa had an idea this might be the day. And if it were so, it were fine-oh! He'd love to sock this fat old run-off-at-the-mouth bitch in the eye. "Do you see any Campbell's Tamater, Tassa o' wherever-you-grew?"

"Can you not bring back a box of tins yourself?" he asked, taking his own step forward; now they were nearly nose-to-nose, and although the woman was large and the young man was willowy, the Master's houseboy showed no sign of fear. Tammy blinked, and for the first time since Tassa had shuffled into the kitchen—wanting no more than a cup of coffee, say thanks—an expression that was not irritation crossed her face. It might have been nervousness; it might even have been fear. "Are you so weak in the arms, Tammy of wherever-*you*-grew, that you can't carry a box of soup-tins out of Stores?"

She drew herself up to her full height, stung. Her jowls (greasy and a-glow with some sort of night-cream) quivered with self-righteousness. "Fetching pantry supplies has ever been the houseboy's job! And thee knows it very well!"

"That don't make it a law that you can't help out. I was mowing his lawn yest'y, as surely you know; I spied you sitting a-kitchen with a glass of cold tea, didn't I, just as comfortable as old Ellie in your favorite chair."

She bristled, losing any fear she might have had in her outrage. "I have as much right to rest as anyone else! I'd just warshed the floor—"

"Looked to me like Dobbie was doing it," he said. Dobbie was the sort of domestic robot known as a "house-elf," old but still quite efficient.

Tammy grew hotter still. "What would you know about house chores, you mincy little queer?"

Color flushed Tassa's normally pale cheeks. He was aware that his hands had rolled themselves into fists, but only because he could feel his carefully cared-for nails biting into his palms. It occurred to him that this sort of petty bitch-and-whistle was downright ludicrous, coming as it did with the end of everything stretching black just beyond them; they were two fools sparring and catcalling on the very lip of the abyss, but he didn't care. Fat old sow had been sniping at him for years, and now here was the real reason. Here it was, finally naked and out in the open.

"Is that what bothers thee about me, sai?" he enquired sweetly. "That I kiss the pole instead of plug the hole, no more than that?"

Now there were torches instead of roses flaring in Tammy Kelly's cheeks. She'd not meant to go so far, but now that she had—that *they* had, for if there was to be a fight, it was his fault as much as hers—she wouldn't back away. Was damned if she would.

"Master's Bible says queerin be a sin," she told him righteously. "I've read it myself, so I have. Book of Leviticracks, Chapter Three, Verse—"

"And what do Leviticracks say about the sin of gluttony?" he enquired. "What do it say about a woman with tits as big as bolsters and an ass as big as a kitchen ta—"

"Never mind the size o' my ass, you little *cocksucker!*"

"At least I can *get* a man," he said sweetly, "and don't have to lie abed with a dustclout—"

"Don't you dare!" she cried shrilly. "Shut your foul mouth before I shut it for you!"

"—to get rid of the cobwebs in my cunny so I can—"

"I'll knock thy teeth out if thee doesn't—"

"—finger my tired old pokeberry pie." Then something which would offend her even more deeply occurred to him. "My tired, *dirty* old pokeberry pie!"

She balled her own fists, which were considerably bigger than his. "At least I've never—"

"Go no further, sai, I beg you."

"—never had some man's nasty old . . . nasty . . . old . . ."

She trailed off, looking puzzled, and sniffed the air. He sniffed it himself, and realized the aroma he was getting wasn't new. He'd been smelling it almost since the argument started, but now it was stronger.

Tammy said, "Do you smell—"

"—smoke!" he finished, and they looked at each other with alarm, their argument forgotten perhaps only five seconds before it would have come to blows. Tammy's eyes fixed on the sampler hung beside the stove. There were similar ones all over Algul Siento, because most of the buildings which made up the compound were wood. *Old* wood. WE ALL MUST WORK TOGETHER TO CREATE A FIRE-FREE ENVIRONMENT, it said.

Somewhere close by—in the back hallway—one of the still-working smoke detectors went off with a loud and frightening bray. Tammy hurried into the pantry to grab the fire-extinguisher in there.

"Get the one in the library!" she shouted, and Tassa ran to do it without a word of protest. Fire was the one thing they all feared.

FIVE

Gaskie o' Tego, the Deputy Security Chief, was standing in the foyer of Feveral Hall, the dormitory directly behind Damli House, talking with James Cagney. Cagney was a redhaired can-toi who favored Western-style shirts and boots that added three inches to his actual five-foot-five. Both had clipboards and were discussing certain necessary changes in the following week's Damli security. Six of the guards who'd been assigned to the second shift had come down with what Gangli, the compound doctor, said was a hume disease called "momps." Sickness was common enough in Thunderclap—it was the air, as everyone knew, and the poisoned leavings of the old people—but it was ever inconvenient. Gangli said they were lucky there had never been an actual plague, like the Black Death or the Hot Shivers.

Beyond them, on the paved court behind Damli House, an early-morning basketball game was going on, several taheen and can-toi guards (who would be officially on duty as soon as the horn blew) against a ragtag team of Breakers. Gaskie watched Joey Rastosovich take a shot from way downtown—*swish.* Trampas snared the ball and took it out of bounds, briefly lifting his cap to scratch beneath it. Gaskie didn't care much for Trampas, who had an entirely inappropriate liking for the talented animals who were his charges. Closer by, sitting on the dorm's steps and also watching the game, was Ted Brautigan. As always, he was sipping at a can of Nozz-A-La.

"Well fuggit," James Cagney said, speaking in the tones of a man who wants to be finished with a boring discussion. "If you don't mind taking a couple of humies off the fence-walk for a day or two—"

"What's Brautigan doing up so early?" Gaskie interrupted. "He almost never rolls out until noon. That kid he pals around with is the same way. What's his name?"

"Earnshaw?" Brautigan also palled around with that half-bright Ruiz, but Ruiz was no kid.

Gaskie nodded. "Aye, Earnshaw, that's the one. He's on duty this morning. I saw him earlier in The Study."

Cag (as his friends called him) didn't give a shit why Brautigan was up with the birdies (not that there were many birdies left, at least in Thunderclap); he only wanted to get this roster business settled so he could stroll across to Damli and get a plate of scrambled eggs. One of the Rods had found fresh chives somewhere, or so he'd heard, and—

"Do'ee smell something, Cag?" Gaskie o' Tego asked suddenly.

The can-toi who fancied himself James Cagney started to enquire if Gaskie had farted, then rethought this humorous riposte. For in fact he did smell something. Was it smoke?

Cag thought it was.

SIX

Ted sat on the cold steps of Feveral Hall, breathing the bad-smelling air and listening to the humes and the taheen trash-talk each other from the basketball court. (Not the can-toi; they refused to indulge in such vulgarity.) His heart was beating hard but not fast. If there was a Rubicon that needed crossing, he realized, he'd crossed it some time ago. Maybe on the night the low men had hauled him back from Connecticut, more likely on the day he'd approached Dinky with the idea of reaching out to the gunslingers that Sheemie Ruiz insisted were nearby. Now he was wound up (to the max, Dinky would have said), but nervous? No. Nerves, he thought, were for people who still hadn't entirely made up their minds.

Behind him he heard one idiot (Gaskie) asking t'other idiot (Cagney) if he smelled something, and Ted knew for sure that Haylis had done his part; the game was afoot. Ted reached into his pocket and brought out a scrap of paper. Written on it was a line of perfect pentameter, although hardly Shakespearian: *GO SOUTH WITH YOUR HANDS UP, YOU WON'T BE HURT.*

He looked at this fixedly, preparing to broadcast.

Behind him, in the Feveral rec room, a smoke detector went off with a loud donkey-bray.

Here we go, here we go, he thought, and looked north, to where he hoped the first shooter—the woman—was hiding.

SEVEN

Three-quarters of the way up the Mall toward Damli House, Master Prentiss stopped with Finli on one side of him and Jakli on the other. The horn still hadn't gone off, but there was a loud braying sound from behind them. They had no more begun to turn toward it when another bray began from the other end of the compound—the dormitory end.

"What the devil—" Pimli began.

—is that was how he meant to finish, but before he could, Tammy Kelly came rushing out through the front door of Warden's House, with Tassa, his houseboy, scampering along right behind her. Both of them were waving their arms over their heads.

"*Fire!*" Tammy shouted. "*Fire!*"

Fire? But that's impossible, Pimli thought. *For if that's the smoke detector I'm hearing in my house and* also *the smoke detector I'm hearing from one of the dorms, then surely—*

"It must be a false alarm," he told Finli. "Those smoke detectors do that when their batteries are—"

Before he could finish this hopeful assessment, a side window of Warden's House exploded outward. The glass was followed by an exhalation of orange flame.

"Gods!" Jakli cried in his buzzing voice. "It *is* fire!"

Pimli stared with his mouth open. And suddenly yet *another* smoke-and-fire alarm went off, this one in a series of loud, hiccuping whoops. Good God, sweet Jesus, that was one of the *Damli House* alarms! Surely nothing could be wrong at—

Finli o' Tego grabbed his arm. "Boss," he said, calmly enough. "We've got real trouble."

Before Pimli could reply, the horn went off, signaling the change of shifts. And suddenly he realized how vulnerable they would be for the next seven minutes or so. Vulnerable to all sorts of things.

He refused to admit the word *attack* into his consciousness. At least not yet.

EIGHT

Dinky Earnshaw had been sitting in the overstuffed easy chair for what seemed like forever, waiting impatiently for the party to begin. Usually being in The Study cheered him up—hell, cheered *everybody* up, it was the "good-mind" effect—but today he only felt the wires of tension inside him winding tighter and tighter, pulling his guts into a ball. He was aware of taheen and can-toi looking down from the balconies every now and again, riding the good-mind wave, but didn't have to worry about being progged by the likes of them; from that, at least, he was safe.

Was that a smoke alarm? From Feveral, perhaps?

Maybe. But maybe not, too. No one else was looking around.

Wait, he told himself. *Ted told you this would be the hard part, didn't he? And at least Sheemie's out of the way. Sheemie's safe in his room, and Corbett Hall's safe from fire. So calm down. Relax.*

That *was* the bray of a smoke alarm. Dinky was sure of it. Well . . . *almost* sure.

A book of crossword puzzles was open in his lap. For the last fifty minutes he'd been filling one of the grids with nonsense-letters, ignoring the definitions completely. Now, across the top, he printed this in large dark block letters: **GO SOUTH WITH YOUR HANDS UP, YOU WON'T BE HU**

That was when one of the upstairs fire alarms, probably the one in the west wing, went off with a loud, warbling bray. Several of the Breakers, jerked rudely from a deep daze of concentration, cried out in surprised alarm. Dinky also cried out, but in relief. Relief and something more. Joy? Yeah, very likely it *was* joy. Because when the fire alarm began to bray, he'd felt the powerful hum of good-mind snap. The eerie combined force of the Breakers had winked out like an overloaded electrical circuit. For the moment, at least, the assault on the Beam had stopped.

Meanwhile, he had a job to do. No more waiting. He stood up, letting the crossword magazine tumble to the Turkish rug, and threw his mind at the Breakers in the room. It wasn't hard; he'd been practicing almost daily for this moment, with Ted's help. And if it worked? If the Breakers picked it up, rebroadcasting it and amping what Dinky could only suggest to the level of a command? Why then it would rise. It would become the dominant chord in a new good-mind gestalt.

At least that was the hope.

(IT'S A FIRE FOLKS THERE'S A FIRE IN THE BUILDING)

As if to underscore this, there was a soft bang-and-tinkle as something imploded and the first puff of smoke seeped from the ventilator panels. Breakers looked around with wide, dazed eyes, some getting to their feet.

And Dinky sent:

(DON'T WORRY DON'T PANIC ALL IS WELL WALK UP THE)

He sent a perfect, practiced image of the north stairway, then added Breakers. Breakers walking up the north stairway. Breakers walking through the kitchen. Crackle of fire, smell of smoke, but both coming from the guards' sleeping area in the west wing. And would anyone question the truth of this mental broadcast? Would anyone wonder who was beaming it out, or why? Not now. Now they were only scared. Now they were *wanting* someone to tell them what to do, and Dinky Earnshaw was that someone.

(NORTH STAIRWAY WALK UP THE NORTH STAIRWAY WALK OUT ONTO THE BACK LAWN)

And it worked. They began to walk that way. Like sheep following a ram or horses following a stallion. Some were picking up the two basic ideas

(NO PANIC NO PANIC)

(NORTH STAIRWAY NORTH STAIRWAY)

and rebroadcasting them. And, even better, Dinky heard it

from above, too. From the can-toi and the taheen who had
been observing from the balconies.

No one ran and no one panicked, but the exodus up the
north stairs had begun.

NINE

Susannah sat astride the SCT in the window of the shed where
she'd been concealed, not worrying about being seen now.
Smoke detectors—at least three of them—were yowling. A
fire alarm was whooping even more loudly; that one was from
Damli House, she was quite sure. As if in answer, a series of loud
electronic goose-honks began from the Pleasantville end of
the compound. This was joined by a multitude of clanging
bells.

With all that happening to their south, it was no wonder
that the woman north of the Devar-Toi saw only the backs of
the three guards in the ivy-covered watchtowers. Three didn't
seem like many, but it was five per cent of the total. A start.

Susannah looked down the barrel of her gun at the one in
her sights and prayed. *God grant me true aim . . . true aim . . .*

Soon.

It would be soon.

TEN

Finli grabbed the Master's arm. Pimli shook him off and started
toward his house again, staring unbelievingly at the smoke
that was now pouring out of all the windows on the left side.

"Boss!" Finli shouted, renewing his grip. "Boss, never mind
that! It's the Breakers we have to worry about! The *Breakers!*"

It didn't get through, but the shocking warble of the Damli
House fire alarm did. Pimli turned back in that direction, and
for a moment he met Jakli's beady little bird's eyes. He saw nothing in them but panic, which had the perverse but welcome
effect of steadying Pimli himself. Sirens and buzzers every-

where. One of them was a regular pulsing honk he'd never heard before. Coming from the direction of Pleasantville?

"Come on, boss!" Finli o' Tego almost pleaded. "We have to make sure the Breakers are okay—"

"Smoke!" Jakli cried, fluttering his dark (and utterly useless) wings. "Smoke from Damli House, smoke from Feveral, too!"

Pimli ignored him. He pulled the Peacemaker from the docker's clutch, wondering briefly what premonition had caused him to put it on. He had no idea, but he was glad for the weight of the gun in his hand. Behind him, Tassa was yelling— Tammy was, too—but Pimli ignored the pair of them. His heart was beating furiously, but he was calm again. Finli was right. The Breakers were the important thing right now. Making sure they didn't lose a third of their trained psychics in some sort of electrical fire or half-assed act of sabotage. He nodded at his Security Chief and they began to run toward Damli House with Jakli squawking and flapping along behind them like a refugee from a Warner Bros. cartoon. Somewhere up there, Gaskie was hollering. And then Pimli o' New Jersey heard a sound that chilled him to the bone, a rapid *chow-chow-chow* sound. Gunfire! If some clown was shooting at his Breakers, that clown's head would finish the day on a high pole, by the gods. That the guards rather than the Breakers might be under attack had at that point still not crossed his mind, nor that of the slightly wilier Finli, either. Too much was happening too fast.

ELEVEN

At the south end of the Devar compound, the syncopated honking sound was almost loud enough to split eardrums. "Christ!" Eddie said, and couldn't hear himself.

In the south watchtowers, the guards were turned away from them, looking north. Eddie couldn't see any smoke yet. Perhaps the guards could from their higher vantage-points.

Roland grabbed Jake's shoulder, then pointed at the SOO LINE boxcar. Jake nodded and scrambled beneath it with Oy at his heels. Roland held both hands out to Eddie—*Stay where you are!*—and then followed. On the other side of the boxcar the boy and the gunslinger stood up, side by side. They would have been clearly visible to the sentries, had the attention of those worthies not been distracted by the smoke detectors and fire alarms inside the compound.

Suddenly the entire front of the Pleasantville Hardware Company descended into a slot in the ground. A robot fire engine, all bright red paint and gleaming chrome, came bolting out of the hitherto concealed garage. A line of red lights pulsed down the center of its elongated body, and an amplified voice bellowed, *"STAND CLEAR! THIS IS FIRE-RESPONSE TEAM BRAVO! STAND CLEAR! MAKE WAY FOR FIRE-RESPONSE TEAM BRAVO!"*

There must be no gunfire from this part of the Devar, not yet. The south end of the compound must seem safe to the increasingly frightened inmates of Algul Siento: don't worry, folks, here's your port in today's unexpected shitstorm.

The gunslinger dipped a 'Riza from Jake's dwindling supply and nodded for the boy to take another. Roland pointed to the guard in the righthand tower, then once more at Jake. The boy nodded, cocked his arm across his chest, and waited for Roland to give him the go.

TWELVE

Once you hear the horn that signals the change of shifts, Roland had told Susannah, *take it to them. Do as much damage as you can, but don't let them see they're only facing a single person, for your father's sake!*

As if he needed to tell her that.

She could have taken the three watchtower guards while the horn was still blaring, but something made her wait. A few seconds later, she was glad she had. The rear door of the Queen Anne burst open so violently it tore off its upper hinge. Breakers piled out, clawing at those ahead of them in their panic (*these are the would-be destroyers of the universe,* she thought, *these sheep*), and among them she saw half a dozen of the freakboys with animal heads and at least four of those creepy humanoids with the masks on.

Susannah took the guard in the west tower first, and had shifted her aim to the pair in the east tower before the first casualty in the Battle of Algul Siento had fallen over the railing and tumbled to the ground with his brains dribbling out of his hair and down his cheeks. The Coyote machine-pistol, switched to the middle setting, fired in low-pitched bursts of three: *Chow! Chow! Chow!*

The taheen and the low man in the east tower spun widdershins to each other, like figures in a dance. The taheen crumpled on the catwalk that skirted the top of the watchtower; the low man was driven into the rail, flipped over it with his bootheels in the sky, then plummeted head-first to the ground. She heard the crack his neck made when it broke.

A couple of the milling Breakers spotted this unfortunate fellow's descent and screamed.

"Put up your hands!" That was Dinky, she recognized his voice. "Put up your hands if you're a Breaker!"

No one questioned the idea; in these circumstances, anyone who sounded like he knew what was going on was in unquestioned charge. Some of the Breakers—but not all, not yet—put their hands up. It made no difference to Susannah. She didn't need raised hands to tell the difference between the sheep and the goats. A kind of haunted clarity had fallen over her vision.

She flicked the fire-control switch from BURST to SINGLE SHOT and began to pick off the guards who'd come up from The Study with the Breakers. *Taheen . . . can-toi, get him . . . a hume but don't shoot her, she's a Breaker even though she doesn't have her hands up . . . don't ask me how I know but I do . . .*

Susannah squeezed the Coyote's trigger and the head of the hume next to the woman in the bright red slacks exploded in a mist of blood and bone. The Breakers screamed like children, staring around with their eyes bulging and their hands up. And now Susannah heard Dinky again, only this time not his physical voice. It was his mental voice she heard, and it was much louder:

(GO SOUTH WITH YOUR HANDS UP, YOU WON'T BE HURT)

Which was her cue to break cover and start moving. She'd gotten eight of the Crimson King's bad boys, counting the three in the towers—not that it was much of an accomplishment, given their panic—and she saw no more, at least for the time being.

Susannah twisted the hand-throttle and scooted the SCT toward one of the other abandoned sheds. The gadget's pickup was so lively that she almost tumbled off the bicycle-style seat. Trying not to laugh (and laughing anyway), she shouted at the top of her lungs, in her best Detta Walker vulture-screech:

"Git outta here, muthafuckahs! Git south! Hands up so we know you fum the bad boys! Everyone doan have their hands up goan get a bullet in the haid! Y'all trus' me on it!"

In through the door of the next shed, scraping a balloon tire of the SCT on the jamb, but not quite hard enough to tip it over. Praise God, for she never would have had enough strength to right it on her own. In here, one of the "lazers" was set on a snap-down tripod. She pushed the toggle-switch marked ON and was wondering if she needed to do something else with the INTERVAL switch when the weapon's muzzle emitted a blinding stream of reddish-purple light that arrowed into the compound above the triple run of fence and made a hole in the top story of Damli House. To Susannah it looked as big as a hole made by a point-blank artillery shell.

This is good, she thought. *I gotta get the other ones going.*

But she wondered if there would be time. Already other Breakers were picking up on Dinky's suggestion, rebroadcasting it and boosting it in the process:

(GO SOUTH! HANDS UP! WON'T BE HURT!)

She flicked the Coyote's fire-switch to FULL AUTO and raked it across the upper level of the nearest dorm to emphasize the point. Bullets whined and ricocheted. Glass broke. Breakers screamed and began to stampede around the side of Damli House with their hands up. Susannah saw Ted come around the same side. He was hard to miss, because he was going against the current. He and Dinky embraced briefly, then raised their hands and joined the southward flow of Breakers, who would soon lose their status as VIPs and become just one more bunch of refugees struggling to survive in a dark and poisoned land.

She'd gotten eight, but it wasn't enough. The hunger was upon her, that dry hunger. Her eyes saw everything. They pulsed and ached in her head, and they saw everything. She hoped that other taheen, low men, or hume guards would come around the side of Damli House.

She wanted more.

THIRTEEN

Sheemie Ruiz lived in Corbett Hall, which happened to be the dormitory Susannah, all unknowing, had raked with at least a hundred bullets. Had he been on his bed, he almost certainly would have been killed. Instead he was on his knees, at the foot of it, praying for the safety of his friends. He didn't even look up when the window blew in but simply redoubled his supplications. He could hear Dinky's thoughts

(GO SOUTH)

pounding in his head, then heard other thought-streams join it,

(WITH YOUR HANDS UP)

making a river. And then *Ted's* voice was there, not just joining the others but amping them up, turning what had been a river

(YOU WON'T BE HURT)

into an ocean. Without realizing it, Sheemie changed his prayer. *Our Father* and *P'teck my pals* became *go south with your hands up, you won't be hurt.* He didn't even stop this when the propane tanks behind the Damli House cafeteria blew up with a shattering roar.

FOURTEEN

Gangli Tristum (that's *Doctor* Gangli to you, say thankya) was in many ways the most feared man in Damli House. He was a can-toi who had—perversely—taken a taheen name instead of a human one, and he ran the infirmary on the third floor of the west wing with an iron fist. And on roller skates.

Things on the ward were fairly relaxed when Gangli was in his office doing paperwork, or off on his rounds (which usually meant visiting Breakers with the sniffles in their dorms), but when he came out, the whole place—nurses and orderlies as well as patients—fell respectfully (and nervously) silent. A newcomer might laugh the first time he saw the squat, dark-complected, heavily jowled man-thing gliding slowly down the center aisle between the beds, arms folded over the stetho-scope which lay on his chest, the tails of his white coat wafting out behind him (one Breaker had once commented, "He looks like John Irving after a bad facelift"). Such a one who was *caught* laughing would never laugh again, however. Dr. Gangli had a sharp tongue, indeed, and no one made fun of his roller skates with impunity.

Now, instead of gliding on them, he went flying up and down the aisles, the steel wheels (for his skating gear far pre-dated rollerblades) rumbling on the hardwood. "All the papers!" he shouted. "Do you hear me? . . . If I lose one file in this fucking mess, *one gods-damned file,* I'll have someone's eyes with my afternoon tea!"

The patients were already gone, of course; he'd had them out of their beds and down the stairs at the first bray of the smoke detector, at the first whiff of smoke. A number of order-lies—gutless wonders, and he knew who each of them was, oh yes, and a complete report would be made when the time came—had fled with the sickfolk, but five had stayed, including his personal assistant, Jack London. Gangli was proud of them, although one could not have told it from his hectoring voice as he skated up and down, up and down, in the thickening smoke.

"Get the papers, d'ye hear? You better, by all the gods that ever walked or crawled! *You better!*"

A red glare shot in through the window. Some sort of weapon, for it blew in the glass wall that separated his office from the ward and set his favorite easy-chair a-smolder.

Gangli ducked and skated under the laser beam, never slowing.

"Gan-a-damn!" cried one of the orderlies. He was a hume, extraordinarily ugly, his eyes bulging from his pale face. "What in the hell was th—"

"Never mind!" Gangli bawled. "Never mind what it was, you pissface clown! Get the papers! *Get my motherfucking papers!*"

From somewhere in front—the Mall?—came the hideous approaching clang-and-yowl of some rescue vehicle. "*STAND CLEAR!*" Gangli heard. "*THIS IS FIRE-RESPONSE TEAM BRAVO!*"

Gangli had never heard of such a thing as Fire-Response Team Bravo, but there was so much they didn't know about this place. Why, he could barely use a third of the equipment in his own surgical suite! Never mind, the thing that mattered right now—

Before he could finish his thought, the gas-pods behind the kitchen blew up. There was a tremendous roar—seemingly from directly beneath them—and Gangli Tristum was thrown into the air, the metal wheels on his roller skates spinning. The others were thrown as well, and suddenly the smoky air was full of flying papers. Looking at them, knowing that the papers would burn and he would be lucky not to burn with them, a clear thought came to Dr. Gangli: the end had come early.

FIFTEEN

Roland heard the telepathic command
(*GO SOUTH WITH YOUR HANDS UP, YOU WON'T BE HURT*)
begin to beat in his mind. It was time. He nodded at Jake and the Orizas flew. Their eerie whistling wasn't loud in the gen-

eral cacophony, yet one of the guards must have heard something coming, because he was beginning to pivot when the plate's sharpened edge took his head off and tumbled it backward into the compound, the eyelashes fluttering in bewildered surprise. The headless body took two steps and then collapsed with its arms over the rail, blood pouring from the neck in a gaudy stream. The other guard was already down.

Eddie rolled effortlessly beneath the SOO LINE boxcar and bounced to his feet on the compound side. Two more automated fire engines had come bolting out of the station hitherto hidden by the hardware store façade. They were wheelless, seeming to run on cushions of compressed air. Somewhere toward the north end of the campus (for so Eddie's mind persisted in identifying the Devar-Toi), something exploded. Good. Lovely.

Roland and Jake took fresh plates from the dwindling supply and used them to cut through the three runs of fence. The high-voltage one parted with a bitter, sizzling crack and a brief blink of blue fire. Then they were in. Moving quickly and without speaking, they ran past the now-unguarded towers with Oy trailing closely at Jake's heels. Here was an alley running between Henry Graham's Drug Store & Soda Fountain and the Pleasantville Book Store.

At the head of the alley, they looked out and saw that Main Street was currently empty, although a tangy electric smell (a subway-station smell, Eddie thought) from the last two fire engines still hung in the air, making the overall stench even worse. In the distance, fire-sirens whooped and smoke detectors brayed. Here in Pleasantville, Eddie couldn't help but think of the Main Street in Disneyland: no litter in the gutters, no rude graffiti on the walls, not even any dust on the plate-glass windows. This was where homesick Breakers came when they needed a little whiff of America, he supposed, but didn't any of them want anything better, anything more *realistic*, than this plastic-fantastic still life? Maybe it looked more inviting with folks on the sidewalks and in the stores, but that was hard to believe. Hard for *him* to believe, at least. Maybe it was only a city boy's chauvinism.

Across from them were Pleasantville Shoes, Gay Paree Fashions, Hair Today, and the Gem Theater (**COME IN IT'S KOOL INSIDE** said the banner hanging from the bottom of the marquee). Roland raised a hand, motioning Eddie and Jake across to that side of the street. It was there, if all went as he hoped (it almost never did), that they would set their ambush. They crossed in a crouch, Oy still scurrying at Jake's heel. So far everything seemed to be working like a charm, and that made the gunslinger nervous, indeed.

SIXTEEN

Any battle-seasoned general will tell you that, even in a small-scale engagement (as this one was), there always comes a point where coherence breaks down, and narrative flow, and any real sense of how things are going. These matters are re-created by historians later on. The need to re-create the myth of coherence may be one of the reasons why history exists in the first place.

Never mind. We have reached that point, the one where the Battle of Algul Siento took on a life of its own, and all I can do now is point here and there and hope you can bring your own order out of the general chaos.

SEVENTEEN

Trampas, the eczema-plagued low man who inadvertently let Ted in on so much, rushed to the stream of Breakers who were fleeing from Damli House and grabbed one, a scrawny ex-carpenter with a receding hairline named Birdie McCann.

"Birdie, what is it?" Trampas shouted. He was currently wearing his thinking-cap, which meant he could not share in the telepathic pulse all around him. "What's happening, do you kn—"

"Shooting!" Birdie yelled, pulling free. "*Shooting!* They're out there!" He pointed vaguely behind him.

"Who? How m—"

"Watch out you idiots it's not slowing down!" yelled Gaskie o' Tego, from somewhere behind Trampas and McCann.

Trampas looked up and was horrified to see the lead fire engine come roaring and swaying along the center of the Mall, red lights flashing, two stainless-steel robot firemen now clinging to the back. Pimli, Finli, and Jakli leaped aside. So did Tassa the houseboy. But Tammy Kelly lay facedown on the grass in a spreading soup of blood. She had been flattened by Fire-Response Team Bravo, which had not actually scrambled to fight a fire in over eight hundred years. Her complaining days were over.

And—

"STAND CLEAR!" blared the fire engine. Behind it, two more engines swerved gaudily around either side of Warden's House. Once again Tassa the houseboy barely leaped in time to save his skin. *"THIS IS FIRE-RESPONSE TEAM BRAVO!"* Some sort of metallic node rose from the center of the engine, split open, and produced a steel whirligig that began to spray high-pressure streams of water in eight different directions. *"MAKE WAY FOR FIRE-RESPONSE TEAM BRAVO!"*

And—

James Cagney—the taheen who was standing with Gaskie in the foyer of the Feveral Hall dormitory when the trouble started, remember him?—saw what was going to happen and began yelling at the guards who were staggering out of Damli's west wing, red-eyed and coughing, some with their pants on fire, a few—oh, praise Gan and Bessa and all the gods—with weapons.

Cag screamed at them to get out of the way and could hardly hear himself in the cacophony. He saw Joey Rastosovich pull two of them aside and watched the Earnshaw kid bump aside another. A few of the coughing, weeping escapees saw the oncoming fire engine and scattered on their own. Then Fire-Response Team Bravo was plowing through the guards from the west wing, not slowing, roaring straight for Damli House, spraying water to every point of the compass.

And—

"Dear Christ, no," Pimli Prentiss moaned. He clapped his hands over his eyes. Finli, on the other hand, was helpless to look away. He saw a low man—Ben Alexander, he was quite sure—chewed beneath the firetruck's huge wheels. He saw another struck by the grille and mashed against the side of Damli House as the engine crashed, spraying boards and glass, then breaking through a bulkhead which had been partially concealed by a bed of sickly flowers. One wheel dropped down into the cellar stairwell and a robot voice began to boom, *"ACCIDENT! NOTIFY THE STATION! ACCIDENT!"*

No shit, Sherlock, Finli thought, looking at the blood on the grass with a kind of sick wonder. How many of his men and his valuable charges had the goddamned malfunctioning firetruck mowed down? Six? Eight? A motherfucking dozen?

From behind Damli House came that terrifying *chow-chow-chow* sound once again, the sound of automatic weapons fire.

A fat Breaker named Waverly jostled him. Finli snared him before Waverly could fly on by. "What happened? Who told you to go south?" For Finli, unlike Trampas, wasn't wearing any sort of thinking-cap and the message

(*GO SOUTH WITH YOUR HANDS UP, YOU WON'T BE HURT*)

was slamming into his head so hard and loud it was nearly impossible to think of anything else.

Beside him, Pimli—struggling to gather his wits—seized on the beating thought and managed one of his own: *That's almost got to be Brautigan, grabbing an idea and amplifying it that way. Who else could?*

And—

Gaskie grabbed first Cag and then Jakli and shouted at them to gather up all the armed guards and put them to work flanking the Breakers who were hurrying south on the Mall and the streets that flanked the Mall. They looked at him with blank, starey eyes—panic-eyes—and he could have screamed with balked fury. And here came the next two engines with their sirens whooping. The larger of the pair struck two of the Breakers, bearing them to the ground and running them over. One of these new casualties was Joey Rastosovich. When the engine had passed, beating at the grass with its compressed-air vents, Tanya fell on her knees beside her dying husband, raising her hands to the sky. She was screaming at the top of her lungs but Gaskie could barely hear her. Tears of frustration and fear prickled the corners of his eyes. *Dirty dogs,* he thought. *Dirty ambushing dogs!*

And—

North of the Algul compound, Susannah broke cover, moving in on the triple run of fence. This wasn't in the plan, but the need to keep shooting, to keep knocking them down, was stronger than ever. She simply couldn't help herself, and Roland would have understood. Besides, the billowing smoke from Damli House had momentarily obscured everything at this end of the compound. Red beams from the "lazers" stabbed into it—on and off, on and off, like some sort of neon sign— and Susannah reminded herself not to get in the way of them, not unless she wanted a hole two inches across all the way through her.

She used bullets from the Coyote to cut her end of the fence—outer run, middle run, inner run—and then vanished into the thickening smoke, reloading as she went.

And—

The Breaker named Waverly tried to pull free of Finli. *Nar, nar, none of that, may it please ya,* Finli thought. He yanked the man—who'd been a bookkeeper or some such thing in his pre-Algul life—closer to him, then slapped him twice across the face, hard enough to make his hand hurt. Waverly screamed in pain and surprise.

"Who the fuck is back there!" Finli roared. *"WHO THE FUCK IS DOING THIS?"* The follow-up fire engines had halted in front of Damli House and were pouring streams of water into the smoke. Finli didn't know if it could help, but probably it couldn't hurt. And at least the damned things hadn't crashed into the building they were supposed to save, like the first one.

"Sir, I don't know!" Waverly sobbed. Blood was streaming from one of his nostrils and the corner of his mouth. *"I don't*

know, but there has to be fifty, maybe a hundred of the devils! Dinky got us out! God bless Dinky Earnshaw!"

Gaskie o' Tego, meanwhile, wrapped one good-sized hand around James Cagney's neck and the other around Jakli's. Gaskie had an idea son of a bitching crowhead Jakli had been on the verge of running, but there was no time to worry about that now. He needed them both.

And—

"Boss!" Finli shouted. "Boss, grab the Earnshaw kid! Something about this smells!"

And—

With Cag's face pressing against one of his cheeks and Jakli's against the other, the Wease (who thought as clearly as anyone that terrible morning) was finally able to make himself heard. Gaskie, meanwhile, repeated his command: divide up the armed guards and put them with the retreating Breakers. *"Don't try to stop them, but stay with them! And for Christ's sake, keep em from getting electrocuted! Keep em off the fence if they go past Main Stree—"*

Before he could finish this admonishment, a figure came plummeting out of the thickening smoke. It was Gangli, the compound doctor, his white coat on fire, his roller skates still on his feet.

And—

Susannah Dean took up a position at the left rear corner of Damli House, coughing. She saw three of the sons of bitches— Gaskie, Jakli, and Cagney, had she but known it. Before she could draw a bead, eddying smoke blotted them out. When it cleared, Jakli and Cag were gone, rounding up armed guards to act as sheepdogs who would at least try to protect their panicked charges, even if they could not immediately stop them. Gaskie was still there, and Susannah took him with a single headshot.

Pimli didn't see it. It was becoming clear to him that all the confusion was on the surface. Quite likely deliberate. The Breakers' decision to move away from the attackers north of the Algul had come a little too quickly and was a little too organized.

Never mind Earnshaw, he thought, Brautigan's *the one I want to talk to.*

But before he could catch up to Ted, Tassa grabbed the Master in a frantic, terrified hug, babbling that Warden's House was on fire, he was afraid, terribly afraid, that all of Master's clothes, his books—

Pimli Prentiss knocked him aside with a hammer-blow to the side of his head. The pulse of the Breakers' unified thought (bad-mind now instead of good-mind), yammered

(WITH YOUR HANDS UP YOU WON'T BE)

crazily in his head, threatening to drive out all thought. Fucking Brautigan had done this, he *knew* it, and the man was too far ahead . . . unless . . .

Pimli looked at the Peacemaker in his hand, considered it, then jammed it back into the docker's clutch under his left arm. He wanted fucking Brautigan alive. Fucking Brautigan had some explaining to do. Not to mention some more goddamned breaking.

Chow-chow-chow. Bullets flicking all around him. Running hume guards, taheen, and can-toi all around him. And Christ, only a few of them were armed, mostly humes who'd been down for fence-patrol. Those who guarded the Breakers didn't really *need* guns, by and large the Breakers were as tame as parakeets and the thought of an outside attack had seemed ludicrous until . . .

Until it happened, he thought, and spied Trampas.

"Trampas!" he bawled. "*Trampas!* Hey, cowboy! Grab Earnshaw and bring him to me! *Grab Earnshaw!*"

Here in the middle of the Mall it was a little less noisy and Trampas heard sai Prentiss quite clearly. He sprinted after Dinky and grabbed the young man by one arm.

And—

Eleven-year-old Daneeka Rostov came out of the rolling smoke that now entirely obscured the lower half of Damli House, pulling two red wagons behind her. Daneeka's face was red and swollen; tears were streaming from her eyes; she was bent over almost double with the effort it was taking her to keep pulling Baj, who sat in one Radio Flyer wagon, and Sej, who sat in the other. Both had the huge heads and tiny, wise eyes of hydrocephalic savants, but Sej was equipped with waving stubs of arms while Baj had none. Both were now foaming at the mouth and making hoarse gagging sounds.

"Help me!" Dani managed, coughing harder than ever. "Help me, someone, before they choke!"

Dinky saw her and started in that direction. Trampas restrained him, although it was clear his heart wasn't in it. "No, Dink," he said. His tone was apologetic but firm. "Let someone else do it. Boss wants to talk to—"

Then Brautigan was there again, face pale, mouth a single stitched line in his lower face. "Let him go, Trampas. I like you, dog, but you don't want to get in our business today."

"Ted? What—"

Dink started toward Dani again. Trampas pulled him back again. Beyond them, Baj fainted and tumbled headfirst from his wagon. Although he landed on the soft grass, his head made a dreadful rotten *splitting* sound, and Dani Rostov shrieked.

Dinky lunged for her. Trampas yanked him back once more, and hard. At the same time he pulled the .38 Colt Woodsman he was wearing in his own docker's clutch.

There was no more time to reason with him. Ted Brautigan hadn't thrown the mind-spear since using it against the wallet-thief in Akron, back in 1935; hadn't even used it when the low men took him prisoner again in the Bridgeport, Connecticut, of 1960, although he'd been sorely tempted. He had promised himself he'd never use it again, and he certainly didn't want to throw it at

(smile *when you say that*)

Trampas, who had always treated him decently. But he had to get to the south end of the compound before order was restored, and he meant to have Dinky with him when he arrived.

Also, he was furious. Poor little Baj, who always had a smile for anyone and everyone!

He concentrated and felt a sick pain rip through his head. The mind-spear flew. Trampas let go of Dinky and gave Ted a look of unbelieving reproach that Ted would remember to the end of his life. Then Trampas grabbed the sides of his head like a man with the worst Excedrin Headache in the universe, and fell dead on the grass with his throat swollen and his tongue sticking out of his mouth.

"Come on!" Ted cried, and grabbed Dinky's arm. Prentiss was looking away for the time being, thank God, distracted by another explosion.

"But Dani . . . and Sej!"

"She can get Sej!" Sending the rest of it mentally:

(*now that she doesn't have to pull Baj too*)

Ted and Dinky fled while behind them Pimli Prentiss turned, looked unbelievingly at Trampas, and bawled for them to stop—to stop in the name of the Crimson King.

Finli o' Tego unlimbered his own gun, but before he could fire, Daneeka Rostov was on him, biting and scratching. She weighed almost nothing, but for a moment he was so surprised to be attacked from this unexpected quarter that she almost bowled him over. He curled a strong, furry arm around her neck and threw her aside, but by then Ted and Dinky were almost out of range, cutting to the left side of Warden's House and disappearing into the smoke.

Finli steadied his pistol in both hands, took in a breath, held it, and squeezed off a single shot. Blood flew from the old man's arm; Finli heard him cry out and saw him swerve. Then the young pup grabbed the old cur and they cut around the corner of the house.

"I'm coming for you!" Finli bellowed after them. "Yar I am, and when I catch you, I'll make you wish you were never born!" But the threat felt horribly empty, somehow.

Now the entire population of Algul Siento—Breakers, taheen, hume guards, can-toi with bloody red spots glaring on their foreheads like third eyes—was in tidal motion, flowing south. And Finli saw something he really did not like at all: the Breakers and *only* the Breakers were moving that way with their arms raised. If there were more harriers down there, they'd have no trouble at all telling which ones to shoot, would they?

And—

In his room on the third floor of Corbett Hall, still on his knees at the foot of his glass-covered bed, coughing on the smoke that was drifting in through his broken window, Sheemie Ruiz had his revelation . . . or was spoken to by his imagination, take your pick. In either case, he leaped to his feet. His eyes, normally friendly but always puzzled by a world he could not quite understand, were clear and full of joy.

"BEAM SAYS THANKYA!" he cried to the empty room.

He looked around, as happy as Ebenezer Scrooge discovering that the spirits have done it all in one night, and ran for the door with his slippers crunching on the broken glass. One sharp spear of glass pierced his foot—carrying his death on its tip, had he but known it, say sorry, say Discordia—but in his joy he didn't even feel it. He dashed into the hall and then down the stairs.

On the second floor landing, Sheemie came upon an elderly female Breaker named Belle O'Rourke, grabbed her, shook her. *"BEAM SAYS THANKYA!"* he hollered into her dazed and uncomprehending face. *"BEAM SAYS ALL MAY YET BE WELL! NOT TOO LATE! JUST IN TIME!"*

He rushed on to spread the glad news (glad to him, anyway), and—

On Main Street, Roland looked first at Eddie Dean, then at Jake Chambers. "They're coming, and this is where we have to take them. Wait for my command, then stand and be true."

EIGHTEEN

First to appear were three Breakers, running full out with their arms raised. They crossed Main Street that way, never seeing Eddie, who was in the box-office of the Gem (he'd knocked out the glass on all three sides with the sandalwood grip of the gun which had once been Roland's), or Jake (sitting inside an engineless Ford sedan parked in front of the Pleasantville Bake Shoppe), or Roland himself (behind a mannequin in the window of Gay Paree Fashions).

They reached the other sidewalk and looked around, bewildered.

Go, Roland thought at them. *Go on and get out of here, take the alley, get away while you can.*

"Come on!" one of them shouted, and they ran down the alley between the drug store and the bookshop. Another appeared, then two more, then the first of the guards, a hume with a pistol raised to the side of his frightened, wide-eyed face. Roland sighted him . . . and then held his fire.

More of the Devar personnel began to appear, running into Main Street from between the buildings. They spread themselves wide apart. As Roland had hoped and expected, they were trying to flank their charges and channel them. Trying to keep the retreat from turning into a rout.

"Form two lines!" a taheen with a raven's head was shouting in a buzzing, out-of-breath voice. *"Form two lines and keep em between, for your fathers' sakes!"*

One of the others, a redheaded taheen with his shirttail out, yelled: *"What about the fence, Jakli? What if they run on the fence?"*

"Can't do nothing about that, Cag, just—"

A shrieking Breaker tried to run past the raven before he could finish, and the raven—Jakli—gave him such a mighty push that the poor fellow went sprawling in the middle of the street. "Stay together, you maggots!" he snarled. "Run if 'ee will, but keep some fucking order about it!" As if there could be any order in this, Roland thought (and not without satisfaction). Then, to the redhead, the one called Jakli shouted: "Let one or two of em fry—the rest'll see and stop!"

It would complicate things if either Eddie or Jake started shooting at this point, but neither did. The three gunslingers watched from their places of concealment as a species of order rose from the chaos. More guards appeared. Jakli and the redhead directed them into the two lines, which was now a corridor running from one side of the street to the other. A few Breakers got past them before the corridor was fully formed, but only a few.

A new taheen appeared, this one with the head of a weasel, and took over for the one called Jakli. He pounded a couple of running Breakers on the back, actually hurrying them up.

From south of Main Street came a bewildered shout: "Fence is cut!" And then another: "I think the guards are dead!" This latter cry was followed by a howl of horror, and Roland knew as surely as if he had seen it that some unlucky Breaker had just come upon a severed watchman's head in the grass.

The terrified babble on the heels of this hadn't run itself out when Dinky Earnshaw and Ted Brautigan appeared from between the bakery and the shoe store, so close to Jake's hiding place that he could have reached out the window of his car and touched them. Ted had been winged. His right shirtsleeve had turned red from the elbow down, but he was moving—with a little help from Dinky, who had an arm around him. Ted turned as the two of them ran through the gauntlet of guards and looked directly at Roland's hiding place for a moment. Then he and Earnshaw entered the alley and were gone.

That made them safe, at least for the time being, and that was good. But where was the big bug? Where was Prentiss, the man in charge of this hateful place? Roland wanted him and yon Weasel-head taheen sai both—cut off the snake's head and the snake dies. But they couldn't afford to wait much longer. The stream of fleeing Breakers was drying up. The gunslinger didn't think sai Weasel would wait for the last stragglers; he'd want to keep his precious charges from escaping through the cut fence. He'd know they wouldn't go far, given the sterile and gloomy countryside all around, but he'd also know that if there were attackers at the north end of the compound, there might be rescuers standing by at the—

And there he was, thank the gods and Gan—sai Pimli Prentiss, staggering and winded and clearly in a state of shock, with a loaded docker's clutch swinging back and forth under his meaty arm. Blood was coming from one nostril and the corner of one eye, as if all this excitement had caused something to rupture inside of his head. He went to the Weasel, weaving slightly from side to side—it was this drunken weave that Roland would later blame in his bitter heart for the final outcome of that morning's work—probably meaning to take command of the operation. Their short but fervent embrace, both giving comfort and taking it, told Roland all he needed to know about the closeness of their relationship.

He leveled his gun on the back of Prentiss's head, pulled the trigger, and watched as blood and hair flew. Master Prentiss's hands shot out, the fingers spread against the dark sky, and he collapsed almost at the stunned Weasel's feet.

As if in response to this, the atomic sun came on, flooding the world with light.

"Hile, you gunslingers, kill them all!" Roland cried, fanning the trigger of his revolver, that ancient murder-machine, with the flat of his right hand. Four had fallen to his fire before the guards, lined up like so many clay ducks in a shooting gallery, had registered the sound of the gunshots, let alone had time to react. *"For Gilead, for New York, for the Beam, for your fathers! Hear me, hear me! Leave not one of them standing! KILL THEM ALL!"*

And so they did: the gunslinger out of Gilead, the former drug addict out of Brooklyn, the lonely child who had once been known to Mrs. Greta Shaw as 'Bama. Coming south from behind them, rolling through thickening banners of smoke on the SCT (diverting from a straight course only once, to swerve around the flattened body of another housekeeper, this one named Tammy), was a fourth: she who had once been instructed in the ways of nonviolent protest by young and earnest men from the N-double A-C-P and who had now embraced, fully and with no regrets, the way of the gun. Susannah picked off three laggard humie guards and one fleeing taheen. The taheen had a rifle slung over one shoulder but never tried for it. Instead he raised his sleek, fur-covered arms— his head was vaguely bearish—and cried for quarter and parole. Mindful of all that had gone on here, not in the least how the pureed brains of children had been fed to the Beam-killers in order to keep them operating at top efficiency, Susannah gave him neither, although neither did she give him cause to suffer or time to fear his fate.

By the time she rolled down the alley between the movie the-ater and the hair salon, the shooting had stopped. Finli and Jakli were dying; James Cagney was dead with his hume mask torn half-off his repulsive rat's head; lying with these were another three dozen, just as dead. The formerly immaculate gutters of Pleasantville ran with their blood.

There were undoubtedly other guards about the com-pound, but by now they'd be in hiding, positive that they had been set upon by a hundred or more seasoned fighters, land-pirates from God only knew where. The majority of Algul Siento's Breakers were in the grassy area between the rear of Main Street and the south watchtowers, huddled like the sheep they were. Ted, unmindful of his bleeding arm, had already begun taking attendance.

Then the entire northern contingent of the harrier army appeared at the head of the alley next to the movieshow: one shor'leg black lady mounted on an ATV. She was steering with one hand and holding the Coyote machine-pistol steady on the handlebars with the other. She saw the bodies heaped in the street and nodded with joyless satisfaction.

Eddie came out of the box-office and embraced her.

"Hey, sugarman, hey," she murmured, fluttering kisses along the side of his neck in a way that made him shiver. Then Jake was there—pale from the killing, but composed—and she slung an arm around his shoulders and pulled him close. Her eyes happened on Roland, standing on the sidewalk behind the three he had drawn to Mid-World. His gun dangled beside his left thigh, and could he feel the expression of longing on his face? Did he even know it was there? She doubted it, and her heart went out to him.

"Come here, Gilead," she said. "This is a *group* hug, and you're part of the group."

For a moment she didn't think he understood the invitation, or was pretending not to understand. Then he came, pausing to re-holster his gun and to pick up Oy. He moved in between Jake and Eddie. Oy jumped into Susannah's lap as though it were the most natural thing in the world. Then the gunslinger put one

arm around Eddie's waist and the other around Jake's. Susannah reached up (the bumbler scrabbling comically for purchase
on her suddenly tilting lap), put her arms around Roland's
neck, and put a hearty smack on his sunburned forehead. Jake
and Eddie laughed. Roland joined them, smiling as we do
when we have been surprised by happiness.

I'd have you see them like this; I'd have you see them very
well. Will you? They are clustered around Suzie's Cruisin Trike,
embracing in the aftermath of their victory. I'd have you see
them this way not because they have won a great battle—they
know better than that, every one of them—but because now
they are ka-tet for the last time. The story of their fellowship
ends here, on this make-believe street and beneath this artificial
sun; the rest of the tale will be short and brutal compared to all
that's gone before. Because when ka-tet breaks, the end always
comes quickly.

Say sorry.

NINETEEN

Pimli Prentiss watched through blood-crusted, dying eyes as the
younger of the two men broke from the group embrace and
approached Finli o' Tego. The young man saw that Finli was still
stirring and dropped to one knee beside him. The woman, now
dismounted from her motorized tricycle, and the boy began to
check the rest of their victims and dispatch the few who still
lived. Even as he lay dying with a bullet in his own head, Pimli
understood this as mercy rather than cruelty. And when the job
was done, Pimli supposed they'd meet with the rest of their cow-
ardly, sneaking friends and search those buildings of the Algul
that were not yet on fire, looking for the remaining guards, and
no doubt shooting out of hand those they discovered. *You
won't find many, my yellowback friends,* he thought. *You've wiped out
two-thirds of my men right here.* And how many of the attackers had
Master Pimli, Security Chief Finli, and their men taken in
return? So far as Pimli knew, not a single one.

But perhaps he could do something about that. His right

hand began its slow and painful journey up toward the docker's clutch, and the Peacemaker holstered there.

Eddie, meanwhile, had put the barrel of the Gilead revolver with the sandalwood grips against the side of Weasel-boy's head. His finger was tightening on the trigger when he saw that Weasel-boy, although shot in the chest, bleeding heavily, and clearly dying fast, was looking at him with complete awareness. And something else, something Eddie did not much care for. He thought it was contempt. He looked up, saw Susannah and Jake checking bodies at the eastern end of the killzone, saw Roland on the far sidewalk, speaking with Dinky and Ted as he knotted a makeshift bandage around the latter's arm. The two former Breakers were listening carefully, and although both of them looked dubious, they were nodding their heads.

Eddie returned his attention to the dying taheen. "You're at the end of the path, my friend," he said. "Plugged in the pump, it looks like to me. Do you have something you want to say before you step into the clearing?"

Finli nodded.

"Say it, then, chum. But I'd keep it short if you want to get it all out."

"Thee and thine are a pack of yellowback dogs," Finli managed. He probably *was* shot in the heart—so it felt, anyway—but he would say this; it needed to be said, and he willed his damaged heart to beat until it was out. Then he'd die and welcome the dark. "Piss-stinking yellowback dogs, killing men from ambush. That's what I'd say."

Eddie smiled humorlessly. "And what about yellowback dogs who'd use children to kill the whole world from ambush, my friend? The whole *universe*?"

The Weasel blinked at that, as if he'd expected no such reply. Perhaps any reply at all. "I had . . . my orders."

"I have no doubt of that," Eddie said. "And followed them to the end. Enjoy hell or Na'ar or whatever you call it." He put the barrel of his gun against Finli's temple and pulled the trigger. The Wease jerked a single time and was still. Grimacing, Eddie got to his feet.

He caught movement from the corner of his eye as he did so and saw another one—the boss of the show—had struggled up onto one elbow. His gun, the Peacemaker .40 that had once executed a rapist, was leveled. Eddie's reflexes were quick, but there was no time to use them. The Peacemaker roared a single time, fire licking from the end of its barrel, and blood flew from Eddie Dean's brow. A lock of hair flipped on the back of his head as the slug exited. He slapped his hand to the hole that had appeared over his right eye, like a man who has remembered something of vital importance just a little too late.

Roland whirled on the rundown heels of his boots, pulling his own gun in a dip too quick to see. Jake and Susannah also turned. Susannah saw her husband standing in the street with the heel of his hand pressed to his brow.

"Eddie? *Sugar?*"

Pimli was struggling to cock the Peacemaker again, his upper lip curled back from his teeth in a doglike snarl of effort. Roland shot him in the throat and Algul Siento's Master snaprolled to his left, the still-uncocked pistol flying out of his hand and clattering to a stop beside the body of his friend the Weasel. It finished almost at Eddie's feet.

"*Eddie!*" Susannah screamed, and began a loping crawl toward him, thrusting herself on her hands. *He's not hurt bad,* she told herself, *not hurt bad, dear God don't let my man be hurt bad—*

Then she saw the blood running from beneath his pressing hand, pattering down into the street, and knew it *was* bad.

"Suze?" he asked. His voice was perfectly clear. "Suzie, where are you? I can't see."

He took one step, a second, a third . . . and then fell facedown in the street, just as Gran-pere Jaffords had known he would, aye, from the first moment he'd laid eyes on him. For the boy was a gunslinger, say true, and it was the only end that one such as he could expect.

CHAPTER XII:
THE TET BREAKS

That night found Jake Chambers sitting disconsolately outside the Clover Tavern at the east end of Main Street in Pleasantville. The bodies of the guards had been carted away by a robot maintenance crew, and that was at least something of a relief. Oy had been in the boy's lap for an hour or more. Ordinarily he would never have stayed so close for so long, but he seemed to understand that Jake needed him. On several occasions, Jake wept into the bumbler's fur.

For most of that endless day Jake found himself thinking in two different voices. This had happened to him before, but not for years; not since the time when, as a very young child, he suspected he might have suffered some sort of weird, below-the-parental-radar breakdown.

Eddie's dying, said the first voice (the one that used to assure him there were monsters in his closet, and soon they would emerge to eat him alive). *He's in a room in Corbett Hall and Susannah's with him and he won't shut up, but he's dying.*

No, denied the second voice (the one that used to assure him—feebly—that there were no such things as monsters). *No, that can't be. Eddie's . . .* Eddie! *And besides, he's ka-tet. He might die when we reach the Dark Tower, we might* all *die when we get there, but not now, not here, that's crazy.*

Eddie's dying, replied the first voice. It was implacable. *He's got a hole in his head almost big enough to stick your fist in, and he's dying.*

To this the second voice could offer only more denials, each weaker than the last.

Not even the knowledge that they had likely saved the Beam

387

(Sheemie certainly seemed to think they had; he'd crisscrossed the weirdly silent campus of the Devar-Toi, shouting the news—*BEAM SAYS ALL MAY BE WELL! BEAM SAYS THANKYA!*—at the top of his lungs) could make Jake feel better. The loss of Eddie was too great a price to pay even for such an outcome. And the breaking of the tet was an even greater price. Every time Jake thought of it, he felt sick to his stomach and sent up inarticulate prayers to God, to Gan, to the Man Jesus, to any or all of them to do a miracle and save Eddie's life.

He even prayed to the writer.

Save my friend's life and we'll save yours, he prayed to Stephen King, a man he had never seen. *Save Eddie and we won't let that van hit you. I swear it.*

Then again he'd think of Susannah screaming Eddie's name, of trying to turn him over, and Roland wrapping his arms around her and saying *You mustn't do that, Susannah, you mustn't disturb him,* and how she'd fought him, her face crazy, her face *changing* as different personalities seemed to inhabit it for a moment or two and then flee. *I have to help him!* she'd sob in the Susannah-voice Jake knew, and then in another, harsher voice she'd shout *Let me go, mahfah! Let me do mah voodoo on him, make mah houngun, he goan git up an walk, you see! Sho!* And Roland holding her through all of it, holding her and rocking her while Eddie lay in the street, but not dead, it would have been better, almost, if he'd been dead (even if being dead meant the end of talking about miracles, the end of hope), but Jake could see his dusty fingers twitching and could hear him muttering incoherently, like a man who talks in his sleep.

Then Ted had come, and Dinky just behind him, and two or three of the other Breakers trailing along hesitantly behind them. Ted had gotten on his knees beside the struggling, screaming woman and motioned for Dinky to get kneebound on the other side of her. Ted had taken one of her hands, then nodded for Dink to take the other. And something had flowed out of them—something deep and soothing. It wasn't meant for Jake, no, not at all, but he caught some of it, anyway, and felt his wildly galloping heart slow. He looked into Ted

Brautigan's face and saw that Ted's eyes were doing their trick, the pupils swelling and shrinking, swelling and shrinking.

Susannah's cries faltered, subsiding to little hurt groans. She looked down at Eddie, and when she bent her head her eyes had spilled tears onto the back of Eddie's shirt, making dark places, like raindrops. That was when Sheemie appeared from one of the alleys, shouting glad hosannahs to all who would hear him— *"BEAM SAYS NOT TOO LATE! BEAM SAYS JUST IN TIME, BEAM SAYS THANKYA AND WE MUST LET HIM HEAL!"*—and limping badly on one foot (none of them thought anything of it then or even noticed it). Dinky murmured to the growing crowd of Breakers looking at the mortally wounded gunslinger, and several went to Sheemie and got him to quiet down. From the main part of the Devar-Toi the alarms continued, but the follow-up fire engines were actually getting the three worst fires (those in Damli House, Warden's House, and Feveral Hall) under control.

What Jake remembered next was Ted's fingers—unbelievably gentle fingers—spreading the hair on the back of Eddie's head and exposing a large hole filled with a dark jelly of blood. There were little white flecks in it. Jake had wanted to believe those flecks were bits of bone. Better than thinking they might be flecks of Eddie's brain.

At the sight of this terrible head-wound Susannah leaped to her feet and began to scream again. Began to struggle. Ted and Dinky (who was paler than paste) exchanged a glance, tightened their grip on her hands, and once more sent the

(*peace ease quiet wait calm slow peace*)

soothing message that was as much colors—cool blue shading to quiet ashes of gray—as it was words. Roland, meanwhile, held her shoulders.

"Can anything be done for him?" Roland asked Ted. "Anything at all?"

"He can be made comfortable," Ted said. "We can do that much, at least." Then he pointed toward the Devar. "Don't you still have work there to finish, Roland?"

For a moment Roland didn't quite seem to understand

that. Then he looked at the bodies of the downed guards, and did. "Yes," he said. "I suppose I do. Jake, can you help me? If the ones left were to find a new leader and regroup . . . that wouldn't do at all."

"What about Susannah?" Jake had asked.

"Susannah's going to help us see her man to a place where he can be at his ease, and die as peacefully as possible," said Ted Brautigan. "Aren't you, dear heart?"

She'd looked at him with an expression that was not quite vacant; the understanding (and the pleading) in that gaze went into Jake's heart like the tip of an icicle. *"Must* he die?" she had asked him.

Ted had lifted her hand to his lips and kissed it. "Yes," he said. "He must die and you must bear it."

"Then you have to do something for me," she said, and touched Ted's cheek with her fingers. To Jake those fingers looked cold. Cold.

"What, love? Anything I can." He took hold of her fingers and wrapped them

(*peace ease quiet wait calm slow peace*)

in his own.

"Stop what you're doing, unless I tell you different," said she.

He looked at her, surprised. Then he glanced at Dinky, who only shrugged. Then he looked back at Susannah.

"You mustn't use your good-mind to steal my grief," Susannah told him, "for I'd open my mouth and drink it to the dregs. Every drop."

For a moment Ted only stood with his head lowered and a frown creasing his brow. Then he looked up and gave her the sweetest smile Jake had ever seen.

"Aye, lady," Ted replied. "We'll do as you ask. But if you need us . . . *when* you need us . . ."

"I'll call," Susannah said, and once more slipped to her knees beside the muttering man who lay in the street.

TWO

As Roland and Jake approached the alley which would take them back to the center of the Devar-Toi, where they would put off mourning their fallen friend by taking care of any who might still stand against them, Sheemie reached out and plucked the sleeve of Roland's shirt.

"Beam says thankya, Will Dearborn that was." He had blown out his voice with shouting and spoke in a hoarse croak. "Beam says all may yet be well. Good as new. *Better.*"

"That's fine," Roland said, and Jake supposed it was. There had been no real joy then, however, as there was no real joy now. Jake kept thinking of the hole Ted Brautigan's gentle fingers had exposed. That hole filled with red jelly.

Roland put an arm around Sheemie's shoulders, squeezed him, gave him a kiss. Sheemie smiled, delighted. "I'll come with you, Roland. Will'ee have me, dear?"

"Not this time," Roland said.

"Why are you crying?" Sheemie asked. Jake had seen the happiness draining from Sheemie's face, being replaced with worry. Meanwhile, more Breakers were returning to Main Street, milling around in little groups. Jake had seen consternation in the expressions they directed toward the gunslinger . . . and a certain dazed curiosity . . . and, in some cases, clear dislike. Hate, almost. He had seen no gratitude, not so much as a speck of gratitude, and for that he'd hated *them.*

"My friend is hurt," Roland had said. "I cry for him, Sheemie. And for his wife, who is my friend. Will you go to Ted and sai Dinky, and try to soothe her, should she ask to be soothed?"

"If you want, aye! Anything for you!"

"Thankee-sai, son of Stanley. And help if they move my friend."

"Your friend Eddie! Him who lays hurt!"

"Aye, his name is Eddie, you say true. Will you help Eddie?"

"Aye!"

"And there's something else—"

"Aye?" Sheemie asked, then seemed to remember something. "Aye! Help you go away, travel far, you and your friends! Ted told me. 'Make a hole,' he said, 'like you did for me.' Only they brought him back. The bad 'uns. They'd not bring you back, for the bad 'uns are gone! Beam's at peace!" And Sheemie laughed, a jarring sound to Jake's grieving ear.

To Roland's too, maybe, because his smile was strained. "In time, Sheemie . . . although I think Susannah may stay here, and wait for us to return."

If we do *return,* Jake thought.

"But I have another chore you may be able to do. Not helping someone travel to that other world, but *like* that, a little. I've told Ted and Dinky, and they'd tell you, once Eddie's been put at his ease. Will you listen?"

"Aye! And help, if I can!"

Roland clapped him on the shoulder. "Good!" Then Jake and the gunslinger had gone in a direction that might have been north, headed back to finish what they had begun.

THREE

They flushed out another fourteen guards in the next three hours, most of them humes. Roland surprised Jake—a little—by only killing the two who shot at them from behind the fire engine that had crashed with one wheel stuck in the cellar bulkhead. The rest he disarmed and then gave parole, telling them that any Devar-Toi guards still in the compound when the late-afternoon change-of-shifts horn blew would be shot out of hand.

"But where will we go?" asked a taheen with a snowy-white rooster's head below a great floppy-red coxcomb (he reminded Jake a little of Foghorn Leghorn, the cartoon character).

Roland shook his head. "I care not where you fetch," he said, "as long as you're not here when the next horn blows, kennit. You've done hell's work here, but hell's shut, and I mean to see it will never open this particular set of doors again."

"What do you mean?" asked the rooster-taheen, almost timidly, but Roland wouldn't say, had only told the creature to pass on the message to any others he might run across.

Most of the remaining taheen and can-toi left Algul Siento in pairs and triplets, going without argument and nervously looking back over their shoulders every few moments. Jake thought they were right to be afraid, because his dinh's face that day had been abstract with thought and terrible with grief. Eddie Dean lay on his deathbed, and Roland of Gilead would not bear crossing.

"What are you going to do to the place?" Jake asked after the afternoon horn had blown. They were making their way past the smoking husk of Damli House (where the robot fire-men had posted signs every twenty feet reading **OFF-LIMITS PENDING FIRE DEPT. INVESTIGATION**), on their way to see Eddie.

Roland only shook his head, not answering the question.

On the Mall, Jake spied six Breakers standing in a circle, holding hands. They looked like folks having a séance. Sheemie was there, and Ted, and Dani Rostov; there also was a young woman, an older one, and a stout, bankerly-looking man. Beyond, lying with their feet sticking out under blankets, was a line of the nearly fifty guards who had died during the brief action.

"Do you know what they're doing?" Jake asked, meaning the séance-*folken*—the ones behind them were just being dead, a job that would occupy them from now on.

Roland glanced toward the circle of Breakers briefly. "Yes."

"What?"

"Not now," said the gunslinger. "Now we're going to pay our respects to Eddie. You're going to need all the serenity you can manage, and that means emptying your mind."

FOUR

Now, sitting with Oy outside the empty Clover Tavern with its neon beer-signs and silent jukebox, Jake reflected on how right

Roland had been, and how grateful Jake himself had been when, after forty-five minutes or so, the gunslinger had looked at him, seen his terrible distress, and excused him from the room where Eddie lingered, giving up his vitality an inch at a time, leaving the imprint of his remarkable will on every last inch of his life's tapestry.

The litter-bearing party Ted Brautigan had organized had borne the young gunslinger to Corbett Hall, where he was laid in the spacious bedroom of the first-floor proctor's suite. The litter-bearers lingered in the dormitory's courtyard, and as the afternoon wore on, the rest of the Breakers joined them. When Roland and Jake arrived, a pudgy red-haired woman stepped into Roland's way.

Lady, I wouldn't do that, Jake had thought. *Not this afternoon.*

In spite of the day's alarums and excursions, this woman — who'd looked to Jake like the Lifetime President of his mother's garden club — had found time to put on a fairly heavy coat of makeup: powder, rouge, and lipstick as red as the side of a Devar fire engine. She introduced herself as Grace Rumbelow (formerly of Aldershot, Hampshire, England) and demanded to know what was going to happen next — where they would go, what they would do, who would take care of them. The same questions the rooster-headed taheen had asked, in other words.

"For we have *been* taken care of," said Grace Rumbelow in ringing tones (Jake had been fascinated with how she said "been," so it rhymed with "seen"), "and are in no position, at least for the time being, to care for ourselves."

There were calls of agreement at this.

Roland looked her up and down, and something in his face had robbed the lady of her measured indignation. "Get out of my road," said the gunslinger, "or I'll push you down."

She grew pale beneath her powder and did as he said without uttering another word. A birdlike clatter of disapproval followed Jake and Roland into Corbett Hall, but it didn't start until the gunslinger was out of their view and they no longer had to fear falling beneath the unsettling gaze of his blue eyes. The

Breakers reminded Jake of some kids with whom he'd gone to school at Piper, classroom nitwits willing to shout out stuff like *this test sucks* or *bite my bag . . .* but only when the teacher was out of the room.

The first-floor hallway of Corbett was bright with fluorescent lights and smelled strongly of smoke from Damli House and Feveral Hall. Dinky Earnshaw was seated in a folding chair to the right of the door marked PROCTOR'S SUITE, smoking a cigarette. He looked up as Roland and Jake approached, Oy trotting along in his usual position just behind Jake's heel.

"How is he?" Roland asked.

"Dying, man," Dinky said, and shrugged.

"And Susannah?"

"Strong. Once he's gone—" Dinky shrugged again, as if to say it could go either way, any way.

Roland knocked quietly on the door.

"Who is it?" Susannah's voice, muffled.

"Roland and Jake," the gunslinger said. "Will you have us?"

The question was met with what seemed to Jake an unusually long pause. Roland, however, didn't seem surprised. Neither did Dinky, for that matter.

At last Susannah said: "Come in."

They did.

FIVE

Sitting with Oy in the soothing dark, waiting for Roland's call, Jake reflected on the scene that had met his eyes in the darkened room. That, and the endless three-quarters of an hour before Roland had seen his discomfort and let him go, saying he'd call Jake back when it was "time."

Jake had seen a lot of death since being drawn to Mid-World; had dealt it; had even experienced his own, although he remembered very little of that. But this was the death of a ka-mate, and what had been going on in the bedroom of the proctor's suite just seemed pointless. And *endless.* Jake wished with all his heart that he'd stayed outside with Dinky; he didn't want to remember his wisecracking, occasionally hot-tempered friend this way.

For one thing, Eddie looked worse than frail as he lay in the proctor's bed with his hand in Susannah's; he looked old and (Jake hated to think of it) stupid. Or maybe the word was *senile.* His mouth had folded in at the corners, making deep dimples. Susannah had washed his face, but the stubble on his cheeks made them look dirty anyway. There were big purple patches beneath his eyes, almost as though that bastard Prentiss had beaten him up before shooting him. The eyes themselves were closed, but they rolled almost ceaselessly beneath the thin veils of his lids, as though Eddie were dreaming.

And he talked. A steady low muttering stream of words. Some of the things he said Jake could make out, some he couldn't. Some of them made at least minimal sense, but a lot of it was what his friend Benny would have called ki'come: utter nonsense. From time to time Susannah would wet a rag in the basin on the table beside the bed, wring it out, and wipe her husband's brow and dry lips. Once Roland got up, took the basin, emptied it in the bathroom, refilled it, and brought it back to her. She thanked him in a low and perfectly pleasant tone of voice. A little later Jake had freshened the water, and she thanked him in the same way. As if she didn't even know they were there.

We go for her, Roland had told Jake. *Because later on she'll remember who was there, and be grateful.*

But would she? Jake wondered now, in the darkness outside the Clover Tavern. *Would* she be grateful? It was down to Roland that Eddie Dean was lying on his deathbed at the age of twenty-five or -six, wasn't it? On the other hand, if not for Roland, she would never have met Eddie in the first place. It was all too confusing. Like the idea of multiple worlds with New Yorks in every one, it made Jake's head ache.

Lying there on his deathbed, Eddie had asked his brother Henry why he never remembered to box out.

He'd asked Jack Andolini who hit him with the ugly-stick.

He'd shouted, "Look out, Roland, it's Big-Nose George, he's back!"

And "Suze, if you can tell him the one about Dorothy and the Tin Woodman, I'll tell him all the rest."

And, chilling Jake's heart: "I do not shoot with my hand; he who aims with his hand has forgotten the face of his father."

At that last one, Roland had taken Eddie's hand in the gloom (for the shades had been drawn) and squeezed it. "Aye, Eddie, you say true. Will you open your eyes and see my face, dear?"

But Eddie hadn't opened his eyes. Instead, chilling Jake's heart more deeply yet, the young man who now wore a useless bandage about his head had murmured, "All is forgotten in the stone halls of the dead. These are the rooms of ruin where the spiders spin and the great circuits fall quiet, one by one."

After that there was nothing intelligible for awhile, only that ceaseless muttering. Jake had refilled the basin of water, and when he had come back, Roland saw his drawn white face and told him he could go.

"But—"

"Go on and go, sugarbunch," Susannah said. "Only be careful. Might still be some of em out there, looking for payback."

"But how will I—"

"I'll call you when it's time," Roland said, and tapped Jake's temple with one of the remaining fingers on his right hand. "You'll hear me."

Jake had wanted to kiss Eddie before leaving, but he was afraid. Not that he might catch death like a cold—he knew better than that—but afraid that even the touch of his lips might be enough to push Eddie into the clearing at the end of the path.

And then Susannah might blame him.

SIX

Outside in the hallway, Dinky asked him how it was going.

"Real bad," Jake said. "Do you have another cigarette?"

Dinky raised his eyebrows but gave Jake a smoke. The boy tamped it on his thumbnail, as he'd seen the gunslinger do with tailor-made smokes, then accepted a light and inhaled deeply. The smoke still burned, but not so harshly as the first time. His head only swam a little and he didn't cough. *Pretty soon I'll be a natural,* he thought. *If I ever make it back to New York, maybe I can go to work for the Network, in my Dad's department. I'm already getting good at The Kill.*

He lifted the cigarette in front of his eyes, a little white missile with smoke issuing from the top instead of the bottom. The word CAMEL was written just below the filter. "I told myself I'd never do this," Jake told Dinky. "Never in life. And here I am with one in my hand." He laughed. It was a bitter laugh, an *adult* laugh, and the sound of it coming out of his mouth made him shiver.

"I used to work for this guy before I came here," Dinky said. "Mr. Sharpton, his name was. He used to tell me that *never*'s the word God listens for when he needs a laugh."

Jake made no reply. He was thinking of how Eddie had talked about the rooms of ruin. Jake had followed Mia into a room like that, once upon a time and in a dream. Now Mia was dead. Callahan was dead. And Eddie was dying. He thought of all the bodies lying out there under blankets while thunder rolled like bones in the distance. He thought of the man who'd shot Eddie snap-rolling to the left as Roland's bullet finished him off. He tried to remember the welcoming party for them back in Calla Bryn Sturgis, the music and dancing and colored torches, but all that came clear was the death of Benny Slightman, another friend. Tonight the world seemed made of death.

He himself had died and come back: back to Mid-World and back to Roland. All afternoon he had tried to believe the same thing might happen to Eddie and knew somehow that it would not. Jake's part in the tale had not been finished. Eddie's was. Jake would have given twenty years of his life—thirty!— not to believe that, but he did. He supposed he had progged it somehow.

The rooms of ruin where the spiders spin and the great circuits fall quiet, one by one.

Jake knew a spider. Was Mia's child watching all of this? Having fun? Maybe rooting for one side or the other, like a fucking Yankee fan in the bleachers?

He is. I know he is. I feel him.

"Are you all right, kiddo?" Dinky asked.

"No," Jake said. "Not all right." And Dinky nodded as if that was a perfectly reasonable answer. *Well,* Jake thought, *probably he expected it. He's a telepath, after all.*

As if to underline this, Dinky had asked who Mordred was.

"You don't want to know," Jake said. "Believe me." He snuffed his cigarette half-smoked ("All your lung cancer's right here, in the last quarter-inch," his father used to say in tones of absolute certainty, pointing to one of his own filterless cigarettes like a TV pitchman) and left Corbett Hall. He used the back door, hoping to avoid the cluster of waiting, anxious Breakers, and in that he had succeeded. Now he was in Pleasantville, sitting on the curb like one of the homeless people you saw back in New York, waiting to be called. Waiting for the end.

He thought about going into the tavern, maybe to draw himself a beer (surely if he was old enough to smoke and to kill people from ambush he was old enough to drink a beer), maybe just to see if the jukebox would play without change. He bet that Algul Siento had been what his Dad had claimed America would become in time, a cashless society, and that old Seeberg was rigged so you only had to push the buttons in order to start the music. And he bet that if he looked at the song-strip next to 19, he'd see "Someone Saved My Life Tonight," by Elton John.

He got to his feet, and that was when the call came. Nor was he the only one who heard it; Oy let go a short, hurt-sounding yip. Roland might have been standing right next to them.

To me, Jake, and hurry. He's going.

SEVEN

Jake hurried back down one of the alleys, skirted the still-smoldering Warden's House (Tassa the houseboy, who had either ignored Roland's order to leave or hadn't been informed of it, was sitting silently on the stoop in a kilt and a sweatshirt, his head in his hands), and began to trot up the Mall, sparing a quick and troubled glance at the long line of dead bodies. The little séance-circle he'd seen earlier was gone.

I won't cry, he promised himself grimly. *If I'm old enough to smoke and think about drawing myself a beer, I'm old enough to control my stupid eyes. I won't cry.*

Knowing he almost certainly would.

EIGHT

Sheemie and Ted had joined Dinky outside the proctor's suite. Dinky had given up his seat to Sheemie. Ted looked tired, but Sheemie looked like shit on a cracker to Jake: eyes bloodshot again, a crust of dried blood around his nose and one ear, cheeks leaden. He had taken off one of his slippers and was massaging his foot as though it pained him. Yet he was clearly happy. Maybe even exalted.

"Beam says all may yet be well, young Jake," Sheemie said. "Beam says not too late. Beam says thankya."

"That's good," Jake said, reaching for the doorknob. He barely heard what Sheemie was saying. He was concentrating

(*won't cry and make it harder for her*)

on controlling his emotions once he was inside. Then Sheemie said something that brought him back in a hurry.

"Not too late in the Real World, either," Sheemie said. "We know. We peeked. Saw the moving sign. Didn't we, Ted?"

"Indeed we did." Ted was holding a can of Nozz-A-La in his lap. Now he raised it and took a sip. "When you get in there, Jake, tell Roland that if it's June 19th of '99 you're interested in, you're still okay. But the margin's commencing to get a little thin."

"I'll tell him," Jake said.

"And remind him that time sometimes slips over there. Slips like an old transmission. That's apt to continue for quite awhile, regardless of the Beam's recovery. And once the 19th is gone . . ."

"It can never come again," Jake said. "Not there. We know." He opened the door and slipped into the darkness of the proctor's suite.

NINE

A single circle of stringent yellow light, thrown by the lamp on the bedtable, lay upon Eddie Dean's face. It cast the shadow of his nose on his left cheek and turned his closed eyes into dark sockets. Susannah was kneeling on the floor beside him, holding both of his hands in both of hers and looking down at him. Her shadow ran long upon the wall. Roland sat on the other side of the bed, in deep shadow. The dying man's long, muttered monologue had ceased, and his respiration had lost all semblance of regularity. He would snatch a deep breath, hold it, then let it out in a lengthy, whistling whoosh. His chest would lie still so long that Susannah would look up into his face, her eyes shining with anxiety until the next long, tearing breath had begun.

Jake sat down on the bed next to Roland, looked at Eddie, looked at Susannah, then looked hesitantly into the gunslinger's face. In the gloom he could see nothing there except weariness.

"Ted says to tell you it's almost June 19th America-side, please and thankya. Also that time could slip a notch."

Roland nodded. "Yet we'll wait for this to be finished, I think. It won't be much longer, and we owe him that."

"How much longer?" Jake murmured.

"I don't know. I thought he might be gone before you got here, even if you ran—"

"I did, once I got to the grassy part—"

"—but, as you see . . ."

"He fights hard," Susannah said, and that this was the only thing left for her to take pride in made Jake cold. "My man fights hard. Mayhap he still has a word to say."

TEN

And so he did. Five endless minutes after Jake had slipped into the bedroom, Eddie's eyes opened. "Sue . . ." He said, "Su . . . sie—"

She leaned close, still holding his hands, smiling into his face, all her concentration fiercely narrowed. And with an effort Jake wouldn't have believed possible, Eddie freed one of his hands, swung it a little to the right, and grasped the tight kinks of her curls. If the weight of his arm pulled at the roots and hurt her, she showed no sign. The smile that bloomed on her mouth was joyous, welcoming, perhaps even sensuous.

"Eddie! Welcome back!"

"Don't bullshit . . . a bullshitter," he whispered. "I'm goin, sweetheart, not comin."

"That's just plain sil—"

"Hush," he whispered, and she did. The hand caught in her hair pulled. She brought her face to his willingly and kissed his living lips one last time. "I . . . will . . . wait for you," he said, forcing each word out with immense effort.

Jake saw beads of sweat surface on his skin, the dying body's last message to the living world, and that was when the boy's heart finally understood what his head had known for hours. He began to cry. They were tears that burned and scoured. When Roland took his hand, Jake squeezed it fiercely. He was frightened as well as sad. If it could happen to Eddie, it could happen to anybody. It could happen to him.

"Yes, Eddie. I know you'll wait," she said.

"In . . ." He pulled in another of those great, wretched, rasping breaths. His eyes were as brilliant as gemstones. "In the clearing." Another breath. Hand holding her hair. Lamplight casting them both in its mystic yellow circle. "The one at the end of the path."

"Yes, dear." Her voice was calm now, but a tear fell on Eddie's cheek and ran slowly down to the line of jaw. "I hear you very well. Wait for me and I'll find you and we'll go together. I'll be walking then, on my own legs."

Eddie smiled at her, then turned his eyes to Jake.

"Jake . . . to me."

No, Jake thought, panicked, *no, I can't, I can't.*

But he was already leaning close, into that smell of the end. He could see the fine line of grit just below Eddie's hairline turning to paste as more tiny droplets of sweat sprang up.

"Wait for me, too," Jake said through numb lips. "Okay, Eddie? We'll all go on together. We'll be ka-tet, just like we were." He tried to smile and couldn't. His heart hurt too much for smiling. He wondered if it might not explode in his chest, the way stones sometimes exploded in a hot fire. He had learned that little fact from his friend Benny Slightman. Benny's death had been bad, but this was a thousand times worse. A *million.*

Eddie was shaking his head. "Not . . . so fast, buddy." He drew in another breath and then grimaced, as if the air had grown quills only he could feel. He whispered then—not from weakness, Jake thought later, but because this was just between them. "Watch . . . for Mordred. Watch . . . Dandelo."

"Dandelion? Eddie, I don't—"

"Dandelo." Eyes widening. Enormous effort. "Protect . . . your . . . dinh . . . from Mordred. From Dandelo. You . . . Oy. *Your* job." His eyes cut toward Roland, then back to Jake. *"Shhh."* Then: "Protect . . ."

"I . . . I will. *We* will."

Eddie nodded a little, then looked at Roland. Jake moved aside and the gunslinger leaned in for Eddie's word to him.

ELEVEN

Never, ever, had Roland seen an eye so bright, not even on Jericho Hill, when Cuthbert had bade him a laughing goodbye.

Eddie smiled. "We had . . . some times."

Roland nodded again.

"You . . . you . . ." But this Eddie couldn't finish. He raised one hand and made a weak twirling motion.

"I danced," Roland said, nodding. "Danced the commala."

Yes, Eddie mouthed, then drew in another of those whooping, painful breaths. It was the last.

"Thank you for my second chance," he said. "Thank you . . . Father."

That was all. Eddie's eyes still looked at him, and they were still aware, but he had no breath to replace the one expended on that final word, that *father.* The lamplight gleamed on the hairs of his bare arms, turning them to gold. The thunder murmured. Then Eddie's eyes closed and he laid his head to one side. His work was finished. He had left the path, stepped into the clearing. They sat around him a-circle, but ka-tet no more.

TWELVE

And so, thirty minutes later.

Roland, Jake, Ted, and Sheemie sat on a bench in the middle of the Mall. Dani Rostov and the bankerly-looking fellow were nearby. Susannah was in the bedroom of the proctor's suite, washing her husband's body for burial. They could hear her from where they were sitting. She was singing. All the songs seemed to be ones they'd heard Eddie singing along the trail. One was "Born to Run." Another was "The Rice Song," from Calla Bryn Sturgis.

"We have to go, and right away," Roland said. His hand had gone to his hip and was rubbing, rubbing. Jake had seen him take a bottle of aspirin (gotten God knew where) from his purse and dry-swallow three. "Sheemie, will you send us on?"

Sheemie nodded. He had limped to the bench, leaning on Dinky for support, and still none of them had had a chance to look at the wound on his foot. His limp seemed so minor compared to their other concerns; surely if Sheemie Ruiz were to die this night it would be as a result of opening a makeshift door between Thunder-side and America. Another strenuous act of teleportation might be lethal to him—what was a sore foot compared to that?

"I'll try," he said. "I'll try my very hardest, so I will."

"Those who helped us look into New York will help us do this," Ted said.

It was Ted who had figured out how to determine the current when on America-side of the Keystone World. He, Dinky, Fred Worthington (the bankerly-looking man), and Dani Rostov had all been to New York, and were all able to summon up clear mental images of Times Square: the lights, the crowds, the movie marquees . . . and, most important, the giant news-ticker which broadcast the events of the day to the crowds below, making a complete circuit of Broadway and Forty-eighth Street every thirty seconds or so. The hole had opened long enough to inform them that UN forensics experts were examining supposed mass graves in Kosovo, that Vice President Gore had spent the day in New York City campaigning for President, that Roger Clemens had struck out thirteen Texas Rangers but the Yankees had still lost the night before.

With the help of the rest, Sheemie could have held the hole open a good while longer (the others had been staring into the brilliance of that bustling New York night with a kind of hungry amazement, not Breaking now but Opening, Seeing), only there turned out to be no need for that. Following the baseball score, the date and time had gone speeding past them in brilliant yellow-green letters a story high: **JUNE 18, 1999 9:19 PM**.

Jake opened his mouth to ask how they could be sure they had been looking into Keystone World, the one where Stephen King had less than a day to live, and then shut it again. The answer was in the time, stupid, as the answer always was: the numbers comprising 9:19 also added up to nineteen.

THIRTEEN

"And how long ago was it that you saw this?" Roland asked.

Dinky calculated. "Had to've been five hours, at least. Based on when the change-of-shifts horn blew and the sun went out for the night."

Which should make it two-thirty in the morning right now on the other side, Jake calculated, counting the hours on his fingers. Thinking was hard now, even simple addition slowed by constant thoughts of Eddie, but he found he could do it if he really tried. *Only you can't depend on its only being five hours, because time goes faster on America-side. That may change now that the Breakers have quit beating up on the Beam— it may equalize— but probably not yet. Right now it's probably still running fast.*

And it might slip.

One minute Stephen King could be sitting in front of his typewriter in his office on the morning of June 19th, fine as paint, and the next . . . boom! Lying in a nearby funeral parlor that evening, eight or twelve hours gone by in a flash, his grieving family sitting in their own circle of lamplight and trying to decide what kind of service King would've wanted, always assuming that information wasn't in his will; maybe even trying to decide where he'd be buried. And the Dark Tower? Stephen King's version of the Dark Tower? Or Gan's version, or the *Prim*'s version? Lost forever, all of them. And that sound you hear? Why, that must be the Crimson King, laughing and laughing and laughing from somewhere deep in the Discordia. And maybe Mordred the Spider-Boy, laughing along with him.

For the first time since Eddie's death, something besides grief came to the forefront of Jake's mind. It was a faint ticking sound, like the one the Sneetches had made when Roland and Eddie programmed them. Just before giving them to Haylis to plant, this had been. It was the sound of time, and time was not their friend.

"He's right," Jake said. "We have to go while we can still do something."

Ted: "Will Susannah—"

"No," Roland said. "Susannah will stay here, and you'll help her bury Eddie. Do you agree?"

"Yes," Ted said. "Of course, if that's how you'd have it."

"If we're not back in . . ." Roland calculated, one eye squinted shut, the other looking off into the darkness. "If we're not back by this time on the night after next, assume that we've come back to End-World at Fedic." *Yes, assume Fedic,* Jake thought. *Of course. Because what good would it do to make the other, even more logical assumption, that we're either dead or lost between the worlds, todash forever?*

"Do'ee ken Fedic?" Roland was asking.

"South of here, isn't it?" asked Worthington. He had wandered over with Dani, the pre-teen girl. "Or what *was* south? Trampas and a few of the other can-toi used to talk of it as though it were haunted."

"It's haunted, all right," Roland said grimly. "Can you put Susannah on a train to Fedic in the event that we're not able to come back here? I know that at least some trains must still run, because of—"

"The Greencloaks?" Dinky said, nodding. "Or the Wolves, as you think of them. All the D-line trains still run. They're automated."

"Are they monos? Do they talk?" Jake asked. He was thinking of Blaine.

Dinky and Ted exchanged a doubtful look, then Dinky returned his attention to Jake and shrugged. "How would we know? I probably know more about D-*cups* than D-lines, and I think that's true of everyone here. The Breakers, at least. I suppose some of the guards might know something more. Or that guy." He jerked a thumb at Tassa, who was still sitting on the stoop of Warden's House, head in hands.

"In any case, we'll tell Susannah to be careful," Roland murmured to Jake. Jake nodded. He supposed that was the best they could do, but he had another question. He made a mental note to ask either Ted or Dinky, if he got a chance to do so without being overheard by Roland. He didn't like the idea of leaving Susannah behind—every instinct of his heart cried out against it—but he knew she would refuse to leave Eddie unburied, and Roland knew it, too. They could make her come, but only by binding and gagging her, and that would only make things worse than they were already.

"It might be," Ted said, "that a few Breakers would be interested in taking the train-trip south with Susannah."

Dani nodded. "We're not exactly loved around here for helping you out," she said. "Ted and Dinky are getting it the worst, but somebody spit at me half an hour ago, while I was in my room, getting this." She held up a battered-looking and clearly much-loved Pooh Bear. "I don't think they'll do anything while you guys are around, but after you go . . ." She shrugged.

"Man, I don't get that," Jake said. "They're *free*."

"Free to do what?" Dinky asked. "Think about it. Most of them were misfits on America-side. Fifth wheels. Over here we were VIPs, and we got the best of everything. Now all that's gone. When you think about it that way, is it so hard to understand?"

"Yes," Jake said bluntly. He supposed he didn't *want* to understand.

"They lost something else, too," Ted told them quietly. "There's a novel by Ray Bradbury called *Fahrenheit 451.* 'It was a pleasure to burn' is that novel's first line. Well, it was a pleasure to Break, as well."

Dinky was nodding. So were Worthington and Dani Rostov.

Even Sheemie was nodding his head.

FOURTEEN

Eddie lay in that same circle of light, but now his face was clean and the top sheet of the proctor's bed had been folded neatly down to his midsection. Susannah had dressed him in a clean white shirt she'd found somewhere (in the proctor's closet was Jake's guess), and she must have found a razor, too, because his cheeks were smooth. Jake tried to imagine her sitting here and shaving the face of her dead husband—singing

"Commala-come-come, the rice has just begun" as she did it—
and at first he couldn't. Then, all at once, the image came to
him, and it was so powerful that he had to struggle once again
to keep from bursting into sobs.

She listened quietly as Roland spoke to her, sitting on the
side of the bed, hands folded in her lap, eyes downcast. To
the gunslinger she looked like a shy virgin receiving a marriage proposal.

When he had finished, she said nothing.

"Do you understand what I've told you, Susannah?"

"Yes," she said, still without looking up. "I'm to bury my man.
Ted and Dinky will help me, if only to keep their friends—" she
gave this word a bitterly sarcastic little twist that actually encouraged Roland a bit; she was in there after all, it seemed "—from
taking him away from me and lynching his body from a sour
apple tree."

"And then?"

"Either you'll find a way to come back here and we'll return
to Fedic together, or Ted and Dinky will put me on the train
and I'll go there alone."

Jake didn't just hate the cold disconnection in her voice; it
terrified him, as well. "You know why we have to go back to the
other side, don't you?" he asked anxiously. "I mean, you *know*,
don't you?"

"To save the writer while there's still time." She had picked
up one of Eddie's hands, and Jake noted with fascination that
his nails were perfectly clean. What had she used to get the dirt
out from beneath them, he wondered—had the proctor had
one of those little nail-care gadgets, like the one his father
always kept on a keychain in his pocket? "Sheemie says we've
saved the Beam of Bear and Turtle. We *think* we've saved the
rose. But there's at least one more job to do. The writer. The
lazybones *writer.*" Now she did look up, and her eyes flashed.
Jake suddenly thought it might be good that Susannah wouldn't
be with them when—if—they met sai Stephen King.

"You *bettah* save him," she said. Both Roland and Jake could
hear old sneak-thief Detta creeping into her voice. "After what's

happened today, you just *bettah.* And this time, Roland, you tell him not to stop with his writin. Not come hell, high water, cancer, or gangrene of the dick. Never mind worryin about the Pulitzer Prize, neither. You tell him to go on and be *done* with his motherfuckin *story.*"

"I will pass the message on," Roland said.

She nodded.

"You'll come to us when this job is finished," Roland said, and his voice rose just slightly on the last word, almost turning it into a question. "You'll come with us and finish the final job, won't you?"

"Yes," she said. "Not because I want to—all the spit and git is out of me—but because *he* wanted me to." Gently, very gently, she put Eddie's hand back on his chest with the other one. Then she pointed a finger at Roland. The tip trembled minutely. "Just don't start up with any of that 'we are ka-tet, we are one from many' crap. Because those days are gone. Ain't they?"

"Yes," Roland said. "But the Tower still stands. And waits."

"Lost my taste for that, too, big boy." Not quite *los' mah tase fo' dat, too,* but almost. "Tell you the truth."

But Jake realized that she was *not* telling the truth. She *hadn't* lost her desire to see the Dark Tower any more than Roland had. Any more than Jake had himself. Their tet might be broken, but ka remained. And she felt it just as they did.

FIFTEEN

They kissed her (and Oy licked her face) before leaving.

"You be careful, Jake," Susannah said. "Come back safe, hear? Eddie would have told you the same."

"I know," Jake said, and then kissed her again. He was smiling because he could hear Eddie telling him to watch his ass, it was cracked already, and starting to cry once more for the same reason. Susannah held him tight a moment longer, then let him go and turned back to her husband, lying so still and cold in the proctor's bed. Jake understood that she had little time for Jake Chambers or Jake Chambers's grief just now. Her own was too big.

SIXTEEN

Outside the suite, Dinky waited by the door. Roland was walking on with Ted, the two of them already at the end of the corridor and deep in conversation. Jake supposed they were headed back to the Mall, where Sheemie (with a little help from the others) would attempt to send them once more to America-side. That reminded him of something.

"The D-line trains go south," Jake said. "Or what's supposed to be south—is that right?"

"More or less, partner," Dinky said. "Some of the engines have got names, like *Delicious Rain* or *Spirit of the Snow Country*, but they've *all* got letters and numbers."

"Does the D stand for Dandelo?" Jake asked.

Dinky looked at him with a puzzled frown. "Dandelo? What in the hell is that?"

Jake shook his head. He didn't even want to tell Dinky where he'd heard the word.

"Well, I don't know, not for sure," Dinky said as they resumed walking, "but I always assumed the D stood for Discordia. Because that's where all the trains supposedly end up, you know—somewhere deep in the universe's baddest Badlands."

Jake nodded. D for Discordia. That made sense. Sort of, anyway.

"You didn't answer my question," Dinky said. "What's a Dandelo?"

"Just a word I saw written on the wall in Thunderclap Station. It probably doesn't mean anything."

SEVENTEEN

Outside Corbett Hall, a delegation of Breakers waited. They looked grim and frightened. *D for Dandelo,* Jake thought. *D for Discordia. Also D for desperate.*

Roland faced them with his arms folded over his chest. "Who speaks for you?" he asked. "If one speaks, let him come forward now, for our time here is up."

A gray-haired gentleman—another bankerly-looking fellow, in truth—stepped forward. He was wearing gray suitpants, a white shirt open at the collar, and a gray vest, also open. The vest sagged. So did the man wearing it.

"You've taken our lives from us," he said. He spoke these words with a kind of morose satisfaction—as if he'd always known it would come to this (or something like this). "The lives we knew. What will you give back in return, Mr. Gilead?"

There was a rumble of approval at this. Jake Chambers heard it and was suddenly more angry than ever before in his life. His hand, seemingly of its own accord, stole to the handle of the Coyote machine-pistol, caressed it, and found a cold comfort in its shape. Even a brief respite from grief. And Roland knew, for he reached behind him without looking and put his hand on top of Jake's. He squeezed until Jake let loose of the gun.

"I'll tell you what I'll give, since you ask," Roland said. "I meant to have this place, where you have fed on the brains of helpless children in order to destroy the universe, burned to the ground; aye, every stick of it. I intended to set certain flying balls that have come into our possession to explode, and blow apart anything that would not burn. I intended to point you the way to the River Whye and the green Callas which lie beyond it, and set you on with a curse my father taught me: may you live long, but not in good health."

A resentful murmur greeted this, but not an eye met Roland's own. The man who had agreed to speak for them (and even in his rage, Jake gave him points for courage) was swaying on his feet, as if he might soon faint away.

"The Callas still lie in that direction," Roland said, and pointed. "If you go, some—many, even—may die on the way, for there are animals out there that are hungry, and what water there is may be poison. I've no doubt the Calla-*folken* will know who you are and what you've been about even if you lie, for they have the Manni among them and the Manni see much. Yet you may find forgiveness there rather than death, for the capacity for forgiveness in the hearts of such people is beyond the capacity of hearts such as yours to understand. Or mine, for that matter.

"That they would put you to work and that the rest of your lives would pass not in the comfort you've known but in toil and sweat I have no doubt, yet I urge you to go, if only to find some redemption for what you have done."

"We didn't *know* what we were doing, ye chary man!" a woman in the back yelled furiously.

"YOU KNEW!" Jake shouted back, screaming so loudly that he saw black dots in front of his eyes, and Roland's hand was once again instantly over his to stay his draw. Would he actually have sprayed the crowd with the Coyote, bringing more death to this terrible place? He didn't know. What he did know was that a gunslinger's hands were sometimes not under his control once a weapon was in them. "Don't you dare say you didn't! *You knew!"*

"I'll give this much, may it do ya," Roland said. "My friends and I — those who survive, although I'm sure the one who lies dead yonder would agree, which is why I speak as I do — will let this place stand. There's food enough to see you through the rest of your lives, I have no doubt, and robots to cook it and wash your clothes and even wipe your asses, if that's what you think you need. If you prefer purgatory to redemption, then stay here. Were I you, I'd make the trek instead. Follow the railroad tracks out of the shadows. Tell them what you did before they can tell you, and get on your knees with your heads bared, and beg their forgiveness."

"Never!" someone shouted adamantly, but Jake thought some of the others looked unsure.

"As you will," said Roland. "I've spoken my last word on it, and the next who speaks back to me may remain silent ever after, for one of my friends is preparing another, her husband, to lie in the ground and I am full of grief and rage. Would you speak more? Would you dare my rage? If so, you dare this." He drew his gun and laid it in the hollow of his shoulder. Jake stepped up beside him, at last drawing his own.

There was a moment of silence, and then the man who had spoken turned away.

"Don't shoot us, mister, you've done enough," someone said bitterly.

Roland made no reply and the crowd began to disperse. Some went running, and the others caught that like a cold. They fled in silence, except for a few who were weeping, and soon the dark had swallowed them up.

"Wow," Dinky said. His voice was soft and respectful.

"Roland," Ted said. "What they did wasn't entirely their fault. I thought I had explained that, but I guess I didn't do a very good job."

Roland holstered his revolver. "You did an excellent job," he said. "That's why they're still alive."

Now they had the Damli House end of the Mall to themselves again, and Sheemie limped up to Roland. His eyes were round and solemn. "Will you show me where you'd go, dear?" he asked. "Can you show me the place?"

The place. Roland had been so fixed on the *when* that he'd scarcely thought of the *where.* And his memories of the road they had traveled in Lovell were pretty skimpy. Eddie had been driving John Cullum's car, and Roland had been deep in his own thoughts, concentrating on the things he would say to convince the caretaker to help them.

"Did Ted show you a place before you sent him on?" he asked Sheemie.

"Aye, so he did. Only he didn't know he was showing me. It was a baby-picture . . . I don't know how to tell you, exactly . . . stupid head! Full of cobwebbies!" Sheemie made a fist and clouted himself between the eyes.

Roland took the hand before Sheemie could hit himself again and unrolled the fingers. He did this with surprising gentleness. "No, Sheemie. I think I understand. You found a thought . . . a memory from when he was a little boy."

Ted had come over to them. "Of course that must be it," he

said. "I don't know why I didn't see it before now. Too simple, maybe. I grew up in Milford, and the place where I came out in 1960 was barely a spit from there in geographical terms. Sheemie must have found a memory of a carriage-ride, or maybe a trip on the Hartford Trolley to see my Uncle Jim and Aunt Molly in Bridgeport. Something in my subconscious." He shook his head. "I *knew* the place where I came out looked familiar, but of course it was years later. The Merritt Parkway wasn't there when I was a boy."

"Can you show me a picture like that?" Sheemie asked Roland hopefully.

Roland thought once more of the place in Lovell where they'd parked on Route 7, the place where he'd called Chevin of Chayven out of the woods, but it simply wasn't sure enough; there was no landmark that made the place only itself and no other. Not one that he remembered, anyway.

Then another idea came. One that had to do with Eddie.

"Sheemie!"

"Aye, Roland of Gilead, Will Dearborn that was!"

Roland reached out and placed his hands on the sides of Sheemie's head. "Close your eyes, Sheemie, son of Stanley."

Sheemie did as he was told, then reached out his own hands and grasped the sides of Roland's head. Roland closed his own eyes.

"See what I see, Sheemie," he said. "See where we would go. See it very well."

And Sheemie did.

EIGHTEEN

While they stood there, Roland projecting and Sheemie seeing, Dani Rostov softly called to Jake.

Once he was before her she hesitated, as if unsure what she would say or do. He began to ask her, but before he could, she stopped his mouth with a kiss. Her lips were amazingly soft.

"That's for good luck," she said, and when she saw his look of amazement and understood the power of what she had done, her timidity lessened. She put her arms around his neck (still holding her scuffed Pooh Bear in one hand; he felt it soft against his back) and did it again. He felt the push of her tiny, hard breasts and would remember the sensation for the rest of his life. Would remember *her* for the rest of his life.

"And that's for me." She retreated to Ted Brautigan's side, eyes downcast and cheeks burning red, before he could speak. Not that he could have, even if his life had depended upon it. His throat was locked shut.

Ted looked at him and smiled. "You judge the rest of them by the first one," he said. "Take it from me. I know."

Jake could still say nothing. She might have punched him in the head instead of kissing him on the lips. He was that dazed.

NINETEEN

Fifteen minutes later, four men, one girl, a billy-bumbler, and one dazed, amazed (and very tired) boy stood on the Mall. They seemed to have the grassy quad to themselves; the rest of the Breakers had disappeared completely. From where he stood, Jake could see the lighted window on the first floor of Corbett Hall where Susannah was tending to her man. Thunder rumbled. Ted spoke now as he had in Thundercap Station's office closet, where the red blazer's brass tag read HEAD OF SHIPPING, back when Eddie's death had been unthinkable: "Join hands. And concentrate."

Jake started to reach for Dani Rostov's hand, but Dinky shook his head, smiling a little. "Maybe you can hold hands with her another day, hero, but right now you're the monkey in the middle. And your dinh's another one."

"You hold hands with each other," Sheemie said. There was a quiet authority in his voice that Jake hadn't heard before. "That'll help."

Jake tucked Oy into his shirt. "Roland, were you able to show Sheemie—"

"Look," Roland said, taking his hands. The others now made a tight circle around them. "Look. I think you'll see."

A brilliant seam opened in the darkness, obliterating Sheemie and Ted from Jake's view. For a moment it trembled and darkened, and Jake thought it would disappear. Then it grew bright again and spread wider. He heard, very faintly (the way you heard things when you were underwater), the sound of a car or truck passing in that other world. And saw a building with a small asphalt lot in front of it. Three cars and a pickup truck were parked there.

Daylight! he thought, dismayed. Because if time never ran backward in the Keystone World, that meant that time *had* slipped. If that was Keystone World, then it was Saturday, the nineteenth of June, in the year—

"Quick!" Ted shouted from the other side of that brilliant hole in reality. "If you're going, go now! He's going to faint! If you're going—"

Roland yanked Jake forward, his purse bouncing on his back as he did so.

Wait! Jake wanted to shout. *Wait, I forgot my stuff!*

But it was too late. There was the sensation of big hands squeezing his chest, and he felt all the air whoosh out of his lungs. He thought, *Pressure change.* There was a sensation of falling *up* and then he was reeling onto the pavement of the parking lot with his shadow tacked to his heels, squinting and grimacing, wondering in some distant part of his mind how long it had been since his eyes had been exposed to plain old natural daylight. Not since entering the Doorway Cave in pursuit of Susannah, maybe.

Very faintly he heard someone—he thought it was the girl who had kissed him—call *Good luck,* and then it was gone. Thunderclap was gone, and the Devar-Toi, and the darkness. They were America-side, in the parking lot of the place to which Roland's memory and Sheemie's power—boosted by the other four Breakers—had taken them. It was the East Stoneham General Store, where Roland and Eddie had been ambushed by

Jack Andolini. Only unless there had been some horrible error, that had been twenty-two years earlier. This was June 19th of 1999, and the clock in the window (IT'S <u>ALWAYS</u> TIME FOR BOAR'S HEAD MEATS! was written in a circle around the face) said it was nineteen minutes of four in the afternoon.

Time was almost up.

PART THREE

IN THIS HAZE OF GREEN AND GOLD

VES'-KA GAN

CHAPTER I:
MRS. TASSENBAUM
DRIVES SOUTH

ONE

The fact of his own almost unearthly speed of hand never occurred to Jake Chambers. All he knew was that when he staggered out of the Devar-Toi and back into America, his shirt—belled out into a pregnant curve by Oy's weight—was pulling out of his jeans. The bumbler, who never had much luck when it came to passing between the worlds (he'd nearly been squashed by a taxicab the last time), tumbled free. Almost anyone else in the world would have been unable to prevent that fall (and in fact it very likely wouldn't have hurt Oy at all), but Jake wasn't almost anyone. Ka had wanted him so badly that it had even found its way around death to put him at Roland's side. Now his hands shot out with a speed so great that they momentarily blurred away to nothing. When they reappeared, one was curled into the thick shag at the nape of Oy's neck and the other into the shorter fur at the rump end of his long back. Jake set his friend down on the pavement. Oy looked up at him and gave a single short bark. It seemed to express not one idea but two: *thanks,* and *don't do that again.*

"Come on," Roland said. "We have to hurry."

Jake followed him toward the store, Oy falling in at his accustomed place by the boy's left heel. There was a sign hanging in the door from a little rubber suction cup. It read WE'RE OPEN, SO COME IN N VISIT, just as it had in 1977. Taped in the window to the left of the door was this:

COME ONE COME ALL
TO THE
1st CONGREGATIONAL CHURCH
BEANHOLE BEAN SUPPER
Saturday June 19th, 1999
Intersection Route 7 & Klatt Road

PARISH HOUSE (In Back)
5 PM–7:30 PM

AT 1st CONGO
"WE'RE ALWAYS GLAD TO SEEYA, NAYBAH!"

Jake thought, *The bean supper will be starting in an hour or so. They'll already be putting down the tablecloths and setting the places.*

Taped to the right of the door was a more startling message to the public:

1st Lovell-Stoneham Church of the Walk-Ins
Will YOU join us for Worship?

Sunday services: 10 AM
Thursday services: 7 PM

EVERY WEDNESDAY IS YOUTH NIGHT!!! 7–9 PM!
Games! Music! Scripture!
AND
NEWS OF WALK-INS!
Hey, Teens!
"Be There or Be Square!!!"
"We Seek the Doorway to Heaven—Will You Seek With Us?"

Jake found himself thinking of Harrigan, the street-preacher on the corner of Second Avenue and Forty-sixth Street, and wondering to which of these two churches he might have been attracted. His head might have told him First Congo, but his *heart*—

"Hurry, Jake," Roland repeated, and there was a jingle as the gunslinger opened the door. Good smells wafted out, reminding Jake (as they had reminded Eddie) of Took's on the Calla high street: coffee and peppermint candy, tobacco and salami, olive oil, the salty tang of brine, sugar and spice and most things nice.

He followed Roland into the store, aware that he had brought at least two things with him, after all. The Coyote machine-pistol was stuffed into the waistband of his jeans, and the bag of Orizas was still slung over his shoulder, hanging on his left side so that the half a dozen plates remaining inside would be within easy reach of his right hand.

TWO

Wendell "Chip" McAvoy was at the deli counter, weighing up a pretty sizable order of sliced honey-cured turkey for Mrs. Tassenbaum, and until the bell over the door rang, once more turning Chip's life upside down (*You've turned turtle*, the oldtimers used to say when your car rolled in the ditch), they had been discussing the growing presence of Jet Skis on Keywadin Pond . . . or rather Mrs. *Tassenbaum* had been discussing it.

Chip thought Mrs. T. was a more or less typical summer visitor: rich as Croesus (or at least her husband, who had one of those new dot-com businesses, was), gabby as a parrot loaded on whiskey, and as crazy as Howard Hughes on a morphine toot. She could afford a cabin cruiser (and two dozen Jet Skis to pull it, if she fancied), but she came down to the market on this end of the lake in a battered old rowboat, tying up right about where John Cullum used to tie his up, until That Day (as the years had refined his story to ever greater purity, burnishing it like an oft-polished piece of teak furniture, Chip had come more and more to convey its capital-letter status with his voice, speaking of That Day in the same reverential tones the Reverend Conveigh used when speaking of Our Lord). La Tassenbaum was talky, meddlesome, good-looking (kinda . . . he supposed . . . if you didn't mind the makeup and the hairspray), loaded with green, and a Republican. Under the circumstances, Chip McAvoy felt perfectly justified in sneaking his thumb onto the corner of the scale . . . a trick he had learned from his father, who had told him you practically had a duty to rook folks from away if they could afford it, but you must never rook folks from the home place, not even if they were as rich as that writer, King, from over in Lovell. Why? Because word got around, and the next thing you knew, out-of-town custom was all a man had to get by on, and try doing *that* in the month of February when the snowbanks on the sides of Route 7 were nine feet high. This wasn't February, however, and Mrs. Tassenbaum—a Daughter of Abraham if he had ever seen one—was not from these parts. No, Mrs. Tassenbaum and her rich-as-Croesus dot-com husband would be gone back to Jew York as soon as they saw the first colored leaf fall. Which was why he felt perfectly comfortable in turning her six-dollar order of turkey into seven dollars and eighty cents with the ball of his thumb on the scale. Nor did it hurt to agree with her when she switched topics and started talking about what a terrible man that Bill Clinton was, although in fact Chip had voted twice for Bubba and would have voted for him a third time, had the Constitution allowed him to run for another term. Bubba was smart, he was good at persuading the ragheads to do what he wanted, he hadn't *entirely* forgotten the working man, and by the Lord Harry he got more pussy than a toilet seat.

"And now *Gore* expects to just . . . ride in on his coattails!" Mrs. Tassenbaum said, digging for her checkbook (the turkey on the scale magically gained another two ounces, and there Chip felt it prudent to lock it in). "Claims he invented the Internet! Huh! I know better! In fact, I know the man who really *did* invent the Internet!" She looked up (Chip's thumb now nowhere near the scales, he had an instinct about such things, damned if he didn't) and gave Chip a roguish little smile. She lowered her voice into its confidential just-we-two register. "I ought to, I've been sleeping in the same bed with him for almost twenty years!"

Chip gave a hearty laugh, took the sliced turkey off the scale, and put it on a piece of white paper. He was glad to leave the subject of Jet Skis behind, as he had one on order from Viking Motors ("The Boys with the Toys") in Oxford himself.

"I know what you mean! That fella Gore, too slick!" Mrs. Tassenbaum was nodding enthusiastically, and so Chip decided to lay on a little more. Never hurt, by Christ. "His hair, for instance—how can you trust a man who puts that much goo in his—"

That was when the bell over the door jingled. Chip looked up. Saw. And froze. A goddamned lot of water had gone under the bridge since That Day, but Wendell "Chip" McAvoy knew the man who'd caused all the trouble the moment he stepped through the door. Some faces you simply never forgot. And hadn't he always known, deep in his heart's most secret place, that the man with the terrible blue eyes hadn't finished his business and would be back?

Back for him?

That idea broke his paralysis. Chip turned and ran. He got no more than three steps along the inside of the counter before a shot rang out, loud as thunder in the store—the place was bigger and fancier than it had been in '77, thank God for his father's insistence on extravagant insurance coverage—and Mrs. Tassenbaum uttered a piercing scream. Three or four people who had been browsing the aisles turned with expressions of astonishment, and one of them hit the floor in a dead faint. Chip had time to register that it was Rhoda Beemer, eldest daughter of one of the two women who'd been killed in here on That Day. Then it seemed to him that time had folded back on itself and it was Ruth herself lying there with a can of creamed corn rolling free of one relaxing hand. He heard a bullet buzz over his head like an angry bee and skidded to a stop, hands raised.

"Don't shoot, mister!" he heard himself bawl in the thin, wavering voice of an old man. "Take whatever's in the register but don't shoot me!"

"Turn around," said the voice of the man who had turned Chip's world turtle on That Day, the man who'd almost gotten him killed (he'd been in the hospital over in Bridgton for two weeks, by the living Jesus) and had now reappeared like an old monster from some child's closet. "The rest of you on the floor, but you turn around, shopkeeper. Turn around and see me.

"See me very well."

THREE

The man swayed from side to side, and for a moment Roland thought he would faint instead of turning. Perhaps some survival-oriented part of his brain suggested that fainting was more likely to get him killed, for the shopkeeper managed to keep his feet and *did* finally turn and face the gunslinger. His dress was eerily similar to what he'd been wearing the last time Roland was here; it could have been the same black tie and butcher's apron, tied up high on his midriff. His hair was still slicked back along his skull, but now it was wholly white instead of salt-and-pepper. Roland remembered the way blood had dashed back from the left side of the shopkeeper's temple as a bullet—one fired by Andolini himself, for all the gunslinger knew—grooved him. Now there was a grayish knot of scar-tissue there. Roland guessed the man combed his hair in a way that would display that mark rather than hide it. He'd either had a fool's luck that day or been saved by ka. Roland thought ka the more likely.

Judging from the sick look of recognition in the shopkeeper's eyes, he thought so, too.

"Do you have a cartomobile, a truckomobile, or a tacksee?" Roland asked, holding the barrel of his gun on the shopkeeper's middle.

Jake stepped up beside Roland. "What are you driving?" he asked the shopkeeper. "That's what he means."

"Truck!" the shopkeeper managed. "International Harvester pickup! It's outside in the lot!" He reached under his apron so suddenly that Roland came within an ace of shooting him. The shopkeeper—mercifully—didn't seem to notice. All of the store's customers were now lying prone, including the woman who'd been at the counter. Roland could smell the meat she had been in the process of trading for, and his stomach rumbled. He was tired, hungry, overloaded with grief, and there were too many things to think about, too many by far. His mind couldn't keep up. Jake would have said he needed to "take a time-out," but he didn't see any time-outs in their immediate future.

The shopkeeper was holding out a set of keys. His fingers were trembling, and the keys jingled. The late-afternoon sun slanting in the windows struck them and bounced complicated reflections into the gunslinger's eyes. First the man in the white apron had plunged a hand out of sight without asking permission (and not slowly); now this, holding up a bunch of reflective metal objects as if to blind his adversary. It was as if he were *trying* to get killed. But it had been that way on the day of the ambush, too, hadn't it? The storekeeper (quicker on his feet then, and without that widower's hump in his back) had followed him and Eddie from place to place like a cat who won't stop getting under your feet, seemingly oblivious to the bullets flying all around them (just as he'd seemed oblivious of the one that grooved the side of his head). At one point, Roland remembered, he had talked about his son, almost like a man in a barbershop making conversation while he waits his turn to sit under the scissors. A ka-mai, then, and such were often safe from harm. At least until ka tired of their antics and swatted them out of the world.

"Take the truck, take it and go!" the shopkeeper was telling him. "It's yours! I'm giving it to you! Really!"

"If you don't stop flashing those damned keys in my eyes, sai, what I'll take is your breath," Roland said. There was another clock behind the counter. He had already noticed that this world was full of clocks, as if the people who lived here thought that by having so many they could cage time. Ten minutes of four, which meant they'd been America-side for nine minutes already. Time was racing, racing. Somewhere nearby Stephen King was almost certainly on his afternoon walk, and in desperate danger, although he didn't know it. Or had it happened already? They—Roland, anyway—had always assumed that the writer's death would hit them hard, like another Beamquake, but maybe not. Maybe the impact of his death would be more gradual.

"How far from here to Turtleback Lane?" Roland rapped at the storekeeper.

The elderly sai only stared, eyes huge and liquid with terror. Never in his life had Roland felt more like shooting a man . . . or at least pistol-whipping him. He looked as foolish as a goat with its foot stuck in a crevice.

Then the woman lying in front of the meat-counter spoke. She was looking up at Roland and Jake, her hands clasped together at the small of her back. "That's in Lovell, mister. It's about five miles from here."

One look in her eyes—large and brown, fearful but not panicky—and Roland decided this was the one he wanted, not the storekeeper. Unless, that was—

He turned to Jake. "Can you drive the shopkeeper's truck five miles?"

Roland saw the boy wanting to say yes, then realizing he couldn't afford to risk ultimate failure by trying to do a thing he—city boy that he was—had never done in his life.

"No," Jake said. "I don't think so. What about you?"

Roland had watched Eddie drive John Cullum's car. It didn't look that hard . . . but there was his hip to consider. Rosa had told him that dry twist moved fast—like a fire driven by strong winds, she'd said—and now he knew what she'd meant. On the trail into Calla Bryn Sturgis, the pain in his hip had been no more than an occasional twinge. Now it was as if the socket had been injected with red-hot lead, then wrapped in strands of barbed wire. The pain radiated all the way down his leg to the right ankle. He'd watched how Eddie manipulated the pedals, going back and forth between the one that made the car speed up and the one that made it slow down, always using the right foot. Which meant the ball of the right hip was always rolling in its socket.

He didn't think he could do that. Not with any degree of safety.

"I think not," he said. He took the keys from the shopkeeper, then looked at the woman lying in front of the meat-counter. "Stand up, sai," he said.

Mrs. Tassenbaum did as she was told, and when she was on her feet, Roland gave her the keys. *I keep meeting useful people in here*, he thought. *If this one's as good as Cullum turned out to be, we might still be all right.*

"You're going to drive my young friend and me to Lovell," Roland said.

"To Turtleback Lane," she said.

"You say true, I say thankya."

"Are you going to kill me after you get to where you want to go?"

"Not unless you dawdle," Roland said.

She considered this, then nodded. "Then I won't. Let's go."

"Good luck, Mrs. Tassenbaum," the shopkeeper told her faintly as she started for the door.

"If I don't come back," she said, "you just remember one thing: it was my husband who invented the Internet—him and his friends, partly at CalTech and partly in their own garages. *Not* Albert Gore."

Roland's stomach rumbled again. He reached over the counter (the shopkeeper cringed away from him as if he suspected Roland of carrying the red plague), grabbed the woman's pile of turkey, and folded three slices into his mouth. The rest he handed to Jake, who ate two slices and then looked down at Oy, who was looking up at the meat with great interest.

"I'll give you your share when we get in the truck," Jake promised.

"Ruck," Oy said; then, with much greater emphasis: "Share!"

"Holy jumping Jesus Christ," the shopkeeper said.

FOUR

The Yankee shopkeeper's accent might have been cute, but his truck wasn't. It was a standard shift, for one thing. Irene Tassenbaum of Manhattan hadn't driven a standard since she had been Irene Cantora of Staten Island. It was also a stick shift, and she had never driven one of those.

Jake was sitting beside her with his feet placed around said stick and Oy (still chewing turkey) on his lap. Roland swung into the passenger seat, trying not to snarl at the pain in his leg. Irene forgot to depress the clutch when she keyed the ignition. The I-H lurched forward, then stalled. Luckily it had been rolling the roads of western Maine since the mid-sixties and it was the sedate jump of an elderly mare rather than the spirited buck of a colt; otherwise Chip McAvoy would once more have lost at least one of his plate-glass windows. Oy scrabbled for balance on Jake's lap and sprayed out a mouthful of turkey along with a word he had learned from Eddie.

Irene stared at the bumbler with wide, startled eyes. "Did that creature just say *fuck*, young man?"

"Never mind what he said," Jake replied. His voice was shaking. The hands of the Boar's Head clock in the window now stood at five to four. Like Roland, the boy had never had a sense of time as a thing so little in their control. "Use the clutch and get us *out* of here."

Luckily, the shifting pattern had been embossed on the head of the stick shift and was still faintly visible. Mrs. Tassenbaum pushed in the clutch with a sneakered foot, ground the gears hellishly, and finally found Reverse. The truck backed out onto Route 7 in a series of jerks, then stalled halfway across the white line. She turned the ignition key, realizing she'd once more forgotten the clutch just a little too late to prevent another series of those spastic leaps. Roland and Jake were now bracing their hands against the dusty metal dashboard, where a faded sticker proclaimed AMERICA! LOVE IT OR LEAVE! in red white and blue. This series of jerks was actually a good thing, for at that moment a truck loaded with logs—it was impossible for Roland not to think of the one that had crashed the last time they'd been here—crested the rise to the north of the store. Had the pickup not jerked its way back into the General Store's parking lot (bashing the fender of a parked car as it came to a stop), they would have been centerpunched. And very likely killed. The logging truck swerved, horn blaring, rear wheels spuming up dust.

The creature in the boy's lap—it looked to Mrs. Tassenbaum like some weird mixture of dog and raccoon—barked again.

Fuck. She was almost sure of it.

The storekeeper and the other patrons were lined up on the other side of the glass, and she suddenly knew what a fish in an aquarium must feel like.

"Lady, can you drive this thing or not?" the boy yelled. He had some sort of bag over his shoulder. It reminded her of a newsboy's bag, only it was leather instead of canvas and there appeared to be plates inside.

"I can drive it, young man, don't you worry." She was terrified, and yet at the same time . . . was she *enjoying* this? She almost thought she was. For the last eighteen years she'd been little more than the great David Tassenbaum's ornament, a supporting character in his increasingly famous life, the lady who said "Try one of *these*" as she passed around *hors d'oeuvres* at parties. Now, suddenly, she was at the center of something, and she had an idea it was something very important indeed.

"Take a deep breath," said the man with the hard sunburned face. His brilliant blue eyes fastened upon hers, and when they did it was hard to think of anything else. Also, the sensation was pleasant. *If this is hypnosis,* she thought, *they ought to teach it in the public schools.* "Hold it, then let it out. And then *drive* us, for your father's sake."

She pulled in a deep breath as instructed, and suddenly the day seemed brighter—nearly brilliant. And she could hear faint singing voices. Lovely voices. Was the truck's radio on, tuned to some opera program? No time to check. But it was nice, whatever it was. As calming as the deep breath.

Mrs. Tassenbaum pushed in the clutch and re-started the engine. This time she found Reverse on the first try and backed into the road almost smoothly. Her first effort at a forward gear netted her Second instead of First and the truck almost stalled when she eased the clutch out, but then the engine seemed to take pity on her. With a wheeze of loose pistons and a manic rapping from beneath the hood, they began rolling north toward the Stoneham-Lovell line.

"Do you know where Turtleback Lane is?" Roland asked her. Ahead of them, near a sign marked MILLION DOLLAR CAMP-GROUND, a battered blue minivan swung out onto the road.

"Yes," she said.

"You're sure?" The last thing the gunslinger wanted was to waste precious time casting about for the back road where King lived.

"Yes. We have friends who live there. The Beckhardts."

For a moment Roland could only grope, knowing he'd heard the name but not where. Then he got it. Beckhardt was the name of the man who owned the cabin where he and Eddie had had their final palaver with John Cullum. He felt a fresh stab of grief in his heart at the thought of Eddie as he'd been on that thundery afternoon, still so strong and vital.

"All right," he said. "I believe you."

She glanced at him across the boy sitting between. "You're in one hell of a hurry, mister—like the white rabbit in *Alice in Wonderland*. What very important date are you almost too late for?"

Roland shook his head. "Never mind, just drive." He looked at the clock on the dashboard, but it didn't work, had stopped in the long-ago with the hands pointed at (of course) 9:19. "It may not be too late yet," he said, while ahead of them, unheeded, the blue van began to pull away. It strayed across the white line of Route 7 into the southbound lane and Mrs. Tassenbaum almost committed a *bon mot*—something about people who started drinking before five—but then the blue van pulled back into the northbound lane, breasted the next hill, and was gone toward the town of Lovell.

Mrs. Tassenbaum forgot about it. She had more interesting things to think about. For instance—

"You don't have to answer what I'm going to ask now if you don't want to," she said, "but I admit that I'm curious: are you boys walk-ins?"

FIVE

Bryan Smith has spent the last couple of nights— along with his rott-weilers, litter-twins he has named Bullet and Pistol— in the Million Dollar Campground, just over the Lovell-Stoneham line. It's nice there by the river (the locals call the rickety wooden structure spanning the water Million Dollar Bridge, which Bryan understands is a joke, and a pretty funny one, by God). Also, folks— hippie-types down from the woods in Sweden, Harrison, and Waterford, mostly— sometimes show up there with drugs to sell. Bryan likes to get mellow, likes to get down, *may it do ya, and he's down this Saturday afternoon . . . not a lot, not the way he likes, but enough to give him a good case of the munchies. They have those Marses' Bars at the Center Lovell Store. Nothing better for the munchies than those.*

He pulls out of the campground and onto Route 7 without so much as a glance in either direction, then says "Whoops, forgot again!" No traffic, though. Later on— especially after the Fourth of July and until Labor Day— there'll be plenty of traffic to contend with, even out here in the boonies, and he'll probably stay closer to home. He knows he isn't much of a driver; one more speeding ticket or fender-bender and he'll probably lose his license for six months. Again.

No problem this time, though; nothing coming but an old pick-em-up, and that baby's almost half a mile back.

"Eat my dust, cowboy!" he says, and giggles. He doesn't know why he said cowboy *when the word in his mind was* muthafuckah, *as in* eat my dust muthafuckah, *but it sounds good. It sounds right. He sees he's drifted into the other lane and corrects his course. "Back on the road again!" he cries, and lets loose another highpitched giggle.* Back on the road again *is a good one, and he always uses it on girls. Another good one is when you twist the wheel from side to side, making your car loop back and forth, and you say* Ahh jeez, musta

had too much cough-syrup! *He knows lots of lines like this, even once thought of writing a book called* Crazy Road Jokes, *wouldn't that be a sketch, Bryan Smith writing a book just like that guy King over in Lovell!*

He turns on the radio (the van yawing onto the soft shoulder to the left of the tarvy, throwing up a rooster-tail of dust, but not quite running into the ditch) and gets Steely Dan, singing "Hey Nineteen." Good one! Yassuh, wicked *good one! He drives a little faster in response to the music. He looks into the rearview mirror and sees his dogs, Bullet and Pistol, looking over the rear seat, bright-eyed. For a moment Bryan thinks they're looking at him, maybe thinking what a good guy he is, then wonders how he can be so stupid. There's a Styrofoam cooler behind the driver's seat, and a pound of fresh hamburger in it. He means to cook it later over a campfire back at Million Dollar. Yes, and a couple more Marses' Bars for dessert, by the hairy old Jesus! Marses' Bars are* wicked *good!*

"You boys ne'mine that cooler," Bryan Smith says, speaking to the dogs he can see in the rear-view mirror. This time the minivan pitches instead of yawing, crossing the white line as it climbs a blind grade at fifty miles an hour. Luckily— or unluckily, depending on your point of view— nothing is coming the other way; nothing puts a stop to Bryan Smith's northward progress.

"You ne'mine that hamburg, that's my supper." He says suppah, *as John Cullum would, but the face looking back at the bright-eyed dogs from the rearview mirror is the face of Sheemie Ruiz. Almost exactly.*

Sheemie could be Bryan Smith's litter-twin.

SIX

Irene Tassenbaum was driving the truck with more assurance now, standard shift or not. She almost wished she didn't have to turn right a quarter of a mile from here, because that would necessitate using the clutch again, this time to downshift. But that was Turtleback Lane right up ahead, and Turtleback was where these boys wanted to go.

Walk-ins! They said so, and *she* believed it, but who else

would? Chip McAvoy, maybe, and surely the Reverend Peterson from that crazy Church of the Walk-Ins down in Stoneham Corners, but anyone else? Her husband, for instance? Nope. Never. If you couldn't engrave a thing on a microchip, David Tassenbaum didn't believe it was real. She wondered—not for the first time lately—if forty-seven was too old to think about a divorce.

She shifted back to Second without grinding the gears *too* much, but then, as she turned off the highway, had to shift all the way down to First when the silly old pickup began to grunt and chug. She thought that one of her passengers would make some sort of smart comment (perhaps the boy's mutant dog would even say *fuck* again), but all the man in the passenger seat said was, "This doesn't look the same."

"When were you here last?" Irene Tassenbaum asked him. She considered shifting up to second gear again, then decided to leave things just as they were. "If it ain't broke, don't fix it," David liked to say.

"It's been awhile," the man admitted. She had to keep sneaking glances at him. There was something strange and exotic about him—especially his eyes. It was as if they'd seen things she'd never even dreamed of.

Stop it, she told herself. *He's probably a drugstore cowboy all the way from Portsmouth, New Hampshire.*

But she kind of doubted that. The boy was odd, as well—him and his exotic crossbreed dog—but they were nothing compared to the man with the haggard face and the strange blue eyes.

"Eddie said it was a loop," the boy said. "Maybe last time you guys came in from the other end."

The man considered this and nodded. "Would the other end be the Bridgton end?" he asked the woman.

"Yes indeed."

The man with the odd blue eyes nodded. "We're going to the writer's house."

"Cara Laughs," she said at once. "It's a beautiful house. I've seen it from the lake, but I don't know which driveway—"

"It's nineteen," the man said. They were currently passing the one marked 27. From this end of Turtleback Lane, the numbers would go down rather than up.

"What do you want with him, if I may I be so bold?"

It was the boy who answered. "We want to save his life."

SEVEN

Roland recognized the steeply descending driveway at once, even though he'd last seen it under black, thundery skies, and much of his attention had been taken by the brilliant flying taheen. There was no sign of taheen or other exotic wildlife today. The roof of the house below had been dressed with copper instead of shingles at some point during the intervening years, and the wooded area beyond it had become a lawn, but the driveway was the same, with a sign reading CARA LAUGHS on the lefthand side and one bearing the number **19** in large numerals on the right. Beyond was the lake, sparkling blue in the strong afternoon light.

From the lawn came the blat of a hard-working small engine. Roland looked at Jake and was dismayed by the boy's pale cheeks and wide, frightened eyes.

"What? What's wrong?"

"He's not here, Roland. Not him, not any of his family. Just the man cutting the grass."

"Nonsense, you can't—" Mrs. Tassenbaum began.

"I *know!*" Jake shouted at her. "I *know,* lady!"

Roland was looking at Jake with a frank and horrified sort of fascination . . . but in his current state, the boy either did not understand the look or missed it entirely.

Why are you lying, Jake? the gunslinger thought. And then, on the heels of that: *He's not.*

"What if it's already happened?" Jake demanded, and yes, he was worried about King, but Roland didn't think that was *all* he was worried about. "What if he's dead and his family's not here because the police called them, and—"

"It hasn't happened," Roland said, but that was all of which he was sure. *What do you know, Jake, and why won't you tell me?*

There was no time to wonder about it now.

EIGHT

The man with the blue eyes sounded calm as he spoke to the boy, but he didn't *look* calm to Irene Tassenbaum; not at all. And those singing voices she'd first noticed outside the East Stoneham General Store had changed. Their song was still sweet, but wasn't there a note of desperation in it now, as well? She thought so. A high, pleading quality that made her temples throb.

"How can you *know* that?" the boy called Jake shouted at the man—his father, she assumed. "How can you be so fucking sure?"

Instead of answering the kid's question, the one called Roland looked at *her*. Mrs. Tassenbaum felt the skin of her arms and back break out in gooseflesh.

"Drive down, sai, may it do ya."

She looked doubtfully at the steep slope of the Cara Laughs driveway. "If I do, I might not get this bucket of bolts back up."

"You'll have to," Roland said.

NINE

The man cutting the grass was King's bondservant, Roland surmised, or whatever passed for such in this world. He was white-haired under his straw hat but straight-backed and hale, wearing his years with little effort. When the truck drove down the steep driveway to the house, the man paused with one arm resting on the handle of the mower. When the passenger door opened and the gunslinger got out, he used the switch to turn the mower off. He also removed his hat—without being exactly aware that he was doing it, Roland thought. Then his eyes registered the gun that hung at Roland's hip, and widened enough to make the crow's-feet around them disappear.

"Howdy, mister," he said cautiously. *He thinks I'm a walk-in,* Roland thought. *Just as she did.*

And they *were* walk-ins of a sort, he and Jake; they just happened to have come to a time and place where such things were common.

And where time was racing.

Roland spoke before the man could go on. "Where are they? Where is *he?* Stephen King? Speak, man, and tell me the truth!"

The hat slipped from the old man's relaxing fingers and fell beside his feet on the newly cut grass. His hazel eyes stared into Roland's, fascinated: the bird looking at the snake.

"Fambly's across the lake, at that place they gut on t'other side," he said. "T'old Schindler place. Havin some kind of pa'ty, they are. Steve said he'd drive over after his walk." And he gestured to a small black car parked on the driveway extension, its nose just visible around the side of the house.

"Where is he walking? Do ya know, tell this lady!"

The old man looked briefly over Roland's shoulder, then back to the gunslinger. "Be easier was I t'drive ya there m'self."

Roland considered this, but only briefly. Easier to begin with, yes. Maybe harder on the other end, where King would either be saved or lost. Because they'd found the woman in ka's road. However minor a role she might have to play, it was her they had found first on the Path of the Beam. In the end it was as simple as that. As for the size of her part, it was better not to judge such things in advance. Hadn't he and Eddie believed John Cullum, met in that same roadside store some three wheels north of here, would have but a minor role to play in their story? Yet it had turned out to be anything but.

All of this crossed his consciousness in less than a second, information (*hunch,* Eddie would have called it) delivered in a kind of brilliant mental shorthand.

"No," he said, and jerked a thumb back over his shoulder. "Tell her. *Now.*"

TEN

The boy—Jake—had fallen back against the seat with his hands lying limp at his sides. The peculiar dog was looking anxiously up into the kid's face, but the kid didn't see him. His eyes were closed, and Irene Tassenbaum at first thought he'd fainted.

"Son? . . . Jake?"

"I have him," the boy said without opening his eyes. "Not Stephen King—I can't touch him—but the other one. I have to slow him down. How can I slow him down?"

Mrs. Tassenbaum had listened to her husband enough at work—holding long, muttered dialogues with himself—to know a self-directed enquiry when she heard one. Also, she had no idea of whom the boy was speaking, only that it wasn't Stephen King. Which left about six billion other possibilities, globally speaking.

Nevertheless, she *did* answer, because she knew what always slowed *her* down.

"Too bad he doesn't need to go to the bathroom," she said.

ELEVEN

Strawberries aren't out in Maine, not this early in the season, but there are raspberries. Justine Anderson (of Maybrook, New York) and Elvira Toothaker (her Lovell friend) are walking along the side of Route 7 (which Elvira still calls The Old Fryeburg Road) with their plastic buckets, harvesting from the bushes which run for at least half a mile along the old rock wall. Garrett McKeen built that wall a hundred years ago, and it is to Garrett's great-grandson that Roland Deschain of Gilead is speaking at this very moment. Ka is a wheel, do ya not kennit.

The two women have enjoyed their hour's walk, not because either of them has any great love of raspberries (Justine reckons she won't even eat hers; the seeds get caught in her teeth) but because it's given them a chance to catch up on their respective families and to laugh a little together about the years when their friendship was new and probably the most important thing in either girl's life. They met at Vassar College (a thousand years ago, so it does seem) and carried the Daisy Chain together at graduation the year they were juniors. This is what they are talking about when the blue minivan—it is a 1985 Dodge Caravan, Justine recognizes the make and model because her oldest son had one just like it when his tribe started growing—comes around the curve by Melder's German Restaurant and Brathaus. It's all over the road, looping from side to side, first spuming up dust from the southbound shoulder, then plunging giddily across the tar and spuming up more from the northbound one. The second time it does this—rolling toward them now, *and coming at a pretty damned good clip—Justine thinks it may actually go into the ditch and turn over ("turn turtle," they used to say back in the forties, when she and Elvira had been at Vassar), but the driver hauls it back on the road just before that can happen.*

"Look out, that person's drunk or something!" Justine says, alarmed. She pulls Elvira back, but they find their way blocked by the old wall with its dressing of raspberry bushes. The thorns catch at their slacks (thank goodness neither of us was wearing shorts, *Justine* will think later . . . *when she has* time *to think) and pull out little puffs of cloth.*

Justine is thinking she should put an arm around her friend's shoulder and tumble them both over the thigh-high wall—do a backflip, just like in gym class all those years ago—but before she can make up her mind to do it, the blue van is by them, and at the moment it passes, it's more or less on the road and not a danger to them.

Justine watches it go by in a muffled blare of rock music, her heart thumping heavily in her chest, the taste of something her body has dumped—adrenaline would be the most likely possibility—flat and metallic on her tongue. And halfway up the hill the little blue van once again lurches across the white line. The driver corrects the drift . . . no, overcorrects. *Once more the blue van is on the righthand shoulder, spuming up yellow dust for fifty yards.*

"Gosh, I hope Stephen King sees that asshole," Elvira says. They have passed the writer half a mile or so back, and said hello. Probably everyone in town has seen him on his afternoon walk, at one time or another.

As if the driver of the blue van has heard Elvira Toothaker call him an asshole, the van's brakelights flare. The van suddenly pulls all the way off the road and stops. When the door opens, the ladies hear a louder blast of rock and roll music. They also hear the driver— a man— yelling at someone (Elvira and Justine just pity the person stuck driving with that guy on such a beautiful June afternoon). "You leave 'at alone!" he shouts. "That ain't yoahs, y'hear?" And then the driver reaches back into the van, brings out a cane, and uses it to help him over the rock wall and into the bushes. The van sits rumbling on the soft shoulder, driver's door open, emitting blue exhaust from one end and rock from the other.

"What's he doing?" Justine asks, a little nervously.

"Taking a leak would be my guess," her friend replies. "But if Mr. King back there is lucky, maybe doing Number Two, instead. That might give him time to get off Route 7 and back onto Turtleback Lane."

Suddenly Justine doesn't feel like picking berries anymore. She wants to go back home and have a strong cup of tea.

The man comes limping briskly out of the bushes and uses his cane to help him back over the rock wall.

"I guess he didn't need to Number Two," Elvira says, and as the bad driver climbs back into his blue van, the two going-on-old women look at each other and burst into giggles.

TWELVE

Roland watched the old man give the woman instructions— something about using Warrington's Road as a shortcut—and then Jake opened his eyes. To Roland the boy looked unutterably weary.

"I was able to make him stop and take a leak," he said. "Now he's fixing something behind his seat. I don't know what it is, but it won't keep him busy for long. Roland, this is bad. We're awfully late. We have to go."

Roland looked at the woman, hoping that his decision not to replace her behind the wheel with the old man had been the right one. "Do you know where to go? Do you understand?"

"Yes," she said. "Up Warrington's to Route 7. We sometimes go to dinner at Warrington's. I know that road."

"Can't guarantee you'll cut his path goin that way," said the caretaker, "but it seems likely." He bent down to pick up his hat and began to brush bits of freshly cut grass from it. He did this with long, slow strokes, like a man caught in a dream. "Ayuh, seems likely t'me." And then, still like a man who dreams awake, he tucked his hat beneath his arm, raised a fist to his forehead, and bent a leg to the stranger with the big revolver on his hip. Why would he not?

The stranger was surrounded by white light.

THIRTEEN

When Roland pulled himself back into the cab of the store-keeper's truck—a chore made more difficult by the rapidly escalating pain in his right hip—his hand came down on Jake's leg, and just like that he knew what Jake had been keeping back, and why. He had been afraid that knowing might cause the gun-slinger's focus to drift. It was not ka-shume the boy had felt, or Roland would have felt it, too. How *could* there be ka-shume among them, with the tet already broken? Their special power, something greater than all of them, perhaps drawn from the Beam itself, was gone. Now they were just three friends (four, counting the bumbler) united by a single purpose. And they could save King. Jake knew it. They could save the writer and come a step closer to saving the Tower by doing so. But one of them was going to die doing it.

Jake knew that, too.

FOURTEEN

An old saying—one taught to him by his father—came to Roland then: *If ka will say so, let it be so.* Yes; all right; let it be so.

During the long years he had spent on the trail of the man in black, the gunslinger would have sworn nothing in the universe could have caused him to renounce the Tower; had he not literally killed his own mother in pursuit of it, back at the start of his terrible career? But in those years he had been friendless, childless, and (he didn't like to admit it, but it was true) heartless. He had been bewitched by that cold romance the loveless mistake for love. Now he had a son and he had been given a second chance and he had changed. Knowing that one of them must die in order to save the writer—that their fellowship must be reduced again, and so soon—would not make him cry off. But he would make sure that Roland of Gilead, not Jake of New York, provided the sacrifice this time.

Did the boy know that he'd penetrated his secret? No time to worry about that now.

Roland slammed the truckomobile's door shut and looked at the woman. "Is your name Irene?" he asked.

She nodded.

"Drive, Irene. Do it as if Lord High Splitfoot were on your trail with rape on his mind, do ya I beg. Out Warrington's Road. If we don't see him there, out the Seven-Road. Will you?"

"You're fucking right," said Mrs. Tassenbaum, and shoved the gearshift into First with real authority.

The engine screamed, but the truck began to roll backward, as if so frightened by the job ahead that it would rather finish up in the lake. Then she engaged the clutch and the old International Harvester leaped ahead, charging up the steep incline of the driveway and leaving a trail of blue smoke and burnt rubber behind.

Garrett McKeen's great-grandson watched them go with his mouth hanging open. He had no idea what had just happened, but he felt sure that a great deal depended on what would happen next.

Maybe everything.

FIFTEEN

Needing to piss that bad was weird, because pissing was the last thing Bryan Smith had done before leaving the Million Dollar Campground. And once he'd clambered over the fucking rock wall, he hadn't been able to manage more than a few drops, even though it had felt like a real bladder-buster at the time. Bryan hopes he's not going to have trouble

with his prostrate; trouble with the old prostrate is the last thing he
needs. He's got enough other problems, by the hairy old Jesus.

Oh well, now that he's stopped he might as well try to fix the Styro-
foam cooler behind the seat— the dogs are still staring at it with their
tongues hanging out. He tries to wedge it underneath the seat, but it
won't go— there's not quite enough clearance. What he does instead is
to point a dirty finger at his rotties and tell them again to ne'mine the
cooler and the meat inside, that's his, that's gonna be his suppah. This
time he even thinks to add a promise that later on he'll mix a little of
the hamburger in with their Purina, if they're good. This is fairly deep
thinking for Bryan Smith, but the simple expedient of swinging the
cooler up front and putting it in the unoccupied passenger seat never
occurs to him.

"You leave it alone!" he tells them again, and hops back behind the
wheel. He slams the door, takes a brief glance in the rearview mirror, sees
two old ladies back there (he didn't notice them before because he wasn't
exactly looking at the road when he passed them), gives them a wave they
never see through the Caravan's filthy rear window, and then pulls back
onto Route 7. Now the radio is playing "Gangsta Dream 19," by Owt-
Ray-Juss, and Bryan turns it up (once more swerving across the white
line and into the northbound lane as he does so— this is the sort of per-
son who simply cannot fix the radio without looking at it). Rap rules!
And metal rules, too! All he needs now to make his day complete is a
tune by Ozzy— "Crazy Train" would be good.

And some of those Marses bars.

SIXTEEN

Mrs. Tassenbaum came bolting out of the Cara Laughs driveway
and onto Turtleback Lane in second gear, the old pickup
truck's engine overcranking (if there'd been an RPM gauge on
the dashboard, the needle would undoubtedly have been red-
lining), the few tools in the back tapdancing crazily in the
rusty bed.

Roland had only a bit of the touch—hardly any at all, compared to Jake—but he had met Stephen King, and taken him
down into the false sleep of hypnosis. That was a powerful

bond to share, and so he wasn't entirely surprised when he touched the mind Jake hadn't been able to reach. It probably didn't hurt that King was thinking about *them*.

He often does on his walks, Roland thought. *When he's alone, he hears the Song of the Turtle and knows that he has a job to do. One he's shirking. Well, my friend, that ends today.*

If, that was, they could save him.

He leaned past Jake and looked at the woman. "Can't you make this gods-cursed thing go faster?"

"Yes," she said. "I believe I can." And then, to Jake: "Can you really read minds, son, or is that only a game you and your friend play?"

"I can't read them, exactly, but I can touch them," Jake said.

"I hope to hell that's the truth," she said, "because Turtle-back's hilly and only one lane wide in places. If you sense someone coming the other way, you have to let me know."

"I will."

"Excellent," said Irene Tassenbaum. She bared her teeth in a grin. Really, there was no longer any doubt: this was the best thing that had ever happened to her. The most *exciting* thing. Now, as well as hearing those singing voices, she could see faces in the leaves of the trees on the sides of the road, as if they were being watched by a multitude. She could feel some tremendous force gathering all around them, and she was possessed by a sudden giddy notion: that if she floored the gas-pedal of Chip McAvoy's old rusty pickup, it might go faster than the speed of light. Powered by the energy she sensed around them, it might outrace time itself.

Well, let's just see about that, she thought. She swung the I-H into the middle of Turtleback Lane, then punched the clutch and yanked the gearshift into Third. The old truck didn't go faster than the speed of light, and it didn't outrace time, but the speedometer needle climbed to fifty . . . and then past. The truck crested a hill, and when it started down the other side it flew briefly into the air.

At least someone was happy; Irene Tassenbaum shouted in excitement.

SEVENTEEN

Stephen King takes two walks, the short one and the long one. The short one takes him out to the intersection of Warrington's Road and Route 7, then back to his house, Cara Laughs, the same way. That one is three miles. The long walk (which also happens to be the name of a book he once wrote under the Bachman name, back before the world moved on) takes him past the Warrington's intersection, down Route 7 as far as the Slab City Road, then all the way back Route 7 to Berry Hill, bypassing Warrington's Road. This walk returns him to his house by way of the north end of Turtleback Lane, and is four miles. This is the one he means to take today, but when he gets back to the intersection of 7 and Warrington's he stops, playing with the idea of going back the short way. He's always careful about walking on the shoulder of the public road, though traffic is light on Route 7, even in summer; the only time this highway ever gets busy is when the Fryeburg Fair's going on, and that doesn't start until the first week of October. Most of the sightlines are good, anyway. If a bad driver's coming (or a drunk) you can usually spot him half a mile away, which gives you plenty of time to vacate the area. There's only one blind hill, and that's the one directly beyond the Warrington's intersection. Yet that's also an aerobic *hill, one that gets the old heart really pumping, and isn't that what he's doing all these stupid walks for? To promote what the TV talking heads call "heart healthiness?" He's quit drinking, he's quit doping, he's almost* quit *smoking, he exercises. What else is there?*

Yet a voice whispers to him just the same. Get off the main road, *it says.* Go on back to the house. You'll have an extra hour before you have to meet the rest of them for the party on the other side of the lake. You can do some work. Maybe start the next *Dark Tower* story; you know it's been on your mind.

Aye, so it has, but he already has a story to work on, and he likes it fine. Going back to the tale of the Tower means swimming in deep water. Maybe drowning there. Yet he suddenly realizes, standing here at this crossroads, that if he goes back early he will *begin. He won't be able to help himself. He'll have to listen to what he sometimes thinks of as Ves'-Ka Gan, the Song of the Turtle (and sometimes as Susannah's Song).*

He'll junk the current story, turn his back on the safety of the land, and swim out into that dark water once again. He's done it four times before, but this time he'll have to swim all the way to the other side.

Swim or drown.

"No," he says. He speaks aloud, and why not? There's no one to hear him out here. He perceives, faintly, the attenuate sound of an approaching vehicle— or is it two? one on Route 7 and one on War-rington's Road?— but that's all.

"No," he says again. "I'm gonna walk, and then I'm gonna party. No more writing today. Especially not that.*"*

And so, leaving the intersection behind, he begins making his way up the steep hill with its short sightline. He begins to walk toward the sound of the oncoming Dodge Caravan, which is also the sound of his oncoming death. The ka of the rational world wants him dead; that of the Prim *wants him alive, and singing his song. So it is that on this sunny afternoon in western Maine, the irresistible force rushes toward the immovable object, and for the first time since the* Prim *receded, all worlds and all existence turn toward the Dark Tower which stands at the far end of Can'-Ka No Rey, which is to say the Red Fields of None. Even the Crimson King ceases his angry screaming. For it is the Dark Tower that will decide.*

"Resolution demands a sacrifice," King says, and although no one hears but the birds and he has no idea what this means, he is not disturbed. He's always muttering to himself; it's as though there is a Cave of Voices in his head, one full of brilliant— but not necessarily intelligent— mimics.

He walks, swinging his arms beside his bluejeaned thighs, unaware that his heart is

(isn't)

finishing its last few beats, that his mind is

(isn't)

thinking its last few thoughts, that his voices are

(aren't)

making their last Delphic pronouncements.

"Ves'-Ka Gan," he says, amused by the sound of it— yet attracted, too. He has promised himself that he'll try not to stuff his Dark Tower fantasies with unpronounceable words in some made-up (not to say

fucked-up) language—his editor, Chuck Verrill in New York, will only cut most of them if he does—but his mind seems to be filling up with such words and phrases all the same: ka, ka-tet, sai, soh, can-toi (that one at least is from another book of his, Desperation), taheen. Can Tolkien's Cirith Ungol and H. P. Lovecraft's Great Blind Fiddler, Nyarlathotep, be far behind?

He laughs, then begins to sing a song one of his voices has given him. He thinks he will certainly use it in the next gunslinger book, when he finally allows the Turtle its voice again. "Commala-come-one," he sings as he walks, "there's a young man with a gun. That young man lost his honey when she took it on the run."

And is that young man Eddie Dean? Or is it Jake Chambers?

"Eddie," he says out loud. "Eddie's the gunny with the honey." He's so deep in thought that at first he doesn't see the roof of the blue Dodge Caravan as it comes over the short horizon ahead of him and so does not realize this vehicle is not on the highway at all, but on the soft shoulder where he is walking. Nor does he hear the oncoming roar of the pickup truck behind him.

EIGHTEEN

Bryan hears the scrape of the cooler's lid even over the funky rip-rap beat of the music, and when he looks in the rearview mirror he's both dismayed and outraged to see that Bullet, always the more forward of the two rotties, has leaped from the storage area at the rear of the van into the passenger compartment. Bullet's rear legs are up on the dirty seat, his stubby tail is wagging happily, and his nose is buried in Bryan's cooler.

At this point any reasonable driver would pull over to the side of the road, stop his vehicle, and take care of his wayward animal. Bryan Smith, however, has never gotten high marks for reason when behind the wheel, and has the driving record to prove it. Instead of pulling over, he twists around to the right, steering with his left hand and shoving ineffectually at the top of the rottweiler's flat head with his right.

"Leave 'at alone!" he shouts at Bullet as his minivan drifts first toward the righthand shoulder and then onto it. "Din' you hear me, Bullet? Are you foolish? Leave 'at alone!" He actually succeeds in shov-

ing the dog's head up for a moment, but there's no fur for his fingers to grasp and Bullet, while no genius, is smart enough to know he has at least one more chance to grab the stuff in the white paper, the stuff radiating that entrancing red smell. He dips beneath Bryan's hand and seizes the wrapped package of hamburger in his jaws.

"Drop it!" Bryan screams. "You drop it right . . . NOW!"

In order to gain the purchase necessary to twist further in the driver's bucket, he presses down firmly with both feet. One of them, unfortunately, is on the accelerator. The van puts on a burst of speed as it rushes toward the top of the hill. At this moment, in his excitement and outrage, Bryan has completely forgotten where he is (Route 7) and what he's supposed to be doing (driving a van). All he cares about is getting the package of meat out of Bullet's jaws.

"Gimme it!" he shouts, tugging. Tail wagging more furiously than ever (to him it's now a game as well as a meal), Bullet tugs back. There's the sound of ripping butcher's paper. The van is now all the way off the road. Beyond it is a grove of old pines lit by lovely afternoon light: a haze of green and gold. Bryan thinks only of the meat. He's not going to eat hamburg with dog-drool on it, and you best believe it.

"Gimme it!" he says, not seeing the man in the path of his van, not seeing the truck that has now pulled up just behind the man, not seeing the truck's passenger door open or the lanky cowboy-type who leaps out, a revolver with big yellow grips spilling from the holster on his hip and onto the ground as he does; Bryan Smith's world has narrowed to one very bad dog and one package of meat. In the struggle for the meat, blood-roses are blooming on the butcher's paper like tattoos.

NINETEEN

"There he is!" the boy named Jake shouted, but Irene Tassenbaum didn't need him to tell her. Stephen King was wearing jeans, a chambray workshirt, and a baseball cap. He was well beyond the place where the road to Warrington's intersected with Route 7, about a quarter of the way up the slope.

She punched the clutch, downshifted to Second like a NASCAR driver with the checkered flag in view, then turned hard left, hauling on the wheel with both hands. Chip McAvoy's pickup truck teetered but did not roll. She saw the twinkle of sun on metal as a vehicle coming the other way reached the top of the hill King was climbing. She heard the man sitting by the door shout, "Pull in behind him!"

She did as he told her, even though she could now see that the oncoming vehicle was off the road and thus apt to broadside them. Not to mention crushing Stephen King in a metal sandwich between them.

The door popped open and the one named Roland half-rolled, half-jumped out of the truck.

After that, things happened very, very fast.

CHAPTER II:
VES'-KA GAN

ONE

What happened was lethally simple: Roland's bad hip betrayed him. He went to his knees with a cry of mingled rage, pain, and dismay. Then the sunlight was blotted out as Jake leaped over him without so much as breaking stride. Oy was barking crazily from the cab of the truck: *"Ake-Ake! Ake-Ake!"*

"Jake, no!" Roland shouted. He saw it all with a terrible clarity. The boy seized the writer around the waist as the blue vehicle—neither a truck nor a car but seemingly a cross between the two—bore down upon them in a roar of dissonant music. Jake turned King to the left, shielding him with his body, and so it was Jake the vehicle struck. Behind the gunslinger, who was now on his knees with his bleeding hands buried in the dirt, the woman from the store screamed.

"JAKE, NO!" Roland bellowed again, but it was too late. The boy he thought of as his son disappeared beneath the blue vehicle. The gunslinger saw one small upraised hand—would never forget it—and then that was gone, too. King, struck first by Jake and then by the weight of the van behind Jake, was thrown to the edge of the little grove of trees, ten feet from the point of impact. He landed on his right side, hitting his head on a stone hard enough to send the cap flying from his head. Then he rolled over, perhaps intending to try for his feet. Or perhaps intending nothing at all; his eyes were shocked zeroes.

The driver hauled on his vehicle's steering wheel and it slipped past on Roland's left, missing him by inches, merely throwing dust into his face instead of running him down. By then it was slowing, the driver perhaps applying the machine's brake now that it was too late. The side squalled across the

451

hood of the pickup truck, slowing the van further, but it was not done doing damage even so. Before coming to a complete stop it struck King again, this time as he lay on the ground. Roland heard the snap of a breaking bone. It was followed by the writer's cry of pain. And now Roland knew for sure about the pain in his own hip, didn't he? It had never been dry twist at all.

He scrambled to his feet, only peripherally aware that his pain was entirely gone. He looked at Stephen King's unnaturally twisted body beneath the left front wheel of the blue vehicle and thought *Good!* with unthinking savagery. *Good! If someone has to die here, let it be you! To hell with Gan's navel, to hell with the stories that come out of it, to hell with the Tower, let it be you and not my boy!*

The bumbler raced past Roland to where Jake lay on his back at the rear of the van with blue exhaust blowing into his open eyes. Oy did not hesitate; he seized the Oriza pouch that was still slung over Jake's shoulder and used it to pull the boy away from the van, doing it inch by inch, his short strong legs digging up puffs of dust. Blood was pouring from Jake's ears and the corners of his mouth. The heels of his shor'boots left a double line of tracks in the dirt and crisp brown pine needles.

Roland staggered to Jake and fell on his knees beside him. His first thought was that Jake was all right after all. The boy's limbs were straight, thank all the gods, and the mark running across the bridge of his nose and down one beardless cheek was oil flecked with rust, not blood as Roland had first assumed. There *was* blood coming out of his ears, yes, and his mouth, too, but the latter stream might only be flowing from a cut in the lining of his cheek, or—

"Go and see to the writer," Jake said. His voice was calm, not at all constricted by pain. They might have been sitting around a little cookfire after a day on the trail, waiting for what Eddie liked to call vittles . . . or, if he happened to be feeling particularly humorous (as he often was), "wittles."

"The writer can wait," Roland said curtly, thinking: *I've been given a miracle. One made by the combination of a boy's yielding, not-*

quite-finished body, and the soft earth that gave beneath him when that
bastard's truckomobile ran over him.

"No," Jake said. "He can't." And when he moved, trying to sit up, his shirt pulled a little tighter against the top half of his body and Roland saw the dreadful concavity of the boy's chest. More blood poured from Jake's mouth, and when he tried to speak again he began to cough, instead. Roland's heart seemed to twist like a rag inside his chest, and there was a moment to wonder how it could possibly go on beating in the face of this.

Oy voiced a moaning cry, Jake's name expressed in a half-howl that made Roland's arms burst out in gooseflesh.

"Don't try to talk," Roland said. "Something may be sprung inside of you. A rib, mayhap two."

Jake turned his head to the side. He spat out a mouthful of blood—some of it ran down his cheek like chewing tobacco—and took a hold on Roland's wrist. His grip was strong; so was his voice, each word clear.

"Everything's sprung. This is dying—I know because I've done it before." What he said next was what Roland had been thinking just before they started out from Cara Laughs: "If ka will say so, let it be so. *See to the man we came to save!"*

It was impossible to deny the imperative in the boy's eyes and voice. It was done, now, the Ka of Nineteen played out to the end. Except, perhaps, for King. The man they had come to save. How much of their fate had danced from the tips of his flying, tobacco-stained fingers? All? Some? This?

Whatever the answer, Roland could have killed him with his bare hands as he lay pinned beneath the machine that had struck him, and never mind that King hadn't been driving the van; if he had been doing what ka had meant him to be doing, he never would have been here when the fool came calling, and Jake's chest wouldn't have that terrible sunken look. It was too much, coming so soon after Eddie had been bushwhacked.

And yet—

"Don't move," he said, getting up. "Oy, don't *let* him move."

"I won't move." Every word still clear, still sure. But now Roland could see blood also darkening the bottom of Jake's shirt and the crotch of his jeans, blooming there like roses. Once before he died and had come back. But not from this world. In this one, death was always for keeps.

Roland turned to where the writer lay.

TWO

When Bryan Smith tried to get out from behind the wheel of his van, Irene Tassenbaum pushed him rudely back in. His dogs, perhaps smelling blood or Oy or both, were barking and capering wildly behind him. Now the radio was pounding out some new and utterly hellish heavy metal tune. She thought her head would split, not from the shock of what had just happened but from pure racket. She saw the man's revolver lying on the ground and picked it up. The small part of her mind still capable of coherent thought was amazed by the weight of the thing. Nevertheless, she pointed it at the man, then reached past him and punched the power button on the radio. With the blaring fuzz-tone guitars gone, she could hear birds as well as two barking dogs and one howling . . . well, one howling whatever-it-was.

"Back your van off the guy you hit," she said. "Slowly. And if you run over the kid again when you do it, I swear I'll blow your jackass head off."

Bryan Smith stared at her with bloodshot, bewildered eyes. "What kid?" he asked.

THREE

When the van's front wheel rolled slowly off the writer, Roland saw that his lower body was twisted unnaturally to the right and a lump pushed out the leg of his jeans on that side. His thigh-bone, surely. In addition, his forehead had been split by the rock against which it had fetched up, and the right side of his face was drowned in blood. He looked worse than Jake, worse by far, but a single glance was enough to tell the gunslinger that if his heart was strong and the shock didn't kill him, he'd probably live through this. Again he saw Jake seizing the man about the waist, shielding him, taking the impact with his own smaller body.

"You again," King said in a low voice.

"You remember me."

"Yes. Now." King licked his lips. "Thirsty."

Roland had nothing to drink, and wouldn't have given more than enough to wet King's lips even if he had. Liquid could induce vomiting in a wounded man, and vomiting could lead to choking. "Sorry," he said.

"No. You're not." He licked his lips again. "Jake?"

"Over there, on the ground. You know him?"

King tried to smile. "*Wrote* him. Where's the one that was with you before? Where's Eddie?"

"Dead," Roland said. "In the Devar-Toi."

King frowned. "Devar . . . ? I don't know that."

"No. That's why we're here. Why we had to come here. One of my friends is dead, another may be dying, and the tet is broken. All because one lazy, fearful man stopped doing the job for which ka intended him."

No traffic on the road. Except for the barking dogs, the howling bumbler, and the chirping birds, the world was silent. They might have been frozen in time. *Perhaps we are,* Roland thought. He had now seen enough to believe that might be possible. *Anything* might be possible.

"I lost the Beam," King said from where he lay on the carpet of needles at the edge of the trees. The light of early summer streamed all around him, that haze of green and gold.

Roland reached under King and helped him to sit up. The writer cried out in pain as the swollen ball of his right hip grated in the shattered, compressed remains of its socket, but he did not protest. Roland pointed into the sky. Fat white fair-weather clouds — *los ángeles,* the cowpokes of Mejis had called them — hung motionless in the blue, except for those directly above them. There they hied rapidly across the sky, as if blown by a narrow wind.

"There!" Roland whispered furiously into the writer's

scraped, dirt-clogged ear. "Directly above you! All around you! Does thee not feel it? Does thee not *see* it?"

"Yes," King said. "I see it now."

"Aye, and 'twas always there. You didn't lose it, you turned your coward's eye away. My friend had to save you for you to see it again."

Roland's left hand fumbled in his belt and brought out a shell. At first his fingers wouldn't do their old, dexterous trick; they were trembling too badly. He was only able to still them by reminding himself that the longer it took him to do this, the greater the chance that they would be interrupted, or that Jake would die while he was busy with this miserable excuse for a man.

He looked up and saw the woman holding his gun on the driver of the van. That was good. *She* was good: why hadn't Gan given the story of the Tower to someone like her? In any case, his instinct to keep her with them had been true. Even the infernal racket of dogs and bumbler had quieted. Oy was licking the dirt and oil from Jake's face, while in the van, Pistol and Bullet were gobbling up the hamburger, this time without interference from their master.

Roland turned back to King, and the shell did its old sure dance across the backs of his fingers. King went under almost immediately, as most people did when they'd been hypnotized before. His eyes were still open, but now they seemed to look through the gunslinger, beyond him.

Roland's heart screamed at him to get through this as quickly as he could, but his head knew better. *You must not botch it. Not unless you want to render Jake's sacrifice worthless.*

The woman was looking at him, and so was the van's driver as he sat in the open door of his vehicle. Sai Tassenbaum was fighting it, Roland saw, but Bryan Smith had followed King into the land of sleep. This didn't surprise the gunslinger much. If the man had the slightest inkling of what he'd done here, he'd be apt to seize any opportunity for escape. Even a temporary one.

The gunslinger turned his attention back to the man who

was, he supposed, his biographer. He started just as he had before. Days ago in his own life. Over two decades ago in the writer's.

"Stephen King, do you see me?"

"Gunslinger, I see you very well."

"When did you last see me?"

"When we lived in Bridgton. When my tet was young. When I was just learning how to write." A pause, and then he gave what Roland supposed was, for him, the most important way of marking time, a thing that was different for every man: "When I was still drinking."

"Are you deep asleep now?"

"Deep."

"Are you under the pain?"

"Under it, yes. I thank you."

The billy-bumbler howled again. Roland looked around, terribly afraid of what it might signify. The woman had gone to Jake and was kneeling beside him. Roland was relieved to see Jake put an arm around her neck and draw her head down so he could speak into her ear. If he was strong enough to do that—

Stop it! You saw the changed shape of him under his shirt. You can't afford to waste time on hope.

There was a cruel paradox here: because he loved Jake, he had to leave the business of Jake's dying to Oy and a woman they had met less than an hour ago.

Never mind. His business now was with King. Should Jake pass into the clearing while his back was turned . . . *if ka will say so, let it be so.*

Roland summoned his will and concentration. He focused them to a burning point, then turned his attention to the writer once more. "Are you Gan?" he asked abruptly, not knowing why this question came to him—only that it was the *right* question.

"No," King said at once. Blood ran into his mouth from the cut on his head and he spat it out, never blinking. "Once I thought I was, but that was just the booze. And pride, I suppose.

No writer is Gan—no painter, no sculptor, no maker of music. We are kas-ka Gan. Not *ka*-Gan but *kas*-ka Gan. Do you understand? Do you . . . do you ken?"

"Yes," Roland said. The prophets of Gan or the singers of Gan: it could signify either or both. And now he knew why he had asked. "And the song you sing is *Ves'*-Ka Gan. Isn't it?"

"Oh, *yes!*" King said, and smiled. "The Song of the Turtle. It's far too lovely for the likes of me, who can hardly carry a tune!"

"I don't care," Roland said. He thought as hard and as clearly as his dazed mind would allow. "And now you've been hurt."

"Am I paralyzed?"

"I don't know." *Nor care.* "All I know is that you'll live, and when you can write again, you'll listen for the Song of the Turtle, Ves'-Ka Gan, as you did before. Paralyzed or not. And this time you'll sing until the song is done."

"All right."

"You'll—"

"And Urs-Ka Gan, the Song of the Bear," King interrupted him. Then he shook his head, although this clearly hurt him despite the hypnotic state he was in. "Urs-*A*-Ka Gan."

The Cry of the Bear? The *Scream* of the Bear? Roland didn't know which. He would have to hope it didn't matter, that it was no more than a writer's quibble.

A car hauling a motor home went past the scene of the accident without slowing, then a pair of large motor-bicycles sped by heading the other way. And an oddly persuasive thought came to Roland: time hadn't stopped, but they were, for the time being, *dim.* Being protected in that fashion by the Beam, which was no longer under attack and thus able to help, at least a little.

FOUR

Tell him again. There must be no misunderstanding. And no weakening, as he weakened before.

He bent down until his face was before King's face, their

noses nearly touching. "This time you'll sing until the song is done, write until the tale is done. Do you truly ken?"

"'And they lived happily ever after until the end of their days,'" King said dreamily. "I wish I could write that."

"So do I." And he did, more than anything. Despite his sorrow, there were no tears yet; his eyes felt like hot stones in his head. Perhaps the tears would come later, when the truth of what had happened here had a chance to sink in a little.

"I'll do as you say, gunslinger. No matter how the tale falls when the pages grow thin." King's voice was itself growing thin. Roland thought he would soon fall into unconsciousness. "I'm sorry for your friends, truly I am."

"Thank you," Roland said, still restraining the urge to put his hands around the writer's neck and choke the life out of him. He started to stand, but King said something that stopped him.

"Did you listen for *her* song, as I told you to do? For the Song of Susannah?"

"I . . . yes."

Now King forced himself up on one elbow, and although his strength was clearly failing, his voice was dry and strong. "She needs you. And you need her. Leave me alone now. Save your hate for those who deserve it more. I didn't make your ka any more than I made Gan or the world, and we both know it. Put your foolishness behind you—and your grief—and do as you'd have me do." King's voice rose to a rough shout; his hand shot out and gripped Roland's wrist with amazing strength. *"Finish the job!"*

At first nothing came out when Roland tried to reply. He had to clear his throat and start again. "Sleep, sai—sleep and forget everyone here except the man who hit you."

King's eyes slipped closed. "Forget everyone here except the man who hit me."

"You were taking your walk and this man hit you."

"Walking . . . and this man hit me."

"No one else was here. Not me, not Jake, not the woman."

"No one else," King agreed. "Just me and him. Will he say the same?"

"Yar. Very soon you'll sleep deep. You may feel pain later, but you feel none now."

"No pain now. Sleep deep." King's twisted frame relaxed on the pine needles.

"Yet before you sleep, listen to me once more," Roland said.

"I'm listening."

"A woman may come to y—wait. Do'ee dream of love with men?"

"Are you asking if I'm gay? Maybe a latent homosexual?" King sounded weary but amused.

"I don't know." Roland paused. "I think so."

"The answer is no," King said. "Sometimes I dream of love with women. A little less now that I'm older . . . and probably not at all for awhile, now. That fucking guy really beat me up."

Not near so bad as he beat up mine, Roland thought bitterly, but he didn't say this.

"If'ee dream only of love with women, it's a woman that may come to you."

"Do you say so?" King sounded faintly interested.

"Yes. If she comes, she'll be fair. She may speak to you about the ease and pleasure of the clearing. She may call herself Morphia, Daughter of Sleep, or Selena, Daughter of the Moon. She may offer you her arm and promise to take you there. You must refuse."

"I must refuse."

"Even if you are tempted by her eyes and breasts."

"Even then," King agreed.

"Why will you refuse, sai?"

"Because the Song isn't done."

At last Roland was satisfied. Mrs. Tassenbaum was kneeling by Jake. The gunslinger ignored both her and the boy and went to the man sitting slumped behind the wheel of the motor-carriage that had done all the damage. This man's eyes were wide and blank, his mouth slack. A line of drool hung from his beard-stubbly chin.

"Do you hear me, sai?"

The man nodded fearfully. Behind him, both dogs had grown silent. Four bright eyes regarded the gunslinger from between the seats.

"What's your name?"

"Bryan, do it please you—Bryan Smith."

No, it didn't please him at all. Here was yet one more he'd like to strangle. Another car passed on the road, and this time the person behind the wheel honked the horn as he or she passed. Whatever their protection might be, it had begun to grow thin.

"Sai Smith, you hit a man with your car or truckomobile or whatever it is thee calls it."

Bryan Smith began to tremble all over. "I ain't never had so much as a parking ticket," he whined, "and I have to go and run into the most famous man in the state! My dogs 'us fightin—"

"Your lies don't anger me," Roland said, "but the fear which brings them forth does. Shut thy mouth."

Bryan Smith did as told. The color was draining slowly but steadily from his face.

"You were alone when you hit him," Roland said. "No one here but you and the storyteller. Do you understand?"

"I was alone. Mister, are you a walk-in?"

"Never mind what I am. You checked him and saw that he was still alive."

"Still alive, good," Smith said. "I didn't mean to hurt nobody, honest."

"He spoke to you. That's how you knew he was alive."

"Yes!" Smith smiled. Then he frowned. "What'd he say?"

"You don't remember. You were excited and scared."

"Scared and excited. Excited and scared. Yes I was."

"You drive now. As you drive, you'll wake up, little by little. And when you get to a house or a store, you'll stop and say there's a man hurt down the road. A man who needs help. Tell it back, and be true."

"Drive," he said. His hands caressed the steering wheel as if he longed to be gone immediately. Roland supposed he did. "Wake up, little by little. When I get to a house or store, tell them

Stephen King's hurt side o' the road and he needs help. I know he's still alive because he talked to me. It was an accident." He paused. "It wasn't my fault. He was walking in the road." A pause. "Probably."

Do I care upon whom the blame for this mess falls? Roland asked himself. In truth he did not. King would go on writing either way. And Roland almost hoped he *would* be blamed, for it was indeed King's fault; he'd had no business being out here in the first place.

"Drive away now," he told Bryan Smith. "I don't want to look at you anymore."

Smith started the van with a look of profound relief. Roland didn't bother watching him go. He went to Mrs. Tassenbaum and fell on his knees beside her. Oy sat by Jake's head, now silent, knowing his howls could no longer be heard by the one for whom he grieved. What the gunslinger feared most had come to pass. While he had been talking to two men he didn't like, the boy whom he loved more than all others—more than he'd loved anyone ever in his life, even Susan Delgado—had passed beyond him for the second time. Jake was dead.

FIVE

"He talked to you," Roland said. He took Jake in his arms and began to rock him gently back and forth. The 'Rizas clanked in their pouch. Already he could feel Jake's body growing cool.

"Yes," she said.

"What did he say?"

"He told me to come back for you 'after the business here is done.' Those were his exact words. And he said, 'Tell my father I love him.'"

Roland made a sound, choked and miserable, deep in his throat. He was remembering how it had been in Fedic, after they had stepped through the door. *Hile, Father,* Jake had said. Roland had taken him in his arms then, too. Only then he had felt the boy's beating heart. He would give anything to feel it beat again.

"There was more," she said, "but do we have time for it now, especially when I could tell you later?"

Roland took her point immediately. The story both Bryan Smith and Stephen King knew was a simple one. There was no place in it for a lank, travel-scoured man with a big gun, nor a woman with graying hair; certainly not for a dead boy with a bag of sharp-edged plates slung over his shoulder and a machine-pistol in the waistband of his pants.

The only question was whether or not the woman would come back at all. She was not the first person he had attracted into doing things they might not ordinarily have done, but he knew things might look different to her once she was away from him. Asking for her promise—*Do you swear to come back for me, sai? Do you swear on this boy's stilled heart?*—would do no good. She could mean every word here and then think better of it once she was over the first hill.

Yet when he'd had a chance to take the shopkeeper who owned the truck, he didn't. Nor had he swapped her for the old man cutting the grass at the writer's house.

"Later will do," he said. "For now, hurry on your way. If for some reason you feel you can't come back here, I'll not hold it against you."

"Where would you go on your own?" she asked him. "Where would you *know* to go? This isn't your world. Is it?"

Roland ignored the question. "If there are people still here the first time you come back—peace officers, guards o' the watch, bluebacks, I don't know—drive past without stopping. Come back again in half an hour's time. If they're still here, drive on again. Keep doing that until they're gone."

"Will they notice me going back and forth?"

"I don't know," he said. "Will they?"

She considered, then almost smiled. "The cops in this part of the world? Probably not."

He nodded, accepting her judgment. "When you feel it's safe, stop. You won't see me, but I'll see you. I'll wait until dark. If you're not here by then, I go."

"I'll come for you, but I won't be driving that miserable

excuse for a truck when I do," she said. "I'll be driving a Mercedes-Benz S600." She said this with some pride.

Roland had no idea what a Mercedes-Bends was, but he nodded as though he did. "Go. We'll talk later, after you come back."

If you come back, he thought.

"I think you may want this," she said, and slipped his revolver back into its holster.

"Thankee-sai."

"You're welcome."

He watched her go to the old truck (which he thought she'd rather come to like, despite her dismissive words) and haul herself up by the wheel. And as she did, he realized there was something he needed, something that might be in the truck. *"Whoa!"*

Mrs. Tassenbaum had put her hand on the key in the ignition. Now she took it off and looked at him inquiringly. Roland settled Jake gently back to the earth beneath which he must soon lie (it was that thought which had caused him to call out) and got to his feet. He winced and put his hand to his hip, but that was only habit. There was no pain.

"What?" she asked as he approached. "If I don't go soon—"

It wouldn't matter if she went at all. "Yes. I know."

He looked in the bed of the truck. Along with the careless scatter of tools there was a square shape under a blue tarpaulin. The edges of the tarp had been folded beneath the object to keep it from blowing away. When Roland pulled the tarp free, he saw eight or ten boxes made of the stiff paper Eddie called "card-board." They'd been pushed together to make the square shape. The pictures printed on the card-board told him they were boxes of beer. He wouldn't have cared if they had been boxes of high explosive.

It was the tarpaulin he wanted.

He stepped back from the truck with it in his arms and said, *"Now* you can go."

She grasped the key that started the engine once more, but did not immediately turn it. "Sir," said she, "I am sorry for your loss. I just wanted to tell you that. I can see what that boy meant to you."

Roland Deschain bowed his head and said nothing.

Irene Tassenbaum looked at him for a moment longer, reminded herself that sometimes words were useless things, then started the engine and slammed the door. He watched her drive into the road (her use of the clutch had already grown smooth and sure), making a tight turn so she could drive north, back toward East Stoneham.

Sorry for your loss.

And now he was alone with that loss. Alone with Jake. For a moment Roland stood surveying the little grove of trees beside the highway, looking at two of the three who had been drawn to this place: a man, unconscious, and a boy dead. Roland's eyes were dry and hot, throbbing in their sockets, and for a moment he was sure that he had again lost the ability to weep. The idea horrified him. If he was incapable of tears after all of this—after what he'd regained and then lost again—what good was any of it? So it was an immense relief when the tears finally came. They spilled from his eyes, quieting their nearly insane blue glare. They ran down his dirty cheeks. He cried almost silently, but there was a single sob and Oy heard it. He raised his snout to the corridor of fast-moving clouds and howled a single time at them. Then he too was silent.

SIX

Roland carried Jake deeper into the woods, with Oy padding at his heel. That the bumbler was also weeping no longer surprised Roland; he had seen him cry before. And the days when he had believed Oy's demonstrations of intelligence (and empathy) might be no more than mimicry had long since passed. Most of what Roland thought about on that short walk was a prayer for the dead he had heard Cuthbert speak on their last campaign together, the one that had ended at Jericho Hill. He doubted that Jake needed a prayer to send him on, but the gunslinger needed to keep his mind occupied, because it did not feel strong just now; if it went too far in the wrong direction, it would certainly break. Perhaps later he could indulge in hysteria—or even irina, the healing madness—but not now. He would not break now. He would not let the boy's death come to nothing.

The hazy green-gold summerglow that lives only in forests (and *old* forests, at that, like the one where the Bear Shardik had rampaged), deepened. It fell through the trees in dusky beams, and the place where Roland finally stopped felt more like a church than a clearing. He had gone roughly two hundred paces from the road on a westerly line. Here he set Jake down and looked about. He saw two rusty beer-cans and a few ejected shell-casings, probably the leavings of hunters. He tossed them further into the woods so the place would be clean. Then he looked at Jake, wiping away his tears so he could see as clearly as possible. The boy's face was as clean as the clearing, Oy had seen to that, but one of Jake's eyes was still open, giving the boy an evil winky look that must not be allowed. Roland rolled the lid closed with a finger, and when it sprang back up again (like a balky windowshade, he thought), he licked the ball of his thumb and rolled the lid shut again. This time it stayed closed.

There was dust and blood on Jake's shirt. Roland took it off, then took his own off and put it on Jake, moving him like a doll in order to get it on him. The shirt came almost to Jake's knees, but Roland made no attempt to tuck it in; this way it covered the bloodstains on Jake's pants.

All of this Oy watched, his gold-ringed eyes bright with tears.

Roland had expected the soil to be soft beneath the thick carpet of needles, and it was. He had a good start on Jake's grave when he heard the sound of an engine from the roadside. Other motor-carriages had passed since he'd carried Jake into the woods, but he recognized the dissonant beat of this one. The man in the blue vehicle had come back. Roland hadn't been entirely sure he would.

"Stay," he murmured to the bumbler. "Guard your master." But that was wrong. "Stay and guard your friend."

It wouldn't have been unusual for Oy to repeat the command (*S'ay!* was about the best he could manage) in the same low voice, but this time he said nothing. Roland watched him lie down beside Jake's head, however, and snap a fly out of the air when it came in for a landing on the boy's nose. Roland nodded, satisfied, then started back the way he had come.

SEVEN

Bryan Smith was out of his motor-carriage and sitting on the rock wall by the time Roland got back in view of him, his cane drawn across his lap. (Roland had no idea if the cane was an affectation or something the man really needed, and didn't care about this, either.) King had regained some soupy version of consciousness, and the two men were talking.

"Please tell me it's just sprained," the writer said in a weak, worried voice.

"Nope! I'd say that leg's broke in six, maybe seven places." Now that he'd had time to settle down and maybe work out a story, Smith sounded not just calm but almost happy.

"Cheer me up, why don't you," King said. The visible side of his face was very pale, but the flow of blood from the gash on his temple had slowed almost to a stop. "Have you got a cigarette?"

"Nope," Smith said in that same weirdly cheerful voice. "Gave em up."

Although not particularly strong in the touch, Roland had enough of it to know this wasn't so. But Smith only had three and didn't want to share them with this man, who could probably afford enough cigarettes to fill Smith's entire van with them. *Besides,* Smith thought—

"Besides, folks who been in a accident ain't supposed to smoke," Smith said virtuously.

King nodded. "Hard to breathe, anyway," he said.

"Prolly bust a rib or two, too. My name's Bryan Smith. I'm the one who hit you. Sorry." He held out his hand and—incredibly—King shook it.

"Nothin like this ever happened to me before," Smith said. "I ain't ever had so much as a parkin ticket."

King might or might not have known this for the lie it was, but chose not to comment on it; there was something else on his mind. "Mr. Smith—Bryan—was anyone else here?"

In the trees, Roland stiffened.

Smith actually appeared to consider this. He reached into his pocket, pulled out a Mars bar and began to unwrap it. Then he shook his head. "Just you n me. But I called 911 and Rescue, up to the store. They said someone was real close. Said they'd be here in no time. Don't you worry."

"You know who I am."

"God *yeah!*" Bryan Smith said, and chuckled. He took a bite of the candy bar and talked through it. "Reckonized you right away. I seen all your movies. My favorite was the one about the Saint Bernard. What was that dog's name?"

"Cujo," King said. This was a word Roland knew, one Susan Delgado had sometimes used when they were alone together. In Mejis, *cujo* meant "sweet one."

"Yeah! That was great! Scary as hell! I'm glad that little boy lived!"

"In the book he died." Then King closed his eyes and lay back, waiting.

Smith took another bite, a humongous one this time. "I liked the show they made about the clown, too! *Very* cool!"

King made no reply. His eyes stayed closed, but Roland thought the rise and fall of the writer's chest looked deep and steady. That was good.

Then a truck roared toward them and swerved to a stop in front of Smith's van. The new motor-carriage was about the size of a funeral bucka, but orange instead of black and equipped with flashing lights. Roland was not displeased to see it roll over the tracks of the storekeeper's truck before coming to a stop.

Roland half-expected a robot to get out of the coach, but it was a man. He reached back inside for a black sawbones' bag. Satisfied that everything here would be as well as it could be, Roland returned to where he had laid Jake, moving with all his old unconscious grace: he cracked not a single twig, surprised not a single bird into flight.

EIGHT

Would it surprise you, after all we've seen together and all the secrets we've learned, to know that at quarter past five that afternoon, Mrs. Tassenbaum pulled Chip McAvoy's old truck into the driveway of a house we've already visited? Probably not, because ka is a wheel, and all it knows how to do is roll. When last we visited here, in 1977, both it and the boathouse on the shore of Keywadin Pond were white with green trim. The Tassenbaums, who bought the place in '94, had painted it an entirely pleasing shade of cream (no trim; to Irene Tassenbaum's way of thinking, trim is for folks who can't make up their minds). They have also put a sign reading SUNSET COTTAGE on a post at the head of the driveway, and as far as Uncle Sam's concerned it's part of their mailing address, but to the local folk, this house at the south end of Keywadin Pond will always be the old John Cullum place.

She parked the truck beside her dark red Benz and went inside, mentally rehearsing what she'd tell David about why she had the local shopkeeper's pickup, but Sunset Cottage hummed with the peculiar silence only empty places have; she picked up on it immediately. She had come back to a lot of empty places— apartments at the beginning, bigger and bigger houses as time went by—over the years. Not because David was out drinking or womanizing, good Lord forbid. No, he and his friends had usually been out in one garage or another, one basement workshop or another, drinking cheap wine and discount beer from the Beverage Barn, creating the Internet plus all the software necessary to support it and make it user-friendly. The profits, although most would not believe it, had only been a side-effect. The silence to which their wives so often came home was another. After awhile all that humming silence kind of got to you, made you *mad,* even, but not today. Today she was delighted the house was just hers.

Are you going to sleep with Marshal Dillon, if he wants you?

It wasn't a question she even had to think about. The

answer was yes, she would sleep with him if he wanted her: side-ways, backward, doggy-style, or straight-up fuck, if that was his pleasure. He wouldn't—even if he hadn't been grieving for his young

(*sai? son?*)

friend, he wouldn't have wanted to sleep with her, she with her wrinkles, she with her hair going gray at the roots, she with the spare tire which her designer clothes could not quite conceal. The very idea was ludicrous.

But yes. If he wanted her, she would.

She looked on the fridge and there, under one of the magnets that dotted it (**WE ARE POSITRONICS, BUILDING THE FUTURE ONE CIRCUIT AT A TIME**, this one said) was a brief note.

> *Ree—*
>   *You wanted me to relax, so I'm relaxing (dammit!).*
> *I.e. gone fishin' with Sonny Emerson, t'other end of the*
> *lake, ayuh, ayuh. Will be back by 7 unless the bugs are too*
> *bad. If I bring you a bass, will you cook & clean?*
>   *D.*
> *PS: Something going on at the store big enuf to rate 3 police*
> *cars. WALK-INS, maybe???? ☺ If you hear, fill me in.*

She'd told him *she* was going to the store this afternoon—eggs and milk that she'd of course never gotten—and he had nodded. *Yes dear, yes dear.* But his note held no hint of worry, no sense that he even remembered what she'd said. Well, what else did she expect? When it came to David, info entered ear A, info exited ear B. Welcome to GeniusWorld.

She turned the note over, plucked a pen from a teacup filled with them, hesitated, then wrote:

> *David,*
>   *Something has happened, and I have to be gone for*
> *awhile. 2 days at least, I think maybe 3 or 4. Please don't*
> *worry about me <u>and don't call anyone.</u> <u>ESPECIALLY*
> *NOT POLICE</u>. It's a stray cat thing.*

Would he understand that? She thought he would if he remembered how they'd met. At the Santa Monica ASPCA, that had been, among the stacked rows of kennels in back: love blooms as the mongrels yap. It sounded like James Joyce to her, by God. He had brought in a stray dog he'd found on a suburban street near the apartment where he was staying with half a dozen egghead friends. She'd been looking for a kitten to liven up what was an essentially friendless life. He'd had all his hair then. As for her, she'd thought women who dyed theirs mildly amusing. Time was a thief, and one of the first things it took was your sense of humor.

She hesitated, then added

Love you,
Ree

Was that true any longer? Well, let it stand, either way. Crossing out what you'd written in ink always looked ugly. She put the note back on the fridge with the same magnet to hold it in place.

She got the keys to the Mercedes out of the basket by the door, then remembered the rowboat, still tied up at the little stub of dock behind the store. It would be all right there. But then she thought of something else, something the boy had told her. *He doesn't know about money.*

She went into the pantry, where they always kept a slim roll of fifties (there were places out here in the boondocks where she would be willing to swear they'd never even *heard* of MasterCard) and took three. She started away, shrugged, went back, and took the other three, as well. Why not? She was living dangerously today.

On her way out, she paused again to look at the note. And then, for absolutely no reason she could understand, she took the Positronics magnet away and replaced it with an orange slice. Then she left.

Never mind the future. For the time being, she had enough to keep her occupied in the present.

NINE

The emergency bucka was gone, bearing the writer to the nearest hospital or infirmary, Roland assumed. Peace officers had come just as it left, and they spent perhaps half an hour talking with Bryan Smith. The gunslinger could hear the palaver from where he was, just over the first rise. The bluebacks' questions were clear and calm, Smith's answers little more than mumbles. Roland saw no reason to stop working. If the blues came back here and found him, he would deal with them. Just incapacitate them, unless they made that impossible; gods knew there had been enough killing. But he would bury his dead, one way or another.

He would bury his dead.

The lovely green-gold light of the clearing deepened. Mosquitoes found him but he did not stop what he was doing in order to slap them, merely let them drink their fill and then lumber off, heavy with their freight of blood. He heard engines starting as he finished hand-digging the grave, the smooth roar of two cars and the more uneven sound of Smith's vanmobile. He had heard the voices of only two peace officers, which meant that, unless there had been a third blueback with nothing to say, they were allowing Smith to drive away by himself. Roland thought this rather odd, but—like the question of whether or not King was paralyzed—it was none of his matter or mind. All that mattered was this; all that mattered was seeing to his own.

He made three trips to collect stones, because a grave dug by hand must necessarily be a shallow one and animals, even in such a tame world as this, are always hungry. He stacked the stones at the head of the hole, a scar lined with earth so rich it could have been black satin. Oy lay by Jake's head, watching the gunslinger come and go, saying nothing. He'd always been different from his kind as they were since the world had moved on; Roland had even speculated that it was Oy's extraordinary chattiness that had caused the others in his tet to expel him, and not gently, either. When they'd come upon this fellow, not too far from the town of River Crossing, he'd been scrawny to the point of starvation, and with a half-healed bite-mark on one flank. The bumbler had loved Jake from the first: "That's as clear as Earth needs," Cort might have said (or Roland's own father, for that matter). And it was to Jake the bumbler had talked the most. Roland had an idea that Oy might fall mostly silent now that the boy was dead, and this thought was another way of defining what was lost.

He remembered the boy standing before the people of Calla Bryn Sturgis in the torchlight, his face young and fair, as if he would live forever. *I am Jake Chambers, son of Elmer, the Line of Eld, the ka-tet of the Ninety and Nine,* he had said, and oh, aye, for here he was in the Ninety and Nine, with his grave all dug, clean and ready for him.

Roland began to weep again. He put his hands over his face and rocked back and forth on his knees, smelling the sweet aromatic needles and wishing he had cried off before ka, that old and patient demon, had taught him the real price of his quest. He would have given anything to change what had happened, anything to close this hole with nothing in it, but this was the world where time ran just one way.

TEN

When he had gained control of himself again, he wrapped Jake carefully in the blue tarpaulin, fashioning a kind of hood around the still, pale face. He would close that face away for good before refilling the grave, but not until.

"Oy?" he asked. "Will you say goodbye?"

Oy looked at Roland, and for a moment the gunslinger wasn't sure he understood. Then the bumbler extended his neck and caressed the boy's cheek a last time with his tongue. "I, Ake," he said: *Bye, Jake* or *I ache,* it came to the same.

The gunslinger gathered the boy up (how light he was, this boy who had jumped from the barn loft with Benny Slightman, and stood against the vampires with Pere Callahan, how curiously light; as if the growing weight of him had departed with his life) and lowered him into the hole. A crumble of dirt spilled down one cheek and Roland wiped it away. That done, he closed his eyes again and thought. Then, at last—haltingly— he began. He knew that any translation into the language of this place would be clumsy, but he did the best he could. If Jake's spirit-man lingered near, it was this language that he would understand.

"Time flies, knells call, life passes, so hear my prayer.

"Birth is nothing but death begun, so hear my prayer.

"Death is speechless, so hear my speech."

The words drifted away into the haze of green and gold. Roland let them, then set upon the rest. He spoke more quickly now.

"This is Jake, who served his ka and his tet. Say true.

"May the forgiving glance of S'mana heal his heart. Say please.

"May the arms of Gan raise him from the darkness of this earth. Say please.

"Surround him, Gan, with light.

"Fill him, Chloe, with strength.

"If he is thirsty, give him water in the clearing.

"If he is hungry, give him food in the clearing.

"May his life on this earth and the pain of his passing become as a dream to his waking soul, and let his eyes fall upon every lovely sight; let him find the friends that were lost to him, and let every one whose name he calls call his in return.

"This is Jake, who lived well, loved his own, and died as ka would have it.

"Each man owes a death. This is Jake. Give him peace."

He knelt a moment longer with his hands clasped between his knees, thinking he had not understood the true power of sorrow, nor the pain of regret, until this moment.

I cannot bear to let him go.

But once again, that cruel paradox: if he didn't, the sacrifice was in vain.

Roland opened his eyes and said, "Goodbye, Jake. I love you, dear."

Then he closed the blue hood around the boy's face against the rain of earth that must follow.

ELEVEN

When the grave was filled and the rocks placed over it, Roland walked back to the clearing by the road and examined the tale the various tracks told, simply because there was nothing else to do. When that meaningless task was finished, he sat down on a fallen log. Oy had stayed by the grave, and Roland had an idea he might bide there. He would call the bumbler when Mrs. Tassenbaum returned, but knew Oy might not come; if he didn't, it meant that Oy had decided to join his friend in the clearing. The bumbler would simply stand watch by Jake's grave until starvation (or some predator) took him. The idea deepened Roland's sorrow, but he would bide by Oy's decision.

Ten minutes later the bumbler came out of the woods on his own and sat down by Roland's left boot. "Good boy," Roland said, and stroked the bumbler's head. Oy had decided to live. It was a small thing, but it was a good thing.

Ten minutes after that, a dark red car rolled almost silently up to the place where King had been struck and Jake killed. It pulled over. Roland opened the door on the passenger side and got in, still wincing against pain that wasn't there. Oy jumped up between his feet without being asked, lay down with his nose against his flank, and appeared to go to sleep.

"Did you see to your boy?" Mrs. Tassenbaum asked, pulling away.

"Yes. Thankee-sai."

"I guess I can't put a marker there," she said, "but later on I could plant something. Is there something you think he might like?"

Roland looked up, and for the first time since Jake's death, he smiled. "Yes," he said. "A rose."

TWELVE

They rode for almost twenty minutes without speaking. She stopped at a small store over the Bridgton town line and pumped gas: MOBIL, a brand Roland recognized from his wanderings. When she went in to pay, he looked up at *los ángeles,* running clear and true across the sky. The Path of the Beam, and stronger already, unless that was just his imagination. He supposed it didn't matter if it was. If the Beam wasn't stronger now, it soon would be. They had succeeded in saving it, but Roland felt no gladness at the idea.

When Mrs. Tassenbaum came out of the store, she was holding a singlet-style shirt with a picture of a bucka-wagon on it—a *real* bucka-wagon—and words written in a circle. He could make out *HOME,* but nothing else. He asked her what the words said.

"BRIDGTON OLD HOME DAYS, JULY 27TH TO JULY 30TH, 1999," she told him. "It doesn't really matter what it says as long as it covers your chest. Sooner or later we'll want to stop, and there's a saying we have in these parts: 'No shirt, no shoes, no service.' Your boots look beat-up and busted down, but I guess they'll get you through the door of most places. But topless? Huh-uh, no way José. I'll get you a better shirt later on—one with a collar—and some decent pants, too. Those jeans are so dirty I bet they'd stand up on their own." She engaged in a brief (but furious) interior debate, then plunged. "You've got I'm going to say roughly two billion scars. And that's just on the part of you I can see."

Roland did not respond to this. "Do you have money?" he asked.

"I got three hundred dollars when I went back to the house to get my car, and I had thirty or forty with me. Also credit cards, but your late friend said to use cash as long as I could. Until you go on by yourself, if possible. He said there might be folks looking for you. He called them 'low men.'"

Roland nodded. Yes, there would be low men out there, and

after all he and his ka-tet had done to thwart the plans of their master, they'd be twice as eager to have his head. Preferably smoking, and on the end of a stick. Also the head of sai Tassenbaum, if they found out about her.

"What else did Jake tell you?" Roland asked.

"That I must take you to New York City, if you wanted to go there. He said there's a door there that will take you to a place called Faydag."

"Was there more?"

"Yes. He said there was another place you might want to go before you used the door." She gave him a timid little sideways glance. "Is there?"

He considered this, then nodded.

"He also spoke to the dog. It sounded as if he was giving the dog . . . orders? Instructions?" She looked at him doubtfully. "Could that be?"

Roland thought it could. The woman Jake could only ask. As for Oy . . . well, it might explain why the bumbler hadn't stayed by the grave, much as he might have wanted to.

For awhile they traveled in silence. The road they were on led to a much busier one, filled with cars and trucks running at high speed in many lanes. She had to stop at a tollbooth and give money to get on. The toll-taker was a robot with a basket for an arm. Roland thought he might be able to sleep, but he saw Jake's face when he closed his eyes. Then Eddie's, with the useless bandage covering his forehead. *If this is what comes when I close my eyes,* he thought, *what will my dreams be like?*

He opened his eyes again and watched as she drove down a smooth, paved ramp, slipping into the heavy flow of traffic without a pause. He leaned over and looked up through the window on his side. There were the clouds, *los ángeles,* traveling above them, in the same direction. They were still on the Path of the Beam.

THIRTEEN

"Mister? Roland?"

She thought he had been dozing with his eyes open. Now he turned to her from where he sat in the passenger bucket seat with his hands in his lap, the good one folded over the mutilated one, hiding it. She thought she had never seen anyone who looked less like he belonged in a Mercedes-Benz. Or any automobile. She also thought she had never seen a man who looked so tired.

But he's not used up. I don't think he's anywhere near used up, although he may think otherwise.

"The animal . . . Oy?"

"Oy, yes." The bumbler looked up at the sound of his name, but didn't repeat it as he might have done only yesterday.

"Is it a dog? It isn't, exactly, is it?"

"He, not it. And no, he's not a dog."

Irene Tassenbaum opened her mouth, then closed it again. This was difficult, because silence in company did not come naturally to her. And she was with a man she found attractive, even in his grief and exhaustion (perhaps to some degree because of those things). A dying boy had asked her to take this man to New York City, and get him to the places he needed to go once they were there. He'd said that his friend knew even less about New York than he did about money, and she believed that was true. But she also believed this man was dangerous. She wanted to ask more questions, but what if he answered them? She understood that the less she knew, the better her chance, once he was gone, of merging into the life she'd been living at quarter to four this afternoon. To merge the way you merged onto the turnpike from a side road. That would be best.

She turned on the radio and found a station playing "Amazing Grace." The next time she looked at her strange companion, she saw that he was looking out at the darkening sky and weeping. Then she chanced to look down and saw something much odder, something that moved her heart as it had not been moved in fifteen years, when she had miscarried her one and only effort to have a child.

The animal, the not-dog, the Oy . . . he was crying, too.

FOURTEEN

She got off 95 just over the Massachusetts state line and checked them into a pair of side-by-side rooms in a dump called the Sea Breeze Inn. She hadn't thought to bring her driving glasses, the ones she called her bug's-asshole glasses (as in "when I'm wearing these things I can see up a bug's asshole"), and she didn't like driving at night, anyway. Bug's-asshole glasses or not, driving at night fried her nerves, and that was apt to bring on a migraine. With a migraine she would be of no use to either of them, and her Imitrex was sitting uselessly in the medicine cabinet back in East Stoneham.

"Plus," she told Roland, "if this Tet Corporation you're looking for is in a business building, you won't be able to get inside until Monday, anyway." Probably not true; this was the sort of man who got into places when he wanted. You couldn't keep him out. She guessed that was part of his attraction to a certain kind of woman.

In any case, he did not object to the motel. No, he would not go out to dinner with her, and so she found the nearest bearable fast-food franchise and brought back a late dinner from KFC. They ate in Roland's room. Irene fixed Oy a plate without being asked. Oy ate a single piece of the chicken, holding it neatly between his paws, then went into the bathroom and appeared to fall asleep on the mat in front of the tub.

"Why do they call this the Sea Breeze?" Roland asked. Unlike Oy, he was eating some of everything, but he did it with no sign of pleasure. He ate like a man doing work. "I get no smell of the ocean."

"Well, probably you can when the wind's in the right quarter and blowing a hurricane," she said. "It's what we call poetic license, Roland."

He nodded, showing unexpected (to her, at least) under-standing. "Pretty lies," he said.

"Yes, I suppose."

She turned on the television, thinking it would divert him, and was shocked by his reaction (although she told herself that what she felt was amusement). When he told her he couldn't see it, she had no idea how to take what he was saying; her first thought that it was some sort of oblique and *teddibly* intellectual criticism of the medium itself. Then she thought he might be speaking (in equally oblique fashion) of his sorrow, his state of mourning. It wasn't until he told her that he heard voices, yes, but saw only lines which made his eyes water that she realized he was telling her the literal truth: he could not see the pic-tures on the screen. Not the rerun of *Roseanne,* not the infomercial for Ab-Flex, not the talking head on the local news. She held on until the story about Stephen King (taken by LifeFlight helicopter to Central Maine General in Lewiston, where an early-evening operation seemed to have saved his right leg—condition listed as fair, more operations ahead, road to recovery expected to be long and uncertain), then turned the TV off.

She bussed up the trash—there was always so much *more* of it from a KFC meal, somehow—bade Roland an uncertain goodnight (which he returned in a distracted, I'm-not-really-here way that made her nervous and sad), then went to her own room next door. There she watched an hour of an old movie in which Yul Brynner played a robot cowboy that had run amok before turning it off and going into the bathroom to brush her teeth. There she realized that she had—of *course,* dollink!—forgotten her toothbrush. She did the best she could with her finger, then lay down on the bed in her bra and panties (no nightgown either). She spent an hour like that before realizing that she was listening for sounds from beyond the paper-thin wall, and for one sound in particular: the crash of the gun he had considerately not worn from the car to the motel room. The single loud shot that would mean he had ended his sorrow in the most direct fashion.

When she couldn't stand the quiet from the other side of the wall any longer she got up, put her clothes back on, and went outside to look at the stars. There, sitting on the curb, she found Roland, with the not-dog at his side. She wanted to ask how he had gotten out of his room without her being aware of it (the walls were so thin and she had been listening so *hard*), but she didn't. She asked him what he was doing out here, instead, and found herself unprepared for both his answer and for the utter nakedness of the face he turned to hers. She kept expecting a patina of civilization from him—a nod in the direction of the niceties—but there was none of that. His honesty was terrifying.

"I'm afraid to go to sleep," he said. "I'm afraid my dead friends will come to me, and that seeing them will kill me."

She looked at him steadily in the mixture of light: that which fell from her room and the horrible heartless Halloween glare of the parking-lot arc sodiums. Her heart was beating hard enough to shake her entire chest, but when she spoke her voice sounded calm enough: "Would it help if I lay down with you?"

He considered this, and nodded. "I think it would."

She took his hand and they went into the room she had rented him. He stripped off his clothes with no sign of embarrassment and she looked, awestruck and afraid, at the scars which lapped and dented his upper body: the red pucker of a knife-slash on one bicep, the milky weal of a burn on another, the white crisscross of lash-marks between and on the shoulderblades, three deep dimples that could only be old bulletholes. And, of course, there were the missing fingers on his right hand. She was curious but knew she'd never dare ask about those.

She took off her own outer clothes, hesitated, then took off her bra, as well. Her breasts hung down, and there was a dented scar of her own on one, from a lumpectomy instead of a bullet. And so what? She never would have been a Victoria's Secret model, even in her prime. And even in her prime she'd never mistaken herself for tits and ass attached to a life-support system.

Nor had ever let anyone else—including her husband—make the same mistake.

She left her panties on, however. If she had trimmed her bush, maybe she would have taken them off. If she'd known, getting up that morning, that she would be lying down with a strange man in a cheap hotel room while some weird animal snoozed on the bathmat in front of the tub. Of course she would have packed a toothbrush and a tube of Crest, too.

When he put her arms around her, she gasped and stiffened, then relaxed. But very slowly. His hips pressed against her bottom and she felt the considerable weight of his package, but it was apparently only comfort he had in mind; his penis was limp.

He clasped her left breast, and ran his thumb into the hollow of the scar left by the lumpectomy. "What's this?" he asked.

"Well," she said (now her voice was no longer even), "according to my doctor, in another five years it would have been cancer. So they cut it out before it could . . . I don't know, exactly—metastasizing comes later, if it comes at all."

"Before it could flower?" he asked.

"Yes. Right. Good." Her nipple was now as hard as a rock, and surely he must feel that. Oh, this was so weird.

"Why is your heart beating so hard?" he asked. "Do I frighten you?"

"I . . . yes."

"Don't be frightened," he said. "Killing's done." A long pause in the dark. They could hear the faint drone of cars on the turnpike. "For now," he added.

"Oh," she said in a small voice. "Good."

His hand on her breast. His breath on her neck. After some endless time that might have been an hour or only five minutes, his breathing lengthened, and she knew he had gone to sleep. She was pleased and disappointed at the same time. A few minutes later she went to sleep herself, and it was the best rest she'd had in years. If he had bad dreams of his gone friends, he did not disturb her with them. When she woke in the morning it was eight o'clock and he was standing naked at the window, looking out through a slit he'd made in the curtains with one finger.

"Did you sleep?" she asked.

"A little. Will we go on?"

FIFTEEN

They could have been in Manhattan by three o'clock in the afternoon, and the drive into the city on a Sunday would have been far easier than during the Monday morning rush hour, but hotel rooms in New York were expensive and even doubling up would have necessitated breaking out a credit card. They stayed at a Motel 6 in Harwich, Connecticut, instead. She took only a single room and that night he made love to her. Not because he exactly wanted to, she sensed, but because he understood it was what she wanted. Perhaps what she needed.

It was extraordinary, although she could not have said precisely how; despite the feel of all those scars beneath her hands—some rough, some smooth—there was the sense of making love to a dream. And that night she *did* dream. It was a field filled with roses she dreamed of, and a huge Tower made of slate-black stone standing at the far end. Partway up, red lamps glowed . . . only she had an idea they weren't lamps at all, but eyes.

Terrible eyes.

She heard many singing voices, thousands of them, and understood that some were the voices of his lost friends. She awoke with tears on her cheeks and a feeling of loss even though he was still beside her. After today she'd see him no more. And that was for the best. Still, she would have given anything in her life to have him make love to her again, even though she understood it had not been really her he had been making love to; even when he came into her, his thoughts had been far away, with those voices.

Those lost voices.

Chapter III:
New York Again
(Roland Shows ID)

On the morning of Monday the 21st of June in the year of '99, the sun shone down on New York City just as if Jake Chambers did not lie dead in one world and Eddie Dean in another; as if Stephen King did not lie in a Lewiston hospital's Intensive Care ward, drifting out into the light of consciousness only for brief intervals; as if Susannah Dean did not sit alone with her grief aboard a train racing on ancient, chancy tracks across the dark wastes of Thunderclap toward the ghost-town of Fedic. There were others who had elected to accompany her on her journey at least that far, but she'd asked them to give her space, and they had complied with her wish. She knew she would feel better if she could cry, but so far she hadn't been able to do that—a few random tears, like meaningless showers in the desert, was the best she had been able to manage—although she had a terrible feeling that things were worse than she knew.

Fuck, dat ain't no "feelin," Detta crowed contemptuously from her place deep inside, as Susannah sat looking out at the dark and rocky wastelands or the occasional ruins of towns and villages that had been abandoned when the world moved on. *You havin a jenna-wine intuition, girl! Only question you cain't answer is whether it be ole long tall and ugly or Young Master Sweetness now visitin wit' yo man in the clearin.*

"Please, no," she murmured. "Please not either of them, God, I can't stand another one."

But God remained deaf to her prayer, Jake remained dead,

485

the Dark Tower remained standing at the end of Can'-Ka No Rey, casting its shadow over a million shouting roses, and in New York the hot summer sun shone down on the just and the unjust alike.

Can you give me hallelujah?

Thankee-sai.

Now somebody yell me a big old God-bomb amen.

TWO

Mrs. Tassenbaum left her car at Sir Speedy-Park on Sixty-third Street (the sign on the sidewalk showed a knight in armor behind the wheel of a Cadillac, his lance sticking jauntily out of the driver's window), where she and David rented two stalls on a yearly basis. They kept an apartment nearby, and Irene asked Roland if he would like to go there and clean up . . . although the man actually didn't look all that bad, she had to admit. She'd bought him a fresh pair of jeans and a white button-up shirt which he had rolled to the elbows; she had also bought a comb and a tube of hair-mousse so strong its molecular makeup was probably closer to Super-Glue than it was to Vitalis. With the unruly mop of gray-flecked hair combed straight back from his brow, she had revealed the spare good looks and angular features of an interesting crossbreed: a mixture of Quaker and Cherokee was what she imagined. The bag of Orizas was once more slung over his shoulder. His gun, the holster wrapped in its shell-belt, was in there, too. He had covered it from enquiring eyes with the Old Home Days tee-shirt.

Roland shook his head. "I appreciate the offer, but I'd as soon do what needs doing and then go back to where I belong." He surveyed the hurrying throngs on the sidewalks bleakly. "If I belong anywhere."

"You could stay at the apartment for a couple of days and rest up," she said. "I'd stay with you." *And fuck thy brains out, do it please ya,* she thought, and could not help a smile. "I mean, I know you won't, but *you* need to know the offer's open."

He nodded. "Thankee, but there's a woman who needs

me to get back to her as soon as I can." It felt like a lie to him, and a grotesque one at that. Based on everything that had happened, part of him thought that Susannah Dean needed Roland of Gilead back in her life almost as much as nursery bah-bos needed rat poison added to their bedtime bottles. Irene Tassenbaum accepted it, however. And part of her was actually anxious to get back to her husband. She had called him last night (using a pay phone a mile from the motel, just to be safe), and it seemed that she had finally gotten David Seymour Tassenbaum's attention again. Based on her encounter with Roland, David's attention was definitely second prize, but it was better than nothing, by God. Roland Deschain would vanish from her life soon, leaving her to find her way back to northern New England on her own and explain what had happened as best she could. Part of her mourned the impending loss, but she'd had enough adventure in the last forty hours or so to last her for the rest of her life, hadn't she? And things to think about, that too. For one thing, it seemed that the world was thinner than she had ever imagined. And reality wider.

"All right," she said. "It's Second Avenue and Forty-sixth Street you want to go to first, correct?"

"Yes." Susannah hadn't had a chance to tell them much about her adventures after Mia had hijacked their shared body, but the gunslinger knew there was a tall building—what Eddie, Jake, and Susannah called a skyscraper—now standing on the site of the former vacant lot, and the Tet Corporation must surely be inside. "Will we need a tack-see?"

"Can you and your furry friend walk seventeen short blocks and two or three long ones? It's your call, but I wouldn't mind stretching my legs."

Roland didn't know how long a long block or how short a short one might be, but he was more than willing to find out now that the deep pain in his right hip had departed. Stephen King had that pain now, along with the one in his smashed ribs and the right side of his split head. Roland did not envy him those pains, but at least they were back with their rightful owner.

"Let's go," he said.

THREE

Fifteen minutes later he stood across from the large dark structure thrusting itself at the summer sky, trying to keep his jaw
from coming unhinged and perhaps dropping all the way to his
chest. It wasn't the Dark Tower, not *his* Dark Tower, at least
(although it wouldn't have surprised him to know there were
people working in yon sky-tower—some of them readers of
Roland's adventures—who called 2 Hammarskjöld Plaza exactly
that), but he had no doubt that it was the Tower's representa-
tive in this Keystone World, just as the rose represented a field
filled with them; the field he had seen in so many dreams.

He could hear the singing voices from here, even over the
jostle and hum of the traffic. The woman had to call his name
three times and finally tug on one sleeve to get his attention.
When he turned to her—reluctantly—he saw it wasn't the
tower across the street that she was looking at (she had grown
up just an hour from Manhattan and tall buildings were an old
story to her) but at the pocket park on their side of the street.
Her expression was delighted. "Isn't it a beautiful little place? I
must have been by this corner a hundred times and I never
noticed it until now. Do you see the fountain? And the turtle
sculpture?"

He did. And although Susannah hadn't told them this part
of her story, Roland knew she had been here—along with
Mia, daughter of none—and sat on the bench closest to the
turtle's wet shell. He could almost see her there.

"I'd like to go in," she said timidly. "May we? Is there time?"

"Yes," he said, and followed her through the little iron gate.

FOUR

The pocket park was peaceful, but not entirely quiet.

"Do you hear people singing?" Mrs. Tassenbaum asked in a
voice that was hardly more than a whisper. "A chorus from
somewhere?"

"Bet your bottom dollar," Roland answered, and was sorry immediately. He'd learned the phrase from Eddie, and saying it hurt. He walked to the turtle and dropped on one knee to examine it more closely. There was a tiny piece gone from the beak, leaving a break like a missing tooth. On the back was a scratch in the shape of a question mark, and fading pink letters.

"What does it say?" she asked. "Something about a turtle, but that's all I can make out."

"'See the TURTLE of enormous girth.'" He knew this without reading it.

"What does it mean?"

Roland stood up. "It's too much to go into. Would you like to wait for me while I go in there?" He nodded in the direction of the tower with its black glass windows glittering in the sun.

"Yes," she said. "I would. I'll just sit on the bench in the sunshine and wait for you. It's . . . refreshing. Does that sound crazy?"

"No," he said. "If someone whose looks you don't trust should speak to you, Irene—I think it unlikely, because this is a safe place, but it's certainly possible—concentrate just as hard as you can, and call for me."

Her eyes widened. "Are you talking ESP?"

He didn't know what ESP stood for, but he understood what she meant, and nodded.

"You'd hear that? Hear *me*?"

He couldn't say for sure that he would. The building might be equipped with damping devices, like the thinking-caps the can-toi wore, that would make it impossible.

"I might. And as I say, trouble's unlikely. This is a safe place."

She looked at the turtle, its shell gleaming with spray from the fountain. "It is, isn't it?" She started to smile, then stopped. "You'll come back, won't you? You wouldn't dump me without at least . . ." She shrugged one shoulder. The gesture made her look very young. "Without at least saying goodbye?"

"Never in life. And my business in yonder tower shouldn't take long." In fact it was hardly business at all . . . unless, that was, whoever was currently running the Tet Corporation had some with him. "We have another place to go, and it's there Oy and I would take our leave of you."

"Okay," she said, and sat on the bench with the bumbler at her feet. The end of it was damp and she was wearing a new pair of slacks (bought in the same quick shopping-run that had netted Roland's new shirt and jeans), but this didn't bother her. They would dry quickly on such a warm, sunny day, and she found she wanted to be near the turtle sculpture. To study its tiny, timeless black eyes while she listened to those sweet voices. She thought that would be very restful. It was not a word she usually thought of in connection with New York, but this was a very un–New York place, with its feel of quiet and peace. She thought she might bring David here, that if they could sit on this bench he might hear the story of her missing three days without thinking her insane. Or *too* insane.

Roland started away, moving easily—moving like a man who could walk for days and weeks without ever varying his pace. *I wouldn't like to have him on my trail,* she thought, and shivered a little at the idea. He reached the iron gate through which he would pass to the sidewalk, then turned to her once more. He spoke in a soft singsong.

> "See the TURTLE of enormous girth!
> On his shell he holds the earth.
> His thought is slow but always kind;
> He holds us all within his mind.
> On his back all vows are made;
> He sees the truth but mayn't aid.
> He loves the land and loves the sea,
> And even loves a child like me."

Then he left her, moving swiftly and cleanly, not looking back. She sat on the bench and watched him wait with the others clustered on the corner for the WALK light, then cross with them, the leather bag slung over his shoulder bouncing lightly against his hip. She watched him mount the steps of 2 Hammarskjöld Plaza and disappear inside. Then she leaned back, closed her eyes, and listened to the voices sing. At some point she realized that at least two of the words they were singing were the ones that made her name.

FIVE

It seemed to Roland that great multitudes of *folken* were streaming into the building, but this was the perception of a man who had spent the latter years of his quest in mostly deserted places. If he'd come at quarter to nine, while people were still arriving, instead of at quarter to eleven, he would have been stunned by the flood of bodies. Now most of those who worked here were settled in their offices and cubicles, generating paper and bytes of information.

The lobby windows were of clear glass and at least two stories high, perhaps three. Consequently the lobby was full of light, and as he stepped inside, the grief that had possessed him ever since kneeling by Eddie in the street of Pleasantville slipped away. In here the singing voices were louder, not a chorus but a great choir. And, he saw, he wasn't the only one who heard them. On the street, people had been hurrying with their heads down and looks of distracted concentration on their faces, as if they were deliberately not seeing the delicate and perishable beauty of the day which had been given them; in here they were helpless not to feel at least some of that to which the gunslinger was so exquisitely attuned, and which he drank like water in the desert.

As if in a dream, he drifted across the rose-marble tile, hearing the echoing clack of his bootheels, hearing the faint and shifting conversation of the Orizas in their pouch. He thought, *People who work here wish they lived here. They may not know it, exactly, but they do. People who work here find excuses to work late. And they will live long and productive lives.*

In the center of the high, echoing room, the expensive marble floor gave way to a square of humble dark earth. It was surrounded by ropes of wine-dark velvet, but Roland knew that even the ropes didn't need to be there. No one would transgress that little garden, not even a suicidal can-toi desperate to make a name for himself. It was holy ground. There were three dwarf palm trees, and plants he hadn't seen since leaving Gilead: Spathiphyllum, he believed they had been called there, although they might not have the same name in this world. There were other plants as well, but only one mattered.

In the middle of the square, by itself, was the rose.

It hadn't been transplanted; Roland saw that at once. No. It was where it had been in 1977, when the place where he was now standing had been a vacant lot, filled with trash and broken bricks, dominated by a sign which announced the coming of Turtle Bay Luxury Condominiums, to be built by Mills Construction and Sombra Real Estate Associates. This building, all one hundred stories of it, had been built instead, and *around* the rose. Whatever business might be done here was secondary to that purpose.

2 Hammarskjöld Plaza was a shrine.

SIX

There was a tap on his shoulder and Roland whirled about so suddenly that he drew glances of alarm. He was alarmed himself. Not for years—perhaps since his early teenage years—had anyone been quiet enough to come within shoulder-tapping distance of him without being overheard. And on this marble floor, he surely should have—

The young (and extremely beautiful) woman who had approached him was clearly surprised by the suddenness of his reaction, but the hands he shot out to seize her shoulders only closed on thin air and then themselves, making a soft clapping sound that echoed back from the ceiling above, a ceiling at least as high as that in the Cradle of Lud. The woman's green eyes were wide and wary, and he would have sworn there was no harm in them, but still, first to be surprised, then to *miss* like that—

He glanced down at the woman's feet and got at least part

of the answer. She was wearing a kind of shoe he'd never seen before, something with deep foam soles and what might have been canvas uppers. Shoes that would move as softly as moccasins on a hard surface. As for the woman herself—

A queer double certainty came to him as he looked at her: first, that he had "seen the boat she came in," as familial resemblance was sometimes expressed in Calla Bryn Sturgis; second, that a society of gunslingers was a-breeding in this world, this special Keystone World, and he had just been accosted by one of them.

And what better place for such an encounter than within sight of the rose?

"I see your father in your face, but can't quite name him," Roland said in a low voice. "Tell me who he was, do it please you."

The woman smiled, and Roland almost had the name he was looking for. Then it slipped away, as such things often did: memory could be bashful. "You never met him . . . although I can understand why you might think you had. I'll tell you later, if you like, but right now I'm to take you upstairs, Mr. Deschain. There's a person who wants . . ." For a moment she looked self-conscious, as if she thought someone had instructed her to use a certain word so she'd be laughed at. Then dimples formed at the corners of her mouth and her green eyes slanted enchantingly up at the corners; it was as if she were thinking *If it's a joke on me, let them have it.* ". . . a person who wants to *palaver* with you," she finished.

"All right," he said.

She touched his shoulder lightly, to hold him where he was yet a moment longer. "I'm asked to make sure that you read the sign in the Garden of the Beam," she said. "Will you do it?"

Roland's response was dry, but still a bit apologetic. "I will if I may," he said, "but I've ever had trouble with your written language, although it seems to come out of my mouth well enough when I'm on this side."

"I think you'll be able to read this," she said. "Give it a try." And she touched his shoulder again, gently turning him back to the square of earth in the lobby floor—not earth that had been brought in wheelbarrows by some crew of gifted gardeners, he knew, but the actual earth of this place, ground which might have been tilled but had not been otherwise changed.

At first he had no more success with the small brass sign in the garden than he'd had with most signs in the shop windows, or the words on the covers of the "magda-seens." He was about to say so, to ask the woman with the faintly familiar face to read it to him, when the letters changed, becoming the Great Letters of Gilead. He was then able to read what was writ there, and easily. When he had finished, it changed back again.

"A pretty trick," he said. "Did it respond to my thoughts?"

She smiled—her lips were coated with some pink candylike stuff—and nodded. "Yes. If you were Jewish, you might have seen it in Hebrew. If you were Russian, it would have been in Cyrillic."

"Say true?"

"True."

The lobby had regained its normal rhythm . . . except, Roland understood, the rhythm of this place would never be like that in other business buildings. Those living in Thunderclap would suffer all their lives from little ailments like boils and eczema and headaches and ear-styke; at the end of it, they would die (probably at an early age) of some big and painful trum, likely the cancers that ate fast and burned the nerves like brushfires as they made their meals. Here was just the opposite: health and harmony, goodwill and generosity. These *folken* did not hear the rose singing, exactly, but they didn't need to. They were the lucky ones, and on some level every one of them knew it . . . which was luckiest of all. He watched them come in and cross to the lift-boxes that were called ele-vaydors, moving briskly, swinging their pokes and packages, their gear and their gunna, and not one course was a perfectly straight line from the doors. A few came to what she'd called the Garden of the Beam, but even those who didn't bent their steps briefly in that direction, as if attracted by a powerful magnet. And if anyone tried to harm the rose? There was a security guard sitting at

a little desk by the elevators, Roland saw, but he was fat and old. And it didn't matter. If anyone made a threatening move, everyone in this lobby would hear a scream of alarm in his or her head, as piercing and imperative as that kind of whistle only dogs can hear. And they would converge upon the would-be assassin of the rose. They would do so swiftly, and with absolutely no regard for their own safety. The rose had been able to protect itself when it had been growing in the trash and the weeds of the vacant lot (or at least draw those who would protect it), and that hadn't changed.

"Mr. Deschain? Are you ready to go upstairs now?"

"Aye," he said. "Lead me as you would."

SEVEN

The familiarity of the woman's face clicked into place for him just as they reached the ele-vaydor. Perhaps it was seeing her in profile that did it, something about the shape of the cheekbone. He remembered Eddie telling him about his conversation with Calvin Tower after Jack Andolini and George Biondi had left the Manhattan Restaurant of the Mind. Tower had been speaking of his oldest friend's family. *They like to boast that they have the most unique legal letterhead in New York, perhaps in the United States. It simply reads "DEEPNEAU."*

"Are you sai Aaron Deepneau's daughter?" he asked her. "Surely not, you're too young. His granddaughter?"

Her smile faded. "Aaron never had children, Mr. Deschain. I'm the granddaughter of his older brother, but my own parents and grandfather died young. Airy was the one who mostly raised me."

"Did you call him so? Airy?" Roland was charmed.

"As a child I did, and it just kind of stuck." She held out a hand, her smile returning. "Nancy Deepneau. And I am so pleased to meet you. A little frightened, but pleased."

Roland shook her hand, but the gesture was perfunctory, hardly more than a touch. Then, with considerably more feeling (for this was the ritual he had grown up with, the one he understood), he placed his fist against his forehead and made a leg. "Long days and pleasant nights, Nancy Deepneau."

Her smile widened into a cheerful grin. "And may you have twice the number, Roland of Gilead! May you have twice the number."

The ele-vaydor came, they got on, and it was to the ninety-ninth floor that they went.

EIGHT

The doors opened on a large round foyer. The floor was carpeted in a dusky pink shade that exactly matched the hue of the rose. Across from the ele-vaydor was a glass door with **THE TET CORPORATION** lettered on it. Beyond, Roland saw another, smaller lobby where a woman sat at a desk, apparently talking to herself. To the right of the outer lobby door were two men wearing business suits. They were chatting to each other, hands in pockets, seemingly relaxed, but Roland saw they were anything but. And they were armed. The coats of their suits were well-tailored, but a man who knows how to look for a gun usually sees one, if a gun is there. These two fellows would stand in this foyer for an hour, maybe two (it was difficult for even good men to remain totally alert for much longer), falling into their little just-chatting routine each time the ele-vaydor came, ready to move instantly if they smelled something wrong. Roland approved.

He didn't spend much time looking at the guards, however. Once he had identified them for what they were, he let his gaze go where it had wanted to be from the moment the ele-vaydor doors opened. There was a large black-and-white picture on the wall to his left. This was a photograph (he had originally thought the word was *fottergraf*) about five feet long and three wide, mounted without a frame, curved so cunningly to the shape of the wall that it looked like a hole into some unnaturally still reality. Three men in jeans and open-necked shirts sat on the top rail of a fence, their boots hooked under the lowest rail. How many times, Roland wondered, had he seen cowboys or *pastorillas* sitting just that way while they watched branding, roping, gelding, or the breaking of wild horses? How many times had he sat so himself, sometimes with one or more of his old tet—Cuthbert, Alain, Jamie DeCurry—sitting to either side of him, as John Cullum and Aaron Deepneau sat flanking the black man with the gold-rimmed spectacles and the tiny white moustache? The remembering made him ache, and this was no mere ache of the mind; his stomach clenched and his heart sped up. The three in the picture had been caught laughing at something, and the result was a kind of timeless perfection, one of those rare moments when men are glad to be what they are and where they are.

"The Founding Fathers," Nancy said. She sounded both amused and sad. "That photo was taken on an executive retreat in 1986. Taos, New Mexico. Three city boys in cow country, how about that. And don't they look like they're having the time of their lives?"

"You say true," Roland said.

"Do you know all three?"

Roland nodded. He knew them, all right, although he had never met Moses Carver, the man in the middle. Dan Holmes's partner, Odetta Holmes's godfather. In the picture he looked to be a robust and healthy seventy, but surely by 1986 he had to be closer to eighty. Perhaps eighty-five. Of course, Roland reminded himself, there was a wild card here: the marvelous thing he'd just seen in the lobby of this building. The rose was no more a fountain of youth than the turtle in the little pocket park across the street was the real Maturin, but did he think it had certain beneficent qualities? Yes he did. Certain healing qualities? Yes he did. Did he believe that the nine years of life Aaron Deepneau had gotten between 1977 and the taking of this picture in 1986 had just been a matter of the *Prim*-replacing pills and medical treatments of the old people? No he did not. These three men—Carver, Cullum, and Deepneau—had come together, almost magically, to fight for the rose in their old age. Their tale, the gunslinger believed, would make a book in itself, very likely a fine and exciting one. What Roland believed was simplicity itself: the rose had shown its gratitude.

"When did they die?" he asked Nancy Deepneau.

"John Cullum went first, in 1989," she said. "Victim of a gunshot wound. He lasted twelve hours in the hospital, long enough for everyone to say goodbye. He was in New York for the annual board meeting. According to the NYPD, it was a streetside mugging gone bad. We believe he was killed by an agent of either Sombra or North Central Positronics. Probably one of the can-toi. There were other attempts that missed."

"Both Sombra and Positronics come to the same thing," said Roland. "They're the agencies of the Crimson King in this world."

"We know," she said, then pointed to the man on the left side of the picture, the one she so strongly resembled. "Uncle Aaron lived until 1992. When you met him . . . in 1977?"

"Yes," Roland said.

"In 1977, no one would have believed he could live so long."

"Did the *fayen-folken* kill him, too?"

"No, the cancer came back, that's all. He died in his bed. I was there. The last thing he said was, 'Tell Roland we did our best.' And so I do tell you."

"Thankee-sai." He heard the roughness in his voice and hoped she would mistake it for curtness. Many had done their best for him, was it not true? A great many, beginning with Susan Delgado, all those years ago.

"Are you all right?" she asked in a low, sympathetic voice.

"Yes," he said. "Fine. And Moses Carver? When did *he* pass?"

She raised her eyebrows, then laughed.

"What—?"

"Look for yourself!"

She pointed toward the glass doors. Now approaching them from the inside, passing the desk-minding woman who had apparently been talking to herself, was a wizened man with fluffy fly-away hair and white eyebrows to match. His skin was dark, but the woman upon whose arm he leaned was even darker. He was tall—perhaps six-and-three, if the bend had been taken out of his spine—but the woman was even taller, at least six-and-six. Her face was not beautiful but almost savagely handsome. The face of a warrior.

The face of a gunslinger.

NINE

Had Moses Carver's spine been straight, he and Roland would have been eye-to-eye. As it was, Carver needed to look up slightly, which he did by cocking his head, birdlike. He seemed incapable of actually bending his neck; arthritis had locked it in place. His eyes were brown, the whites so muddy it was difficult to tell where the irises ended, and they were full of merry laughter behind their gold-rimmed spectacles. He still had the tiny white moustache.

"Roland of Gilead!" said he. "How I've longed to meet you, sir! I b'lieve it's what's kept me alive so long after John and Aaron passed. Let loose of me a minute, Marian, let loose! There's something I have to do!"

Marian Carver let go of him and looked at Roland. He didn't hear her voice in his head and didn't need to; what she wanted to tell him was clear in her eyes: *Catch him if he falls, sai.*

But the man Susannah had called Daddy Mose didn't fall. He put his loosely clenched, arthritic fist to his forehead, then bent his right knee, taking all of his weight on his trembling right leg. "Hile you last gunslinger, Roland Deschain out of Gilead, son of Steven and true descendent of Arthur Eld. I, the last of what was called among ourselves the Ka-Tet of the Rose, salute you."

Roland put his own fisted hand to his forehead and did more than make a leg; he went to his knee. "Hile Daddy Mose, godfather of Susannah, dinh of the Ka-Tet of the Rose, I salute you with my heart."

"Thankee," said the old man, and then laughed like a boy. "We're well met in the House of the Rose! What was once meant to be the Grave of the Rose! Ha! Tell me we're not! Can you?"

"Nay, for it would be a lie."

"Speak it!" the old man cried, then uttered that cheery go-to-hell laugh once again. "But I'm f'gettin my manners in my awe, gunslinger. This handsome stretch of woman standing beside me, it'd be natural for you to call her my granddaughter, 'cause I was sem'ty in the year she was born, which was nineteen-and-sixty-nine. But the truth is"—*But'na troof is* was what reached Roland's ear—"that sometimes the best things in life are started late, and having children"—*Chirrun*—"is one of'm, in my opinion. Which is a long-winded way of saying this is my daughter, Marian Odetta Carver, President of the Tet Corporation since I stepped down in '97, at the age of ninety-eight. And do you think it would frost some country-club balls, Roland, to know that this business, now worth just about ten billion dollars, is run by a Negro?" His accent, growing deeper as his excitement and joy grew, turned the last into *Dis bid'ness, now wuth jus 'bout tin binnion dolla, is run bah NEE-grow?*

"Stop, Dad," the tall woman beside him said. Her voice was kind but brooked no denial. "You'll have that heart monitor you wear sounding the alarm if you don't, and this man's time is short."

"She run me like a ray'road!" the old man cried indignantly. At the same time he turned his head slightly and dropped Roland a wink of inexpressible slyness and good humor with the eye his daughter could not see.

As if she wasn't onto your tricks, old man, Roland thought, amused even in his sorrow. *As if she hasn't been on to them for many and many a year—say delah.*

Marian Carver said, "We'd palaver with you for just a little while, Roland, but first there's something I need to see."

"Ain't a bit o' need for that!" the old man said, his voice cracking with indignation. "Not a bit o' need, and you know it! Did I raise a jackass?"

"He's very likely right," Marian said, "but always safe—"

"—never sorry," the gunslinger said. "It's a good rule, aye. What is it you'd see? What will tell you that I am who I say I am, and you believe I am?"

"Your gun," she said.

Roland took the Old Home Days shirt out of the leather bag, then pulled out the holster. He unwrapped the shell-belt and pulled out his revolver with the sandalwood grips. He heard Marian Carver draw in a sharp, awed breath and chose to ignore it. He noticed that the two guards in their well-cut suits had drawn close, their eyes wide.

"You see it!" Moses Carver shouted. "Aye, every one of you here! Say *God*! Might as well tell your gran-babbies you saw Excalibur, the Sword of Arthur, for't comes to the same!"

Roland held his father's revolver out to Marian. He knew she would need to take it in order to confirm who he was, that she must do this before leading him into the Tet Corporation's soft belly (where the wrong someone could do terrible damage), but for a moment she was unable to fulfill her responsibility. Then she steeled herself and took the gun, her eyes widening at the weight of it. Careful to keep all of her fingers away from the trigger, she brought the barrel up to her eyes and then traced a bit of the scrollwork near the muzzle:

"Will you tell me what this means, Mr. Deschain?" she asked him.

"Yes," he said, "if you will call me Roland."

"If you ask, I'll try."

"This is Arthur's mark," he said, tracing it himself. "The only mark on the door of his tomb, do ya. 'Tis his dinh mark, and means WHITE."

The old man held out his trembling hands, silent but imperative.

"Is it loaded?" she asked Roland, and then, before he could answer: "Of course it is."

"Give it to him," Roland said.

Marian looked doubtful, the two guards even more so, but Daddy Mose still held his hands out for the widowmaker, and

Roland nodded. The woman reluctantly held the gun out to her father. The old man took it, held it in both hands, and then did something that both warmed and chilled the gunslinger's heart: he kissed the barrel with his old, folded lips.

"What does thee taste?" Roland asked, honestly curious.

"The years, gunslinger," Moses Carver said. "So I do." And with that he held the gun out to the woman again, butt first.

She handed it back to Roland as if glad to be rid of its grave and killing weight, and he wrapped it once more in its belt of shells.

"Come in," she said. "And although our time is short, we'll make it as joyful as your grief will allow."

"Amen to that!" the old man said, and clapped Roland on the shoulder. "She's still alive, my Odetta—she you call Susannah. There's that. Thought you'd be glad to know it, sir."

Roland *was* glad, and nodded his thanks.

"Come now, Roland," Marian Carver said. "Come and be welcome in our place, for it's your place as well, and we know the chances are good that you'll never visit it again."

TEN

Marian Carver's office was on the northwest corner of the ninety-ninth floor. Here the walls were all glass unbroken by a single strut or muntin, and the view took the gunslinger's breath away. Standing in that corner and looking out was like hanging in midair over a skyline more fabulous than any mind could imagine. Yet it was one he had seen before, for he recognized yonder suspension bridge as well as some of the tall buildings on this side of it. He *should* have recognized the bridge, for they'd almost died on it in another world. Jake had been kidnapped off it by Gasher, and taken to the Tick-Tock Man. This was the City of Lud as it must have been in its prime.

"Do you call it New York?" he asked. "You do, yes?"

"Yes," Nancy Deepneau said.

"And yonder bridge, that swoops?"

"The George Washington," Marian Carver said. "Or just the GWB, if you're a native."

So yonder lay not only the bridge which had taken them into Lud but the one beside which Pere Callahan had walked when he left New York to start his wandering days. That Roland remembered from his story, and very well.

"Would you care for some refreshment?" Nancy asked.

He began to say no, took stock of how his head was swimming, and changed his mind. Something, yes, but only if it would sharpen wits that needed to be sharp. "Tea, if you have it," he said. "Hot, strong tea, with sugar or honey. Can you?"

"We can," Marian said, and pushed a button on her desk. She spoke to someone Roland couldn't see, and all at once the woman in the outer office—the one who had appeared to be talking to herself—made more sense to him.

When the ordering of hot drinks and sandwiches (what Roland supposed he would always think of as popkins) was done, Marian leaned forward and captured Roland's eye. "We're well-met in New York, Roland, so I hope, but our time here isn't . . . isn't *vital*. And I suspect you know why."

The gunslinger considered this, then nodded. A trifle cautiously, but over the years he had built a degree of caution into his nature. There were others—Alain Johns had been one, Jamie DeCurry another—for whom a sense of caution had been inbred, but that had never been the case with Roland, whose tendency had been to shoot first and ask questions later.

"Nancy told you to read the plaque in the Garden of the Beam," Marian said. "Did—"

"Garden of the Beam, say *Gawd!*" Moses Carver interjected. On the walk down the corridor to his daughter's office, he had picked a cane out of a faux elephant-foot stand, and now he thumped it on the expensive carpet for emphasis. Marian bore this patiently. "Say *Gawd*-bomb!"

"My father's recent friendship with the Reverend Harrigan, who holds court down below, has not been the high point in my life," Marian said with a sigh, "but never mind. Did you read the plaque, Roland?"

He nodded. Nancy Deepneau had used a different word—sign or sigul—but he understood it came to the same. "The letters changed into Great Letters. I could read it very well."

"And what did it say?"

"GIVEN BY THE TET CORPORATION, IN HONOR OF EDWARD CANTOR DEAN AND JOHN "JAKE" CHAMBERS." He paused. "Then it said 'Cam-a-cam-mal, Pria-toi, Gan delah,' which you might say as WHITE OVER RED, THUS GAN WILLS EVER."

"And to us it says GOOD OVER EVIL, THIS IS THE WILL OF GOD," Marian said.

"God be praised!" Moses Carver said, and thumped his cane. "May the *Prim* rise!"

There was a perfunctory knock at the door and then the woman from the outer desk came in, carrying a silver tray. Roland was fascinated to see a small black knob suspended in front of her lips, and a narrow black armature that disappeared into her hair. Some sort of far-speaking device, surely. Nancy Deepneau and Marian Carver helped her set out steaming cups of tea and coffee, bowls of sugar and honey, a crock of cream. There was also a plate of sandwiches. Roland's stomach rumbled. He thought of his friends in the ground—no more popkins for them—and also of Irene Tassenbaum, sitting in the little park across the street, patiently waiting for him. Either thought alone should have been enough to kill his appetite, but his stomach once more made its impudent noise. Some parts of a man were conscienceless, a fact he supposed he had known since childhood. He helped himself to a popkin, dumped a heaping spoonful of sugar into his tea, then added honey for good measure. He would make this as brief as possible and return to Irene as soon as he could, but in the meantime . . .

"May it do you fine, sir," Moses Carver said, and blew across his coffee cup. "Over the teeth, over the gums, look out guts, here it comes! Hee!"

"Dad and I have a house on Montauk Point," said Marian, pouring cream into her own coffee, "and we were out there this past weekend. At around five-fifteen on Saturday afternoon, I got a call from one of the security people here. The Hammarskjöld Plaza Association employs them, but the Tet Corporation pays them a bonus so we may know . . . certain things of interest, let's say . . . as soon as they occur. We've been watching that plaque in the lobby with extraordinary interest as the nineteenth of June approached, Roland. Would it surprise you to know that, until roughly quarter of five on that day, it read GIVEN BY THE TET CORPORATION, IN HONOR OF THE BEAM FAMILY, AND IN MEMORY OF GILEAD?"

Roland considered this, sipped his tea (it was hot and strong and good), then shook his head. "No."

She leaned forward, eyes gleaming. "And why do you say so?"

"Because until Saturday afternoon between four and five o'clock, nothing was sure. Even with the Breakers stopped, nothing was sure until Stephen King was safe." He glanced around at them. "Do you know about the Breakers?"

Marian nodded. "Not the details, but we know the Beam they were working to destroy is safe from them now, and that it wasn't so badly damaged it can't regenerate." She hesitated, then said: "And we know of your loss. Both of your losses. We're ever so sorry, Roland."

"Those boys are safe in the arms of Jesus," Marian's father said. "And even if they ain't, they're together in the clearing."

Roland, who wanted to believe this, nodded and said thankya. Then he turned back to Marian. "The thing with the writer was very close. He was hurt, and badly. Jake died saving him. He put his body between King and the van-mobile that would have taken his life."

"King is going to live," Nancy said. "And he's going to write again. We have that on very good authority."

"Whose?"

Marian leaned forward. "In a minute," she said. "The point is, Roland, we believe it, we're sure of it, and King's safety over the next few years means that your work in the matter of the Beams is done: Ves'-Ka Gan."

Roland nodded. The song would continue.

"There's plenty of work for us ahead," Marian went on, "thirty years' worth at least, we calculate, but—"

"But it's *our* work, not yours," Nancy said.

"You have this on the same 'good authority'?" Roland asked, sipping his tea. Hot as it was, he'd gotten half of the large cup inside of him already.

"Yes. Your quest to defeat the forces of the Crimson King has been successful. The Crimson King himself—"

"That wa'n't *never* this man's quest and you know it!" the centenarian sitting next to the handsome black woman said, and he once more thumped his cane for emphasis. "His quest—"

"Dad, that's enough." Her voice was hard enough to make the old man blink.

"Nay, let him speak," Roland said, and they all looked at him, surprised by (and a little afraid of) that dry whipcrack. "Let him speak, for he says true. If we're going to have it out, let us have it all out. For me, the Beams have always been no more than means to an end. Had they broken, the Tower would have fallen. Had the Tower fallen, I should never have gained it, and climbed to the top of it."

"You're saying you cared more for the Dark Tower than for the continued existence of the universe," Nancy Deepneau said. She spoke in a just-let-me-make-sure-I've-got-this-right voice and looked at Roland with a mixture of wonder and contempt. "For the continued existence of *all* the universes."

"The Dark Tower *is* existence," Roland said, "and I have sacrificed many friends to reach it over the years, including a boy who called me father. I have sacrificed my own soul in the bargain, lady-sai, so turn thy impudent glass another way. May you do it soon and do it well, I beg."

His tone was polite but dreadfully cold. All the color was dashed from Nancy Deepneau's face, and the teacup in her hands trembled so badly that Roland reached out and plucked it from her hand, lest it spill and burn her.

"Take me not amiss," he said. "Understand me, for we'll never speak more. What was done was done in both worlds, well and ill, for ka and against it. Yet there's more beyond all worlds than you know, and more behind them than you could ever guess. My time is short, so let's move on."

"Well said, sir!" Moses Carver growled, and thumped his cane again.

"If I offended, I'm truly sorry," Nancy said.

To this Roland made no reply, for he knew she was not sorry a bit—she was only afraid of him. There was a moment of uncomfortable silence that Marian Carver finally broke. "We don't have any Breakers of our own, Roland, but at the ranch in Taos we employ a dozen telepaths and precogs. What they make together is sometimes uncertain but always greater than the sum of its parts. Do you know the term 'good-mind'?"

The gunslinger nodded.

"They make a version of that," she said, "although I'm sure it's not so great or powerful as that the Breakers in Thunderclap were able to produce."

"B'cause they had hundreds," the old man grumped. "*And* they were better fed."

"Also because the servants of the King were more than willing to kidnap any who were particularly powerful," Nancy said, "they always had what we'd call 'the pick of the litter.' Still, ours have served us well enough."

"Whose idea was it to put such folk to work for you?" Roland asked.

"Strange as it might seem to you, partner," Moses said, "it was Cal Tower. He never contributed much—never did much but c'lect his books and drag his heels, greedy highfalutin whitebread sumbitch that he was—"

His daughter gave him a warning look. Roland found he had to struggle to keep a straight face. Moses Carver might be a hundred years old, but he had pegged Calvin Tower in a single phrase.

"Anyway, he read about putting tellypaths to work in a bunch of science fiction books. Do you know about science fiction?"

Roland shook his head.

"Well, ne'mine. Most of it's bullshit, but every now and then a good idear crops up. Listen to me and I'll tell you a good 'un. You'll understand if you know what Tower and your friend Mist' Dean talked about twenty-two years ago, when Mist' Dean come n saved Tower from them two honky thugs."

"Dad," Marian said warningly. "You quit with the nigger talk, now. You're old but not stupid."

He looked at her; his muddy old eyes gleamed with malicious good cheer; he looked back at Roland and once more came that sly droop of a wink. "Them two honky *dago* thugs!"

"Eddie spoke of it, yes," Roland said.

The slur disappeared from Carver's voice; his words became crisp. "Then you know they spoke of a book called *The Hogan,* by Benjamin Slightman. The title of the book was misprinted, and so was the writer's name, which was just the sort of thing that turned old fatty's dials."

"Yes," Roland said. The title misprint had been *The Dogan,* a phrase that had come to have great meaning to Roland and his tet.

"Well, after your friend came to visit, Cal Tower got interested in that fella all over again, and it turned out he'd written four other books under the name of *Daniel Holmes.* He was as white as a Klansman's sheet, this Slightman, but the name he chose to write his other books under was the name of Odetta's father. And I bet that don't surprise you none, does it?"

"No," Roland said. It was just one more faint click as the combination-dial of ka turned.

"And all the books he wrote under the Holmes name were science fiction yarns, about the government hiring tellypaths and precogs to find things out. And that's where *we* got the idea." He looked at Roland and gave his cane a triumphant thump. "There's more to the tale, a good deal, but I don't guess you've got the time. That's what it all comes back to, isn't it? Time. And in this world it only runs one way." He looked wistful. "I'd give a great lot, gunslinger, to see my goddaughter again, but I don't guess that's in the cards, is it? Unless we meet in the clearing."

"I think you say true," Roland told him, "but I'll take her word of you, and how I found you still full of hot spit and fire—"

"Say *God,* say *Gawd*-bomb!" the old man interjected, and thumped his cane. "Tell it, brother! And see that you tell *her!*"

"So I will." Roland finished the last of his tea, then put the cup on Marian Carver's desk and stood with a supporting hand on his right hip as he did. It would take him a long time to get used to the lack of pain there, quite likely more time than he had. "And now I must take my leave of you. There's a place not far from here where I need to go."

"We know where," Marian said. "There'll be someone to meet you when you arrive. The place has been kept safe for you, and if the door you seek is still there and still working, you'll go through it."

Roland made a slight bow. "Thankee-sai."

"But sit a few moments longer, if you will. We have gifts for you, Roland. Not enough to pay you back for all you've done— whether doing it was your first purpose or not—but things you may want, all the same. One's news from our good-mind folk in Taos. One's from more . . ." She considered. ". . . more normal researchers, folks who work for us in this very building. They call themselves the Calvins, but not because of any religious bent. Perhaps it's a little homage to Mr. Tower, who died of a heart attack in his new shop nine years ago. Or perhaps it's only a joke."

"A bad one if it is," Moses Carver grumped.

"And then there are two more . . . from us. From Nancy, and me, and my Dad, and one who's gone on. Will you sit a little longer?"

And although he was anxious to be off, Roland did as he was asked. For the first time since Jake's death, a true emotion other than sorrow had risen in his mind.

Curiosity.

ELEVEN

"First, the news from the folks in New Mexico," Marian said when Roland had resumed his seat. "They have watched you as well as they can, and although what they saw Thunder-side was hazy at best, they believe that Eddie told Jake Chambers something—perhaps something of importance—not long before he died. Likely as he lay on the ground, and before he . . . I don't know . . ."

"Before he slipped into twilight?" Roland suggested.

"Yes," Nancy Deepneau agreed. "We think so. That is to say, *they* think so. Our version of the Breakers."

Marian gave her a little frown that suggested this was a lady who did not appreciate being interrupted. Then she returned her attention to Roland. "Seeing things on this side is easier for our people, and several of them are quite sure—not positive but quite sure—that Jake may have passed this message on before he himself died." She paused. "This woman you're traveling with, Mrs. Tannenbaum—"

"Tassenbaum," Roland corrected. He did it without thinking, because his mind was otherwise occupied. Furiously so.

"Tassenbaum," Marian agreed. "She's undoubtedly told you some of what Jake told her before he passed on, but there may be something else. Not a thing she's holding back, but something she didn't recognize as important. Will you ask her to go over what Jake said to her once more before you and she part company?"

"Yes," Roland said, and of course he would, but he didn't believe Jake had passed on Eddie's message to Mrs. Tassenbaum. No, not to her. He realized that he'd hardly thought of Oy since they'd parked Irene's car, but Oy had been with them, of course; would now be lying at Irene's feet as she sat in the little park across the street, lying in the sun and waiting for him.

"All right," she said. "That's good. Let's move on."

Marian opened the wide center drawer of her desk. From it she brought out a padded envelope and a small wooden box.

IN THIS HAZE OF GREEN AND GOLD

The envelope she handed to Nancy Deepneau. The box she placed on the desktop in front of her.

"This next is Nancy's to tell," she said. "And I'd just ask you to be brief, Nancy, because this man looks very anxious to be off."

"Tell it," Moses said, and thumped his cane.

Nancy glanced at him, then at Roland . . . or in the vicinity of him, anyway. Color was climbing in her cheeks, and she looked flustered. "Stephen King," she said, then cleared her throat and said it again. From there she didn't seem to know how to go on. Her color burned even deeper beneath her skin.

"Take a deep breath," Roland said, "and hold it."

She did as he told her.

"Now let it out."

And this, too.

"Now tell me what you would, Nancy niece of Aaron."

"Stephen King has written nearly forty books," she said, and although the color remained in her cheeks (Roland supposed he would find out what it signified soon enough), her voice was calmer now. "An amazing number of them, even the very early ones, touch on the Dark Tower in one way or another. It's as though it was always on his mind, from the very first."

"You say what I know is true," Roland told her, folding his hands, "I say thankya."

This seemed to calm her even further. "Hence the Calvins," she said. "Three men and two women of a scholarly bent who do nothing from eight in the morning until four in the afternoon but read the works of Stephen King."

"They don't just read them," Marian said. "They cross-reference them by settings, by characters, by themes—such as they are—even by mention of popular brand-name products."

"Part of their work is looking for references to people who live or did live in the Keystone World," Nancy said. "Real people, in other words. And references to the Dark Tower, of course." She handed him the padded envelope and Roland felt the corners of what could only be a book inside. "If King ever wrote a keystone *book,* Roland—outside the Dark Tower series itself, I mean—we think it must be this one."

The flap of the envelope was held by a clasp. Roland looked askance at both Marian and Nancy. They nodded. The gunslinger opened the clasp and pulled out an extremely thick volume with a cover of red and white. There was no picture on it, only Stephen King's name and a single word.

Red for the King, White for Arthur Eld, he thought. *White over Red, thus Gan wills ever.*

Or perhaps it was just a coincidence.

"What is this word?" Roland asked, tapping the title.

"*Insomnia,*" Nancy said. "It means—"

"I know what it means," Roland said. "Why do you give me the book?"

"Because the story hinges on the Dark Tower," Nancy said, "and because there's a character in it named Ed Deepneau. He happens to be the villain of the piece."

The villain of the piece, Roland thought. *No wonder her color rose.*

"Do you have anyone by that name in your family?" he asked her.

"We did," she said. "In Bangor, which is the town King is writing about when he writes about Derry, as he does in this book. The real Ed Deepneau died in 1947, the year King was born. He was a bookkeeper, as inoffensive as milk and cookies. The one in *Insomnia* is a lunatic who falls under the power of the Crimson King. He attempts to turn an airplane into a bomb and crash it into a building, killing thousands of people."

"Pray it never happens," the old man said gloomily, looking out at the New York City skyline. "God knows it could."

"In the story the plan fails," Nancy said. "Although some people *are* killed, the main character in the book, an old man named Ralph Roberts, manages to keep the absolute worst from happening."

Roland was looking intently at Aaron Deepneau's grand-niece. "The Crimson King is mentioned in here? By *actual name?*"

"Yes," she said. "The Ed Deepneau in Bangor—the *real* Ed Deepneau—was a cousin of my father's, four or five times removed. The Calvins could show you the family tree if you wanted, but there really isn't much of a connection to Uncle Aaron's part of it. We think King may have used the name in the book as a way of getting your attention—or ours—without even realizing what he was doing."

"A message from his undermind," the gunslinger mused.

Nancy brightened. "His subconscious, yes! Yes, that's exactly what we think!"

It *wasn't* exactly what Roland was thinking. The gunslinger had been recalling how he had hypnotized King in the year of 1977; how he had told him to listen for Ves'-Ka Gan, the Song of the Turtle. Had King's undermind, the part of him that would never have stopped trying to obey the hypnotic command, put part of the Song of the Turtle in this book? A book the Servants of the King might have neglected because it wasn't part of the "Dark Tower Cycle"? Roland thought that could be, and that the name Deepneau might indeed be a sigul. But—

"I can't read this," he said. "A word here and a word there, perhaps, but no more."

"You can't, but my girl can," Moses Carver said. "My girl Odetta, that you call Susannah."

Roland nodded slowly. And although he had already begun to have his doubts, his mind nevertheless cast up a brilliant image of the two of them sitting close by a fire—a large one, for the night was cold—with Oy between. In the rocks above them the wind howled bitter notes of winter, but they cared not, for their bellies were full, their bodies were warm, dressed in the skins of animals they had killed themselves, and they had a story to entertain them.

Stephen King's story of insomnia.

"She'll read it to you on the trail," Moses said. "On your last trail, say God!"

Yes, Roland thought. *One last story to hear, one last trail to follow. The one that leads to Can'-Ka No Rey, and the Dark Tower. Or it would be nice to think so.*

Nancy said, "In the story, the Crimson King is using Ed Deepneau to kill one single child, a boy named Patrick Danville. Just before the attack, while Patrick and his mother are waiting for a woman to make a speech, the boy draws a picture, one that shows you, Roland, and the Crimson King, apparently imprisoned at the top of the Dark Tower."

Roland started in his seat. "The *top*? Imprisoned at the *top*?"

"Easy," Marian said. "Take it easy, Roland. The Calvins have been analyzing King's work for years, every word and every reference, and everything they produce gets forwarded to the good-mind *folken* in New Mexico. Although these two groups have never seen each other, it would be perfectly correct to say that they work together."

"Not that they're always in agreement," Nancy said.

"They sure *aren't!*" Marian spoke in the exasperated tone of one who's had to referee more than her share of squabbles. "But one thing that they *are* in agreement about is that King's references to the Dark Tower are almost always masked, and sometimes mean nothing at all."

Roland nodded. "He speaks of it because his undermind is always thinking of it, but sometimes he lapses into gibberish."

"Yes," Nancy said.

"But obviously you don't think this entire book is a false trail, or you would not want to give it to me."

"Indeed we do not," Nancy said. "But that doesn't mean the Crimson King is necessarily imprisoned at the *top* of the Tower. Although I suppose it might."

Roland thought of his own belief that the Red King was locked out of the Tower, on a kind of balcony. Was it a genuine intuition, or just something he wanted to believe?

"In any case, we think you should watch for this Patrick Danville," Marian said. "The consensus is that he's a real person, but we haven't been able to find any trace of him here. Perhaps you may find him in Thunderclap."

"Or beyond it," Moses put in.

Marian was nodding. "According to the story King tells in

Insomnia—you'll see for yourself—Patrick Danville dies as a young man. *But that may not be true.* Do you understand?"

"I'm not sure I do."

"When you find Patrick Danville—or when he finds you—he may still be the child described in this book," Nancy said, "or he could be as old as Uncle Mose."

"Bad luck f'him if that be true!" said the old man, and chortled.

Roland lifted the book, stared at the red and white cover, traced the slightly raised letters that made a word he could not read. "Surely it's just a story?"

"From the spring of 1970, when he typed the line *The man in black fled across the desert and the gunslinger followed,*" Marian Carver said, "very few of the things Stephen King wrote were 'just stories.' He may not believe that; we do."

But years of dealing with the Crimson King may have left you with a way of jumping at shadows, do it please ya, Roland thought. Aloud he said, "If not stories, what?"

It was Moses Carver who answered. "We think maybe messages in bottles." In the way he spoke this word—*boh'uls,* almost—Roland heard a heartbreaking echo of Susannah, and suddenly wanted to see her and know she was all right. This desire was so strong it left a bitter taste on his tongue.

"—that great sea."

"Beg your pardon," the gunslinger said. "I was wool-gathering."

"I said we believe that Stephen King's cast his bottles upon that great sea. The one we call the *Prim.* In hopes that they'll reach you, and the messages inside will make it possible for you and my Odetta to gain your goal."

"Which brings us to our final gifts," Marian said. "Our true gifts. First . . ." She handed him the box.

It opened on a hinge. Roland placed his left hand splayed over the top, meaning to swing it back, then paused and studied his interlocutors. They were looking at him with hope and suspenseful interest, an expression that made him uneasy. A mad (but surprisingly persuasive) idea came to him: that these were in truth agents of the Crimson King, and when he opened the box, the last thing he'd see would be a primed sneetch, counting down the last few clicks to red zero. And the last sound he'd hear before the world blew up around him would be their mad laughter and a cry of *Hile the Red King!* It wasn't impossible, either, but a point came where one had to trust, because the alternative was madness.

If ka will say so, let it be so, he thought, and opened the box.

TWELVE

Within, resting on dark blue velvet (which they might or might not have known was the color of the Royal Court of Gilead), was a watch within a coiled chain. Engraved upon its gold cover were three objects: a key, a rose, and—between and slightly above them—a tower with tiny windows marching around its circumference in an ascending spiral.

Roland was amazed to find his eyes once more filling with tears. When he looked at the others again—two young women and one old man, the brains and guts of the Tet Corporation—he at first saw six instead of three. He blinked the phantom doubles away.

"Open the cover and look inside," Moses Carver said. "And there's no need to hide your tears in this company, you son of Steven, for we're not the machines the others would replace us with, if they had their way."

Roland saw that the old man spoke true, for tears were slipping down the weathered darkness of his cheeks. Nancy Deepneau was also weeping freely. And although Marian Carver no doubt prided herself on being made of sterner stuff, her eyes held a suspicious gleam.

He depressed the stem protruding from the top of the case, and the lid sprang up. Inside, finely scrolled hands told the hour and the minute, and with perfect accuracy, he had no doubt. Below, in its own small circle, a smaller hand raced away the seconds. Carved on the inside of the lid was this:

To the Hand of ROLAND DESCHAIN
From Those of
MOSES ISAAC CARVER
MARIAN ODETTA CARVER
NANCY REBECCA DEEPNEAU

With Our Gratitude

White Over Red, Thus GOD Wills Ever

"Thankee-sai," Roland said in a hoarse and trembling voice. "I thank you, and so would my friends, were they here to speak."

"In our hearts they *do* speak, Roland," Marian said. "And in your face we see them very well."

Moses Carver was smiling. "In our world, Roland, giving a man a gold watch has a special significance."

"What would that be?" Roland asked. He held the watch—easily the finest timepiece he'd ever had in his life—up to his ear and listened to the precise and delicate ticking of its machinery.

"That his work is done and it's time for him to go fishing or play with his grandchildren," Nancy Deepneau said. "But we gave it to you for a different reason. May it count the hours to your goal and tell you when you near it."

"How can it do that?"

"We have one exceptional good-mind fellow in New Mexico," Marian said. "His name is Fred Towne. He sees a great deal and is rarely if ever mistaken. This watch is a Patek Philippe, Roland. It cost nineteen thousand dollars, and the makers guarantee a full refund of the price if it's ever fast or slow. It needs no winding, for it runs on a battery—*not* made by North Central Positronics or any subsidiary thereof, I can assure you—that will last a hundred years. According to Fred, when you near the Dark Tower, the watch may nevertheless stop."

"Or begin to run backward," Nancy said. "Watch for it."

Moses Carver said, "I believe you will, won't you?"

"Aye," Roland agreed. He put the watch carefully in one

pocket (after another long look at the carvings on the golden cover) and the box in another. "I will watch this watch very well."

"You must watch for something else, too," Marian said. "Mordred."

Roland waited.

"We have reason to believe that he's murdered the one you called Walter." She paused. "And I see that does not surprise you. May I ask why?"

"Walter's finally left my dreams, just as the ache has left my hip and my head," Roland said. "The last time he visited them was in Calla Bryn Sturgis, the night of the Beamquake." He would not tell them how terrible those dreams had been, dreams in which he wandered, lost and alone, down a dank castle corridor with cobwebs brushing his face; the scuttering sound of something approaching from the darkness behind him (or perhaps above him), and, just before waking up, the gleam of red eyes and a whispered, inhuman voice: "*Father.*"

They were looking at him grimly. At last Marian said: "Beware him, Roland. Fred Towne, the fellow I mentioned, says 'Mordred be a-hungry.' He says that's a literal hunger. Fred's a brave man, but he's afraid of your . . . your enemy."

My son, why don't you say it? Roland thought, but believed he knew. She withheld out of care for his feelings.

Moses Carver stood and set his cane beside his daughter's desk. "I have one more thing for you," he said, "on'y it was yours all along—yours to carry and lay down when you get to where you're bound."

Roland was honestly perplexed, and more perplexed still when the old man began to slowly unbutton his shirt down the front. Marian made as if to help him and he motioned her away brusquely. Beneath his dress-shirt was an old man's strap-style undershirt, what the gunslinger thought of as a slinkum. Beneath it was a shape that Roland recognized at once, and his heart seemed to stop in his chest. For a moment he was cast back to the cabin on the lake—Beckhardt's cabin, Eddie by his side—and heard his own words: *Put Auntie's cross around your neck, and when you meet with sai Carver, show it to him. It may go a long way toward convincing him you're on the straight. But first . . .*

The cross was now on a chain of fine gold links. Moses Carver pulled it free of his slinkum by this, looked at it for a moment, looked up at Roland with a little smile on his lips, then down at the cross again. He blew upon it. Faint and faint, raising the hair on the gunslinger's arms, came Susannah's voice:

"We buried Pimsey under the apple tree . . ."

Then it was gone. For a moment there was nothing, and Carver, frowning now, drew in breath to blow again. There was no need. Before he could, John Cullum's Yankee drawl arose, not from the cross itself, but seemingly from the air just above it.

"We done our best, partner"—*paaa't-nuh*—"and I hope 'twas good enough. Now, I always knew this was on loan to me, and here it is, back where it belongs. You know where it finishes up, I . . ." Here the words, which had been fading ever since *here it is*, became inaudible even to Roland's keen ears. Yet he had heard enough. He took Aunt Talitha's cross, which he had promised to lay at the foot of the Dark Tower, and donned it once more. It had come back to him, and why would it not have done? Was ka not a wheel?

"I thank you, sai Carver," he said. "For myself, for my ka-tet that was, and on behalf of the woman who gave it to me."

"Don't thank me," Moses Carver said. "Thank Johnny Cullum. He give it to me on his deathbed. That man had some hard bark on him."

"I—" Roland began, and for a moment could say no more. His heart was too full. "I thank you all," he said at last. He bowed his head to them with the palm of his right fist against his brow and his eyes closed.

When he opened them again, Moses Carver was holding out his thin old arms. "Now it's time for us to go our way and you to go yours," he said. "Put your arms around me, Roland, and kiss my cheek in farewell if you would, and think of my girl as you do, for I'd say goodbye to her if I may."

Roland did as he was bid, and in another world, as she

dozed aboard a train bound for Fedic, Susannah put a hand to
her cheek, for it seemed to her that Daddy Mose had come to
her, and put an arm around her, and bid her goodbye, good
luck, good journey.

THIRTEEN

When Roland stepped out of the ele-vaydor in the lobby, he
wasn't surprised to see a woman in a gray-green pullover and
slacks the color of moss standing in front of the garden with a
few other quietly respectful *folken*. An animal which was not
quite a dog sat by her left shoe. Roland crossed to her and
touched her elbow. Irene Tassenbaum turned to him, her eyes
wide with wonder.

"Do you hear it?" she asked. "It's like the singing we heard
in Lovell, only a hundred times sweeter."

"I hear it," he said. Then he bent and picked up Oy. He
looked into the bumbler's bright gold-ringed eyes as the voices
sang. "Friend of Jake," he said, "what message did he give?"

Oy tried, but the best he could manage was something that
sounded like *Dandy-o,* a word Roland vaguely remembered
from an old drinking song, where it rimed with *Adelina says she's
randy-o.*

Roland put his forehead down against Oy's forehead and
closed his eyes. He smelled the bumbler's warm breath. And
more: a scent deep in his fur that was the hay into which Jake
and Benny Slightman had taken turns jumping not so long
before. In his mind, mingled with the sweet singing of those
voices, he heard the voice of Jake Chambers for the last time:

Tell him Eddie says, "Watch for Dandelo." Don't forget!
And Oy had not.

FOURTEEN

Outside, as they descended the steps of 2 Hammarskjöld Plaza,
a deferential voice said, "Sir? Madam?"

It was a man in a black suit and a soft black cap. He stood by the longest, blackest car Roland had ever seen. Looking at it made the gunslinger uneasy.

"Who's sent us a funeral bucka?" he asked.

Irene Tassenbaum smiled. The rose had refreshed her—excited and exhilarated her, as well—but she was still tired. And concerned to get in touch with David, who would likely be out of his mind with worry by this time.

"It's not a hearse," she said. "It's a limousine. A car for special people . . . or people who think they're special." Then, to the driver: "While we're riding, can you have someone in your office check some airline info for me?"

"Of course, madam. May I ask your carrier of choice and your destination?"

"My destination's Portland, Maine. My carrier of choice is Rubberband Airlines, if they're going there this afternoon."

The limousine's windows were smoked glass, the interior dim and ringed with colored lights. Oy jumped up on one of the seats and watched with interest as the city rolled past. Roland was mildly amazed to see that there was a completely stocked liquor-bar on one side of the long passenger compartment. He thought of having a beer and decided that even such a mild drink would be enough to dim his own lights. Irene had no such worries. She poured herself what looked like whiskey from a small bottle and then held the glass toward him.

"May your road wind ever upward and the wind be ever at your back, me foine bucko," she said.

Roland nodded. "A good toast. Thankee-sai."

"These have been the most amazing three days of my life. I want to thankee-sai *you*. For choosing me." *Also for laying me*, she thought but did not add. She and Dave still enjoyed the occasional snuggle, but not like that of the previous night. It had never been like that. And if Roland hadn't been distracted? Very likely she would have blown her silly self up, like a Black Cat firecracker.

Roland nodded and watched the streets of the city—a version of Lud, but still young and vital—go by. "What about your car?" he asked.

"If we want it before we come back to New York, we'll have someone drive it up to Maine. Probably David's Beemer will do us. It's one of the advantages of being wealthy—why are you looking at me that way?"

"You have a cartomobile called a *Beamer?*"

"It's slang," she said. "It's actually BMW. Stands for Bavarian Motor Works."

"Ah." Roland tried to look as if he understood.

"Roland, may I ask you a question?"

He twirled his hand for her to go ahead.

"When we saved the writer, did we also save the world? We did, somehow, didn't we?"

"Yes," he said.

"How does it happen that a writer who's not even very good—and I can say that, I've read four or five of his books— gets to be in charge of the world's destiny? Or of the entire universe's?"

"If he's not very good, why didn't you stop at one?"

Mrs. Tassenbaum smiled. *"Touché.* He *is* readable, I'll give him that—tells a good story, but has a tin ear for language. I answered your question, now answer mine. God knows there are writers who feel that the whole world hangs on what they say. Norman Mailer comes to mind, also Shirley Hazzard and John Updike. But apparently in this case the world really does. How did it happen?"

Roland shrugged. "He hears the right voices and sings the right songs. Which is to say, ka."

It was Irene Tassenbaum's turn to look as though she understood.

FIFTEEN

The limousine drew up in front of a building with a green awning out front. Another man in another well-cut suit was standing by the door. The steps leading up from the sidewalk were blocked with yellow tape. There were words printed on it which Roland couldn't read.

"It says CRIME SCENE, DO NOT ENTER," Mrs. Tassenbaum told him. "But it looks like it's been there awhile. I think they usually take the tape down once they're finished with their cameras and little brushes and things. You must have powerful friends."

Roland was sure the tape had indeed been there awhile; three weeks, give or take. That was when Jake and Pere Callahan had entered the Dixie Pig, positive they were going to their deaths but pushing ahead anyway. He saw there was a little puddle of liquor left in Irene's glass and swallowed it, grimacing at the hot taste of the alcohol but relishing the burn on the way down.

"Better?" she asked.

"Aye, thanks." He reset the bag with the Orizas in it more firmly on his shoulder and got out with Oy at his heel. Irene paused to talk to the driver, who seemed to have been successful in making her travel arrangements. Roland ducked beneath the tape and then just stood where he was for a moment, listening to the honk and pound of the city on this bright June day, relishing its adolescent vitality. He would never see another city, of that much he was almost positive. And perhaps that was just as well. He had an idea that after New York, all others would be a step down.

The guard—obviously someone who worked for the Tet Corporation and not this city's constabulary—joined him on the walk. "If you want to go in there, sir, there's something you should show me."

Roland once more took his gunbelt from the pouch, once more unwrapped it from the holster, once more drew his father's gun. This time he did not offer to hand it over, nor did that gentleman ask to take it. He only examined the scrollwork, particularly that at the end of the barrel. Then he nodded respectfully and stepped back. "I'll unlock the door. Once you go inside, you're on your own. You understand that, don't you?"

Roland, who had been on his own for most of his life, nodded.

Irene took his elbow before he could move forward, turned him, and put her arms around his neck. She had also bought herself a pair of low-heeled shoes, and only needed to tilt her head back slightly in order to look into his eyes.

"You take care of yourself, cowboy." She kissed him briefly on the mouth—the kiss of a friend—and then knelt to stroke Oy. "And take care of the little cowboy, too."

"I'll do my best," Roland said. "Will you remember your promise about Jake's grave?"

"A rose," she said. "I'll remember."

"Thankee." He looked at her a moment longer, consulted the workings of his own inner instincts—hunch-think—and came to a decision. From the bag containing the Orizas, he took the envelope containing the bulky book . . . the one Susannah would never read to him on the trail, after all. He put it in Irene's hands.

She looked at it, frowning. "What's in here? Feels like a book."

"Yar. One by Stephen King. *Insomnia,* it's called. Has thee read that one?"

She smiled a bit. "No, thee hasn't. Has thee?"

"No. And won't. It feels tricksy to me."

"I don't understand you."

"It feels . . . thin." He was thinking of Eyebolt Canyon, in Mejis.

She hefted it. "Feels pretty goddamned thick to me. A Stephen King book for sure. He sells by the inch, America buys by the pound."

Roland only shook his head.

Irene said, "Never mind. I'm being smart because Ree doesn't do goodbyes well, never has. You want me to keep this, right?"

"Yes."

"Okay. Maybe when Big Steve gets out of the hospital, I'll get him to sign it. The way I look at it, he owes me an autograph."

"Or a kiss," Roland said, and took another for himself. With the book out of his hands, he felt somehow lighter. Freer. *Safer.* He drew her fully into his arms and hugged her. Irene Tassenbaum returned his strength with her own.

Then Roland let her go, touched his forehead lightly with his fist, and turned to the door of the Dixie Pig. He opened it and slipped inside with no look back. That, he had found, was ever the easiest way.

SIXTEEN

The chrome post which had been outside on the night Jake and Pere Callahan had come here had been put in the lobby for safekeeping. Roland stumbled against it, but his reflexes were as quick as ever and he grabbed it before it could fall over. He read the sign on top slowly, sounding the words out and getting the sense of only one: CLOSED. The orange electric *flambeaux* which had lit the dining room were off but the battery-powered emergency lights were on, filling the area beyond the lobby and the bar with a flat glare. To the left was an arch and another dining room beyond it. There were no emergency lights there; that part of the Dixie Pig was as dark as a cave. The light from the main dining room seemed to creep in about four feet—just far enough to illuminate the end of a long table—and then fall dead. The tapestry of which Jake had spoken was gone. It might be in the evidence room of the nearest police station, or it might already have joined some collector's trove of oddities. Roland could smell the faint aroma of charred meat, vague and unpleasant.

In the main dining room, two or three tables were overturned. Roland saw stains on the red rug, several dark ones that were almost certainly blood and a yellowish curd that was . . . something else.

H'row it aside! Nasty bauble of the 'heep-God, h'row it aside if you dare!

And the Pere's voice, echoing dimly in Roland's ears, unafraid: *I needn't stake my faith on the challenge of such a thing as you, sai.*

The Pere. Another of those he had left behind.

Roland thought briefly of the scrimshaw turtle that had been hidden in the lining of the bag they had found in the vacant lot, but didn't waste time looking for it. If it had been here, he thought he would have heard its voice, calling to him in the silence. No, whoever had appropriated the tapestry of the vampire-knights at dinner had very likely taken the *sköldpadda* as well, not knowing what it was, only knowing it was something strange and wonderful and otherworldly. Too bad. It might have come in handy.

The gunslinger moved on, weaving his way among the tables with Oy trotting at his heel.

SEVENTEEN

He paused in the kitchen long enough to wonder what the constabulary of New York had made of it. He was willing to bet they had never seen another like it, not in this city of clean machinery and bright electric lights. This was a kitchen in which Hax, the cook he remembered best from his youth (and beneath whose dead feet he and his best friend had once scattered bread for the birds), would have felt at home. The cookfires had been out for weeks, but the smell of the meat that had been roasted here—some of the variety known as long pork—was strong and nasty. There were more signs of trouble here, as well (a scum-caked pot lying on the green tiles of the floor, blood which had been burned black on one of the stovetops), and Roland could imagine Jake fighting his way through the kitchen. But not in panic; no, not he. Instead he had paused to demand directions of the cook's boy.

What's your name, cully?

Jochabim, that be I, son of Hossa.

Jake had told them this part of his story, but it was not memory that spoke to Roland now. It was the voices of the dead. He had heard such voices before, and knew them for what they were.

EIGHTEEN

Oy took the lead as he had done the last time he had been here. He could still smell Ake's scent, faint and sorrowful. Ake had gone on ahead now, but not so very far; he was good, Ake was good, Ake would wait, and when the time came—when the job Ake had given him was done—Oy would catch up and go with him as before. His nose was strong, and he would find fresher scent than this when the time came to search for it. Ake had saved him from death, which did not matter. Ake had saved him from loneliness and shame after Oy had been cast out by the tet of his kind, and that did.

In the meantime, there was this job to finish. He led the man Olan into the pantry. The secret door to the stairs had been closed, but the man Olan felt patiently along the shelves of cans and boxes until he found the way to open it. All was as it had been, the long, descending stair dimly lit by overhead bulbs, the scent damp and overlaid with mold. He could smell the rats which scuttered in the walls; rats and other things, too, some of them bugs of the sort he had killed the last time he and Ake had come here. That had been good killing, and he would gladly have more, if more were offered. Oy wished the bugs would show themselves again and challenge him, but of course they didn't. They were afraid, and they were right to be afraid, for ever had his kind stood enemy to theirs.

He started down the stairs with the man Olan following behind.

NINETEEN

They passed the deserted kiosk with its age-yellowed signs (NEW YORK SOUVENIRS, LAST CHANCE, and VISIT SEPTEMBER 11, 2001), and fifteen minutes later—Roland checked his new watch to be sure of the time—they came to a place where there was a good deal of broken glass on the dusty corridor floor. Roland picked Oy up so he wouldn't cut the pads of his feet. On both walls he

saw the shattered remains of what had been glass-covered
hatches of some kind. When he looked in, he saw complicated
machinery. They had almost caught Jake here, snared him in
some kind of mind-trap, but once again Jake had been clever
enough and brave enough to get through. *He survived everything
but a man too stupid and too careless to do the simple job of driving his
bucka on an empty road,* Roland thought bitterly. *And the man who
brought him there—that man, too.* Then Oy barked at him and
Roland realized that in his anger at Bryan Smith (and at himself), he was squeezing the poor little fellow too tightly.

"Cry pardon, Oy," he said, and put him down.

Oy trotted on without making any reply, and not long
after Roland came to the scattered bodies of the boogers who
had harried his boy from the Dixie Pig. Here also, printed in
the dust that coated the floor of this ancient corridor, were the
tracks he and Eddie had made when they arrived. Again he
heard a ghost-voice, this time that of the man who had been
the harriers' leader.

*I know your name by your face, and your face by your mouth. 'Tis
the same as the mouth of your mother, who did suck John Farson with
such glee.*

Roland turned the body over with the toe of his boot (a
hume named Flaherty, whose da' had put a fear of dragons in
his head, had the gunslinger known or cared . . . which he did
not) and looked down into the dead face, which was already
growing a crop of mold. Next to him was the stoat-head taheen
whose final proclamation had been *Be damned to you, then,
chary-ka.* And beyond the heaped bodies of these two and their
mates was the door that would take him out of the Keystone
World for good.

Assuming that it still worked.

Oy trotted to it and sat down before it, looking back at
Roland. The bumbler was panting, but his old, amiably fiendish
grin was gone. Roland reached the door and placed his hands
against the close-grained ghostwood. Deep within he felt a low
and troubled vibration. This door was still working but might
not be for much longer.

He closed his eyes and thought of his mother bending over him as he lay in his little bed (how soon before he had been promoted from the cradle he didn't know, but surely not long), her face a patchwork of colors from the nursery windows, Gabrielle Deschain who would later die at those hands which she caressed so lightly and lovingly with her own; daughter of Candor the Tall, wife of Steven, mother of Roland, singing him to sleep and dreams of those lands only children know.

> *Baby-bunting, baby-dear,*
> *Baby, bring your berries here.*
> *Chussit, chissit, chassit!*
> *Bring enough to fill your basket!*

So far I've traveled, he thought with his hands splayed on the ghostwood door. *So far I've traveled and so many I've hurt along the way, hurt or killed, and what I may have saved was saved by accident and can never save my soul, do I have one. Yet there's this much: I've come to the head of the last trail, and I need not travel it alone, if only Susannah will go with me. Mayhap there's still enough to fill my basket.*

"Chassit," Roland said, and opened his eyes as the door opened. He saw Oy leap nimbly through. He heard the shrill scream of the void between the worlds, and then stepped through himself, sweeping the door shut behind him and still without a backward look.

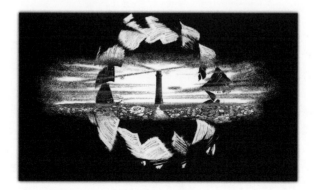

CHAPTER IV:
FEDIC (TWO VIEWS)

ONE

Look at how brilliant it is here!

When we came before, Fedic was shadowless and dull, but there was a reason for that: it wasn't the real Fedic but only a kind of todash substitute; a place Mia knew well and remembered well (just as she remembered the castle allure, where she went often before circumstances—in the person of Walter o' Dim—gave her a physical body) and could thus re-create. Today, however, the deserted village is almost too bright to look at (although we'll no doubt see better once our eyes have adjusted from the murk of Thunderclap and the passage beneath the Dixie Pig). Every shadow is crisp; they might have been cut from black felt and laid upon the oggan. The sky is a sharp and cloudless blue. The air is chill. The wind whining around the eaves of the empty buildings and through the battlements of Castle Discordia is autumnal and somehow introspective. Sitting in Fedic Station is an atomic locomotive—what was called a hot-enj by the old people—with the words **SPIRIT OF TOPEKA** written on both sides of the bullet nose. The slim pilot-house windows have been rendered almost completely opaque by centuries of desert grit flung against the glass, but little does that matter; the *Spirit of Topeka* has made her last trip, and even when she *did* run regularly, no mere hume ever guided her course. Behind the engine are only three cars. There were a dozen when she set out from Thunderclap Station on her last run, and there were a dozen when she arrived in sight of this ghost town, but . . .

Ah, well, that's Susannah's tale to tell, and we will listen as she tells it to the man she called dinh when there was a ka-tet for

531

him to guide. And here is Susannah herself, sitting where we saw her once before, in front of the Gin-Puppy Saloon. Parked at the hitching rail is her chrome steed, which Eddie dubbed Suzie's Cruisin Trike. She's cold and hasn't so much as a sweater to pull close around her, but her heart tells her that her wait is almost over. And how she hopes her heart is right, for this is a haunted place. To Susannah, the whine of the wind sounds too much like the bewildered cries of the children who were brought here to have their bodies roont and their minds murdered.

Beside the rusty Quonset hut up the street (the Arc 16 Experimental Station, do ya not recall it) are the gray cyborg horses. A few more have fallen over since the last time we visited; a few more click their heads restlessly back and forth, as if trying to see the riders who will come and untether them. But that will never happen, for the Breakers have been set free to wander and there's no more need of children to feed their talented heads.

And now, look you! At last comes what the lady has waited for all this long day, and the day before, and the day before that, when Ted Brautigan, Dinky Earnshaw, and a few others (not Sheemie, he's gone into the clearing at the end of the path, say sorry) bade her goodbye. The door of the Dogan opens, and a man comes out. The first thing she sees is that his limp is gone. Next she notices his new bluejeans and shirt. Nifty duds, but he's otherwise as ill-prepared for this cold weather as she is. In his arms the newcomer holds a furry animal with its ears cocked. That much is well, but the boy who should be holding the animal is absent. No boy, and her heart fills with sorrow. Not surprise, however, because she has known, just as yonder man (yonder chary man) would have known had she been the one to pass from the path.

She slips down from her seat on her hands and the stumps of her legs; she hoists herself off the boardwalk and into the street. There she raises a hand and waves it over her head. "Roland!" she cries. "Hey, gunslinger! I'm over here!"

He sees her and waves back. Then he bends and puts down the animal. Oy races toward her hellbent for election, head down, ears flat against his skull, running with the speed and low-slung, leaping grace of a weasel on a crust of snow. While he's still seven feet away from her (seven at least), he jumps into the air, his shadow flying fleetly over the packed dirt of the street. She grabs him like a deep receiver hauling in a Hail Mary pass. The force of his forward motion knocks the breath from her and bowls her over in a puff of dust, but the first breath she's able to take in goes back out as laughter. She's still laughing as he stands with his stubby front legs on her chest and his stubby rear ones on her belly, ears up, squiggly tail wagging, licking her cheeks, her nose, her eyes.

"Let up on it!" she cries. "Let up on it, honey, 'fore you kill me!"

She hears this, so lightly meant, and her laughter stops. Oy steps off her, sits, tilts his snout at the empty blue socket of the sky, and lets loose a single long howl that tells her everything she would need to know, had she not known already. For Oy has more eloquent ways of speaking than his few words.

She sits up, slapping puffs of dust out of her shirt, and a shadow falls over her. She looks up but at first cannot see Roland's face. His head is directly in front of the sun, and it makes a fierce corona around him. His features are lost in blackness.

But he's holding out his hands.

Part of her doesn't want to take them, and do ya not kennit? Part of her would end it here and send him into the Badlands alone. No matter what Eddie wanted. No matter what Jake undoubtedly wanted, too. This dark shape with the sun blazing around its head has dragged her out of a mostly comfortable life (oh yes, she had her ghosts—and at least one mean-hearted demon, as well—but which of us don't?). He has introduced her first to love, then to pain, then to horror and loss. The deal's run pretty much downhill, in other words. It is his balefully talented hand that has authored her sorrow, this dusty knight-errant who has come walking out of the old world in his old boots and with an old death-engine on each hip. These are melodramatic thoughts, purple images, and the old Odetta, patron of The Hungry i and all-around cool kitty, would no doubt have laughed at them. But she has changed, he has changed her, and she reckons that if anyone is entitled to melodramatic thoughts and purple images, it is Susannah, daughter of Dan.

Part of her would turn him away, not to end his quest or break his spirit (only death will do those things), but to take such light as remains out of his eyes and punish him for his relentless unmeaning cruelty. But ka is the wheel to which we all are bound, and when the wheel turns we must perforce turn with it, first with our heads up to heaven and then revolving hellward again, where the brains inside them seem to burn. And so, instead of turning away —

TWO

Instead of turning away, as part of her wanted to do, Susannah took Roland's hands. He pulled her up, not to her feet (for she had none, although for awhile a pair had been given her on loan) but into his arms. And when he tried to kiss her cheek, she turned her face so that his lips pressed on hers. *Let him understand it's no halfway thing,* she thought, breathing her air into him and then taking his back, changed. *Let him understand that if I'm in it, I'm in to the end. God help me, I'm in with him to the end.*

THREE

There were clothes in the Fedic Millinery & Ladies' Wear, but they fell apart at the touch of their hands — the moths and the years had left nothing usable. In the Fedic Hotel (QUIET ROOMS, GUD BEDS) Roland found a cabinet with some blankets that would do them at least against the afternoon chill. They wrapped up in them — the afternoon breeze was just enough to make their musty smell bearable — and Susannah asked about Jake, to have the immediate pain of it out of the way.

"The writer again," she said bitterly when he had finished, wiping away her tears. "God damn the man."

"My hip let go and the . . . and Jake never hesitated."

Roland had almost called him *the boy*, as he had taught himself to think of Elmer's son as they closed in on Walter. Given a second chance, he had promised himself he would never do that again.

"No, of course he didn't," she said, smiling. "He never would. He had a yard of guts, our Jake. Did you take care of him? Did you do him right? I'd hear that part."

So he told her, not failing to include Irene Tassenbaum's promise of the rose. She nodded, then said: "I wish we could do the same for your friend, Sheemie. He died on the train. I'm sorry, Roland."

Roland nodded. He wished he had tobacco, but of course there was none. He had both guns again and they were seven Oriza plates to the good, as well. Otherwise they were stocked with little-going-on-none.

"Did he have to push again, while you were coming here? I suppose he did. I knew one more might kill him. Sai Brautigan did, too. And Dinky."

"But that wasn't it, Roland. It was his foot."

The gunslinger looked at her, not understanding.

"He cut it on a piece of broken glass during the fight to take Blue Heaven, and the air and dirt of that place was *poison!*" It was Detta who spat the last word, her accent so thick that the gunslinger barely understood it: *Pizen!* "Goddam foot swole up . . . toes like sausages . . . then his cheeks and throat went all dusky, like a bruise . . . he took fever . . ." She pulled in a deep breath, clutching the two blankets she wore tighter around her. "He was delirious, but his head cleared at the end. He spoke of you, and of Susan Delgado. He spoke with such love and such regret . . ." She paused, then burst out: "We *will* go there, Roland, we *will*, and if it isn't worth it, your Tower, somehow we'll make it worth it!"

"We'll go," he said. "We'll find the Dark Tower, and nothing will stand against us, and before we go in, we'll speak their names. All of the lost."

"Your list will be longer than mine," she said, "but mine will be long enough."

To this Roland did not reply, but the robot huckster, perhaps startled out of its long sleep by the sound of their voices, did. "Girls, girls, *girls!*" it cried from inside the batwing doors of the Gaiety Bar and Grill. "Some are humie and some are cybie, but who cares, you can't tell, who cares, they give, you tell, girls tell, you tell . . ." There was a pause and then the robot huckster shouted one final word—"*SATISFACTION!*"—and fell silent.

"By the gods, but this is a sad place," he said. "We'll stay the night and then see it no more."

"At least the sun's out, and that's a relief after Thunderclap, but isn't it *cold!*"

He nodded, then asked about the others.

"They've gone on," she said, "but there was a minute there when I didn't think any of us were going anywhere except to the bottom of yonder crevasse."

She pointed to the end of the Fedic high street furthest from the castle wall.

"There are TV screens that still work in some of the train-cars, and as we came up on town we got a fine view of the bridge that's gone. We could see the ends sticking out over the hole, but the gap in the middle had to be a hundred yards across. Maybe more. We could see the train trestle, too. That was still intact. The train was slowing down by then, but not enough so any of us could have jumped off. By then there was no time. And the jump would likely have killed anyone who tried. We were going, oh I'm gonna say fifty miles an hour. And as soon as we were on the trestle, the fucking thing started to creak and groan. Or to queel and grale, if you've ever read your James Thurber, which I suppose you have not. The train was playing music. Like Blaine did, do you remember?"

"Yes."

"But we could hear the trestle getting ready to let go even over that. Then everything started shaking from side to side. A voice—very calm and soothing—said, 'We are experiencing minor difficulties, please take your seats.' Dinky was holding that little Russian girl, Dani. Ted took my hands and said, 'I want to tell you, madam, that it has been a pleasure to know you.'

There was a lurch so hard it damn near threw me out of my seat—would have, if Ted hadn't been holding onto me—and I thought 'That's it, we're gone, please God let me be dead before whatever's down there gets its teeth into me,' and for a second or two we were going backward. *Backward,* Roland! I could see the whole car—we were in the first one behind the loco—tilting up. There was the sound of tearing metal. Then the good old *Spirit of Topeka* put on a burst of speed. Say what you want to about the old people, I know they got a lot of things wrong, but they built machines that had some *balls.*

"The next thing I knew, we were coasting into the station. And here comes that same soothing voice, this time telling us to look around our seats and make sure we've got all our personals—our gunna, you ken. Like we were on a damn TWA flight landing at Idlewild! It wasn't until we were out on the platform that we saw the last nine cars of the train were gone. Thank God they were all empty." She cast a baleful (but frightened) eye toward the far end of the street. "Hope whatever's down there chokes on em."

Then she brightened.

"There's one good thing—at speeds of up to three hundred miles an hour, which is what that ain't-we-happy voice said the *Spirit of Topeka* was doing, we must have left Master Spider-Boy in the dust."

"I wouldn't count on it," Roland said.

She rolled her eyes wearily. "Don't tell me that."

"I *do* tell you. But we'll deal with Mordred when the time comes, and I don't think that will be today."

"Good."

"Have you been beneath the Dogan again? I take it you have."

Susannah's eyes grew round. "Isn't it *something*? Makes Grand Central look like a train station someplace out in Sticksville, U.S.A. How long did it take you to find your way up?"

"If it had just been me, I'd still be wandering around down there," Roland admitted. "Oy found the way out. I assumed he was following your scent."

Susannah considered this. "Maybe he was. Jake's, more likely. Did you cross a wide passage with a sign on the wall reading SHOW ORANGE PASS ONLY, BLUE PASS NOT ACCEPTED?"

Roland nodded, but the fading sign painted on the wall had meant little to him. He had identified the passage which the Wolves took at the beginning of their raids by the sight of two motionless gray horses far down the passage, and another of those snarling masks. He had also seen a moccasin he remembered quite well, one that had been made from a chunk of rubber. One of Ted's or Dinky's, he decided; Sheemie Ruiz had no doubt been buried in his.

"So," he said. "You got off the train—how many were you?"

"Five, with Sheemie gone," she said. "Me, Ted, Dinky, Dani Rostov, and Fred Worthington—do you remember Fred?"

Roland nodded. The man in the bankerly suit.

"I gave them the guided tour of the Dogan," she said. "As much as I could, anyway. The beds where they stole the brains out of the kids and the one where Mia finally gave birth to her monster; the one-way door between Fedic and the Dixie Pig in New York that still works; Nigel's apartment.

"Ted and his friends were pretty amazed by the rotunda where all the doors are, especially the one going to Dallas in 1963, where President Kennedy was killed. We found another door two levels down—this is where most of the passages are— that goes to Ford's Theater, where President Lincoln was assassinated in 1865. There's even a poster for the play he was watching when Booth shot him. *Our American Cousin,* it was called. What kind of people would want to go and watch things like that?"

Roland thought a lot of people might, actually, but knew better than to say so.

"It's all very old," she said. "And very hot. And very fucking scary, if you want to know the truth. Most of the machinery has quit, and there are puddles of water and oil and God knows what everywhere. Some of the puddles gave off a glow, and Dinky said he thought it might be radiation. I don't like to think what I got growin on my bones or when my hair'll start fallin out. There were doors where we could hear those awful chimes . . . the ones that set your teeth on edge."

"Todash chimes."

"Yep. And *things* behind some of em. Slithery things. Was it you or was it Mia who told me there are monsters in the todash darkness?"

"I might have," he said. Gods knew there were.

"There are things in that crack beyond town, too. Was Mia told me that. 'Monsters that cozen, diddle, increase, and plot to escape,' she said. And then Ted, Dinky, Dani, and Fred joined hands. They made what Ted called 'the little good-mind.' I could feel it even though I wasn't in their circle, and I was *glad* to feel it, because that's one spooky old place down there." She clutched her blankets more tightly. "I don't look forward to going again."

"But you believe we have to."

"There's a passage that goes deep under the castle and comes out on the other side, in the Discordia. Ted and his friends located it by picking up old thoughts, what Ted called ghost-thoughts. Fred had a piece of chalk in his pocket and he marked it for me, but it'll still be hard to find again. What it's like down there is the labyrinth in an old Greek story where this bull-monster was supposed to run. I *guess* we can find it again . . ."

Roland bent and stroked Oy's rough fur. "We'll find it. This fella will backtrail your scent. Won't you, Oy?"

Oy looked up at him with his gold-ringed eyes but said nothing.

"Anyway," she went on, "Ted and the others touched the minds of the things that live in that crack outside of town. They didn't mean to, but they did. Those things are neither for the Crimson King nor against him, they're only for themselves, but they *think*. And they're telepathic. They knew we were there, and once the contact was made, they were glad to palaver. Ted and his friends said that they've been tunneling their way toward the catacombs under the Experimental Station for a long long time, and now they're close to breaking through. Once they do, they'll be free to roam wherever they want."

Roland considered this silently for a few moments, rocking back and forth on the eroded heels of his boots. He hoped he and Susannah would be long gone before that breakthrough happened . . . but perhaps it would happen before Mordred got here, and the halfling would have to face them, if he wanted to follow. Baby Mordred against the ancient monsters from under the earth—that was a happy thought.

At last he nodded for Susannah to go on.

"We heard todash chimes coming from some of the passages, too. Not just from behind the doors but from passages with no doors to block em off! Do you see what that means?"

Roland did. If they picked the wrong one—or if Ted and his friends were wrong about the passageway they had marked—he, Susannah, and Oy would likely disappear forever instead of coming out on the far side of Castle Discordia.

"They wouldn't leave me down there—they took me back as far as the infirmary before going on themselves—and I was damned glad. I wasn't looking forward to finding my way alone, although I guess I probably could've."

Roland put an arm around her and gave her a hug. "And their plan was to use the door that the Wolves used?"

"Uh-huh, the one at the end of the ORANGE PASS corridor. They'll come out where the Wolves did, find their way to the River Whye, and then across it to Calla Bryn Sturgis. The Calla-*folken* will take them in, won't they?"

"Yes."

"And once they hear the whole story, they won't . . . won't lynch them or anything?"

"I'm sure not. Henchick will know they're telling the truth and stand up for them, even if no one else will."

"They're hoping to use the Doorway Cave to get back America-side." She sighed. "I hope it works for them, but I have my doubts."

Roland did, as well. But the four of them were powerful, and Ted had struck him as a man of extraordinary determination and resource. The Manni-folk were also powerful, in their way, and great travelers between the worlds. He thought that, sooner or later, Ted and his friends probably *would* get back to America. He considered telling Susannah that it would happen if ka willed it, then thought better of it. Ka was not her favorite word just now, and he could hardly blame her for that.

"Now hear me very well and think hard, Susannah. Does the word *Dandelo* mean anything to you?"

Oy looked up, eyes bright.

She thought about it. "It might have some faint ring," she said, "but I can't do better than that. Why?"

Roland told her what he believed: that as Eddie lay dying, he had been granted some sort of vision about a thing . . . or a place . . . or a person. Something named Dandelo. Eddie had passed this on to Jake, Jake had passed it to Oy, and Oy had passed it on to Roland.

Susannah was frowning doubtfully. "It's maybe been handed around too much. There was this game we used to play when we were kids. Whisper, it was called. The first kid would think something up, a word or a phrase, and whisper it to the next kid. You could only hear it once, no repeats allowed. The next kid would pass on what he thought *he'd* heard, and the next, and the next. By the time it got to the last kid in line, it was something entirely different, and everyone would have a good laugh. But if this is wrong, I don't think we'll be laughing."

"Well," Roland said, "we'll keep a lookout and hope that I got it right. Mayhap it means nothing at all." But he didn't really believe that.

"What are we going to do for clothes, if it gets colder than this?" she asked.

"We'll make what we need. I know how. It's something else we don't need to worry about today. What we *do* need to worry about is finding something to eat. I suppose if we have to, we can find Nigel's pantry—"

"I don't want to go back under the Dogan until we have to," Susannah said. "There's got to be a kitchen near the infirmary; they must have fed those poor kids something."

Roland considered this, then nodded. It was a good idea.

"Let's do it now," she said. "I don't even want to be on the top floor of that place after dark."

FOUR

On Turtleback Lane, in the year of '02, month of August, Stephen King awakes from a waking dream of Fedic. He types *"I don't even want to be on the top floor of that place after dark."* The words appear on the screen before him. It's the end of what he calls a subchapter, but that doesn't always mean he's done for the day. Being done for the day depends on what he hears. Or, more properly, on what he doesn't. What he listens for is Ves'-Ka Gan, the Song of the Turtle. This time the music, which is faint on some days and so loud on others that it almost deafens him, seems to have ceased. It will return tomorrow. At least, it always has.

He pushes the control-key and the S-key together. The computer gives a little chime, indicating that the material he's written today has been saved. Then he gets up, wincing at the pain in his hip, and walks to the window of his office. It looks out on the driveway slanting up at a steep angle to the road where he now rarely walks. (And on the main road, Route 7, never.) The hip is very bad this morning, and the big muscles of his thigh are on fire. He rubs the hip absently as he stands looking out.

Roland, you bastard, you gave me back the pain, he thinks. It runs down his right leg like a red-hot rope, can ya not say Gawd, can ya not say Gawd-bomb, and he's the one who got stuck with it in the end. It's been three years since the accident that almost took his life and the pain is still there. It's less now, the human body has an amazing engine of healing inside it (*a hot-enj,* he thinks, and smiles), but sometimes it's still bad. He doesn't think about it much when he's writing, writing's a sort of benign todash, but it's always stiff after he's spent a couple of hours at his desk.

He thinks of Jake. He's sorry as hell that Jake died, and he guesses that when this last book is published, the readers are going to be just *wild*. And why not? Some of them have known Jake Chambers for twenty years, almost twice as long as the boy actually lived. Oh, they'll be wild, all right, and when he writes back and says he's as sorry as they are, as *surprised* as they are, will they believe him? Not on your tintype, as his grandfather used to say. He thinks of *Misery*—Annie Wilkes calling Paul Sheldon a cockadoodie brat for trying to get rid of silly, bubbleheaded Misery Chastain. Annie shouting that Paul was the *writer* and the writer is God to his characters, he doesn't have to kill any of them if he doesn't want to.

But he's *not* God. At least not in this case. He knows damned well that Jake Chambers wasn't there on the day of his accident, nor Roland Deschain, either—the idea's laughable, they're make-believe, for Christ's sake—but he also knows that at some point the song he hears when he sits at his fancy Macintosh writing-machine became Jake's death-song, and to ignore that would have been to lose touch with Ves'-Ka Gan entirely, and he must not do that. Not if he is to finish. That song is the only thread he has, the trail of breadcrumbs he must follow if he is ever to emerge from this bewildering forest of plot he has planted, and—

Are you sure you *planted it?*

Well . . . no. In fact he is not. So call for the men in the white coats.

And are you completely sure Jake wasn't there that day? After all, how much of the damned accident do you actually remember?

Not much. He remembers seeing the top of Bryan Smith's van appear over the horizon, and realizing it's not on the road, where it should be, but on the soft shoulder. After that he remembers Smith sitting on a rock wall, looking down at him, and telling him that his leg was broke in at least six places, maybe seven. But between these two memories—the one of the approach and the one of the immediate aftermath—the film of his memory has been burned red.

Or *almost* red.

But sometimes in the night, when he awakes from dreams he can't quite remember . . .

Sometimes there are . . . well . . .

"Sometimes there are voices," he says. "Why don't you just say it?"

And then, laughing: "I guess I just did."

He hears the approaching click of toenails down the hall, and Marlowe pokes his long nose into the office. He's a Welsh Corgi, with short legs and big ears, and a pretty old guy now, with his own aches and pains, not to mention the eye he lost to cancer the previous year. The vet said he probably wouldn't make it back from that one, but he did. What a good guy. What a *tough* guy. And when he raises his head from his necessarily low perspective to look at the writer, he's wearing his old fiendish grin. *How's it goin, bubba?* that look seems to say. *Gettin any good words today? How do ya?*

"I do fine," he tells Marlowe. "Hangin in. How are *you* doin?"

Marlowe (sometimes known as The Snoutmaster) waggles his arthritic rear end in response.

"You again." That's what I said to him. And he asked, "Do you remember me?" Or maybe he said it— "You remember me." I told him I was thirsty. He said he didn't have anything to drink, he said sorry, and I called him a liar. And I was right to call him a liar because he wasn't sorry a bit. He didn't care a row of pins if I was thirsty because Jake was dead and he tried to put it on me, son of a bitch tried to put the blame on me—

"But none of that actually happened," King says, watching Marlowe waddle back toward the kitchen, where he will check his dish again before taking one of his increasingly long naps. The house is empty except for the two of them, and under those circumstances he often talks to himself. "I mean, you *know* that, don't you? That none of it actually happened?"

He supposes he does, but it was so *odd* for Jake to die like that. Jake is in all his notes, and no surprise there, because Jake was supposed to be around until the very end. All of them were, in fact. Of course no story except a bad one, one that arrives DOA, is ever *completely* under the writer's control, but this one is so *out* of control it's ridiculous. It really *is* more like watching something happen—or listening to a song—than writing a damned made-up story.

He decides to make himself a peanut butter and jelly sandwich for lunch and forget the whole damned thing for another day. Tonight he will go to see the new Clint Eastwood movie, *Bloodwork,* and be glad he can go anywhere, do anything. Tomorrow he'll be back at his desk, and something from the film may slip out into the book—certainly Roland himself was partly Clint Eastwood to start with, Sergio Leone's Man with No Name.

And . . . speaking of books . . .

Lying on the coffee-table is one that came via FedEx from his office in Bangor just this morning: *The Complete Poetical Works of Robert Browning.* It contains, of course, "Childe Roland to the Dark Tower Came," the narrative poem that lies at the root of King's long (and trying) story. An idea suddenly occurs to him, and it brings an expression to his face that stops just short of outright laughter. As if reading his feelings (and possibly he can; King has always suspected dogs are fairly recent émigrés from that great I-know-just-how-you-feel country of Empathica), Marlowe's own fiendish grin appears to widen.

"One place for the poem, old boy," King says, and tosses the book back onto the coffee-table. It's a big 'un, and lands with a thud. "One place and one place only." Then he settles deeper in the chair and closes his eyes. *Just gonna sit here like this for a minute or two,* he thinks, knowing he's fooling himself, knowing he'll almost certainly doze off. As he does.

PART FOUR:
THE WHITE LANDS
OF EMPATHICA

DANDELO

CHAPTER I:
THE THING UNDER THE CASTLE

ONE

They did indeed find a good-sized kitchen and an adjoining pantry at ground-level in the Arc 16 Experimental Station, and not far from the infirmary. They found something else, as well: the office of sai Richard P. Sayre, once the Crimson King's Head of Operations, now in the clearing at the end of the path courtesy of Susannah Dean's fast right hand. Lying atop Sayre's desk were amazingly complete files on all four of them. These they destroyed, using the shredder. There were photographs of Eddie and Jake in the folders that were simply too painful to look at. Memories were better.

On Sayre's wall were two framed oil-paintings. One showed a strong and handsome boy. He was shirtless, barefooted, tousle-haired, smiling, dressed only in jeans and wearing a docker's clutch. He looked about Jake's age. This picture had a not-quite-pleasant sensuality about it. Susannah thought that the painter, sai Sayre, or both might have been part of the Lavender Hill Mob, as she had sometimes heard homosexuals called in the Village. The boy's hair was black. His eyes were blue. His lips were red. There was a livid scar on his side and a birthmark on his left heel as crimson as his lips. A snow-white horse lay dead before him. There was blood on its snarling teeth. The boy's marked left foot rested on the horse's flank, and his lips were curved in a smile of triumph.

"That's Llamrei, Arthur Eld's horse," Roland said. "Its image was carried into battle on the pennons of Gilead, and was the sigul of all In-World."

"So according to this picture, the Crimson King wins?" she asked. "Or if not him then Mordred, his son?"

549

Roland raised his eyebrows. "Thanks to John Farson, the Crimson King's men won the In-World lands long ago," he said. But then he smiled. It was a sunny expression so unlike his usual look that seeing it always made Susannah feel dizzy. "But I think *we* won the only battle that matters. What's shown in this picture is no more than someone's wishful fairy-tale." Then, with a savagery that startled her, he smashed the glass over the frame with his fist and yanked the painting free, ripping it most of the way down the middle as he did so. Before he could tear it to pieces, as he certainly meant to do, she stopped him and pointed to the bottom. Written there in small but nonetheless extravagant calligraphy was the artist's name: *Patrick Danville.*

The other painting showed the Dark Tower, a sooty-gray black cylinder tapering upward. It stood at the far end of Can'-Ka No Rey, the field of roses. In their dreams the Tower had seemed taller than the tallest skyscraper in New York (to Susannah this meant the Empire State Building). In the painting it looked to be no more than six hundred feet high, yet this robbed it of none of its dreamlike majesty. The narrow windows rose in an ascending spiral around it just as in their dreams. At the top was an oriel window of many colors—each, Roland knew, corresponding to one of the Wizard's glasses. The inmost circle but one was the pink of the ball that had been left for awhile in the keeping of a certain witch-woman named Rhea; the center was the dead ebony of Black Thirteen.

"The room behind that window is where I would go," Roland said, tapping the glass over the picture. "That is where my quest ends." His voice was low and awestruck. "This picture wasn't done from any dream, Susannah. It's as if I could touch the texture of every brick. Do you agree?"

"Yes." It was all she could say. Looking at it here on the late Richard Sayre's wall robbed her breath. Suddenly it all seemed possible. The end of the business was, quite literally, in sight.

"The person who painted it must have been there," Roland mused. "Must have set up his easel in the very roses."

"Patrick Danville," she said. "It's the same signature as on the one of Mordred and the dead horse, do you see?"

"I see it very well."

"And do you see the path through the roses that leads to the steps at the base?"

"Yes. Nineteen steps, I have no doubt. Chassit. And the clouds overhead—"

She saw them, too. They formed a kind of whirlpool before streaming away from the Tower, and toward the Place of the Turtle, at the other end of the Beam they had followed so far. And she saw another thing. Outside the barrel of the Tower, at what might have been fifty-foot intervals, were balconies encircled with waist-high wrought-iron railings. On the second of these was a blob of red and three tiny blobs of white: a face that was too small to see, and a pair of upraised hands.

"Is that the Crimson King?" she asked, pointing. She didn't quite dare put the tip of her finger on the glass over that tiny figure. It was as if she expected it to come to life and snatch her into the picture.

"Yes," Roland said. "Locked out of the only thing he ever wanted."

"Then maybe we could go right up the stairs and past him. Give him the old raspberry on the way by." And when Roland looked puzzled at that, she put her tongue between her lips and demonstrated.

This time the gunslinger's smile was faint and distracted. "I don't think it will be so easy," he said.

Susannah sighed. "Actually I don't, either."

They had what they'd come for—quite a bit more, in fact—but they still found it hard to leave Sayre's office. The picture held them. Susannah asked Roland if he didn't want to take it along. Certainly it would be simple enough to cut it out of the frame with the letter-opener on Sayre's desk and roll it up. Roland considered the idea, then shook his head. There was a kind of malevolent life in it that might attract the wrong sort of attention, like moths to a bright light. And even if that were not the case, he had an idea that both of *them* might spend too much time looking at it. The picture might distract them or, even worse, hypnotize them.

In the end, maybe it's just another mind-trap, he thought. *Like Insomnia.*

"We'll leave it," he said. "Soon enough—in months, maybe even weeks—we'll have the real thing to look at."

"Do you say so?" she asked faintly. "Roland, do you really say so?"

"I do."

"All three of us? Or will Oy and I have to die, too, in order to open your way to the Tower? After all, you *started* alone, didn't you? Maybe you have to finish that way. Isn't that how a writer would want it?"

"That doesn't mean he can *do* it," Roland said. "Stephen King's not the water, Susannah—he's only the pipe the water runs through."

"I understand what you're saying, but I'm not sure I entirely believe it."

Roland wasn't completely sure he did, either. He thought of pointing out to Susannah that Cuthbert and Alain had been with him at the true beginning of his quest, in Mejis, and when they set out from Gilead the next time, Jamie DeCurry had joined them, making the trio a quartet. But the quest had really started after the battle of Jericho Hill, and yes, by then he had been on his own.

"I started lone-john, but that's not how I'll finish," he said. She had been making her way quite handily from place to place in a rolling office-chair. Now he plucked her out of it and settled her on his right hip, the one that no longer pained him. "You and Oy will be with me when I climb the steps and enter the door, you'll be with me when I climb the stairs, you'll be with me when I deal with yon capering red goblin, and you'll be with me when I enter the room at the top."

Although Susannah did not say so, this felt like a lie to her. In truth it felt like a lie to both of them.

TWO

They brought canned goods, a skillet, two pots, two plates, and two sets of utensils back to the Fedic Hotel. Roland had added a flashlight that provided a feeble glow from nearly dead batteries, a butcher's knife, and a handy little hatchet with a rubber grip. Susannah had found a pair of net bags in which to store this little bit of fresh gunna. She also found three cans of jelly-like stuff on a high shelf in the pantry adjacent to the infirmary kitchen.

"It's Sterno," she told the gunslinger when he inquired. "Good stuff. You can light it up. It burns slow and makes a blue flame hot enough to cook on."

"I thought we'd build a little fire behind the hotel," he said. "I won't need this smelly stuff to make one, certainly." He said it with a touch of contempt.

"No, I suppose not. But it might come in handy."

"How?"

"I don't know, but . . ." She shrugged.

Near the door to the street they passed what appeared to be a janitor's closet filled with piles of rickrack. Susannah had had enough of the Dogan for one day and was anxious to be out, but Roland wanted to have a look. He ignored the mop buckets and brooms and cleaning supplies in favor of a jumble of cords and straps heaped in a corner. Susannah guessed from the boards on top of which they lay that this stuff had once been used to build temporary scaffoldings. She also had an idea what Roland wanted the strappage for, and her heart sank. It was like going all the way back to the beginning.

"Thought I was done with piggybackin'," she said crossly, and with more than a touch of Detta in her voice.

"It's the only way, I think," Roland said. "I'm just glad I'm whole enough again to carry your weight."

"And that passage underneath's the only way through? You're sure of that?"

"I suppose there might be a way through the castle—" he began, but Susannah was already shaking her head.

"I've been up top with Mia, don't forget. The drop into the Discordia on the far side's at least five hundred feet. Probably more. There might have been stairs in the long-ago, but they're gone now."

"Then we're for the passage," he said, "and the passage is for us. Mayhap we'll find something for you to ride in once we're on the other side. In another town or village."

Susannah was shaking her head again. "I think this is where civilization ends, Roland. And I think we better bundle up as much as we can, because it's gonna get *cold.*"

Bundling-up materials seemed to be in short supply, however, unlike the foodstuffs. No one had thought to store a few extra sweaters and fleece-lined jackets in vacuum-packed cans. There were blankets, but even in storage they had grown thin and fragile, just short of useless.

"I don't give a bedbug's ass," she said in a wan voice. "Just as long as we get out of this place."

"We will," he said.

THREE

Susannah is in Central Park, and it's cold enough to see her breath. The sky overhead is white from side to side, a snow-sky. She's looking down at the polar bear (who's rolling around on his rocky island, seeming to enjoy the cold just fine) when a hand snakes around her waist. Warm lips smack her cold cheek. She turns and there stand Eddie and Jake. They are wearing identical grins and nearly identical red stocking caps. Eddie's says MERRY *across the front and Jake's says* CHRISTMAS. *She opens her mouth to tell them "You boys can't be here, you boys are dead," and then she realizes, with a great and singing relief, that all that business was just a dream she had. And really, how could you doubt it? There are no talking animals called billy-bumblers, not really, no taheen-creatures with the bodies of humans and the heads of animals, no places called Fedic or Castle Discordia.*

*Most of all, there are no gunslingers. John Kennedy was the last,
her chauffeur Andrew was right about that.*

*"Brought you hot chocolate," Eddie says and holds it out to her. It's
the perfect cup of hot chocolate,* mit schlag *on top and little sprinkles
of nutmeg dotting the cream; she can smell it, and as she takes it she can
feel his fingers inside his gloves and the first flakes of that winter's snow
drift down between them. She thinks how good it is to be alive in plain
old New York, how great that reality is reality, that they are together in
the Year of Our Lord—*

What *Year of Our Lord?*

*She frowns, because this is a serious question, isn't it? After all,
Eddie's an eighties man and she never got any further than 1964 (or
was it '65?). As for Jake, Jake Chambers with the word* CHRISTMAS
*printed on the front of his happy hat, isn't he from the seventies? And
if the three of them represent three decades from the second half of the
twentieth century, what is their commonality? What year is this?*

"NINETEEN," *says a voice out of the air (perhaps it is the voice of
Bango Skank, the Great Lost Character),* "this is NINETEEN, this is
CHASSIT. All your friends are dead."

*With each word the world becomes more unreal. She can see through
Eddie and Jake. When she looks down at the polar bear she sees it's lying
dead on its rock island with its paws in the air. The good smell of hot
chocolate is fading, being replaced by a musty smell: old plaster, ancient
wood. The odor of a hotel room where no one has slept for years.*

No, *her mind moans.* No, I want Central Park, I want Mr.
MERRY and Mr. CHRISTMAS, I want the smell of hot chocolate and the sight of December's first hesitant snowflakes, I've
had enough of Fedic, In-World, Mid-World, and End-World. I
want *My*-World. I don't care if I ever see the Dark Tower.

*Eddie's and Jake's lips move in unison, as if they are singing a
song she can't hear, but it's not a song; the words she reads on their lips
just before the dream breaks apart are*

FOUR

"Watch out for Dandelo."

She woke up with these words on her own lips, shivering in the early not-quite-dawn light. And the breath-seeing part of her dream was true, if no other. She felt her cheeks and wiped away the wetness there. It wasn't quite cold enough to freeze the tears to her skin, but just-a-damn-bout.

She looked around the dreary room here in the Fedic Hotel, wishing with all her heart that her dream of Central Park had been true. For one thing, she'd had to sleep on the floor—the bed was basically nothing but a rust-sculpture waiting to disintegrate—and her back was stiff. For another, the blankets she'd used as a makeshift mattress and the ones she'd wrapped around her had all torn to rags as she tossed and turned. The air was heavy with their dust, tickling her nose and coating her throat, making her feel like she was coming down with the world's worst cold. Speaking of cold, she was shivering. And she needed to pee, which meant dragging herself down the hall on her stumps and half-numbed hands.

And none of that was really what was wrong with Susannah Odetta Holmes Dean this morning, all right? The problem was that she had just come from a beautiful dream to a world

(*this is NINETEEN all your friends are dead*)

where she was now so lonely that she felt half-crazy with it. The problem was that the place where the sky was brightening was not necessarily the east. The problem was that she was tired and sad, homesick and heartsore, griefstruck and depressed. The problem was that, in this hour before dawn, in this frontier museum-piece of a hotel room where the air was full of musty blanket-fibers, she felt as if all but the last two ounces of fuck-you had been squeezed out of her. She wanted the dream back.

She wanted Eddie.

"I see you're up, too," said a voice, and Susannah whirled

around, pivoting on her hands so quickly she picked up a splinter.

The gunslinger leaned against the door between the room and the hall. He had woven the straps into the sort of carrier with which she was all too familiar, and it hung over his left shoulder. Hung over his right was a leather sack filled with their new possessions and the remaining Orizas. Oy sat at Roland's feet, looking at her solemnly.

"You scared the living Jesus out of me, sai Deschain," she said.

"You've been crying."

"Isn't any of your nevermind if I have been or if I haven't."

"We'll feel better once we're out of here," he said. "Fedic's curdled."

She knew exactly what he meant. The wind had kicked up fierce in the night, and when it screamed around the eaves of the hotel and the saloon next door, it had sounded to Susannah like the screams of children—wee ones so lost in time and space they would never find their way home.

"All right, but Roland—before we cross the street and go into that Dogan, I want your promise on one thing."

"What promise would you have?"

"If something looks like getting us—some monster out of the Devil's Arse or one from the todash between-lands—you put a bullet in my head before it happens. When it comes to yourself you can do whatever you want, but . . . what? What are you holding that out for?" It was one of his revolvers.

"Because I'm only really good with one of them these days. And because I won't be the one to take your life. If you should decide to do it yourself, however—"

"Roland, your fucked-up scruples never cease to amaze me," she said. Then she took the gun with one hand and pointed to the harness with the other. "As for that thing, if you think I'm gonna ride in it before I have to, you're crazy."

A faint smile touched his lips. "It's better when it's the two of us, isn't it?"

She sighed, then nodded. "A little bit, yeah, but far from perfect. Come on, big fella, let's blow this place. My ass is an ice-cube and the smell is killing my sinuses."

FIVE

He put her in the rolling office-chair once they were back in the Dogan and pushed her in it as far as the first set of stairs, Susannah holding their gunna and the bag of Orizas in her lap. At the stairs the gunslinger booted the chair over the edge and then stood with Susannah on his hip, both of them wincing at the crashing echoes as the chair tumbled over and over to the bottom.

"That's the end of *that*," she said when the echoes had finally ceased. "You might as well have left it at the top for all the good it's going to do me now."

"We'll see," Roland said, starting down. "You might be surprised."

"That thing ain't gonna work fo' shit an we bofe know it," Detta said. Oy uttered a short, sharp bark, as if to say *That's right.*

SIX

The chair *did* survive its tumble, however. And the next, as well. But when Roland hunkered to examine the poor battered thing after being pushed down a third (and extremely long) flight of stairs, one of the casters was bent badly out of true. It reminded him a little of how her abandoned wheelchair had looked when they'd come upon it after the battle with the Wolves on the East Road.

"There, now, dint I tell you?" she asked, and cackled. "Reckon it's time to start totin dat barge, Roland!"

He eyed her. "Can you make Detta go away?"

She looked at him, surprised, then used her memory to replay the last thing she had said. She flushed. "Yes," she said in a remarkably small voice. "Say sorry, Roland."

He picked her up and got her settled into the harness. Then they went on. As unpleasant as it was beneath the Dogan—as *creepy* as it was beneath the Dogan—Susannah was glad that they were putting Fedic behind them. Because that meant they were putting the rest of it behind them, too: Lud, the Callas, Thunderclap, Algul Siento; New York City and western Maine, as well. The castle of the Red King was ahead, but she didn't think they had to worry much about it, because its most celebrated occupant had run mad and decamped for the Dark Tower.

The extraneous was slipping away. They were closing in on the end of their long journey, and there was little else to worry about. That was good. And if she should happen to fall on her way to Roland's obsession? Well, if there was only darkness on the other side of existence (as she had for most of her adult life believed), then nothing was lost, as long as it wasn't *todash* darkness, a place filled with creeping monsters. And, hey! Perhaps there *was* an afterlife, a heaven, a reincarnation, maybe even a resurrection in the clearing at the end of the path. She liked that last idea, and had now seen enough wonders to believe it might be so. Perhaps Eddie and Jake would be waiting for her there, all bundled up and with the first down-drifting snowflakes of winter getting caught in their eyebrows: Mr. MERRY and Mr. CHRISTMAS, offering her hot chocolate. *Mit schlag.*

Hot chocolate in Central Park! What was the Dark Tower compared to that?

SEVEN

They passed through the rotunda with its doors to everywhere; they came eventually to the wide passage with the sign on the wall reading SHOW ORANGE PASS ONLY, BLUE PASS NOT ACCEPTED. A little way down it, in the glow of one of the still-working fluorescent lights (and near the forgotten rubber moccasin), they saw something printed on the tile wall and detoured down to read it.

Roland, Susannah: We are on our way! Wish us good luck!
                        Good luck to you!
                        May God bless you!
             We will never forget you!

Under the main message they had signed their names: Fred Worthington, Dani Rostov, Ted Brautigan, and Dinky Earnshaw. Below the names were two more lines, written in another hand. Susannah thought it was Ted's, and reading them made her feel like crying:

We go to seek a better world.
May you find one, as well

"God love em," Susannah said hoarsely. "May God love and keep em all."

"Keep-um," said a small and rather timid voice from Roland's heel. They looked down.

"Decided to talk again, sugarpie?" Susannah asked, but to this Oy made no reply. It was weeks before he spoke again.

EIGHT

Twice they got lost. Once Oy rediscovered their way through the maze of tunnels and passages—some moaning with distant drafts, some alive with sounds that were closer and more menacing—and once Susannah came back to the route herself, spotting a Mounds Bar wrapper Dani had dropped. The Algul had been well-stocked with candy, and the girl had brought plenty with her. ("Although not one single change of clothes," Susannah said with a laugh and a shake of her head.) At one point, in front of an ancient ironwood door that looked to Roland like the ones he'd found on the beach, they heard an unpleasant *chewing* sound. Susannah tried to imagine what might be making such a noise and could think of nothing but a giant, disembodied mouth full of yellow fangs streaked with dirt. On the door was an indecipherable symbol. Just looking at it made her uneasy.

"Do you know what that says?" she asked. Roland—although he spoke over half a dozen languages and was familiar with many more—shook his head. Susannah was relieved. She had an idea that if you knew the sound that symbol stood for, you'd want to say it. Might *have* to say it. And then the door would open. Would you want to run when you saw the thing that was chewing on the other side? Probably. Would you be *able* to?

Maybe not.

Shortly after passing this door they went down another, shorter, flight of stairs. "I guess I forgot this one when we were talking yesterday, but I remember it now," she said, and pointed to the dust on the risers, which was disturbed. "Look, there's our tracks. Fred carried me going down, Dinky when we came back up. We're almost there now, Roland, promise you."

But she got lost again in the warren of diverging passages at the bottom of the stairs and this was when Oy put them right, trotting down a dim, tunnel-like passage where the gunslinger had to walk bent-over with Susannah clinging to his neck.

"I don't know—" Susannah began, and that was when Oy led them into a brighter corridor (*comparatively* brighter: half of the overhead fluorescents were out, and many of the tiles had fallen from the walls, revealing the dark and oozy earth beneath). The bumbler sat down on a scuffed confusion of tracks and looked at them as if to say, *Is this what you wanted?*

"Yeah," she said, obviously relieved. "Okay. Look, just like I told you." She pointed to a door marked FORD'S THEATER, 1865 SEE THE LINCOLN ASSASSINATION. Beside it, under glass, was a poster for *Our American Cousin* that looked as if it had been printed the day before. "What we want's just down here a little way. Two lefts and then a right—I think. Anyway, I'll know it when I see it."

Through it all Roland was patient with her. He had a nasty idea which he did not share with Susannah: that the maze of passageways and corridors down here might be in drift, just as the points of the compass were, in what he was already thinking of as "the world above." If so, they were in trouble.

It was hot down here, and soon they were both sweating freely. Oy panted harshly and steadily, like a little engine, but kept a steady pace beside the gunslinger's left heel. There was no dust on the floor, and the tracks they'd seen off and on earlier were gone. The noises from behind the doors were louder, however, and as they passed one, something on the other side thumped it hard enough to make it shudder in its frame. Oy barked at it, laying his ears back against his skull, and Susannah voiced a little scream.

"Steady-oh," Roland said. "It can't break through. None of them can break through."

"Are you sure of that?"

"Yes," said the gunslinger firmly. He wasn't sure at all. A phrase of Eddie's occurred to him: *All bets are off.*

They skirted the puddles, being careful not even to touch the ones that were glowing with what might have been radiation or witchlight. They passed a broken pipe that was exhaling a listless plume of green steam, and Susannah suggested they hold their breath until they were well past it. Roland thought that an extremely good idea.

Thirty or forty yards further along she bid him stop. "I don't know, Roland," she said, and he could hear her struggling to keep the panic out of her voice. "I thought we had it made in the shade when I saw the Lincoln door, but now this . . . this here . . ." Her voice wavered and he felt her draw a deep breath, struggling to get herself under control. "This all looks different. And the *sounds* . . . how they get in your head . . ."

He knew what she meant. On their left was an unmarked door that had settled crookedly against its hinges, and from the gap at the top came the atonal jangle of todash chimes, a sound that was both horrible and fascinating. With the chimes came a steady draft of stinking air. Roland had an idea she was about to suggest they go back while they still could, maybe rethink this whole going-under-the-castle idea, and so he said, "Let's see what's up there. It's a little brighter, anyway."

As they neared an intersection from which passages and tiled corridors rayed off in all directions, he felt her shift against him, sitting up. "There!" she shouted. "That pile of rubble! We walked around that! We walked around that, Roland, *I remember!*"

Part of the ceiling had fallen into the middle of the inter-section, creating a jumble of broken tiles, smashed glass, snags of wire, and plain old dirt. Along the edge of it were tracks.

"Down there!" she cried. "Straight ahead! Ted said, 'I think this is the one they called Main Street' and Dinky said he thought so, too. Dani Rostov said that a long time ago, around the time the Crimson King did whatever it was that darkened Thunderclap, a whole bunch of people used that way to get out. Only they left some of their thoughts behind. I asked her what feeling that was like and she said it was a little like seeing dirty soap-scum on the sides of the tub after you let out the water. 'Not nice,' she said. Fred marked it and then we went all the way back up to the infirmary. I don't want to brag and queer the deal, but I think we're gonna be okay."

And they were, at least for the time being. Eighty paces beyond the pile of rubble they came upon an arched opening. Beyond it, flickering white balls of radiance hung down from the ceiling, leading off at a downward-sloping angle. On the wall, in four chalkstrokes that had already started to run because of the moisture seeping through the tiles, was the last message left for them by the liberated Breakers:

They rested here for awhile, eating handfuls of raisins from a vacuum-sealed can. Even Oy nibbled a few, although it was clear from the way he did it that he didn't care for them much. When they'd all eaten their fill and Roland had once more stored the can in the leather sack he'd found along the way, he asked her: "Are you ready to go on?"

"Yes. Right away, I think, before I lose my— *my God, Roland, what was that?*"

From behind them, probably from one of the passages leading away from the rubble-choked intersection, had come a low thudding sound. It had a liquid quality to it, as if a giant in water-filled rubber boots had just taken a single step.

"I don't know," he said.

Susannah was looking uneasily back over her shoulder but could see only shadows. Some of them were moving, but that could have been because some of the lights were flickering.

Could have been.

"You know," she said, "I think it might be a good idea if we vacated this area just about as fast as we can."

"I think you're right," he said, resting on one knee and the splayed tips of his fingers, like a runner getting ready to burst from the blocks. When she was back in the harness, he got to his feet and moved past the arrow on the wall, setting a pace that was just short of a jog.

NINE

They had been moving at that near-jog for about fifteen minutes when they came upon a skeleton dressed in the remains of a rotting military uniform. There was still a flap of scalp on its head and tuft of listless black hair sprouting from it. The jaw grinned, as if welcoming them to the underworld. Lying on the floor beside the thing's naked pelvis was a ring that had finally slipped from one of the moldering fingers of the dead man's right hand. Susannah asked Roland if she could have a closer look. He picked it up and handed it to her. She examined it just long enough to confirm what she had thought, then cast it aside. It made a little clink and then there were only the sounds of dripping water and the todash chimes, fainter now but persistent.

"What I thought," she said.

"And what was that?" he asked, moving on again.

"The guy was an Elk. My father had the same damn ring."

"An elk? I don't understand."

"It's a fraternal order. A kind of good-ole-boy ka-tet. But what in the hell would an Elk be doing down here? A Shriner, now, that I could understand." And she laughed, a trifle wildly.

The hanging bulbs were filled with some brilliant gas that pulsed with a rhythmic but not quite constant beat. Susannah knew there was something there to get, and after a little while she got it. While Roland was hurrying, the pulse of the guide-lights was rapid. When he slowed down (never stopping but conserving his energy, all the same), the pulse in the globes also slowed down. She didn't think they were responding to his heartbeat, exactly, or hers, but that was part of it. (Had she known the term *biorhythm,* she would have seized upon it.) Fifty yards or so ahead of their position at any given time, Main Street was dark. Then, one by one, the lights would come on as they approached. It was mesmerizing. She turned to look back—only once, she didn't want to throw him off his stride—and saw that, yes, the lights were going dark again fifty yards or so behind. These lights were much brighter than the flickering globes at the entrance to Main Street, and she guessed that those ran off some other power-source, one that was (like almost everything else in this world) starting to give out. Then she noticed that one of the globes they were approaching remained dark. As they neared and then passed under it, she saw that it wasn't *completely* dead; a dim core of illumination burned feebly deep inside, twitching to the beat of their bodies and brains. It reminded her of how you'd sometimes see a neon sign with one or more letters on the fritz, turning PABST into PA ST or TASTY BRATWURST into TASTY RATWURST. A hundred feet or so further on they came to another burnt-out bulb, then another, then two in a row.

"Chances are good we're gonna be in the dark before long," she said glumly.

"I know," Roland said. He was starting to sound the teensiest bit out of breath.

The air was still dank, and a chill was gradually replacing the heat. There were posters on the walls, most rotted far beyond the point of readability. On a dry stretch of wall she saw one that depicted a man who had just lost an arena battle to a tiger. The big cat was yanking a bloody snarl of intestines from the screaming man's belly while the crowd went nuts. There was one line of copy in half a dozen different languages. English was second from the top. VISIT CIRCUS MAXIMUS! **YOU WILL CHEER!** it said.

"Christ, Roland," Susannah said. "Christ almighty, what *were* they?"

Roland did not reply, although he knew the answer: they were *folken* who had run mad.

TEN

At hundred-yard intervals, little flights of stairs—the longest was only ten risers from top to bottom—took them gradually deeper into the bowels of the earth. After they'd gone what Susannah estimated to be a quarter of a mile, they came to a gate that had been torn away, perhaps by some sort of vehicle, and smashed to flinders. Here were more skeletons, so many that Roland had to tread upon some in order to pass. They did not crunch but made a damp puttering sound that was somehow worse. The smell that arose from them was sallow and wet. Most of the tiles had been torn away above these bodies, and those that were still on the walls had been pocked with bullet-holes. A firefight, then. Susannah opened her mouth to say something about it, but before she could, that low thudding sound came again. She thought it was a little louder this time. A little closer. She looked behind her again and saw nothing. The lights fifty yards back were still going dark in a line.

"I don't like to sound paranoid, Roland, but I think we are being followed."

"I know we are."

"You want me to throw a shot at it? Or a plate? That whistling can be pretty spooky."

"No."

"Why not?"

"It may not know what we are. If you shoot . . . it will."

It took her a moment to realize what he was really saying: he wasn't sure bullets—or an Oriza—would stop whatever was back there. Or, worse, perhaps he *was* sure.

When she spoke again, she worked very hard to sound calm, and thought she succeeded tolerably well. "It's something from that crack in the earth, do you think?"

"It might be," Roland said. "Or it might be something that got through from todash space. Now hush."

The gunslinger went on more quickly, finally reaching jogging pace and then passing it. She was amazed by his mobility now that the pain that had troubled his hip was gone, but she could hear his breathing as well as feel it in the rise and fall of his back—quick, gasping intakes followed by rough expulsions that sounded almost like cries of annoyance. She would have given anything to be running beside him on her own legs, the strong ones Jack Mort had stolen from her.

The overhead globes pulsed faster now, the pulsation easier to see because there were fewer of them. In between, their combined shadow would stretch long ahead of them, then shorten little by little as they approached the next light. The air was cooler; the ceramic stuff which floored the passage less and less even. In places it had split apart and pieces of it had been tossed aside, leaving traps for the unwary. These Oy avoided with ease, and so far Roland had been able to avoid them, too.

She was about to tell him that she hadn't heard their follower for awhile when something behind them pulled in a great gasping breath. She felt the air around her reverse direction; felt the tight curls on her head spring wildly about as the air was sucked backward. There was an enormous slobbering noise that made her feel like screaming. Whatever was back there, it was big.

No.

Enormous.

ELEVEN

They pelted down another of those short stairways. Fifty yards beyond it, three more of the pulsing globes bloomed with unsteady light, but after that there was just darkness. The ragged tiled sides of the passage and its uneven, decaying floor melted into a void so deep that it looked like a physical substance: great clouds of loosely packed black felt. They would run into it, she thought, and at first their momentum would continue to carry them forward. Then the stuff would shove them backward like a spring, and whatever was back there would be on them. She would catch a glimpse of it, something so awful and alien her mind would not be able to recognize it, and that might be a mercy. Then it would pounce, and—

Roland ran into the darkness without slowing, and of course they did not bounce back. At first there was a little light, some from behind them and some from the globes overhead (a few were still giving off a last dying core of radiance). Just enough to see another short stairway, its upper end flanked by crumbling skeletons wearing a few wretched rags of clothing. Roland hurried down the steps—there were nine in this flight—without stopping. Oy ran at his side, ears back against his skull, fur rippling sleekly, almost dancing his way down. Then they were in pure dark.

"Bark, Oy, so we don't run into each other!" Roland snapped. "Bark!"

Oy barked. A thirty-count later, he snapped the same order and Oy barked again.

"Roland, what if we come to another stairway?"

"We will," he said, and a ninety-count after that, they did. She felt him tip forward, feet stuttering. She felt the muscles in his shoulders jump as he put his hands out before him, but they did not fall. Susannah could only marvel at his reflexes. His boots rapped unhesitatingly downward in the dark. Twelve steps this time? Fourteen? They were back on the flat surface of the passageway before she could get a good count. So now she knew he was capable of negotiating stairs even in the dark, even at a dead run. Only what if he stuck his foot in a hole? God knew it was possible, given the way the flooring had rotted. Or suppose they came to a stacked bone-barrier of skeletons? In the flat passageway, at the speed he was now running, that would mean a nasty tumble at the very least. Or suppose they ran into a jumble of bones at the head of one of the little stairways? She tried to block the vision of Roland swooping out into blackness like a crippled high-diver and couldn't quite do it. How many of *their* bones would be broken when they crash-landed at the bottom? *Shit, sugar, pick a number,* Eddie might have said. This flat-out run was insanity.

But there was no choice. She could hear the thing behind them all too clearly now, not just its slobbering breath but a sandpapery rasping sound as something slid across one of the passageway walls—or maybe both. Every now and then she'd also hear a clink and a clitter as a tile was torn off. It was impossible not to construct a picture from these sounds, and what Susannah began to see was a great black worm whose segmented body filled the passage from side to side, occasionally ripping off loose ceramic squares and crushing them beneath its gelatinous body as it rushed ever onward, hungry, closing the gap between it and them.

And closing it much more rapidly now. Susannah thought she knew why. Before, they had been running in a moving island of light. Whatever that thing behind them was, it didn't like the light. She thought of the flashlight Roland had added to their gunna, but without fresh batteries, it would be next to useless. Twenty seconds after flicking the switch on its long barrel, the damn thing would be dead.

Except . . . wait a minute.

Its barrel.

Its long barrel!

Susannah reached into the leather bag bouncing around at Roland's side, finding tins of food, but those weren't the tins she wanted. At last she found one that she did, recognizing it by the circular gutter running around the lid. There was no time to

wonder why it should feel so immediately and intimately familiar; Detta had her secrets, and something to do with Sterno was
probably one of them. She held the can up to smell and be sure,
then promptly bashed herself on the bridge of the nose with it
when Roland stumbled over something—maybe a chunk of
flooring, maybe another skeleton—and had to battle again for
balance. He won this time, too, but eventually he'd lose and the
thing back there might be on them before he could get up.
Susannah felt warm blood begin to course down her face and
the thing behind them, perhaps smelling it, let loose an enormous damp cry. She thought of a gigantic alligator in a Florida
swamp, raising its scaly head to bay at the moon. And it was so
close.

Oh dear God give me time, she thought. *I don't want to go like
this, getting shot's one thing, but getting eaten alive in the dark—*

That was another.

"Go *faster!*" she snarled at Roland, and thumped at his
sides with her thighs, like a rider urging on a weary horse.

Somehow, Roland did. His respiration was now an agonized roar. He had not breathed so even after dancing the
commala. If he kept on, his heart would burst in his chest. But—

"*Faster,* Tex! Let it all out, goddammit! I might have a trick
up my sleeve, but in the meantime you give it every-damn-
everything you got!"

And there in the dark beneath Castle Discordia, Roland
did.

TWELVE

She plunged her free hand once more into the bag and it
closed on the flashlight's barrel. She pulled it out and tucked it
under her arm (knowing if she dropped it they were gone for
sure), then snapped back the tab-release on the Sterno can,
relieved to hear the momentary hiss as the vacuum-seal broke.
Relieved but not surprised—if the seal had been broken, the
flammable jelly inside would have evaporated long ago and the
can would have been lighter.

"Roland!" she shouted. "Roland, I need matches!"

"Shirt . . . pocket!" he panted. "Reach for them!"

But first she dropped the flashlight into the seam where her crotch met the middle of his back, then snatched it up just before it could slide away. Now, with a good hold on it, she plunged the barrel into the can of Sterno. To grab one of the matches while holding the can and the jelly-coated flashlight would have taken a third hand, so she jettisoned the can. There were two others in the bag, but if this didn't work she'd never have a chance to reach for one of them.

The thing bellowed again, sounding as if it were *right behind them.* Now she could smell it, the aroma like a load of fish rotting in the sun.

She reached over Roland's shoulder and plucked a single match from his pocket. There might be time to light one; not for two. Roland and Eddie were able to pop them alight with their thumbnails, but Detta Walker had known a trick worth two of that, had used it on more than one occasion to impress her whiteboy victims in the roadhouses where she'd gone trolling. She grimaced in the dark, peeling her lips away from her teeth, and placed the head of the match between the two front ones on top. *Eddie, if you're there, help me, sugar— help me do right.*

She struck the match. Something hot burned the roof of her mouth and she tasted sulfur on her tongue. The head of the match nearly blinded her dark-adapted eyes, but she could see well enough to touch it to the jelly-coated barrel of the flashlight. The Sterno caught at once, turning the barrel into a torch. It was weak but it was *something.*

"*Turn around!*" she screamed.

Roland skidded to a stop immediately—no questions, no protest—and pivoted on his heels. She held the burning flashlight out before her and for a moment they both saw the head of something wet and covered with pink albino eyes. Below them was a mouth the size of a trapdoor, filled with squirming tentacles. The Sterno didn't burn brightly, but in this Stygian blackness it was bright enough to make the thing recoil. Before it disappeared into the blackness again, she saw all those eyes squeezing shut and had a moment to think of how sensitive they must be if even a little guttering flame like this could—

Lining the floor of the passageway on both sides were jumbled heaps of bones. In her hand, the bulb end of the flashlight was already growing warm. Oy was barking frantically, looking back into the dark with his head down and his short legs splayed, every hair standing on end.

"Squat down, Roland, squat!"

He did and she handed him the makeshift torch, which was already beginning to gutter, the yellow flames running up and down the stainless steel barrel turning blue. The thing in the dark let out another deafening roar, and now she could see its shape again, weaving from side to side. It was creeping closer as the light faltered.

If the floor's wet here, we're most likely done, she thought, but the touch of her fingers as she groped for a thighbone suggested it was not. Perhaps that was a false message sent by her hopeful senses—she could certainly hear water dripping from the ceiling somewhere up ahead—but she didn't think so.

She reached into the bag for another can of Sterno, but at first the release-ring defied her. The thing was coming and now she could see any number of short, misshapen legs beneath its raised lump of a head. Not a worm after all but some kind of giant centipede. Oy placed himself in front of her, still barking, every tooth on display. It was Oy the thing would take first if she couldn't—

Then her finger slipped into the ring lying almost flat against the lid of the can. There was a *pop-hissh* sound. Roland was waving the flashlight back and forth, trying to fan a little life into the guttering flames (which might have worked had there been fuel for them), and she saw their fading shadows rock deliriously back and forth on the decaying tile walls.

The circumference of the bone was too big for the can. Now lying in an awkward sprawl, half in and half out of the harness, she dipped into it, brought out a handful of jelly, and slathered it up and down the bone. If the bone was wet, this would only buy them a few more seconds of horror. If it was dry, however, then maybe . . . just maybe . . .

The thing was creeping ever closer. Amid the tentacles sprouting from its mouth she could see jutting fangs. In another moment it would be close enough to lunge at Oy, taking him with the speed of a gecko snatching a fly out of the air. Its rotted-fish aroma was strong and nauseating. And what might be behind it? What other abominations?

No time to think about that now.

She touched her thighbone torch to the fading flames licking along the barrel of the flashlight. The bloom of fire was greater than she had expected—far greater—and the thing's scream this time was filled with pain as well as surprise. There was a nasty squelching sound, like mud being squeezed in a vinyl raincoat, and it lashed backward.

"Git me more bones," she said as Roland cast the flashlight aside. "And make sure they're dem *drah* bones." She laughed at her own wit (since nobody else would), a down-and-dirty Detta cackle.

Still gasping for breath, Roland did as she told him.

THIRTEEN

They resumed their progress along the passage, Susannah now riding backward, a position that was difficult but not impossible. If they got out of here, her back would ache a bitch for the next day or two. *And I'll relish every single throb,* she told herself. Roland still had the Bridgton Old Home Days tee-shirt Irene Tassenbaum had bought him. He handed it up to Susannah. She wrapped it around the bottom of the bone and held it out as far as she possibly could while still keeping her balance. Roland wasn't able to run—she would have surely tumbled out of the harness had he tried doing that—but he maintained a good fast walking pace, pausing every now and then to pick up a likely-looking arm- or legbone. Oy soon got the idea and began bringing them to the gunslinger in his mouth. The thing continued to follow them. Every now and then Susannah caught a glimpse of its slick-gleaming skin, and even when it drew back beyond the chancy light of her current torch they would hear those liquid stomping sounds, like a giant in mud-filled boots. She began to think it was the sound of the thing's tail. This filled her with a horror that was unreasoning and private and almost powerful enough to undo her mind.

That it should have a tail! her mind nearly raved. *A tail that sounds like it's filled with water or jelly or half-coagulated blood! Christ! My God! My Christ!*

It wasn't just light keeping it from attacking them, she reckoned, but fear of fire. The thing must have hung back while they were in the part of the passage where the glow-globes still worked, thinking (if it *could* think) that it would wait and take them once they were in the dark. She had an idea that if it had known they had access to fire, it might simply have closed some or all of its many eyes and pounced on them where a few of the globes were out and the light was dimmer. Now it was at least temporarily out of luck, because the bones made surprisingly good torches (the idea that they were being helped by the recovering Beam in this regard did not cross her mind). The only question was whether or not the Sterno would hold out. She was able to conserve now because the bones burned on their own once they were going—except for a couple of damp ones that she had to cast aside after lighting her next torches from their guttering tips—but you *did* have to get them going, and she was already deep into the third and last can. She bitterly regretted the one she'd tossed away when the thing had been closing in on them, but didn't know what else she could have done. She also wished Roland would go faster, although she guessed he now couldn't have maintained much speed even if she'd been faced around the right way and holding onto him. Maybe a short burst, but surely no more. She could feel his muscles trembling under his shirt. He was close to blown out.

Five minutes later, while getting a handful of canned heat to slather on a bony bulb of knee atop a shinbone, her fingers touched the bottom of the Sterno can. From the darkness behind them came another of those watery stomping sounds. The tail of their friend, her mind insisted. It was keeping pace. Waiting for them to run out of fuel and for the world to go dark again. Then it would pounce.

Then it would eat.

FOURTEEN

They were going to need a fallback position. She became sure of that almost as soon as the tips of her fingers touched the bottom of the can. Ten minutes and three torches later, Susannah prepared to tell the gunslinger to stop when—and if—they came to another especially large ossuary. They could make a bonfire of rags and bones, and once it was going hot and bright, they'd simply run like hell. When—and if—they heard the thing on their side of the fire-barrier again, Roland could lighten his load and speed his heels by leaving her behind. She saw this idea not as self-sacrificing but merely logical—there was no reason for the monstrous centipede to get both of them if they could avoid it. And she had no plans to let it take her, as far as that went. Certainly not alive. She had his gun, and she'd use it. Five shots for Sai Centipede; if it kept coming after that, the sixth for herself.

Before she could say any of these things, however, Roland got in three words that stopped all of hers. "Light," he panted. "Up ahead."

She craned around and at first saw nothing, probably because of the torch she'd been holding out. Then she did: a faint white glow.

"More of those globes?" she asked. "A stretch of them that are still working?"

"Maybe. I don't think so."

Five minutes later she realized she could see the floor and walls in the light of her latest torch. The floor was covered with a fine scrim of dust and pebbles such as could only have been blown in from outside. Susannah threw her arms up over her head, one hand holding a blazing bone wrapped in a shirt, and gave a scream of triumph. The thing behind her answered with a roar of fury and frustration that did her heart good even as it pebbled her skin with goosebumps.

"Goodbye, honey!" she screamed. "Goodbye, you eye-covered muthafuck!"

It roared again and thrust itself forward. For one moment she saw it plain: a huge round lump that couldn't be called a face in spite of the lolling mouth; the segmented body, scratched and oozing from contact with the rough walls; a quartet of stubby armlike appendages, two on each side. These ended in snapping pincers. She shrieked and thrust the torch back at it, and the thing retreated with another deafening roar.

"Did your mother never teach you that it's wrong to tease the animals?" Roland asked her, and his tone was so dry she couldn't tell if he was kidding her or not.

Five minutes after that they were out.

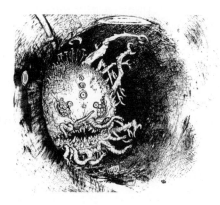

Chapter II:
On Badlands Avenue

They exited through a crumbling hillside arch beside a Quonset hut similar in shape but much smaller than the Arc 16 Experimental Station. The roof of this little building was covered with rust. There were piles of bones scattered around the front in a rough ring. The surrounding rocks had been blackened and splintered in places; one boulder the size of the Queen Anne house where the Breakers had been kept was split in two, revealing an interior filled with sparkling minerals. The air was cold and they could hear the restless whine of the wind, but the rocks blocked the worst of it and they turned their faces up to the sharp blue sky with wordless gratitude.

"There was some kind of battle here, wasn't there?" she asked.

"Yes, I'd say so. A big one, long ago." He sounded utterly whipped.

A sign lay facedown on the ground in front of the Quonset's half-open door. Susannah insisted that he put her down so she could turn it over and read it. Roland did as she asked and then sat with his back propped against a rock, staring at Castle Discordia, which was now behind them. Two towers jutted into the blue, one whole and the other shattered off near what he judged had been the top. He concentrated on getting his breath back. The ground under him was very cold, and he knew already that their trek through the Badlands was going to be difficult.

Susannah, meanwhile, had lifted the sign. She held it with one hand and wiped off an ancient scrum of dirt with the other. The words she uncovered were in English, and gave her a deep chill:

THIS CHECKPOINT IS CLOSED.
FOR-EVER.

Below it, in red, seeming to glare at her, was the Eye of the King.

TWO

There was nothing in the Quonset's main room but jumbles of equipment that had been blasted to ruin and more skeletons, none whole. In the adjoining storeroom, however, she found delightful surprises: shelves and shelves of canned food—more than they could possibly carry—and also more Sterno. (She did not think Roland would sneer at the idea of canned heat anymore, and she was right.) She poked her head out of the storeroom's rear door almost as an afterthought, not expecting to find anything except maybe a few more skeletons, and there *was* one. The prize was the vehicle in which this loose agglomeration of bones was resting: a dogcart a bit like the one she'd found herself sitting in atop the castle, during her palaver with Mia. This one was both smaller and in much better shape. Instead of wood, the wheels were metal coated with thin rinds of some synthetic stuff. Pull-handles jutted from the sides, and she realized it wasn't a dogcart at all, but a kind of rickshaw.

Git ready to pull yo sweetie, graymeat!

This was a typically nasty Detta Walker thought, but it surprised a laugh out of her, all the same.

"What have you found that's amusing?" Roland called.

"You'll see," she called back, straining to keep Detta out of her voice, at least. In this she did not entirely succeed. "You gonna see soon enough, sho."

THREE

There was a small motor at the rear of the rickshaw, but both saw at a glance it had been ages since it had run. In the storeroom Roland found a few simple tools, including an adjustable wrench. It was frozen with its jaw open, but an application of oil (in what was to Susannah a very familiar red-and-black 3-In-1 can) got it working again. Roland used the wrench to unbolt the motor from its mounts and then tumbled it off the side. While he worked and Susannah did what Daddy Mose would have called the heavy looking-on, Oy sat forty paces outside the arch through which they had exited, clearly on guard against the thing that had followed them in the dark.

"No more than fifteen pounds," Roland said, wiping his hands on his jeans and looking at the tumbled motor, "but I reckon I'll be glad we got rid of it by the time we're done with this thing."

"When do we start?" she asked.

"As soon as we've loaded as much canned stuff into the back as I think I can carry," he said, and fetched a heavy sigh. His face was pale and stubbly. There were dark circles beneath his eyes, new lines carving his cheeks and descending to his jaw from the corners of his mouth. He looked as thin as a whip.

"Roland, you can't! Not so soon! You're done up!"

He gestured at Oy, sitting so patiently, and at the maw of darkness forty paces beyond him. "Do you want to be this close to that hole when dark comes?"

"We can build a fire—"

"It may have friends," he said, "that aren't shy of fire. While we were in yonder shaft, that thing wouldn't have wanted to share us because it didn't think it *had* to share. Now it might not care, especially if it's vengeance-minded."

"A thing like that can't think. Surely not." This was easier to believe now that they were out. But she knew she might change her mind once the shadows began to grow long and pool together.

"I don't think it's a chance we can afford to take," Roland said.

She decided, very reluctantly, that he was right.

FOUR

Luckily for them, this first stretch of the narrow path winding into the Badlands was mostly level, and when they *did* come to an uphill stretch, Roland made no objection to Susannah's getting out and hopping gamely along behind what she had dubbed Ho Fat's Luxury Taxi until they reached the crest of the hill. Little by little, Castle Discordia fell behind them. Roland kept going after the rocks had blocked the blasted tower from their view, but when the other one was gone as well, he pointed to a stony bower beside the path and said, "That's where we'll camp tonight, unless you have objections."

She had none. They'd brought along enough bones and khaki rags to make a fire, but Susannah knew the fuel wouldn't last long. The bits of cloth would burn as rapidly as newspaper and the bones would be gone before the hands of Roland's fancy new watch (which he had shown her with something like reverence) stood together at midnight. And tomorrow night there would likely be no fire at all and cold food eaten directly from the cans. She was aware that things could have been ever so much worse—she put the daytime temperature at forty-five degrees, give or take, and they *did* have food—but she would have given a great deal for a sweater; even more for a pair of longjohns.

"Probably we'll find more stuff we can use for fuel as we go along," she said hopefully once the fire was lit (the burning bones gave off a nasty smell, and they were careful to sit downwind). "Weeds . . . bushes . . . more bones . . . maybe even deadwood."

"I don't think so," he said. "Not on this side of the Crimson King's castle. Not even devilgrass, which grows damned near anywhere in Mid-World."

"You don't know that. Not for sure." She couldn't bear

thinking about days and days of unvarying chill, with the two of them dressed for nothing more challenging than a spring day in Central Park.

"I think he murdered this land when he darkened Thunderclap," Roland mused. "It probably wasn't much of a shake to begin with, and it's sterile now. But count your blessings." He reached over and touched a pimple that had popped out of her skin beside her full lower lip. "A hundred years ago this might have darkened and spread and eaten your skin right off your bones. Gotten into your brain and run you mad before you died."

"Cancer? Radiation?"

Roland shrugged as if to say it didn't matter. "Somewhere beyond the Crimson King's castle we may come to grasslands and even forests again, but the grass will likely be buried under snow when we get there, for the season's wrong. I can feel it in the air, see it in the way the day's darkening so quickly."

She groaned, striving for comic effect, but what came out was a sound of fear and weariness so real that it frightened her. Oy pricked up his ears and looked around at them. "Why don't you cheer me up a little, Roland?"

"You need to know the truth," he said. "We can get on as we are for a good long while, Susannah, but it isn't going to be pleasant. We have food enough in yonder cart to keep us for a month or more, if we stretch it out . . . and we will. When we come again to land that's alive, we'll find animals even if there *is* snow. And that's what I want. Not because we'll be hungry for fresh meat by then, although we will be, but because we'll need the hides. I hope we won't need them desperately, that it won't be that near a thing, but—"

"But you're afraid it will."

"Yes," he said. "I'm afraid it will. For over a long period of time there's little in life so disheartening as constant cold—not deep enough to kill, mayhap, but always there, stealing your energy and your will and your body-fat, an ounce at a time. I'm afraid we're in for a very hard stretch. You'll see."

She did.

FIVE

There's little in life that's so disheartening as constant cold.

The days weren't so bad. They were on the move, at least, exercising and keeping their blood up. Yet even during the days she began to dread the open areas they sometimes came to, where the wind howled across miles of broken bushless rock and between the occasional butte or mesa. These stuck up into the unvarying blue sky like the red fingers of otherwise buried stone giants. The wind seemed to grow ever sharper as they trudged below the milky swirls of cloud moving along the Path of the Beam. She would hold her chapped hands up to shield her face from it, hating the way her fingers would never go completely numb but instead turned into dazed things full of buried buzzings. Her eyes would well up with water, and then the tears would gush down her cheeks. These tear-tracks never froze; the cold wasn't that bad. It was just deep enough to make their lives a slowly escalating misery. For what pittance would she have sold her immortal soul during those unpleasant days and horrible nights? Sometimes she thought a single sweater would have purchased it; at other times she thought *No, honey, you got too much self-respect, even now. Would you be willing to spend an eternity in hell— or maybe in the todash darkness—for a single sweater? Surely not!*

Well, *maybe* not. But if the devil tempting her were to throw in a pair of earmuffs—

And it would have taken so little, really, to make them comfortable. She thought of this constantly. They had the food, and they had water, too, because at fifteen-mile intervals along the path they came to pumps that still worked, pulling great cold gushes of mineral-tasting water from deep under the Badlands.

Badlands. She had hours and days and, ultimately, weeks to meditate on that word. What made lands bad? Poisoned water? The water out here wasn't sweet, not by any means, but it wasn't poisoned, either. Lack of food? They had food, although she guessed it might become a problem later on, if they didn't find more. In the meantime she was getting almighty tired of corned beef hash, not to mention raisins for breakfast and raisins if you wanted dessert. Yet it was food. Body-gasoline. What made the Badlands bad when you had food and water? Watching the sky turn first gold and then russet in the west; watching it turn purple and then starshot black in the east. She watched the days end with increasing dread: the thought of another endless night, the three of them huddled together while the wind whined and twined its way through the rocks and the stars glared down. Endless stretches of cold purgatory while your feet and fingers buzzed and you thought *If I only had a sweater and a pair of gloves, I could be comfortable. That's all it would take, just a sweater and a pair of gloves. Because it's really not that cold.*

Exactly how cold *did* it get after sundown? Never below thirty-two degrees Fahrenheit, she knew, because the water she put out for Oy never froze solid. She guessed that the temperature dropped to around forty in the hours between midnight and dawn; on a couple of nights it might have fallen into the thirties, because she saw tiny spicules of ice around the edge of the pot that served Oy as a dish.

She began to eye his fur coat. At first she told herself this was nothing but a speculative exercise, a way of passing the time — exactly how hot did the bumbler's metabolism run, and exactly how warm did that coat (that thick, *luxuriantly* thick, that *amazingly* thick coat) keep him? Little by little she recognized her feelings for what they were: jealousy that muttered in Detta's voice. *L'il buggah doan feel no pain after the sun go down, do he? No, not him! You reckon you could git two sets o' mittens outta that hide?*

She would thrust these thoughts away, miserable and horrified, wondering if there was any lower limit to the human spirit at its nasty, calculating, self-serving worst, not wanting to know.

Deeper and deeper that cold worked into them, day by day and night by night. It was like a splinter. They would sleep huddled together with Oy between them, then turn so the sides of them that had been facing the night were turned inward again. Real restorative sleep never lasted long, no matter how tired they were. When the moon began to wax, brightening the dark, they spent two weeks walking at night and sleeping in the day-time. That was a little better.

The only wildlife they saw were large black birds either fly-ing against the southeastern horizon or gathered in a sort of convention atop the mesas. If the wind was right, Roland and Susannah could hear their shrill, gabby conversation.

"You think those things'd be any good to eat?" Susannah asked the gunslinger once. The moon was almost gone and they had reverted to traveling during the daytime so they could see any potential hazards (on several occasions deep crevasses had crossed the path, and once they came upon a sinkhole that appeared to be bottomless).

"What do *you* think?" Roland asked her.

"Prob'ly not, but I wouldn't mind tryin one and finding out." She paused. "What do you reckon they live on?"

Roland only shook his head. Here the path wound through a fantastic petrified garden of needle-sharp rock formations. Further off, a hundred or more black, crowlike birds either cir-cled a flat-topped mesa or sat on its edge looking in Roland and Susannah's direction, like a beady-eyed panel of jurors.

"Maybe we ought to make a detour," she said. "See if we can't find out."

"If we lost the path, we might not be able to find it again," Roland said.

"That's bullshit! Oy would—"

"Susannah, I don't want to hear any more about it!" He spoke in a sharply angry tone she had never heard before. Angry, yes, she had heard Roland angry many times. But there was a pettiness in this, a sulkiness that worried her. And fright-ened her a little, as well.

They went on in silence for the next half an hour, Roland pulling Ho Fat's Luxury Taxi and Susannah riding. Then the narrow path (Badlands Avenue, she'd come to call it) tilted upward and she hopped down, catching up with him and then going along beside. For such forays she'd torn his Old Home Days tee-shirt in half and wore it wrapped around her hands. It protected her from sharp stones, and also warmed her fingers, at least a little.

He glanced down at her, then back at the path ahead. His lower lip was stuck out a bit and Susannah thought that surely he couldn't know how absurdly willful that expression was—like a three-year-old who has been denied a trip to the beach. He couldn't know and she wouldn't tell him. Later, maybe, when they could look back on this nightmare and laugh. When they could no longer remember what, exactly, was so terrible about a night when the temperature was forty-one degrees and you lay awake, shivering on the cold ground, watching the occasional meteor scrape cold fire across the sky, thinking *Just a sweater, that's all I need. Just a sweater and I'd go along as happy as a parakeet at feeding time.* And wondering if there was enough hide on Oy to make them each a pair of underdrawers and if killing him might not actually be doing the poor little beastie a favor; he'd just been so *sad* since Jake passed into the clearing.

"Susannah," Roland said. "I was sharp with you just now, and I cry your pardon."

"There's no need," she said.

"I think there is. We've enough problems without making problems between us. Without making resentments between us."

She was quiet. Looking up at him as he looked off into the southeast, at the circling birds.

"Those rooks," he said.

She was quiet, waiting.

"In my childhood, we sometimes called them Gan's Blackbirds. I told you and Eddie about how my friend Cuthbert and I spread bread for the birds after the cook was hanged, didn't I?"

"Yes."

"They were birds exactly like those, named Castle Rooks by some. Never Royal Rooks, though, for they were scavenger birds. You asked what yonder rooks live on. Could be they're scavenging in the yards and streets of *his* castle, now that he's departed."

"Le Casse Roi Russe, or Roi Rouge, or whatever you call it."

"Aye. I don't say for sure, but . . ."

Roland didn't finish and didn't need to. After that she kept an eye on the birds, and yes, they seemed to be both coming and going from the southeast. The birds might mean that they were making progress after all. It wasn't much, but enough to buoy her spirits for the rest of that day and deep into another shivering rotten-cold night.

SIX

The following morning, as they were eating another cold breakfast in another fireless camp (Roland had promised that tonight they would use some of the Sterno and have food that was at least warm), Susannah asked if she could look at the watch he had been given by the Tet Corporation. Roland passed it over to her willingly enough. She looked long at the three siguls cut into the cover, especially the Tower with its ascending spiral of windows. Then she opened it and looked inside. Without looking up at Roland she said, "Tell me again what they said to you."

"They were passing on what one of their good-minds told them. An especially talented one, by their accounts, although I don't remember his name. According to him, the watch may stop when we near the Dark Tower, or even begin to run backward."

"Hard to imagine a Patek Philippe running backward," she said. "According to this, it's eight-sixteen AM or PM back in New York. Here it looks about six-thirty AM, but I don't guess that means much, one way or the other. How're we supposed to know if this baby is running fast or slow?"

Roland had stopped storing goods in his gunna and was considering her question. "Do you see the tiny hand at the bottom? The one that runs all by himself?"

"The second-hand, yes."

"Tell me when he's straight up."

She looked at the second-hand racing around in its own circle, and when it was in the noon position, she said, "Right now."

Roland was hunkered down, a position he could accomplish easily now that the pain in his hip was gone. He closed his eyes and wrapped his arms around his knees. Each breath he exhaled emerged in a thin mist. Susannah tried not to look at this; it was as if the hated cold had actually grown strong enough to appear before them, still ghostlike but visible.

"Roland, what're you d—"

He raised a hand to her, palm out, not opening his eyes, and she hushed.

The second-hand hurried around its circle, first dipping down, then rising until it was straight up again. And when it had arrived there—

Roland opened his eyes and said, "That's a minute. A *true* minute, as I live beneath the Beam."

Her mouth dropped open. "How in the name of heaven did you do that?"

Roland shook his head. He didn't know. He only knew that Cort had told them they must always be able to keep time in their heads, because you couldn't depend on watches, and a sundial was no good on a cloudy day. Or at midnight, for that matter. One summer he had sent them out into the Baby Forest west of the castle night after uncomfortable night (and it was scary out there, too, at least when one was on one's own, although of course none of them would ever have said so out loud, even to each other), until they could come back to the yard behind the Great Hall at the very minute Cort had specified. It was strange how that clock-in-the-head thing worked. The thing was, at first it didn't. And didn't. And didn't. Down would come Cort's callused hand, down it would come a-clout, and Cort would growl *Arr, maggot, back to the woods tomorrow night! You must like it out there!* But once that headclock started ticking, it always seemed to run true. For awhile Roland had lost it, just as the world had lost its points of the compass, but now it was back and that cheered him greatly.

"Did you count the minute?" she asked. "Mississippi-one, Mississippi-two, like that?"

He shook his head. "I just know. When a minute's up, or an hour."

"Bol-she-*vecky!*" she scoffed. "You guessed!"

"If I'd guessed, would I have spoken after exactly one revolution of the hand?"

"You mought got lucky," Detta said, and eyed him shrewdly with one eye mostly closed, an expression Roland detested. (But never said so; that would only cause Detta to goad him with it on those occasions when she peeked out.)

"Do you want to try it again?" he asked.

"No," Susannah said, and sighed. "I take your word for it that your watch is keeping perfect time. And that means we're not close to the Dark Tower. Not yet."

"Perhaps not close enough to affect the watch, but closer than I've ever been," Roland said quietly. "Comparatively speaking, we're now almost in its shadow. Believe me, Susannah—I know."

"But—"

From over their heads came a cawing that was both harsh and oddly muffled: *Croo, croo!* instead of *Caw, caw!* Susannah looked up and saw one of the huge blackbirds—the sort Roland had called Castle Rooks—flying overhead low enough so that they could hear the labored strokes of its wings. Dangling from its long hooked bill was a limp strand of something yellowy-green. To Susannah it looked like a piece of dead seaweed. Only not *entirely* dead.

She turned to Roland, looked at him with excited eyes.

He nodded. "Devilgrass. Probably bringing it back to feather his mate's nest. Certainly not for the babies to eat. Not *that* stuff. But devilgrass always goes last when you're walking into the Nowhere Lands, and always shows up first when you're walking back out of them, as we are. As we finally are. Now listen to me, Susannah, I'd have you listen, and I'd have you push that tiresome bitch Detta as far back as possible. Nor would I have you waste my time by telling me she's not there when I can see her dancing the commala in your eyes."

Susannah looked surprised, then piqued, as if she would protest. Then she looked away without saying anything. When she looked back at him again, she could no longer feel the presence of the one Roland had called "that tiresome bitch." And Roland must no longer have detected her presence, because he went on.

"I think it will soon look like we're coming out of the Badlands, but you'd do well not to trust what you see—a few buildings and maybe a little paving on the roads doesn't make for safety or civilization. And before too long we're going to come to his castle, Le Casse Roi Russe. The Crimson King is almost certainly gone from there, but he may have left a trap for us. I want you to look and listen. If there's talking to be done, I want you to let me do it."

"What do you know that I don't?" she asked. "What are you holding back?"

"Nothing," he said (with what was, for him, a rare earnestness). "It's only a feeling, Susannah. We're close to our goal now, no matter what the watch may say. Close to winning our way to the Dark Tower. But my teacher, Vannay, used to say that there's just one rule with no exceptions: *before victory comes temptation.* And the greater the victory to win, the greater the temptation to withstand."

Susannah shivered and put her arms around herself. "All I want is to be warm," she said. "If nobody offers me a big load of firewood and a flannel union suit to cry off the Tower, I guess we'll be all right awhile longer."

Roland remembered one of Cort's most serious maxims— *Never speak the worst aloud!*—but kept his own mouth shut, at least on that subject. He put his watch away carefully and then rose, ready to move on.

But Susannah paused a moment longer. "I've dreamed of the other one," she said. There was no need for her to say of whom she was speaking. "Three nights in a row, scuttering along our backtrail. Do you think he's really there?"

"Oh yes," Roland said. "And I think he's got an empty belly."

"Hungry, Mordred's a-hungry," she said, for she had also heard these words in her dream.

Susannah shivered again.

SEVEN

The path they walked widened, and that afternoon the first scabby plates of pavement began to show on its surface. It widened further still, and not long before dark they came to a place where another path (which had surely been a road in the long-ago) joined it. Here stood a rusty rod that had probably supported a street-sign, although there was nothing atop it now. The next day they came to the first building on this side of Fedic, a slumped wreck with an overturned sign on the remains of the porch. There was a flattened barn out back. With Roland's help Susannah turned the sign over, and they could make out one word: **LIVERY**. Below it was the red eye they had come to know so well.

"I think the track we've been following was once a coach-road between Castle Discordia and the Le Casse Roi Russe," he said. "It makes sense."

They began to pass more buildings, more intersecting roads. It was the outskirts of a town or village—perhaps even a city that had once spread around the Crimson King's castle. But unlike Lud, there was very little of it left. Sprigs of devilgrass grew in list-less clumps around the remains of some of the buildings, but nothing else alive. And the cold clamped down harder than ever. On their fourth night after seeing the rooks, they tried camping in the remains of a building that was still standing, but both of them heard whispering voices in the shadows. Roland identified these—with a matter-of-factness Susannah found eerie—as the voices of ghosts of what he called "housies," and suggested they move back out into the street.

"I don't believe they could do harm to us, but they might hurt the little fellow," Roland said, and stroked Oy, who had crept into his lap with a timidity very unlike his usual manner.

Susannah was more than willing to retreat. The building in which they had tried to camp had a chill that she thought was worse than physical cold. The things they had heard whispering in there might be old, but she thought they were still hungry.

And so the three of them huddled together once more for warmth in the middle of Badlands Avenue, beside Ho Fat's Luxury Taxi, and waited for dawn to raise the temperature a few degrees. They tried making a fire from the boards of one of the collapsed buildings, but all they succeeded in doing was wasting a double handful of Sterno. The jelly guttered along the splintered pieces of a broken chair they had used for kindling, then went out. The wood simply refused to burn.

"Why?" Susannah asked as she watched the last few wisps of smoke dissipate. *"Why?"*

"Are you surprised, Susannah of New York?"

"No, but I want to know why. Is it too old? Petrified, or something?"

"It won't burn because it hates us," Roland said, as if this should have been obvious to her. "This is *his* place, still his even though he's moved on. Everything here hates us. But . . . listen, Susannah. Now that we're on an actual road, still more paved than not, what do you say to walking at night again? Will you try it?"

"Sure," she said. "Anything's got to be better than lying out on the tarvy and shivering like a kitten that just got a ducking in a waterbarrel."

So that was what they did—the rest of that first night, all the next, and the two after that. She kept thinking, *I'm gonna get sick, I can't go on like this without coming down with something,* but she didn't. Neither of them did. There was just that pimple to the left of her lower lip, which sometimes popped its top and trickled a little flow of blood before clotting and scabbing over again. Their only sickness was the constant cold, eating deeper and deeper into the center of them. The moon had begun to fatten once more, and one night she realized that they had been trekking southeast from Fedic nearly a month.

Slowly, a deserted village replaced the fantastic needle-gardens of rock, but Susannah had taken what Roland had said to heart: they were still in the Badlands, and although they could now read the occasional sign which proclaimed this to be THE KING'S WAY (with the eye, of course; always there was the red eye), she understood they were really still on Badlands Avenue.

It was a weirding village, and she could not begin to imagine what species of freakish people might once have lived here. The sidestreets were cobbled. The cottages were narrow and steep-roofed, the doorways thin and abnormally high, as if made for the sort of narrow folk seen in the distorted curves of funhouse mirrors. They were Lovecraft houses, Clark Ashton Smith houses, William Hope Hodgson borderlands houses, all crammed together under a Lee Brown Coye sickle moon, the houses all a-tilt and a-lean on the hills that grew up gradually around the way they walked. Here and there one had collapsed, and there was an unpleasantly *organic* look to these ruins, as if they were torn and rotted flesh instead of ancient boards and glass. Again and again she caught herself seeing dead faces peering at her from some configuration of boards and shadow, faces that seemed to rotate in the rubble and follow their course with terrible zombie eyes. They made her think of the Door-keeper on Dutch Hill, and that made her shiver.

On their fourth night on The King's Way, they came to a major intersection where the main road made a crooked turn, bending more south than east and thus off the Path of the Beam. Ahead, less than a night's walk (or ride, if one happened to be aboard Ho Fat's Luxury Taxi), was a high hill with an enormous black castle dug into it. In the chancy moonlight it had a vaguely Oriental look to Susannah. The towers bulged at the tops, as if wishing they could be minarets. Fantastic walkways flew between them, crisscrossing above the courtyard in front of the castle proper. Some of these walkways had fallen to ruin, but most still held. She could also hear a vast, low rumbling sound. Not machinery. She asked Roland about it.

"Water," he said.

"What water? Do you have any idea?"

He shook his head. "But I'd not drink what flowed close to that castle, even were I dying of thirst."

"This place is bad," she muttered, meaning not just the castle but the nameless village of leaning

(*leering*)

houses that had grown up all around it. "And Roland—it's not empty."

"Susannah, if thee feels spirits knocking for entrance into thy head—knocking or gnawing—then bid them away."

"Will that work?"

"I'm not sure it will," he admitted, "but I've heard that such things must be granted entry, and that they're wily at gaining it by trick and by ruse."

She had read *Dracula* as well as heard Pere Callahan's story of Jerusalem's Lot, and understood what Roland meant all too well.

He took her gently by the shoulders and turned her away from the castle—which might not be naturally black after all, she had decided, but only tarnished by the years. Daylight would tell. For the present their way was lit by a cloud-scummed quarter-moon.

Several other roads led away from the place where they had stopped, most as crooked as broken fingers. The one Roland wanted her to look upon was straight, however, and Susannah realized it was the only *completely* straight street she had seen since the deserted village began to grow silently up around their way. It was smoothly paved rather than cobbled and pointed southeast, along the Path of the Beam. Above it flowed the moon-gilded clouds like boats in a procession.

"Does thee glimpse a darkish blur at the horizon, dear?" he murmured.

"Yes. A dark blur and a whitish band in front of it. What is it? Do you know?"

"I have an idea, but I'm not sure," Roland said. "Let's have us a rest here. Dawn's not far off, and then we'll both see. And besides, I don't want to approach yonder castle at night."

"If the Crimson King's gone, and if the Path of the Beam lies that way—" She pointed. "Why do we need to go to his damn old castle at all?"

"To make sure he *is* gone, for one thing," Roland said. "And we may be able to trap the one behind us. I doubt it—he's wily—but there's a chance. He's also young, and the young are sometimes careless."

"You'd kill him?"

Roland's smile was wintry in the moonlight. Merciless. "Without a moment's hesitation," said he.

EIGHT

In the morning Susannah woke from an uncomfortable doze amid the scattered supplies in the back of the rickshaw and saw Roland standing in the intersection and looking along the Path of the Beam. She got down, moving with great care because she was stiff and didn't want to fall. She imagined her bones cold and brittle inside her flesh, ready to shatter like glass.

"What do you see?" he asked her. "Now that it's light, what do you see over that way?"

The whitish band was snow, which did not surprise her given the fact that those were true uplands. What did surprise her—and gladdened her heart more than she would have believed possible—were the trees beyond the band of snow. Green fir-trees. *Living things.*

"Oh, Roland, they look lovely!" she said. "Even with their feet in the snow, they look lovely! Don't they?"

"Yes," he said. He lifted her high and turned her back the way they had come. Beyond the nasty crowding suburb of dead houses she could see some of the Badlands they'd come through, all those crowding spines of rock broken by the occasional butte or mesa.

"Think of this," he said. "Back yonder as you look is Fedic. Beyond Fedic, Thunderclap. Beyond Thunderclap, the Callas and the forest that marks the borderland between Mid-World and End-World. Lud is further back that way, and River Crossing further still; the Western Sea and the great Mohaine Desert, too. Somewhere back there, lost in the leagues and lost in time as well is what remains of In-World. The Baronies. Gilead. Places where even now there are people who remember love and light."

"Yes," she said, not understanding.

"That was the way the Crimson King turned to cast his petulance," Roland said. "*He* meant to go the other way, ye must ken, to the Dark Tower, and even in his madness he knew better than to kill the land he must pass through, he and whatever band of followers he took with him." He drew her toward him and kissed her forehead with a tenderness that made her feel like crying. "We three will visit his castle, and trap Mordred there if our fortune is good and his is ill. Then we'll go on, and back into living lands. There'll be wood for fires and game to provide fresh food and hides to wrap around us. Can you go on a little longer, dear? Can *thee?*"

"Yes," she said. "Thank you, Roland."

She hugged him, and as she did, she looked toward the red castle. In the growing light she could see that the stone of which it had been made, although darkened by the years, had once been the color of spilled blood. This called forth a memory of her palaver with Mia on the Castle Discordia allure, a memory of steadily pulsing crimson light in the distance. Almost from where they now were, in fact.

Come to me now, if you'd come at all, Susannah, Mia had told her. *For the King can fascinate, even at a distance.*

It was that pulsing red glow of which she had been speaking, but—

"It's gone!" she said to Roland. "The red light from the castle—Forge of the King, she called it! It's gone! *We haven't seen it once in all this time!*"

"No," he said, and this time his smile was warmer. "I believe it must have stopped at the same time we ended the Breakers' work. The Forge of the King has gone out, Susannah. Forever, if the gods are good. That much we have done, although it has cost us much."

That afternoon they came to Le Casse Roi Russe, which turned out not to be entirely deserted, after all.

CHAPTER III:
THE CASTLE OF THE CRIMSON KING

ONE

They were a mile from the castle and the roar of the unseen river had become very loud when bunting and posters began to appear. The bunting consisted of red, white, and blue swags—the kind Susannah associated with Memorial Day parades and small-town Main Streets on the Fourth of July. On the façades of these narrow, secretive houses and the fronts of shops long closed and emptied from basement to attic, such decoration looked like rouge on the cheeks of a decaying corpse.

The faces on the posters were all too familiar to her. Richard Nixon and Henry Cabot Lodge flashed V's-for-victory and car-salesmen grins (NIXON/LODGE, BECAUSE THE WORK'S NOT DONE, these read). John Kennedy and Lyndon Johnson stood with their arms around each other and their free hands raised. Below their feet was the bold proclamation WE STAND ON THE EDGE OF A NEW FRONTIER.

"Any idea who won?" Roland asked over his shoulder. Susannah was currently riding in Ho Fat's Luxury Taxi, taking in the sights (and wishing for a sweater: even a light cardigan would do her just fine, by God).

"Oh, yes," she said. There was no doubt in her mind that these posters had been mounted for her benefit. "Kennedy did."

"He became your dinh?"

"Dinh of the entire United States. And Johnson got the job when Kennedy was gunned down."

"Shot? Do you say so?" Roland was interested.

"Aye. Shot from hiding by a coward named Oswald."

"And your United States was the most powerful country in the world."

597

"Well, Russia was giving us a run for our money when you grabbed me by the collar and yanked me into Mid-World, but yes, basically."

"And the folk of your country choose their dinh for themselves. It's not done on account of fathership."

"That's right," she said, a little warily. She half-expected Roland to blast the democratic system. Or laugh at it.

Instead he surprised her by saying, "To quote Blaine the Mono, that sounds pretty swell."

"Do me a favor and don't quote him, Roland. Not now, not ever. Okay?"

"As you like," he said, then went on without a pause, but in a much lower voice. "Keep my gun ready, may it do ya."

"Does me fine," she agreed at once, and in the same low voice. It came out *Does 'ee 'ine*, because she didn't even want to move her lips. She could feel that they were now being watched from within the buildings that crowded this end of The King's Way like shops and inns in a medieval village (or a movie set of one). She didn't know if they were humans, robots, or maybe just still-operating TV cameras, but she hadn't mistrusted the feeling even before Roland spoke up and confirmed it. And she only had to look at Oy's head, tick-tocking back and forth like the pendulum in a grandfather clock, to know he felt it, too.

"And was he a good dinh, this Kennedy?" Roland asked, resuming his normal voice. It carried well in the silence. Susannah realized a rather lovely thing: for once she wasn't cold, even though this close to the roaring river the air was dank as well as chill. She was too focused on the world around her to be cold. At least for the present.

"Well, not everyone thought so, certainly the nut who shot him didn't, but I did," she said. "He told folks when he was running that he meant to change things. Probably less than half the voters thought he meant it, because most politicians lie for the same reason a monkey swings by his tail, which is to say because he can. But once he was elected, he started in doin the things he'd promised to do. There was a showdown over a place called Cuba, and he was just as brave as . . . well, let's just say you would have been pleased to ride with him. When some folks saw just how serious he was, the motherfucks hired the nut to shoot him."

"Oz-walt."

She nodded, not bothering to correct him, thinking that there was nothing to correct, really. *Oz-walt. Oz.* It all came around again, didn't it?

"And Johnson took over when Kennedy fell."

"Yep."

"How did *he* do?"

"Was too early to tell when I left, but he was more the kind of fella used to playing the game. 'Go along to get along,' we used to say. Do you ken it?"

"Yes, indeed," he said. "And Susannah, I think we've arrived." Roland brought Ho Fat's Luxury Taxi to a stop. He stood with the handles wrapped in his fists, looking at Le Casse Roi Russe.

TWO

Here The King's Way ended, spilling into a wide cobbled fore-court that had once no doubt been guarded as assiduously by the Crimson King's men as Buckingham Palace was by the Beefeaters of Queen Elizabeth. An eye that had faded only slightly over the years was painted on the cobbles in scarlet. From ground-level, one could only assume what it was, but from the upper levels of the castle itself, Susannah guessed, the eye would dominate the view to the northwest.

Same damn thing's probably painted at every other point of the compass, too, she thought.

Above this outer courtyard, stretched between two deserted guard-towers, was a banner that looked freshly painted. Stenciled upon it (also in red, white, and blue) was this:

WELCOME, ROLAND AND SUSANNAH!
(OY, TOO!)
KEEP ON ROCKIN' IN THE FREE WORLD!

The castle beyond the inner courtyard (and the caged river which here served as a moat) was indeed of dark red stone blocks that had darkened to near-black over the years. Towers and turrets burst upward from the castle proper, swelling in a way that hurt the eye and seemed to defy gravity. The castle within these gaudy brackets was sober and undecorated except for the staring eye carved into the keystone arch above the main entrance. Two of the overhead walkways had fallen, littering the main courtyard with shattered chunks of stone, but six others remained in place, crisscrossing at different levels in a way that made her think of turnpike entrances and exits where a number of major highways met. As with the houses, the doors and windows were oddly narrow. Fat black rooks were perched on the sills of the windows and lined up along the overhead walkways, peering at them.

Susannah swung down from the rickshaw with Roland's gun stuffed into her belt, within easy reach. She joined him, looking at the main gate on this side of the moat. It stood open. Beyond it, a humped stone bridge spanned the river. Beneath the bridge, dark water rushed through a stone throat forty feet wide. The water smelled harsh and unpleasant, and where it flowed around a number of fangy black rocks, the foam was yellow instead of white.

"What do we do now?" she asked.

"Listen to those fellows, for a start," he said, and nodded toward the main doors on the far side of the castle's cobbled forecourt. The portals were ajar and through them now came two men—perfectly ordinary men, not narrow funhouse fellows, as she had rather expected. When they were halfway across the forecourt, a third slipped out and scurried along after. None appeared to be armed, and as the two in front approached the bridge, she was not exactly flabbergasted to see they were identical twins. And the one behind looked the same: Caucasian, fairly tall, long black hair. Triplets, then: two to meet, and one for good luck. They were wearing jeans and heavy pea-coats of which she was instantly (and achingly) jealous. The two in front carried large wicker baskets by leather handles.

"Put spectacles and beards on them, and they'd look exactly like Stephen King as he was when Eddie and I first met him," Roland said in a low voice.

"Really? Say true?"

"Yes. Do you remember what I told you?"

"Let you do the talking."

"And before victory comes temptation. Remember that, too."

"I will. Roland, are you afraid of em?"

"I think there's little to fear from those three. But be ready to shoot."

"They don't look armed." Of course there were those wicker baskets; anything might be in those.

"All the same, be ready."

"Count on it," said she.

THREE

Even with the roar of the river rushing beneath the bridge, they could hear the steady tock-tock of the strangers' bootheels. The two with the baskets advanced halfway across the bridge and stopped at its highest point. Here they put down their burdens side by side. The third man stopped on the castle side and stood with his empty hands clasped decorously before him. Now Susannah could smell the cooked meat that was undoubtedly in one of the boxes. Not long pork, either. Roast beef and chicken all mingled was what it smelled like to her, an aroma that was heaven-sent. Her mouth began to water.

"Hile, Roland of Gilead!" said the dark-haired man on their right. "Hile, Susannah of New York! Hile, Oy of Mid-World! Long days and pleasant nights!"

"One's ugly and the others are worse," his companion remarked.

"Don't mind him," said the righthand Stephen King look-alike.

"'Don't mind him,'" mocked the other, screwing his face up in a grimace so purposefully ugly that it was funny.

"May you have twice the number," Roland said, responding to the more polite of the two. He cocked his heel and made a perfunctory bow over his outstretched leg. Susannah curtsied in the Calla fashion, spreading imaginary skirts. Oy sat by Roland's left foot, only looking at the two identical men on the bridge.

"We are uffis," said the man on the right. "Do you ken uffis, Roland?"

"Yes," he said, and then, in an aside to Susannah: "It's an old word . . . ancient, in fact. He claims they're shape-changers." To this he added in a much lower voice that could surely not be heard over the roar of the river: "I doubt it's true."

"Yet it is," said the one on the right, pleasantly enough.

"Liars see their own kind everywhere," observed the one on the left, and rolled a cynical blue eye. Just one. Susannah didn't believe she had ever seen a person roll just one eye before.

The one behind said nothing, only continued to stand and watch with his hands clasped before him.

"We can take any shape we like," continued the one on the right, "but our orders were to assume that of someone you'd recognize and trust."

"I'd not trust sai King much further than I could throw his heaviest grandfather," Roland remarked. "As troublesome as a trousers-eating goat, that one."

"We did the best we could," said the righthand Stephen King. "We could have taken the shape of Eddie Dean, but felt that might be too painful to the lady."

"The 'lady' looks as if she'd be happy to fuck a rope, could she make it stand up between her thighs," remarked the left-hand Stephen King, and leered.

"Uncalled-for," said the one behind, he with his hands crossed in front of him. He spoke in the mild tones of a contest referee. Susannah almost expected him to sentence Badmouth King to five minutes in the penalty box. She wouldn't have minded, either, for hearing Badmouth King crack wise hurt her heart; it reminded her of Eddie.

Roland ignored all the byplay.

"Could the three of you take three different shapes?" he inquired of Goodmouth King. Susannah heard the gunslinger swallow quite audibly before asking this question, and knew she wasn't the only one struggling to keep from drooling over the smells from the food-basket. "Could one of you have been sai King, one sai Kennedy, and one sai Nixon, for instance?"

"A good question," said Goodmouth King on the right.

"A stupid question," said Badmouth King on the left. "Nothing at all to the point. Off we go into the wild blue yonder. Oh well, was there ever an action hero who was an intellectual?"

"Prince Hamlet of Denmark," said Referee King quietly from behind them. "But since he's the only one who comes immediately to mind, he may be no more than the exception that proves the rule."

Goodmouth and Badmouth both turned to look at him. When it was clear that he was done, they turned back to Roland and Susannah.

"Since we're actually one being," said Goodmouth, "and of fairly limited capabilities at that, the answer is no. We could all be Kennedy, or we could all be Nixon, but—"

" 'Jam yesterday, jam tomorrow, but never jam today,' " said Susannah. She had no idea why this had popped into her head (even less why she should have said it out loud), but Referee King said "Exactly!" and gave her a go-to-the-head-of-the-class nod.

"Move on, for your father's sake," said Badmouth King on the left. "I can barely look at these traitors to the Lord of the Red wi'out puking."

"Very well," said his partner. "Although calling them traitors seems rather unfair, at least if one adds ka to the equation. Since the names we give ourself would be unpronounceable to you—"

"Like Superman's rival, Mr. Mxyzptlk," said Badmouth.

"—you may as well use those Los' used. Him being the one you call the Crimson King. I'm ego, roughly speaking, and go by the name of Feemalo. This fellow beside me is Fumalo. He's our id."

"So the one behind you must be Fimalo," Susannah said, pronouncing it *Fie*-ma-lo. "What's he, your superego?"

"Oh brilliant!" Fumalo exclaimed. "I bet you can even say Freud so it doesn't rhyme with lewd!" He leaned forward and gave her his knowing leer. "But can you *spell* it, you shor'-leg New York blackbird?"

"Don't mind him," said Feemalo, "he's always been threatened by women."

"Are you Stephen King's ego, id, and superego?" Susannah asked.

"What a good question!" Feemalo said approvingly.

"What a *dumb* question!" Fumalo said, disapprovingly. "Did your parents have any kids that lived, Blackbird?"

"You don't want to start in playing the dozens with me," Susannah said, "I'll bring out Detta Walker and shut you down."

Referee King said, "I have nothing to do with sai King other than having appropriated some of his physical characteristics for a short time. And I understand that short time is really all the time you have. I have no particular love for your cause and no intention of going out of my way to help you—not *far* out of my way, at least—and yet I understand that you two are largely responsible for the departure of Los'. Since he kept me prisoner and treated me as little more than his court jester—or even his pet monkey—I'm not at all sorry to see him go. I'd help you if I can—a little, at least—but no, I won't go out of my way to do so. 'Let's get that up front,' as your late friend Eddie Dean might have said."

Susannah tried not to wince at this, but it hurt. It hurt.

As before, Feemalo and Fumalo had turned to look at Fimalo when he spoke. Now they turned back to Roland and Susannah.

"Honesty's the best policy," said Feemalo, with a pious look. "Cervantes."

"Liars prosper," said Fumalo, with a cynical grin. "Anonymous."

Feemalo said, "There were times when Los' would make us divide into six, or even seven, and for no other reason than because it *hurt.* Yet we could leave no more than anyone else in the castle could, for he'd set a dead-line around its walls."

"We thought he'd kill us all before he left," Fumalo said, and with none of his previous fuck-you cynicism. His face wore the long and introspective expression of one who looks back on a disaster perhaps averted by mere inches.

Feemalo: "He *did* kill a great many. Beheaded his Minister of State."

Fumalo: "Who had advanced syphilis and no more idea what was happening to him than a pig in a slaughterhouse chute, more's the pity."

Feemalo: "He lined up the kitchen staff and the women o' work—"

Fumalo: "All of whom had been very loyal to him, very loyal indeed—"

Feemalo: "And made them take poison as they stood in front of him. He could have killed them in their sleep if he'd wanted to—"

Fumalo: "And by no more than wishing it on them."

Feemalo: "But instead he made them take poison. *Rat* poison. They swallowed large brown chunks of it and died in convulsions right in front of him as he sat on his throne—"

Fumalo: "Which is made of skulls, do ye ken—"

Feemalo: "He sat there with his elbow on his knee and his fist on his chin, like a man thinking long thoughts, perhaps about squaring the circle or finding the Ultimate Prime Number, all the while watching them writhe and vomit and convulse on the floor of the Audience Chamber."

Fumalo (with a touch of eagerness Susannah found both prurient and *extremely* unattractive): "Some died begging for water. It was a *thirsty* poison, aye! And we thought *we* were next!"

At this Feemalo at last betrayed, if not anger, then a touch of pique. "Will you let me tell this and have done with it so they can go on or back as they please?"

"Bossy as ever," Fumalo said, and dropped into a sulky silence. Above them, the Castle Rooks jostled for position and looked down with beady eyes. *No doubt hoping to make a meal of those who don't walk away,* Susannah thought.

"He had six of the surviving Wizard's Glasses," Feemalo said. "And when you were still in Calla Bryn Sturgis, he saw something in them that finished the job of running him mad. We don't know for sure what it was, for we didn't see, but we have an idea it was your victory not just in the Calla but further on, at Algul Siento. If so, it meant the end of his scheme to bring down the Tower from afar, by breaking the Beams."

"Of course that's what it was," Fimalo said quietly, and once more both Stephen Kings on the bridge turned to look at him. "It could have been nothing else. What brought him to the brink of madness in the first place were two conflicting compulsions in his mind: to bring the Tower down, and to get there before *you* could get there, Roland, and mount to the top. To destroy it . . . or to rule it. I'm not sure he has ever cared overmuch about *understanding* it—just about beating you to something you want, and then snatching it away from you. About such things he'd care much."

"It'd no doubt please you to know how he raved about you, and cursed your name in the weeks before he smashed his precious playthings," said Fumalo. "How he came to fear you, insofar as he *can* fear."

"Not this one," Feemalo contradicted, and rather glumly, Susannah thought. "It wouldn't please this one much at all. He wins with no better grace than he loses."

Fimalo said: "When the Red King saw that the Algul would fall to you, he understood that the working Beams would regenerate. More! That eventually those two working Beams would re-create the *other* Beams, knitting them forth mile by mile and wheel by wheel. If that happens, then eventually . . ."

Roland was nodding. In his eyes Susannah saw an entirely new expression: glad surprise. *Maybe he does know how to win,* she thought. "Then eventually what has moved on might return again," the gunslinger said. "Perhaps Mid-World and In-World." He paused. "Perhaps even Gilead. The light. The *White.*"

"No perhaps about it," Fimalo said. "For ka is a wheel, and if a wheel be not broken, it will always roll. Unless the Crimson King can become either Lord of the Tower or its Lord High Executioner, all that was will eventually return."

"Lunacy," said Fumalo. "And *destructive* lunacy, at that. But of course Big Red always *was* Gan's crazy side." He gave Susannah an ugly smirk and said, "That's *Frooood,* Lady Blackbird."

Feemalo resumed. "And after the Balls were smashed and the killing was done—"

"This is what we'd have you understand," said Fumalo. "If, that is, your heads aren't too thick to get the sense of it."

"After those chores were finished, he killed *himself,*" Fimalo said, and once more the other two turned to him. It was as if they were helpless to do otherwise.

"Did he do it with a spoon?" Roland asked. "For that was the prophecy my friends and I grew up with. 'Twas in a bit of doggerel."

"Yes indeed," said Fimalo. "I thought he'd cut his throat with it, for the edge of the spoon's bowl had been sharpened (like certain plates, ye ken—ka's a wheel, and always comes around to where it started), but he swallowed it. *Swallowed* it, can you imagine? Great gouts of blood poured from his mouth. *Freshets!* Then he mounted the greatest of the gray horses—he calls it Nis, after the land of sleep and dreams—and rode southeast into the white lands of Empathica with his little bit of gunna before him on the saddle." He smiled. "There are great stores of food here, but *he* has no need of it, as you may ken. Los' no longer eats."

"Wait a minute, time out," Susannah said, raising her hands

in a T-shape (it was a gesture she'd picked up from Eddie, although she didn't realize it). "If he swallowed a sharpened spoon and cut himself open as well as choking—"

"Lady Blackbird begins to see the light!" Fumalo exulted, and shook his hands at the sky.

"—then how could he do *anything*?"

"Los' cannot die," Feemalo said, as if explaining something obvious to a three-year-old. "And *you*—"

"You poor *saps*—" his partner put in with good-natured viciousness.

"You can't kill a man who's already dead," Fimalo finished. "As he was, Roland, your guns might have ended him . . ."

Roland was nodding. "Handed down from father to son, with barrels made from Arthur Eld's great sword, Excalibur. Yes, that's also part of the prophecy. As he of course would know."

"But now he's safe from them. Has put himself *beyond* them. He is Un-dead."

"We have reason to believe that he's been shunted onto a balcony of the Tower," Roland said. "Un-dead or not, he never could have gained the top without some sigul of the Eld; surely if he knew so much prophecy, then he knew that."

Fimalo was smiling grimly. "Aye, but as Horatio held the bridge in a story told in Susannah's world, so Los', the Crimson King, now holds the Tower. He has found his way into its mouth but cannot climb to the top, 'tis true. Yet while he holds it hard, neither can you."

"It seems old King Red wasn't entirely mad, after all," Feemalo said.

"Cray-zee lak-a de *focks!*" Fumalo added. He tapped his temple gravely . . . and then burst out laughing.

"But if you go on," said Fimalo, "you bring to him the siguls of the Eld he needs to gain possession of that which now holds him captive."

"He'd have to take them from me first," Roland said. "From *us*." He spoke without drama, as if merely commenting on the weather.

"True," Fimalo agreed, "but consider, Roland. You cannot

kill him with them, but it *is* possible that he might be able to take them from you, for his mind is devious and his reach is long. If he were to do so . . . well! Imagine a dead king, and mad, at the top of the Dark Tower, with a pair of the great old guns in his possession! He might rule from there, but I think that, given his insanity, he'd choose to bring it down, instead. Which he might be able to do, Beams or no Beams."

Fimalo studied them gravely from his place on the far side of the bridge.

"And then," he said, "all would be darkness."

FOUR

There was a pause during which those gathered in that place considered the idea. Then Feemalo said, almost apologetically: "The cost might not be so great if one were just to consider this world, which we might call Tower Keystone, since the Dark Tower exists here not as a rose, as it does on many, or an immortal tiger, as it does on some, or the ur-dog Rover, as it does on at least one—"

"A dog named *Rover*?" Susannah asked, bemused. "Do you really say so?"

"Lady, you have all the imagination of a half-burnt stick," Fumalo said in a tone of deep disgust.

Feemalo paid no heed. "In this world, the Tower is itself. In the world where you, Roland, have most lately been, most species still breed true and many lives are sweet. There is still energy and hope. Would you risk destroying that world as well as this, and the other worlds sai King has touched with his imagination, and drawn from? For it was not he that created them, you know. To peek in Gan's navel does not make one Gan, although many creative people seem to think so. Would you risk it all?"

"We're just asking, not trying to convince you," Fimalo said. "But the truth is bald: now this is only your quest, gunslinger. That's *all* it is. Nothing sends you further. Once you pass beyond this castle and into the White Lands, you and your friends pass beyond ka itself. And you need not do it. All you have been through was set in motion so that you might save the Beams, and by saving them ensure the eternal existence of the Tower, the axle upon which all worlds and all life spins. That is done. If you turn back now, the dead King will be trapped forever where he is."

"Sez *you*," Susannah put in, and with a rudeness worthy of sai Fumalo.

"Whether you speak true or speak false," Roland said, "I will push on. For I have promised."

"To *whom* have you given your promise?" Fimalo burst out. For the first time since stopping on the castle side of the bridge, he unclasped his hands and used them to push his hair back from his brow. The gesture was small but expressed his frustration with perfect eloquence. "For there's no prophecy of such a promise; I tell you so!"

"There wouldn't be. For it's one I made myself, and one I mean to keep."

"This man is as crazy as Los' the Red," Fumalo said, not without respect.

"All right," Fimalo said. He sighed and once more clasped his hands before him. "I have done what *I* can do." He nodded to his other two thirds, who were looking attentively back at him.

Feemalo and Fumalo each dropped to one knee: Feemalo his right, Fumalo his left. They lifted away the lids of the wicker boxes they had carried and tilted them forward. (Susannah was fleetingly reminded of how the models on *The Price Is Right* and *Concentration* showed off the prizes.)

Inside one was food: roasts of chicken and pork, joints of beef, great pink rounds of ham. Susannah felt her stomach expand at the sight, as if making ready to swallow all of it, and it was only with a great effort that she stopped the sensual moan rising in her throat. Her mouth flooded with saliva and she raised a hand to wipe it away. They would know what she was doing, she supposed there was no help for that, but she could at least keep them from the satisfaction of seeing the physical evidence of her hunger gleaming on her lips and chin. Oy barked, but kept his seat by the gunslinger's left heel.

Inside the other basket were big cable-knit sweaters, one green and one red: Christmas colors.

"There's also long underwear, coats, fleece-lined shor'-boots, and gloves," said Feemalo. "For Empathica's deadly cold at this time of year, and you'll have months of walking ahead."

"On the outskirts of town we've left you a light aluminum sledge," Fimalo said. "You can throw it in the back of your little cart and then use it to carry the lady and your gunna, once you reach the snowlands."

"You no doubt wonder why we do all this, since we disapprove of your journey," said Feemalo. "The fact is, we're grateful for our survival—"

"We really did think we were done for," Fumalo broke in. "'The quarterback is toast,' Eddie might have said."

And this, too, hurt her . . . but not as much as looking at all that food. Not as much as imagining how it would feel to slip one of those bulky sweaters over her head and let the hem fall all the way to the middle of her thighs.

"My decision was to try and talk you out of going if I could," said Fimalo—the only one who spoke of himself in the first-person singular, Susannah had noticed. "And if I couldn't, I'd give you the supplies you'd need to go on with."

"You can't kill him!" Fumalo burst out. "Don't you see that, you wooden-headed killing machine, don't you *see*? All you can do is get overeager and play into his dead hands! How can you be so *stu*—"

"Hush," Fimalo said mildly, and Fumalo hushed at once. "He's taken his decision."

"What will you do?" Roland asked. "Once we've pushed on, that is?"

The three of them shrugged in perfect mirror unison, but it was Fimalo—the so-called uffi's superego—who answered. "Wait here," he said. "See if the matrix of creation lives or dies. In the meanwhile, try to refurbish Le Casse and bring it to some of its previous glory. It was a beautiful place once. It can be beautiful again. And now I think our palaver's done. Take your gifts with our thanks and good wishes."

"*Grudging* good wishes," said Fumalo, and actually smiled. Coming from him, that smile was both dazzling and unexpected.

Susannah almost started forward. Hungry as she was for fresh food (for fresh *meat*), it was the sweaters and the thermal underwear that she really craved. Although supplies were getting thin (and would surely run out before they were past the place the uffi called Empathica), there were still cans of beans and tuna and corned beef hash rolling around in the back of Ho Fat's Luxury Taxi, and their bellies were currently full. It was the cold that was killing her. That was what it felt like, at least; cold working its way inward toward her heart, one painful inch at a time.

Two things stopped her. One was the realization that a single step forward was all it would take to destroy what little remained of her will; she'd run to the center of the bridge and fall on her knees before that deep basket of clothes and go grubbing through it like a predatory housewife at the annual Filene's white-sale. Once she took that first step, nothing would stop her. And losing her will wouldn't be the worst of it; she would also lose the self-respect Odetta Holmes had labored all her life to win, despite the barely suspected saboteur lurking in her mind.

Yet even that wouldn't have been enough to hold her back. What did was a memory of the day they'd seen the crow with the green stuff in its beak, the crow that had been going *Croo, croo!* instead of *Caw, caw!* Only devilgrass, true, but green stuff, all the same. Living stuff. That was the day Roland had told her to hold her tongue, had told her—what was it? *Before victory comes temptation.* She never would have suspected that her life's greatest temptation would be a cable-knit fisherman's sweater, but—

She suddenly understood what the gunslinger must have known, if not from the first then from soon after the three Stephen Kings appeared: this whole thing was a shuck. She didn't know what, exactly, was in those wicker baskets, but she doubted like hell that it was food and clothes.

She settled within herself.

"Well?" Fimalo asked patiently. "Will you come and take the

presents I'd give you? You must come, if you'd have them, for halfway across the bridge is as far as I can go myself. Just beyond Feemalo and Fumalo is the King's dead-line. You and she may pass both ways. We may not."

Roland said, "We thank you for your kindness, sai, but we're going to refuse. We have food, and clothing is waiting for us up ahead, still on the hoof. Besides, it's really not that cold."

"No," Susannah agreed, smiling into the three identical—and identically dumbfounded—faces. "It's really not."

"We'll be pushing on," Roland said, and made another bow over his cocked leg.

"Say thankya, say may ya do well," Susannah put in, and once more spread her invisible skirts.

She and Roland began to turn away. And that was when Feemalo and Fumalo, still down on their knees, reached inside the open baskets before them.

Susannah needed no instruction from Roland, not so much as a shouted word. She drew the revolver from her belt and shot down the one on her left—Fumalo—just as he swung a long-barreled silver gun out of the basket. What looked like a scarf was hanging from it. Roland drew from his holster, as blindingly fast as ever, and fired a single shot. Above them the rooks took wing, cawing affrightedly, turning the blue sky momentarily black. Feemalo, also holding one of the silver guns, collapsed slowly forward across his basket of food with a dying expression of surprise on his face and a bullet-hole dead center in his forehead.

FIVE

Fimalo stood where he was, on the far side of the bridge. His hands were still clasped in front of him, but he no longer looked like Stephen King. He now wore the long, yellow-complexioned face of an old man who is dying slowly and not well. What hair he had was a dirty gray rather than luxuriant black. His skull was a peeling garden of eczema. His cheeks, chin, and forehead were lumped with pimples and open sores, some pustulating and some bleeding.

"What are you, really?" Roland asked him.

"A hume, just as you are," said Fimalo, resignedly. "Rando Thoughtful was my name during my years as the Crimson King's Minister of State. Once upon a time, however, I was plain old Austin Cornwell, from upstate New York. Not the Keystone World, I regret to say, but another. I ran the Niagara Mall at one time, and before that I had a successful career in advertising. You might be interested to know I worked on accounts for both Nozz-A-La and the Takuro Spirit."

Susannah ignored this bizarre and unexpected résumé. "So he *didn't* have his top boy beheaded, after all," she said. "What about the three Stephen Kings?"

"Just a glammer," said the old man. "Are you going to kill me? Go ahead. All I ask is that you make quick work of it. I'm not well, as you must see."

"Was any of what you told us true?" Susannah asked.

His old eyes looked at her with watery amazement. "*All* of it was," he said, and advanced onto the bridge, where two other old men—his assistants, once upon a time, she had no doubt—lay sprawled. "All of it, anyway, save for one lie . . . and this." He kicked the baskets over so that the contents spilled out.

Susannah gave an involuntary shout of horror. Oy was up in a flash, standing protectively in front of her with his short legs spread and his head lowered.

"It's all right," she said, but her voice was still trembling. "I was just . . . startled."

The wicker basket which had seemed to contain all sorts of freshly cooked roasts was actually filled with decaying human limbs—long pork, after all, and in bad shape even considering what it was. The flesh was mostly blue-black and a-teem with maggots.

And there were no clothes in the other basket. What Fimalo had spilled out of it was actually a shiny knot of dying snakes. Their beady eyes were dull; their forked tongues flickered list-lessly in and out; several had already ceased to move.

"You would have refreshed them wonderfully, if you'd pressed them against your skin," Fimalo said regretfully.

"You didn't really expect that to happen, did you?" Roland asked.

"No," the old man admitted. He sat on the bridge with a weary sigh. One of the snakes attempted to crawl into his lap and he pushed it away with a gesture that was both absent and impatient. "But I had my orders, so I did."

Susannah was looking at the corpses of the other two with horrified fascination. Feemalo and Fumalo, now just a couple of dead old men, were rotting with unnatural rapidity, their parchment skins deflating toward the bone and oozing slack rivulets of pus. As she watched, the sockets of Feemalo's skull surfaced like twin periscopes, giving the corpse a momentary expression of shock. Some of the snakes crawled and writhed around these decaying corpses. Others were crawling into the basket of maggoty limbs, seeking the undoubtedly warmer regions at the bottom of the heap. Decay brought its own temporary fevers, and she supposed that she herself might be tempted to luxuriate in it while she could. If she were a snake, that was.

"Are you going to kill me?" Fimalo asked.

"Nay," Roland said, "for your duties aren't done. You have another coming along behind."

Fimalo looked up, a gleam of interest in his rheumy old eyes. "Your son?"

"Mine, and your master's, as well. Would you give him a word for me during your palaver?"

"If I'm alive to give it, sure."

"Tell him that I'm old and crafty, while he's but young. Tell him that if he lies back, he may live awhile yet with his dreams of revenge . . . although what I've done to him requiring his vengeance, I know not. And tell him that if he comes forward, I'll kill him as I intend to kill his Red Father."

"Either you listen and don't hear or hear and don't believe," Fimalo said. Now that his own ruse had been exposed (nothing so glamorous as an uffi, Susannah thought; just a retreaded adman from upstate New York), he seemed unutterably weary. "You cannot kill a creature that has killed itself. Nor can you enter the Dark Tower, for there is only one entrance, and the balcony upon which Los' is imprisoned commands it. And he's armed with a sufficiency of weapons. The sneetches alone would seek you out and slay you before you'd crossed halfway through the field of roses."

"That's our worry," Roland said, and Susannah thought he'd rarely spoken a truer word: she was worrying about it already. "As for you, will you pass my message on to Mordred, when you see him?"

Fimalo made a gesture of acquiescence.

Roland shook his head. "Don't just flap thy hand at me, cully—let me hear from your mouth."

"I'll pass along your message," said Fimalo, then added: "*If* I see him, and we palaver."

"You will. 'Day to you, sir." Roland began to turn away, but Susannah caught his arm and he turned back.

"Swear to me that all you told us was true," she bade the ugly ancient sitting on the cobbled bridge and below the cold gaze of the crows, who were beginning to settle back to their former places. What she meant to learn or prove by this she had not the slightest idea. Would she know this man's lies, even now? Probably not. But she pressed on, just the same. "Swear it on the name of your father, and on his face, as well."

The old man raised his right hand to her, palm out, and Susannah saw there were open sores even there. "I swear it on the name of Andrew John Cornwell, of Tioga Springs, New York. And on his face, too. The King of this castle really did run mad, and really did burst those Wizard's Glasses that had come into his hands. He really did force the staff to take poison and he really did watch them die." He flung out the hand he'd held up in pledge to the box of severed limbs. "Where do you think I got those, Lady Blackbird? Body Parts R Us?"

She didn't understand the reference, and remained still.

"He really has gone on to the Dark Tower. He's like the dog in some old fable or other, wanting to make sure that if *he* can't get any good from the hay, no one else will, either. I didn't even lie to you about what was in these boxes, not really. I simply

showed you the goods and let you draw your own conclusions."
His smile of cynical pleasure made Susannah wonder if she
ought to remind him that Roland, at least, had seen through
this trick. She decided it wasn't worth it.

"I told you only one outright lie," said the former Austin
Cornwell. "That he'd had me beheaded."

"Are you satisfied, Susannah?" Roland asked her.

"Yes," she said, although she wasn't; not really. "Let's go."

"Climb up in Ho Fat, then, and don't turn thy back on
him when thee does. He's sly."

"Tell me about it," Susannah said, and then did as she was
asked.

"Long days and pleasant nights," said the former sai Cornwell from where he sat amid the squirming, dying snakes. "May
the Man Jesus watch over you and all your clan-fam. And may
you show sense before it's too late for sense and *stay away from
the Dark Tower!*"

SIX

They retraced their path to the intersection where they had
turned away from the Path of the Beam to go to the Crimson
King's castle, and here Roland stopped to rest for a few minutes.
A little bit of a breeze had gotten up, and the patriotic bunting
flapped. She saw it now looked old and faded. The pictures of
Nixon, Lodge, Kennedy, and Johnson had been defaced by graffiti which was itself ancient. All the glammer—such ragged
glammer as the Crimson King had been able to manage, at any
rate—was gone.

Masks off, masks off, she thought tiredly. *It was a wonderful
party, but now it's finished . . . and the Red Death holds sway over all.*

She touched the pimple beside her mouth, then looked at
the tip of her finger. She expected to see blood or pus or both.
There was neither, and that was a relief.

"How much of it do you believe?" Susannah asked him.

"Pretty much all of it," Roland replied.

"So he's up there. In the Tower."

"Not *in* it. Trapped *outside* it." He smiled. "There's a big difference."

"Is there really? And what will you do to him?"

"I don't know."

"Do you think that if he did get control of your guns, that he could get back inside the Tower and climb to the top?"

"Yes." The reply was immediate.

"What will you do about it?"

"Not let him get either of them." He spoke as if this should have been self-evident, and Susannah supposed it should have been. What she had a way of forgetting was how goddamned *literal* he was. About everything.

"You were thinking of trapping Mordred, back at the castle."

"Yes," Roland agreed, "but given what we found there—and what we were told—it seemed better to move on. Simpler. Look."

He took out the watch and snapped open the lid. They both observed the second-hand racing its solitary course. But at the same speed as before? Susannah didn't know for sure, but she didn't think so. She looked up at Roland with her eyebrows raised.

"Most of the time it's still right," Roland said, "but no longer *all* of the time. I think that it's losing at least a second every sixth or seventh revolution. Perhaps three to six minutes a day, all told."

"That's not very much."

"No," Roland admitted, putting the watch away, "but it's a start. Let Mordred do as he will. The Dark Tower lies close beyond the white lands, and I mean to reach it."

Susannah could understand his eagerness. She only hoped it wouldn't make him careless. If it did, Mordred Deschain's youth might no longer matter. If Roland made the right mistake at the wrong moment, she, he, and Oy might never see the Dark Tower at all.

Her thoughts were interrupted by a great fluttering from behind them. Not quite lost within it came a human sound that began as a howl and quickly rose to a shriek. Although distance diminished that cry, the horror and pain in it were all too clear. At last, mercifully, it faded.

"The Crimson King's Minister of State has entered the clearing," Roland said.

Susannah looked back toward the castle. She could see its blackish-red ramparts, but nothing else. She was *glad* she could see nothing else.

Mordred's a-hungry, she thought. Her heart was beating fast and she thought she had never been so frightened in her whole life—not lying next to Mia as she gave birth, not even in the blackness under Castle Discordia.

Mordred's a-hungry . . . but now he'll be fed.

SEVEN

The old man who had begun life as Austin Cornwell and who would end it as Rando Thoughtful sat at the castle end of the bridge. The rooks waited above him, perhaps sensing that the day's excitement was not yet done. Thoughtful was warm enough thanks to the pea-coat he was wearing, and he had helped himself to a mouthful of brandy before leaving to meet Roland and his blackbird ladyfriend. Well . . . perhaps that wasn't *quite* true. Perhaps it was Brass and Compson (also known as Feemalo and Fumalo) who'd had the mouthfuls of the King's best brandy, and Los's ex-Minister of State who had polished off the last third of the bottle.

Whatever the cause, the old man fell asleep, and the coming of Mordred Red-Heel didn't wake him. He sat with his chin on his chest and drool trickling from between his pursed lips, looking like a baby who has fallen asleep in his highchair. The birds on the parapets and walkways were gathered more thickly than ever. Surely they would have flown at the approach of the young Prince, but he looked up at them and made a gesture in the air: the open right hand waved brusquely across the face, then curled into a fist and pulled downward. *Wait,* it said.

Mordred stopped on the town side of the bridge, sniffing

delicately at the decayed meat. That smell had been charming enough to bring him here even though he knew Roland and Susannah had continued along the Path of the Beam. Let them and their pet bumbler get fairly back on their way, was the boy's thinking. This wasn't the time to close the gap. Later, perhaps. Later his White Daddy would let down his guard, if only for a moment, and then Mordred would have him.

For dinner, he hoped, but lunch or breakfast would do almost as well.

When we last saw this fellow, he was only

(*baby-bunting baby-dear baby bring your berries here*)

an infant. The creature standing beyond the gates of the Crimson King's castle had grown into a boy who looked about nine years old. Not a handsome boy; not the sort anyone (except for his lunatic mother) would have called comely. This had less to do with his complicated genetic inheritance than with plain starvation. The face beneath the dry spall of black hair was haggard and far too thin. The flesh beneath Mordred's blue bombardier's eyes was a discolored, pouchy purple. His complexion was a birdshot blast of sores and blemishes. These, like the pimple beside Susannah's mouth, could have been the result of his journey through the poisoned lands, but surely Mordred's diet had something to do with it. He could have stocked up on canned goods before setting out from the checkpoint beyond the tunnel's mouth—Roland and Susannah had left plenty behind—but he hadn't thought to do so. He was, as Roland knew, still learning the tricks of survival. The only thing Mordred had taken from the checkpoint Quonset was a rotting railwayman's pillowtick jacket and a pair of serviceable boots. Finding the boots was good fortune indeed, although they had mostly fallen apart as the trek continued.

Had he been a hume—or even a more ordinary were-creature, for that matter—Mordred would have died in the Badlands, coat or no coat, boots or no boots. Because he was what he was, he had called the rooks to him when he was hungry, and the rooks had no choice but to come. The birds made nasty eating and the bugs he summoned from beneath the parched (and still faintly radioactive) rocks were even worse, but he had choked them down. One day he had touched the mind of a weasel and bade it come. It had been a scrawny, wretched thing, on the edge of starvation itself, but it tasted like the world's finest steak after the birds and the bugs. Mordred had changed into his other self and gathered the weasel into his seven-legged embrace, sucking and eating until there was nothing left but a torn piece of fur. He would have gladly eaten another dozen, but that had been the only one.

And now there was a whole basket of food set before him. It was well-aged, true, but what of that? Even the maggots would provide nourishment. More than enough to carry him into the snowy woods southeast of the castle, which would be teeming with game.

But before them, there was the old man.

"Rando," he said. "Rando Thoughtful."

The old man jerked and mumbled and opened his eyes. For a moment he looked at the scrawny boy standing before him with a total lack of understanding. Then his rheumy eyes filled with fright.

"Mordred, son of Los'," he said, trying a smile. "Hile to you, King that will be!" He made a shuffling gesture with his legs, then seemed to realize that he was sitting down and it wouldn't do. He attempted to find his feet, fell back with a bump that amused the boy (amusement had been hard to come by in the Badlands, and he welcomed it), then tried again. This time he managed to get up.

"I see no bodies except for those of two fellows who look like they died even older than you," Mordred remarked, looking around in exaggerated fashion. "I certainly see no dead gunslingers, of either the long-leg or shor'-leg variety."

"You say true—and I say thankya, o'course I do—but I can explain that, sai, and quite easily—"

"Oh, but wait! Hold thy explanation, excellent though I'm sure it is! Let me guess, instead! Is it that the snakes have bound the gunslinger and his lady, long fat snakes, and you've had them removed into yonder castle for safekeeping?"

"My lord—"

"If so," Mordred continued, "there must have been an almighty lot of snakes in thy basket, for I still see many out here. Some appear to be dining on what should have been my supper." Although the severed, rotting limbs in the basket would still be his supper—part of it, anyway—Mordred gave the old fellow a reproachful look. "*Have* the gunslingers been put away, then?"

The old man's look of fright departed and was replaced by one of resignation. Mordred found this downright infuriating. What he wanted to see in old sai Thoughtful's face was not fright, and certainly not resignation, but hope. Which Mordred would snatch away at his leisure. His shape wavered. For a moment the old man saw the unformed blackness which lurked beneath, and the many legs. Then it was gone and the boy was back. For the moment, at least.

May I not die screaming, the former Austin Cornwell thought. *At least grant me that much, you gods that be. May I not die screaming in the arms of yonder monstrosity.*

"You know what's happened here, young sai. It's in my mind, and so it's in yours. Why not take the mess in that basket—the snakes, too, do ya like em—and leave an old man to what little life he has left? For your father's sake, if not your own. I served him well, even at the end. I could have simply hunkered in the castle and let them go their course. But I didn't. I *tried.*"

"You had no choice," Mordred replied from his end of the bridge. Not knowing if it was true or not. Nor caring. Dead flesh was only nourishment. Living flesh and blood still rich with the air of a man's last breath . . . ah, that was something else. That was *fine dining!* "Did he leave me a message?"

"Aye, you know he did."

"Tell me."

"Why don't you just pick it out of my mind?"

Again there came that fluttering, momentary change. For a moment it was neither a boy nor a boy-sized spider standing on the far end of the bridge but something that was both at the

same time. Sai Thoughtful's mouth went dry even while the drool that had escaped during his nap still gleamed on his chin. Then the boy-version of Mordred solidified again inside his torn and rotting coat.

"Because it pleases me to hear it from your drooping old stew-hole," he told Thoughtful.

The old man licked his lips. "All right; may it do ya fine. He said that he's crafty while you're young and without so much as a sip of guile. He said that if you don't stay back where you belong, he'll have your head off your shoulders. He said he'd like to hold it up to your Red Father as he stands trapped upon his balcony."

This was quite a bit more than Roland actually said (as we should know, having been there), and more than enough for Mordred.

Yet *not* enough for Rando Thoughtful. Perhaps only ten days before it would have accomplished the old man's purpose, which was to goad the boy into killing him quickly. But Mordred had seasoned in a hurry, and now withstood his first impulse to simply bolt across the bridge into the castle courtyard, changing as he charged, and tearing Rando Thoughtful's head from his body with the swipe of one barbed leg.

Instead he peered up at the rooks—hundreds of them, now—and they peered back at him, as intent as pupils in a classroom. The boy made a fluttering gesture with his arms, then pointed at the old man. The air was at once filled with the rising whir of wings. The King's Minister turned to flee, but before he'd gotten a single step, the rooks descended on him in an inky cloud. He threw his arms up to protect his face as they lit on his head and shoulders, turning him into a scarecrow. This instinctive gesture did no good; more of them alit on his upraised arms until the very weight of the birds forced them down. Bills nipped and needled at the old man's face, drawing blood in tiny tattoo stipples.

"*No!*" Mordred shouted. "Save the skin for me . . . but you may have his eyes."

It was then, as the eager rooks tore Rando Thoughtful's eyes from their living sockets, that the ex-Minister of State uttered the rising howl Roland and Susannah heard as they neared the edge of Castle-town. The birds who couldn't find a roosting-place hung around him in a living thunderhead. They turned him on his levitating heels and carried him toward the changeling, who had now advanced to the center of the bridge and squatted there. The boots and rotted pillowtick coat had been left behind for the nonce on the town side of the bridge; what waited for sai Thoughtful, reared up on its back legs, forelegs pawing the air, red mark on its hairy belly all too visible, was Dan-Tete, the Little Red King.

The man floated to his fate, shrieking and eyeless. He thrust his hands out in front of him, making warding-off gestures, and the spider's front legs seized one of them, guided it into the bristling maw of its mouth, and bit it off with a candy-cane crunch.

Sweet!

EIGHT

That night, beyond the last of the oddly narrow, oddly unpleasant townhouses, Roland stopped in front of what had probably been a smallhold farm. He stood facing the ruin of the main building, sniffing.

"What, Roland? What?"

"Can you smell the wood of that place, Susannah?"

She sniffed. "I can, as a matter of fact—what of it?"

He turned to her, smiling. "If we can smell it, we can burn it."

This turned out to be correct. They had trouble kindling the fire, even aided by Roland's slyest tricks of trailcraft and half a can of Sterno, but in the end they succeeded. Susannah sat as close to it as she could, turning at regular intervals in order to toast both sides equally, relishing the sweat that popped out first on her face and her breasts, then on her back. She had forgotten what it was to be warm, and went on feeding wood to the flames until the campfire was a roaring bonfire. To animals in the open lands further along the Path of the healing Beam, that fire must have looked like a comet that had fallen to Earth, still blazing. Oy sat beside her, ears cocked, looking into the fire as if mesmerized. Susannah kept expecting Roland to object—to tell her to stop feeding the damned thing and start letting it burn down, for her father's sake—but he didn't. He only sat with his disassembled guns before him, oiling the pieces. When the fire grew too hot, he moved back a few feet. His shadow danced a skinny, wavering commala in the firelight.

"Can you stand one or two more nights of cold?" he asked her at last.

She nodded. "If I have to."

"Once we start climbing toward the snowlands, it will be *really* cold," he said. "And while I can't promise you we'll have to go fireless for only a single night, I don't believe it'll be any longer than two."

"You think it'll be easier to take game if we don't build a fire, don't you?"

Roland nodded and began putting his guns back together.

"Will there be game as early as day after tomorrow?"

"Yes."

"How do you know?"

He considered this, then shook his head. "I can't say—but I do."

"Can you smell it?"

"No."

"Touch their minds?"

"It's not that, either."

She let it go. "Roland, what if Mordred sends the birds against us tonight?"

He smiled and pointed to the flames. Below them, a deepening bed of bright red coals waxed and waned like dragon's breath. "They'll not come close to thy bonfire."

"And tomorrow?"

"Tomorrow we'll be further from Le Casse Roi Russe than even Mordred can persuade them to go."

"And how do you know *that?*"

He shook his head yet again, although he thought he knew

the answer to her question. What he knew came from the Tower. He could feel the pulse of it awakening in his head. It was like green coming out of a dry seed. But it was too early to say so.

"Lie down, Susannah," he said. "Take your rest. I'll watch until midnight, then wake you."

"So now we keep a watch," she said.

He nodded.

"Is he watching *us?*"

Roland wasn't sure, but thought that Mordred was. What his imagination saw was a skinny boy (but with a potbelly pooched out in front of him now, for he'd have eaten well), naked inside the rags of a filthy, torn coat. A skinny boy laid up in one of those unnaturally skinny houses, perhaps on the third floor, where the sightline was good. He sits at a window with his knees pulled up against his chest for warmth, the scar on his side perhaps aching in the bony cold, looking out at the flare of their fire, jealous of it. Jealous of their companionship, as well. Half-mother and White Father, with their backs turned to him.

"It's likely," he said.

She started to lie down, then stopped. She touched the sore beside her mouth. "This isn't a pimple, Roland."

"No?" He sat quiet, watching her.

"I had a friend in college who got one just like it," Susannah said. "It'd bleed, then stop, then almost heal up, then darken and bleed a little more. At last she went to see a doctor—a special kind we call a dermatologist—and he said it was an angioma. A blood-tumor. He gave her a shot of novocaine and took it off with a scalpel. He said it was a good thing she came when she did, because every day she waited that thing was sinking its roots in a little deeper. Eventually, he said, it would have worked its way right through the roof of her mouth, and maybe into her sinuses, too."

Roland was silent, waiting. The term she had used clanged in his head: *blood-tumor.* He thought it might have been coined to describe the Crimson King himself. Mordred, as well.

"We don't have no novocaine, Baby-Boots," Detta Walker said, "and Ah know dat, sho! But if de time come and Ah tell you, you goan whip out yo' knife and cut dat ugly mahfah right off'n me. Goan do it faster than yon bum'blah c'n snatch a fly out de air. You unnerstand me? Kitch mah drift?"

"Yes. Now lie over. Take some rest."

She lay over. Five minutes after she had appeared to go to sleep, Detta Walker opened her eyes and gave him

(*I watchin you, white boy*)

a glare. Roland nodded to her and she closed her eyes again. A minute or two later, they opened a second time. Now it was Susannah who looked at him, and this time when her eyes closed, they didn't open again.

He had promised to wake her at midnight, but let her sleep two hours longer, knowing that in the heat of the fire her body was *really* resting, at least for this one night. At what his fine new watch said was one o' the clock, he finally felt the gaze of their pursuer slip away. Mordred had lost his fight to stay awake through the darkest watches of the night, as had innumerable children before him. Wherever his room was, the unwanted, lonely child now slept in it with his wreck of a coat pulled around him and his head in his arms.

And does his mouth, still caked with sai Thoughtful's blood, purse and quiver, as if dreaming of the nipple it knew but once, the milk it never tasted?

Roland didn't know. Didn't particularly want to know. He was only glad to be awake in the stillwatch of the night, feeding the occasional piece of wood to the lowering fire. It would die quickly, he thought. The wood was newer than that of which the townhouses were constructed, but it was still ancient, hardened to a substance that was nearly stone.

Tomorrow they would see trees. The first since Calla Bryn Sturgis, if one set aside those growing beneath Algul Siento's artificial sun and those he'd seen in Stephen King's world. That would be good. Meanwhile, the dark held hard. Beyond the circle of the dying fire a wind moaned, lifting Roland's hair from his temples and bringing a faint, sweet smell of snow. He tilted his head back and watched the clock of the stars turn in the blackness overhead.

CHAPTER IV:
HIDES

They had to go fireless three nights instead of one or two. The last was the longest, most wretched twelve hours of Susannah's life. *Is it worse than the night Eddie died?* she asked herself at one point. *Are you really saying this is worse than lying awake in one of those dormitory rooms, knowing that was how you'd be lying from then on? Worse than washing his face and hands and feet? Washing them for the ground?*

Yes. This *was* worse. She hated knowing it, and would never admit it to anyone else, but the deep, endless cold of that last night was *far* worse. She came to dread every light breath of breeze from the snowlands to the east and south. It was both terrible and oddly humbling to realize how easily physical discomfort could take control, expanding like poison gas until it owned all the floor-space, took over the entire playing field. Grief? Loss? What were those things when you could feel cold on the march, moving in from your fingers and toes, crawling up your motherfucking *nose*, and moving where? Toward the brain, do it please ya. And toward the heart. In the grip of cold like that, grief and loss were nothing but words. No, not even that. Only *sounds*. So much meaningless quack as you sat shuddering under the stars, waiting for a morning that would never come.

What made it worse was knowing there were potential bonfires all around them, for they'd reached the live region Roland called "the undersnow." This was a series of long, grassy slopes (most of the grass now white and dead) and shallow valleys where there were isolated stands of trees, and brooks now plugged with ice. Earlier, in daylight, Roland had pointed out several holes in the ice and told her they'd been made by deer.

629

He pointed out several piles of scat, as well. In daylight such sign had been interesting, even hopeful. But in this endless ditch of night, listening to the steady low click of her chattering teeth, it meant nothing. Eddie meant nothing. Jake, neither. The Dark Tower meant nothing, nor did the bonfire they'd had out the outskirts of Castle-town. She could remember the look of it, but the feel of heat warming her skin until it brought an oil of sweat was utterly lost. Like a person who has died for a moment or two and has briefly visited some shining afterlife, she could only say that it had been wonderful.

Roland sat with his arms around her, sometimes voicing a dry, harsh cough. Susannah thought he might be getting sick, but this thought also had no power. Only the cold.

Once—shortly before dawn finally began to stain the sky in the east, this was—she saw orange lights swirl-dancing far ahead, past the place where the snow began. She asked Roland if he had any idea what they were. She had no real interest, but hearing her voice reassured her that she wasn't dead. Not yet, at least.

"I think they're hobs."

"W-What are th-they?" She now stuttered and stammered everything.

"I don't know how to explain them to you," he said. "And there's really no need. You'll see them in time. Right now if you listen, you'll hear something closer and more interesting."

At first she heard only the sigh of the wind. Then it dropped and her ears picked up the dry swish of the grass below as something walked through it. This was followed by a low crunching sound. Susannah knew exactly what it was: a hoof stamping through thin ice, opening the running water to the cold world above. She also knew that in three or four days' time she might be wearing a coat made from the animal that was now drinking nearby, but this also had no meaning. Time was a useless concept when you were sitting awake in the dark, and in constant pain.

Had she thought she had been cold before? That was quite funny, wasn't it?

"What about Mordred?" she asked. "Is he out there, do you think?"

"Yes."

"And does he feel the cold like we do?"

"I don't know."

"I can't stand much more of this, Roland—I really can't."

"You won't have to. It'll be dawn soon, and I expect we'll have a fire tomorrow come dark." He coughed into his fist, then put his arm back around her. "You'll feel better once we're up and in the doings. Meantime, at least we're together."

TWO

Mordred *was* as cold as they were, every bit, and he had no one.

He was close enough to hear them, though: not the actual words, but the sound of their voices. He shuddered uncontrollably, and had lined his mouth with dead grass when he became afraid that Roland's sharp ears might pick up the sound of his chattering teeth. The railwayman's jacket was no help; he had thrown it away when it had fallen into so many pieces that he could no longer hold it together. He'd worn the arms of it out of Castle-town, but then they had fallen to pieces as well, starting at the elbows, and he'd cast them into the low grass beside the old road with a petulant curse. He was only able to go on wearing the boots because he'd been able to weave long grass into a rough twine. With it he'd bound what remained of them to his feet.

He'd considered changing back to his spider-form, knowing that body would feel the cold less, but his entire short life had been plagued by the specter of starvation, and he supposed that part of him would always fear it, no matter how much food he had at hand. The gods knew there wasn't much now; three severed arms, four legs (two partially eaten), and a piece of a torso from the wicker basket, that was all. If he changed, the spider would gobble that little bit up by daylight. And while there was game out here—he heard the deer moving around just as clearly as his White Daddy did—Mordred wasn't entirely confident of his ability to trap it, or run it down.

So he sat and shivered and listened to the sound of their voices until the voices ceased. Maybe they slept. He might have dozed a little, himself. And the only thing that kept him from giving up and going back was his hatred of them. That they should have each other when he had no one. No one at all.

Mordred's a-hungry, he thought miserably. *Mordred's a-cold. And Mordred has no one. Mordred's alone.*

He slipped his wrist into his mouth, bit deep, and sucked the warmth that flowed out. In the blood he tasted the last of Rando Thoughtful's life . . . but so little! So soon gone! And once it was, there was nothing but the useless, recycled taste of himself.

In the dark, Mordred began to cry.

THREE

Four hours after dawn, under a white sky that promised rain or sleet (perhaps both at the same time), Susannah Dean lay shivering behind a fallen log, looking down into one of the little valleys. *You'll hear Oy,* the gunslinger had told her. *And you'll hear me, too. I'll do what I can, but I'll be driving them ahead of me and you'll have the best shooting. Make every shot count.*

What made things worse was her creeping intuition that Mordred was very close now, and he might try to bushwhack her while her back was turned. She kept looking around, but they had picked a relatively clear spot, and the open grass behind her was empty each time save once, when she had seen a large brown rabbit lolloping along with its ears dragging the ground.

At last she heard Oy's high-pitched barking from the copse of trees on her left. A moment later, Roland began to yell. "H'yah! H'yah! Get on brisk! Get on brisk, I tell thee! Never tarry! Never tarry a single—" Then the sound of him coughing. She didn't like that cough. No, not at all.

Now she could see movement in the trees, and for one of the few times since Roland had forced her to admit there was another person hiding inside of her, she called on Detta Walker.

I need you. If you want to be warm again, you settle my hands so I can shoot straight.

And the ceaseless shivering of her body stopped. As the herd of deer burst out of the trees—not a small herd, either; there had to be at least eighteen of them, led by a buck with a magnificent rack—her hands also stopped their shaking. In the right one she held Roland's revolver with the sandalwood grips.

Here came Oy, bursting out of the woods behind the final straggler. This was a mutie doe, running (and with eerie grace) on four legs of varying sizes with a fifth waggling bonelessly from the middle of her belly like a teat. Last of all came Roland, not really running at all, not anymore, but rather staggering onward at a grim jog. She ignored him, tracking the buck with the gun as the big fellow ran across her field of fire.

"This way," she whispered. "Break to your right, honey-child, let's see you do it. Commala-come-come."

And while there was no reason why he should have, the buck leading his little fleeing herd did indeed veer slightly in Susannah's direction. Now she was filled with the sort of coldness she welcomed. Her vision seemed to sharpen until she could see the muscles rippling under the buck's hide, the white crescent as his eye rolled, the old wound on the nearest doe's foreleg, where the fur had never grown back. She had a moment to wish Eddie and Jake were lying on either side of her, feeling what she was feeling, seeing what she was seeing, and then that was gone, too.

I do not kill with my gun; she who kills with her gun has forgotten the face of her father.

"I kill with my heart," she murmured, and began shooting.

The first bullet took the lead buck in the head and he crashed over on his left side. The others ran past him. A doe leaped over his body and Susannah's second bullet took her at the height of her leap, so that she crashed down dead on the other side, one leg splayed and broken, all grace gone.

She heard Roland fire three times, but didn't look to see how he'd done; she had her own business to attend to, and she attended to it well. Each of the last four bullets in the cylinder took down a deer, and only one was still moving when he fell. It didn't occur to her that this was an amazing piece of shooting, especially with a pistol; she was a gunslinger, after all, and shooting was her business.

Besides, the morning was windless.

Half the herd now lay dead in the grassy valley below. All the remainder save one wheeled left and pelted away downslope toward the stream. A moment later they were lost in a screen of willows. The last one, a yearling buck, ran directly toward her. Susannah didn't bother trying to reload from the little pile of bullets lying beside her on a square of buckskin but took one of the 'Riza plates instead, her hand automatically finding the dull gripping-place.

"'Riza!" she screamed, and flung it. It flew across the dry grass, elevating slightly as it did, giving off that weird moaning sound. It struck the racing buck at mid-neck. Droplets of blood flew in a garland around its head, black against the white sky. A butcher's cleaver could not have done a neater job. For a moment the buck ran on, heedless and headless, blood jetting from the stump of its neck as its racing heart gave up its last half a dozen beats. Then it crashed to its splayed forelegs less than ten yards in front of her hide, staining the dry yellow grass a bright red.

The previous night's long misery was forgotten. The numbness had departed her hands and her feet. There was no grief in her now, no sense of loss, no fear. For the moment Susannah was exactly the woman that ka had made her. The mixed smell of gunpowder and blood from the downed buck was bitter; it was also the world's sweetest perfume.

Standing up straight on her stumps, Susannah spread her arms, Roland's pistol clenched in her right hand, and made a *Y* against the sky. Then she screamed. There were no words in it, nor could there have been. Our greatest moments of triumph are always inarticulate.

FOUR

Roland had insisted that they eat a huge breakfast, and her protests that cold corned beef tasted like so much lumpy mush cut zero ice with him. By two that afternoon according to his fancy-schmancy pocket-watch—right around the time the steady cold rain fattened into an icy drizzle, in other words—she was glad. She had never done a harder day of physical labor, and the day wasn't finished. Roland was by her all the while, matching her in spite of his worsening cough. She had time (during their brief but crazily delicious noon meal of seared deer-steaks) to consider how strange he was, how remarkable. After all this time and all these adventures, she had still not seen the bottom of him. Not even close. She had seen him laughing and crying, killing and dancing, she'd seen him sleeping and on the squat behind a screen of bushes with his pants down and his ass hung over what he called the Log of Ease. She'd never slept with him as a woman does with a man, but she thought she'd seen him in every other circumstance, and . . . no. Still no bottom.

"That cough's sounding more and more like pneumonia to me," Susannah remarked, not long after the rain had started. They were then in the part of the day's activities Roland called aven-car: carrying the kill and preparing to make it into something else.

"Never let it worry you," Roland said. "I have what I need here to cure it."

"Say true?" she asked doubtfully.

"Yar. And these, which I never lost." He reached into his pocket and showed her a handful of aspirin tablets. She thought the expression on his face was one of real reverence, and why not? It might be that he owed his life to what he called *astin*. *Astin* and *cheflet*.

They loaded their kill into the back of Ho Fat's Luxury Taxi and dragged it down to the stream. It took three trips in all. After they'd stacked the carcasses, Roland carefully placed the head of the yearling buck atop the pile, where it looked at them from its glazed eyes.

"What you want that for?" Susannah asked, with a trace of Detta in her voice.

"We're going to need all the brains we can get," Roland said, and coughed dryly into his curled fist again. "It's a dirty way to do the job, but it's quick, and it works."

FIVE

When they had their kill piled beside the icy stream ("At least we don't have the flies to worry about," Roland said), the gunslinger began gathering deadwood. Susannah looked forward to the fire, but her terrible need of the previous night had departed. She had been working hard, and for the time being, at least, was warm enough to suit her. She tried to remember the depth of her despair, how the cold had crept into her bones, turning them to glass, and couldn't do it. Because the body had a way of forgetting the worst things, she supposed, and without the body's cooperation, all the brain had were memories like faded snapshots.

Before beginning his wood-gathering chore, Roland inspected the bank of the icy stream and dug out a piece of rock. He handed it to her, and Susannah rubbed a thumb over its milky, water-smoothed surface. "Quartz?" she asked, but she didn't think it was. Not quite.

"I don't know that word, Susannah. We call it chert. It makes tools that are primitive but plenty useful: axe-heads, knives, skewers, scrapers. It's scrapers we'll want. Also at least one hand-hammer."

"I know what we're going to scrape, but what are we going to hammer?"

"I'll show you, but first will you join me here for a moment?" Roland got down on his knees and took her cold hand in one of his. Together they faced the deer's head.

"We thank you for what we are about to receive," Roland told the head, and Susannah shivered. It was exactly how her father began when he was giving the grace before a big meal, one where all the family was gathered.

Our own family is broken, she thought, but did not say; done was done. The response she gave was the one she had been taught as a young girl: "Father, we thank thee."

"Guide our hands and guide our hearts as we take life from death," Roland said. Then he looked at her, eyebrows raised, asking without speaking a word if she had more to say.

Susannah found that she did. "Our Father, Who art in heaven, hallow'd be Thy name. Thy kingdom come, Thy will be done, on Earth as it is in heaven. Forgive us our trespasses, as we forgive those who trespass against us. Lead us not into temptation; deliver us from evil; Thou art the kingdom, and the power, and the glory, now and forever."

"That's a lovely prayer," he said.

"Yes," she agreed. "I didn't say it just right—it's been a long time—but it's still the best prayer. Now let's do our business, while I can still feel my hands."

Roland gave her an amen.

SIX

Roland took the severed head of the yearling deer (the antler-nubs made lifting it easy), set it in front of him, then swung the fist-sized chunk of rock against the skull. There was a muffled cracking sound that made Susannah's stomach cringe. Roland gripped the antlers and pulled, first left and then right. When Susannah saw the way the broken skull wiggled under the hide, her stomach did more than cringe; it did a slow loop-the-loop.

Roland hit twice more, wielding the piece of chert with near-surgical precision. Then he used his knife to cut a circle in the head-hide, which he pulled off like a cap. This revealed the cracked skull beneath. He worked the blade of his knife into the widest crack and used it as a lever. When the deer's brain was exposed, he took it out, set it carefully aside, and looked at Susannah. "We'll want the brains of every deer we killed, and that's what we need a hammer for."

"Oh," she said in a choked voice. "Brains."

"To make a tanning slurry. But there's more use for chert than that. Look." He showed her how to bang two chunks together until one or both shattered, leaving large, nearly even pieces instead of jagged lumps. She knew that metamorphic rocks broke that way, but schists and such were generally too weak to make good tools. This stuff was *strong*.

"When you get chunks that break thick enough to hold on one side but thin to an edge on the other," Roland said, "lay them by. Those will be our scrapers. If we had more time we could make handles, but we don't. Our hands will be plenty sore by bedtime."

"How long do you think it will take to get enough scrapers?"

"Not so long," Roland said. "Chert breaks lucky, or so I used to hear."

While Roland dragged deadwood for a fire into a copse of mixed willows and alders by the edge of the frozen stream, Susannah inspected her way along the embankments, looking for chert. By the time she'd found a dozen large chunks, she had also located a granite boulder rising from the ground in a smooth, weather-worn curve. She thought it would make a fine anvil.

The chert did indeed break lucky, and she had thirty potential scrapers by the time Roland was bringing back his third large load of firewood. He made a little pile of kindling which Susannah shielded with her hands. By then it was sleeting, and although they were working beneath a fairly dense clump of trees, she thought it wouldn't be long before both of them were soaked.

When the fire was lit, Roland went a few steps away, once more fell on his knees, and folded his hands.

"Praying again?" she asked, amused.

"What we learn in our childhood has a way of sticking," he said. He closed his eyes for a few moments, then brought his clasped hands to his mouth and kissed them. The only word she heard him say was *Gan*. Then he opened his eyes and lifted his hands, spreading them and making a pretty gesture that looked to her like birds flying away. When he spoke again, his voice was dry and matter-of-fact: Mr. Taking-Care-of-Business. "That's very well, then," he said. "Let's go to work."

SEVEN

They made twine from grass, just as Mordred had done, and hung the first deer—the one already headless—by its back legs from the low branch of a willow. Roland used his knife to cut its belly open, then reached into the guts, rummaged, and removed two dripping red organs that she thought were kidneys.

"These for fever and cough," he said, and bit into the first one as if it were an apple. Susannah made a gurking noise and turned away to consider the stream until he was finished. When he was, she turned back and watched him cut circles around the hanging legs close to where they joined the body.

"Are you any better?" she asked him uneasily.

"I will be," he said. "Now help me take the hide off this fellow. We'll want the first one with the hair still on it—we need to make a bowl for our slurry. Now watch."

He worked his fingers into the place where the deer's hide still clung to the body by the thin layer of fat and muscle beneath, then pulled. The hide tore easily to a point halfway down the deer's midsection. "Now do your side, Susannah."

Getting her fingers underneath was the only hard part. This time they pulled together, and when they had the hide all the way down to the dangling forelegs, it vaguely resembled a shirt. Roland used his knife to cut it off, then began to dig in the ground a little way from the roaring fire but still beneath the shelter of the trees. She helped him, relishing the way the sweat rolled down her face and body. When they had a shallow bowl-shaped depression two feet across and eighteen inches deep, Roland lined it with the hide.

All that afternoon they took turns skinning the eight other deer they had killed. It was important to do it as quickly as possible, for when the underlying layer of fat and muscle dried up, the work would become slower and harder. The gunslinger kept the fire burning high and hot, every now and then leaving her to rake ashes out onto the ground. When they had cooled enough so they would not burn holes in their bowl-liner, he pushed them into the hole they'd made. Susannah's back and arms were aching fiercely by five o'clock, but she kept at it. Roland's face, neck, and hands were comically smeared with ash.

"You look like a fella in a minstrel show," she said at one point. "Rastus Coon."

"Who's that?"

"Nobody but the white folks' fool," she said. "Do you suppose Mordred's out there, watching us work?" All day she'd kept an eye peeled for him.

"No," he said, pausing to rest. He brushed his hair back from his forehead, leaving a fresh smear and now making her think of penitents on Ash Wednesday. "I think he's gone off to make his own kill."

"Mordred's a-hungry," she said. And then: "You can touch him a little, can't you? At least enough to know if he's here or if he's gone."

Roland considered this, then said simply: "I'm his father."

EIGHT

By dark, they had a large heap of deerskins and a pile of skinned, headless carcasses that surely would have been black with flies in warmer weather. They ate another huge meal of sizzling venison steaks, utterly delicious, and Susannah spared another thought for Mordred, somewhere out in the dark, probably eating his own supper raw. He might have matches, but he wasn't stupid; if they saw another fire in all this darkness, they would rush down upon it. And him. Then, bang-bang-bang, goodbye Spider-Boy. She felt a surprising amount of sympathy for him and told herself to beware of it. Certainly he would have felt none for either her or Roland, had the shoe been on the other foot.

When they were done eating, Roland wiped his greasy fingers on his shirt and said, "That tasted fine."

"You got *that* right."

"Now let's get the brains out. Then we'll sleep."

"One at a time?" Susannah asked.

"Yes—so far as I know, brains only come one to a customer."

For a moment she was too surprised at hearing Eddie's phrase

(*one to a customer*)

coming from Roland's mouth to realize he'd made a joke. Lame, yes, but a *bona fide* joke. Then she managed a token laugh. "Very funny, Roland. You know what I meant."

Roland nodded. "We'll sleep one at a time and stand a watch, yes. I think that would be best."

Time and repetition had done its work; she'd now seen too many tumbling guts to feel squeamish about a few brains. They cracked heads, used Roland's knife (its edge now dull) to pry open skulls, and removed the brains of their kill. These they put carefully aside, like a clutch of large gray eggs. By the time the last deer was debrained, Susannah's fingers were so sore and swollen she could hardly bend them.

"Lie over," Roland said. "Sleep. I'll take the first watch."

She didn't argue. Given her full belly and the heat of the fire, she knew sleep would come quickly. She also knew that when she woke up tomorrow, she was going to be so stiff that even sitting up would be difficult and painful. Now, though, she didn't care. A feeling of vast contentment filled her. Some of it was having eaten hot food, but by no means all. The greater part of her well-being stemmed from a day of hard work, no more or less than that. The sense that they were not just floating along but *doing for themselves.*

Jesus, she thought, *I think I'm becoming a Republican in my old age.*

Something else occurred to her then: how quiet it was. No sounds but the sough of the wind, the whispering sleet (now starting to abate), and the crackle of the blessed fire.

"Roland?"

He looked at her from his place by the fire, eyebrows raised.

"You've stopped coughing."

He smiled and nodded. She took his smile down into sleep, but it was Eddie she dreamed of.

NINE

They stayed three days in the camp by the stream, and during that time Susannah learned more about making hide garments than she would ever have believed (and much more than she really wanted to know).

By casting a mile or so in either direction along the stream they found a couple of logs, one for each of them. While they looked, they used their makeshift pot to soak their hides in a dark soup of ash and water. They set their logs at an angle against the trunks of two willow trees (close, so they could work side by side) and used chert scrapers to dehair the hides. This took one day. When it was done, they bailed out the "pot," turned the hide liner over and filled it up again, this time with a mixture of water and mashed brains. This "cold-weather hiding" was new to her. They put the hides in this slurry to soak overnight and, while Susannah began to make thread from strings of gristle and sinew, Roland re-sharpened his knife, then used it to whittle half a dozen bone needles. When he was done, all of his fingers were bleeding from dozens of shallow cuts. He coated them with wood-ash soak and slept with them that way, his hands looking as if they were covered with large and clumsy gray-black gloves. When he washed them off in a stream the following day, Susannah was amazed to see the cuts already well on their way to healing. She tried dabbing some of the wood-ash stuff on the persistent sore beside her mouth, but it stung horribly and she washed it away in a hurry.

"I want you to whop this goddam thing off," she said.

Roland shook his head. "We'll give it a little longer to heal on its own."

"Why?"

"Cutting on a sore's a bad idea unless you absolutely have to do it. Especially out here, in what Jake would have called 'the boondogs.'"

She agreed (without bothering to correct his pronunciation), but unpleasant images crept into her head when she lay down: visions of the pimple beginning to spread, erasing her face inch by inch, turning her entire head into a black, crusted, bleeding tumor. In the dark, such visions had a horrible persuasiveness, but luckily she was too tired for them to keep her awake long.

On their second day in what Susannah was coming to think of as the Hide Camp, Roland built a large and rickety frame over a new fire, one that was low and slow. They smoked the hides two by two and then laid them aside. The smell of the finished product was surprisingly pleasant. *It smells like leather,* she thought, holding one to her face, and then had to laugh. That was, after all, exactly what it was.

The third day they spent "making," and here Susannah finally outdid the gunslinger. Roland sewed a wide and barely serviceable stitch. She thought that the vests and leggings he made would hold together for a month, two at the most, then begin to pull apart. She was far more adept. Sewing was a skill she'd learned from her mother and both grandmothers. At first she found Roland's bone needles maddeningly clumsy, and she paused long enough to cover both the thumb and forefinger of her right hand with little deerskin caps which she tied in place. After that it went faster, and by mid-afternoon of making-day she was taking garments from Roland's pile and oversewing his stitches with her own, which were finer and closer. She thought he might object to this—men were proud—but he didn't, which was probably wise. It quite likely would have been Detta who replied to any whines and queasies.

By the time their third night in Hide Camp had come, they each had a vest, a pair of leggings, and a coat. They also had a pair of mittens each. These were large and laughable, but would keep their hands warm. And, speaking of hands, Susannah was once more barely able to bend hers. She looked doubtfully at the remaining hides and asked Roland if they would spend another making-day here.

He considered the idea, then shook his head. "We'll load the ones that are left into the Ho Fat Tack-see, I think, along with some of the meat and chunks of ice from the stream to keep it cool and good."

"The Taxi won't be any good when we come to the snow, will it?"

"No," he admitted, "but by then the rest of the hides will be clothing and the meat will be eaten."

"You just can't stay here any longer, that's what it comes down to, isn't it? You hear it calling. The Tower."

Roland looked into the snapping fire and said nothing. Nor had to.

"What'll we do about hauling our gunna when we come to the white lands?"

"Make a travois. And there'll be plenty of game."

She nodded and started to lie down. He took her shoulders and turned her toward the fire, instead. His face came close to hers, and for a moment Susannah thought he meant to kiss her goodnight. He looked long and hard at the crusted sore beside her mouth, instead.

"Well?" she finally asked. She could have said more, but he would have heard the tremor in her voice.

"I think it's a little smaller. Once we leave the Badlands behind, it may heal on its own."

"Do you really say so?"

The gunslinger shook his head at once. "I say *may.* Now lie over, Susannah. Take your rest."

"All right, but don't you let me sleep late this time. I want to watch my share."

"Yes. Now lie over."

She did as he said, and was asleep even before her eyes closed.

TEN

She's in Central Park and it's cold enough to see her breath. The sky overhead is white from side to side, a snow-sky, but she's not cold. No, not in her new deerskin coat, leggings, vest, and funny deerskin mittens. There's something on her head, too, pulled down over her ears and keeping them as toasty as the rest of her. She takes the cap off, curious, and sees it's not deerskin like the rest of her new clothing, but a red-and-green stocking cap. Written across the front is MERRY CHRISTMAS.

She looks at it, startled. Can you have déjà vu *in a dream? Apparently so. She looks around and there are Eddie and Jake, grinning at her. Their heads are bare and she realizes she has in her hands a combination of the caps they were wearing in some other dream. She feels a great, soaring burst of joy, as if she has just solved some supposedly insoluble problem: squaring the circle, let us say, or finding the Ultimate Prime Number (take* that, *Blaine, may it bust ya brain, ya crazy choochoo train).*

Eddie is wearing a sweatshirt that says I DRINK NOZZ-A-LA!

Jake is wearing one that says I DRIVE THE TAKURO SPIRIT!

Both have cups of hot chocolate, the perfect kind mit schlag *on top and little sprinkles of nutmeg dotting the cream.*

"What world is this?" she asks them, and realizes that somewhere nearby carolers are singing "What Child Is This."

"You must let him go his course alone," says Eddie.

"Yar, and you must beware of Dandelo," says Jake.

"I don't understand," Susannah says, and holds out her stocking cap to them. "Wasn't this yours? Didn't you share it?"

"It could be your hat, if you want it," says Eddie, and then holds out his cup. "Here, I brought you hot chocolate."

"No more twins," says Jake. "There's only one hat, do ya not see."

Before she can reply, a voice speaks out of the air and the dream begins to unravel. "NINETEEN," *says the voice.* "This is NINETEEN, this is CHASSIT."

With each word the world becomes more unreal. She can see through

Eddie and Jake. The good smell of hot chocolate is fading, being replaced by the smell of ash

(wednesday)

and leather. She sees Eddie's lips moving and she thinks he's saying a name, and then

ELEVEN

"Time to get up, Susannah," Roland said. "It's your watch."

She sat up, looking around. The campfire had burned low.

"I heard him moving out there," Roland said, "but that was some time ago. Susannah, are you all right? Were you dreaming?"

"Yes," she said. "There was only one hat in this dream, and I was wearing it."

"I don't understand you."

Nor did she understand herself. The dream was already fading, as dreams do. All she knew for sure was that the name on Eddie's lips just before he faded away for good had been that of Patrick Danville.

Chapter V:
Joe Collins of Odd's Lane

ONE

Three weeks after the dream of one hat, three figures (two large, one small) emerged from a tract of upland forest and began to move slowly across a great open field toward more woods below. One of the large figures was pulling the other on a contraption that was more sled than travois.

Oy raced back and forth between Roland and Susannah, as if keeping a constant watch. His fur was thick and sleek from cold weather and a constant diet of deermeat. The land the three of them were currently covering might have been a meadow in the warmer seasons, but now the ground was buried under five feet of snow. The pulling was easier, because their way was finally leading downward. Roland actually dared hope the worst was over. And crossing the White Lands had not been too bad—at least, not yet. There was plenty of game, there was plenty of wood for their nightly fire, and on the four occasions when the weather turned nasty and blizzards blew, they had simply laid up and waited for the storms to wear themselves out on the wooded ridges that marched southeast. Eventually they did, although the angriest of these blizzards lasted two full days, and when they once more took to the Path of the Beam, they found another three feet of new snow on the ground. In the open places where the shrieking nor'east wind had been able to rage fully, there were drifts like ocean waves. Some of these had buried tall pines almost to their tops.

After their first day in the White Lands, with Roland struggling to pull her (and then the snow had been less than a foot deep), Susannah saw that they were apt to spend months crossing those high, forested ridges unless Roland had a pair of snowshoes, so that first night she'd set out to make him a pair. It was a trial-and-error process ("By guess and by gosh" was how Susannah put it), but the gunslinger pronounced her third effort a success. The frames were made of limber birch branches, the centers of woven, overlapping deerskin strips. To Roland they looked like teardrops.

"How did you know to do this?" he asked her after his first day of wearing them. The increase in distance covered was nothing short of amazing, especially once he had learned to walk with a kind of rolling, shipboard stride that kept the snow from accumulating on the latticed surfaces.

"Television," Susannah said. "There used to be this program I watched when I was a kid, *Sergeant Preston of the Yukon*. Sergeant Preston didn't have a billy-bumbler to keep him company, but he *did* have his faithful dog, King. Anyway, I closed my eyes and tried to remember what the guy's snowshoes looked like." She pointed to the ones Roland was wearing. "That's the best I could do."

"You did fine," he said, and the sincerity she heard in his simple compliment made her tingle all over. This was not necessarily the way she wanted Roland (or any other man, for that matter) to make her feel, but she seemed stuck with it. She wondered if that was nature or nurture, and wasn't sure she wanted to know.

"They'll be all right as long as they don't fall apart," she allowed. Her first effort had done just that.

"I don't feel the strips loosening," he told her. "Stretching a little, maybe, but that's all."

Now, as they crossed the great open space, that third pair of snowshoes was still holding together, and because she felt as though she'd made some sort of contribution, Susannah was able to let Roland pull her along without too much guilt. She *did* wonder about Mordred from time to time, and one night about ten days after they had crossed the snow-boundary, she came out and asked Roland to tell her what he knew. What prompted her was his declaration that there was no need to set a watch, at least for awhile; they could both get a full ten hours' worth of sleep, if that's what their bodies could use. Oy would wake them if they needed waking.

Roland had sighed and looked into the fire for nearly a full minute, his arms around his knees and his hands clasped loosely between them. She had just about decided he wasn't going to answer at all when he said, "Still following, but falling further and further behind. Struggling to eat, struggling to catch up, struggling most of all to stay warm."

"To stay *warm?*" To Susannah this seemed hard to believe. There were trees all around them.

"He has no matches and none of the Sterno stuff, either. I believe that one night—early on, this would have been—he came upon one of our fires with live coals still under the ash, and he was able to carry some with him for a few days after that and so have a fire at night. It's how the ancient rock-dwellers used to carry fire on their journeys, or so I was told."

Susannah nodded. She had been taught roughly the same thing in a high school science class, although the teacher had admitted a lot of what they knew about how Stone Age people got along wasn't true knowledge at all, but only informed guesswork. She wondered how much of what Roland had just told her was also guesswork, and so she asked him.

"It's not guessing, but I can't explain it. If it's the touch, Susannah, it's not such as Jake had. Not seeing and hearing, or even dreaming. Although . . . do you believe we have dreams sometimes we don't remember after we awaken?"

"Yes." She thought of telling him about rapid eye movement, and the REM sleep experiments she'd read about in *Look* magazine, then decided it would be too complex. She contented herself with saying that she was sure folks had dreams every single night that they didn't remember.

"Mayhap I see him and hear him in those," Roland said. "All I know is that he's struggling to keep up. He knows so little about the world that it's really a wonder he's still alive at all."

"Do you feel sorry for him?"

"No. I can't afford pity, and neither can you."

But his eyes had left hers when he said that, and she thought he was lying. Maybe he didn't *want* to feel sorry for Mordred, but she was sure he did, at least a little. Maybe he wanted to hope that Mordred would die on their trail—certainly there were plenty of chances it would happen, with hypothermia being the most likely cause—but Susannah didn't think he was quite able to do it. They might have outrun ka, but she reckoned that blood was still thicker than water.

There was something else, however, more powerful than even the blood of relation. She knew, because she could now feel it beating in her own head, both sleeping and waking. It was the Dark Tower. She thought that they were very close to it now. She had no idea what they were going to do about its mad guardian when and if they got there, but she found she no longer cared. For the present, all she wanted was to see it. The idea of entering it was still more than her imagination could deal with, but seeing it? Yes, she could imagine that. And she thought that seeing it would be enough.

TWO

They made their way slowly down the wide white downslope with Oy first hurrying at Roland's heel, then dropping behind to check on Susannah, then bounding back to Roland again. Bright blue holes sometimes opened above them. Roland knew that was the Beam at work, constantly pulling the cloud-cover southeast. Otherwise, the sky was white from horizon to horizon, and had a low *full* look both of them now recognized. More snow was on the come, and the gunslinger had an idea this storm might be the worst they'd seen. The wind was getting up, and the moisture in it was enough to numb all his exposed skin (after three weeks of diligent needlework, that amounted to not much more than his forehead and the tip of his nose). The gusts lifted long diaphanous scarves of white. These raced past them and then on down the slope like fantastical, shape-changing ballet-dancers.

"They're beautiful, aren't they?" Susannah asked from behind him, almost wistfully.

Roland of Gilead, no judge of beauty (except once, in the outland of Mejis), grunted. He knew what would be beautiful to him: decent cover when the storm overtook them, something more than just a thick grove of trees. So he almost doubted what he saw when the latest gust of wind blew itself out and the snow settled. He dropped the tow-band, stepped out of it, went back to Susannah (their gunna, now on the increase again, was strapped to the sledge behind her), and dropped on one knee next to her. Dressed in hides from top to toe, he looked more like a mangy bigfoot than a man.

"What do you make of that?" he asked her.

The wind kicked up again, harder than ever, at first obscuring what he had seen. When it dropped, a hole opened above them and the sun shone briefly through, lighting the snowfield with billions of diamond-chip sparkles. Susannah shaded her eyes with one hand and looked long downhill. What she saw was an inverted *T* carved in the snow. The cross arm, closest to them (but still at least two miles away) was relatively short, perhaps two hundred feet on either side. The long arm, however, was *very* long, going all the way to the horizon and then disappearing over it.

"Those are roads!" she said. "Someone's plowed a couple of roads down there, Roland!"

He nodded. "I thought so, but I wanted to hear you say it. I see something else, as well."

"What? Your eyes are sharper than mine, and by a lot."

"When we get a little closer, you'll see for yourself."

He tried to rise and she tugged impatiently at his arm. "Don't you play that game with me. What is it?"

"Roofs," he said, giving in to her. "I think there are cottages down there. Mayhap even a town."

"People? Are you saying *people*?"

"Well, it looks like there's smoke coming from one of the houses. Although it's hard to tell for sure with the sky so white."

She didn't know if she wanted to see people or not. Certainly such would complicate things. "Roland, we'll have to be careful."

"Yes," he said, and went back to the tow-band again. Before he picked it up, he paused to readjust his gunbelt, dropping the holster a bit so it lay more comfortably near his left hand.

An hour later they came to the intersection of the lane and the road. It was marked by a snowbank easily eleven feet high, one that had been built by some sort of plow. Susannah could see tread-marks, like those made by a bulldozer, pressed into the packed snow. Rising out of this hardpack was a pole. The street sign on top was no different from those she'd seen in all sorts of towns; at intersections in New York City, for that matter. The one indicating the short road said

ODD'S LANE.

It was the other that thrilled her heart, however.

TOWER ROAD,

it read.

THREE

All but one of the cottages clustered around the intersection were deserted, and many lay in half-buried heaps, broken beneath the weight of accumulating snow. One, however—it was about three-quarters of the way down the lefthand arm of Odd's Lane—was clearly different from the others. The roof had been mostly cleared of its potentially crushing weight of snow, and a path had been shoveled from the lane to the front door. It was from the chimney of this quaint, tree-surrounded cottage that the smoke was issuing, feather-white. One window was lit a wholesome butter-yellow, too, but it was the smoke that captured Susannah's eye. As far as she was concerned, it was the final touch. The only question in her mind was who would answer the door when they knocked. Would it be Hansel or his sister Gretel? (And were those two twins? Had anyone ever researched the matter?) Perhaps it would be Little Red Riding Hood, or Goldilocks, wearing a guilty goatee of porridge.

"Maybe we should just pass it by," she said, aware that she had dropped her voice to a near-whisper, even though they were still on the high snowbank created by the plow. "Give it a miss and say thank ya." She gestured to the sign reading **TOWER ROAD**. "We've got a clear way, Roland—maybe we ought to take it."

"And if we should, do you think that Mordred will?" Roland asked. "Do you think he'll simply pass by and leave whoever lives there in peace?"

Here was a question that hadn't even occurred to her, and of course the answer was no. If Mordred decided he could kill whoever was in the cottage, he'd do it. For food if the inhabitants were edible, but food would only be a secondary consideration. The woods behind them had been teeming with game, and even if Mordred hadn't been able to catch his own supper (and in his spider form, Susannah was sure he would have been perfectly capable of doing that), they had left the remains of their own meals at a good many camps. No, he would come out of the snowy uplands fed . . . but not happy. Not happy at all. And so woe to whoever happened to be in his path.

On the other hand, she thought . . . only there *was* no other hand, and all at once it was too late, anyway. The front door of the cottage opened, and an old man came out onto the stoop. He was wearing boots, jeans, and a heavy parka with a fur-lined hood. To Susannah this latter garment looked like something that might have been purchased at the Army-Navy Surplus Store in Greenwich Village.

The old man was rosy-cheeked, the picture of wintry good health, but he limped heavily, depending on the stout stick in his left hand. From behind his quaint little cottage with its fairy-tale plume of smoke came the piercing whinny of a horse.

"Sure, Lippy, I see em!" the old man cried, turning in that direction. "I got a'least one good eye left, ain't I?" Then he turned back to where Roland stood on the snowbank with Susannah and Oy flanking him. He raised his stick in a salute that seemed both merry and unafraid. Roland raised his own hand in return.

"Looks like we're in for some palaver whether we want it or not," said Roland.

"I know," she replied. Then, to the bumbler: "Oy, mind your manners now, you hear?"

Oy looked at her and then back at the old man without making a sound. On the subject of minding his manners he'd keep his own counsel awhile, it seemed.

The old man's bad leg was clearly *very* bad—"Next door to nuthin," Daddy Mose Carver would have said—but he got on well enough with his stick, moving in a sideways hopping gait that Susannah found both amusing and admirable. "Spry as a cricket" was another of Daddy Mose's many sayings, and perhaps this one fit yonder old man better. Certainly she saw no harm or danger in a white-haired fellow (the hair was long and baby-fine, hanging to the shoulders of his anorak) who had to hop along on a stick. And, as he drew closer, she saw that one of his eyes was filmed white with a cataract. The pupil, which was faintly visible, seemed to look dully off to their left. The other, however, regarded the newcomers with lively interest as the inhabitant of the cottage hopped down Odd's Lane toward them.

The horse whinnied again and the old man waved his stick wildly against the white, low-lying sky. "Shut up ya haybox, ya turd-factory, y'old clap-cunt gammer-gurt, ain't you ever seen cump'ny before? Was ya born in a barn, hee-hee? (For if y'wasn't, I'm a blue-eyed baboon, which there ain't no such thing!)"

Roland snorted with genuine laughter, and the last of Susannah's watchful apprehension departed. The horse whinnied again from the outbuilding behind the cottage—it was nowhere near grand enough to be called a barn—and the old man waved his stick at it once more, almost falling to the snowpack in the process. His awkward but nonetheless rapid gait had now brought him halfway to their location. He saved himself from what would have been a nasty tumble, took a large sidle-hop using the stick for a prop, then waved it cheerily in their direction.

"Hile, gunslingers!" the old man shouted. His lungs, at least, were admirable. "Gunslingers on pilgrimage to the Dark Tower, so y'are, so ya must be, for don't I see the big irons with the yaller grips? And the Beam be back, fair and strong, for I feel it and Lippy do, too! Spry as a colt she's been ever since Christmas, or what I call Christmas, not having a calendar nor seen Sainty Claus, which I wouldn't expect, for have I been a good boy? Never! Never! Good boys go to heaven, and all my friends be in t'other place, toastin marshmallows and drinkin Nozzy spiked with whiskey in the devil's den! Arrr, ne'mine, my tongue's caught in the middle and runs on both ends! Hile to one, hile to t'other, and hile to the little furry gobbins in between! Billy-bumbler as I live and breathe! *Yow*, ain't it good to see ya! Joe Collins is my name, Joe Collins of Odd's Lane, plenty odd m'self, one-eyed and lame I am, but otherwise at your service!"

He had now reached the snowbank marking the spot where Tower Road ended . . . or where it began, depending on your point of view and the direction you were traveling, Susannah supposed. He looked up at them, one eye bright as a bird's, the other looking off into the white wastes with dull fascination.

"Long days and pleasant nights, yar, so say I, and anyone who'd say different, they ain't here anyway, so who gives a good goddam what they say?" From his pocket he took what could only be a gumdrop and tossed it up. Oy grabbed it out of the air easily: *Snap!* and gone.

At this both Roland *and* Susannah laughed. It felt strange to laugh, but it was a good feeling, like finding something of value long after you were sure it was lost forever. Even Oy appeared to be grinning, and if the horse bothered him (it trumpeted again as they looked down on sai Collins from their snowbank perch), it didn't show.

"I got a million questions for yer," Collins said, "but I'll start with just one: how in the hell are yers gonna get down offa that snowbank?"

FOUR

As it turned out, Susannah slid down, using their travois as a sled. She chose the place where the northwestern end of Odd's Lane disappeared beneath the snow, because the embankment was a little shallower there. Her trip was short but not smooth. She hit a large and crusted snow-boulder three quarters of the way down, fell off the travois, and made the rest of her descent in a pair of gaudy somersaults, laughing wildly as she fell. The travois turned over—turned turtle, may it do ya—and spilled their gunna every whichway and hell to breakfast.

Roland and Oy came leaping down behind. Roland bent over her at once, clearly concerned, and Oy sniffed anxiously at her face, but Susannah was still laughing. So was the codger. Daddy Mose would have called his laughter "gay as old Dad's hatband."

"I'm fine, Roland—took worse tumbles off my Flexible Flyer when I was a kid, tell ya true."

"All's well that ends well," Joe Collins agreed. He gave her a look with his good eye to make sure she was indeed all right, then began to pick up some of the scattered goods, leaning laboriously over on his stick, his fine white hair blowing around his rosy face.

"Nah, nah," Roland said, reaching out to grasp his arm. "I'll do that, thee'll fall on thy thiddles."

At this the old man roared with laughter, and Roland joined him willingly enough. From behind the cottage, the horse gave another loud whinny, as if protesting all this good humor.

"'Fall on thy thiddles'! Man, that's a good one! I don't have the veriest clue under heaven what my thiddles are, yet it's a good one! Ain't it just!" He brushed the snow off Susannah's hide coat while Roland quickly picked up the spilled goods and stacked them back on their makeshift sled. Oy helped, bringing several wrapped packages of meat in his jaws and dropping them on the back of the travois.

"That's a smart little beastie!" Joe Collins said admiringly.

"He's been a good trailmate," Susannah agreed. She was now very glad they had stopped; would not have deprived herself of this good-natured old man's acquaintance for worlds. She offered him her clumsily clad right hand. "I'm Susannah Dean—Susannah of New York. Daughter of Dan."

He took her hand and shook it. His own hand was ungloved, and although the fingers were gnarled with arthritis, his grip was strong. "New York, is it! Why, I once hailed from there, myself. Also Akron, Omaha, and San Francisco. Son of Henry and Flora, if it matters to you."

"You're from America-side?" Susannah asked.

"Oh God yes, but long ago and long," he said. "What'chee might call delah." His good eye sparkled; his bad eye went on regarding the snowy wastes with that same dead lack of interest. He turned to Roland. "And who might you be, my friend? For I'll call you my friend same as I would anyone, unless they prove different, in which case I'd belt em with Bessie, which is what I call my stick."

Roland was grinning. Was helpless not to, Susannah thought. "Roland Deschain, of Gilead. Son of Steven."

"Gilead! *Gilead!*" Collins's good eye went round with amazement. "There's a name out of the past, ain't it? One for the books! Holy Pete, you must be older'n God!"

"Some would say so," Roland agreed, now only smiling . . . but warmly.

"And the little fella?" he asked, bending forward. From his pocket, Collins produced two more gumdrops, one red and one green. Christmas colors, and Susannah felt a faint touch of *déjà vu.* It brushed her mind like a wing and then was gone. "What's your name, little fella? What do they holler when they want you to come home?"

"He doesn't—"

—*talk anymore, although he did once* was how Susannah meant to finish, but before she could, the bumbler said: "Oy!" And he said it as brightly and firmly as ever in his time with Jake.

"Good fella!" Collins said, and tumbled the gumdrops into

Oy's mouth. Then he reached out with that same gnarled hand, and Oy raised his paw to meet it. They shook, well-met near the intersection of Odd's Lane and Tower Road.

"I'll be damned," Roland said mildly.

"So won't we all in the end, I reckon, Beam or no Beam," Joe Collins remarked, letting go of Oy's paw. "But not today. Now what I say is that we ort to get in where it's warm and we can palaver over a cup of coffee—for I have some, so I do—or a pot of ale. I even have sumpin I call eggnog, if it does ya. It does me pretty fine, especially with a teensy piss o' rum in it, but who knows? I ain't really *tasted* nuffink in five years or more. Air outta the Discordia's done for my taste-buds and for my nose, too. Anyro', what do you say?" He regarded them brightly.

"I'd say that sounds pretty damned fine," Susannah told him. Rarely had she said anything she meant more.

He slapped her companionably on the shoulder. "A good woman is a pearl beyond price! Don't know if that's Shakespeare, the Bible, or a combination of the t—

"Arrr, Lippy, goddam what used to be yer eyes, where do you think *you're* going? Did yer want to meet these folks, was that it?"

His voice had fallen into the outrageous croon that seems the exclusive property of people who live alone except for a pet or two. His horse had blundered its way to them and Collins grabbed her around the neck, petting her with rough affection, but Susannah thought the beast was the ugliest quadruped she'd seen in her whole life. Some of her good cheer melted away at the sight of the thing. Lippy was blind—not in one eye but in both—and scrawny as a scarecrow. As she walked, the rack of her bones shifted back and forth so clearly beneath her mangy coat that Susannah almost expected some of them to poke through. For a moment she remembered the black corridor under Castle Discordia with a kind of nightmarish total recall: the slithering sound of the thing that had followed them, and the bones. All those bones.

Collins might have seen some of this on her face, for when he spoke again he sounded almost defensive. "Her an ugly old thing, I know, but when you get as old as she is, I don't reckon you'll be winnin many beauty contests yourself!" He patted the horse's chafed and sore-looking neck, then seized her scant mane as if to pull the hair out by the roots (although Lippy showed no pain) and turned her in the road so she was facing the cottage again. As he did this, the first flakes of the coming storm skirled down.

"Come on, Lippy, y'old ki'-box and gammer-gurt, ye sway-back nag and lost four-legged leper! Can't ye smell the snow in the air? Because I can, and my nose went south years ago!"

He turned back to Roland and Susannah and said, "I hope y'prove partial to my cookin, so I do, because I think this is gonna be a three-day blow. Aye, three at least before Demon Moon shows er face again! But we're well-met, so we are, and I set my watch and warrant on it! Ye just don't want to judge my hospitality by my *horse*-pitality! Hee!"

I should hope not, Susannah thought, and gave a little shiver. The old man had turned away, but Roland gave her a curious look. She smiled and shook her head as if to say *It's nothing*— which, of course, it was. She wasn't about to tell the gunslinger that a spavined nag with cataracts on her eyes and her ribs show-ing had given her a case of the whim-whams. Roland had never called her a silly goose, and by God she didn't mean to give him cause to do so n—

As if hearing her thoughts, the old nag looked back and bared her few remaining teeth at Susannah. The eyes in Lippy's bony wedge of a head were pus-rimmed plugs of blindness above her somehow gruesome grin. She whinnied at Susan-nah as if to say *Think what you will, blackbird; I'll be here long after thee's gone thy course and died thy death.* At the same time the wind gusted, swirling snow in their faces, soughing in the snow-laden firs, and hooting beneath the eaves of Collins's little house. It began to die away and then strengthened again for a moment, making a brief, grieving cry that sounded almost human.

FIVE

The outbuilding consisted of a chicken-coop on one side, Lippy's stall on the other, and a little loft stuffed with hay. "I can get up there and fork it down," Collins said, "but I take my life in my hands ever time I do, thanks to this bust hip of mine. Now, I can't make you help an old man, sai Deschain, but if you would . . . ?"

Roland climbed the ladder resting a-tilt against the edge of the loft floor and tossed down hay until Collins told him it was good, plenty enough to last Lippy through even four days' worth of blow. ("For she don't eat worth what'chee might call a Polish fuck, as you can see lookin at her," he said.) Then the gunslinger came back down and Collins led them along the short back walk to his cottage. The snow piled on either side was as high as Roland's head.

"Be it ever so humble, et cet'ra," Joe said, and ushered them into his kitchen. It was paneled in knotty pine which was actually plastic, Susannah saw when she got closer. And it was delightfully warm. The name on the electric stove was Rossco, a brand she'd never heard of. The fridge was an Amana and had a special little door set into the front, above the handle. She leaned closer and saw the words MAGIC ICE. "This thing makes ice cubes?" she asked, delighted.

"Well, no, not exactly," Joe said. "It's the *freezer* that makes em, beauty; that thing on the front just drops em into your drink."

This struck her funny, and she laughed. She looked down, saw Oy looking up at her with his old fiendish grin, and that made her laugh harder than ever. Mod cons aside, the smell of the kitchen was wonderfully nostalgic: sugar and spice and everything nice.

Roland was looking up at the fluorescent lights and Collins nodded. "Yar, yar, I got all the 'lectric," he said. "Hot-air furnace, too, ain't it nice? And nobody ever sends me a bill! The genny's in a shed round to t'other side. It's a Honda, and quiet as Sunday morning! Even when you get right up on top of its little shed, you don't hear nuffink but *mmmmmm*. Stuttering Bill changes the propane tank and does the maintenance when it needs maintaining, which hasn't been but twice in all the time I've been here. Nawp, Joey's lyin, he'll soon be dyin. Three times, it's been. Three in all."

"Who's Stuttering Bill?" Susannah asked, just as Roland was asking "How long have you been here?"

Joe Collins laughed. "One at a time, me foine new friends, one at a time!" He had set his stick aside to struggle out of his coat, put his weight on his bad leg, made a low snarling sound, and nearly fell over. *Would* have fallen over, had Roland not steadied him.

"Thankee, thankee, thankee," Joe said. "Although I tell you what, it wouldn't have been the first time I wound up with my nose on that lernoleum! But, as you saved me a tumble, it's your question I'll answer first. I've been here, Odd Joe of Odd's Lane, just about seb'nteen years. The only reason I can't tell you bang-on is that for awhile there, time got pretty goddam funny, if you know what I mean."

"We do," Susannah said. "Believe me, we do."

Collins was now divesting himself of a sweater, and beneath it was another. Susannah's first impression had been of a stout old man who stopped just short of fat. Now she saw that a lot of what she'd taken for fat was nothing but padding. He wasn't as desperately scrawny as his old horse, but he was a long shout from stout.

"Now Stuttering Bill," the old man continued, removing the second sweater, "he be a robot. Cleans the house as well as keepin my generator runnin . . . and a-course he's the one that does the plowin. When I first come here, he only stuttered once in awhile; now it's every second or third word. What I'll do when he finally runs down I dunno." To Susannah's ear, he sounded singularly unworried about it.

"Maybe he'll get better, now that the Beam's working right again," she said.

"He might last a little *longer*, but I doubt like hell that he'll get any *better,*" Joe said. "Machines don't heal the way living things do." He'd finally reached his thermal undershirt, and here the stripdown stopped. Susannah was grateful. Looking at the somehow ghastly barrel of the horse's ribs, so close beneath the short gray fur, had been enough. She had no wish to see the master's, as well.

"Off with yer coats and your leggings," Joe said. "I'll get yez eggnog or whatever else ye'd like in a minute or two, but first I'd show yer my livin room, for it's my pride, so it is."

SIX

There was a rag rug on the living room floor that would have looked at home in Gramma Holmes's house, and a La-Z-Boy recliner with a table beside it. The table was heaped with magazines, paperback books, a pair of spectacles, and a brown bottle containing God knew what sort of medicine. There was a television, although Susannah couldn't imagine what old Joe might possibly watch on it (Eddie and Jake would have recognized the VCR sitting on the shelf beneath). But what took all of Susannah's attention—and Roland's, as well—was the photograph on one of the walls. It had been thumbtacked there slightly askew, in a casual fashion that seemed (to Susannah, at least) almost sacrilegious.

It was a photograph of the Dark Tower.

Her breath deserted her. She worked her way over to it, barely feeling the knots and nubbles of the rag rug beneath her palms, then raised her arms. "Roland, pick me up!"

He did, and she saw that his face had gone dead pale except for two hard balls of color burning in his thin cheeks. His eyes were blazing. The Tower stood against the darkening sky with sunset painting the hills behind it orange, the slitted windows rising in their eternal spiral. From some of those windows there spilled a dim and eldritch glow. She could see balconies jutting out from the dark stone sides at every two or three stories, and the squat doors that opened onto them, all shut. Locked as well, she had no doubt. Before the Tower was the field of roses, Can'-Ka No Rey, dim but still lovely in the shadows. Most of the roses were closed against the coming dark but a few still peeped out like sleepy eyes.

"Joe!" she said. Her voice was little more than a whisper. She felt faint, and it seemed she could hear singing voices, far and wee. "Oh, Joe! This *picture* . . . !"

"Aye, mum," he said, clearly pleased by her reaction. "It's a good 'un, ain't it? Which is why I pinned it up. I've got others, but this is the best. Right at sunset, so the shadow seems to lie forever back along the Path of the Beam. Which in a way it does, as I'm sure ye both must know."

Roland's breathing in her right ear was rapid and ragged, as if he'd just run a race, but Susannah barely noticed. For it was not just the *subject* of the picture that had filled her with awe.

"This is a *Polaroid!*"

"Well . . . yar," he said, sounding puzzled at the level of her excitement. "I suppose Stuttering Bill could have brung me a Kodak if I'd ast for one, but how would I ever have gotten the fillum developed? And by the time I thought of a video camera— for the gadget under the TV'd play such things—I was too old to go back, and yonder nag 'uz too old to carry me. Yet I would if I could, for it's lovely there, a place of warm-hearted ghosts. I heard the singing voices of friends long gone; my Ma and Pa, too. I allus—"

A paralysis had seized Roland. She felt it in the stillness of his muscles. Then it broke and he turned from the picture so fast that it made Susannah dizzy. "You've been there?" he asked. "*You've been to the Dark Tower?*"

"Indeed I have," said the old man. "For who else do ye think took that pitcher? Ansel Fuckin Adams?"

"*When* did you take it?"

"That's from my last trip," he said. "Two year ago, in the summer—although that's lower land, ye must know, and if the snow ever comes to it, I've never seen it."

"How long from here?"

Joe closed his bad eye and calculated. It didn't take him long, but to Roland and Susannah it *seemed* long, very long indeed. Outside, the wind gusted. The old horse whinnied as if in protest at the sound. Beyond the frost-rimmed window, the falling snow was beginning to twist and dance.

"Well," he said, "ye're on the downslope now, and Stuttering Bill keeps Tower Road plowed for as far as ye'd go; what else does the old whatchamacallit have to do with his time? O' course ye'll want to wait here until this new nor'east jeezer blows itself out—"

"How long once we're on the move?" Roland asked.

"Rarin t'go, ain'tcha? Aye, hot n rarin, and why not, for if you've come from In-World ye must have been many long years gettin this far. Hate to think how many, so I do. I'm gonna say it'd take you six days to get out of the White Lands, maybe seven—"

"Do you call these lands Empathica?" Susannah asked.

He blinked, then gave her a puzzled look. "Why no, ma'am—I've never heard this part of creation called anything but the White Lands."

The puzzled look was bogus. She was almost sure of it. Old Joe Collins, cheery as Father Christmas in a children's play, had just lied to her. She wasn't sure why, and before she could pursue it, Roland asked sharply: "Would you let that go for now? Would you, for your father's sake?"

"Yes, Roland," she said meekly. "Of course."

Roland turned back to Joe, still holding Susannah on his hip.

"Might take you as long as nine days, I guess," Joe said, scratching his chin, "for that road can be plenty slippery, especially after Bill packs down the snow, but you can't get him to stop. He's got his orders to follow. His *programmin,* he calls it." The old man saw Roland getting ready to speak and raised his hand. "Nay, nay, I'm not drawrin it out to irritate cher, sir or sai or whichever you prefer—it's just that I'm not much used to cump'ny.

"Once you get down b'low the snowline it must be another ten or twelve days a-walkin, but ain't no need in the world to walk unless you fancy it. There's another one of those Positronics huts down there with any number a' wheelie vehicles parked inside. Like golf-carts, they are. The bat'tries are all dead, natcherly—flat as yer hat—but there's a gennie there, too, Honda just like mine, and it was a-workin the last time I was down there, for Bill keeps things in trim as much as he can. If you could charge up one of those wheelies, why that'd cut your time down to four days at most. So here's what I think: if you had to hoof it the whole way, it might take you as long as nineteen days. If you can go the last leg in one o' them hummers— that's what I call em, hummers, for that's the sound they make when they're runnin—I should say ten days. Maybe eleven."

The room fell silent. The wind gusted, throwing snow against the side of the cottage, and Susannah once more marked how it sounded almost like a human cry. A trick of the angles and eaves, no doubt.

"Less than three weeks, even if we had to walk," Roland said. He reached out toward the Polaroid photograph of the dusky stone tower standing against the sunset sky, but did not quite touch it. It was as if, Susannah thought, he were afraid to touch it. "After all the years and all the miles."

Not to mention the gallons of spilled blood, Susannah thought, but she would not have said this even if the two of them had been alone. There was no need to; he knew how much blood had been spilled as well as she did. But there was something off-key here. Off-key or downright wrong. And the gunslinger did *not* seem to know *that.*

Sympathy was to respect the feelings of another. Empathy was to actually *share* those feelings. Why would folks call any land Empathica?

And why would this pleasant old man lie about it?

"Tell me something, Joe Collins," Roland said.

"Aye, gunslinger, if I can."

"Have you been right up *to* it? Laid your hand on the stone of it?"

The old man looked at first to see if Roland was joshing him. When he was sure that wasn't the case, he looked shocked. "No," he said, and for the first time sounded as American as Susannah herself. "That pitcher's as close as I dared go. The edge of the rosefield. I'm gonna say two, two hundred and fifty yards away. What the robot'd call five hundred arcs o' the wheel."

Roland nodded. "And why not?"

"Because I thought to go closer might kill me, but I wouldn't be able to stop. The voices would draw me on. So I thought then, and so I do think, even today."

SEVEN

After dinner—surely the finest meal Susannah had had since being hijacked into this other world, and possibly the best in her entire life—the sore on her face burst wide open. It was Joe Collins's fault, in a way, but even later, when they had much to hold against the only inhabitant of Odd's Lane, she did not blame him for that. It was the last thing he would have wanted, surely.

He served chicken, roasted to a turn and especially tasty after all the venison. With it, Joe brought to table mashed potatoes with gravy, cranberry jelly sliced into thick red discs, green peas ("Only canned, say sorry," he told them), and a dish of little boiled onions bathing in sweet canned milk. There was also eggnog. Roland and Susannah drank it with childish greed, although both passed on "the teensy piss o' rum." Oy had his own dinner; Joe fixed a plate of chicken and potatoes for him and then set it on the floor by the stove. Oy made quick work of it and then lay in the doorway between the kitchen and the combination living room/dining room, licking his chops to get every taste of giblet gravy out of his whiskers while watching the humes with his ears up.

"I couldn't eat dessert so don't ask me," Susannah said when she'd finished cleaning her plate for the second time, sopping up the remains of the gravy with a piece of bread. "I'm not sure I can even get down from this chair."

"Well, that's all right," Joe said, looking disappointed, "maybe later. I've got a chocolate pudding and a butterscotch one."

Roland raised his napkin to muffle a belch and then said, "I could eat a dab of both, I think."

"Well, come to that, maybe I could, too," Susannah allowed. How many eons since she'd tasted butterscotch?

When they were done with the pudding, Susannah offered to help with the cleaning-up but Joe waved her away, saying he'd just put the pots and plates in the dishwasher to rinse and then run "the whole happy bunch of em" later. He seemed spryer to her as he and Roland went back and forth into the kitchen, less dependent on the stick. Susannah guessed that the little piss o' rum (or maybe several of them, adding up to one large piss by the end of the meal) might have had something to do with it.

He poured coffee and the three of them (four, counting Oy) sat down in the living room. Outside it was growing dark and the wind was screaming louder than ever. *Mordred's out there someplace, hunkered down in a snow-hollow or a grove of trees,* she thought, and once again had to stifle pity for him. It would have been easier if she hadn't known that, murderous or not, he must still be a child.

"Tell us how you came to be here, Joe," Roland invited.

Joe grinned. "That's a hair-raising story," he said, "but if you really want to hear it, I guess I don't mind tellin it." The grin mellowed to a wistful smile. "It's nice, havin folks to talk to for a little bit. Lippy does all right at listenin, but she never says nuffink back."

He'd started off trying to be a teacher, Joe said, but quickly discovered that life wasn't for him. He liked the kids—loved them, in fact—but hated all the administrative bullshit and the way the system seemed set up to make sure no square pegs escaped the relentless rounding process. He quit teaching after only three years and went into show business.

"Did you sing or dance?" Roland wanted to know.

"Neither one," Joe replied. "I gave em the old stand-up."

"Stand-up?"

"He means he was a comedian," Susannah said. "He told jokes."

"Correct!" Joe said brightly. "Some folks actually thought they were funny, too. Course, they were the minority."

He got an agent whose previous enterprise, a discount men's clothing store, had gone bankrupt. One thing led to another, he said, and one *gig* led to another, too. Eventually he found himself working second- and third-rate nightclubs from coast to coast, driving a battered but reliable old Ford pickup truck and going where Shantz, his agent, sent him. He almost never worked the weekends; on the weekends, even the third-rate clubs wanted to book rock-and-roll bands.

This was in the late sixties and early seventies, and there'd been no shortage of what Joe called "current events material": hippies and yippies, bra-burners and Black Panthers, movie-stars, and, as always, politics—but he said he had been more of a traditional joke-oriented comedian. Let Mort Sahl and George Carlin do the current-events shtick if they wanted it; he'd stick to *Speaking of my mother-in-law* and *They say our Polish friends are dumb but let me tell you about this Irish girl I met.*

During his recitation, an odd (and—to Susannah, at least—rather poignant) thing happened. Joe Collins's Mid-World accent, with its yers and yars and if-it-does-yas began to cross-fade into an accent she could only identify as Wiseguy Ameri-can. She kept expecting to hear *bird* come out of his mouth as *boid, heard* as *hoid,* but she guessed that was only because she'd spent so much time with Eddie. She thought Joe Collins was one of those odd natural mimics whose voices are the auditory equivalent of Silly Putty, taking impressions that fade as quickly as they rise to the surface. Doing a club in Brooklyn, it probably *was boid* and *hoid;* in Pittsburgh it would be *burrd* and *hurrd;* the Giant Eagle supermarket would become *Jaunt Iggle.*

Roland stopped him early on to ask if a comic was like a court jester, and the old man laughed heartily. "You got it. Just think of a bunch of people sitting around in a smoky room with drinks in their hands instead of the king and his courtiers."

Roland nodded, smiling.

"There are advantages to being a funnyman doing one-nighters in the Midwest, though," he said. "If you tank in

Dubuque, all that happens is you end up doing twenty minutes instead of forty-five and then it's on to the next town. There are probably places in Mid-World where they'd cut off your damn head for stinking up the joint."

At this the gunslinger burst out laughing, a sound that still had the power to startle Susannah (although she was laughing herself). "You say true, Joe."

In the summer of 1972, Joe had been playing a nightclub called Jango's in Cleveland, not far from the ghetto. Roland interrupted again, this time wanting to know what a ghetto was.

"In the case of Hauck," Susannah said, "it means a part of the city where most of the people are black and poor, and the cops have a habit of swinging their billyclubs first and asking questions later."

"Bing!" Joe exclaimed, and rapped his knuckles on the top of his head. "Couldn't have said it better myself!"

Again there came that odd, babyish crying sound from the front of the house, but this time the wind was in a relative lull. Susannah glanced at Roland, but if the gunslinger heard, he gave no sign.

It was *the wind,* Susannah told herself. *What else* could *it be?*

Mordred, her mind whispered back. *Mordred out there, freezing. Mordred out there dying while we sit in here with our hot coffee.*

But she said nothing.

There had been trouble in Hauck for a couple of weeks, Joe said, but he'd been drinking pretty heavily ("Hitting it hard" was how he put it) and hardly realized that the crowd at his second show was about a fifth the size of the one at the first. "Hell, I was on a roll," he said. "I don't know about anyone else, but I was knocking *myself* dead, rolling me in the aisles."

Then someone had thrown a Molotov cocktail through the club's front window (*Molotov cocktail* was a term Roland understood), and before you could say *Take my mother-in-law . . . please,* the place was on fire. Joe had boogied out the back, through the stage door. He'd almost made it to the street when three men ("all very black, all roughly the size of NBA centers") grabbed him. Two held; the third punched. Then someone swung a bottle. Boom-boom, out go the lights. He had awakened on a grassy hillside near a deserted town called Stone's Warp, according to the signs in the empty buildings along Main Street. To Joe Collins it had looked like the set of a Western movie after all the actors had gone home.

It was around this time that Susannah decided she did not believe much of sai Collins's story. It was undoubtedly entertaining, and given Jake's first entry into Mid-World, after being run over in the street and killed while on his way to school, it was not totally implausible. But she still didn't believe much of it. The question was, did it matter?

"You couldn't call it heaven, because there were no clouds and no choirs of angels," Joe said, "but I decided it was some sort of an afterlife, just the same." He had wandered about. He found food, he found a horse (Lippy), and moved on. He had met various roving bands of people, some friendly, some not, some true-threaded, some mutie. Enough so he'd picked up some of the lingo and a little Mid-World history; certainly he knew about the Beams and the Tower. At one point he'd tried to cross the Badlands, he said, but he'd gotten scared and turned back when his skin began to break out in all sorts of sores and weird blemishes.

"I got a boil on my ass, and that was the final touch," he said. "Six or eight years ago, this might have been. Me n Lippy said the hell with going any further. That was when I found this place, which is called Westring, and when Stuttering Bill found me. He's got a little doctorin, and he lanced the boil on my bottom."

Roland wanted to know if Joe had witnessed the passage of the Crimson King as that mad creature made his final pilgrimage to the Dark Tower. Joe said he had not, but that six months ago there had been a terrible storm ("a real boilermaker") that drove him down into his cellar. While he was there the electric lights had failed, genny or no genny, and as he cowered in the dark, a sense had come to him that some terrible creature was close by, and that it might at any moment touch Joe's mind and follow his thoughts to where he was hiding.

"You know what I felt like?" he asked them.

Roland and Susannah shook their heads. Oy did the same, in perfect imitation.

"Snack-food," Joe said. "Potential snack-food."

This part of his story's true, Susannah thought. *He may have changed it around a little, but basically it's true.* And if she had any reason to think that, it was only because the idea of the Crimson King traveling in his own portable storm seemed horribly plausible.

"What did you do?" Roland asked.

"Went to sleep," he said. "It's a talent I've always had, like doing impressions—although I don't do famous voices in my act, because they never go over out in the sticks. Not unless you're Rich Little, at least. Strange but true. I can sleep pretty much on command, so that's what I did down in the cellar. When I woke up again the lights were back on and the . . . the whatever-it-was was gone. I know about the Crimson King, of course, I see folks from time to time still—nomads like you three, for the most part—and they talk about him. Usually they fork the sign of the evil eye and spit between their fingers when they do. You think that was him, huh? You think the Crimson King actually passed by Odd's Lane on his way to the Tower." Then, before they had a chance to answer: "Well, why not? Tower Road's the main throughfare, after all. It goes all the way there."

You know it was him, Susannah thought. *What game are you playing, Joe?*

The thin cry that was most definitely not the wind came again. She no longer thought it was Mordred, though. She thought that maybe it was coming from the cellar where Joe had gone to hide from the Crimson King . . . or so he'd said. Who was down there now? And was he hiding, as Joe had done, or was he a prisoner?

"It hasn't been a bad life," Joe was saying. "Not the life I expected, not by any manner or means, but I got a theory—the folks who end up living the lives they expected are more often than not the ones who end up takin sleepin pills or stickin the barrel of a gun in their mouths and pullin the trigger."

Roland seemed still to be a few turns back, because he said, "You were a court jester and the customers in these inns were your court."

Joe smiled, showing a lot of white teeth. Susannah frowned. Had she seen his teeth before? They had been doing a lot of laughing and she *should* have seen them, but she couldn't remember that she actually had. Certainly he didn't have the mush-mouth sound of someone whose teeth are mostly gone (such people had consulted with her father on many occasions, most of them in search of artificial replacements). If she'd had to guess earlier on, she would have said he *had* teeth but they were down to nothing but pegs and nubbins, and—

And what's the matter with you, girl? He might be lying about a few things, but he surely didn't grow a fresh set of teeth since you sat down to dinner! You're letting your imagination run away with you.

Was she? Well, it was possible. And maybe that thin cry was nothing but the sound of the wind in the eaves at the front of the house, after all.

"I'd hear some of your jokes and stories," Roland said. "As you told them on the road, if it does ya."

Susannah looked at him closely, wondering if the gunslinger had some ulterior motive for this request, but he seemed genuinely interested. Even before seeing the Polaroid of the Dark Tower tacked to the living room wall (his eyes returned to it constantly as Joe told his story), Roland had been invested by a kind of hectic good cheer that was really not much like him at all. It was almost as if he were ill, edging in and out of delirium.

Joe Collins seemed surprised by the gunslinger's request, but not at all displeased. "Good God," he said. "I haven't done any stand-up in what seems like a thousand years . . . and considering the way time stretched there for awhile, maybe it *has* been a thousand. I'm not sure I'd know how to begin."

Susannah surprised herself by saying, "Try."

EIGHT

Joe thought about it and then stood up, brushing a few errant crumbs from his shirt. He limped to the center of the room, leaving his crutch leaning against his chair. Oy looked up at him with his ears cocked and his old grin on his chops, as if anticipating the entertainment to come. For a moment Joe looked uncertain. Then he took a deep breath, let it out, and gave them a smile. "Promise you won't throw no tomatoes if I stink up the joint," he said. "Remember, it's been a long time."

"Not after you took us in and fed us," Susannah said. "Never in life."

Roland, always literal, said, "We have no tomatoes, in any case."

"Right, right. Although there are some canned ones in the pantry . . . forget I said that!"

Susannah smiled. So did Roland.

Encouraged, Joe said: "Okay, let's go back to that magical place called Jango's in that magical city some folks call the mistake on the lake. Cleveland, Ohio, in other words. Second show. The one I never got to finish, and I was on a roll, take my word for it. Give me just a second . . ."

He closed his eyes. Seemed to gather himself. When he opened them again, he somehow looked ten years younger. It was astounding. And he didn't just *sound* American when he began to speak, he *looked* American. Susannah couldn't have explained that in words, but she knew it was true: here was one Joe Collins, Made in U.S.A.

"Hey, ladies and gentlemen, welcome to Jango's, I'm Joe Collins and you're not."

Roland chuckled and Susannah smiled, mostly to be polite—that was a pretty old one.

"The management has asked me to remind you that this is two-beers-for-a-buck night. Got it? Good. With them the motive is profit, with me it's self-interest. Because the more you drink, the funnier I get."

Susannah's smile widened. There was a rhythm to comedy, even *she* knew that, although she couldn't have done even five minutes of stand-up in front of a noisy nightclub crowd, not if her life had depended on it. There was a *rhythm,* and after an uncertain beginning, Joe was finding his. His eyes were half-lidded, and she guessed he was seeing the mixed colors of the gels over the stage—so like the colors of the Wizard's Rainbow, now that she thought of it—and smelling the smoke of fifty smoldering cigarettes. One hand on the chrome pole of the mike; the other free to make any gesture it liked. Joe Collins playing Jango's on a Friday night—

No, not a Friday. He said all the clubs book rock-and-roll bands on the weekends.

"Ne'mine all that mistake-on-the-lake stuff, Cleveland's a beautiful city," Joe said. He was picking up the pace a little now. Starting to rap, Eddie might have said. "My folks are from Cleveland, but when they were seventy they moved to Florida. They didn't want to, but shitfire, it's the law. Bing!" Joe rapped his knuckles against his head and crossed his eyes. Roland chuckled again even though he couldn't have the slightest idea where (or even what) Florida was. Susannah's smile was wider than ever.

"Florida's a helluva place," Joe said. *"Helluva* place. Home of the newly wed and the nearly dead. My grandfather retired to Florida, God rest his soul. When I die, I want to go peacefully, in my sleep, like Grampa Fred. Not screaming, like the passengers in his car."

Roland roared with laughter at that one, and Susannah did, too. Oy's grin was wider than ever.

"My grandma, she was great, too. She said she learned how to swim when someone took her out on the Cuyahoga River and threw her off the boat. I said, 'Hey, Nana, they weren't trying to teach you how to swim.'"

Roland snorted, wiped his nose, then snorted again. His cheeks had bloomed with color. Laughter elevated the entire metabolism, put it almost on a fight-or-flight basis; Susannah had read that somewhere. Which meant her own must be rising, because she was laughing, too. It was as if all the horror and sorrow were gushing out of an open wound, gushing out like—

Well, like blood.

She heard a faint alarm-bell start to ring, far back in her mind, and ignored it. What was there to be alarmed about? They were *laughing*, for goodness' sake! Having a good time!

"Can I be serious a minute? No? Well, fuck you and the nag you rode in on—tomorrow when I wake up, I'll be sober, but you'll still be ugly.

"And bald."

(Roland roared.)

"I'm gonna be serious, okay? If you don't like it, stick it where you keep your change-purse. My Nana was a great lady. Women in general are great, you know it? But they have their flaws, just like men. If a woman has to choose between catching a fly ball and saving a baby's life, for instance, she'll save the baby without even considering how many men are on base. Bing!" He rapped his head with his knuckles and popped his eyes in a way that made them both laugh. Roland tried to put his coffee cup down and spilled it. He was holding his stomach. Hearing him laugh so hard—to surrender to laughter so completely— was funny in itself, and Susannah burst out in a fresh gale.

"Men are one thing, women are another. Put em together and you've got a whole new taste treat. Like Oreos. Like Peanut Butter Cups. Like raisin cake with snot sauce. Show me a man and a woman and I'll show you the Peculiar Institution—not slavery, marriage. But I repeat myself. Bing!" He rapped his head. Popped his eyes. This time they seemed to come ka-sproing halfway out of their sockets

(*how does he* do *that*)

and Susannah had to clutch her stomach, which was beginning to ache with the force of her laughter. And her temples were beginning to pound. It hurt, but it was a *good* hurt.

"Marriage is having a wife or a husband. Yeah! Check Webster's! Bigamy is having a wife or husband too many. Of course, that's also monogamy. Bing!"

If Roland laughed any harder, Susannah thought, he would

go sliding right out of his chair and into the puddle of spilled coffee.

"Then there's divorce, a Latin term meaning 'to rip a man's genitals out through the wallet.'"

"But I was talking about Cleveland, remember? You know how Cleveland got started? A bunch of people in New York said, 'Gee I'm starting to enjoy the crime and the poverty, but it's not quite cold enough. Let's go west.'"

Laughter, Susannah would reflect later, is like a hurricane: once it reaches a certain point, it becomes self-feeding, self-supporting. You laugh not because the *jokes* are funny but because your own *condition* is funny. Joe Collins took them to this point with his next sally.

"Hey, remember in elementary school, you were told that in case of fire you have to line up quietly with the smallest people in front and the tallest people at the end of the line? What's the logic in that? Do tall people burn slower?"

Susannah shrieked with laughter and slapped the side of her face. This produced a sudden and unexpected burst of pain that drove all the laughter out of her in a moment. The sore beside her mouth had been growing again, but hadn't bled in two or three days. When she inadvertently struck it with her flailing hand, she knocked away the blackish-red crust covering it. The sore did not just bleed; it *gushed.*

For a moment she was unaware of what had just happened. She only knew that slapping the side of her face hurt *much* more than it should have done. Joe also seemed unaware (his eyes were mostly closed again), *must* have been unaware, because he rapped faster than ever: "Hey, and what about that seafood restaurant they have at Sea World? I got halfway through my fishburger and wondered if I was eating a slow learner! Bing! And speaking of fish —"

Oy barked in alarm. Susannah felt sudden wet warmth run down the side of her neck and onto her shoulder.

"Stop, Joe," Roland said. He sounded out of breath. Weak. With laughter, Susannah supposed. Oh, but the side of her face hurt, and —

Joe opened his eyes, looking annoyed. "What? Jesus Christ, you wanted it and I was *giving* it to ya!"

"Susannah's hurt herself." The gunslinger was up and looking at her, laughter lost in concern.

"I'm not hurt, Roland, I just slapped myself upside the head a little harder than I m—" Then she looked at her hand and was dismayed to see it was wearing a red glove.

NINE

Oy barked again. Roland snatched the napkin from beside his overturned cup. One end was brown and soaking with coffee, but the other was dry. He pressed it against the gushing sore and Susannah winced away from his touch at first, her eyes filling with tears.

"Nay, let me stop the bleeding at least," Roland murmured, and grasped her head, working his fingers gently into the tight cap of her curls. "Hold steady." And for him she managed to do it.

Through her watering eyes Susannah thought Joe still looked pissed that she had interrupted his comedy routine in such drastic (not to mention messy) fashion, and in a way she didn't blame him. He'd been doing a really good job; she'd gone and spoiled it. Aside from the pain, which was abating a little now, she was horribly embarrassed, remembering the time she had started her period in gym class and a little trickle of blood had run down her thigh for the whole world to see—that part of it with whom she had third-period PE, at any rate. Some of the girls had begun chanting *Plug it UP!*, as if it were the funniest thing in the world.

Mixed with this memory was fear concerning the sore itself. What if it was cancer? Before, she'd always been able to thrust this idea away before it was fully articulated in her mind. This time she couldn't. What if she'd caught her stupid self a cancer on her trek through the Badlands?

Her stomach knotted, then heaved. She kept her fine dinner in its place, but perhaps only for the time being.

Suddenly she wanted to be alone, *needed* to be alone. If she was going to vomit, she didn't want to do it in front of Roland and this stranger. Even if she wasn't, she wanted some time to get herself back under control. A gust of wind strong enough to shake the entire cottage roared past like a hot-enj in full flight; the lights flickered and her stomach knotted again at the seasick motion of the shadows on the wall.

"I've got to go . . . the bathroom . . ." she managed to say. For a moment the world wavered, but then it steadied down again. In the fireplace a knot of wood exploded, shooting a flurry of crimson sparks up the chimney.

"You sure?" Joe asked. He was no longer angry (if he had been), but he was looking at her doubtfully.

"Let her go," Roland said. "She needs to settle herself down, I think."

Susannah began to give him a grateful smile, but it hurt the sore place and started it bleeding again, too. She didn't know what else might change in the immediate future thanks to the dumb, unhealing sore, but she *did* know she was done listening to jokes for awhile. She'd need a transfusion if she did much more laughing.

"I'll be back," she said. "Don't you boys go and eat all the rest of that pudding on me." The very thought of food made her feel ill, but it was something to say.

"On the subject of pudding, I make no promise," Roland said. Then, as she began to turn away: "If thee feels lightheaded in there, call me."

"I will," she said. "Thank you, Roland."

TEN

Although Joe Collins lived alone, his bathroom had a pleasantly feminine feel to it. Susannah had noticed that the first time she'd used it. The wallpaper was pink, with green leaves and— what else?—wild roses. The john looked perfectly modern except for the ring, which was wood instead of plastic. Had he carved it himself? She didn't think it was out of the question, although probably the robot had brought it from some forgotten store of stuff. Stuttering Carl? Was that what Joe called the robot? No, Bill. Stuttering Bill.

On one side of the john there was a stool, on the other a claw-foot tub with a shower attachment that made her think of Hitchcock's *Psycho* (but *every* shower made her think of that damned movie since she'd seen it in Times Square). There was also a porcelain washstand set in a waist-high wooden cabinet—good old plainoak rather than ironwood, she judged. There was a mirror above it. She presumed you swung it out and there were your pills and potions. All the comforts of home.

She removed the napkin with a wince and a little hissing cry. It had stuck in the drying blood, and pulling it away hurt. She was dismayed by the amount of blood on her cheeks, lips, and chin—not to mention her neck and the shoulder of her shirt. She told herself not to let it make her crazy; you ripped the top off something and it was going to bleed, that was all. Especially if it was on your stupid *face.*

In the other room she heard Joe say something, she couldn't tell what, and Roland's response: a few words with a chuckle tacked on at the end. *So weird to hear him do that,* she thought. *Almost like he's drunk.* Had she ever seen Roland drunk? She realized she had not. Never falling-down drunk, never mother-naked, never fully caught by laughter . . . until now.

Ten' yo business, woman, Detta told her.

"All right," she muttered. "All right, all right."

Thinking drunk. Thinking naked. Thinking lost in laughter. Thinking they were all so close to being the same thing.

Maybe they *were* the same thing.

Then she got up on the stool and turned on the water. It came in a gush, blotting out the sounds from the other room.

She settled for cold, splashing it gently on her face, then using a facecloth—even more gently—to clean the skin around the sore. When that was done, she patted the sore itself. Doing it didn't hurt as much as she'd been afraid it might. Susannah was a little encouraged. When she was done, she rinsed out Joe's facecloth before the bloodstains could set and leaned close to the mirror. What she saw made her breathe a sigh of relief. Slapping her hand incautiously to her face like that had torn the entire top off the sore, but maybe in the end that would turn out to be for the best. One thing was for sure: if Joe had a bottle of hydrogen peroxide or some kind of antibiotic cream in his medicine cabinet, she intended to give the damned mess a good cleaning-out while it was open. And ne'mine how much it might sting. Such a cleansing was due and overdue. Once it was finished, she'd bandage it over and then just hope for the best.

She spread the facecloth on the side of the basin to dry, then plucked a towel (it was the same shade of pink as the wallpaper) from a fluffy stack on a nearby shelf. She got it halfway to her face, then froze. There was a piece of notepaper lying on the next towel in the stack. It was headed with a flower-decked bench being lowered by a pair of happy cartoon angels. Beneath was this printed, bold-face line:

☺ ☹ RELAX! HERE COMES THE ☺ ☹
DEUS EX MACHINA!

And, in faded fountain pen ink:

Odd's Lane

Odd Lane

Turn this over after you think about it.

Frowning, Susannah plucked the sheet of notepaper from the stack of towels. Who had left it here? Joe? She doubted it like hell. She turned the paper over. Here the same hand had written:

> You didn't <u>think</u> about it!
>
> what a bad girl!
>
> I've left you something in the medicine cabinet,
>
> but first
>
> ✱✱ THINK ABOUT IT! ✱✱
>
> (Hint: Comedy + Tragedy = MAKE BELIEVE)

In the other room, Joe continued to speak and this time Roland burst out laughing instead of just chuckling. It sounded to Susannah as if Joe had resumed his monologue. In a way she could understand that—he'd been doing something he loved, something he hadn't had a chance to do in a good long stretch of years—but part of her didn't like the idea at all. That Joe would resume while she was in the bathroom tending to herself, that Roland would *let* him resume. Would listen and laugh while she was shedding blood. It seemed like a rotten, boysclubby kind of thing to do. She supposed she had gotten used to better from Eddie.

Why don't you forget the boys for the time being and concentrate on what's right in front of you? What does it mean?

One thing seemed obvious: someone had expected her to come in here and find that note. Not Roland, not Joe. *Her. What a bad girl,* it said. *Girl.*

But who could have known? Who could have been sure? It wasn't as if she made a habit of slapping her face (or her chest, or her knee) when she laughed; she couldn't remember a single other instance when—

But she could. Once. At a Dean Martin–Jerry Lewis movie.

Dopes at Sea, or something like that. She'd been caught up in the same fashion then, laughing simply because the laughter had reached some point of critical mass and become self-feeding. The whole audience—at the Clark in Times Square, for all she knew—doing the same, rocking and rolling, swinging and swaying, spraying popcorn from mouths that were no longer their own. Mouths that belonged, at least for a few minutes, to Martin and Lewis, those dopes at sea. But it had only happened that once.

Comedy plus tragedy equals make-believe. But there's no tragedy here, is there?

She didn't expect an answer to this, but she got one. It came in the cold voice of intuition.

Not yet, there isn't.

For no reason whatsoever she found herself thinking of Lippy. Grinning, gruesome Lippy. Did the *folken* laugh in hell? Susannah was somehow sure they did. They grinned like Lippy the Wonder-Nag when Satan began his

(*take my horse . . . please*)

routine, and then they laughed. Helplessly. Hopelessly. For all of eternity, may it please ya not at all.

What in the hell's wrong with you, woman?

In the other room, Roland laughed again. Oy barked, and that also sounded like laughter.

Odd's Lane, Odd Lane . . . think about it.

What was there to think about? One was the name of the street, the other was the same thing, only without the—

"Whoa-back, wait a minute," she said in a low voice. Little more than a whisper, really, and who did she think would hear her? Joe was talking—pretty much nonstop, it sounded like—and Roland was laughing. So who did she think might be listening? The cellar-dweller, if there really was one?

"Whoa-on a minute, just wait."

She closed her eyes and once more saw the two street-signs on their pole, signs that were actually a little below the pilgrims, because the newcomers had been standing on a snowbank nine feet high. **TOWER ROAD**, one of the signs had read—

that one pointing to the plowed road that disappeared over the horizon. The other, the one indicating the short lane with the cottages on it, had said **ODD'S LANE,** only . . .

"Only it *didn't,*" she murmured, clenching the hand that wasn't holding the note into a fist. "It *didn't.*"

She could see it clearly enough in her mind's eye: **ODD'S LANE,** with the apostrophe and the *S added,* and why would somebody do that? Was the sign-changer maybe a compulsive neatnik who couldn't stand—

What? Couldn't stand what?

Beyond the closed bathroom door, Roland roared louder than ever. Something fell over and broke. *He's not used to laughing like that,* Susannah thought. *You best look out, Roland, or you'll do yourself damage. Laugh yourself into a hernia, or something.*

Think about it, her unknown correspondent had advised, and she was trying. Was there something about the words *odd* and *lane* that someone didn't want them to see? If so, that person had no need to worry, because she sure wasn't seeing it. She wished Eddie was here. Eddie was the one who was good at the funky stuff: jokes and riddles and . . . an . . .

Her breath stopped. An expression of wide-eyed comprehension started to dawn her face, and on the face of her twin in the mirror. She had no pencil and was terrible at the sort of mental rearrangements that she now had to—

Balanced on the stool, Susannah leaned over the waist-high washstand and blew on the mirror, fogging it. She printed **ODD LANE.** Looked at it with growing understanding and dismay. In the other room, Roland laughed harder than ever and now she recognized what she should have seen thirty valuable seconds ago: that laughter wasn't merry. It was jagged and out of control, the laughter of a man struggling for breath. Roland was laughing the way the *folken* laughed when comedy turned to tragedy. The way *folken* laughed in hell.

Below **ODD LANE** she used the tip of her finger to print **DANDELO,** the anagram Eddie might have seen right away, and surely once he realized the apostrophe-*S* on the sign had been added to distract them.

In the other room the laughter dropped and changed, becoming a sound that was alarming instead of amusing. Oy was barking crazily, and Roland—

Roland was choking.

CHAPTER VI:
PATRICK DANVILLE

ONE

She wasn't wearing her gun. Joe had insisted she take the La-Z-Boy recliner when they'd returned to the living room after dinner, and she'd put the revolver on the magazine-littered end-table beside it, after rolling the cylinder and drawing the shells. The shells were in her pocket.

Susannah tore open the bathroom door and scrambled back into the living room. Roland was lying on the floor between the couch and the television, his face a terrible purple color. He was scratching at his swollen throat and still laughing. Their host was standing over him, and the first thing she saw was that his hair—that baby-fine, shoulder-length white hair—was now almost entirely black. The lines around his eyes and mouth had been erased. Instead of ten years younger, Joe Collins now looked twenty or even thirty years younger.

The son of a bitch.

The *vampire* son of a bitch.

Oy leaped at him and seized Joe's left leg just above the knee. "Twenny-five, sissy-four, nineteen, *hike!*" Joe cried merrily, and kicked out, now as agile as Fred Astaire. Oy flew through the air and hit the wall hard enough to knock a plaque reading GOD BLESS OUR HOME to the floor. Joe turned back to Roland.

"What I think," he said, "is that women need a reason to have sex." Joe put one foot on Roland's chest—like a big-game hunter with his trophy, Susannah thought. "Men, on the other hand, only need a *place*! Bing!" He popped his eyes. "The thing about sex is that God gives men a brain and a dick, but only enough blood to operate one at a—"

685

He never heard her approach or lift herself into the La-Z-Boy in order to gain the necessary height; he was concentrating too completely on what he was doing. Susannah laced her hands together into a single fist, raised them to the height of her right shoulder, then brought them down and sideways with all the force she could manage. The fist struck the side of Joe's head hard enough to knock him away. She had connected with solid bone, however, and the pain in her hands was excruciating.

Joe staggered, waving his arms for balance and looking around at her. His upper lip rose, exposing his teeth—perfectly ordinary teeth, and why not? He wasn't the sort of vampire who survived on blood. This was Empathica, after all. And the face around those teeth was changing: darkening, contracting, turning into something that was no longer human. It was the face of a psychotic clown.

"*You,*" he said, but before he could say anything else, Oy had raced forward again. There was no need for the bumbler to use his teeth this time because their host was still staggering. Oy crouched behind the thing's ankle and Dandelo simply fell over him, his curses ceasing abruptly when he struck his head. The blow might have put him out if not for the homey rag rug covering the hardwood. As it was he forced himself to a sitting position almost at once, looking around groggily.

Susannah knelt by Roland, who was also trying to sit up but not doing as well. She seized his gun in its holster, but he closed a hand around her wrist before she could pull it out. Instinct, of course, and to be expected, but Susannah felt close to panic as Dandelo's shadow fell over them.

"You bitch, I'll teach you to interrupt a man when he's on a—"

"*Roland, let it go!*" she screamed, and he did.

Dandelo dropped, meaning to land on her and crush the gun between them, but she was an instant too quick. She rolled aside and he landed on Roland, instead. Susannah heard the tortured *Owuff!* as the gunslinger lost whatever breath he had managed to regain. She raised herself on one arm, panting, and pointed the gun at the one on top, the one undergoing some horridly busy change inside his clothes. Dandelo raised his hands, which were empty. Of course they were, it wasn't his hands he used to kill with. As he did so, his features began to pull together, becoming more and more surface things—not features at all but markings on some animal's hide or an insect's carapace.

"Stop!" he cried in a voice that was dropping in pitch and becoming something like a cicada's buzz. "I want to tell you the one about the archbishop and the chorus girl!"

"Heard it," she said, and shot him twice, one bullet following another into his brain from just above what had been his right eye.

TWO

Roland floundered to his feet. His hair was matted to the sides of his swollen face. When she tried to take his hand, he waved her away and staggered to the front door of the little cottage, which now looked dingy and ill-lit to Susannah. She saw there were food-stains on the rug, and a large water-blemish on one wall. Had those things been there before? And dear Lord in heaven, what exactly had they eaten for supper? She decided she didn't want to know, as long as it didn't make her sick. As long as it wasn't poisonous.

Roland of Gilead pulled open the door. The wind ripped it from his grasp and threw it against the wall with a bang. He staggered two steps into the screaming blizzard, bent forward with his hands placed on his lower thighs, and vomited. She saw the jet of egested material, and how the wind whipped it away into the dark. When Roland came back in, his shirt and the side of his face were rimed with snow. It was fiercely hot in the cottage; that was something else Dandelo's glammer had hidden from them until now. She saw that the thermostat—a plain old Honeywell not much different from the one in her New York apartment—was still on the wall. She went to it and examined it. It was twisted as far as it would go, beyond the eighty-five-degree mark. She pushed it back to seventy with the tip of a finger, then turned to survey the room. The fireplace was actually twice the size it had appeared to them, and filled with enough logs to make it roar like a steel-furnace. There was nothing she could do about that for the time being, but it would eventually die down.

The dead thing on the rug had mostly burst out of its clothes. To Susannah it now looked like some sort of bug with misshapen appendages—almost arms and legs—sticking out of the sleeves of its shirt and the legs of its jeans. The back of the shirt had split down the middle and what she saw in the gap was a kind of shell on which rudimentary human features were printed. She would not have believed anything could be worse than Mordred in his spider-form, but this thing was. Thank God it was dead.

The tidy, well-lit cottage—like something out of a fairy-tale, and hadn't she seen that from the first?—was now a dim and smoky peasant's hut. There were still electric lights, but they looked old and long-used, like the kind of fixtures one might find in a flophouse hotel. The rag rug was dark with dirt as well as splotched with spilled food, and unraveling in places.

"Roland, are you all right?"

Roland looked at her, and then, slowly, went to his knees before her. For a moment she thought he was fainting, and she was alarmed. When she realized, only a second later, what was really happening, she was more alarmed still.

"Gunslinger, I was 'mazed," Roland said in a husky, trembling voice. "I was taken in like a child, and I cry your pardon."

"Roland, no! Git up!" That was Detta, who always seemed to come out when Susannah was under great strain. She thought, *It's a wonder I didn't say "Git up, honky,"* and had to choke back a cry of hysterical laughter. He would not have understood.

"Give me pardon, first," Roland said, not looking at her.

She fumbled for the formula and found it, which was a relief. She couldn't stand to see him on his knees like that. "Rise, gunslinger, I give you pardon in good heart." She paused, then added: "If I save your life another nine times, we'll be somewhere close to even."

He said, "Your kind heart makes me ashamed of my own," and rose to his feet. The terrible color was fading from his cheeks. He looked at the thing on the rug, casting its grotesquely misshapen shadow up the wall in the firelight. Looked around at the close little hut with its ancient fixtures and flickering electric bulbs.

"What he fed us was all right," he said. It was as if he'd read her mind and seen the worst fear that it held. "He'd never poison what he meant to . . . eat."

She was holding his gun out to him, butt first. He took it and reloaded the two empty chambers before dropping it back into the holster. The hut's door was still open and snow came blowing in. It had already created a white delta in the little entryway, where their makeshift hide coats hung. The room was a little cooler now, a little less like a sauna.

"How did you know?" he asked.

She thought back to the hotel where Mia had left Black Thirteen. Later on, after they'd left, Jake and Callahan had been able to get into Room 1919 because someone had left them a note and

(*dad-a-chee*)

a key. Jake's name and *This is the truth* had been written on the envelope in a hybrid of cursive script and printing. She was sure that if she had that envelope with its brief message and compared it to the message she'd found in the bathroom, she would find the same hand made both.

According to Jake, the desk-clerk at the New York Plaza–Park Hotel had told them the message had been left by a man named Stephen King.

"Come with me," she said. "Into the bathroom."

THREE

Like the rest of the hut, the bathroom was smaller now, not much more than a closet. The tub was old and rusty, with a thin layer of dirt in the bottom. It looked like it had last been used . . .

Well, the truth was that it looked to Susannah like it had *never* been used. The shower-head was clotted with rust. The pink wallpaper was dull and dirty, peeling in places. There were no roses. The mirror was still there, but a crack ran down the middle of it, and she thought it was sort of a wonder that she hadn't cut the pad of her finger, writing on it. The vapor of her breath had faded but the words were still there, visible in the grime: **ODD LANE**, and, below that, **DANDELO**.

"It's an anagram," she said. "Do you see?"

He studied the writing, then shook his head, looking a bit ashamed.

"Not your fault, Roland. They're our letters, not the ones you know. Take my word for it, it's an anagram. Eddie would have seen it right away, I bet. I don't know if it was Dandelo's idea of a joke, or if there are some sort of rules glammer things like him have to follow, but the thing is, we figured it out in time, with a little help from Stephen King."

"*You* figured it out," he said. "I was busy laughing myself to death."

"We both would have done that," she said. "You were just a little more vulnerable because your sense of humor . . . forgive me, Roland, but as a rule, it's pretty lame."

"I know that," he said bleakly. Then he suddenly turned and left the room.

A horrid idea came to Susannah, and it seemed a very long time before the gunslinger came back. "Roland, is he still . . . ?"

He nodded, smiling a little. "Still as dead as ever was. You shot true, Susannah, but all at once I needed to be sure."

"I'm glad," she said simply.

"Oy's standing guard. If anything *were* to happen, I'm sure he'd let us know." He picked the note up from the floor and carefully puzzled out what was written on the back. The only term she had to help him with was *medicine cabinet*. "'I've left you something.' Do you know what?"

She shook her head. "I didn't have time to look."

"Where is this medicine cabinet?"

She pointed at the mirror and he swung it out. It squalled

on its hinges. There were indeed shelves behind it, but instead of the neat rows of pills and potions she had imagined, there were only two more brown bottles, like the one on the table beside the La-Z-Boy, and what looked to Susannah like the world's oldest box of Smith Brothers Wild Cherry Cough Drops. There was also an envelope, however, and Roland handed it to her. Written on the front, in that same distinctive half-writing, half-printing, was this:

Childe Roland, of Gilead
Susannah Dean, of New York

You saved my life.
I've saved yours.
All debts are paid.

S.K.

"Childe?" she asked. "Does that mean anything to you?"

He nodded. "It's a term that describes a knight—or a gunslinger—on a quest. A formal term, and ancient. We never used it among ourselves, you must ken, for it means holy, chosen by ka. We never liked to think of ourselves in such terms, and I haven't thought of myself so in many years."

"Yet you are Childe Roland?"

"Perhaps once I was. We're beyond such things now. Beyond ka."

"But still on the Path of the Beam."

"Aye." He traced the last line on the envelope: *All debts are paid.* "Open it, Susannah, for I'd see what's inside."

She did.

FOUR

It was a photocopy of a poem by Robert Browning. King had written the poet's name in his half-script, half-printing above the title. Susannah had read some of Browning's dramatic monologues in college, but she wasn't familiar with this poem. She was, however, *extremely* familiar with its subject; the title of the poem was "Childe Roland to the Dark Tower Came." It was narrative in structure, the rhyme-scheme balladic (a-b-b-a-a-b), and thirty-four stanzas long. Each stanza was headed with a Roman numeral. Someone—King, presumably—had circled stanzas I, II, XIII, XIV, and XVI.

"Read the marked ones," he said hoarsely, "because I can only make out a word here and there, and I would know what they say, would know it very well."

"Stanza the First," she said, then had to clear her throat. It was dry. Outside the wind howled and the naked overhead bulb flickered in its flyspecked fixture.

> *"My first thought was, he lied in every word,*
> *That hoary cripple, with malicious eye*
> *Askance to watch the working of his lie*
> *On mine, and mouth scarce able to afford*
> *Suppression of the glee, that pursed and scored*
> *Its edge, at one more victim gained thereby."*

"Collins," Roland said. "Whoever wrote that spoke of Collins as sure as King ever spoke of our ka-tet in his stories! 'He lied in every word!' Aye, so he did!"

"Not Collins," she said. "Dandelo."

Roland nodded. "Dandelo, say true. Go on."

"Okay; Stanza the Second.

> *"What else should he be set for, with his staff?*
> *What, save to waylay with his lies, ensnare*
> *All travellers who might find him posted there,*

> *And ask the road? I guessed what skull-like laugh*
> *Would break, what crutch 'gin write my epitaph*
> *For pastime in the dusty thoroughfare. "*

"Does thee remember his stick, and how he waved it?" Roland asked her.

Of course she did. And the thoroughfare had been snowy instead of dusty, but otherwise it was the same. *Otherwise it was a description of what had just happened to them.* The idea made her shiver.

"Was this poet of your time?" Roland asked. "Your when?"

She shook her head. "Not even of my country. He died at least sixty years before my when."

"Yet he must have seen what just passed. A version of it, anyway."

"Yes. And Stephen King knew the poem." She had a sudden intuition, one that blazed too bright to be anything but the truth. She looked at Roland with wild, startled eyes. "It was this poem that got King going! *It was his inspiration!*"

"Do you say so, Susannah?"

"Yes!"

"Yet this Browning must have seen *us.*"

She didn't know. It was too confusing. Like trying to figure out which came first, the chicken or the egg. Or being lost in a hall of mirrors. Her head was swimming.

"Read the next one marked, Susannah! Read ex-eye-eye-eye."

"That's Stanza Thirteen," she said.

> *"As for the grass, it grew as scant as hair*
> *In leprosy; thin dry blades pricked the mud*
> *Which underneath looked kneaded up with blood.*
> *One stiff blind horse, his every bone a-stare,*
> *Stood stupefied, however he came there;*
> *Thrust out past service from the devil's stud!*

"Now Stanza the Fourteenth I read thee.

"Alive? He might be dead for aught I know,
    With that red gaunt and colloped neck a-strain,
    And shut eyes underneath the rusty mane;
Seldom went such grotesqueness with such woe;
I never saw a brute I hated so;
    He must be wicked to deserve such pain."

"Lippy," the gunslinger said, and jerked a thumb back over his shoulder. "Yonder's pluggit, colloped neck and all, only female instead of male."

She made no reply—needed to make none. Of course it was Lippy: blind and bony, her neck rubbed right down to the raw pink in places. *Her an ugly old thing, I know,* the old man had said . . . the thing that had *looked* like an old man. *Ye old ki'-box and gammer-gurt, ye lost four-legged leper!* And here it was in black and white, a poem written long before sai King was even born, perhaps eighty or even a hundred years before: . . . *as scant as hair/In leprosy.*

"Thrust out past service from the devil's stud!" Roland said, smiling grimly. "And while she'll never stud nor ever did, we'll see she's back with the devil before we leave!"

"No," she said. "We won't." Her voice sounded drier than ever. She wanted a drink, but was now afraid to take anything flowing from the taps in this vile place. In a little bit she would get some snow and melt it. Then she would have her drink, and not before.

"Why do you say so?"

"Because she's gone. She went out into the storm when we got the best of her master."

"How does thee know it?"

Susannah shook her head. "I just do." She shuffled to the next page in the poem, which ran to over two hundred lines. "Stanza the Sixteenth.

"Not it! I fancied . . ."

She ceased.

"Susannah? Why do you—" Then his eyes fixed on the

next word, which he could read even in English letters. "Go on," he said. His voice was low, the words little more than a whisper.

"Are you positive?"

"Read, for I would hear."

She cleared her throat. "Stanza the Sixteenth.

> *"Not it! I fancied Cuthbert's reddening face*
> *Beneath its garniture of curly gold,*
> *Dear fellow, till I almost felt him fold*
> *An arm in mine to fix me to the place,*
> *That way he used. Alas, one night's disgrace!*
> *Out went my heart's new fire and left it cold."*

"He writes of Mejis," Roland said. His fists were clenched, although she doubted that he knew it. "He writes of how we fell out over Susan Delgado, for after that it was never the same between us. We mended our friendship as best we could, but no, it was never quite the same."

"After the woman comes to the man or the man to the woman, I don't think it ever is," she said, and handed him the photocopied sheets. "Take this. I've read all the ones he mentioned. If there's stuff in the rest about coming to the Dark Tower—or not—puzzle it out by yourself. You can do it if you try hard enough, I reckon. As for me, I don't want to know."

Roland, it seemed, did. He shuffled through the pages, looking for the last one. The pages weren't numbered, but he found the end easily enough by the white space beneath that stanza marked XXXIV. Before he could read, however, that thin cry came again. This time the wind was in a complete lull and there was no doubt about where it came from.

"That's someone below us, in the basement," Roland said.

"I know. And I think I know who it is."

He nodded.

She was looking at him steadily. "It all fits, doesn't it? It's like a jigsaw puzzle, and we've put in all but the last few pieces."

The cry came again, thin and lost. The cry of someone

who was next door to dead. They left the bathroom, drawing their guns. Susannah didn't think they'd need them this time.

FIVE

The bug that had made itself look like a jolly old joker named Joe Collins lay where it had lain, but Oy had backed off a step or two. Susannah didn't blame him. Dandelo was beginning to stink, and little trickles of white stuff were beginning to ooze through its decaying carapace. Nevertheless, Roland bade the bumbler remain where he was, and keep watch.

The cry came again when they reached the kitchen, and it was louder, but at first they saw no way down to the cellar. Susannah moved slowly across the cracked and dirty linoleum, looking for a hidden trapdoor. She was about to tell Roland there was nothing when he said, "Here. Behind the cold-box."

The refrigerator was no longer a top-of-the-line Amana with an icemaker in the door but a squat and dirty thing with the cooling machinery on top, in a drum-shaped casing. Her mother had had one like it when Susannah had been a little girl who answered to the name of Odetta, but her mother would have died before ever allowing her own to be even a tenth as dirty. A hundredth.

Roland moved it aside easily, for Dandelo, sly monster that he'd been, had put it on a little wheeled platform. She doubted that he got many visitors, not way out here in End-World, but he had been prepared to keep his secrets if someone *did* drop by. As she was sure *folken* did, every once and again. She imagined that few if any got any further along their way than the little hut on Odd Lane.

The stairs leading down were narrow and steep. Roland felt around inside the door and found a switch. It lit two bare bulbs, one halfway down the stairs and one below. As if in response to the light, the cry came again. It was full of pain and fear, but there were no words in it. The sound made her shiver.

"Come to the foot of the stairs, whoever you are!" Roland called.

No response from below. Outside the wind gusted and whooped, driving snow against the side of the house so hard that it sounded like sand.

"Come to where we can see you, or we'll leave you where you are!" Roland called.

The inhabitant of the cellar didn't come into the scant light but cried out again, a sound that was loaded with woe and terror and—Susannah feared it—madness.

He looked at her. She nodded and spoke in a whisper. "Go first. I'll back your play, if you have to make one."

"'Ware the steps that you don't take a tumble," he said in the same low voice.

She nodded again and made his own impatient twirling gesture with one hand: *Go on, go on.*

That raised a ghost of a smile on the gunslinger's lips. He went down the stairs with the barrel of his gun laid into the hollow of his right shoulder, and for a moment he looked so like Jake Chambers that she could have wept.

SIX

The cellar was a maze of boxes and barrels and shrouded things hanging from hooks. Susannah had no wish to know what the dangling things were. The cry came again, a sound like sobbing and screaming mingled together. Above them, dim and muffled now, came the whoop and gasp of the wind.

Roland turned to his left and threaded his way down a zigzag aisle with crates stacked head-high on either side. Susannah followed, keeping a good distance between them, looking constantly back over her shoulder. She was also alert for the sound of Oy raising the alarm from above. She saw one stack of crates that was labeled TEXAS INSTRUMENTS and another stack with HO FAT CHINESE FORTUNE COOKIE CO. stenciled on the side. She was not surprised to see the joke name of their long-abandoned taxi; she was far beyond surprise.

Ahead of her, Roland stopped. "Tears of my mother," he said in a low voice. She had heard him use this phrase once before, when they had come upon a deer that had fallen into a ravine and lay there with both back legs and one front one broken, starving and looking up at them sightlessly, for the flies had eaten the unfortunate animal's living eyes out of their sockets.

She stayed where she was until he gestured for her to join him, and then moved quickly up to his right side, boosting herself along on the palms of her hands.

In the stonewalled far corner of Dandelo's cellar—the southeast corner, if she had her directions right—there was a makeshift prison cell. Its door was made of crisscrossing steel bars. Nearby was the welding rig Dandelo must have used to construct it . . . but long ago, judging from the thick layer of dust on the acetylene tank. Hanging from an S-shaped hook pounded into the stone wall, just out of the prisoner's reach— left close by to mock him, Susannah had no doubt—was a large and old-fashioned

(*dad-a-chum dad-a-chee*)

silver key. The prisoner in question stood at the bars of his detainment, holding his filthy hands out to them. He was so scrawny that he reminded Susannah of certain terrible concentration-camp photos she had seen, images of those who had survived Auschwitz and Bergen-Belsen and Buchenwald, living (if barely) indictments of mankind as a whole with their striped uniforms hanging off them and their ghastly bellboy's pillbox hats still on their heads and their terrible bright eyes, so full of awareness. *We wish we did not know what we have become*, those eyes said, *but unfortunately we do.*

Something like that was in Patrick Danville's eyes as he held out his hands and made his inarticulate pleading noises. Close up, they sounded to her like the mocking cries of some jungle bird on a movie soundtrack: *I-yeee, I-yeee, I-yowk, I-yowk!*

Roland took the key from its hook and went to the door. One of Danville's hands clutched at his shirt and the gunslinger pushed it off. It was a gesture entirely without anger, she thought, but the scrawny thing in the cell backed away with his eyes bulging in their sockets. His hair was long—it hung all the way to his shoulders—but there was only the faintest haze of beard on his cheeks. It was a little thicker on his chin and upper lip. Susannah thought he might be seventeen, but surely not much older.

"No offense, Patrick," Roland said in a purely conversational voice. He put the key in the lock. "Is thee Patrick? Is thee Patrick Danville?"

The scrawny thing in the dirty jeans and billowing gray shirt (it hung nearly to his knees) backed into the corner of his triangular cell without replying. When his back was against the stone, he slid slowly to a sitting position beside what Susannah assumed was his slop-bucket, the front of his shirt first bunching together and then flowing into his crotch like water as his knees rose to nearly frame his emaciated, terrified face. When Roland opened the cell door and pulled it outward as far as it would go (there were no hinges), Patrick Danville began to make the bird-sound again, only this time louder: *I-YEEE! I-YOWK! I-YEEEEEE!* Susannah gritted her teeth. When Roland made as if to enter the cell, the boy uttered an even louder shriek, and began to beat the back of his head against the stones. Roland stepped back out of the cell. The awful head-banging ceased, but Danville looked at the stranger with fear and mistrust. Then he held out his filthy, long-fingered hands again, as if for succor.

Roland looked to Susannah.

She swung herself on her hands so she was in the door of the cell. The emaciated boy-thing in the corner uttered its weird bird-shriek again and pulled the supplicating hands back, crossing them at the wrists, turning their gesture into one of pathetic defense.

"No, honey." This was a Detta Walker Susannah had never heard before, nor suspected. "No, honey, Ah ain' goan hurt you, if Ah meant t'do dat, Ah'd just put two in yo' haid, like Ah did that mahfah upstairs."

She saw something in his eyes—perhaps just a minute widening that revealed more of the bloodshot whites. She smiled and nodded. "Dass ri'! Mistuh Collins, he *daid!* He ain' nev' goan come down he' no mo an . . . whuh? Whut he do to you, Patrick?"

Above them, muffled by the stone, the wind gusted. The lights flickered; the house creaked and groaned in protest.

"Whuh he do t'you, boy?"

It was no good. He didn't understand. She had just made up her mind to this when Patrick Danville put his hands to his stomach and held it. He twisted his face into a cramp that she realized was supposed to indicate laughter.

"He make you laugh?"

Patrick, crouched in his corner, nodded. His face twisted even more. Now his hands became fists that rose to his face. He rubbed his cheeks with them, then screwed them into his eyes, then looked at her. Susannah noticed there was a little scar on the bridge of his nose.

"He make you cry, too."

Patrick nodded. He did the laughing mime again, holding the stomach and going ho-ho-ho; he did the crying mime, wiping tears from his fuzzy cheeks; this time he added a third bit of mummery, scooping his hands toward his mouth and making *smack-smack* sounds with his lips.

From above and slightly behind her, Roland said: "He made you laugh, he made you cry, he made you eat."

Patrick shook his head so violently it struck the stone walls that were the boundaries of his corner.

"*He* ate," Detta said. "Dass whut you trine t'say, ain't it? *Dandelo* ate."

Patrick nodded eagerly.

"He made you laugh, he made you cry, and den he ate whut came out. Cause dass what he do!"

Patrick nodded again, bursting into tears. He made inarticulate wailing sounds. Susannah worked her way slowly into the cell, pushing herself along on her palms, ready to retreat if the head-banging started again. It didn't. When she reached the boy in the corner, he put his face against her bosom and wept. Susannah turned, looked at Roland, and told him with her eyes that he could come in now.

When Patrick looked up at her, it was with dumb, doglike adoration.

"Don't you worry," Susannah said—Detta was gone again, probably worn out from all that nice. "He's not going to get you, Patrick, he's dead as a doornail, dead as a stone in the river. Now I want you to do something for me. I want you to open your mouth."

Patrick shook his head at once. There was fear in his eyes again, but something else she hated to see even more. It was shame.

"Yes, Patrick, yes. Open your mouth."

He shook his head violently, his greasy long hair whipping from side to side like the head of a mop.

Roland said, "What—"

"Hush," she told him. "Open your mouth, Patrick, and show us. Then we'll take you out of here and you'll never have to be down here again. Never have to be Dandelo's dinner again."

Patrick looked at her, pleading, but Susannah only looked back at him. At last he closed his eyes and slowly opened his mouth. His teeth were there, but his tongue was not. At some point, Dandelo must have tired of his prisoner's voice—or the words it articulated, anyway—and had pulled it out.

SEVEN

Twenty minutes later, the two of them stood in the kitchen doorway, watching Patrick Danville eat a bowl of soup. At least half of it was going down the boy's gray shirt, but Susannah reckoned that was all right; there was plenty of soup, and there were more shirts in the hut's only bedroom. Not to mention Joe Collins's heavy parka hung on the hook in the entry, which she expected Patrick would wear hence from here. As for the remains of Dandelo—Joe Collins that was—they had wrapped them in three blankets and tossed them unceremoniously out into the snow.

She said, "Dandelo was a vampire that fed on emotions instead of blood. Patrick, there . . . Patrick was his cow. There's two ways you can take nourishment from a cow: meat or milk.

The trouble with meat is that once you eat the prime cuts, the not-so-prime cuts, and then the stew, it's gone. If you just take the milk, though, you can go on forever . . . always assuming you give the cow something to eat every now and then."

"How long do you suppose he had him penned up down there?" Roland asked.

"I don't know." But she remembered the dust on the acetylene tank, remembered it all too well. "A fairly long time, anyway. What must have seemed like forever to him."

"And it hurt."

"Plenty. Much as it must have hurt when Dandelo pulled the poor kid's tongue out, I bet the emotional bloodsucking hurt more. You see how he is."

Roland saw, all right. He saw something else, as well. "We can't take him out in this storm. Even if we dressed him up in three layers of clothes, I'm sure it would kill him."

Susannah nodded. She was sure, too. Of that, and something else: she could not stay in the house. *That* might kill *her.*

Roland agreed when she said so. "We'll camp out in yonder barn until the storm finishes. It'll be cold, but I see a pair of possible gains: Mordred may come, and Lippy may come back."

"You'd kill them both?"

"Aye, if I could. Do'ee have a problem with that?"

She considered it, then shook her head.

"All right. Let's put together what we'd take out there, for we'll have no fire for the next two days, at least. Maybe as long as four."

EIGHT

It turned out to be three nights and two days before the blizzard choked on its own fury and blew itself out. Near dusk of the second day, Lippy came limping out of the storm and Roland put a bullet in the blind shovel that was her head. Mordred never showed himself, although she had a sense of him lurking close on the second night. Perhaps Oy did, too, for he stood at the mouth of the barn, barking hard into the blowing snow.

During that time, Susannah found out a good deal more about Patrick Danville than she had expected. His mind had been badly damaged by his period of captivity, and that did not surprise her. What did was his capacity for recovery, limited though it might be. She wondered if she herself could have come back at all after such an ordeal. Perhaps his talent had something to do with it. She had seen his talent for herself, in Sayre's office.

Dandelo had given his captive the bare minimum of food necessary to keep him alive, and had stolen emotions from him on a regular basis: two times a week, sometimes three, once in awhile even four. Each time Patrick became convinced that the next time would kill him, someone would happen by. Just lately, Patrick had been spared the worst of Dandelo's depredations, because "company" had been more frequent than ever before. Roland told her later that night, after they'd bedded down in the hayloft, that he believed many of Dandelo's most recent victims must have been exiles fleeing either from Le Casse Roi Russe or the town around it. Susannah could certainly sympathize with the thinking of such refugees: *The King is gone, so let's get the hell out of here while the getting's good. After all, Big Red might take it into his head to come back, and he's off his chump, round the bend, possessed of an elevator that no longer goes to the top floor.*

On some occasions, Joe had assumed his true Dandelo form in front of his prisoner, then had eaten the boy's resulting terror. But he had wanted much more than terror from his captive cow. Susannah guessed that different emotions must produce different flavors: like having pork one day, chicken the next, and fish the day after that.

Patrick couldn't talk, but he could gesture. And he could do more than that, once Roland showed them a queer find he'd come upon in the pantry. On one of the highest shelves was a stack of oversized drawing pads marked MICHELANGELO, FINE FOR CHARCOAL. They had no charcoal, but near the pads was a clutch of brand-new Eberhard-Faber #2 pencils held together by a rubber band. What qualified the find as especially queer was the fact that someone (presumably Dandelo) had carefully cut the eraser off the top of each pencil. These were stored in a canning jar next to the pencils, along with a few paper clips and a pencil-sharpener that looked like the whistles on the undersides of the few remaining Oriza plates from Calla Bryn Sturgis. When Patrick saw the pads, his ordinarily dull eyes lit up and he stretched both hands longingly toward them, making urgent hooting sounds.

Roland looked at Susannah, who shrugged and said, "Let's see what he can do. I have a pretty good idea already, don't you?"

It turned out that he could do a lot. Patrick Danville's drawing ability was nothing short of amazing. And his pictures gave him all the voice he needed. He produced them rapidly, and with clear pleasure; he did not seem disturbed at all by their harrowing clarity. One showed Joe Collins chopping into the back of an unsuspecting visitor's head with a hatchet, his lips pulled back in a snarling grin of pleasure. Beside the point of impact, the boy had printed **CHUNT!** And **SPLOOSH!** in big comic-book letters. Above Collins's head, Patrick drew a thought-balloon with the words **Take that, ya lunker!** in it. Another picture showed Patrick himself, lying on the floor, reduced to helplessness by laughter that was depicted with terrible accuracy (no need of the **Ha! Ha! Ha!** scrawled above his head), while Collins stood over him with his hands on his hips, watching. Patrick then tossed back the sheet of paper with that drawing on it and quickly produced another picture which showed Collins on his knees, with one hand twined in Patrick's hair while his pursed lips hovered in front of Patrick's laughing, agonized mouth. Quickly, in a single practiced movement (the tip of the pencil never left the paper), the boy made another comic-strip thought-balloon over the old man's head and then put seven letters and two exclamation points inside.

"What does it say?" Roland asked, fascinated.

"'YUM! Good!'" Susannah answered. Her voice was small and sickened.

Subject matter aside, she could have watched him draw for

hours; in fact, she did. The speed of the pencil was eerie, and neither of them ever thought to give him one of the amputated erasers, for there seemed to be no need. So far as Susannah could see, the boy either never made a mistake, or incorporated the mistakes into his drawings in a way that made them—well, why stick at the words if they were the right words?—little acts of genius. And the resulting pictures weren't sketches, not really, but finished works of art in themselves. She knew what Patrick—this one or another Patrick from another world along the path of the Beam—would later be capable of with oil paints, and such knowledge made her feel cold and hot at the same time. What did they have here? A tongueless Rembrandt? It occurred to her that this was their second idiot-savant. Their third, if you counted Oy as well as Sheemie.

Only once did his lack of interest in the erasers cross Susannah's mind, and she put it down to the arrogance of genius. Not a single time did it occur to her—or to Roland—that this young version of Patrick Danville might not yet know that such things as erasers even existed.

NINE

Near the end of the third night, Susannah awoke in the loft, looked at Patrick lying asleep beside her, and descended the ladder. Roland was standing in the doorway of the barn, smoking a cigarette and looking out. The snow had stopped. A late moon had made its appearance, turning the fresh snow on Tower Road into a sparkling land of silent beauty. The air was still and so cold she felt the moisture in her nose crackle. Far in the distance she heard the sound of a motor. As she listened, it seemed to her that it was drawing closer. She asked Roland if he had any idea what it was or what it might mean to them.

"I think it's likely the robot he called Stuttering Bill, out doing his after-storm plowing," he said. "He may have one of those antenna-things on his head, like the Wolves. You remember?"

She remembered very well, and said so.

"It may be that he holds some special allegiance to Dandelo," Roland said. "I don't think that's likely, but it wouldn't be the strangest thing I ever ran across. Be ready with one of your plates if he shows red. And I'll be ready with my gun."

"But you don't think so." She wanted to be a hundred per cent clear on this point.

"No," Roland said. "He could give us a ride, perhaps all the way to the Tower itself. Even if not, he might take us to the far edge of the White Lands. That would be good, for the boy's still weak."

This raised a question in her mind. "We call him the boy, because he looks like a boy," she said. "How old do you think he is?"

Roland shook his head. "Surely no younger than sixteen or seventeen, but he might be as old as thirty. Time was strange when the Beams were under attack, and it took strange hops and twists. I can attest to that."

"Did Stephen King put him in our way?"

"I can't say, only that he knew of him, sure." He paused. "The Tower is so close! Do you feel it?"

She did, and all the time. Sometimes it was a pulsing, sometimes it was singing, quite often it was both. And the Polaroid still hung in Dandelo's hut. That, at least, had not been part of the glammer. Each night in her dreams, at least once, she saw the Tower in that photograph standing at the end of its field of roses, sooty gray-black stone against a troubled sky where the clouds streamed out in four directions, along the two Beams that still held. She knew what the voices sang—*commala! commala! commala-come-come!*—but she did not think that they sang to her, or for her. No, say no, say never in life; this was Roland's song, and Roland's alone. But she had begun to hope that that didn't necessarily mean she was going to die between here and the end of her quest.

She had been having her own dreams.

TEN

Less than an hour after the sun rose (firmly in the east, and we all say thankya), an orange vehicle—combination truck and bulldozer—appeared over the horizon and came slowly but steadily toward them, pushing a big wing of fresh snow to its right, making the high bank even higher on that side. Susannah guessed that when it reached the intersection of Tower Road and Odd Lane, Stuttering Bill (almost surely the plow's operator) would swing it around and plow back the other way. Maybe he stopped here, as a rule, not for coffee but for a fresh squirt of oil, or something. She smiled at the idea, and at something else, as well. There was a loudspeaker mounted on the cab's roof and a rock and roll song she actually knew was issuing forth. Susannah laughed, delighted. "'California Sun'! The Rivieras! Oh, doesn't it sound *fine!*"

"If you say so," Roland agreed. "Just keep hold of thy plate."

"You can count on that," she said.

Patrick had joined them. As always since Roland had found them in the pantry, he had a pad and a pencil. Now he wrote a single word in capital letters and held it out to Susannah, knowing that Roland could read very little of what he wrote, even if it was printed in letters that were big-big. The word in the lower quadrant of the sketch-pad was **BILL**. This was below an amazing drawing of Oy, with a comic-strip speech-balloon over his head reading **YARK! YARK!** All this he had casually crossed out so she wouldn't think it was what he wanted her to look at. The slashed X sort of broke her heart, because the picture beneath its crossed lines was Oy to the life.

ELEVEN

The plow pulled up in front of Dandelo's hut, and although the engine continued to run, the music cut off. Down from the driver's seat there galumphed a tall (eight feet at the very least), shiny-headed robot who looked quite a lot like Nigel from the

Arc 16 Experimental Station and Andy from Calla Bryn Sturgis. He cocked his metal arms and put his metal hands on his hips in a way that would likely have reminded Eddie of George Lucas's C3P0, had Eddie been there. The robot spoke in an amplified voice that rolled away across the snowfields:

"*HELLO, J-JOE! WHAT DO YOU NUH-NUH-KNOW? HOW ARE TRICKS IN KUH-KUH-KOKOMO?*"

Roland stepped out of the late Lippy's quarters. "Hile, Bill," he said mildly. "Long days and pleasant nights."

The robot turned. His eyes flashed bright blue. That looked like surprise to Susannah. He showed no alarm that she could see, however, and didn't appear to be armed, but she had already marked the antenna rising from the center of his head—twirling and twirling in the bright morning light—and she felt confident she could clip it with an Oriza if she needed to. Easy-peasy-Japaneezy, Eddie would have said.

"Ah!" said the robot. "A gudda-gah, gunna-gah, g-g-g—" He raised an arm that had not one elbow-joint but two and smacked his head with it. From inside came a little whistling noise— *Wheeep!*—and then he finished: "A gunslinger!"

Susannah laughed. She couldn't help it. They had come all this way to meet an oversized electronic version of Porky Pig. *T'beya-t'beya-t'beya, that's all, folks!*

"I had heard rumors of such on the l-l-l-land," the robot said, ignoring her laughter. "Are you Ruh-Ruh-Roland of G-Gilead?"

"So I am," Roland said. "And you?"

"William, D-746541-M, Maintenance Robot, Many Other Functions. Joe Collins calls me Stuh-huttering B-Bill. I've got a f-f-fried sir-hirkit somewhere inside. I could fix it, but he fuh-fuh-forbade me. And since he's the only h-human around . . . or was . . ." He stopped. Susannah could quite clearly hear the clit-ter-clack of relays somewhere inside and what *she* thought of wasn't C3P0, who she'd of course never seen, but Robby the Robot from *Forbidden Planet*.

Then Stuttering Bill quite touched her heart by putting one metal hand to his forehead and bowing . . . but not to either

her or to Roland. He said, "Hile, Patrick D-Danville, son of S-S-Sonia! It's good to see you out and in the c-c-clear, so it is!" And Susannah could hear the emotion in Stuttering Bill's voice. It was genuine gladness, and she felt more than okay about lowering her plate.

TWELVE

They palavered in the yard. Bill would have been quite willing to go into the hut, for he had but rudimentary olfactory equipment. The humes were better equipped and knew that the hut stank and had not even warmth to recommend it, for the furnace and the fire were both out. In any case, the palaver didn't take long. William the Maintenance Robot (Many Other Functions) had counted the being that sometimes called itself Joe Collins as his master, for there was no longer anyone else to lay claim to the job. Besides, Collins/Dandelo had the necessary code-words.

"I w-was nuh-not able to g-give him the c-code wuh-wuh-hurds when he a-asked," said Stuttering Bill, "but my p-pro-gramming did not pruh-prohibit bringing him cer-hertain m-manuals that had the ih-information he needed."

"Bureaucracy is so wonderful," Susannah said.

Bill said he had stayed away from "J-J-Joe" as often (and as long) as he could, although he had to come when Tower Road needed plowing—that was also in his programming—and once a month to bring provisions (canned goods, mostly) from what he called "the Federal." He also liked to see Patrick, who had once given Bill a wonderful picture of himself that he looked at often (and of which he had made many copies). Yet every time he came, he confided, he was sure he would find Patrick gone—killed and thrown casually into the woods somewhere back toward what Bill called "the Buh-Buh-Bads," like an old piece of trash. But now here he was, alive and free, and Bill was delighted.

"For I do have r-r-rudimentary em-m-motions," he said, sounding to Susannah like someone owning up to a bad habit.

"Do you need the code-words from us, in order to accept our orders?" Roland asked.

"Yes, sai," Stuttering Bill said.

"*Shit,*" Susannah muttered. They had had similar problems with Andy, back in Calla Bryn Sturgis.

"H-H-However," said Stuttering Bill, "if you were to c-c-couch your orders as suh-huh-hugestions, I'm sure I'd be huh-huh-huh-huh—" He raised his arm and smacked his head again. The *Wheep!* sound came once more, not from his mouth but from the region of his chest, Susannah thought. "—happy to oblige," he finished.

"My first suggestion is that you fix that fucking stutter," Roland said, and then turned around, amazed. Patrick had collapsed to the snow, holding his belly and voicing great, blurry cries of laughter. Oy danced around him, barking, but Oy was harmless; this time there was no one to steal Patrick's joy. It belonged only to him. And to those lucky enough to hear it.

THIRTEEN

In the woods beyond the plowed intersection, back toward what Bill would have called "the Bads," a shivering adolescent boy wrapped in stinking, half-scraped hides watched the quartet standing in front of Dandelo's hut. *Die,* he thought at them. *Die, why don't you all do me a favor and just die?* But they didn't die, and the cheerful sound of their laughter cut him like knives.

Later, after they had all piled into the cab of Bill's plow and driven away, Mordred crept down to the hut. There he would stay for at least two days, eating his fill from the cans in Dandelo's pantry—and eating something else as well, something he would live to regret. He spent those days regaining his strength, for the big storm *had* come close to killing him. He believed it was his hate that had kept him alive, that and no more.

Or perhaps it was the Tower.

For he felt it, too—that pulse, that singing. But what Roland and Susannah and Patrick heard in a major key, Mordred heard in a minor. And where they heard many voices, he heard only one. It was the voice of his Red Father, telling him to come. Telling him to kill the mute boy, and the blackbird bitch, and especially the gunslinger out of Gilead, the uncaring White Daddy who had left him behind. (Of course his Red Daddy had also left him behind, but this never crossed Mordred's mind.)

And when the killing was done, the whispering voice promised, they would destroy the Dark Tower and rule todash together for eternity.

So Mordred ate, for Mordred was a-hungry. And Mordred slept, for Mordred was a-weary. And when Mordred dressed himself in Dandelo's warm clothes and set out along the freshly plowed Tower Road, pulling a rich sack of gunna on a sled behind him—canned goods, mostly—he had become a young man who looked to be perhaps twenty years old, tall and straight and as fair as a summer sunrise, his human form marked only by the scar on his side where Susannah's bullet had winged him, and the blood-mark on his heel. That heel, he had promised himself, would rest on Roland's throat, and soon.

PART FIVE:

THE SCARLET FIELD OF CAN'-KA NO REY

CHAPTER I:

THE SORE AND THE DOOR
(GOODBYE, MY DEAR)

ONE

In the final days of their long journey, after Bill—just Bill now, no longer Stuttering Bill—dropped them off at the Federal, on the edge of the White Lands, Susannah Dean began to suffer frequent bouts of weeping. She would feel these impending cloudbursts and would excuse herself from the others, saying she had to go into the bushes and do her necessary. And there she would sit on a fallen tree or perhaps just the cold ground, put her hands over her face, and let her tears flow. If Roland knew this was happening—and surely he must have noted her red eyes when she returned to the road—he made no comment. She supposed he knew what she did.

Her time in Mid-World—and End-World—was almost at an end.

TWO

Bill took them in his fine orange plow to a lonely Quonset hut with a faded sign out front reading

FEDERAL OUTPOST 19
TOWER WATCH
TRAVEL BEYOND THIS POINT IS FORBIDDEN!

She supposed Federal Outpost 19 was still technically in the White Lands of Empathica, but the air had warmed considerably as Tower Road descended, and the snow on the ground was

715

little more than a scrim. Groves of trees dotted the ground ahead, but Susannah thought the land would soon be almost entirely open, like the prairies of the American Midwest. There were bushes that probably supported berries in warm weather—perhaps even pokeberries—but now they were bare and clattering in the nearly constant wind. Mostly what they saw on either side of Tower Road—which had once been paved but had now been reduced to little more than a pair of broken ruts—were tall grasses poking out of the thin snow-cover. They whispered in the wind and Susannah knew their song: *Commala-come-come, journey's almost done.*

"I may go no further," Bill said, shutting down the plow and cutting off Little Richard in mid-rave. "Tell ya sorry, as they say in the Arc o' the Borderlands."

Their trip had taken one full day and half of another, and during that time he had entertained them with a constant stream of what he called "golden oldies." Some of these were not old at all to Susannah; songs like "Sugar Shack" and "Heat Wave" had been current hits on the radio when she'd returned from her little vacation in Mississippi. Others she had never heard at all. The music was stored not on records or tapes but on beautiful silver discs Bill called "ceedees." He pushed them into a slot in the plow's instrument-cluttered dashboard and the music played from at least eight different speakers. Any music would have sounded fine to her, she supposed, but she was especially taken by two songs she had never heard before. One was a deliriously happy little rocker called "She Loves You." The other, sad and reflective, was called "Hey Jude." Roland actually seemed to know the latter one; he sang along with it, although the words he knew were different from the ones coming out of the plow's multiple speakers. When she asked, Bill told her the group was called The Beetles.

"Funny name for a rock-and-roll band," Susannah said.

Patrick, sitting with Oy in the plow's tiny rear seat, tapped her on the shoulder. She turned and he held up the pad through which he was currently working his way. Beneath a picture of Roland in profile, he had printed: **BEATLES, not Beetles.**

"It's a funny name for a rock-and-roll band no matter which way you spell it," Susannah said, and that gave her an idea. "Patrick, do you have the touch?" When he frowned and raised his hands—*I don't understand,* the gesture said—she rephrased the question. "Can you read my mind?"

He shrugged and smiled. This gesture said *I don't know,* but she thought Patrick did know. She thought he knew very well.

THREE

They reached "the Federal" near noon, and there Bill served them a fine meal. Patrick wolfed his and then sat off to one side with Oy curled at his feet, sketching the others as they sat around the table in what had once been the common room. The walls of this room were covered with TV screens—Susannah guessed there were three hundred or more. They must have been built to last, too, because some were still operating. A few showed the rolling hills surrounding the Quonset, but most broadcast only snow, and one showed a series of rolling lines that made her feel queasy in her stomach if she looked at it too long. The snow-screens, Bill said, had once shown pictures from satellites in orbit around the Earth, but the cameras in those had gone dead long ago. The one with the rolling lines was more interesting. Bill told them that, until only a few months ago, that one had shown the Dark Tower. Then, suddenly, the picture had dissolved into nothing but those lines.

"I don't think the Red King liked being on television," Bill told them. "Especially if he knew company might be coming. Won't you have another sandwich? There are plenty, I assure you. No? Soup, then? What about you, Patrick? You're too thin, you know—far, *far* too thin."

Patrick turned his pad around and showed them a picture of Bill bowing in front of Susannah, a tray of neatly cut sandwiches in one metal hand, a carafe of iced tea in the other. Like all of Patrick's pictures, it went far beyond caricature, yet had been produced with a speed of hand that was eerie. Susannah applauded. Roland smiled and nodded. Patrick grinned, holding his teeth together so that the others wouldn't have to look at the empty hole behind them. Then he tossed the sheet back and began something new.

"There's a fleet of vehicles out back," Bill said, "and while many of them no longer run, some still do. I can give you a truck with four-wheel drive, and while I cannot assure you it will run smoothly, I believe you can count on it to take you as far as the Dark Tower, which is no more than one hundred and twenty wheels from here."

Susannah felt a great and fluttery lift-drop in her stomach. One hundred and twenty wheels was a hundred miles, perhaps even a bit less. They *were* close. So close it was scary.

"You would not want to come upon the Tower after dark," Bill said. "At least I shouldn't think so, considering the new resident. But what's one more night camped at the side of the road to such great travelers as yourselves? Not much, I should say! But even with one last night on the road (and barring breakdowns, which the gods know are always possible), you'd have your goal in sight by mid-morning of tomorrowday."

Roland considered this long and carefully. Susannah had to tell herself to breathe while he did so, because part of her didn't want to.

I'm not ready, that part thought. And there was a deeper part—a part that remembered every nuance of what had become a recurring (and evolving) dream—that thought something else: *I'm not meant to go at all. Not all the way.*

At last Roland said: "I thank you, Bill—we all say thank you, I'm sure—but I think we'll pass on your kind offer. Were you to ask me why, I couldn't say. Only that part of me thinks that tomorrowday's too soon. That part of me thinks we should go the rest of the way on foot, just as we've already traveled so far." He took a deep breath, let it out. "I'm not ready to be there yet. Not quite ready."

You too, Susannah marveled. *You too.*

"I need a little more time to prepare my mind and my heart. Mayhap even my soul." He reached into his back pocket and brought out the photocopy of the Robert Browning poem that had been left for them in Dandelo's medicine chest. "There's something writ in here about remembering the old times before coming to the last battle . . . or the last stand. It's well-said. And perhaps, really, all I need is what this poet speaks of—a draught of earlier, happier sights. I don't know. But unless Susannah objects, I believe we'll go on foot."

"Susannah doesn't object," she said quietly. "Susannah thinks it's just what the doctor ordered. Susannah only objects to being dragged along behind like a busted tailpipe."

Roland gave her a grateful (if distracted) smile—he seemed to have gone away from her somehow during these last few days—and then turned back to Bill. "I wonder if you have a cart I could pull? For we'll have to take at least some gunna . . . and there's Patrick. He'll have to ride part of the time."

Patrick looked indignant. He cocked an arm in front of him, made a fist, and flexed his muscle. The result—a tiny goose-egg rising on the biceps of his drawing-arm—seemed to shame him, for he dropped it quickly.

Susannah smiled and reached out to pat his knee. "Don't look like that, sugar. It's not your fault that you spent God knows how long caged up like Hansel and Gretel in the witch's house."

"I'm sure I have such a thing," Bill said, "and a battery-powered version for Susannah. What I don't have, I can make. It would take an hour or two at most."

Roland was calculating. "If we leave here with five hours of daylight ahead of us, we might be able to make twelve wheels by sunset. What Susannah would call nine or ten miles. Another five days at that rather leisurely speed would bring us to the Tower I've spent my life searching for. I'd come to it around sunset if possible, for that's when I've always seen it in my dreams. Susannah?"

And the voice inside—that deep voice—whispered: *Four nights. Four nights to dream. That should be enough. Maybe more than enough.* Of course, ka would have to intervene. If they had indeed outrun its influence, that wouldn't— *couldn't*—happen. But Susannah now thought ka reached everywhere, even to the Dark Tower. Was, perhaps, embodied *by* the Dark Tower.

"That's fine," she told him in a faint voice.

"Patrick?" Roland asked. "What do you say?"

Patrick shrugged and flipped a hand in their direction, hardly looking up from his pad. Whatever they wanted, that gesture said. Susannah guessed that Patrick understood little about the Dark Tower, and cared less. And why would he care? He was free of the monster, and his belly was full. Those things were enough for him. He had lost his tongue, but he could sketch to his heart's content. She was sure that to Patrick, that seemed like more than an even trade. And yet . . . and yet . . .

He's not meant to go, either. Not him, not Oy, not me. But what is to become of us, then?

She didn't know, but she was queerly unworried about it. Ka would tell. Ka, and her dreams.

FOUR

An hour later the three humes, the bumbler, and Bill the robot stood clustered around a cut-down wagon that looked like a slightly larger version of Ho Fat's Luxury Taxi. The wheels were tall but thin, and spun like a dream. Even when it was full, Susannah thought, it would be like pulling a feather. At least while Roland was fresh. Pulling it uphill would undoubtedly rob him of his energy after awhile, but as they ate the food they were carrying, Ho Fat II would grow lighter still . . . and she thought there wouldn't be many hills, anyway. They had come to the open lands, the prairie-lands; all the snow- and tree-covered ridges were behind them. Bill had provided her with an electric runabout that was more scooter than golf-cart. Her days of being dragged along behind ("like a busted tailpipe") were done.

"If you'll give me another half an hour, I can smooth this off," Bill said, running a three-fingered steel hand along the edge where he had cut off the front half of the small wagon that was now Ho Fat II.

"We say thankya, but it won't be necessary," Roland said. "We'll lay a couple of hides over it, just so."

He's impatient to be off, Susannah thought, *and after all this time, why wouldn't be be? I'm anxious to be off, myself.*

"Well, if you say so, let it be so," Bill said, sounding unhappy about it. "I suppose I just hate to see you go. When will I see humes again?"

None of them answered that. They didn't know.

"There's a mighty loud horn on the roof," Bill said, pointing at the Federal. "I don't know what sort of trouble it was meant to signal—radiation leaks, mayhap, or some sort of attack—but I do know the sound of it will carry across a hundred wheels at least. More, if the wind's blowing in the right direction. If I should see the fellow you think is following you, or if such motion-sensors as still work pick him up, I'll set it off. Perhaps you'll hear."

"Thank you," Roland said.

"Were you to drive, you could outrun him easily," Bill pointed out. "You'd reach the Tower and never have to see him."

"That's true enough," Roland said, but he showed absolutely no sign of changing his mind, and Susannah was glad.

"What will you do about the one you call his Red Father, if he really does command Can'-Ka No Rey?"

Roland shook his head, although he had discussed this probability with Susannah. He thought they might be able to circle the Tower from a distance and come then to its base from a direction that was blind to the balcony on which the Crimson King was trapped. Then they could work their way around to the door beneath him. They wouldn't know if that was possible until they could actually see the Tower and the lay of the land, of course.

"Well, there'll be water if God wills it," said the robot formerly known as Stuttering Bill, "or so the old people did say. And mayhap I'll see you again, in the clearing at the end of the path, if nowhere else. If robots are allowed to go there. I hope it's so, for there's many I've known that I'd see again."

He sounded so forlorn that Susannah went to him and

raised her arms to be picked up, not thinking about the absurdity of wanting to hug a robot. But he did and she did—quite fervently, too. Bill made up for the malicious Andy, back in Calla Bryn Sturgis, and was worth hugging for that, if nothing else. As his arms closed around her, it occurred to Susannah that Bill could break her in two with those titanium-steel arms if he wanted to. But he didn't. He was gentle.

"Long days and pleasant nights, Bill," she said. "May you do well, and we all say so."

"Thank you, madam," he said and put her down. "I say thudda-thank, thumma-thank, thukka—" *Wheep!* And he struck his head, producing a bright clang. "I say thank ya kindly." He paused. "I *did* fix the stutter, say true, but as I may have told you, I am not entirely without emotions."

FIVE

Patrick surprised them both by walking for almost four hours beside Susannah's electric scooter before tiring and climbing into Ho Fat II. They listened for the horn warning them that Bill had seen Mordred (or that the instruments in the Federal had detected him), but did not hear it . . . and the wind was blowing their way. By sunset, they had left the last of the snow. The land continued to flatten out, casting their shadows long before them.

When they finally stopped for the night, Roland gathered enough brush for a fire and Patrick, who had dozed off, woke up long enough to eat an enormous meal of Vienna sausage and baked beans. (Susannah, watching the beans disappear into Patrick's tongueless mouth, reminded herself to spread her hides upwind of him when she finally laid down her weary head.) She and Oy also ate heartily, but Roland hardly touched his own food.

When dinner was done, Patrick took up his pad to draw, frowned at his pencil, and then held out a hand to Susannah. She knew what he wanted, and took the glass canning jar from the little bag of personals she kept slung over her shoulder. She held onto this because there was only the one pencil sharpener, and she was afraid that Patrick might lose it. Of course Roland could sharpen the Eberhard-Fabers with his knife, but it would change the quality of the points somewhat. She tipped the jar, spilling erasers and paperclips and the required object into her cupped palm. Then she handed it to Patrick, who sharpened his pencil with a few quick twists, handed it back, and immediately fell to his work. For a moment Susannah looked at the pink erasers and wondered again why Dandelo had bothered to cut them off. As a way of teasing the boy? If so, it hadn't worked. Later in life, perhaps, when the sublime connections between his brain and his fingers rusted a little (when the small but undeniably brilliant world of his talent had moved on), he might require erasers. For now even his mistakes continued to be inspirations.

He didn't draw long. When Susannah saw him nodding over his pad in the orange glare of the fading sunset, she took it from his unprotesting fingers, bedded him down in the back of the cart (propped level with the front end on a convenient boulder jutting from the ground), covered him with hides, and kissed his cheek.

Sleepily, Patrick reached up and touched the sore below her own cheek. She winced, then held steady at his gentle touch. The sore had clotted over again, but it throbbed painfully. Even smiling hurt her these days. The hand fell away and Patrick slept.

The stars had come out. Roland was looking raptly up at them.

"What do you see?" she asked him.

"What do *you* see?" he asked in turn.

She looked at the brightening celestial landscape. "Well," she said, "there's Old Star and Old Mother, but they seem to have moved west. And that there—oh my goodness!" She placed her hands on his stubbly cheeks (he never seemed to grow an actual beard, only a bristly scruff) and turned it. "That wasn't there back when we left from the Western Sea, I know it wasn't. That one's in *our* world, Roland—we call it the Big Dipper!"

He nodded. "And once, according to the oldest books in my father's library, it was in the sky of our world, as well. Lydia's Dipper, it was called. And now here it is again." He turned to her, smiling. "Another sign of life and renewal. How the Crimson King must hate to look up from his entrapment and see it riding the sky again!"

SIX

Not long after, Susannah slept. And dreamed.

SEVEN

She's in Central Park again, under a bright gray sky from which the first few snowflakes are once more drifting; carolers nearby are singing not "Silent Night" or "What Child Is This" but the Rice Song: "Rice be a green-o, See what we seen-o, Seen-o the green-o, Come-come-commala!" She takes off her cap, afraid it will have changed somehow, but it still says MERRY CHRISTMAS! and
(no twins here)
she is comforted.

She looks around and there stand Eddie and Jake, grinning at her. Their heads are bare; she has gotten their hats. She has combined their hats.

Eddie is wearing a sweatshirt that says I DRINK NOZZ-A-LA!
Jake is wearing one that says I DRIVE THE TAKURO SPIRIT!

None of this is precisely new. What she sees behind them, standing near a carriage-path leading back to Fifth Avenue, most certainly is. It's a door about six and a half feet high, and made of solid ironwood, from the look of it. The doorknob's of solid gold, and filigreed with a shape the lady gunslinger finally recognizes: two crossed pencils. Eberhard-Faber #2's, she has no doubt. And the erasers have been cut off.

Eddie holds out a cup of hot chocolate. It's the perfect kind mit schlag *on top, and a little sprinkling of nutmeg dotting the cream. "Here," he says, "I brought you hot chocolate."*

She ignores the outstretched cup. She's fascinated by the door. "It's like the ones along the beach, isn't it?" she asks.

"Yes," Eddie says.

"No," Jake says at the same time.

"You'll figure it out," they say together, and grin at each other, delighted.

She walks past them. Writ upon the doors through which Roland drew them were THE PRISONER *and* THE LADY OF SHADOWS *and* THE PUSHER. *Writ upon this one is* ⬡⬡⬡ ⬡⬡. *And below that:*

THE ARTIST

She turns back to them and they are gone.

Central Park is gone.

She is looking at the ruination of Lud, gazing upon the waste lands.

On a cold and bitter breeze she hears four whispered words: "Time's almost up . . . hurry . . ."

EIGHT

She woke in a kind of panic, thinking *I have to leave him . . . and best I do it before I can s'much as see his Dark Tower on the horizon. But where do I go? And how can I leave him to face both Mordred and the Crimson King with only Patrick to help him?*

This idea caused her to reflect on a bitter certainty: come a showdown, Oy would almost certainly be more valuable to Roland than Patrick. The bumbler had proved his mettle on more than one occasion and would have been worthy of the title *gunslinger,* had he but a gun to sling and a hand to sling it with. Patrick, though . . . Patrick was a . . . well, a pencil-slinger. Faster than blue blazes, but you couldn't kill much with an Eberhard-Faber unless it was *very* sharp.

She'd sat up. Roland, leaning against the far side of her little scooter and keeping the watch, hadn't noticed. And she didn't *want* him to notice. That would lead to questions. She lay back down, pulling her hides around her and thinking of their first hunt. She remembered how the yearling buck had swerved and run right at her, and how she'd decapitated it with the

Oriza. She remembered the whistling sound in the chilly air, the one that resulted when the wind blew through the little attachment on the bottom of the plate, the attachment that looked so much like Patrick's pencil sharpener. She thought her mind was trying to make some sort of connection here, but she was too tired to know what it might be. And maybe she was trying too hard, as well. If so, what was she to do about that?

There was at least one thing she *did* know, from her time in Calla Bryn Sturgis. The meaning of the symbols writ upon the door was UNFOUND.

Time's almost up. Hurry.

The next day her tears began.

NINE

There were still plenty of bushes behind which she could go to do her necessary (and cry her tears, when she could no longer hold them back), but the land continued to flatten and open. Around noon of their second full day on the road, Susannah saw what she at first thought was a cloud-shadow moving across the land far up ahead, only the sky above was solid blue from horizon to horizon. Then the great dark patch began to veer in a very un-cloudlike way. She caught her breath and brought her little electric scooter to a stop.

"Roland!" she said. "Yonder's a herd of buffalo, or maybe they're bison! Sure as death n taxes!"

"Aye, do you say so?" Roland asked, with only passing interest. "We called em bannock, in the long ago. It's a good-sized herd."

Patrick was standing in the back of Ho Fat II, sketching madly. He switched his grip on the pencil he was using, now holding the yellow barrel against his palm and shading with the tip. She could almost smell the dust boiling up from the herd as he shaded it with his pencil. Although it seemed to her that he'd taken the liberty of moving the herd five or even ten miles closer, unless his vision was a good deal sharper than her own. That, she supposed, was entirely possible. In any case, her eyes had adjusted and she could see them better herself. Their great shaggy heads. Even their black eyes.

"There hasn't been a herd of buffalo that size in America for almost a hundred years," she said.

"Aye?" Still only polite interest. "But they're in plenty here, I should say. If a little tet of em comes within pistol-shot range, let's take a couple. I'd like to taste some fresh meat that isn't deer. Would you?"

She let her smile answer for her. Roland smiled back. And it occurred to her again that soon she would see him no more, this man she'd believed was either a mirage or a daemon before she had come to know him both an-tet and dan-dinh. Eddie was dead, Jake was dead, and soon she would see Roland of Gilead no more. Would he be dead, as well? Would she?

She looked up into the glare of the sun, wanting him to mistake the reason for her tears if he saw them. And they moved on into the southeast of that great and empty land, into the ever-strengthening beat-beat-beat that was the Tower at the axis of all worlds and time itself.

Beat-beat-beat.

Commala-come-come, journey's almost done.

That night she stood the first watch, then awakened Roland at midnight.

"I think he's out there someplace," she said, pointing into the northwest. There was no need to be more specific; it could only be Mordred. Everyone else was gone. "Watch well."

"I will," he said. "And if you hear a gunshot, *wake* well. And fast."

"You can count on it," said she, and lay down in the dry winter grass behind Ho Fat II. At first she wasn't sure she'd be able to sleep; she was still jazzed from the sense of an unfriendly other in the vicinity. But she *did* sleep.

And dreamed.

TEN

The dream of the second night is both like and unlike the dream of the first. The main elements are exactly the same: Central Park, gray sky, spits of snow, choral voices (this time harmonizing "Come Go With Me," the old Del-Vikings hit), Jake (I DRIVE THE TAKURO SPIRIT!) and Eddie (this time wearing a sweatshirt reading CLICK! IT'S A SHINNARO CAMERA!). Eddie has hot chocolate but doesn't offer it to her. She can see the anxiety not only in their faces but in the tensed-up set of their bodies. That is the main difference in this dream: there is something to see, or something to do, or perhaps it's both. Whatever it is, they expected her to see it or do it by now and she is being backward.

A rather terrible question occurs to her: is she being purposely *backward? Is there something here she doesn't want to confront? Could it even be possible that the Dark Tower is fucking up communications? Surely that's a stupid idea—these people she sees are but figments of her longing imagination, after all; they are* dead! *Eddie killed by a bullet, Jake as a result of being run over by a car—one slain in this world, one in the Keystone World where fun is fun and done is done (must be done, for there time always runs in one direction) and Stephen King is their poet laureate.*

Yet she cannot deny that look on their faces, that look of panic that seems to tell her You *have it, Suze—you have what we want to show you, you have what you need to know. Are you going to let it slip away? It's the fourth quarter. It's the fourth quarter and the clock is ticking and will continue to tick, *must* continue to tick because all your time-outs are gone. You have to hurry . . . hurry . . .

ELEVEN

She snapped awake with a gasp. It was almost dawn. She wiped a hand across her brow, and it came away wet with sweat.

What do you want me to know, Eddie? What is it you'd have me know?

To this question there was no answer. How could there be?

Mistuh Dean, he daid, she thought, and lay back down. She lay that way for another hour, but couldn't get back to sleep.

TWELVE

Like Ho Fat I, Ho Fat II was equipped with handles. Unlike those on Ho Fat I, these handles were adjustable. When Patrick felt like walking, the handles could be moved apart so he could pull one and Roland the other. When Patrick felt like riding, Roland moved the handles together so he could pull on his own.

They stopped at noon for a meal. When it was done, Patrick crawled into the back of Ho Fat II for a snooze. Roland waited until he heard the boy (for so they continued to think of him, no matter what his age) snoring, then turned to her.

"What fashes thee, Susannah? I'd have you tell me. I'd have you tell me dan-dinh, even though there's no longer a tet and I'm your dinh no more." He smiled. The sadness in that smile broke her heart and she could hold her tears back no more. Nor the truth.

"If I'm still with you when we see your Tower, Roland, things have gone all wrong."

"*How* wrong?" he asked her.

She shook her head, beginning to weep harder. "There's supposed to be a door. It's the Unfound Door. But I don't know how to find it! Eddie and Jake come to me in my dreams and tell me I know—they tell me with their eyes—but I don't! *I swear I don't!*"

He took her in his arms and held her and kissed the hollow of her temple. At the corner of her mouth, the sore throbbed and burned. It wasn't bleeding, but it had begun to grow again.

"Let be what will be," said the gunslinger, as his own mother had once told him. "Let be what will be, and hush, and let ka work."

"You said we'd outrun it."

He rocked her in his arms, rocked her, and it was good. It was soothing. "I was wrong," he said. "As thee knows."

THIRTEEN

It was her turn to watch early on the third night, and she was looking back behind them, northwest along the Tower Road, when a hand grasped her shoulder. Terror sprang up in her mind like a jack-in-the-box and she whirled

(*he's behind me oh dear God Mordred's got around behind me and it's the spider!*)

with her hand going to the gun in her belt and yanking it free.

Patrick recoiled from her, his own face long with terror, raising his hands in front of him. If he'd cried out he would surely have awakened Roland, and then everything might have been different. But he was too frightened to cry out. He made a low sound in his throat and that was all.

She put the gun back, showed him her empty hands, then pulled him to her and hugged him. At first he was stiff against her—still afraid—but after a little he relaxed.

"What is it, darling?" she asked him, *sotto voce.* Then, using Roland's phrase without even realizing it: "What fashes thee?"

He pulled away from her and pointed dead north. For a moment she still didn't understand, and then she saw the orange lights dancing and darting. She judged they were at least five miles away, and she could hardly believe she hadn't seen them before.

Still speaking low, so as not to wake Roland, she said: "They're nothing but foo-lights, sugar—they can't hurt you. Roland calls em hobs. They're like St. Elmo's fire, or something."

But he had no idea of what St. Elmo's fire was; she could see that in his uncertain gaze. She settled again for telling him they couldn't hurt him, and indeed, this was the closest the hobs had ever come. Even as she looked back at them, they began to dance away, and soon most of them were gone. Perhaps she had *thought* them away. Once she would have scoffed at such an idea, but no longer.

Patrick began to relax.

"Why don't you go back to sleep, honey? You need to take your rest." And she needed to take hers, but she dreaded it. Soon she would wake Roland, and sleep, and the dream would come. The ghosts of Jake and Eddie would look at her, more frantic than ever. Wanting her to know something she didn't, couldn't know.

Patrick shook his head.

"Not sleepy yet?"

He shook his head again.

"Well then, why don't you draw awhile?" Drawing always relaxed him.

Patrick smiled and nodded and went at once to Ho Fat for his current pad, walking in big exaggerated sneak-steps so as not to wake Roland. It made her smile. Patrick was always willing to draw; she guessed that one of the things that kept him alive in the basement of Dandelo's hut had been knowing that every now and then the rotten old fuck would give him a pad and one of the pencils. He was as much an addict as Eddie had been at his worst, she reflected, only Patrick's dope was a narrow line of graphite.

He sat down and began to draw. Susannah resumed her watch, but soon felt a queer tingling all over her body, as if *she* were the one being watched. She thought of Mordred again, and then smiled (which hurt; with the sore growing fat again, it always did now). Not Mordred; Patrick. Patrick was watching her.

Patrick was *drawing* her.

She sat still for nearly twenty minutes, and then curiosity overcame her. For Patrick, twenty minutes would be long enough to do the *Mona Lisa*, and maybe St. Paul's Basilica in the background for good measure. That tingling sense was so *queer*, almost not a mental thing at all but something physical.

She went to him, but Patrick at first held the pad against his chest with unaccustomed shyness. But he *wanted* her to look; that was in his eyes. It was almost a love-look, but she thought it was the drawn Susannah he'd fallen in love with.

"Come on, honeybunch," she said, and put a hand on the

pad. But she would not tug it away from him, not even if he wanted her to. He was the artist; let it be wholly his decision whether or not to show his work. "Please?"

He held the pad against him a moment longer. Then—shyly, not looking at her—he held it out. She took it, and looked down at herself. For a moment she could hardly breathe, it was that good. The wide eyes. The high cheekbones, which her father had called "those jewels of Ethiopia." The full lips, which Eddie had so loved to kiss. It was her, it was her to the very life . . . but it was also *more* than her. She would never have thought love could shine with such perfect nakedness from the lines made with a pencil, but here that love was, oh say true, say so true; love of the boy for the woman who had saved him, who had pulled him from the dark hole where he otherwise would surely have died. Love for her as a mother, love for her as a woman.

"Patrick, it's wonderful!" she said.

He looked at her anxiously. Doubtfully. *Really?* his eyes asked her, and she realized that only he—the poor needy Patrick inside, who had lived with this ability all his life and so took it for granted—could doubt the simple beauty of what he had done. Drawing made *him* happy; this much he'd always known. That his pictures could make *others* happy . . . that idea would take some getting used to. She wondered again how long Dandelo had had him, and how the mean old thing had come by Patrick in the first place. She supposed she'd never know. Meantime, it seemed very important to convince him of his own worth.

"Yes," she said. "Yes, it *is* wonderful. You're a fine artist, Patrick. Looking at this makes me feel good."

This time he forgot to hold his teeth together. And that smile, tongueless or not, was so wonderful she could have eaten it up. It made her fears and anxieties seem small and silly.

"May I keep it?"

Patrick nodded eagerly. He made a tearing motion with one hand, then pointed at her. *Yes! Tear it off! Take it! Keep it!*

She started to do so, then paused. His love (and his pencil) had made her beautiful. The only thing to spoil that beauty was the black splotch beside her mouth. She turned the drawing toward him, tapped the sore on it, then touched it on her own face. And winced. Even the lightest touch hurt. "This is the only damned thing," she said.

He shrugged, raising his open hands to his shoulders, and she had to laugh. She did it softly so as not to wake Roland, but yes, she did have to laugh. A line from some old movie had occurred to her: *I paint what I see.*

Only this wasn't paint, and it suddenly occurred to her that he could take care of the rotten, ugly, painful thing. As it existed on paper, at least.

Then she'll be my twin, she thought affectionately. *My better half; my pretty twin sis—*

And suddenly she understood—

Everything? Understood *everything?*

Yes, she would think much later. Not in any coherent fashion that could be written down—if $a + b = c$, then $c - b = a$ and $c - a = b$—but yes, she understood everything. *Intuited* everything. No wonder the dream-Eddie and dream-Jake had been impatient with her; it was so obvious.

Patrick, *drawing* her.

Nor was this the first time she had been drawn.

Roland had drawn her to his world . . . with magic.

Eddie had drawn her to himself with love.

As had Jake.

Dear God, had she been here so long and been through so much without knowing what ka-tet *was,* what it meant? Ka-tet was family.

Ka-tet was love.

To *draw* is to make a picture with a pencil, or maybe charcoal.

To *draw* is also to fascinate, to compel, and to bring forward. *To bring one out of one's self.*

The *drawers* were where Detta went to fulfill herself.

Patrick, that tongueless boy genius, pent up in the wilderness. Pent up in the drawers. And now? Now?

Now he my forspecial, thought Susanna/Odetta/Detta, and reached into her pocket for the glass jar, knowing exactly what she was going to do and why she was going to do it.

When she handed back the pad without tearing off the sheet that now held her image, Patrick looked badly disappointed.

"Nar, nar," said she (and in the voice of many). "Only there's something I'd have you do before I take it for my pretty, for my precious, for my ever, to keep and know how I was at this where, at this when."

She held out one of the pink rubber pieces, understanding now why Dandelo had cut them off. For he'd had his reasons.

Patrick took what she offered and turned it over between his fingers, frowning, as if he had never seen such a thing before. Susannah was sure he had, but how many years ago? How close might he have come to disposing of his tormentor, once and for all? And why hadn't Dandelo just killed him then?

Because once he took away the erasers he thought he was safe, she thought.

Patrick was looking at her, puzzled. Beginning to be upset.

Susannah sat down beside him and pointed at the blemish on the drawing. Then she put her fingers delicately around Patrick's wrist and drew it toward the paper. At first he resisted, then let his hand with the pink nubbin in it be tugged forward.

She thought of the shadow on the land that hadn't been a shadow at all but a herd of great, shaggy beasts Roland called bannock. She thought of how she'd been able to smell the dust when Patrick began to *draw* the dust. And she thought of how, when Patrick had drawn the herd closer than it actually was (artistic license, and we all say thankya), it had actually *looked* closer. She remembered thinking that her eyes had adjusted and now marveled at her own stupidity. As if eyes could adjust to distance the way they could adjust to the dark.

No, Patrick had moved them closer. Had moved them closer by *drawing* them closer.

When the hand holding the eraser was almost touching the paper, she took her own hand away—this had to be all Patrick, she was somehow sure of it. She moved her fingers back and forth, miming what she wanted. He didn't get it. She did it again, then pointed to the sore beside the full lower lip.

"Make it gone, Patrick," she said, surprised by the steadiness of her own voice. "It's ugly, make it gone." Again she made that rubbing gesture in the air. "Erase it."

This time he got it. She saw the light in his eyes. He held the pink nubbin up to her. *Perfectly* pink it was—not a smudge of graphite on it. He looked at her, eyebrows raised, as if to ask if she was sure.

She nodded.

Patrick lowered the eraser to the sore and began to rub it on the paper, tentatively at first. Then, as he saw what was happening, he worked with more spirit.

FOURTEEN

She felt the same queer tingling sensation, but when he'd been drawing, it had been all over her. Now it was in only one place, to the right side of her mouth. As Patrick got the hang of the eraser and bore down with it, the tingling became a deep and monstrous itch. She had to clutch her hands deep into the dirt on either side of her to keep from reaching up and clawing at the sore, scratching it furiously, and never mind if she tore it wide open and sent a pint of blood gushing down her deerskin shirt.

It be over in a few more seconds, it have to be, it have to be, oh dear God please LET IT END—

Patrick, meanwhile, seemed to have forgotten all about her. He was looking down at his picture, his hair hanging to either side of his face and obscuring most of it, completely absorbed by this wonderful new toy. He erased delicately . . . then a little harder (the itch intensified) . . . then more softly again. Susannah felt like shrieking. That itch was suddenly everywhere. It burned in her forebrain, buzzed across the wet surfaces of her eyes like twin clouds of gnats, it shivered at the very tips of her nipples, making them hopelessly hard.

I'll scream, I can't help it, I have to scream—

She was drawing in her breath to do just that when suddenly the itch was gone. The pain was gone, as well. She reached toward the side of her mouth, then hesitated.

I don't dare.

You better *dare!* Detta responded indignantly. *After all you been through—all we been through—you must have enough backbone left to touch yo' own damn face, you yella bitch!*

She brought her fingers down to the skin. The *smooth* skin. The sore which had so troubled her since Thunderclap was gone. She knew that when she looked in a mirror or a still pool of water, she would not even see a scar.

FIFTEEN

Patrick worked a little longer—first with the eraser, then with the pencil, then with the eraser again—but Susannah felt no itch and not even a faint tingle. It was as though, once he had passed some critical point, the sensations just ceased. She wondered how old Patrick had been when Dandelo snipped all the erasers off the pencils. Four? Six? Young, anyway. She was sure that his original look of puzzlement when she showed him one of the erasers had been unfeigned, and yet once he began, he used it like an old pro.

Maybe it's like riding a bicycle, she thought. *Once you learn how, you never forget.*

She waited as patiently as she could, and after five very long minutes, her patience was rewarded. Smiling, Patrick turned the pad around and showed her the picture. He had erased the blemish completely and then faintly shaded the area so that it looked like the rest of her skin. He had been careful to brush away every single crumb of rubber.

"Very nice," she said, but that was a fairly shitty compliment to offer genius, wasn't it?

So she leaned forward, put her arms around him, and kissed him firmly on the mouth. "Patrick, it's *beautiful.*"

The blood rushed so quickly and so strongly into his face that she was alarmed at first, wondering if he might not have a stroke in spite of his youth. But he was smiling as he held out the pad to her with one hand, making tearing gestures again with the other. Wanting her to take it. Wanting her to have it.

Susannah tore it off very carefully, wondering in a dark back corner of her mind what would happen if she tore it—tore *her*—right down the middle. She noted as she did that there was no amazement in his face, no astonishment, no fear. He had to have seen the sore beside her mouth, because the nasty thing had pretty much dominated her face for all the time he'd known her, and he had drawn it in near-photographic detail. Now it was gone—her exploring fingers told her so—yet Patrick wasn't registering any emotion, at least in regard to that. The conclusion seemed clear enough. When he'd erased it from his drawing, he'd also erased it from his own mind and memory.

"Patrick?"

He looked at her, smiling. Happy that she was happy. And Susannah was *very* happy. The fact that she was also scared to death didn't change that in the slightest.

"Will you draw something else for me?"

He nodded. Made a mark on his pad, then turned it around so she could see:

?

She looked at the question-mark for a moment, then at him. She saw he was clutching the eraser, his wonderful new tool, very tightly.

Susannah said: "I want you to draw me something that isn't there."

He cocked his head quizzically to the side. She had to smile a little in spite of her rapidly thumping heart—Oy looked that way sometimes, when he wasn't a hundred per cent sure what you meant.

"Don't worry, I'll tell you."

And she did, very carefully. Patrick listened. At some point Roland heard Susannah's voice and awoke. He came over, looked at her in the dim red light of the embering campfire, started to look away, then snapped back, eyes widening. Until that moment, she hadn't been sure Roland would see what was no longer there, either. She thought it at least possible that Patrick's magic would have been strong enough to erase it from the gunslinger's memory, too.

"Susannah, thy face! What's happened to thy—"

"Hush, Roland, if you love me."

The gunslinger hushed. Susannah returned her attention to Patrick and began to speak again, quietly but urgently. Patrick listened, and as he did, she saw the light of understanding begin to enter his gaze.

Roland replenished the fire without having to be asked, and soon their little camp was bright under the stars.

Patrick wrote a question, putting it thriftily to the left of the question-mark he had already drawn:

How tall?

Susannah took Roland by the elbow and positioned him in front of Patrick. The gunslinger stood about six-foot-three. She had him pick her up, then held a hand roughly three inches over his head. Patrick nodded, smiling.

"And look you at something that has to be on it," she said, and took a branch from their little pile of brush. She broke it over her knee, creating a point of her own. She could remember the symbols, but it would be best if she didn't think about them overmuch. She sensed they had to be absolutely right or the door she wanted him to make for her would either open on some place she didn't want to go, or would not open at all. Therefore once she began to draw in the mixed dirt and ash by the campfire, she did it as rapidly as Patrick himself might have done, not pausing long enough to cast her eye back upon a single symbol. For if she looked back at one she would surely look back at all, and she would see something that looked wrong to her, and uncertainty would set in like a sickness. Detta—brash, foul-mouthed Detta, who had turned out on more than one occasion to be her savior—might step in and take over, finish for her, but she couldn't count on that. On her heart's deepest level, she still did not entirely trust Detta not to send everything to blazes at a crucial moment, and for no other reason than the black joy of the thing. Nor did she fully trust Roland, who might want to keep her for reasons he did not fully understand himself.

So she drew quickly in the dirt and ashes, not looking back, and these were the symbols that flowed away beneath the flying tip of her makeshift implement:

"Unfound," Roland breathed. "Susannah, what—how—"

"Hush," she repeated.

Patrick bent over his pad and began to draw.

SIXTEEN

She kept looking around for the door, but the circle of light thrown by their fire was very small even after Roland had set it to blazing. Small compared to the vast darkness of the prairie, at least. She saw nothing. When she turned to Roland she could see the unspoken question in his eyes, and so, while Patrick kept working, she showed him the picture of her the young man had drawn. She indicated the place where the blemish had been. Holding the page close to his face, Roland at last saw the eraser's marks. Patrick had concealed what few traces he'd left behind with great cunning, and Roland had found them only with the closest scrutiny; it was like casting for an old trail after many days of rain.

"No wonder the old man cut off his erasers," he said, giving the picture back to her.

"That's what I thought."

From there she skipped ahead to her single true intuitive leap: that if Patrick could (in this world, at least) un-create by erasing, he might be able to create by drawing. When she mentioned the herd of bannock that had seemed mysteriously closer, Roland rubbed his forehead like a man who has a nasty headache.

"I should have seen that. Should have realized what it meant, too. Susannah, I'm getting old."

She ignored that—she'd heard it before—and told him about the dreams of Eddie and Jake, being sure to mention the product-names on the sweatshirts, the choral voices, the offer of hot chocolate, and the growing panic in their eyes as the nights passed and still she did not see what the dream had been sent to show her.

"Why didn't you tell me this dream before now?" Roland asked. "Why didn't you ask for help in interpreting it?"

She looked at him steadily, thinking she had been right not to ask for his help. Yes—no matter how much that might hurt him. "You've lost two. How eager would you have been to lose me, as well?"

He flushed. Even in the firelight she could see it. "Thee speaks ill of me, Susannah, and have thought worse."

"Perhaps I have," she said. "If so, I say sorry. I wasn't sure of what I wanted myself. Part of me wants to see the Tower, you know. Part of me wants that very badly. And even if Patrick can draw the Unfound Door into existence and I can open it, it's not the real world it opens on. That's what the names on the shirts mean, I'm sure of it."

"You mustn't think that," Roland said. "Reality is seldom a thing of black and white, I think, of is and isn't, be and not be."

Patrick made a hooting sound and they both looked. He was holding his pad up, turned toward them so they could see what he had drawn. It was a perfect representation of the Unfound Door, she thought. THE ARTIST wasn't printed on it, and the doorknob was plain shiny metal—no crossed pencils adorned it—but that was all right. She hadn't bothered to tell him about those things, which had been for her benefit and understanding.

They did everything but draw me a map, she thought. She wondered why everything had to be so damn hard, so damn
(*riddle-de-dum*)

mysterious, and knew that was a question to which she would never find a satisfactory answer . . . except it was the human condition, wasn't it? The answers that mattered never came easily.

Patrick made another of those hooting noises. This time it had an interrogative quality. She suddenly realized that the poor kid was practically dying of anxiety, and why not? He had just executed his first commission, and wanted to know what his *patrono d'arte* thought of it.

"It's great, Patrick—terrific."

"Yes," Roland agreed, taking the pad. The door looked to him exactly like those he'd found as he staggered along the beach of the Western Sea, delirious and dying of the lobstrosity's poisoned bite. It was as if the poor tongueless creature had looked into his head and seen an actual picture of that door— a fottergraff.

Susannah, meanwhile, was looking around desperately. And when she began to swing along on her hands toward the edge of the firelight, Roland had to call her back sharply, reminding her that Mordred might be out there anywhere, and the darkness was Mordred's friend.

Impatient as she was, she retreated from the edge of the light, remembering all too well what had happened to Mordred's body-mother, and how quickly it had happened. Yet it hurt to pull back, almost physically. Roland had told her that he expected to catch his first glimpse of the Dark Tower toward the end of the coming day. If she was still with him, if she saw it with him, she thought its power might prove too strong for her. Its glammer. Now, given a choice between the door and the Tower, she knew she could still choose the door. But as they drew closer and the power of the Tower grew stronger, its pulse deeper and more compelling in her mind, the singing voices ever sweeter, choosing the door would be harder to do.

"I don't see it," she said despairingly. "Maybe I was wrong. Maybe there *is* no damn door. Oh, Roland—"

"I don't think you were wrong," Roland told her. He spoke with obvious reluctance, but as a man will when he has a job to do, or a debt to repay. And he did owe this woman a debt, he reckoned, for had he not pretty much seized her by the scruff of the neck and hauled her into this world, where she'd learned the art of murder and fallen in love and been left bereaved? Had he not kidnapped her into this present sorrow? If he could make that right, he had an obligation to do so. His desire to keep her with him—and at the risk of her own life—was pure selfishness, and unworthy of his training.

More important than that, it was unworthy of how much he had come to love and respect her. It broke what remained of his heart to think of bidding her goodbye, the last of his strange and wonderful ka-tet, but if it was what she wanted, what she *needed,* then he must do it. And he thought he *could* do it, for he had seen something about the young man's drawing that Susannah had missed. Not something that was there; something that wasn't.

"Look thee," he said gently, showing her the picture. "Do you see how hard he's tried to please thee, Susannah?"

"Yes!" she said. "Yes, of course I do, but—"

"It took him ten minutes to do this, I should judge, and most of his drawings, good as they are, are the work of three or four at most, wouldn't you say?"

"I don't understand you!" She nearly screamed this.

Patrick drew Oy to him and wrapped an arm around the bumbler, all the while looking at Susannah and Roland with wide, unhappy eyes.

"He worked so hard to give you what you want that there's only the Door. It stands by itself, all alone on the paper. It has no . . . no . . . "

He searched for the right word. Vannay's ghost whispered it dryly into his ear.

"It has no context!"

For a moment Susannah continued to look puzzled, and then the light of understanding began to break in her eyes. Roland didn't wait; he simply dropped his good left hand on Patrick's shoulder and told him to put the door behind Susannah's little electric golf-cart, which she had taken to calling Ho Fat III.

Patrick was happy to oblige. For one thing, putting Ho Fat III in front of the door gave him a reason to use his eraser. He worked much more quickly this time—almost carelessly, an observer might have said—but the gunslinger was sitting right next to him and didn't think Patrick missed a single stroke in his depiction of the little cart. He finished by drawing its single front wheel and putting a reflected gleam of firelight in the hubcap. Then he put his pencil down, and as he did, there was a disturbance in the air. Roland felt it push against his face. The flames of the fire, which had been burning straight up in the windless dark, streamed briefly sideways. Then the feeling was gone. The flames once more burned straight up. And standing not ten feet from that fire, behind the electric cart, was a door Roland had last encountered in Calla Bryn Sturgis, in the Cave of the Voices.

SEVENTEEN

Susannah waited until dawn, at first passing the time by gathering up her gunna, then putting it aside again—what would her few possessions (not to mention the little hide bag in which they were stored) avail her in New York City? People would laugh. They would probably laugh anyway . . . or scream and run at the very sight of her. The Susannah Dean who suddenly appeared in Central Park would look to most folks not like a college graduate or an heiress to a large fortune; not even like Sheena, Queen of the Jungle, say sorry. No, to civilized city people she'd probably look like some kind of freak-show escapee. And once she went through *this* door, would there be any going back? Never. Never in life.

So she put her gunna aside and simply waited. As dawn began to show its first faint white light on the horizon, she called Patrick over and asked him if he wanted to go along with her. Back to the world you came from or one very much like it, she told him, although she knew he didn't remember that world at all—either he'd been taken from it too young, or the trauma of being snatched away had erased his memory.

Patrick looked at her, then at Roland, who was squatted on his hunkers, looking at him. "Either way, son," the gunslinger said. "You can draw in either world, tell ya true. Although where she's going, there'll be more to appreciate it."

He wants him to stay, she thought, and was angry. Then Roland looked at her and gave his head a minute shake. She wasn't sure, but she thought that meant—

And no, she didn't just think. She knew what it meant. Roland wanted her to know he was hiding his thoughts from Patrick. His desires. And while she'd known the gunslinger to lie (most spectacularly at the meeting on the Calla Bryn Sturgis common-ground before the coming of the Wolves), she had never known him to lie to *her*. To Detta, maybe, but not to her. Or Eddie. Or Jake. There had been times when he hadn't told them all he knew, but outright lie . . . ? No. They'd been ka-tet, and Roland had played them straight. Give the devil his due.

Patrick suddenly took up his pad and wrote quickly on the clean sheet. Then he showed it to them:

I will stay. Scared to go sumplace new.

As if to emphasize exactly what he meant, he opened his lips and pointed into his tongueless mouth.

And did she see relief on Roland's face? If so, she hated him for it.

"All right, Patrick," she said, trying to show none of her feelings in her voice. She even reached over and patted his hand. "I understand how you feel. And while it's true that people can be cruel . . . cruel and mean . . . there's plenty who are kind. Listen, thee: I'm not going until dawn. If you change your mind, the offer is open."

He nodded quickly. *Grateful I ain't goan try no harder t'change his mine,* Detta thought angrily. *Ole white man probably grateful, too!*

Shut up, Susannah told her, and for a wonder, Detta did.

EIGHTEEN

But as the day brightened (revealing a medium-sized herd of grazing bannock not two miles away), she let Detta back into her mind. More: she let Detta take over. It was easier that way, less painful. It was Detta who took one more stroll around the campsite, briskly breathing the last of this world for both of them, and storing away the memory. It was Detta who went around the door, rocking first one way and then the other on the toughened pads of her palms, and saw the nothing at all on the other side. Patrick walked on one side of her, Roland on the other. Patrick hooted with surprise when he saw the door was gone. Roland said nothing. Oy walked up to the place where the door had been, sniffed at the air . . . and then walked through the place where it was, if you were looking from the other side. *If we was over there,* Detta thought, *we'd see him walk right through it, like a magic trick.*

She returned to Ho Fat III, which she had decided to ride through the door. Always assuming it would open, that was. This whole business would be quite a joke if it turned out it wouldn't. Roland made to help her up into the seat; she brushed him brusquely away and mounted on her own. She pushed the red button beside the wheel, and the cart's electric motor started with a faint hum. The needle marked CHG still swung well over into the green. She turned the throttle on the right handlebar and rolled slowly toward the closed door with the symbols meaning UNFOUND marching across the front. She stopped with the cart's little bullet nose almost touching it.

She turned to the gunslinger with a fixed make-believe smile.

"All ri', Roland—Ah'll say g'bye to you, then. Long days n pleasant nights. May you reach y'damn Tower, and—"

"No," he said.

She looked at him, *Detta* looked at him with her eyes both blazing and laughing. Challenging him to turn this into something she didn't want it to be. Challenging him to turn her out now that she was in. *C'mon, honky white boy, lessee you do it.*

"What?" she asked. "What's on yo' mine, big boy?"

"I'd not say goodbye to you like this, after all this time," he said.

"What do you mean?" Only in Detta's angry burlesque, it came out *Whatchu mean?*

"You know."

She shook her head defiantly. *Doan.*

"For one thing," he said, taking her trail-toughened left hand gently in his mutilated right one, "there's another who should have the choice to go or stay, and I'm not speaking of Patrick."

For a moment she didn't understand. Then she looked down at a certain pair of gold-ringed eyes, a certain pair of cocked ears, and did. She had forgotten about Oy.

"If Detta asks him, he'll surely stay, for she's never been to his liking. If Susannah asks him . . . why, then I don't know."

Just like that, Detta was gone. She would be back—Susannah understood now that she would never be entirely free of Detta Walker, and that was all right, because she no longer wanted to be—but for now she was gone.

"Oy?" she said gently. "Will you come with me, honey? It may be we'll find Jake again. Maybe not quite the same, but still . . ."

Oy, who had been almost completely silent during their trek across the Badlands and the White Lands of Empathica and the open rangelands, now spoke. "Ake?" he said. But he spoke doubtfully, as one who barely remembers, and her heart broke. She had promised herself she wouldn't cry, and Detta all but *guaranteed* she wouldn't cry, but now Detta was gone and the tears were here again.

"*Jake,*" she said. "You remember Jake, honeybunch, I know you do. Jake and Eddie."

"Ake? Ed?" With a little more certainty now. He *did* remember.

"Come with me," she urged, and Oy started forward as if he would jump up in the cart beside her. Then, with no idea at all why she should say it, she added: "There are other worlds than these."

Oy stopped as soon as the words were out of her mouth. He sat down. Then he got up again, and she felt a moment of hope: perhaps there could still be some little ka-tet, a dan-tete-tet, in some version of New York where folks drove Takuro Spirits and took pictures of each other drinking Nozz-A-La with their Shin-naro cameras.

Instead, Oy trotted back to the gunslinger and sat beside one battered boot. They had walked far, those boots, far. Miles and wheels, wheels and miles. But now their walking was almost done.

"Olan," said Oy, and the finality in his strange little voice rolled a stone against her heart. She turned bitterly to the old man with the big iron on his hip.

"There," she said. "You have your own glammer, don't you? Always did. You drew Eddie on to one death, and Jake to a pair of em. Now Patrick, and even the bumbler. Are you happy?"

"No," said he, and she saw he truly was not. She believed she had never seen such sadness and such loneliness on a human face. "Never was I farther from happy, Susannah of New York. Will you change your mind and stay? Will thee come the last little while with me? That would make me happy."

For a wild moment she thought she would. That she would simply turn the little electric cart from the door—which was one-sided and made no promises—and go with him to the Dark Tower. Another day would do it; they could camp at mid-afternoon and thus arrive tomorrow at sunset, as he wanted.

Then she remembered the dream. The singing voices. The young man holding out the cup of hot chocolate—the good kind, *mit schlag.*

"No," she said softly. "I'll take my chance and go."

For a moment she thought he would make it easy on her, just agree and let her go. Then his anger—no, his *despair*—broke in a painful burst. "But you can't be *sure!* Susannah, what if the dream itself is a trick and a glammer? What if the things you see even when the door's open are nothing but tricks and glammers? What if you roll right through and into todash space?"

"Then I'll light the darkness with thoughts of those I love."

"And that might work," said he, speaking in the bitterest voice she had ever heard. "For the first ten years . . . or twenty . . . or even a hundred. And then? What about the rest of eternity? Think of Oy! Do you think he's forgotten Jake? Never! Never! Never in your life! Never in his! He senses something wrong! Susannah, don't. I beg you, don't go. I'll get on my knees, if that will help." And to her horror, he began to do exactly that.

"It won't," she said. "And if this is to be my last sight of you—my heart says it is—then don't let it be of you on your knees. You're not a kneeling man, Roland, son of Steven, never were, and I don't want to remember you that way. I want to see you on your feet, as you were in Calla Bryn Sturgis. As you were with your friends at Jericho Hill."

He got up and came to her. For a moment she thought he meant to restrain her by force, and she was afraid. But he only put his hand on her arm for a moment, and then took it away. "Let me ask you again, Susannah. *Are you sure?*"

She conned her heart and saw that she was. She understood the risks, but yes—she was. And why? Because Roland's way was the way of the gun. Roland's way was death for those who rode or walked beside him. He had proved it over and over again, since the earliest days of his quest—no, even before, since overhearing Hax the cook plotting treachery and thus assuring his death by the rope. It was all for the good (for what he called the White), she had no doubt of it, but Eddie still lay in his grave in one world and Jake in another. She had no doubt that much the same fate was waiting for Oy, and for poor Patrick.

Nor would their deaths be long in coming.

"I'm sure," said she.

"All right. Will you give me a kiss?"

She took him by the arm and pulled him down and put her lips on his. When she inhaled, she took in the breath of a thousand years and ten thousand miles. And yes, she tasted death.

But not for you, gunslinger, she thought. *For others, but never for you. May I escape your glammer, and may I do fine.*

She was the one who broke their kiss.

"Can you open the door for me?" she asked.

Roland went to it, and took the knob in his hand, and the knob turned easily within his grip.

Cold air puffed out, strong enough to blow Patrick's long hair back, and with it came a few flakes of snow. She could see grass that was still green beneath light frost, and a path, and an iron fence. Voices were singing "What Child Is This," just as in her dream.

It could be Central Park. Yes, it *could* be; Central Park of some other world along the axis, perhaps, and not the one she came from, but close enough so that in time she would know no difference.

Or perhaps it was, as he said, a glammer.

Perhaps it was the todash darkness.

"It could be a trick," he said, most certainly reading her mind.

"*Life* is a trick, love a glammer," she replied. "Perhaps we'll meet again, in the clearing at the end of the path."

"As you say so, let it be so," he told her. He put out one leg, the rundown heel of his boot planted in the earth, and bowed to her. Oy had begun to weep, but he sat firmly beside the gunslinger's left boot. "Goodbye, my dear."

"Goodbye, Roland." Then she faced ahead, took in a deep breath, and twisted the little cart's throttle. It rolled smoothly forward.

"*Wait!*" Roland cried, but she never turned, nor looked at him again. She rolled through the door. It slammed shut behind her at once with a flat, declamatory clap he knew all too well, one he'd dreamed of ever since his long and feverish walk along the edge of the Western Sea. The sound of the singing was gone and now there was only the lonely sound of the prairie wind.

Roland of Gilead sat in front of the door, which already looked tired and unimportant. It would never open again. He put his face in his hands. It occurred to him that if he had never loved them, he would never have felt so alone as this. Yet of all his many regrets, the re-opening of his heart was not among them, even now.

NINETEEN

Later—because there's always a later, isn't there?—he made breakfast and forced himself to eat his share. Patrick ate heartily, then withdrew to do his necessary while Roland packed up.

There was a third plate, and it was still full. "Oy?" Roland asked, tipping it toward the billy-bumbler. "Will'ee not have at least a bite?"

Oy looked at the plate, then backed away two firm steps. Roland nodded and tossed away the uneaten food, scattering it into the grass. Mayhap Mordred would come along in good time, and find something to his liking.

At mid-morning they moved on, Roland pulling Ho Fat II and Patrick walking along beside with his head hung low. And soon the beat of the Tower filled the gunslinger's head again. Very close now. That steady, pulsing power drove out all thoughts of Susannah, and he was glad. He gave himself to the steady beating and let it sweep away all his thoughts and all his sorrow.

Commala-come-come, sang the Dark Tower, now just over the horizon. *Commala-come-come, gunslinger may ya come.*

Commala-come-Roland, the journey's nearly done.

Chapter II:
Mordred

The dan-tete was watching when the long-haired fellow they were now traveling with grabbed Susannah's shoulder to point out the dancing orange hobs in the distance. Mordred watched as she whirled, pulling one of the White Daddy's big revolvers. For a moment the far-seeing glass eyes he'd found in the house on Odd's Lane trembled in Mordred's hand, that was how hard he was rooting for his Blackbird Mommy to shoot the Artist. How the guilt would have bitten into her! Like the blade of a dull hatchet, yar! It was even possible that, overcome by the horror of what she had done, she'd've put the barrel of the gun to her own head and pulled the trigger a second time, and how would Old White Daddy like waking up to *that?*

Ah, children are such dreamers.

It didn't happen, of course, but there had been much more to watch. Some of it was hard to see, though. Because it wasn't just excitement that made the binoculars tremble. He was dressed warmly now, in layers of Dandelo's hume clothes, but he was still cold. Except when he was hot. And either way, hot or cold, he trembled like a toothless old gaffer in a chimney corner. This state of affairs had been growing gradually worse since he left Joe Collins's house behind. Fever roared in his bones like a blizzard wind. Mordred was no longer a-hungry (for Mordred no longer had an appetite), but Mordred was a-sick, a-sick, a-sick.

In truth, he was afraid Mordred might be a-dying.

Nonetheless he watched Roland's party with great interest, and once the fire was replenished, he saw even better. Saw the door come into being, although he could not read the symbols

751

there writ upon. He understood that the Artist had somehow drawn it into being—what a godlike talent that was! Mordred longed to eat him just on the chance such a talent might be transmittable! He doubted it, the spiritual side of cannibalism was greatly overrated, but what harm in seeing for one's self?

He watched their palaver. He saw—and also understood—her plea to the Artist and the Mutt, her whining entreaties

(*come with me so I don't have to go alone, come on, be a sport, in fact be a* couple *of sports, oh boo-hoo*)

and rejoiced in her sorrow and fury when the plea was rejected by both boy and beast; Mordred rejoiced even though he knew it would make his own job harder. (A *little* harder, anyway; how much trouble could a mute young man and a billy-bumbler really give him, once he changed his shape and made his move?) For a moment he thought that, in her anger, she might shoot Old White Daddy with his own gun, and that Mordred did *not* want. Old White Daddy was meant to be *his*. The voice from the Dark Tower had told him so. A-sick he surely was, a-dying he might be, but Old White Daddy was still meant to be *his* meal, not the Blackbird Mommy's. Why, she'd leave the meat to rot without taking a single bite! But she didn't shoot him. Instead she *kissed* him. Mordred didn't want to see that, it made him feel sicker than ever, and so he put the binoculars aside. He lay in the grass amid a little clump of alders, trembling, hot and cold, trying not to puke (he had spent the entire previous day puking and shitting, it seemed, until the muscles of his midsection ached with the strain of sending such heavy traffic in two directions at once and nothing came up his throat but thick, mucusy strings and nothing out of his backside but brown stew and great hollow farts), and when he looked through the binoculars again, it was just in time to see the back end of the little electric cart disappear as the Blackbird Mommy drove it through the door. Something swirled out around it. Dust, maybe, but he thought snow. There was also singing. The sound of it made him feel almost as sick as seeing her kiss Old White Gunslinger Daddy. Then the door slammed shut behind her and the singing was gone and the gunslinger just sat there near it, with his face in his hands, boo-hoo, sob-sob. The bumbler went to him and put its long snout on one of his boots as if to offer comfort, how sweet, how puking sweet. By then it was dawn, and Mordred dozed a little. When he woke up, it was to the sound of Old White Daddy's voice. Mordred's hiding place was downwind, and the words came to him clearly: "Oy? Will'ee not have at least a bite?" The bumbler would not, however, and the gunslinger had scattered the food that had been meant for the little furry houken. Later, after they moved on (Old White Gunslinger Daddy pulling the cart the robot had made for them, plodding slowly along the ruts of Tower Road with his head down and his shoulders all a-slump), Mordred crept to the campsite. He did indeed eat some of the scattered food—surely it had not been poisoned if Roland had hoped it would go down the bumbler's gullet—but he stopped after only three or four chunks of meat, knowing that if he went on eating, his guts would spew everything back out, both north and south. He couldn't have that. If he didn't hold onto at least *some* nourishment, he would be too weak to follow them. And he *must* follow, had to stay close a little while longer. It would have to be tonight. It would have to be, because tomorrow Old White Daddy would reach the Dark Tower, and then it would almost certainly be too late. His heart told him so. Mordred plodded as Roland had, but even more slowly. Every now and then he would double over as cramps seized him and his human shape wavered, that blackness rising and receding under his skin, his heavy coat bulging restlessly as the other legs tried to burst free, then hanging slack again as he willed them back inside, gritting his teeth and groaning with effort. Once he shit a pint or so of stinky brown fluid in his pants, and once he managed to get his trousers down, and he cared little either way. No one had invited him to the Reap Ball, ha-ha! Invitation lost in the mail, no doubt! Later, when it came time to attack, he would let the little Red King free. But if it happened now, he was almost positive he wouldn't be able to change back again. He wouldn't have the strength. The spider's faster metabolism would fan the sickness the way a strong wind fans a low ground-fire into a forest-gobbling blaze. What was killing him slowly would kill him rapidly, instead. So he fought it, and by afternoon he felt a little better. The pulse from the Tower was growing rapidly now, growing in strength and urgency. So was his Red Daddy's voice, urging him on, urging him to stay within striking distance. Old White Gunslinger Daddy had gotten no more than four hours' sleep a night for weeks now, because he had been standing watch-and-watch with the now-departed Blackbird Mommy. But Blackbird Mommy hadn't ever had to pull that cart, had she? No, just rode in it like Queen Shit o' Turd Hill did she, hee! Which meant Old White Gunslinger Daddy was plenty tired, even with the pulse of the Dark Tower to buoy him up and pull him onward. Tonight Old White Daddy would either have to depend on the Artist and the Mutt to stand the first watch or try to do the whole thing on his own. Mordred thought he could stand one more wakeful night himself, simply because he knew he'd never have to have another. He would creep close, as he had the previous night. He would watch their camp with the old man-monster's glass eyes for far-seeing. And when they were all asleep, he would change for the last time and rush down upon them. Scrabble-de-dee comes me, hee! Old White Daddy might never even wake up, but Mordred hoped he would. At the very end. Just long enough to realize what was happening to him. Just long enough to know that his son was snatching him into the land of death only hours before he would have reached his precious Dark Tower. Mordred clenched his fists and watched the fingers turn black. He felt the terrible but pleasurable itching up the sides of his body as the spider-legs tried to burst through—seven instead of eight, thanks to the terrible-nastyawful Blackbird Mommy who had been both preg and not-preg at the same time, and might she rot screaming in todash space forever (or at least until one of the Great Ones who lurked there found her). He fought and encouraged the change with equal ferocity. At last he only fought it, and the urge to change subsided. He gave out a victory-fart, but although this one was long and smelly, it was silent. His asshole was now a broken squeezebox that could no longer make music but only gasp. His fingers returned to their normal pinkish-white shade and the itching up and down the sides of his body disappeared. His head swam and slithered with fever; his thin arms (little more than sticks) ached with chills. The voice of his Red Daddy was sometimes loud and sometimes faint, but it was always there: *Come to me. Run to me. Hie thy doubleton self. Come-commala, you good son of mine. We'll bring the Tower down, we'll destroy all the light there is, and then rule the darkness together.*

Come to me.

Come.

TWO

Surely those three who remained (four, counting himself) had outrun ka's umbrella. Not since the *Prim* receded had there been such a creature as Mordred Deschain, who was part hume and part of that rich and potent soup. Surely such a creature could never have been meant by ka to die such a mundane death as the one that now threatened: fever brought on by food-poisoning.

Roland could have told him that eating what he found in the snow around to the side of Dandelo's barn was a bad idea; so could Robert Browning, for that matter. Wicked or not, actual *horse* or not, Lippy (probably named after another, and better-known, Browning poem called "Fra Lippo Lippi") had been a sick animal herself when Roland ended her life with a bullet to the head. But Mordred had been in his spider-form when he'd come upon the thing which at least *looked* like a horse, and almost nothing would have stopped him from eating the meat. It wasn't until he'd resumed his human form again that he wondered uneasily how there could be so much meat on Dandelo's bony old nag and why it had been so soft and warm, so full of uncoagulated blood. It had been in a snowdrift, after all, and had been lying there for some days. The mare's remains should have been frozen stiff.

Then the vomiting began. The fever came next, and with it the struggle not to change until he was close enough to his Old

White Daddy to rip him limb from limb. The being whose coming had been prophesied for thousands of years (mostly by the Manni-folk, and usually in frightened whispers), the being who would grow to be half-human and half-god, the being who would oversee the end of humanity and the return of the *Prim* . . . that being had finally arrived as a naïve and bad-hearted child who was now dying from a bellyful of poisoned horsemeat.

Ka could have had no part in this.

THREE

Roland and his two companions didn't make much progress on the day Susannah left them. Even had he not planned to travel short miles so that they could come to the Tower at sunset of the day following, Roland wouldn't have been able to go far. He was disheartened, lonely, and tired almost to death. Patrick was also tired, but *he* at least could ride if he chose to, and for most of that day he did so choose, sometimes napping, sometimes sketching, sometimes walking a little while before climbing back into Ho Fat II and napping some more.

The pulse from the Tower was strong in Roland's head and heart, and its song was powerful and lovely, now seemingly composed of a thousand voices, but not even these things could take the lead from his bones. Then, as he was looking for a shady spot where they could stop and eat a little midday meal (by now it was actually mid-afternoon), he saw something that momentarily made him forget both his weariness and his sorrow.

Growing by the side of the road was a wild rose, seemingly the exact twin of the one in the vacant lot. It bloomed in defiance of the season, which Roland put as very early spring. It was a light pink shade on the outside and darkened to a fierce red on the inside; the exact color, he thought, of heart's desire. He fell on his knees before it, tipped his ear toward that coral cup, and listened.

The rose was singing.

The weariness stayed, as weariness will (on this side of the grave, at least), but the loneliness and the sadness departed, at least for a little while. He peered into the heart of the rose and saw a yellow center so bright he couldn't look directly at it.

Gan's gateway, he thought, not sure exactly what that was but positive that he was right. *Aye, Gan's gateway, so it is!*

This was unlike the rose in the vacant lot in one crucial way: the feeling of sickness and the faint voices of discord were gone. This one was rich with health as well as full of light and love. It and all the others . . . they . . . they must . . .

They feed the Beams, don't they? With their songs and their perfume. As the Beams feed them. It's a living force-field, a giving and taking, all spinning out from the Tower. And this is only the first, the farthest outrider. In Can'-Ka No Rey there are tens of thousands, just like this.

The thought made him faint with amazement. Then came another that filled him with anger and fear: the only one with a view of that great red blanket was insane. Would blight them all in an instant, if allowed free rein to do so.

There was a hesitant tap on his shoulder. It was Patrick, with Oy at his heel. Patrick pointed to the grassy area beside the rose, then made eating gestures. Pointed at the rose and made drawing motions. Roland wasn't very hungry, but the boy's other idea pleased him a great deal.

"Yes," he said. "We'll have a bite here, then maybe I'll take me a little siesta while you draw the rose. Will you make two pictures of it, Patrick?" He showed the two remaining fingers on his right hand to make sure Patrick understood.

The young man frowned and cocked his head, still not understanding. His hair hung to one shoulder in a bright sheaf. Roland thought of how Susannah had washed that hair in a stream in spite of Patrick's hooted protests. It was the sort of thing Roland himself would never have thought to do, but it made the young fellow look a lot better. Looking at that sheaf of shining hair made him miss Susannah in spite of the rose's song. She had brought grace to his life. It wasn't a word that had occurred to him until she was gone.

Meanwhile, here was Patrick, wildly talented but awfully slow on the uptake.

Roland gestured to his pad, then to the rose. Patrick nodded—that part he got. Then Roland raised two of the fingers on his good hand and pointed to the pad again. This time the light broke on Patrick's face. He pointed to the rose, to the pad, to Roland, and then to himself.

"That's right, big boy," Roland said. "A picture of the rose for you and one for me. It's nice, isn't it?"

Patrick nodded enthusiastically, setting to work while Roland rustled the grub. Once again Roland fixed three plates, and once again Oy refused his share. When Roland looked into the bumbler's gold-ringed eyes he saw an emptiness there—a kind of loss—that hurt him deep inside. And Oy couldn't stand to miss many meals; he was far too thin already. Trail-frayed, Cuthbert would have said, probably smiling. In need of some hot sassafras and salts. But the gunslinger had no sassy here.

"Why do'ee look so?" Roland asked the bumbler crossly. "If'ee wanted to go with her, thee should have gone when thee had the chance! Why will'ee cast thy sad houken's eyes on me now?"

Oy looked at him a moment longer, and Roland saw that he had hurt the little fellow's feelings; ridiculous but true. Oy walked away, little squiggle of tail drooping. Roland felt like calling him back, but that would have been more ridiculous yet, would it not? What plan did he have? To apologize to a billy-bumbler?

He felt angry and ill at ease with himself, feelings he had never suffered before hauling Eddie, Susannah, and Jake from America-side into his life. Before they'd come he'd felt almost nothing, and while that was a narrow way to live, in some ways it wasn't so bad; at least you didn't waste time wondering if you should apologize to animals for taking a high tone to them, by the gods.

Roland hunkered by the rose, leaning into the soothing power of its song and the blaze of light—*healthy* light—from its center. Then Patrick hooted at him, gesturing for Roland to move away so he could see it and draw it. This added to Roland's sense of dislocation and annoyance, but he moved back without a word of protest. He had, after all, asked Patrick to draw it, hadn't he? He thought of how, if Susannah had been here, their eyes would have met with amused understanding, as the eyes of parents do over the antics of a small child. But she wasn't here, of course; she'd been the last of them and now she was gone, too.

"All right, can'ee see howgit rosen-gaff a tweakit better?" he asked, striving to sound comic and only sounding cross—cross and tired.

Patrick, at least, didn't react to the harshness in the gunslinger's tone; *probably didn't even ken what I said,* Roland thought. The mute boy sat with his ankles crossed and his pad balanced on his thighs, his half-finished plate of food set off to one side.

"Don't get so busy you forget to eat that," Roland said. "You mind me, now." He got another distracted nod for his pains and gave up. "I'm going to snooze, Patrick. It'll be a long afternoon." *And an even longer night,* he added to himself . . . and yet he had the same consolation as Mordred: tonight would likely be the last. He didn't know for sure what waited for him in the Dark Tower at the end of the field of roses, but even if he managed to put paid to the Crimson King, he felt quite sure that this was his last march. He didn't believe he would ever leave Can'-Ka No Rey, and that was all right. He was very tired. And, despite the power of the rose, sad.

Roland of Gilead put an arm over his eyes and was asleep at once.

FOUR

He didn't sleep for long before Patrick woke him with a child's enthusiasm to show him the first picture of the rose he'd drawn—the sun suggested no more than ten minutes had passed, fifteen at most.

Like all of his drawings, this one had a queer power. Patrick had captured the rose almost to the life, even though he had nothing but a pencil to work with. Still, Roland would much have preferred another hour's sleep to this exercise in art appreciation. He nodded his approval, though—no more grouch and grump in the presence of such a lovely thing, he promised himself—and Patrick smiled, happy even with so little. He tossed back the sheet and began drawing the rose again. One picture for each of them, just as Roland had asked.

Roland could have slept again, but what was the point? The mute boy would be done with the second picture in a matter of minutes and would only wake him again. He went to Oy instead, and stroked the bumbler's dense fur, something he rarely did.

"I'm sorry I spoke rough to'ee, fella," Roland said. "Will you not set me on with a word?"

But Oy would not.

Fifteen minutes later, Roland re-packed the few things he'd taken out of the cart, spat into his palms, and hoisted the handles again. The cart was lighter now, had to be, but it felt heavier.

Of course it's heavier, he thought. *It's got my grief in it. I pull it along with me everywhere I go, so I do.*

Soon Ho Fat II had Patrick Danville in it, as well. He crawled up, made himself a little nest, and fell asleep almost at once. Roland plodded on, head down, shadow growing longer at his heels. Oy walked beside him.

One more night, the gunslinger thought. *One more night, one more day to follow, and then it's done. One way or t' other.*

He let the pulse of the Tower and its many singing voices fill his head and lighten his heels . . . at least a little. There were more roses now, dozens scattered on either side of the road and brightening the otherwise dull countryside. A few were growing in the road itself and he was careful to detour around them. Tired though he might be, he would not crush a single one, or roll a wheel over a single fallen petal.

FIVE

He stopped for the night while the sun was still well above the horizon, too weary to go farther even though there would be at least another two hours of daylight. Here was a stream that had gone dry, but in its bed grew a riot of those beautiful wild roses. Their songs didn't diminish his weariness, but they revived his spirit to some extent. He thought this was true for Patrick and Oy, as well, and that was good. When Patrick had awakened he'd looked around eagerly at first. Then his face had darkened, and Roland knew he was realizing all over again that Susannah was gone. The boy had cried a little then, but perhaps there would be no crying here.

There was a grove of cottonwood trees on the bank—at least the gunslinger thought they were cottonwoods—but they had died when the stream from which their roots drank had disappeared. Now their branches were only bony, leafless snarls against the sky. In their silhouettes he could make out the number nineteen over and over again, in both the figures of Susannah's world and those of his own. In one place the branches seemed to clearly spell the word *CHASSIT* against the deepening sky.

Before making a fire and cooking them an early supper—canned goods from Dandelo's pantry would do well enough tonight, he reckoned—Roland went into the dry streambed and smelled the roses, strolling slowly among the dead trees and listening to their song. Both the smell and the sound were refreshing.

Feeling a little better, he gathered wood from beneath the trees (snapping off a few of the lower branches for good measure, leaving dry, splintered stumps that reminded him a little of Patrick's pencils) and piled kindling in the center. Then he struck a light, speaking the old catechism almost without hearing it: "Spark-a-dark, who's my sire? Will I lay me? Will I stay me? Bless this camp with fire."

While he waited for the fire to first grow and then die down to a bed of rosy embers, Roland took out the watch he had been given in New York. Yesterday it had stopped, although he had been assured the battery that ran it would last for fifty years.

Now, as late afternoon faded to evening, the hands had very slowly begun to move backward.

He looked at this for a little while, fascinated, then closed the cover and looked at the siguls inscribed there: key and rose and Tower. A faint and eldritch blue light had begun to gleam from the windows that spiraled upward.

They didn't know it would do that, he thought, and then put the watch carefully back in his lefthand front pocket, checking first (as he always did) that there was no hole for it to fall through. Then he cooked. He and Patrick ate well.

Oy would touch not a single bite.

SIX

Other than the night he had spent in palaver with the man in black—the night during which Walter had read a bleak fortune from an undoubtedly stacked deck—those twelve hours of dark by the dry stream were the longest of Roland's life. The weariness settled over him ever deeper and darker, until it felt like a cloak of stones. Old faces and old places marched in front of his heavy eyes: Susan, riding hellbent across the Drop with her blond hair flying out behind; Cuthbert running down the side of Jericho Hill in much the same fashion, screaming and laughing; Alain Johns raising a glass in a toast; Eddie and Jake wrestling in the grass, yelling, while Oy danced around them, barking.

Mordred was somewhere out there, and close, yet again and again Roland found himself drifting toward sleep. Each time he jerked himself awake, staring around wildly into the dark, he knew he had come nearer to the edge of unconsciousness. Each time he expected to see the spider with the red mark on its belly bearing down on him and saw nothing but the hobs, dancing orange in the distance. Heard nothing but the sough of the wind.

But he waits. He bides. And if I sleep—when *I sleep*—*he'll be on us.*

Around three in the morning he roused himself by willpower alone from a doze that was on the very verge of tumbling him into deeper sleep. He looked around desperately, rubbing his eyes with the heels of his palms hard enough to make mirks and fouders and sankofites explode across his field of vision. The fire had burned very low. Patrick lay about twenty feet from it, at the twisted base of a cottonwood tree. From where Roland sat, the boy was no more than a hide-covered hump. Of Oy there was no immediate sign. Roland called to the bumbler and got no response. The gunslinger was about to try his feet when he saw Jake's old friend a little beyond the edge of the failing firelight—or at least the gleam of his gold-ringed eyes. Those eyes looked at Roland for a moment, then disappeared, probably when Oy put his snout back down on his paws.

He's tired, too, Roland thought, *and why not?*

The question of what would become of Oy after tomorrow tried to rise to the surface of the gunslinger's troubled, tired mind, and Roland pushed it away. He got up (in his weariness his hands slipped down to his formerly troublesome hip, as if expecting to find the pain still there), went to Patrick, and shook him awake. It took some doing, but at last the boy's eyes opened. That wasn't good enough for Roland. He grasped Patrick's shoulders and pulled him up to a sitting position. When the boy tried to slump back down again, Roland shook him. *Hard.* He looked at Roland with dazed incomprehension.

"Help me build up the fire, Patrick."

Doing that should wake him up at least a little. And once the fire was burning bright again, Patrick would have to stand a brief watch. Roland didn't like the idea, knew full well that leaving Patrick in charge of the night would be dangerous, but trying to watch the rest of it on his own would be even more dangerous. He needed sleep. An hour or two would be enough, and surely Patrick could stay awake that long.

Patrick was willing enough to gather up some sticks and put

them on the fire, although he moved like a bougie—a reanimated corpse. And when the fire was blazing, he slumped back down in his former place with his arms between his bony knees, already more asleep than awake. Roland thought he might actually have to slap the boy to bring him around, and would later wish—bitterly—that he had done just that.

"Patrick, listen to me." He shook Patrick by the shoulders hard enough to make his long hair fly, but some of it flopped back into his eyes. Roland brushed it away. "I need you to stay awake and watch. Just for an hour . . . just until . . . look up, Patrick! Look! Gods, don't you *dare* go to sleep on me again! Do you see that? The brightest star of all those close to us!"

It was Old Mother Roland was pointing to, and Patrick nodded at once. There was a gleam of interest in his eye now, and the gunslinger thought that was encouraging. It was Patrick's "I want to draw" look. And if he sat drawing Old Mother as she shone in the widest fork of the biggest dead cottonwood, then the chances were good that he'd stay awake. Maybe until dawn, if he got fully involved.

"Here, Patrick." He made the boy sit against the base of the tree. It was bony and knobby and—Roland hoped—uncomfortable enough to prohibit sleep. All these movements felt to Roland like the sort you made underwater. Oh, he was tired. *So* tired. "Do you still see the star?"

Patrick nodded eagerly. He seemed to have thrown off his sleepiness, and the gunslinger thanked the gods for this favor.

"When it goes behind that thick branch and you can't see it or draw it anymore without getting up . . . you call me. Wake me up, no matter how hard it is. Do you understand?"

Patrick nodded at once, but Roland had now traveled with him long enough to know that such a nod meant little or nothing. Eager to please, that's what he was. If you asked him if nine and nine made nineteen, he would nod with the same instant enthusiasm.

"When you can't see it anymore from where you're sitting . . ." His own words seemed to be coming from far away, now. He'd just have to hope that Patrick understood. The tongueless boy had taken out his pad, at least, and a freshly sharpened pencil.

That's my best protection, Roland's mind muttered as he stumbled back to his little pile of hides between the campfire and Ho Fat II. *He won't fall asleep while he's drawing, will he?*

He hoped not, but supposed he didn't really know. And it didn't matter, because he, Roland of Gilead, was going to sleep in any case. He'd done the best he could, and it would have to be enough.

"An hour," he muttered, and his voice was far and wee in his own ears. "Wake me in an hour . . . when the star . . . when Old Mother goes behind . . ."

But Roland was unable to finish. He didn't even know what he was saying anymore. Exhaustion grabbed him and bore him swiftly away into dreamless sleep.

SEVEN

Mordred saw it all through the far-seeing glass eyes. His fever had soared, and in its bright flame, his own exhaustion had at least temporarily departed. He watched with avid interest as the gunslinger woke the mute boy—the Artist—and bullied him into helping him build up the fire. He watched, rooting for the mute to finish this chore and then go back to sleep before the gunslinger could stop him. That didn't happen, unfortunately. They had camped near a grove of dead cottonwoods, and Roland led the Artist to the biggest tree. Here he pointed up at the sky. It was strewn with stars, but Mordred reckoned Old White Gunslinger Daddy was pointing to Old Mother, because she was the brightest. At last the Artist, who didn't seem to be rolling a full barrow (at least not in the brains department) seemed to understand. He got out his pad and had already set to sketching as Old White Daddy stumbled a little way off, still muttering instructions and orders to which the Artist was pretty clearly paying absolutely no attention at all. Old White Daddy collapsed so suddenly that for a moment Mordred feared that perhaps the strip of jerky that served the son of a bitch as a heart had finally given up beating. Then Roland stirred in the grass, resettling himself, and Mordred, lying on a knoll about ninety yards west of the dry streambed, felt his own heartbeat slow. And deep though the Old White Gunslinger Daddy's exhaustion might be, his training and his long lineage, going all the way back to the Eld himself, would be enough to wake him with his gun in his hand the second the Artist gave one of his wordless but devilishly loud cries. Cramps seized Mordred, the deepest yet. He doubled over, fighting to hold his human shape, fighting not to scream, fighting not to die. He heard another of those long flabbering noises from below and felt more of the lumpy brown stew begin coursing down his legs. But his preternaturally keen nose smelled more than excreta in this new mess; this time he smelled blood as well as shit. He thought the pain would never end, that it would go on deepening until it tore him in two, but at last it began to let up. His looked at his left hand and was not entirely surprised to see that the fingers had blackened and fused together. They would never come back to human again, those fingers; he believed he had but only one more change left in him. Mordred wiped sweat from his brow with his right hand and raised the bin-doculars to his eyes again, praying to his Red Daddy that the stupid mutie boy would be asleep. But he was not. He was leaning against the cottonwood tree and looking up between the branches and drawing Old Mother. That was the moment when Mordred Deschain came closest to despair. Like Roland, he thought drawing was the one thing that would likely keep the idiot boy awake. Therefore, why not give in to the change while he had the heat of this latest fever-spike to fuel him with its destructive energy? Why not take his chance? It was Roland he wanted, after all, not the boy; surely he could, in his spider form, sweep down on the gunslinger rapidly enough to grab him and pull him against the spider's craving mouth. Old White Daddy might get off one shot, possibly even two, but Mordred thought he could take one or two, if the flying bits of lead didn't find the white node on the spider's back: his dual body's brain. *And once I pull him in, I'll never let him go until he's sucked dry, nothing but a dust-mummy like the other one, Mia.*

He relaxed, ready to let the change sweep over him, and then another voice spoke from the center of his mind. It was the voice of his Red Daddy, the one who was imprisoned on the side of the Dark Tower and needed Mordred alive, at least one more day, in order to set him free.

Wait a little longer, this voice counseled. *Wait a little more. I might have another trick up my sleeve. Wait . . . wait just a little longer . . .*

Mordred waited. And after a moment or two, he felt the pulse from the Dark Tower change.

EIGHT

Patrick felt that change, too. The pulse became soothing. And there were words in it, ones that blunted his eagerness to draw. He made another line, paused, then put his pencil aside and only looked up at Old Mother, who seemed to pulse in time with the words he heard in his head, words Roland would have recognized. Only these were sung in an old man's voice, quavering but sweet:

> *"Baby-bunting, darling one,*
> *Now another day is done.*
> *May your dreams be sweet and merry,*
> *May you dream of fields and berries.*
>
> *Baby-bunting, baby-dear,*
> *Baby, bring your berries here.*
> *Oh chussit, chissit, chassit!*
> *Bring enough to fill your basket!"*

Patrick's head nodded. His eyes closed . . . opened . . . slipped closed again.

Enough to fill my basket, he thought, and slept in the firelight.

NINE

Now, my good son, whispered the cold voice in the middle of Mordred's hot and melting brains. *Now. Go to him and make sure he never rises from his sleep. Murder him among the roses and we'll rule together.*

Mordred came from hiding, the binoculars tumbling from a hand that was no longer a hand at all. As he changed, a feeling of huge confidence swept through him. In another minute it would be done. They both slept, and there was no way he could fail.

He rushed down on the camp and the sleeping men, a black nightmare on seven legs, his mouth opening and closing.

TEN

Somewhere, a thousand miles away, Roland heard barking, loud and urgent, furious and savage. His exhausted mind tried to turn away from it, to blot it out and go deeper. Then there was a horrible scream of agony that awoke him in a flash. He knew that voice, even as distorted by pain as it was.

"*Oy!*" he cried, leaping up. "*Oy, where are you? To me! To m—*"

There he was, twisting in the spider's grip. Both of them were clearly visible in the light of the fire. Beyond them, sitting propped against the cottonwood tree, Patrick gazed stupidly through a curtain of hair that would soon be dirty again, now that Susannah was gone. The bumbler wriggled furiously to and fro, snapping at the spider's body with foam flying from his jaws even as Mordred bent him in a direction his back was never meant to go.

If he'd not rushed out of the tall grass, Roland thought, *that would be me in Mordred's grip.*

Oy sent his teeth deep into one of the spider's legs. In the firelight Roland could see the coin-sized dimples of the bumbler's jaw-muscles as he chewed deeper still. The thing squalled and its grip loosened. At that moment Oy might have gotten free, had he chosen to do so. He did not. Instead of jumping down and leaping away in the momentary freedom granted him before Mordred was able to re-set his grip, Oy used the time to extend his long neck and seize the place where one of the thing's legs joined its bloated body. He bit deep, bringing a flood of blackish-red liquor that ran freely from the sides of his muzzle. In the firelight it gleamed with orange sparks. Mordred squalled louder still. He had left Oy out of his calculations, and was now paying the price. In the firelight, the two writhing forms were figures out of a nightmare.

Somewhere nearby, Patrick was hooting in terror.

Worthless whoreson fell asleep after all, Roland thought bitterly. But who had set him to watch in the first place?

"Put him down, Mordred!" he shouted. "Put him down and I'll let you live another day! I swear it on my father's name!"

Red eyes, full of insanity and malevolence, peered at him over Oy's contorted body. Above them, high on the curve of the spider's back, were tiny blue eyes, hardly more than pin-holes. They stared at the gunslinger with a hate that was all too human.

My own eyes, Roland thought with dismay, and then there was a bitter crack. It was Oy's spine, but in spite of this mortal injury he never loosened his grip on the joint where Mordred's leg joined his body, although the steely bristles had torn away much of his muzzle, baring sharp teeth that had sometimes closed on Jake's wrist with gentle affection, tugging him toward something Oy wanted the boy to see. *Ake!* he would cry on such occasions. *Ake-Ake!*

Roland's right hand dropped to his holster and found it empty. It was only then, hours after she had taken her leave, that he realized Susannah had taken one of his guns with her into the other world. *Good,* he thought. *Good. If it is the darkness she found, there would have been five for the things in it and one for herself. Good.*

But this thought was also dim and distant. He pulled the other revolver as Mordred crouched on his hindquarters and used his remaining middle leg, curling it around Oy's midsection and pulling the animal, still snarling, away from his torn and bleeding leg. The spider twirled the furry body upward in a terrible spiral. For a moment it blotted out the bright beacon that was Old Mother. Then he hurled Oy away from him and Roland had a moment of *déjà vu,* realizing he had seen this long ago, in the Wizard's Glass. Oy arced across the fireshot dark and was impaled on one of the cottonwood branches the gun-slinger himself had broken off for firewood. He gave an awful hurt cry—a death-cry—and then hung, suspended and limp, above Patrick's head.

Mordred came at Roland without a pause, but his charge was a slow, shambling thing; one of his legs had been shot away only minutes after his birth, and now another hung limp and broken, its pincers jerking spasmodically as they dragged on the grass. Roland's eye had never been clearer, the chill that surrounded him at moments like this never deeper. He saw the white node and the blue bombardier's eyes that were *his* eyes. He saw the face of his only son peering over the back of the abomination and then it was gone in a spray of blood as his first bullet tore it off. The spider reared up, legs clashing at the black and star-shot sky. Roland's next two bullets went into its revealed belly and exited through the back, pulling dark sprays of liquid with it. The spider slewed to one side, perhaps trying to run away, but its remaining legs would not support it. Mordred Deschain fell into the fire, casting up a flume of red and orange sparks. It writhed in the embers, the bristles on its belly beginning to burn, and Roland, grinning bitterly, shot it again. The dying spider rolled out of the now scattered fire on its back, its remaining legs twitching together in a knot and then spreading apart. One fell back into the fire and began to burn. The smell was atrocious.

Roland started forward, meaning to stamp out the little fires the scattered embers had started in the grass, and then a howl of outraged fury rose in his head.

My son! My only son! You've murdered him!

"He was mine, too," Roland said, looking at the smoldering

monstrosity. He could own the truth. Yes, he could do that much.

Come then! Come, son-killer, and look at your Tower, but know this—you'll die of old age at the edge of the Can'-Ka before you ever so much as touch its door! I will never let you pass! Todash space itself will pass away before I let you pass! Murderer! Murderer of your mother, murderer of your friends—aye, every one, for Susannah lies dead with her throat cut on the other side of the door you sent her through—and now murderer of your own son!

"Who sent him to me?" Roland asked the voice in his head. "Who sent yonder child—for that's what he is, inside that black skin—to his death, ye red boggart?"

To this there was no answer, so Roland re-holstered his gun and put out the patches of fire before they could spread. He thought of what the voice had said about Susannah, decided he didn't believe it. She might be dead, aye, *might* be, but he thought Mordred's Red Father knew for sure no more than Roland himself did.

The gunslinger let that thought go and went to the tree, where the last of his ka-tet hung, impaled . . . but still alive. The gold-ringed eyes looked at Roland with what might almost have been weary amusement.

"Oy," Roland said, stretching out his hand, knowing it might be bitten and not caring in the least. He supposed that part of him—and not a small one, either—wanted to be bitten. "Oy, we all say thank you. *I* say thank you, Oy."

The bumbler did not bite, and spoke but one word. *"Olan,"* said he. Then he sighed, licked the gunslinger's hand a single time, hung his head down, and died.

ELEVEN

As dawn strengthened into the clear light of morning, Patrick came hesitantly to where the gunslinger sat in the dry streambed, amid the roses, with Oy's body spread across his lap like a stole. The young man made a soft, interrogative hooting sound.

"Not now, Patrick," Roland said absently, stroking Oy's fur. It was dense but smooth to the touch. He found it hard to believe that the creature beneath it had gone, in spite of the stiffening muscles and the tangled places where the blood had now clotted. He combed these smooth with his fingers as best he could. "Not now. We have all the livelong day to get there, and we'll do fine."

No, there was no need to hurry; no reason why he should not leisurely mourn the last of his dead. There had been no doubt in the old King's voice when he had promised that Roland should die of old age before he so much as touched the door in the Tower's base. They would go, of course, and Roland would study the terrain, but he knew even now that his idea of coming to the Tower on the old monster's blind side and then working his way around was not an idea at all, but a fool's hope. There had been no doubt in the old villain's voice; no doubt hiding behind it, either.

And for the time being, none of that mattered. Here was another one he had killed, and if there was consolation to be had, it was this: Oy would be the last. Now he was alone again except for Patrick, and Roland had an idea Patrick was immune to the terrible germ the gunslinger carried, for he had never been ka-tet to begin with.

I only kill my family, Roland thought, stroking the dead billy-bumbler.

What hurt most was remembering how unpleasantly he had spoken to Oy the day before. *If 'ee wanted to go with her, thee should have gone when thee had thy chance!*

Had he stayed because he knew that Roland would need him? That when push came down to shove (it was Eddie's phrase, of course), Patrick would fail?

Why will 'ee cast thy sad houken's eyes on me now?

Because he had known it was to be his last day, and his dying would be hard?

"I think you knew both things," Roland said, and closed his eyes so he could feel the fur beneath his hands better. "I'm so sorry I spoke to'ee so—would give the fingers on my good left hand if I could take the words back. So I would, every one, say true."

But here as in the Keystone World, time only ran one way. Done was done. There would be no taking back.

Roland would have said there was no anger left, that every bit of it had been burned away, but when he felt the tingling all over his skin and understood what it meant, he felt fresh fury rise in his heart. And he felt the coldness settle into his tired but still talented hands.

Patrick was *drawing* him! Sitting beneath the cottonwood just as if a brave little creature worth ten of him—no, a hundred!— hadn't died in that very tree, and for both of them.

It's his way, Susannah spoke up calmly and gently from deep in his mind. *It's all he has, everything else has been taken from him—his home world as well as his mother and his tongue and whatever brains he might once have had. He's mourning, too, Roland. He's frightened, too. This is the only way he has of soothing himself.*

Undoubtedly all true. But the truth of it actually fed his rage instead of damping it down. He put his remaining gun aside (it lay gleaming between two of the singing roses) because having it close to hand wouldn't do, no, not in his current mood. Then he rose to his feet, meaning to give Patrick the scolding of his life, if for no other reason than it would make Roland feel a little bit better himself. He could already hear the first words: *Do you enjoy drawing those who saved your mostly worthless life, stupid boy? Does it cheer your heart?*

He was opening his mouth to begin when Patrick put his pencil down and seized his new toy, instead. The eraser was half-gone now, and there were no others; as well as Roland's gun, Susannah had taken the little pink nubbins with her, probably for no other reason than that she'd been carrying the jar in her pocket and her mind had been studying other, more important, matters. Patrick poised the eraser over his drawing, then looked up—perhaps to make sure he really wanted to erase at all—and saw the gunslinger standing in the streambed and frowning at him. Patrick knew immediately that Roland was angry, although he probably had no idea under heaven as to *why,* and his face cramped with fear and unhappiness. Roland saw him now as Dandelo must have seen him time and time again, and his anger collapsed at the thought. He would not have Patrick fear him—for Susannah's sake if not his own, he would not have Patrick fear him.

And discovered that it *was* for his own sake, after all.

Why not kill him, then? asked the sly, pulsing voice in his head. *Kill him and put him out of his misery, if thee feels so tender toward him? He and the bumbler can enter the clearing together. They can make a place there for you, gunslinger.*

Roland shook his head and tried to smile. "Nay, Patrick, son of Sonia," he said (for that was how Bill the robot had called the boy). "Nay, I was wrong—again—and will not scold thee. But . . ."

He walked to where Patrick was sitting. Patrick cringed away from him with a doglike, placatory smile that made Roland angry all over again, but he quashed the emotion easily enough this time. Patrick had loved Oy too, and this was the only way he had of dealing with his sorrow.

Little that mattered to Roland now.

He reached down and gently plucked the eraser out of the boy's fingers. Patrick looked at him questioningly, then reached out his empty hand, asking with his eyes that the wonderful (and useful) new toy be given back.

"Nay," Roland said, as gently as he could. "You made do for the gods only know how many years without ever knowing such things existed; you can make do the rest of this one day, I think. Mayhap there'll be something for you to draw—and then undraw—later on. Do'ee ken, Patrick?"

Patrick did not, but once the eraser was safely deposited in Roland's pocket along with the watch, he seemed to forget about it and just went back to his drawing.

"Put thy picture aside for a little, too," Roland told him.

Patrick did so without argument. He pointed first to the cart, then to the Tower Road, and made his interrogative hooting sound.

"Aye," Roland said, "but first we should see what Mordred

had for gunna—there may be something useful there—and bury our friend. Will'ee help me see Oy into the ground, Patrick?"

Patrick was willing, and the burial didn't take long; the body was far smaller than the heart it had held. By mid-morning they had begun to cover the last few miles on the long road which led to the Dark Tower.

CHAPTER III:
THE CRIMSON KING
AND THE DARK TOWER

ONE

The road and the tale have both been long, would you not say so? The trip has been long and the cost has been high . . . but no great thing was ever attained easily. A long tale, like a tall Tower, must be built a stone at a time. Now, however, as the end draws closer, you must mark yon two travelers walking toward us with great care. The older man—he with the tanned, lined face and the gun on his hip—is pulling the cart they call Ho Fat II. The younger one—he with the oversized drawing pad tucked under his arm that makes him look like a student in days of old—is walking along beside it. They are climbing a long, gently upsloping hill not much different from hundreds of others they have climbed. The overgrown road they follow is lined on either side with the remains of rock walls; wild roses grow in amiable profusion amid the tumbles of fieldstone. In the open, brush-dotted land beyond these fallen walls are strange stone edifices. Some look like the ruins of castles; others have the appearance of Egyptian obelisks; a few are clearly Speaking Rings of the sort where demons may be summoned; one ancient ruin of stone pillars and plinths has the look of Stonehenge. One almost expects to see hooded Druids gathered in the center of that great circle, perhaps casting the runes, but the keepers of these monuments, these precursors of the Great Monument, are all gone. Only small herds of bannock graze where once they worshipped.

Never mind. It's not old ruins we've come to observe near

the end of our long journey, but the old gunslinger pulling the handles of the cart. We stand at the crest of the hill and wait as he comes toward us. He comes. And comes. Relentless as ever, a man who always learns to speak the language of the land (at least some of it) and the customs of the country; he is still a man who would straighten pictures in strange hotel rooms. Much about him has changed, but not that. He crests the hill, so close to us now that we can smell the sour tang of his sweat. He looks up, a quick and automatic glance he shoots first ahead and then to either side as he tops any hill — *Always con yer vantage* was Cort's rule, and the last of his pupils has still not forgotten it. He looks up without interest, looks down . . . and stops. After a moment of staring at the broken, weed-infested paving of the road, he looks up again, more slowly this time. Much more slowly. As if in dread of what he thinks he has seen.

And it's here we must join him — sink into him — although how we will ever con the vantage of Roland's heart at such a moment as this, when the single-minded goal of his lifetime at last comes in sight, is more than this poor excuse for a storyman can ever tell. Some moments are beyond imagination.

TWO

Roland glanced up quickly as he topped the hill, not because he expected trouble but because the habit was too deeply ingrained to break. *Always con yer vantage,* Cort had told them, drilling it into their heads from the time when they had been little more than babbies. He looked back down at the road — it was becoming more and more difficult to swerve among the roses without crushing any, although he had managed the trick so far — and then, belatedly, realized what he had just seen.

What you thought *you saw,* Roland told himself, still looking down at the road. *It's probably just another of the strange ruins we've been passing ever since we started moving again.*

But even then Roland knew it wasn't so. What he'd seen was not to either side of the Tower Road, but dead ahead.

He looked up again, hearing his neck creak like hinges in an old door, and there, still miles ahead but now visible on the horizon, real as roses, was the top of the Dark Tower. That which he had seen in a thousand dreams he now saw with his living eyes. Sixty or eighty yards ahead, the road rose to a higher hill with an ancient Speaking Ring moldering in the ivy and honeysuckle on one side and a grove of ironwood trees on the other. At the center of this near horizon, the black shape rose in the near distance, blotting out a tiny portion of the blue sky.

Patrick came to a stop beside Roland and made one of his hooting sounds.

"Do you see it?" Roland asked. His voice was dusty, cracked with amazement. Then, before Patrick could answer, the gunslinger pointed to what the boy wore around his neck. In the end, the binoculars had been the only item in Mordred's little bit of gunna worth taking.

"Give them over, Pat."

Patrick did, willingly enough. Roland raised them to his eyes, made a minute adjustment to the knurled focus knob, and then caught his breath as the top of the Tower sprang into view, seemingly close enough to touch. How much was visible over the horizon? How much was he looking at? Twenty feet? Perhaps as much as fifty? He didn't know, but he could see at least three of the narrow slit-windows which ascended the Tower's barrel in a spiral, and he could see the oriel window at the top, its many colors blazing in the spring sunshine, the black center seeming to peer back down the binoculars at him like the very Eye of Todash.

Patrick hooted and held out a hand for the binoculars. He wanted his own look, and Roland handed the glasses over without a murmur. He felt light-headed, not really there. It occurred to him that he had sometimes felt like that in the weeks before his battle with Cort, as though he were a dream or a moonbeam. He had sensed something coming, some vast change, and that was what he felt now.

Yonder it is, he thought. *Yonder is my destiny, the end of my life's road. And yet my heart still beats (a little faster than before, 'tis true), my blood still courses, and no doubt when I bend over to grasp the han-*

dles of this becurst cart my back will groan and I may pass a little gas. Nothing at all has changed.

He waited for the disappointment this thought surely presaged—the letdown. It didn't come. What he felt instead was a queer, soaring brightness that seemed to begin in his mind and then spread to his muscles. For the first time since setting out at mid-morning, thoughts of Oy and Susannah left his mind. He felt free.

Patrick lowered the binoculars. When he turned to Roland, his face was excited. He pointed to the black thumb jutting above the horizon and hooted.

"Yes," Roland said. "Someday, in some world, some version of you will paint it, along with Llamrei, Arthur Eld's horse. That I know, for I've seen the proof. As for now, it's where we must go."

Patrick hooted again, then pulled a long face. He put his hands to his temples and swayed his head back and forth, like someone who has a terrible headache.

"Yes," Roland said. "I'm afraid, too. But there's no help for it. I have to go there. Would you stay here, Patrick? Stay and wait for me? If you would, I give you leave to do so."

Patrick shook his head at once. And, just in case Roland didn't take the point, the mute boy seized his arm in a hard grip. The right hand, the one with which he drew, was like iron.

Roland nodded. Even tried to smile. "Yes," he said, "that's fine. Stay with me as long as you like. As long as you understand that in the end I'll have to go on alone."

THREE

Now, as they rose from each dip and topped each hill, the Dark Tower seemed to spring closer. More of the spiraling windows which ran around its great circumference became visible. Roland could see two steel posts jutting from the top. The clouds which followed the Paths of the two working Beams seemed to flow away from the tips, making a great *X*-shape in the sky. The voices grew louder, and Roland realized they were singing the names of the world. Of *all* the worlds. He didn't know how he could know that, but he was sure of it. That lightness of being continued to fill him up. Finally, as they crested a hill with great stone men marching away to the north on their left (the remains of their faces, painted in some blood-red stuff, glared down upon them), Roland told Patrick to climb up into the cart. Patrick looked surprised. He made a series of hooting noises Roland took to mean *But aren't you tired?*

"Yes, but I need an anchor, even so. Without one I'm apt to start running toward yonder Tower, even though part of me knows better. And if plain old exhaustion doesn't burst my heart, the Red King's apt to take my head off with one of his toys. Get in, Patrick."

Patrick did so. He rode sitting hunched forward, with the binoculars pressed against his eyes.

FOUR

Three hours later, they came to the foot of a much steeper hill. It was, Roland's heart told him, the last hill. Can'-Ka No Rey was beyond. At the top, on the right, was a cairn of boulders that had once been a small pyramid. What remained stood about thirty feet high. Roses grew around its base in a rough crimson ring. Roland set this in his sights and took the hill slowly, pulling the cart by its handles. As he climbed, the top of the Dark Tower once more appeared. Each step brought a greater length of it into view. Now he could see the balconies with their waist-high railings. There was no need of the binoculars; the air was preternaturally clear. He put the distance remaining at no more than five miles. Perhaps only three. Level after level rose before his not-quite-disbelieving eye.

Just shy of this hill's top, with the crumbling rock pyramid twenty paces ahead of them on the right, Roland stopped, bent, and set the handles of the cart on the road for the last time. Every nerve in his body spoke of danger.

"Patrick? Hop down."

Patrick did so, looking anxiously into Roland's face and hooting.

The gunslinger shook his head. "I can't say why just yet. Only it's not safe." The voices sang in a great chorus, but the air around them was still. Not a bird soared overhead or sang in the distance. The wandering herds of bannock had all been left behind. A breeze soughed around them, and the grasses rippled. The roses nodded their wild heads.

The two of them walked on together, and as they did, Roland felt a timid touch against the side of his two-fingered right hand. He looked at Patrick. The mute boy looked anxiously back, trying to smile. Roland took his hand, and they crested the hill in that fashion.

Below them was a great blanket of red that stretched to the horizon in every direction. The road cut through it, a dusty white line perfectly straight and perhaps twelve feet wide. In the middle of the rose-field stood the sooty dark gray Tower, just as it had stood in his dreams; its windows gleamed in the sun. Here the road split and made a perfect white circle around the Tower's base to continue on the other side, in a direction Roland believed was now dead east instead of south-by-east. Another road ran off at right angles to the Tower Road: to the north and south, if he was right in believing that the points of the compass had been re-established. From above, the Dark Tower would look like the center of a blood-filled gunsight.

"It's—" Roland began, and then a great, crazed shriek floated to them on the breeze, weirdly undiminished by the distance of miles. *It comes on the Beam,* Roland thought. *And it's carried by the roses.*

"*GUNSLINGER!*" screamed the Crimson King. "*NOW YOU DIE!*"

There was a whistling sound, thin at first and then growing, cutting through the combined song of the Tower and the roses like the keenest blade ever ground on a wheel dusted with diamonds. Patrick stood transfixed, peering dumbly at the Tower; he would have been blown out of his boots if not for Roland, whose reflexes were as quick as ever. He pulled the mute boy behind the heaped stone of the pyramid by their joined hands. There were other stones hidden in the high grass of dock and

jimson; they stumbled over these and went sprawling. Roland felt the corner of one digging painfully into his ribs.

The whistle continued to rise, becoming an earsplitting whine. Roland saw a golden something flash past in the air— one of the sneetches. It struck the cart and it blew up, scattering their gunna every which way. Most of the stuff settled back to the road, cans rattling and bouncing, some of them burst.

Then came high, chattering laughter that set Roland's teeth on edge; beside him, Patrick covered his ears. The lunacy in that laughter was almost unbearable.

"COME OUT!" urged that distant, mad, laughing voice. *"COME OUT AND PLAY, ROLAND! COME TO ME! COME TO YOUR TOWER, AFTER ALL THE LONG YEARS WILL YOU NOT?"*

Patrick looked at him, his eyes desperate and frightened. He was holding his drawing pad against his chest like a shield.

Roland peered carefully around the edge of the pyramid, and there, on a balcony two levels up from the Tower's base, he saw exactly what he had seen in sai Sayre's painting: one blob of red and three blobs of white; a face and two upraised hands. But this was no painting, and one of the hands moved rapidly forward in a throwing gesture and there came another hellish, rising whine. Roland rolled back against the tumble of the pyramid. There was a pause that seemed endless, and then the sneetch struck the pyramid's other side and exploded. The concussion threw them forward onto their faces. Patrick screamed in terror. Rocks flew to either side in a spray. Some of them rattled down on the road, but Roland saw not a single piece of shrapnel strike so much as a single rose.

The boy scrambled to his knees and would have run— likely back into the road—but Roland grabbed him by the collar of his hide coat and yanked him down again.

"We're safe enough here," he murmured to Patrick. "Look." He reached into a hole revealed by the falling rock, knocked on the interior with his knuckles, produced a dull ringing noise, and showed his teeth in a strained grin. "Steel! Yar! He can hit this thing with a dozen of his flying fireballs and not knock it down. All he can do is blast away the rocks and blocks and expose what lies beneath. Kennit? And I don't think he'll waste his ammunition. He can't have much more than a donkey's carry."

Before Patrick could reply, Roland peered around the pyramid's ragged edge once more. He cupped his hands around his mouth and screamed: *"TRY AGAIN, SAI! WE'RE STILL HERE, BUT PERHAPS YOUR NEXT THROW WILL BE LUCKY!"*

There was a moment of silence, then an insane scream: *"EEEEEEEEEEE! YOU DON'T DARE MOCK ME! YOU DON'T DARE! EEEEEEEEEEE!"*

Now came another of those rising whistles. Roland grabbed Patrick and fell on top of him, behind the pyramid but not against it. He was afraid it might vibrate hard enough when the sneetch struck to give them concussion injuries, or turn their soft insides to jelly.

Only this time the sneetch didn't strike the pyramid. It flew past it instead, soaring above the road. Roland rolled off Patrick and onto his back. His eyes picked up the golden blur and marked the place where it buttonhooked back toward its targets. He shot it out of the air like a clay plate. There was a blinding flash and then it was gone.

"OH DEAR, STILL HERE!" Roland called, striving to put just the right note of mocking amusement into his voice. It wasn't easy when you were screaming at the top of your lungs.

Another crazed scream in response— *"EEEEEEEEE!"* Roland was amazed that the Red King didn't split his own head wide open with such cries. He reloaded the chamber he'd emptied—he intended to keep a full gun just as long as he could— and this time there was a double whine. Patrick moaned, rolled over onto his belly, and plunged his face into the rock-strewn grass, covering his head with his hands. Roland sat with his back against the pyramid of rock and steel, the long barrel of his six-gun lying on his thigh, relaxed and waiting. At the same time he bent all of his willpower toward one object. His eyes wanted water in response to that high, approaching whistle, and he must not let them. If he ever needed the preternaturally keen eyesight for which he'd been famous in his time, this was it.

Those blue eyes were still clear when the sneetches bolted past above the road. This time one buttonhooked left and the other right. They took evasive action, jigging crazily first one way and then another. It made no difference. Roland waited, sitting with his legs outstretched and his old broken boots cocked into a relaxed V, his heart beating slow and steady, his eye filled with all the world's clarity and color (had he seen better on that last day, he believed he would have been able to see the wind). Then he snapped his gun up, blew both sneetches out of the air, and was once more reloading the empty chambers while the afterimages still pulsed with his heartbeat in front of his eyes.

He leaned to the corner of the pyramid, plucked up the binoculars, braced them on a convenient spur of rock, and looked through them for his enemy. The Crimson King almost jumped at him, and for once in his life Roland saw exactly what he had imagined: an old man with an enormous nose, hooked and waxy; red lips that bloomed in the snow of a luxuriant beard; snowy hair that spilled down the Crimson King's back almost all the way to his scrawny bottom. His pink-flushed face peered toward the pilgrims. The King wore a robe of brilliant red, dotted here and about with lightning strokes and cabalistic symbols. To Susannah, Eddie, and Jake, he would have looked like Father Christmas. To Roland he looked like what he was: Hell, incarnate.

"HOW SLOW YOU ARE!" the gunslinger cried in a tone of mock amazement. *"TRY THREE, PERHAPS THREE AT ONCE WILL DO YA!"*

Looking into the binoculars was like looking into a magic hourglass tipped on its side. Roland watched the Big Red King leaping up and down, shaking his hands beside his face in a way that was almost comic. Roland thought he could see a crate at that robed figure's feet, but wasn't entirely sure; the scrolled iron staves between the balcony's floor and its railing obscured it.

Must be his ammunition supply, he thought. Must *be. How many can he have in a crate that size? Twenty? Fifty?* It didn't matter. Unless the Red King could throw more than twelve at a time, Roland was confident he could shoot anything out of the air the old daemon sent his way. This was, after all, what he'd been made for.

Unfortunately, the Crimson King knew it as well as Roland did.

The thing on the balcony gave another gruesome, ear-splitting cry (Patrick plugged his dirty ears with his dirty fingers) and made as if to dip down for fresh ammunition. Then, however, he stopped himself. Roland watched him advance to the balcony's railing . . . and then peer directly into the gunslinger's eyes. That glare was red and burning. Roland lowered the binoculars at once, lest he be fascinated.

The King's call drifted to him. *"WAIT THEN, A BIT—AND MEDITATE ON WHAT YOU'D GAIN, ROLAND! THINK HOW CLOSE IT IS! AND . . . LISTEN! HEAR THE SONG YOUR DARLING SINGS!"*

He fell silent then. No more whistling; no more whines; no more oncoming sneetches. What Roland heard instead was the sough of the wind . . . and what the King wanted him to hear.

The call of the Tower.

Come, Roland, sang the voices. They came from the roses of Can'-Ka No Rey, they came from the strengthening Beams overhead, they came most of all from the Tower itself, that for which he had searched all his life, that which was now in reach . . . that which was being held away from him, now, at the last. If he went to it, he would be killed in the open. Yet the call was like a fishhook in his mind, drawing him. The Crimson King knew it would do his work if he only waited. And as the time passed, Roland came to know it, too. Because the calling voices weren't constant. At their current level he could withstand them. *Was* withstanding them. But as the afternoon wore on, the level of the call grew stronger. He began to understand—and with growing horror—why in his dreams and visions he had always seen himself coming to the Dark Tower at sunset, when the light in the western sky seemed to reflect the field of roses, turning the whole world into a bucket of blood held up by one single stanchion, black as midnight against the burning horizon.

He had seen himself coming at sunset because that was when the Tower's strengthening call would finally overcome his willpower. He would go. No power on Earth would be able to stop him.

Come . . . come . . . became *COME . . . COME . . .* and then *COME! COME!* His head ached with it. And *for* it. Again and again he found himself getting to his knees and forced himself to sit down once more with his back against the pyramid.

Patrick was staring at him with growing fright. He was partly or completely immune to that call—Roland understood this—but he knew what was happening.

FIVE

They had been pinned down for what Roland judged to be an hour when the King tried another pair of sneetches. This time they flew on either side of the pyramid and hooked back almost at once, coming at him in perfect formation but twenty feet apart. Roland took the one on the right, snapped his wrist to the left, and blew the other one out of the sky. The explosion of the second one was close enough to buffet his face with warm air, but at least there was no shrapnel; when they blew, they blew completely, it seemed.

"TRY AGAIN!" he called. His throat was rough and dry now, but he knew the words were carrying—the air in this place was made for such communication. And he knew each one was a dagger pricking the old lunatic's flesh. But he had his own problems. The call of the Tower was growing steadily stronger.

"COME, GUNSLINGER!" the madman's voice coaxed. *"PER-HAPS I'LL LET THEE COME, AFTER ALL! WE COULD AT LEAST PALAVER ON THE SUBJECT, COULD WE NOT?"*

To his horror, Roland thought he sensed a certain sincerity in that voice.

Yes, he thought grimly. *And we'll have coffee. Perhaps even a little fry-up.*

He fumbled the watch out of his pocket and snapped it open. The hands were running briskly backward. He leaned against the pyramid and closed his eyes, but that was worse. The call of the Tower

(*come, Roland come, gunslinger, commala-come-come, now the journey's done*)

was louder, more insistent than ever. He opened them again and looked up at the unforgiving blue sky and the clouds that raced across it in columns to the Tower at the end of the rose-field.

And the torture continued.

SIX

He hung on for another hour while the shadows of the bushes and the roses growing near the pyramid lengthened, hoping against hope that something would occur to him, some brilliant idea that would save him from having to put his life and his fate in the hands of the talented but soft-minded boy by his side. But as the sun began to slide down the western arc of the sky and the blue overhead began to darken, he knew there was nothing else. The hands of the pocket-watch were turning backward ever faster. Soon they would be spinning. And when they began to spin, he would go. Sneetches or no sneetches (and what else might the madman be holding in reserve?), he would go. He would run, he would zig-zag, he would fall to the ground and crawl if he had to, and no matter what he did, he knew he would be lucky to make it even half the distance to the Dark Tower before he was blown out of his boots.

He would die among the roses.

"Patrick," he said. His voice was husky.

Patrick looked up at him with desperate intensity. Roland stared at the boy's hands—dirty, scabbed, but in their way as incredibly talented as his own—and gave in. It occurred to him that he'd only held out as long as this from pride; he had wanted to kill the Crimson King, not merely send him into some null zone. And of course there was no guarantee that Patrick could do to the King what he'd done to the sore on Susannah's face. But the pull of the Tower would soon be too strong to resist, and all his other choices were gone.

"Change places with me, Patrick."

Patrick did, scrambling carefully over Roland. He was now at the edge of the pyramid nearest the road.

"Look through the far-seeing instrument. Lay it in that notch—yes, just so—and look."

Patrick did, and for what seemed to Roland a very long time. The voice of the Tower, meanwhile, sang and chimed and cajoled. At long last, Patrick looked back at him.

"Now take thy pad, Patrick. Draw yonder man." Not that he *was* a man, but at least he looked like one.

At first, however, Patrick only continued to gaze at Roland, biting his lip. Then, at last, he took the sides of the gunslinger's head in his hands and brought it forward until they were brow to brow.

Very hard, whispered a voice deep in Roland's mind. It was not the voice of a boy at all, but of a grown man. A powerful man. *He's not entirely there. He darkles. He tincts.*

Where had Roland heard those words before?

No time to think about it now.

"Are you saying you can't?" Roland asked, injecting (with an effort) a note of disappointed incredulity into his voice. "That *you* can't? That *Patrick* can't? The *Artist* can't?"

Patrick's eyes changed. For a moment Roland saw in them the expression that would be there permanently if he grew to be a man . . . and the paintings in Sayre's office said that he would do that, at least on some track of time, in some world. Old enough, at least, to paint what he had seen this day. That expression would be hauteur, if he grew to be an old man with a little wisdom to match his talent; now it was only arrogance. The look of a kid who knows he's faster than blue blazes, the best, and cares to know nothing else. Roland knew that look, for had he not seen it gazing back at him from a hundred mirrors and still pools of water when he had been as young as Patrick Danville was now?

I can, came the voice in Roland's head. *I only say it won't be easy. I'll need the eraser.*

Roland shook his head at once. In his pocket, his hand closed around what remained of the pink nubbin and held it tight.

"No," he said. "Thee must draw cold, Patrick. Every line right the first time. The erasing comes later."

For a moment the look of arrogance faltered, but only for a moment. When it returned, what came with it pleased the gunslinger mightily, and eased him a little, as well. It was a look of hot excitement. It was the look the talented wear when, after years of just moving sleepily along from pillar to post, they are finally challenged to do something that will tax their abilities, stretch them to their limits. Perhaps even beyond them.

Patrick rolled to the binoculars again, which he'd left propped aslant just below the notch. He looked long while the voices sang their growing imperative in Roland's head.

And at last he rolled away, took up his pad, and began to draw the most important picture of his life.

SEVEN

It was slow work compared to Patrick's usual method—rapid strokes that produced a completed and compelling drawing in only minutes. Roland again and again had to restrain himself from shouting at the boy: *Hurry up! For the sake of all the gods, hurry up! Can't you see that I'm in agony here?*

But Patrick didn't see and wouldn't have cared in any case. He was totally absorbed in his work, caught up in the unknowing greed of it, pausing only to go back to the binoculars now and then for another long look at his red-robed subject. Sometimes he slanted the pencil to shade a little, then rubbed with his thumb to produce a shadow. Sometimes he rolled his eyes back in his head, showing the world nothing but the waxy gleam of the whites. It was as if he were conning some version of the Red King that stood a-glow in his brain. And really, how did Roland know that was not possible?

I don't care what it is. Just let him finish before I go mad and sprint to what the Old Red King so rightly called "my darling."

Half an hour at least three days long passed in this fashion. Once the Crimson King called more coaxingly than ever to Roland, asking if he would not come to the Tower and palaver, after all. Perhaps, he said, if Roland were to free him from his balcony prison, they might bury an arrow together and then climb to the top room of the Tower in that same spirit of friendliness. It was not impossible, after all. A hard rain made for queer bedfellows at the inn; had Roland never heard that saying?

The gunslinger knew the saying well. He also knew that the Red King's offer was essentially the same false request as before, only this time dressed up in morning coat and cravat. And this time Roland heard worry lurking in the old monster's voice. He wasted no energy on reply.

Realizing his coaxing had failed, the Crimson King threw another sneetch. This one flew so high over the pyramid it was only a spark, then dove down upon them with the scream of a falling bomb. Roland took care of it with a single shot and reloaded from a plentitude of shells. He wished, in fact, that the King would send more of the flying grenados against him, because they took his mind temporarily off the dreadful call of the Tower.

It's been waiting for me, he thought with dismay. *That's what makes it so hard to resist, I think— it's calling me in particular. Not to Roland, exactly, but to the entire line of Eld . . . and of that line, only I am left.*

EIGHT

At last, as the descending sun began to take on its first hues of orange and Roland felt he could stand it no longer, Patrick put his pencil aside and held the pad out to Roland, frowning. The look made Roland afraid. He had never seen that particular expression in the mute boy's repertoire. Patrick's former arrogance was gone.

Roland took the pad, however, and for a moment was so amazed by what he saw there that he looked away, as if even the eyes in Patrick's drawing might have the power to fascinate him; might perhaps compel him to put his gun to his temple and blow out his aching brains. It was that good. The greedy and questioning face was long, the cheeks and forehead marked by creases so deep they might have been bottomless. The lips within the foaming beard were full and cruel. It was the mouth of a man who would turn a kiss into a bite if the spirit took him, and the spirit often would.

"WHAT DO YOU THINK YOU'RE DOING?" came that screaming, lunatic voice. *"IT WON'T DO YOU ANY GOOD, WHATEVER IT IS! I HOLD THE TOWER—EEEEEEEE!—I'M LIKE THE DOG WITH THE GRAPES, ROLAND! IT'S MINE EVEN IF I CAN'T CLIMB IT! AND YOU'LL COME! EEEEE! SAY TRUE! BEFORE THE SHADOW OF THE TOWER REACHES YOUR PALTRY HIDING-PLACE, YOU'LL COME! EEEEEEEE! EEEEEEEE!* **EEEEEEEE!***"*

Patrick covered his ears, wincing. Now that he had finished drawing, he registered those terrible screams again.

That the picture was the greatest work of Patrick's life Roland had absolutely no doubt. Challenged, the boy had done more than rise above himself; he had *soared* above himself and committed genius. The image of the Crimson King was haunting in its clarity. *The far-seeing instrument can't explain this, or not all of it,* Roland thought. *It's as if he has a third eye, one that looks out from his imagination and sees everything. It's that eye he looks through when he rolls the other two up. To own such an ability as this . . . and to express it with something as humble as a pencil! Ye gods!*

He almost expected to see the pulse begin to beat in the hollows of the old man's temples, where clocksprings of veins had been delineated with only a few gentle, feathered shadings. At the corner of the full and sensuous lips, the gunslinger could see the wink of a single sharp

(*tusk*)

tooth, and he thought the lips of the drawing might come to
life and part as he looked, revealing a mouthful of fangs: one
mere wink of white (which was only a bit of unmarked paper,
after all) made the imagination see all the rest, and even to smell
the reek of meat that would accompany each outflow of breath.
Patrick had perfectly captured a tuft of hair curling from one of
the King's nostrils, and a tiny thread of scar that wove in and out
of the King's right eyebrow like a bit of string. It was a marvelous
piece of work, better by far than the portrait the mute boy
had done of Susannah. Surely if Patrick had been able to erase
the sore from that one, then he could erase the Crimson King
from this one, leaving nothing but the balcony railing before
him and the closed door to the Tower's barrel behind. Roland
almost expected the Crimson King to breathe and move, and so
surely it was done! Surely . . .

But it was not. It was not, and wanting would not make it so.
Not even needing would make it so.

It's his eyes, Roland thought. They were wide and terrible, the
eyes of a dragon in human form. They were dreadfully good,
but they weren't right. Roland felt a kind of desperate, miserable certainty and shuddered from head to toe, hard enough to
make his teeth chatter. *They're not quite r—*

Patrick took hold of Roland's elbow. The gunslinger had
been concentrating so fiercely on the drawing that he nearly
screamed. He looked up. Patrick nodded at him, then touched
his fingers to the corners of his own eyes.

Yes. His eyes. I know that! But what's wrong with them?

Patrick was still touching the corners of his eyes. Overhead,
a flock of rusties flew through a sky that would soon be more
purple than blue, squalling the harsh cries that had given them
their name. It was toward the Dark Tower that they flew; Roland
arose to follow them so they should not have what he could not.

Patrick grabbed him by his hide coat and pulled him back.
The boy shook his head violently, and this time pointed toward
the road.

"I SAW THAT, ROLAND!" came the cry. *"YOU THINK THAT
WHAT'S GOOD ENOUGH FOR THE BIRDS IS GOOD ENOUGH*

FOR YOU, DO YOU NOT? EEEEEEEEE! AND IT'S TRUE, SURE! SURE AS SUGAR, SURE AS SALT, SURE AS RUBIES IN KING DANDO'S VAULT—EEEEEEEE, HA! I COULD HAVE HAD YOU JUST NOW, BUT WHY BOTHER? I THINK I'D RATHER SEE YOU COME, PISSING AND SHAKING AND UNABLE TO STOP YOURSELF!"

As I will, Roland thought. *I won't be able to help myself. I may be able to hold here another ten minutes, perhaps even another twenty, but in the end . . .*

Patrick interrupted his thoughts, once more pointing at the road. Pointing back the way they had come.

Roland shook his head wearily. "Even if I could fight the pull of the thing—and I couldn't, it's all I can do to bide here—retreat would do us no good. Once we're no longer in cover, he'll use whatever else he has. He has something, I'm sure of it. And whatever it is, the bullets of my revolver aren't likely to stop it."

Patrick shook his head hard enough to make his long hair fly from side to side. The grip on Roland's arm tightened until the boy's fingernails bit into the gunslinger's flesh even through three layers of hide clothing. His eyes, always gentle and usually puzzled, now peered at Roland with a look close to fury. He pointed again with his free hand, three quick jabbing gestures with the grimy forefinger. *Not* at the road, however.

Patrick was pointing at the roses.

"What about them?" Roland asked. "Patrick, what about them?"

This time Patrick pointed first to the roses, then to the eyes in his picture.

And this time Roland understood.

NINE

Patrick didn't want to get them. When Roland gestured to him to go, the boy shook his head at once, whipping his hair once more from side to side, his eyes wide. He made a whistling noise between his teeth that was a remarkably good imitation of an oncoming sneetch.

"I'll shoot anything he sends," Roland said. "You've seen me do it. If there was one close enough so that I could pick it myself, I would. But there's not. So it has to be you who picks the rose and me who gives you cover."

But Patrick only cringed back against the ragged side of the pyramid. Patrick would not. His fear might not have been as great as his talent, but it was surely a close thing. Roland calculated the distance to the nearest rose. It was beyond their scant cover, but perhaps not by too much. He looked at his diminished right hand, which would have to do the plucking, and asked himself how hard it could be. The fact, of course, was that he didn't know. These were not ordinary roses. For all he knew, the thorns growing up the green stem might have a poison in them that would drop him paralyzed into the tall grass, an easy target.

And Patrick would not. Patrick knew that Roland had once had friends, and that now all his friends were dead, and Patrick would not. If Roland had had two hours to work on the boy—possibly even one—he might have broken through his terror. But he didn't have that time. Sunset had almost come.

Besides, it's close. I can do it if I have to . . . and I must.

The weather had warmed enough so there was no need for the clumsy deerskin gloves Susannah had made them, but Roland had been wearing his that morning, and they were still tucked in his belt. He took one of them and cut off the end, so his two remaining fingers would poke through. What remained would at least protect his palm from the thorns. He put it on, then rested on one knee with his remaining gun in his other hand, looking at the nearest rose. Would one be enough? It would have to be, he decided. The next was fully six feet further away.

Patrick clutched his shoulder, shaking his head frantically.

"I have to," Roland said, and of course he did. This was his job, not Patrick's, and he had been wrong to try and make the boy do it in the first place. If he succeeded, fine and well. If he failed and was blown apart here at the edge of Can'-Ka No Rey, at least that dreadful *pulling* would cease.

The gunslinger took a deep breath, then leaped from cover and at the rose. At the same moment, Patrick clutched at him again, trying to hold him back. He grabbed a fold of Roland's coat and twisted him off-true. Roland landed clumsily on his side. The gun flew out of his hand and fell in the tall grass. The Crimson King screamed (the gunslinger heard both triumph and fury in that voice) and then came the approaching whine of another sneetch. Roland closed his mittened right hand around the stem of the rose. The thorns bit through the tough deerskin as if it were no more than a coating of cobwebs. Then into his hand. The pain was enormous, but the song of the rose was sweet. He could see the blaze of yellow deep in its cup, like the blaze of a sun. Or a million of them. He could feel the warmth of blood filling the hollow of his palm and running between the remaining fingers. It soaked the deerskin, blooming another rose on its scuffed brown surface. And here came the sneetch that would kill him, blotting out the rose's song, filling his head and threatening to split his skull.

The stem never did break. In the end, the rose tore free of the ground, roots and all. Roland rolled to his left, grabbed his gun, and fired without looking. His heart told him there was no longer time to look. There was a shattering explosion, and the warm air that buffeted his face this time was like a hurricane.

Close. Very close, that time.

The Crimson King screamed his frustration— *"EEEEEEEEEEE!"*—and the cry was followed by multiple approaching whistles. Patrick pressed himself against the pyramid, face-first. Roland, clutching the rose in his bleeding right hand, rolled onto his back, raised his gun, and waited for the sneetches to make their turn. When they did, he took care of them: one and two and three.

"STILL HERE!" he cried at the old Red King. *"STILL HERE, YOU OLD COCKSUCKER, MAY IT DO YA FINE!"*

The Crimson King gave another of his terrible howls, but sent no more sneetches.

"SO NOW YOU HAVE A ROSE!" he screamed. *"LISTEN TO IT, ROLAND! LISTEN WELL, FOR IT SINGS THE SAME SONG! LISTEN AND COMMALA-COME-COME!"*

Now that song was all but imperative in Roland's head. It

burned furiously along his nerves. He grasped Patrick and turned him around. "Now," he said. "For my life, Patrick. For the lives of every man and woman who ever died in my place so I could go on."

And child, he thought, seeing Jake in the eye of his memory. Jake first hanging over darkness, then falling into it.

He stared into the mute boy's terrified eyes. "Finish it! *Show me that you can.*"

TEN

Now Roland witnessed an amazing thing: when Patrick took the rose, he wasn't cut. Not so much as scratched. Roland pulled his own lacerated glove off with his teeth and saw that not only was his palm badly slashed, but one of his remaining fingers now hung by a single bloody tendon. It drooped like something that wants to go to sleep. But Patrick was not cut. The thorns did not pierce him. And the terror had gone out of his eyes. He was looking from the rose to his drawing, back and forth with tender calculation.

"ROLAND! WHAT ARE YOU DOING? COME, GUNSLINGER, FOR SUNSET'S ALMOST NIGH!"

And yes, he would come. One way or the other. Knowing it was so eased him somewhat, enabled him to remain where he was without trembling too badly. His right hand was numb to the wrist, and Roland suspected he would never feel it again. That was all right; it hadn't been much of a shake since the lobstrosities had gotten at it.

And the rose sang *Yes, Roland, yes—you'll have it again. You'll be whole again. There will be renewal. Only come.*

Patrick plucked a petal from the rose, judged it, then plucked another to go with it. He put them in his mouth. For a moment his face went slack with a peculiar sort of ecstasy, and Roland wondered what the petals might taste like. Overhead the sky was growing dark. The shadow of the pyramid that had been hidden by the rocks stretched nearly to the road. When the point of that shadow touched the way that had brought him here, Roland supposed he would go whether the Crimson King still held the Tower approach or not.

"WHAT'S THEE DOING? EEEEEEEEE! WHAT DEVILTRY WORKS IN THY MIND AND THY HEART?"

You're a great one to speak of deviltry, Roland thought. He took out his watch and snapped back the cover. Beneath the crystal, the hands now sped backward, five o'clock to four, four to three, three to two, two to one, and one to midnight.

"Patrick, hurry," he said. "Quick as you can, I beg, for my time is almost up."

Patrick cupped a hand beneath his mouth and spat out a red paste the color of fresh blood. The color of the Crimson King's robe. And the exact color of his lunatic's eyes.

Patrick, on the verge of using color for the first time in his life as an artist, made to dip the tip of his right forefinger into this paste, and then hesitated. An odd certainty came to Roland then: the thorns of these roses only pricked when their roots still tied the plant to Mim, or Mother Earth. Had he gotten his way with Patrick, Mim would have cut those talented hands to ribbons and rendered them useless.

It's still ka, the gunslinger thought. *Even out here in End-W—*

Before he could finish the thought, Patrick took the gunslinger's right hand and peered into it with the intensity of a fortune-teller. He scooped up some of the blood that flowed there and mixed it with his rose-paste. Then, carefully, he took a tiny bit of this mixture upon the second finger of his right hand. He lowered it to his painting . . . hesitated . . . looked at Roland. Roland nodded to him and Patrick nodded in return, as gravely as a surgeon about to make the first cut in a dangerous operation, then applied his finger to the paper. The tip touched down as delicately as the beak of a hummingbird dipping into a flower. It colored the Crimson King's left eye and then lifted away. Patrick cocked his head, looking at what he had done with a fascination Roland had never seen on a human face in all his long and wandering time. It was as if the boy were some Manni prophet, finally granted a glimpse of Gan's face after twenty years of waiting in the desert.

Then he broke into an enormous, sunny grin.

The response from the Dark Tower was more immediate and—to Roland, at least—immensely gratifying. The old creature pent on the balcony howled in pain.

"WHAT'S THEE DOING? EEEEEEE! EEEEEEEE! STOP! IT BURNS! BURRRRNS! EEEEEEEEEEEEEEEEEEEEE!"

"Now finish the other," Roland said. "Quickly! For your life and mine!"

Patrick colored the other eye with the same delicate dip of the finger. Now two brilliant crimson eyes looked out of Patrick's black-and-white drawing, eyes that had been colored with attar of rose and the blood of Eld; eyes that burned with Hell's own fire.

It was done.

Roland produced the eraser at last, and held it out to Patrick. "Make him gone," he said. "Make yonder foul hob gone from this world and every world. Make him gone at last."

ELEVEN

There was no question it would work. From the moment Patrick first touched the eraser to his drawing—to that curl of nostril-hair, as it happened—the Crimson King began to scream in fresh pain and horror from his balcony redoubt. And in *understanding.*

Patrick hesitated, looking at Roland for confirmation, and Roland nodded. "Aye, Patrick. His time has come and you're to be his executioner. Go on with it."

The Old King threw four more sneetches, and Roland took care of them all with calm ease. After that he threw no more, for he had no hands with which to throw. His shrieks rose to gibbering whines that Roland thought would surely never leave his ears.

The mute boy erased the full, sensuous mouth from within its foam of beard, and as he did it, the screams first grew muffled and then ceased. In the end Patrick erased everything but the eyes, and these the remaining bit of rubber would not even blur.

They remained until the piece of pink gum (originally part of a Pencil-Pak bought in a Norwich, Connecticut, Woolworth's during a back-to-school sale in August of 1958) had been reduced to a shred the boy could not even hold between his long, dirty nails. And so he cast it away and showed the gunslinger what remained: two malevolent blood-red orbs floating three-quarters of the way up the page.

All the rest of him was gone.

TWELVE

The shadow of the pyramid's tip had come to touch the road; now the sky in the west changed from the orange of a reaptide bonfire to that cauldron of blood Roland had seen in his dreams ever since childhood. When it did, the call of the Tower doubled, then trebled. Roland felt it reach out and grasp him with invisible hands. The time of his destiny was come.

Yet there was this boy. This friendless boy. Roland would not leave him to die here at the end of End-World if he could help it. He had no interest in atonement, and yet Patrick had come to stand for all the murders and betrayals that had finally brought him to the Dark Tower. Roland's family was dead; his misbegotten son had been the last. Now would Eld and Tower be joined.

First, though—or last—this.

"Patrick, listen to me," he said, taking the boy's shoulder with his whole left hand and his mutilated right. "If you'd live to make all the pictures ka has stored away in your future, ask me not a single question nor ask me to repeat a single thing."

The boy looked at him, large-eyed and silent in the red and dying light. And the Song of the Tower rose around them to a mighty shout that was nothing but *commala*.

"Go back to the road. Pick up all the cans that are whole. That should be enough to feed you. Go back the way we came. Never leave the road. You'll do fine."

Patrick nodded with perfect understanding. Roland saw he believed, and that was good. Belief would protect him even more surely than a revolver, even one with the sandalwood grips.

"Go back to the Federal. Go back to the robot, Stuttering Bill that was. Tell him to take you to a door that swings open on America-side. If it won't open to your hand, *draw* it open with thy pencil. Do'ee understand?"

Patrick nodded again. Of course he understood.

"If ka should eventually lead you to Susannah in any where or when, tell her Roland loves her still, and with all his heart." He drew Patrick to him and kissed the boy's mouth. "Give her that. Do'ee understand?"

Patrick nodded.

"All right. I go. Long days and pleasant nights. May we meet in the clearing at the end of the path when all worlds end."

Yet even then he knew this would not happen, for the worlds would never end, not now, and for him there would be no clearing. For Roland Deschain of Gilead, last of Eld's line, the path ended at the Dark Tower. And that did him fine.

He rose to his feet. The boy looked up at him with wide, wondering eyes, clutching his pad. Roland turned. He drew in breath to the bottom of his lungs and let it out in a great cry.

"NOW COMES ROLAND TO THE DARK TOWER! I HAVE BEEN TRUE AND I STILL CARRY THE GUN OF MY FATHER AND YOU WILL OPEN TO MY HAND!"

Patrick watched him stride to where the road ended, a black silhouette against that bloody burning sky. He watched as Roland walked among the roses, and sat shivering in the shadows as Roland began to cry the names of his friends and loved ones and ka-mates; those names carried clear in that strange air, as if they would echo forever.

"I come in the name of Steven Deschain, he of Gilead!

"I come in the name of Gabrielle Deschain, she of Gilead!

"I come in the name of Cortland Andrus, he of Gilead!

"I come in the name of Cuthbert Allgood, he of Gilead!

"I come in the name of Alain Johns, he of Gilead!

"I come in the name of Jamie DeCurry, he of Gilead!

"I come in the name of Vannay the Wise, he of Gilead!

"I come in the name of Hax the Cook, he of Gilead!

"I come in the name of David the hawk, he of Gilead and the sky!

"I come in the name of Susan Delgado, she of Mejis!

"I come in the name of Sheemie Ruiz, he of Mejis!

"I come in the name of Pere Callahan, he of Jerusalem's Lot, and the roads!

"I come in the name of Ted Brautigan, he of America!

"I come in the name of Dinky Earnshaw, he of America!

"I come in the name of Aunt Talitha, she of River Crossing, and will lay her cross here, as I was bid!

"I come in the name of Stephen King, he of Maine!

"I come in the name of Oy, the brave, he of Mid-World!

"I come in the name of Eddie Dean, he of New York!

"I come in the name of Susannah Dean, she of New York!

"I come in the name of Jake Chambers, he of New York, whom I call my own true son!

"I am Roland of Gilead, and I come as myself; *you will open to me.*"

After that came the sound of a horn. It simultaneously chilled Patrick's blood and exalted him. The echoes faded into silence. Then, perhaps a minute later, came a great, echoing boom: the sound of a door swinging shut forever.

And after that came silence.

THIRTEEN

Patrick sat where he was at the base of the pyramid, shivering, until Old Star and Old Mother rose in the sky. The song of the roses and the Tower hadn't ceased, but it had grown low and sleepy, little more than a murmur.

At last he went back to the road, gathered as many whole cans as he could (there was a surprising number of them, considering the force of the explosion that had demolished the cart), and found a deerskin sack that would hold them. He realized he had forgotten his pencil and went back to get it.

Beside the pencil, gleaming in the starlight, was Roland's watch.

The boy took it with a small (and nervous) hoot of glee. He put it in his pocket. Then he went back to the road and slung his little sack of gunna over his shoulder.

I can tell you that he walked until nearly midnight, and that he looked at the watch before taking his rest. I can tell you that the watch had stopped completely. I can tell you that, come noon of the following day, he looked at it again and saw that it had begun to run in the correct direction once more, albeit very slowly. But of Patrick I can tell you no more, not whether he made it back to the Federal, not whether he found Stuttering Bill that was, not whether he eventually came once more to America-side. I can tell you none of these things, say sorry. Here the darkness hides him from my storyteller's eye and he must go on alone.

SUSANNAH IN NEW YORK

EPILOGUE

Susannah in New York
(Epilogue)

No one takes alarm as the little electric cart slides out of nowhere an inch at a time until it's wholly here in Central Park; no one sees it but us. Most of those here are looking skyward, as the first snowflakes of what will prove to be a great pre-Christmas snowstorm come skirling down from a white sky. The Blizzard of '87, the newspapers will call it. Visitors to the park who aren't watching the snowfall begin are watching the carolers, who are from public schools far uptown. They are wearing either dark red blazers (the boys) or dark red jumpers (the girls). This is the Harlem School Choir, sometimes called The Harlem Roses in the *Post* and its rival tabloid, the New York *Sun*. They sing an old hymn in gorgeous doo-wop harmony, snapping their fingers as they make their way through the staves, turning it into something that sounds almost like early Spurs, Coasters, or Dark Diamonds. They are standing not too far from the environment where the polar bears live their city lives, and the song they're singing is "What Child Is This."

One of those looking up into the snow is a man Susannah knows well, and her heart leaps straight up to heaven at the sight of him. In his left hand he's holding a large paper cup and she's sure it contains hot chocolate, the good kind *mit schlag.*

For a moment she's unable to touch the controls of the little cart, which came from another world. Thoughts of Roland and Patrick have left her mind. All she can think of is Eddie — Eddie in front of her right here and now, Eddie alive again. And if this is not the Keystone World, not quite, what of that? If Co-Op City is in Brooklyn (or even in Queens!) and Eddie drives a Takuro Spirit instead of a Buick Electra, what of those things? It

807

doesn't matter. Only one thing would, and it's that which keeps her hand from rising to the throttle and trundling the cart toward him.

What if he doesn't recognize her?

What if when he turns he sees nothing but a homeless black lady in an electric cart whose battery will soon be as flat as a sat-on hat, a black lady with no money, no clothes, no address (not in *this* where and when, say thankee sai) and no legs? A homeless black lady with no connection to him? Or what if he *does* know her, somewhere far back in his mind, yet still denies her as completely as Peter denied Jesus, because remembering is just too hurtful?

Worse still, what if he turns to her and she sees the burned-out, fucked-up, empty-eyed stare of the longtime junkie? What if, what if, and here comes the snow that will soon turn the whole world white.

Stop thy grizzling and go to him, Roland tells her. *You didn't face Blaine and the taheen of Blue Heaven and the thing under Castle Discordia just to turn tail and run now, did you? Surely you've got a moit more guts than that.*

But she isn't sure she really does until she sees her hand rise to the throttle. Before she can twist it, however, the gunslinger's voice speaks to her again, this time sounding wearily amused.

Perhaps there's something you want to get rid of first, Susannah?

She looks down and sees Roland's weapon stuck through her crossbelt, like a Mexican *bandido*'s *pistola,* or a pirate's cutlass. She pulls it free, amazed at how good it feels in her hand . . . how brutally right. Parting from this, she thinks, will be like parting from a lover. And she doesn't *have* to, does she? The question is, what does she love more? The man or the gun? All other choices will flow from this one.

On impulse she rolls the cylinder and sees that the rounds inside look old, their casings dull.

These'll never fire, she thinks . . . and, without knowing why, or precisely what it means: *These are wets.*

She sights up the barrel and is queerly saddened—but not surprised—to find that the barrel lets through no light. It's plugged. Has been for decades, from the look of it. This gun will never fire again. There is no choice to be made, after all. This gun is over.

Susannah, still holding the revolver with the sandalwood grips in one hand, twists the throttle with the other. The little electric cart—the one she named Ho Fat III, although that is already fading in her mind—rolls soundlessly forward. It passes a green trash barrel with **KEEP LITTER IN ITS PLACE!** stenciled on the side. She tosses Roland's revolver into this litter barrel. Doing it hurts her heart, but she never hesitates. It's heavy, and sinks into the crumpled fast-food wrappers, advertising circulars, and discarded newspapers like a stone into water. She is still enough of a gunslinger to bitterly regret throwing away such a storied weapon (even if the final trip between worlds has spoiled it), but she's already become enough of the woman who's waiting for her up ahead not to pause or look back once the job is done.

Before she can reach the man with the paper cup, he turns. He is indeed wearing a sweatshirt that says I DRINK NOZZ-A-LA!, but she barely registers that. It's him: that's what she registers. It's Edward Cantor Dean. And then even that becomes secondary, because what she sees in his eyes is all she has feared. It's total puzzlement. He doesn't know her.

Then, tentatively, he smiles, and it is the smile she remembers, the one she always loved. Also he's clean, she knows it at once. She sees it in his face. Mostly in his eyes. The carolers from Harlem sing, and he holds out the cup of hot chocolate.

"Thank God," he says. "I'd just about decided I'd have to drink this myself. That the voices were wrong and I was going crazy after all. That . . . well . . ." He trails off, looking more than puzzled. He looks afraid. "Listen, you are here for *me*, aren't you? Please tell me I'm not making an utter ass of myself. Because, lady, right now I feel as nervous as a long-tailed cat in a roomful of rocking chairs."

"You're not," she says. "Making an ass of yourself, I mean." She's remembering Jake's story about the voices he heard arguing in his mind, one yelling that he was dead, the other that he was alive. Both of them utterly convinced. She has at least some idea of how terrible that must be, because she knows a little about other voices. Strange voices.

"Thank God," he says. "Your name is Susannah?"

"Yes," she says. "My name is Susannah."

Her throat is terribly dry, but the words come out, at least. She takes the cup from him and sips the hot chocolate through the cream. It is sweet and good, a taste of this world. The sound of the honking cabs, their drivers hurrying to make their day before the snow shuts them down, is equally good. Grinning, he reaches out and wipes a tiny dab of the cream from the tip of her nose. His touch is electric, and she sees that he feels it, too. It occurs to her that he is going to kiss her again for the first time, and sleep with her again for the first time, and fall in love with her again for the first time. He may know those things because voices have told him, but she knows them for a far better reason: because those things have already happened. Ka is a wheel, Roland said, and now she knows it's true. Her memories of

(*Mid-World*)

the gunslinger's where and when are growing hazy, but she thinks she will remember just enough to know it's *all* happened before, and there is something incredibly sad about this.

But at the same time, it's good.

It's a damn miracle, is what it is.

"Are you cold?" he asks.

"No, I'm okay. Why?"

"You shivered."

"It's the sweetness of the cream." Then, looking at him as she does it, she pokes her tongue out and licks a bit of the nutmeg-dusted foam.

"If you aren't cold now, you will be," he says. "WRKO says the temperature's gonna drop twenty degrees tonight. So I bought you something." From his back pocket he takes a knitted cap, the kind you can pull down over your ears. She looks at the front of it and sees the words there printed in red: MERRY CHRISTMAS.

"Bought it in Brendio's, on Fifth Avenue," he says.

Susannah has never heard of Brendio's. *Brentano's,* maybe—the bookstore—but not Brendio's. But of course in the America where she grew up, she never heard of Nozz-A-La or Takuro Spirit automobiles, either. "Did your voices tell you to buy it?" Teasing him a little now.

He blushes. "Actually, you know, they sort of did. Try it on."

It's a perfect fit.

"Tell me something," she says. "Who's the President? You're not going to tell me it's Ronald Reagan, are you?"

He looks at her incredulously for a moment, and then smiles. "What? That old actor who used to host *Death Valley Days* on TV? You're kidding, right?"

"Nope. I always thought *you* were the one who was kidding about Ronnie Reagan, Eddie."

"I don't know what you mean."

"That's okay, just tell me who the President is."

"Gary Hart," he says, as if speaking to a child. "From Colorado. He almost dropped out of the race in 1980—as I'm sure you know—over that *Monkey Business* business. Then he said 'Fuck em if they can't take a joke' and hung on in there. Ended up winning in a landslide."

His smile fades a little as he studies her.

"You're not kidding me, are you?"

"Are you kidding *me* about the voices? The ones you hear in our head? The ones that wake you up at two in the morning?"

Eddie looks almost shocked. "How can you know *that?*"

"It's a long story. Maybe someday I'll tell you." *If I can still remember,* she thinks.

"It's not just the voices."

"No?"

"No. I've been dreaming of you. For months now. I've been waiting for you. Listen, we don't know each other . . . this is crazy . . . but do you have a place to stay? You don't, do you?"

She shakes her head. Doing a passable John Wayne (or maybe it's Blaine the train she's imitating), she says: "Ah'm a stranger here in Dodge, pilgrim."

Her heart is pounding slowly and heavily in her chest, but she feels a rising joy. This is going to be all right. She doesn't know how it can be, but yes, it's going to be just fine. This time ka is working in her favor, and the force of ka is enormous. This she knows from experience.

"If I asked how I know you . . . or where you come from . . ." He pauses, looking at her levelly, and then says the rest of it. "Or how I can possibly love you already . . . ?"

She smiles. It feels good to smile, and it no longer hurts the side of her face, because whatever was there (some sort of scar, maybe—she can't quite remember) is gone. "Sugar," she tells him, "it's what I said: a long story. You'll get some of it in time, though . . . what I remember of it. And it could be that we still have some work to do. For an outfit called the Tet Corporation." She looks around and then says, "What year is this?"

"1987," he says.

"And do you live in Brooklyn? Or maybe the Bronx?"

The young man whose dreams and squabbling voices have led him here—with a cup of hot chocolate in his hand and a MERRY CHRISTMAS hat in his back pocket—bursts out laughing. "God, no! I'm from White Plains! I came in on the train with my brother. He's right over there. He wanted a closer look at the polar bears."

The brother. Henry. The great sage and eminent junkie. Her heart sinks.

"Let me introduce you," he says.

"No, really, I—"

"Hey, if we're gonna be friends, you gotta be friends with my kid brother. We're *tight*. Jake! Hey, Jake!"

She hasn't noticed the boy standing down by the railing which guards the sunken polar bears' environment from the rest of the park, but now he turns and her heart takes a great, giddy leap in her chest. Jake waves and ambles toward them.

"Jake's been dreaming about you, too," Eddie tells her. "It's the only reason I know I'm not going crazy. Any crazier than usual, at least."

She takes Eddie's hand—that familiar, well-loved hand.

And when the fingers close over hers, she thinks she will die of joy. She will have many questions—so will they—but for the time being she has only one that feels important. As the snow begins to fall more thickly around them, landing in his hair and in his lashes and on the shoulders of his sweatshirt, she asks it.

"You and Jake—what's your last name?"

"Toren," he says. "It's German."

Before either of them can say anything else, Jake joins them. And will I tell you that these three lived happily ever after? I will not, for no one ever does. But there *was* happiness.

And they *did* live.

Beneath the flowing and sometimes glimpsed glammer of the Beam that connects Shardik the Bear and Maturin the Turtle by way of the Dark Tower, they *did* live.

That's all.

That's enough.

Say thankya.

CODA

FOUND

FOUND
(CODA)

ONE

I've told my tale all the way to the end, and am satisfied. It was
(I set my watch and warrant on it) the kind only a good God
would save for last, full of monsters and marvels and voyaging
here and there. I can stop now, put my pen down, and rest my
weary hand (although perhaps not forever; the hand that tells
the tales has a mind of its own, and a way of growing restless).
I can close my eyes to Mid-World and all that lies beyond Mid-
World. Yet some of you who have provided the ears without
which no tale can survive a single day are likely not so willing.
You are the grim, goal-oriented ones who will not believe that
the joy is in the journey rather than the destination no matter
how many times it has been proven to you. You are the unfortunate ones who still get the lovemaking all confused with the
paltry squirt that comes to end the lovemaking (the orgasm is,
after all, God's way of telling us we've finished, at least for the
time being, and should go to sleep). You are the cruel ones who
deny the Grey Havens, where tired characters go to rest. You say
you want to know how it all comes out. You say you want to follow Roland into the Tower; you say that is what you paid your
money for, the show you came to see.

I hope most of you know better. *Want* better. I hope you
came to hear the tale, and not just munch your way through the
pages to the ending. For an ending, you only have to turn to the
last page and see what is there writ upon. But endings are
heartless. An ending is a closed door no man (or Manni) can
open. I've written many, but most only for the same reason that
I pull on my pants in the morning before leaving the bedroom—because it is the custom of the country.

817

And so, my dear Constant Reader, I tell you this: You can stop here. You can let your last memory be of seeing Eddie, Susannah, and Jake in Central Park, together again for the first time, listening to the children's choir sing "What Child Is This." You can be content in the knowledge that sooner or later Oy (probably a canine version with a long neck, odd gold-ringed eyes, and a bark that sometimes sounds eerily like speech) will also enter the picture. That's a pretty picture, isn't it? *I* think so. And pretty close to happily ever after, too. Close enough for government work, as Eddie would say.

Should you go on, you will surely be disappointed, perhaps even heartbroken. I have one key left on my belt, but all it opens is that final door, the one marked ⏀⏀⏀ ⏀⏀. What's behind it won't improve your love-life, grow hair on your bald spot, or add five years to your natural span (not even five minutes). There is no such thing as a happy ending. I never met a single one to equal "Once upon a time."

Endings are heartless.

Ending is just another word for goodbye.

TWO

Would you still?

Very well, then, come. (Do you hear me sigh?) Here is the Dark Tower, at the end of End-World. See it, I beg.

See it very well.

Here is the Dark Tower at sunset.

THREE

He came to it with the oddest feeling of remembrance; what Susannah and Eddie called *déjà vu.*

The roses of Can'-Ka No Rey opened before him in a path to the Dark Tower, the yellow suns deep in their cups seeming to regard him like eyes. And as he walked toward that gray-black column, Roland felt himself begin to slip from the world as he had always known it. He called the names of his friends and loved ones, as he had always promised himself he would; called them in the gloaming, and with perfect force, for no longer was there any need to reserve energy with which to fight the Tower's pull. To give in—finally—was the greatest relief of his life.

He called the names of his *compadres* and *amoras,* and although each came from deeper in his heart, each seemed to have less business with the rest of him. His voice rolled away to the darkening red horizon, name upon name. He called Eddie's and Susannah's. He called Jake's, and last of all he called his own. When the sound of it had died out, the blast of a great horn replied, not from the Tower itself but from the roses that lay in a carpet all around it. That horn was the *voice* of the roses, and cried him welcome with a kingly blast.

In my dreams the horn was always mine, he thought. *I should have known better, for mine was lost with Cuthbert, at Jericho Hill.*

A voice whispered from above him: *It would have been the work of three seconds to bend and pick it up. Even in the smoke and the death. Three seconds. Time, Roland—it always comes back to that.*

That was, he thought, the voice of the Beam—the one they had saved. If it spoke out of gratitude it could have saved its breath, for what good were such words to him now? He remembered a line from Browning's poem: *One taste of the old times sets all to rights.*

Such had never been his experience. In his own, memories brought only sadness. They were the food of poets and fools, sweets that left a bitter aftertaste in the mouth and throat.

Roland stopped for a moment still ten paces from the ghostwood door in the Tower's base, letting the voice of the roses—that welcoming horn—echo away to nothing. The feeling of *déjà vu* was still strong, almost as though he had been here after all. And of course he had been, in ten thousand premonitory dreams. He looked up at the balcony where the Crimson King had stood, trying to defy ka and bar his way. There, about six feet above the cartons that held the few remaining sneetches (the old lunatic had had no other weapons after all, it seemed), he saw two red eyes, floating in the darkening air, looking down at him with eternal hatred. From their backs, the thin silver of the optic nerves (now tinted red-orange with the light of the leaving sun) trailed away to nothing. The gunslinger supposed the Crimson King's eyes would remain up there forever, watching Can'-Ka No Rey while their owner wandered the world to which Patrick's eraser and enchanted Artist's eye had sent him. Or, more likely, to the space *between* the worlds.

Roland walked on to where the path ended at the steel-banded slab of black ghostwood. Upon it, a sigul that he now knew well was engraved three-quarters of the way up:

$$\text{\textvisiblespace}$$

Here he laid two things, the last of his gunna: Aunt Talitha's cross, and his remaining sixgun. When he stood up, he saw the first two hieroglyphics had faded away:

$$\text{\textvisiblespace}$$

UNFOUND had become FOUND.

He raised his hand as if to knock, but the door swung open of its own accord before he could touch it, revealing the bottom steps of an ascending spiral stairway. There was a sighing voice— *Welcome, Roland, thee of Eld.* It was the Tower's voice. This edifice was not stone at all, although it might look like stone; this was a living thing, Gan himself, likely, and the pulse he'd felt deep in his head even thousands of miles from here had always been Gan's beating life-force.

Commala, gunslinger. Commala-come-come.

And wafting out came the smell of alkali, bitter as tears. The smell of . . . what? What, exactly? Before he could place it the odor was gone, leaving Roland to surmise he had imagined it.

He stepped inside and the Song of the Tower, which he had always heard—even in Gilead, where it had hidden in his mother's voice as she sang him her cradle songs—finally ceased. There was another sigh. The door swung shut with a boom, but he was not left in blackness. The light that remained was that of the shining spiral windows, mixed with the glow of sunset.

Stone stairs, a passage just wide enough for one person, ascended.

"Now comes Roland," he called, and the words seemed to spiral up into infinity. "Thee at the top, hear and make me welcome if you would. If you're my enemy, know that I come unarmed and mean no ill."

He began to climb.

Nineteen steps brought him to the first landing (and to each one thereafter). A door stood open here and beyond it was a small round room. The stones of its wall were carved with thousands of overlapping faces. Many he knew (one was the face of Calvin Tower, peeping slyly over the top of an open book). The faces looked at him and he heard their murmuring.

Welcome Roland, you of the many miles and many worlds; welcome thee of Gilead, thee of Eld.

On the far side of the room was a door flanked by dark red swags traced with gold. About six feet up from the door—at the exact height of his eyes—was a small round window, little bigger than an outlaw's peekhole. There was a sweet smell, and this one he could identify: the bag of pine sachet his mother had placed first in his cradle, then, later, in his first real bed. It brought back those days with great clarity, as aromas always do; if any sense serves us as a time machine, it's that of smell.

Then, like the bitter call of the alkali, it was gone.

The room was unfurnished, but a single item lay on the floor. He advanced to it and picked it up. It was a small cedar clip, its bow wrapped in a bit of blue silk ribbon. He had seen such things long ago, in Gilead; must once have worn one himself. When the sawbones cut a newly arrived baby's umbilical cord, separating mother from child, such a clip was put on above the baby's navel, where it would stay until the remainder of the cord fell off, and the clip with it. (The navel itself was called tet-ka can Gan.) The bit of silk on this one told that it had belonged to a boy. A girl's clip would have been wrapped with pink ribbon.

'Twas my own, he thought. He regarded it a moment longer, fascinated, then put it carefully back where it had been. Where it belonged. When he stood up again, he saw a baby's face

(*Can this be my darling bah-bo? If you say so, let it be so!*)

among the multitude of others. It was contorted, as if its first breath of air outside the womb had not been to its liking, already fouled with death. Soon it would pronounce judgment on its new situation with a squall that would echo throughout the apartments of Steven and Gabrielle, causing those friends and servants who heard it to smile with relief. (Only Marten Broadcloak would scowl.) The birthing was done, and it had been a livebirth, tell Gan and all the gods thankya. There was an heir to the Line of Eld, and thus there was still the barest outside chance that the world's rueful shuffle toward ruin might be reversed.

Roland left that room, his sense of *déjà vu* stronger than ever. So was the sense that he had entered the body of Gan himself.

He turned to the stairs and once more began to climb.

FOUR

Another nineteen steps took him to the second landing and the second room. Here bits of cloth were scattered across the circular floor. Roland had no question that they had once been an infant's clout, torn to shreds by a certain petulant interloper, who had then gone out onto the balcony for a look back at the field of roses and found himself betaken. He was a creature of monumental slyness, full of evil wisdom . . . but in the end he had slipped, and now he would pay forever and ever.

If it was only a look he wanted, why did he bring his ammunition with him when he stepped out?

Because it was his only gunna, and slung over his back, whispered one of the faces carved into the curve of the wall. This was the face of Mordred. Roland saw no hatefulness there now but only the lonely sadness of an abandoned child. That face was as lonesome as a train-whistle on a moonless night. There had been no clip for Mordred's navel when he came into the world, only the mother he had taken for his first meal. No clip, never in life, for Mordred had never been part of Gan's tet. No, not he.

My Red Father would never go unarmed, whispered the stone boy. *Not once he was away from his castle. He was mad, but never that mad.*

In this room was the smell of talc put on by his mother while he lay naked on a towel, fresh from his bath and playing with his newly discovered toes. She had soothed his skin with it, singing as she caressed him: *Baby-bunting, baby dear, baby bring your basket here!*

This smell too was gone as quickly as it had come.

Roland crossed to the little window, walking among the shredded bits of diaper, and looked out. The disembodied eyes sensed him and rolled over giddily to regard him. That gaze was poisonous with fury and loss.

Come out, Roland! Come out and face me one to one! Man to man! An eye for an eye, may it do ya!

"I think not," Roland said, "for I have more work to do. A little more, even yet."

It was his last word to the Crimson King. Although the lunatic screamed thoughts after him, he screamed in vain, for Roland never looked back. He had more stairs to climb and more rooms to investigate on his way to the top.

FIVE

On the third landing he looked through the door and saw a corduroy dress that had no doubt been his when he'd been only a year old. Among the faces on this wall he saw that of his father, but as a much younger man. Later on that face had become cruel—events and responsibilities had turned it so. But not here. Here, Steven Deschain's eyes were those of a man looking on something that pleases him more than anything else ever has, or ever could. Here Roland smelled a sweet and husky aroma he knew for the scent of his father's shaving soap. A phantom voice whispered, *Look, Gabby, look you! He's smiling! Smiling at me! And he's got a new tooth!*

On the floor of the fourth room was the collar of his first dog, Ring-A-Levio. Ringo, for short. He'd died when Roland was three, which was something of a gift. A boy of three was still allowed to weep for a lost pet, even a boy with the blood of Eld in his veins. Here the gunslinger that was smelled an odor that was wonderful but had no name, and knew it for the smell of the Full Earth sun in Ringo's fur.

Perhaps two dozen floors above Ringo's Room was a scattering of breadcrumbs and a limp bundle of feathers that had once belonged to a hawk named David—no pet he, but certainly a friend. The first of Roland's many sacrifices to the Dark Tower. On one section of the wall Roland saw David carved in flight, his stubby wings spread above all the gathered court of Gilead (Marten the Enchanter not least among them). And to the left of the door leading onto the balcony, David was carved again. Here his wings were folded as he fell upon Cort like a blind bullet, heedless of Cort's upraised stick.

Old times.

Old times and old crimes.

Not far from Cort was the laughing face of the whore with whom the boy had sported that night. The smell in David's Room was her perfume, cheap and sweet. As the gunslinger drew it in, he remembered touching the whore's pubic curls and was shocked to remember now what he had remembered then, as his fingers slid toward her slicky-sweet cleft: being fresh out of his baby's bath, with his mother's hands upon him.

He began to grow hard, and Roland fled that room in fear.

SIX

There was no more red to light his way now, only the eldritch blue glow of the windows—glass eyes that were alive, glass eyes that looked upon the gunless intruder. Outside the Dark Tower, the roses of Can'-Ka No Rey had closed for another day. Part of his mind marveled that he should be here at all; that he had one by one surmounted the obstacles placed in his path, as dreadfully single-minded as ever. *I'm like one of the old people's robots,* he thought. *One that will either accomplish the task for which it has been made or beat itself to death trying.*

Another part of him was not surprised at all, however. This was the part that dreamed as the Beams themselves must, and this darker self thought again of the horn that had fallen from Cuthbert's fingers—Cuthbert, who had gone to his death laughing. The horn that might to this very day lie where it had fallen on the rocky slope of Jericho Hill.

And of course I've seen these rooms before! They're telling my life, after all.

Indeed they were. Floor by floor and tale by tale (not to mention death by death), the rising rooms of the Dark Tower recounted Roland Deschain's life and quest. Each held its memento; each its signature aroma. Many times there was more than a single floor devoted to a single year, but there was always at least one. And after the thirty-eighth room (which is nineteen doubled, do ya not see it), he wished to look no more. This one contained the charred stake to which Susan Delgado had been bound. He did not enter, but looked at the face upon the wall. That much he owed her. *Roland, I love thee!* Susan Delgado had screamed, and he knew it was the truth, for it was only her love that rendered her recognizable. And, love or no love, in the end she had still burned.

This is a place of death, he thought, *and not just here. All these rooms. Every floor.*

Yes, gunslinger, whispered the Voice of the Tower. *But only because your life has made it so.*

After the thirty-eighth floor, Roland climbed faster.

SEVEN

Standing outside, Roland had judged the Tower to be roughly six hundred feet high. But as he peered into the hundredth room, and then the two hundredth, he felt sure he must have climbed eight times six hundred. Soon he would be closing in on the mark of distance his friends from America-side had called a mile. That was more floors than there possibly could be—no Tower could be a mile high!—but still he climbed, climbed until he was nearly running, yet never did he tire. It once crossed his mind that he'd never reach the top; that the Dark Tower was infinite in height as it was eternal in time. But after a moment's consideration he rejected the idea, for it was his life the Tower was telling, and while that life had been long, it had by no means been eternal. And as it had had a beginning (marked by the cedar clip and the bit of blue silk ribbon), so it would have an ending.

Soon now, quite likely.

The light he sensed behind his eyes was brighter now, and did not seem so blue. He passed a room containing Zoltan, the bird from the weed-eater's hut. He passed a room containing the atomic pump from the Way Station. He climbed more stairs, paused outside a room containing a dead lobstrosity, and by now the light he sensed was *much* brighter and no longer blue.

It was . . .

He was quite sure it was . . .

It was sunlight. Past twilight it might be, with Old Star and Old Mother shining from above the Dark Tower, but Roland was quite sure he was seeing—or sensing—*sunlight.*

He climbed on without looking into any more of the rooms, without bothering to smell their aromas of the past. The stairwell narrowed until his shoulders nearly touched its curved stone sides. No songs now, unless the wind was a song, for he heard it soughing.

He passed one final open door. Lying on the floor of the tiny room beyond it was a pad from which the face had been erased. All that remained were two red eyes, glaring up.

I have reached the present. I have reached now.

Yes, and there was sunlight, commala sunlight inside his eyes and waiting for him. It was hot and harsh upon his skin. The sound of the wind was louder, and that sound was also harsh. Unforgiving. Roland looked at the stairs curving upward; now his shoulders *would* touch the walls, for the passage was no wider than the sides of a coffin. Nineteen more stairs, and then the room at the top of the Dark Tower would be his.

"I come!" he called. "If'ee hear me, hear me well! *I come!*"

He took the stairs one by one, walking with his back straight and his head held up. The other rooms had been open to his eye. The final one was closed off, his way blocked by a ghost-wood door with a single word carved upon it. That word was

ROLAND.

He grasped the knob. It was engraved with a wild rose wound around a revolver, one of those great old guns from his father and now lost forever.

Yet it will be yours again, whispered the voice of the Tower and the voice of the roses—these voices were now one.

What do you mean?

To this there was no answer, but the knob turned beneath his hand, and perhaps that was an answer. Roland opened the door at the top of the Dark Tower.

He saw and understood at once, the knowledge falling upon him in a hammerblow, hot as the sun of the desert that was the apotheosis of all deserts. How many times had he climbed these stairs only to find himself peeled back, curved back, turned back? Not to the beginning (when things might have been changed and time's curse lifted), but to that moment in the Mohaine Desert when he had finally understood that his thoughtless, questionless quest would ultimately succeed? How many times had he traveled a loop like the one in the clip that had once pinched off his navel, his own tet-ka can Gan? How many times *would* he travel it?

"Oh, no!" he screamed. "*Please, not again! Have pity! Have mercy!*"

The hands pulled him forward regardless. The hands of the Tower knew no mercy.

They were the hands of Gan, the hands of ka, and they knew no mercy.

He smelled alkali, bitter as tears. The desert beyond the door was white; blinding; waterless; without feature save for the faint, cloudy haze of the mountains which sketched themselves on the horizon. The smell beneath the alkali was that of the devil-grass which brought sweet dreams, nightmares, death.

But not for you, gunslinger. Never for you. You darkle. You tinct. May I be brutally frank? You go on.

And each time you forget the last time. For you, each time is the first time.

He made one final effort to draw back: hopeless. Ka was stronger.

Roland of Gilead walked through the last door, the one he always sought, the one he always found. It closed gently behind him.

EIGHT

The gunslinger paused for a moment, swaying on his feet. He thought he'd almost passed out. It was the heat, of course; the damned heat. There was a wind, but it was dry and brought no relief. He took his waterskin, judged how much was left by the heft of it, knew he shouldn't drink—it wasn't time to drink— and had a swallow, anyway.

For a moment he had felt he was somewhere else. In the Tower itself, mayhap. But of course the desert was tricky, and full of mirages. The Dark Tower still lay thousands of wheels ahead. That sense of having climbed many stairs and looked into many rooms where many faces had looked back at him was already fading.

I will reach it, he thought, squinting up at the pitiless sun. *I swear on the name of my father that I will.*

And perhaps this time if you get there it will be different, a voice whispered—surely the voice of desert delirium, for what other time had there ever been? He was what he was and where he was, just that, no more than that, no more. He had no sense of humor and little imagination, but he was steadfast. He was a gunslinger. And in his heart, well-hidden, he still felt the bitter romance of the quest.

You're the one who never changes, Cort had told him once, and in his voice Roland could have sworn he heard fear . . . although why Cort should have been afraid of him—a boy—Roland couldn't tell. *It'll be your damnation, boy. You'll wear out a hundred pairs of boots on your walk to hell.*

And Vannay: *Those who do not learn from the past are condemned to repeat it.*

And his mother: *Roland, must you always be so serious? Can you never rest?*

Yet the voice whispered it again

(*different this time mayhap different*)

and Roland *did* seem to smell something other than alkali and devil-grass. He thought it might be flowers.

He thought it might be roses.

He shifted his gunna from one shoulder to the other, then touched the horn that rode on his belt behind the gun on his right hip. The ancient brass horn had once been blown by Arthur Eld himself, or so the story did say. Roland had given it to Cuthbert Allgood at Jericho Hill, and when Cuthbert fell, Roland had paused just long enough to pick it up again, knocking the deathdust of that place from its throat.

This is your sigul, whispered the fading voice that bore with it the dusk-sweet scent of roses, the scent of home on a summer evening—O lost!—a stone, a rose, an unfound door; a stone, a rose, a door.

This is your promise that things may be different, Roland—that there may yet be rest. Even salvation.

A pause, and then:

If you stand. If you are true.

He shook his head to clear it, thought of taking another sip of water, and dismissed the idea. Tonight. When he built his campfire over the bones of Walter's fire. Then he would drink. As for now . . .

As for now, he would resume his journey. Somewhere ahead

was the Dark Tower. Closer, however, much closer, was the man (*was* he a man? was he really?) who could perhaps tell him how to get there. Roland would catch him, and when he did, that man would talk—aye, yes, yar, tell it on the mountain as you'd hear it in the valley: Walter would be caught, and Walter would talk.

Roland touched the horn again, and its reality was oddly comforting, as if he had never touched it before.

Time to get moving.

The man in black fled across the desert, and the gunslinger followed.

June 19, 1970–April 7, 2004:
I tell God thankya.

APPENDIX

ROBERT BROWNING

"CHILDE ROLAND TO THE DARK TOWER CAME"

I

My first thought was, he lied in every word,
That hoary cripple, with malicious eye
Askance to watch the workings of his lie
On mine, and mouth scarce able to afford
Suppression of the glee, that pursed and scored
Its edge, at one more victim gained thereby.

II

What else should he be set for, with his staff?
What, save to waylay with his lies, ensnare
All travellers who might find him posted there,
And ask the road? I guessed what skull-like laugh
Would break, what crutch 'gin write my epitaph
For pastime in the dusty thoroughfare.

III

If at his counsel I should turn aside
Into that ominous tract which, all agree,
Hides the Dark Tower. Yet acquiescingly

I did turn as he pointed, neither pride
Nor hope rekindling at the end descried,
So much as gladness that some end might be.

IV

For, what with my whole world-wide wandering,
What with my search drawn out through years, my hope
Dwindled into a ghost not fit to cope
With that obstreperous joy success would bring,
I hardly tried now to rebuke the spring
My heart made, finding failure in its scope.

V

As when a sick man very near to death
Seems dead indeed, and feels begin and end
The tears and takes the farewell of each friend,
And hears one bid the other go, draw breath
Freelier outside, ('since all is o'er,' he saith
'And the blow fallen no grieving can amend;')

VI

When some discuss if near the other graves
Be room enough for this, and when a day
Suits best for carrying the corpse away,
With care about the banners, scarves and staves
And still the man hears all, and only craves
He may not shame such tender love and stay.

VII

Thus, I had so long suffered in this quest,
Heard failure prophesied so oft, been writ
So many times among 'The Band' to wit,
The knights who to the Dark Tower's search addressed
Their steps — that just to fail as they, seemed best,
And all the doubt was now — should I be fit?

VIII

So, quiet as despair I turned from him,
That hateful cripple, out of his highway
Into the path he pointed. All the day
Had been a dreary one at best, and dim
Was settling to its close, yet shot one grim
Red leer to see the plain catch its estray.

IX

For mark! No sooner was I fairly found
Pledged to the plain, after a pace or two,
Than, pausing to throw backwards a last view
O'er the safe road, 'twas gone; grey plain all round:
Nothing but plain to the horizon's bound.
I might go on, naught else remained to do.

X

So on I went. I think I never saw
Such starved ignoble nature; nothing throve:
For flowers — as well expect a cedar grove!

But cockle, spurge, according to their law
Might propagate their kind with none to awe,
You'd think; a burr had been a treasure trove.

XI

No! penury, inertness and grimace,
In some strange sort, were the land's portion. 'See
Or shut your eyes,' said Nature peevishly,
'It nothing skills: I cannot help my case:
'Tis the Last Judgement's fire must cure this place
Calcine its clods and set my prisoners free.'

XII

If there pushed any ragged thistle-stalk
Above its mates, the head was chopped, the bents
Were jealous else. What made those holes and rents
In the dock's harsh swarth leaves, bruised as to baulk
All hope of greenness? 'tis a brute must walk
Pashing their life out, with a brute's intents.

XIII

As for the grass, it grew as scant as hair
In leprosy; thin dry blades pricked the mud
Which underneath looked kneaded up with blood.
One stiff blind horse, his every bone a-stare,
Stood stupefied, however he came there:
Thrust out past service from the devil's stud!

XIV

Alive? he might be dead for aught I know,
With that red gaunt and colloped neck a-strain.
And shut eyes underneath the rusty mane;
Seldom went such grotesqueness with such woe;
I never saw a brute I hated so;
He must be wicked to deserve such pain.

XV

I shut my eyes and turned them on my heart,
As a man calls for wine before he fights,
I asked one draught of earlier, happier sights,
Ere fitly I could hope to play my part.
Think first, fight afterwards, the soldier's art:
One taste of the old time sets all to rights.

XVI

Not it! I fancied Cuthbert's reddening face
Beneath its garniture of curly gold,
Dear fellow, till I almost felt him fold
An arm to mine to fix me to the place,
The way he used. Alas, one night's disgrace!
Out went my heart's new fire and left it cold.

XVII

Giles then, the soul of honour—there he stands
Frank as ten years ago when knighted first,
What honest man should dare (he said) he durst.

Good—but the scene shifts—faugh! what hangman hands
Pin to his breast a parchment? His own bands
Read it. Poor traitor, spit upon and curst!

XVIII

Better this present than a past like that:
Back therefore to my darkening path again!
No sound, no sight as far as eye could strain.
Will the night send a howlet or a bat?
I asked: when something on the dismal flat
Came to arrest my thoughts and change their train.

XIX

A sudden little river crossed my path
As unexpected as a serpent comes.
No sluggish tide congenial to the glooms;
This, as it frothed by, might have been a bath
For the fiend's glowing hoof—to see the wrath
Of its black eddy bespate with flakes and spumes.

XX

So petty yet so spiteful! All along,
Low scrubby alders kneeled down over it;
Drenched willows flung them headlong in a fit
Of mute despair, a suicidal throng:
The river which had done them all the wrong,
Whate'er that was, rolled by, deterred no whit.

XXI

Which, while I forded—good saints, how I feared
To set my foot upon a dead man's cheek,
Each step, or feel the spear I thrust to seek
For hollows, tangled in his hair or beard!
—It may have been a water-rat I speared,
But, ugh! it sounded like a baby's shriek.

XXII

Glad was I when I reached the other bank.
Now for a better country. Vain presage!
Who were the strugglers, what war did they wage,
Whose savage trample thus could pad the dank
Soil to a plash? Toads in a poisoned tank
Or wild cats in a red-hot iron cage—

XXIII

The fight must so have seemed in that fell cirque,
What penned them there, with all the plain to choose?
No footprint leading to that horrid mews,
None out of it. Mad brewage set to work
Their brains, no doubt, like galley-slaves the Turk
Pits for his pastime, Christians against Jews.

XXIV

And more than that—a furlong on—why, there!
What bad use was that engine for, that wheel,
Or brake, not wheel—that harrow fit to reel

Men's bodies out like silk? With all the air
Of Tophet's tool, on earth left unaware
Or brought to sharpen its rusty teeth of steel.

XXV

Then came a bit of stubbed ground, once a wood,
Next a marsh it would seem, and now mere earth
Desperate and done with; (so a fool finds mirth,
Makes a thing and then mars it, till his mood
Changes and off he goes!) within a rood—
Bog, clay and rubble, sand, and stark black dearth.

XXVI

Now blotches rankling, coloured gay and grim,
Now patches where some leanness of the soil's
Broke into moss, or substances like boils;
Then came some palsied oak, a cleft in him
Like a distorted mouth that splits its rim
Gaping at death, and dies while it recoils.

XXVII

And just as far as ever from the end!
Naught in the distance but the evening, naught
To point my footstep further! At the thought,
A great black bird, Apollyon's bosom friend,
Sailed past, not best his wide wing dragon-penned
That brushed my cap—perchance the guide I sought.

XXVIII

For, looking up, aware I somehow grew,
'Spite of the dusk, the plain had given place
All round to mountains—with such name to grace
Mere ugly heights and heaps now stolen in view.
How thus they had surprised me—solve it, you!
How to get from them was no clearer case.

XXIX

Yet half I seemed to recognise some trick
Of mischief happened to me, God knows when—
In a bad dream perhaps. Here ended, then
Progress this way. When, in the very nick
Of giving up, one time more, came a click
As when a trap shuts—you're inside the den.

XXX

Burningly it came on me all at once,
This was the place! those two hills on the right,
Crouched like two bulls locked horn in horn in fight;
While to the left a tall scalped mountain . . . Dunce,
Dotard, a-dozing at the very nonce,
After a life spent training for the sight!

XXXI

What in the midst lay but the Tower itself?
The round squat turret, blind as the fool's heart,
Built of brown stone, without a counterpart

In the whole world. The tempest's mocking elf
Points to the shipman thus the unseen shelf
He strikes on, only when the timbers start.

XXXII

Not see? because of night perhaps?—why day
Came back again for that! before it left
The dying sunset kindled through a cleft:
The hills, like giants at a hunting, lay,
Chin upon hand, to see the game at bay, —
'Now stab and end the creature—to the heft!'

XXXIII

Not hear? When noise was everywhere! it tolled
Increasing like a bell. Names in my ears
Of all the lost adventurers, my peers—
How such a one was strong, and such was bold,
And such was fortunate, yet each of old
Lost, lost! one moment knelled the woe of years.

XXXIV

There they stood, ranged along the hillsides, met
To view the last of me, a living frame
For one more picture! In a sheet of flame
I saw them and I knew them all. And yet
Dauntless the slug-horn to my lips I set,
And blew. 'Childe Roland to the Dark Tower came.'

AUTHOR'S NOTE

Sometimes I think I have written more about the Dark Tower *books* than I have written about the Dark Tower itself. These related writings include the ever-growing synopsis (known by the quaint old word *Argument*) at the beginning of each of the first five volumes, and afterwords (most totally unnecessary and some actually embarrassing in retrospect) at the end of all the volumes. Michael Whelan, the extraordinary artist who illustrated both the first volume and this last, proved himself to be no slouch as a literary critic as well when, after reading a draft of Volume Seven, he suggested—in refreshingly blunt terms— that the rather lighthearted afterword I'd put at the end was jarring and out of place. I took another look at it and realized he was right.

The first half of that well-meant but off-key essay can now be found as an introduction to the first four volumes of the series; it's called "On Being Nineteen." I thought of leaving Volume Seven without any afterword at all; of letting Roland's discovery at the top of his Tower be my last word on the matter. Then I realized that I had one more thing to say, a thing that actually *needed* to be said. It has to do with my presence in my own book.

There's a smarmy academic term for this—"metafiction." I hate it. I hate the pretentiousness of it. I'm in the story only because I've known for some time now (consciously since writing *Insomnia* in 1995, unconsciously since temporarily losing track of Father Donald Callahan near the end of *'Salem's Lot*) that many of my fictions refer back to Roland's world and Roland's story. Since I was the one who wrote them, it seemed logical that I was part of the gunslinger's ka. My idea was to use the *Dark Tower* stories as a kind of summation, a way of unifying as many of my previous stories as possible beneath the arch of some *über*-tale. I never meant that to be pretentious (and I hope it isn't), but only as a way of showing how life influences art (and vice-versa). I think that, if you have read these last three *Dark Tower* volumes, you'll see that my talk of retirement makes more sense in this context. In a sense, there's nothing left to say now that Roland has reached his goal . . . and I hope the reader will see that by discovering the Horn of Eld, the gunslinger may finally be on the way to his own resolution. Possibly even to redemption. It was *all* about reaching the Tower, you see—mine as well as Roland's—and that has finally been accomplished. You may not like what Roland found at the top, but that's a different matter entirely. And don't write me any angry letters about it, either, because I won't answer them. There's nothing left to say on the subject. I wasn't exactly crazy about the ending, either, if you want to know the truth, but it's the *right* ending. The *only* ending, in fact. You have to remember that I don't make these things up, not exactly; I only write down what I see.

Readers will speculate on how "real" the Stephen King is who appears in these pages. The answer is "not very," although the one Roland and Eddie meet in Bridgton (*Song of Susannah*) is very close to the Stephen King I remember being at that time. As for the Stephen King who shows up in this final volume . . . well, let's put it this way: my wife asked me if I would kindly not give fans of the series very precise directions to where we live or who we really are. I agreed to do that. Not because I wanted to, exactly—part of what makes this story go, I think, is the sense of the fictional world bursting through into the real one—but because this happens to be my wife's life as well as mine, and she should not be penalized for either loving me, or living with me. So I have fictionalized the geography of western Maine to a great extent, trusting readers to grasp the intent of the fiction and to understand why I treated my own part in it as I did. And if you feel a need to drop in and say hello, please think again. My family and I have a good deal less privacy than we used to, and I have no wish to give up any more, may it do ya fine. My books are my way of knowing you. Let them be your way of knowing me, as well. It's enough. And on behalf of Roland and all his ka-tet—now scattered, say sorry—I thank you for coming along, and sharing this adventure with me. I never worked harder on a project in my life, and I know—none better, alas—that it has not been entirely successful. What work of make-believe ever is? And yet for all of that, I would not give back a single minute of the time that I have lived in Roland's where and when. Those days in Mid-World and End-World were quite extraordinary. Those were days when my imagination was so clear I could smell the dust and hear the creak of leather.

Stephen King
August 21, 2003